FRANKI AMATO MYSTERIES BOX SET

(BOOKS 1–3)

TRACI ANDRIGHETTI

Limoncello
Press

FRANKI AMATO MYSTERIES BOX SET
(BOOKS 1–3)

by

TRACI ANDRIGHETTI

***

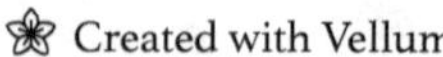 Created with Vellum

Limoncello Yellow

USA TODAY BESTSELLING AUTHOR

Traci Andrighetti

LIMONCELLO YELLOW

by

TRACI ANDRIGHETTI

***

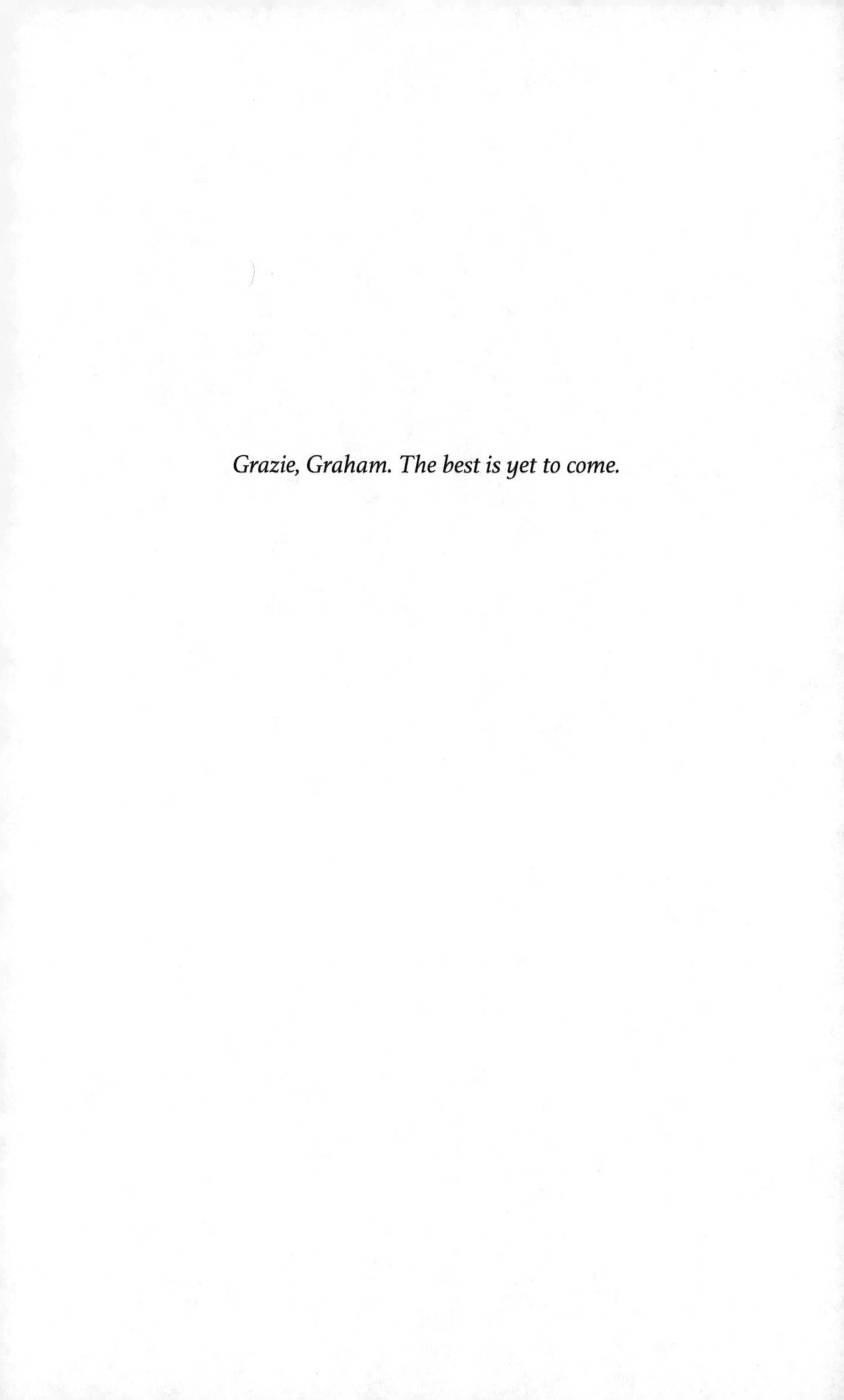

Grazie, Graham. The best is yet to come.

1

———

"This place makes the Bates Motel look like a freakin' spa resort." My sarcastic quip wasn't intended for my partner, Officer Stan Stubbs. It was for me. Because I was shaking so badly from the cold and fear that I was afraid the gun in my holster would fire on its own. I longed for the cozy fire and protective embrace of my boyfriend that I'd felt as we'd exchanged Christmas presents just hours before.

"Folks, you need to go back to your rooms immediately," Stan announced to the crowd of curious motel guests.

The onlookers began to disperse, and the woman in room six moaned again. According to 911 dispatch, she had been in distress for at least half an hour.

I shivered and wondered what kind of psycho had harmed the woman.

Stan drew his gun. "Something about this doesn't feel like a regular domestic abuse situation. We need urgent backup, Franki."

I nodded and grabbed the radio from my belt. "I have a 10-39 at the Twilight Motel on Manor Road. Request backup."

Stan began his approach to room six.

I put the device away and drew my gun. I took my place on the opposite side of the door from Stan.

"I'm goin' in on the count of three." He used his dire tone to match the circumstances. "I need to get to the john, and quick like."

I gasped. "*Now*, Stan?"

Stan was my partner on the Austin PD. As a rookie on the force, I'd been paired with a seasoned veteran of the department. Even though we'd spent the past six months together, I'd learned little from Stan except that he had a "wifey" named Juanita who worshipped the ground he walked on, he valued his handgun collection more than he did his adult children, and he suffered from acute, chronic gastrointestinal distress. And despite his self-proclaimed "legendary instinct" for cracking cases, he was perpetually baffled by his stomach issues even though the culprit was clear—a steady diet of jelly donuts and chorizo-bean-and-cheese breakfast tacos that he washed down with a gallon or so of coffee and Gatorade because he was also chronically dehydrated from the diarrhea. Needless to say, he spent the better part of every shift visiting the nearest men's room.

Ignoring my concern, Stan grasped his gun with both hands and slammed his right shoulder into the door. It flew open, and he stormed into the room. "Police! Hands in the air!"

I rushed in behind him, my gun drawn, and the woman let out a hair-raising scream.

"What in the hell?" Stan shouted.

I followed his gaze to the bed, and a chill went through my body.

Stan snorted. "Why, it's just a couple goin' at it."

I blinked hard. *Was it my imagination playing tricks on me at 4:30 a.m., or was one member of that couple horribly familiar? As in, exchanging-gifts-by-a-cozy-fire familiar?*

"Vince?" My voice was barely above a whisper as I stared at my boyfriend of over two years.

He looked at me like a deer caught in the headlights. "Franki?"

Make that, like a cheating rat caught in the act.

Stan looked from Vince to me. "You two know each other?"

I nodded, unable to speak. The chill that I'd felt had turned to a dull aching pain, and all I wanted to do was run from the room and cry. But I couldn't because I was on duty.

"I'll let you take it from here." Stan rushed into the bathroom and slammed the door.

No sooner had he left than the woman leapt from the bed—all 6' 5" or so of her—wearing nothing but her outrage. "Zis invazion iz illegal in *Deutschland*."

"All right, Franki." Vince's tone was patronizing. "No crime has been committed, so why don't you put the gun down? Then we can all talk about this like rational adults."

No crime? Rational adults? The dull pain turned to red-hot anger. Before I could think it through, I shouted, "If you think for one minute that I'm going to sit down to chat with you and your German whore here—"

The furious *fräulein* kicked the gun from my hand, and I watched in what seemed like slow motion as it flew under the bed.

"Be careful, Franki," Vince warned. "She's here from Munich on a semi-pro wrestling tour."

"Oh, so *now* you're worried about my well-being?" I backed away from the German giantess. Now that I'd mentioned it, I was a little worried about me too. She was squatting down low with her hands raised, like she was going to make mincemeat of me.

"For you, ze 'tilt-a-whirl slam.'" She lunged for my waist.

From over her shoulder, I saw Vince leap from the bed to

tackle her. Without even so much as a glance over her shoulder, she laid him out cold with an elbow to the jaw.

"Ze 'discus elbow shmash,'" she explained, raising her chin and jutting out her King Kong-like chest.

It was clear that the crazed Kraut was a force to be reckoned with. Unfortunately for me, she was refusing to recognize that *I* was a force to be reckoned with too—a member of the *police* force. Before I knew what was happening, she had heaved all 5' 10" and 170 pounds of me over her right shoulder and begun to spin. Then she let go.

I landed on the floor with a thud and desperately tried to remember what the police academy had taught me to do in such situations. But the truth was that the trainers hadn't covered how to extricate oneself from a female German wrestler with a serious case of roid rage.

"*Und* now ze 'fist drop.'" She fell onto me while driving her fist into my belly.

I writhed on the ground in agony, gasping for breath. Then I saw the Munich Monster rise up from the floor like Godzilla from the sea. Clutching my stomach, I scrambled to my feet and did my best to mimic her sparring moves.

I dodged another lunge and glanced in the direction of the bathroom. "I really need you out here, Stan."

"Just another minute." I heard the toilet flush.

I had to reason with the raging wrestler. "Listen, Greta or Helga or whatever your name is—"

"*Mein* name is Petra. Petra ze Pretzelmaker." Her face contorted with rage as the veins bulged from her thick, manly neck. "It iz not *whore*."

"Well, whoever you are," I wheezed, "you're under arrest."

"*Nein. You* are under arrest. Prepare for ze 'body avalanche.'" She flew through the air, knocked me flat on my back, and pinned me beneath her hulking frame.

Trying to protect my stomach from another fist drop, I rolled over just as she introduced a "hair pull" move that jerked me backward into an upward facing dog position.

With my gaze locked on the ceiling, I frantically tried to visualize what a good cop would do in a situation she hadn't been trained for when her partner's in the bathroom and she'd already called for backup, but nothing was coming to me. In the meantime, Petra, as her wrestling named implied, was twisting me into a pretzel. I had to buy time until backup arrived, or she was going to turn me into *spaetzle.*

"Petra, you need to release me. In the U.S., assaulting a police officer is a felony offense. You could go to prison for a long time."

To my relief, she abruptly let go of my hair. But as I fell forward, she used her brawn to lift me into the air by my belt loops and sling me over her shoulder yet again. I heard the distinct sound of the seat of my uniform pants splitting.

Wunderbar, I thought as I remembered that I'd gone commando that day for lack of clean underwear.

"*Und* now I shpank."

"Don't you dare."

The full force of her giant paw came down on my bare behind.

I mentally swore at the backup team for taking so long to arrive, and I cursed my pants for splitting. I'd spent years avoiding my large butt, both visually and mentally. Since it was behind me, I'd never had to look at it or think about it. Ever. And that had been my strategy—until then.

I heard a wet smacking sound as her palm struck my bottom for the second time. My eyes filled with angry tears.

The toilet flushed again.

"I'm coming, Franki." Stan rushed from the bathroom,

fumbling with the buckle on his oversized pants. He drew his gun and aimed it at Petra. "Freeze! You're under arrest!"

Petra stopped in mid-spank, leaving my bare bottom directly under the glow of the only light in the dim room.

"Drop the officer, boy," Stan commanded.

To my chagrin, Petra promptly did as she was told, and I hit the floor with the full force of my weight on my right knee. I was almost positive that it was either dislocated or broken.

Stan waved the gun at Petra. "Now lie down on your belly real slow-like, son, and put your hands behind your back."

I rolled onto my back and clutched my knee. "She's the female, Stan. Vince is unconscious on the other side of the bed."

He sauntered over to Petra and squinted at her in the soft light. "Well I'll be damned."

After he cuffed the then astonishingly docile *Deutschländer* and pulled her to her feet, he whistled in amazement. "You're a real nutcracker, aren't ya?"

Despite my loathing for the woman, I rolled my eyes at Stan's remark. The guy had no filter.

I looked on angrily as he led the placid Petra out the door to the squad car, protecting her head with his right hand as he helped her into the backseat with the other.

From the corner of my eye, I noticed that Vince was regaining consciousness across the room. If I could have walked or even crawled to his side, I would've knocked him out again.

Vince sat up and rubbed his jaw where he'd been elbowed. "Are you okay, babe?"

I stared at him in disbelief. "You mean after finding you in bed with a woman who just tried to kill me? Yeah, Vince. Doin' great."

"I can explain..."

"That's classic." I turned my head to hide my tears. "Do us both a favor and shut your mouth."

Stan popped his head into the room. "Uh, Vince, can I talk to you outside for a minute?"

Vince nodded and followed Stan out the door. I couldn't hear what they were saying, but I would have sworn that I heard them chuckle. I watched furious as they solidified their male bonding moment over a handshake before Vince got into his car and drove away.

Stan reentered the room, and he nonchalantly pulled out his report pad and started to write.

I looked at him from my supine position on the floor. "Um, Stan? Do you think maybe you could help me up? Since I'm injured?"

"Huh? Oh sure. One sec." He finished writing his sentence and ambled over to me. He put his hands on his hips. "You looked pretty funny hanging upside down over Suzy Schwarzenegger's shoulder. Did you know your butt was showin'?"

"Yeah, thanks," I replied through clenched teeth. I was forever on the receiving end of his asinine comments.

"Sure, Franki. That's what partners are for."

I snorted. Since starting this job, Stan had been about as helpful to me as a ball and chain around my ankle and a noose around my neck. I had watched in frustration as the other rookies flourished under the watchful eyes of their respective partners while I had languished under the disinterested gaze of mine. And when I'd finally gotten up the nerve to privately request a new partner, I'd been publicly branded as a trouble-maker and earned the nickname "Finicky Franki," as though I were a petulant child or, even worse, a cat.

Stan helped me off the ground, and he let out a loud, greasy fart. "Hooo! That felt goooood."

I closed my eyes—and my nostrils—and promised myself that I would learn how to meditate.

"You know, I've really got to see somebody about my stomach," he said for what must have been the hundredth time since I had met him. "I think I might have some kind of problem, but I don't know why. Hell, I'm in the best shape of my life."

Stan patted his spare tire belly as he walked—and I hopped, unassisted—to the squad car.

As soon as he climbed into the seat, he emitted three resounding sausage-scented belches. "Ugh, this heartburn is a killer. I feel like Old Faithful's eruptin' in my gut. Hey, could you hand me my antacids? They're in the glove box."

By this time, I knew very well where he kept his antacids, anti-diarrheals, and anti-gas tablets, all of which I regularly replenished out of my own pocket unbeknownst to Stan. I opened the glove compartment and handed him the box of antacids. Then I rolled down my window for life-sustaining oxygen. He'd already left me to die a violent slamming death. I'd be damned if I was going to let him suffocate me too.

"You okay, Franki?"

"I'm fine."

"Well, you rolled down your window like you needed some air. You feelin' dizzy?"

Oh indeed I am, but not because you let the Teutonic Titan spin me around the motel room for half a freakin' hour. He had absolutely no concept that his bodily functions might present a problem for me, both in terms of my physical safety on calls and my ability to breathe.

We arrived at the station and took Petra to booking. After she was processed and taken to her cell, Stan turned to me for his customary end-of-the-shift lecture. "You know, you've really got to pay attention when you're out there on the street. This isn't the first time I've had to come to your rescue."

"Stan, I—"

"I mean, I'm not bragging or anything," he interrupted, "but

I'm the best of the best. If you can't learn from me, then I don't know if you're gonna make it on the force."

"Stan, you—"

"You know I have to write this in my report, Franki. You put me in real danger out there. I had no backup. I could've been killed."

That did it. Although I was mostly mad at Vince, Stan was about to find out what it was like when I lost *my* filter. And it's not like he didn't have it coming. "Let me get this straight. I put *you* in danger? Are you freakin' kidding me? You put *me* in danger when you left me alone with the *Deutsch* Destroyer. And this was hardly the first time. I mean, I'm always covering my ass while yours is parked on a toilet seat."

Stan smirked. "Well, you didn't do such a good job of covering your ass tonight, now did you?"

Why *did I have to mention my ass?* I'd practically handed it to him on a platter with that remark.

"And that's the problem." He gestured toward a window overlooking the street. "You can't protect yourself out there, and you can't be relied on to protect your partner from loonies like Schotsie the Sausagestuffer, either."

"Petra the Pretzelmaker."

"And if you really want to know something," he said in an offended tone, "it's inappropriate for you to discuss my bathroom habits."

Me? I'd had to endure play-by-play reenactments of the ins and outs of his bowels—make that the outs—on a daily basis since the first day of our partnership. But Stan was too self-absorbed to ever be able to realize that, much less admit it. Our conversation hadn't amounted to anything, just like my career. There was nothing more to say. Actually, there was *one* thing.

"I quit."

~

I SHOVED the crutch that the emergency room doctor had given me into the backseat of my 1965 cherry red Mustang convertible and winced as I climbed into the front seat. The pain in my sprained knee was intense, but it was nothing compared to the ache in my heart. I reached into my bag for my car keys but pulled out my phone instead. I glanced at the time on the display—seven thirty a.m. If I knew my workaholic best friend Veronica Maggio, she was already toiling away at her new detective agency. I debated waiting to call her until after I'd had some time to sleep on the painful events of the night shift, but I decided that I'd rest a whole lot easier knowing how she was going to react to my news. I scrolled through my contacts, tapped her name, and held my breath.

"Private Chicks, Incorporated." Veronica's phone voice was clipped and professional. "If you give us the time, we'll solve your crime. What can I help you with?"

I tried to pretend she was next door instead of five hundred lonely miles away in New Orleans. "Do you always answer the phone that way?"

"In this economic climate, you have to be aggressive. So I answer with my phone version of the thirty-second elevator pitch." Unlike me, Veronica was extremely practical and all business. Though, no one could tell that about her at first glance because she looked and acted a lot like Elle Woods in *Legally Blonde*—petite, blonde, perky and perfectly put together—only she had a cream Pomeranian named Hercules instead of a tan Chihuahua named Bruiser. Veronica was everything I wasn't, and that was putting it mildly.

"I guess that's a good idea," I said. "But I don't know about the 'If you give us the time' part. It makes it sound like it could take you a while to solve a case."

"It's an expression, Franki. It means that if you hire us, we'll solve your case."

"I suppose."

An awkward pause ensued.

"So?" Veronica prodded. "What's wrong?"

I did my utmost to feign surprise. "Why would you think something's wrong?"

"Because you're doing everything you can to avoid telling me why you called."

I straightened in my seat. "I called because I've decided to take you up on your offer to join your PI firm. I'm moving to New Orleans."

"Really? What about Vince? And your job?"

"Vince and I aren't together anymore." *There. I said it. And it had hurt.*

"Do you want to talk about it?"

Her tone had softened, prompting self-pity to prick at my eyelids. "Let's just say that I was in a committed relationship, but he wasn't."

"I'm sorry, Franki."

"Me too." I leaned my head against the headrest and wiped away tears with the back of my hand.

"But I hope you're not leaving your job because of Vince."

"He's got nothing to do with it." It was a fib, but if I had told her that I discovered Vince's betrayal thanks to a 911 call, she would've never believed that I was leaving the force because it was the right thing to do. "The hard truth is that I'm not cut out for the police force. I gave my two weeks' notice this morning."

"Are you kidding?" Her pitch rose with each syllable. "You're a born cop. I mean, you still need some experience and all, but you come from a Sicilian family, and you grew up in Houston. If you don't know crime, who does?"

"Verrrry funny. Need I remind you that you're half Sicilian too?" I asked, half-heartedly playing along.

"Yeah, but I'm also half Swedish, which tempers the Italian-ness considerably. You've got it on both sides, so you're screwed."

"You're a laugh a minute, you know that? I tell you what, let's leave ethnicity out of this," I said, as though I believed that were possible. Veronica and I had bonded as pre-law students at the University of Texas, and not over our criminology classes but over all things Italian—our Italian language courses, our fami-lies, endless bottles of Chianti and, of course, Gucci, Prada, Armani, and Dolce and Gabbana (in *Cosmopolitan* and *Vogue*, that is). "I might have the makings of a good cop, but that doesn't mean I belong on the police force."

"This doesn't have anything to do with your trusty partner, does it? What happened this time? Did the diarrhea king leave you high and dry again?"

"Something like that." I looked out the driver window and thought of Petra heaving me repeatedly into the air and rubbed my wounded knee. "But Stan's not really the issue. I need to get off the night shift and return to the world of the living. And I want a job that's a little more predictable. As a private investiga-tor, I'd have some say in the cases I take." *And the situations I find myself in.*

"Do you regret going to the police academy after UT?"

"You know I had no choice. I wanted to prove to my family that women could do more than make pasta and birth babies."

"I know," Veronica said. "But I still say that becoming a cop was taking rebellion to the extreme."

"It was the best way I could think of to show them that I was as tough and capable as any man. Besides," I said, eager to change the subject from my family, "you weren't happy as an attorney, and I knew that I wouldn't have been either, especially not as a criminal defense attorney. I want to catch criminals, not defend or prosecute them. If I work for you, I can still do that but in a less restrictive environment. I can be my own boss. You know, call my own shots and that sort of thing."

"I certainly understand wanting to be your own boss. But aren't you going to feel like you've proven your family right by leaving the force?"

"They'll probably see it that way. But I'm just going to have to figure out a way to prove them wrong."

"O-kay." She drew the word out, unconvinced. "As long as you're *sure* that you're leaving Austin for the right reasons, then I could really use your help down here."

"I'm sure, Veronica." I gripped the gear shift and gathered my resolve. "Austin was a great place to go to school, but now I need to move on. And with the New Year just two weeks away, it's the perfect time to start a new life."

"And just in time for Mardi Gras. *Laissez les bons temps rouler!*"

"*Oui, cher,*" I cheered in the Cajun custom—but with a *joie de vivre* that I definitely didn't feel.

2

Sitting on the floor of my empty apartment, I stared at my cell phone. I wasn't waiting for Vince to call. I was avoiding calling my parents—for the past two weeks. Joe and Brenda Amato were as open to change as the Catholic Church, so the news of my breakup with Vince and the police force was going to hit them and my live-in Sicilian *nonna* like a divorce *and* an excommunication. As for the news that I was moving to New Orleans instead of home to Houston, they would view that as nothing short of my eternal damnation in hell. And based on what I knew about NOLA summers, that judgment might've been fairly accurate.

But since I was leaving in the morning, I sucked up my courage and sucked in a breath. Then I tapped their number and imagined that each ring was the toll of a death knell.

"Hello?" My mother's voice was so loud and shrill that Napoleon, my brindle cairn terrier who'd been sleeping in a corner, raised an ear.

"Hi, Mom."

"Francesca? Is that you?"

I rolled my eyes. "Yes, it's me. Your only daughter?"

"Well, I know *that*, dear."

A conversation with Petra the Pretzelmaker would be easier.

"Is everything all right, Francesca? It's a Wednesday."

"I know it's a Wednesday, Mom."

"You usually call on a Sunday, dear."

"Ah." I hadn't realized I was so predictable. "Listen, I'm calling because I have some things to tell you and Dad."

"Well, I hope they're good things. You know how your father worries about you. He just can't sleep at night if he thinks the slightest thing is wrong with his baby. And then he's absolutely *miserable* at the deli the next day. He acts like Anthony and me and the customers don't matter."

I could make the case that he was right about my brother Anthony. "Mom, can you just tell Dad to get on the line?"

"Of course, dear. All you had to do was ask." She slammed the phone down onto what was undoubtedly the kitchen counter. "Joe! Get on the other line. Francesca's calling from Austin." She picked up the receiver again. "Franki?"

"Still here, Mom." I sighed. "Dad knows where I live, by the way. I've been here for fourteen years."

"Well, you know your father can't hear anymore. I told him to have his ears checked, but he won't listen to me. He's got that wax build up that older men get. One second, dear." She slammed down the phone again. "Joe!"

To my relief, I heard my father pick up another line.

"I'm here, Brenda." He'd used his irritated, this-had-better-be-good-news voice. "What's going on, Franki?"

"Hey, Dad. I was just calling to tell you guys about some things that are in the works." I'd added the spunky "in the works" line in a desperate attempt to put a preemptive, positive spin on my news.

"I hope everything's okay." His tone was unhopeful.

"Everything's fine," I lied through my teeth.

"Well, that's good because thanks to your brothers, I just don't know how much more bad news we can take around here." His tone had gone from unhopeful to downright unhappy. "It's looking like Michael's going to get laid off from the accounting firm, and Anthony's decided that the deli's not good enough for him anymore. He wants to go and manage a *bar*, of all things. Sometimes I don't know what's wrong with that boy. Amato's Deli is a solid business. I built it from the ground up, and I'm proud to go to work there every day with our family name on that sign. Besides, you don't just up and leave a good job on a whim in times like these, whether your family owns the place or not."

"Y-you're right, Dad." I leaned my back against the wall. "But anyway, my news is definitely good. I've got a new job as a PI at Veronica's agency and a new place to live...and I'm single again."

The other end of the line went silent for what seemed that eternal damnation in hell as we all searched for something to say.

My mom, who'd long suspected that I was solely to blame for the fact that I was pushing thirty and unmarried, cleared her throat in preparation to take the call to a dark place. "What did you do to Vince, Francesca?"

I decided to dispense with the pleasantries and make it painfully clear that I'd had nothing to do with *this* breakup, unlike a few others I could think of. "I caught him in bed with another woman, Mom."

"Now Francesca, are you *sure* it was Vince?" she asked with her characteristic talent for denial. "You know how quick you are to jump to conclusions."

I mentally replayed the scene of bursting into that motel room and seeing Vince's naked backside in bed with pair of long and not-so-feminine legs wrapped around his waist. "Yeah. I'm sure."

My dad, who'd never spoken to me of sex in his entire life and who'd taken great pains to feign sleep during unexpected sex scenes while watching TV with me, cleared his throat in preparation to shift the focus of the conversation. "You couldn't hack fighting crime with the protection of the law on your side in a nice college town like Austin, so now you're going to go it alone as a PI in a dangerous city like New Orleans. Is that what you're telling us, Franki?"

"Dad, I made it onto the force, so clearly I *can* hack it. I just don't like the rigid structure of police work. And you'll be glad to know that being a PI is actually safer than being a cop. Instead of going toe-to-toe with drug dealers, armed robbers, and murderers, I'll be investigating things like insurance fraud, infidelity, and missing persons cases."

"While you're out-a there looking for all-a those-a missing-a persons, maybe you find-a that husband you're missing," my nonna Carmela interjected.

I silently cursed my parents for having three phones in their house. "Hi, Nonna."

"Don't-a hi-a me. Now, I have-a no problem that you're gonna go to New Orleans. You know that your *nonnu*, God rest-a his soul, and I raised your *patri* and his-a four brothers there. There are still a lotta nice Sicilian boys in New Orleans, even for a *zitella* like-a you."

The back of my head hit the wall. My nonna had been calling me a zitella, the Italian word for "old maid," since I was sixteen. She'd also been telling me that she had one thing left to do before she could die—see to it that I was properly *sistemata*, or settled, and making lots of babies and home-cooked meals for my husband.

"I still have-a some good friends there with-a some sons," Nonna said. "They might-a be divorced once or twice, and they might-a have-a some kids. And maybe they don't have-a no job.

But remember, a zitella can't-a be choosy. I'll make-a some calls and get-a back-a to you."

I swallowed a lump the size of a calzone. "Thanks, Nonna. But I'd really rather meet men on my own."

My mother gave an unamused laugh. "Well, we can see where that's gotten you, dear."

"Franki, when is this move?" My dad had once again shifted the conversation away from men. "I can help you, if you'd like. I wouldn't mind going down to the French Quarter to check in with everyone at Central Grocery. That's where I got my start in the deli business, you know. Making muffulettas."

"Yeah, I know, Dad." As if I could've forgotten that Central Grocery's famous muffuletta sandwich was indirectly responsible for me and my two brothers' entire existence. "But that won't be necessary. I'm leaving tomorrow with only what I can put in my car. I got rid of most of my stuff because the apartment's fully furnished."

"*What*?" My mom and nonna shouted in unison.

"You gonna sleep in someone else's-a bed?" My nonna had genuine fear in her voice. "*Porta iella!*"

I'd heard her use this phrase, which was Italian for "It brings bad luck," at least twice a week throughout my childhood. To my nonna, practically every single action, if done improperly or in the wrong frame of mind, would either bring bad luck or invoke *malocchiu*, the dreaded "evil eye."

"And besides bad luck," my mother said, "it's just plain dirty, Francesca. You don't know anything about the people who slept in that bed before you. Some people don't bathe. And they might have had bedbugs. Or maybe—"

"Okay, well, thanks for the advice, everyone. I'd love to keep talking, but I've got packing to do before I leave tomorrow. *Ciao ciao!*"

I hung up without giving them a chance to respond—a technique I'd learned the first time I'd called home after moving away to go to college. Then I let out a long, slow exhale. To think I'd considered moving back home to Houston instead of New Orleans.

AFTER EIGHT HOURS OF DRIVING—FOR Napoleon, eight hours of dozing—we turned onto our new street in the Uptown neighborhood of New Orleans. We were greeted by a crowd of people, who had their backs to us. I heard a live brass band playing "When the Saints Go Marching In" and realized that the crowd was walking in procession in time with the music. The people in the back of the procession wore casual clothes. Some twirled parasols, others shook handkerchiefs. Those in the front, however, were dressed more elegantly and mostly in black.

"Oh, hell no. We're following a jazz funeral."

Napoleon's ears shot up as though he too understood that it wasn't an auspicious beginning to our new life.

As I inched down Maple Street, I caught glimpses of the horse-drawn hearse carrying a casket behind glass, and I watched as the funeral-goers danced joyously to the music. My father had once told me that the people in the front, the family and friends of the deceased, were called the "first line." Those in the back were called the "second line" because they weren't part of the funeral but instead were passersby following along and enjoying the music. Life was certainly different in New Orleans, and so was death.

I glanced at the street addresses on my left and saw that they were odd-numbered. I looked at the next address and discovered that we were close to 7445. "We're almost there, boy."

Napoleon cocked his head, no doubt wondering whether he

would ever crack the mysteries of human speech, and I gave his head an affectionate scratch.

A few minutes later, the funeral procession entered a large cemetery.

I looked to my left again and saw 7445, an old two-story house that had been converted into a fourplex.

And I shuddered in horror.

My new home was right smack across the street from that cemetery.

I was going to have to kill Veronica for not telling me about it. And after I did, I knew exactly where I would bury her. She was well aware that cemeteries—particularly creepy New Orleans ones with their assortment of tombs, sarcophagi, obelisks, gothic statues, and voodoo rituals—made my skin crawl.

The good news was that next to the cemetery was a tavern named Thibodeaux's, which it looked like I was going to need.

I parked on the street in front of the house. Before I could get out of the car, Veronica came out her front door, smiling and waving with Hercules in tow in a turquoise fuzzy sweater that matched hers perfectly. Despite her Sicilian father, Veronica looked Swedish like her ex-ballerina mother, with long blonde hair, cornflower blue eyes, and pale skin.

"Franki!" She squealed.

I climbed from the car and bent over—at the waist—to hug her. I'd forgotten how tiny she was, and I wondered for at least the hundredth time how her internal organs could function in such a small frame.

She looked at me and smiled. "How does it feel to be in New Orleans?"

I glanced over at the cemetery and then back at her. "At the moment, it feels fairly morbid."

"Oh, come on. You don't still have that weird cemetery issue, do you?"

"Yes, Veronica. And I can't believe you didn't tell me that there's one right across the street. Lots of people would find it disturbing to go to sleep at night with a cemetery in their front yard, especially a *New Orleans* cemetery."

Veronica shook her head in mock disgust as she grabbed a box from my back seat.

"Thank God there's a bar right next to it, in case I need to drink myself to death from despair."

She gave a sweet smile. "Well, if you do drink yourself to death, I wouldn't have to carry you very far for your burial."

I pointed my index and pinky fingers downward—the opposite of the University of Texas hook 'em horns gesture—like my nonna had taught me to ward off the threat of death, which Veronica had so carelessly cast upon me.

She rolled her eyes. "You still do that silly *scongiuri* gesture? God, Franki, you make me *so* glad my nonna stayed in Sicily. You're so superstitious."

"I do it just in case," I snapped. "I mean, you never know..."

Veronica walked to my new front door, which was next to hers, and pulled a key from the front pocket of her designer jeans. "Glenda—our landlady—told me to let you in. She'll come downstairs to meet you in a few minutes."

With the box balanced on her left hip, Veronica unlocked my front door and shoved it open with her shoulder. She turned to me and bowed. "Welcome to your humble abode."

Excited, I entered the apartment with Napoleon at my heels. As I surveyed the living room, a number of adjectives came to mind, but humble was *not* one of them.

The room was the home-decor equivalent of Amsterdam's Red Light District. The walls were covered in fuzzy, blood-red wallpaper with shiny gold *fleurs-de-lis*, and hanging from the ceiling was a baroque red-and-black crystal chandelier. The couch was a rococo chaise lounge in velvet zebra print, and next to it was a lilac velour armchair with gold fringe that matched the drapery to perfection. On the opposite wall there was a mahogany wood fireplace with a hearth covered in white candles of various sizes and shapes. In front of the fireplace, a bearskin rug replete with a bear head covered the hardwood floors. The only thing missing was the red fluorescent light in the living room window signaling my availability for prospective clients.

"Wow. So...this Glenda... Is she a prostitute?" It was a joke. Sort of.

"Former stripper, actually," Veronica said. "And she's really touchy about the difference, so don't use the word prostitute in front of her."

I gaped at my best friend. "You're serious?"

She blinked as though renting me an apartment from a former *stripper* across from a *cemetery* was normal. "You know, I was reading that the brothel look is really popular. I believe it's called 'bordello chic.'" She paced as she tried to reconcile her unusually conflicted sense of fashion. "But now that I think about it, Lenny Kravitz redecorated his house here in New Orleans, and designers call his style 'bordello modern.'"

"Something tells me that Lenny didn't decorate this place. And I wouldn't exactly call this 'bordello modern.' It's more like 'bordello seventies.'"

"Well, at least you won't have to add any touches of color."

"I'll say. Speaking of color, any idea of the backstory on this furniture?" I eyed the chaise lounge nervously. "I mean, I know it's used. But do you have any idea *where* it was used?"

Veronica shrugged. "Glenda's a collector. She's always going on some trip or other to buy antique furniture. You'll have to ask her where she got it."

I considered Glenda's potential sources and then immediately resolved to get a new couch. And a new bed.

"She also collects stripper costumes." Veronica took a seat on the lilac armchair.

"I guess you could say she's the Debbie Reynolds of the stripping world."

"How do you mean?" I was dying to hear the rationale behind that analogy.

"She collects stripper costumes like Debbie collected Hollywood costumes. She's got an Anna Nicole Smith, a Dita Von Teese, and a Gypsy Rose Lee. You know, Glenda was quite the local celebrity back in the sixties and seventies. She stripped for all the famous singers, actors, and politicians. She even danced for President John F. Kennedy. She made a fortune and invested it all in real estate, antiques, and strip memorabilia."

"What did you say her last name was?" I was determined to google her.

"O'Brien. But her stage name was Lorraine Lamour."

"Oh, solid choice." I was truly impressed.

"Do you want to go see the *boudoir*?"

"Okay. But promise me that it doesn't have a heart-shaped bed or a mirrored ceiling."

"Lord, no. I don't go in for the tacky look," a raspy voice said behind me.

I turned and saw standing in the doorway a short, wiry, sixty-something woman with a deeply lined face, platinum boob-length hair, and the longest false eyelashes I had ever seen. From the outfit she was wearing, I had no doubt whatsoever that it was Glenda. She was dressed in a sheer black robe with gold sequins, a ruffled leopard print corset with a matching ultra mini skirt, black satin stripper slippers with feathers, and a bright yellow boa. In her left hand, she held a Mae West-style cigarette holder, and in her right was a glass of champagne.

"You must be Miss Franki. I can see that you're Italian because you look like that actress from the 1960s, Claudia Cardinale. You've got her tits too." She sized up my chest as she took a drag from her cigarette. "My name's Glenda, but I also answer to Lorraine. Welcome to New Orleans, sugar."

"Thanks, uh, Miss Glenda." I threw in the *Miss* because I was uncertain of proper Southern stripper forms of address and whether I was supposed to throw in a *honey* or a *doll*. "It's a pleasure to meet you."

"Likewise, I'm sure." She inelegantly exhaled a puff of smoke. "I see that Miss Ronnie here has shown you the place. In case she didn't mention it, the laundry room is downstairs in the basement. And if you need more storage space, there's a walk-in closet down there you're free to use. I used to keep my costumes in it, but after the post-Katrina floods I moved them to the apartment upstairs."

"Veron—, I mean, Miss Ronnie, told me that you collect costumes."

"I still have every one I wore on stage, except one made of packing tape—they had to cut me out of that one, child." She laughed with a hacking sound typical of smoker's cough. "Anyway, I dropped a wad of strippin' tips on those costumes, so I've gotta look after my investment."

"Of course." I did my best to sound empathetic.

"Now. I don't mind your furry friend here as long as he doesn't poop and pee on my chaise lounge. I had to search all over Louisiana to find one in faux zebra."

I glanced at Napoleon, who was hiking his leg on Hercules, and nudged him with my foot. "Oh, he's house trained."

"Good. One last thing—The Visitor Policy. I don't allow my female tenants to have more than two male friends spend the night at one time. I've got a reputation to protect, and I don't want people to think I rent to whores."

"Certainly not," I said with conviction.

"Let me know if you have any questions."

I started to ask Glenda about the origin of the furniture and then decided to keep my mouth shut. "No, I think it's all painfu —, er, very clear for now."

"All right then, you ladies have a good evening. And when you're all settled in, Miss Franki, I'll take you over to Thibodeaux's for a Harvey Wallbanger. *Au revoir.*"

I turned to Veronica. "What's a Harvey Wallbanger? Or is that a who?"

"It's some drink from the seventies."

"That's funny. I'd sort of taken her for a Fuzzy Navel or Slippery Nipple drinker."

She gave me a sideways look. "You know, Glenda's a little rough around the edges, but she's whip smart."

"An interesting choice of adjectives to describe her intelligence."

Veronica leaned over to pick up Hercules, who, despite his mighty name, had been having a tough time fending off Napoleon's skillful battle techniques. "So, what do you say, Franki?"

"I say that people think Austin is weird, but it's got nothing on NOLA."

"Are you ready to start work tomorrow?" She adjusted Hercules's sweater.

I took a seat on the chaise lounge. "After today, I'm ready for anything."

~

MY PHONE RANG on the nightstand.

Thinking it was my mom or my nonna calling to make sure that I'd encased the mattress in plastic, which I had seriously considered doing, I rolled onto my side in the black French bordello-style bed and pulled the hot pink duvet over my ear.

But I could still hear Napoleon snoring beside me.

And my phone continued to ring.

I opened my eyes and glared at the hot pink canopy, Then I sat up and looked at the display.

Vince.

He'd called every day since I'd caught him in bed with the wrathful wrestler, but I never answered. I had also promptly deleted all of the messages he'd left for me without listening to a single one of them. Deep down I was thinking that if I just avoided him, I wouldn't really have to face the fact that it was over, that I was alone yet again. But I knew that the time had come to hear him out and then tell him in no uncertain terms that we were through. Otherwise, I was never really going to be able to reassemble the shattered pieces of my life—not to mention my pride—and move on.

I tapped *Answer.* "What do you want, Vince?"

"Franki, finally. Why haven't you returned any of my calls? I've missed you, babe."

"Oh, I'm sure you haven't missed me that much. You seem to be perfectly capable of finding other women to keep you company when I'm not around."

"Babe, listen. That...it was all a misunderstanding."

"*Really?* So, you're telling me that I didn't see the Munich Maniac's legs wrapped around your waist? Or, maybe I did, but she was just giving you private wrestling lessons? Is that it?"

"Look, the guys dragged me to one of those nude oil-wrestling joints—"

"Spare me the sordid details. I don't care anymore."

He sighed.

I punched a pillow.

Napoleon stopped snoring, but he didn't wake up.

"Okay, babe." Vince spoke with a note of surrender. "I admit it. I made a mistake. Haven't you ever made a mistake?"

"Yeah. I have. The day I decided to trust a cheat like you. And while we're on the subject of mistakes, did you happen to notice that Petra looked a lot like a Peter?"

"Damn it, Franki. Why are you being so harsh? Lots of couples deal with cheating, and they come through it stronger, babe."

I snorted a laugh. "First of all, stop calling me 'babe.' And second, don't try to make it sound like cheating is a normal part of a relationship. I don't have to accept womanizing, and I'm not going to."

"Yeah, because you're so damned perfect, aren't you? It's time to grow up and deal with reality instead of running away to New Orleans like a child."

I stiffened. "Wait. How did you know I left Austin? Have you been spying on me, or something?"

"I'm a lot of things, but I'm not a stalker, Franki. When you wouldn't answer my calls I got worried, so I called Nonna Carmela. She told me you'd moved."

I'm sure she also told you to remind me that I wasn't getting any younger and that zitelle couldn't be choosers. "Vince, please leave my family out of this. This is between you and me—at least it *was*. There's no you and me anymore. Not now, not ever."

"So, you're going to throw away everything we had over an indiscretion?"

"We're not talking about an *indiscretion*. It's a huge *betrayal*. And yes, I most certainly am." I was proud of myself for holding my ground, even though my legs would've been shaking had I been standing on actual ground. I had a history of looking the other way where men were concerned. But not this time.

"If that's what you want, you've got it. You won't hear from me again. But let me make something clear." His tone had turned lowdown, like him. "If you're waiting for Prince Charming or for a knight in shining armor, he ain't gonna come. Especially not at your age. So you'd best think about that long and hard, *principessa*, or you're gonna end up old and alone."

The call ended.

Vince had hung up.

I sat with the phone frozen to my ear. Not even a minute before I'd been so proud of myself, thinking that I'd come a long way from the insecure woman who would forgive a man practically anything. Then in ten seconds flat Vince had reduced me to a stubborn and naïve zitella with one foot in the grave—make that the cemetery across the street. And just like that all of my insecurities rushed back.

I nestled into my pillows and pulled the duvet to my chin. I certainly didn't think I was waiting for a fairy-tale guy, especially since I'd dated Vince. But the hard truth was that every relationship I'd ever been in had ended in disaster. And after spending roughly half my life dating unsuccessfully, it seemed like I might have some sort of problem. The question was, did I come to New Orleans to solve my problem? Or to run from it?

3

———————

"What's that look for?" I glared at Napoleon, who'd lowered his ears at the sight of my first-day-on-the-job turtleneck and jeans.

He rose from the bearskin rug and hopped onto the chaise lounge.

"If you're suggesting I wear animal print like that tacky faux zebra, forget it."

He swallowed and rested his chin on his paws.

"Besides, a brown turtleneck is kind of an animal style."

Napoleon sighed and closed his eyes.

Anyone who thought I was crazy for talking to a dog hadn't met my cairn terrier. He had a way of communicating that was almost human.

I entered the kitchen, which was attached to the living room by a half-wall with a breakfast counter, and pulled a cold piece of pizza from the fridge. It was eight thirty a.m., which was the time Veronica and I had agreed we'd leave for the office.

Taking a seat at the kitchen table, I tried to quell my excitement and anxiety. Mostly, I couldn't wait to see the office building. Before establishing Private Chicks, Inc. two years before,

Veronica had settled a personal injury case fresh out of Tulane Law School that netted her a cool one point five million after taxes. Calling that payout her "ticket out of law," she paid off her student loans, maxed out her 401K, bought the Audi, and put a huge down payment on an old office building at 1200 Decatur Street. The thought of working in a French Quarter office with my best friend—as opposed to a smelly squad car with Stan—was exhilarating. But I was also nervous because I wasn't sure how I was going to handle the freedom of working as a PI after the rigid schedule and structure of police work.

Would I actually get any work done? Or would I just sit at the nearby Café du Monde drinking chicory coffee and stuffing my face full of beignets?

A knock at the front door interrupted a fantasy I was about to have that involved burning enough calories from all of my investigative legwork to eat a daily half-dozen or so of the pastries—with extra powdered sugar. But the split in my patrol pants weighed heavily on my mind—and my behind—because I was pretty sure I couldn't blame that on Petra.

I tossed the pizza in the fridge and opened the door to Veronica, who wore a pink-and-black Chanel suit with a vintage black Chanel handbag.

Napoleon might've been right about my outfit.

As if to confirm my suspicion, he sat up and wagged his tail when she entered the living room. The traitor.

She flashed her eyes. "I hope you're ready to get to work, because I just got a call from a new client. He's going to meet us at four o'clock."

"Who is he?" "A financial advisor named Ryan Hunter. He's the primary suspect in the murder of his ex-girlfriend, Jessica Evans. She was found strangled to death at the LaMarca store she managed on Canal Street. The poor woman was only twenty-six."

"There's a LaMarca here? I love that store." I thought back to a trip to Italy I'd taken several years before and the fabulous black leather handbag I'd splurged on at the original LaMarca on Rome's chic Via Condotti. "You know, I think I heard something about the murder on the radio when I was coming into town."

"Yeah, it's been all over the local media for weeks. Come on. I'll tell you about it on the way to the office."

After assuring Napoleon that I would be back soon, I locked my apartment door and then got into Veronica's waiting white Audi convertible.

"So, here's what I know." Veronica started the engine of her car and then backed out of the driveway. "Keep in mind that I haven't seen the police report yet. But from what Ryan told me, and from what I've heard on the news, a salesgirl found Jessica's body when she came to work on the morning of December 13th. She said the back door was unlocked, and Jessica was lying on the floor in the middle of some racks of scarves. Nothing had been taken from the store."

"You said she was strangled, right?"

"Yeah, with a scarf."

"Was she killed that morning? Or the day before?"

Veronica took a left turn. "Sometime the night before. Apparently, she'd stayed late after the store closed. The police didn't release the information about the murder weapon being a scarf, by the way. Someone leaked that to the press. Anyway, Franki, this is big. If we can help clear this guy or even solve the case, we're golden. Private Chicks, Inc. will be a household name in NOLA."

"That would be amazing." I looked out the passenger window so that she wouldn't see my concern. Everything was happening so fast, and solving a high-profile murder in The Big Easy wouldn't be easy at all. I hoped I was up to the job.

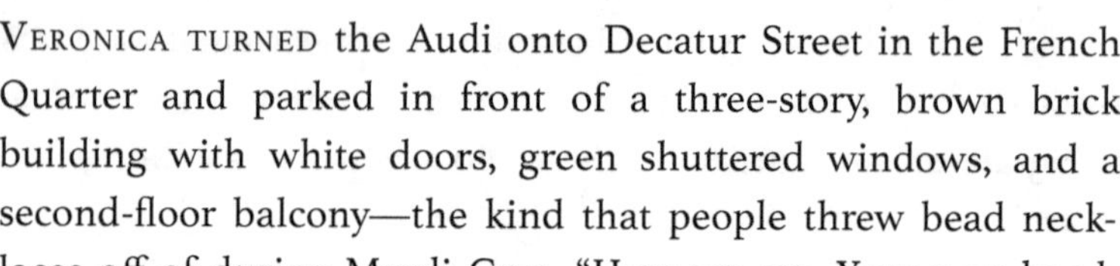

VERONICA TURNED the Audi onto Decatur Street in the French Quarter and parked in front of a three-story, brown brick building with white doors, green shuttered windows, and a second-floor balcony—the kind that people threw bead necklaces off of during Mardi Gras. "Here we are. Your new headquarters."

The smell of marinara teased my nostrils as I exited the car and looked around. "I smell my nonna's kitchen, but I don't see Private Chicks."

She giggled. "It's on the top floor. I rent the first two floors to Nizza, an Italian restaurant and bar."

My jaw dropped—while salivating. It was classic Veronica— her mind was always so focused on work that she would forget to tell me some of the pertinent details of her life, no matter how momentous they might have been.

I followed her up three long, thigh-busting flights of stairs. By the time we got to the top, I felt certain that each flight would burn off a beignet.

"Our conference room." She gestured to an unmarked door. "And across the stairwell here is our office." She led me through an old detective movie-style door that had "Private Chicks" in black letters on frosted glass. "It used to be an apartment, so I turned the living room into the lobby, kept the kitchen and bathroom, and made the two bedrooms down the hall into offices."

"Nice." And it was, especially the old brick walls and the two overstuffed couches that faced one another in the center of the room. As soon as I got situated in my new digs, I was going to get situated on those couches.

She pulled her phone from her purse. "Oh, shoot. I need to make a call. Your office is the first door on the right down the hallway. Why don't you start getting set up?"

"Glad to." I was so excited to have my own office that I almost bounced down the hallway. And I spent the rest of the day organizing my desk and learning how to use Veronica's case management software for private investigators.

The lobby bell sounded at a quarter till four as someone entered the living room that served as our lobby. Thinking it was Ryan Hunter, I walked out to greet him. I was met by a young man with a thin, angular face and lanky frame. He looked no more than sixteen or seventeen. *He's clearly not Ryan—that is, unless Jessica Evans was into jailbait.*

Veronica walked into the lobby with her handbag and her laptop. "Franki Amato, this is David Savoie. David, Franki is our new investigator."

He extended a hand with long spindly fingers. "Nice to meet you, Miss Amato."

"Call me Franki. Please." I said the last word with a wince—David had a powerful handshake for such a skinny kid.

"Sure thing, Franki." He flashed a toothy smile.

Veronica perched on a couch. "David is our computer Boy Friday. He can do anything from programming to research. We have him fifteen to twenty hours per week, depending on his school load."

"Oh, you're in college?" I'd assumed he was barely in high school.

"Yeah, I go to Tulane. But I can see how you'd be confused. People think I'm *much* older than I really am." David straightened his posture. "I'm nineteen, but I can pass for twenty-three easy."

"I can see that," I lied.

Veronica and I shared a smile at his boyish confidence.

David slid out of his backpack and then his jacket, both of which he tossed onto a nearby desk. He looked like a boy who had grown two feet over the course of a summer, and he was so thin that I was tempted to order him a couple of large pizzas from Nizza.

His gaze went to the laptop on my desk, and he ran over to pick it up. "*Dude!* That's *your* computer? Awwwesooome. Can I help you connect that to the printer, or anything?"

I watched anxiously as he turned my laptop over in his hands. I still owed the credit card company over two thousand dollars for that computer and would never be able to replace it. I snatched it from his grasp. "Thanks, but I took care of that this morning. Right now, Veronica and I are just waiting on a client—"

Our conversation was cut short as a tall, muscular man in his mid-to-late thirties entered the office.

Speak of the devil. Wait. Is Ryan Hunter the devil? I could sense a darkness about the guy, and it wasn't because he was under police suspicion. His ice blue eyes and cruel mouth spoke volumes about his character.

Veronica rose to greet him. "Ryan Hunter?"

"Yes. Are you Veronica Maggio?"

"I am, and this is my colleague, Franki Amato, and our IT consultant, David Savoie. Franki and I will be handling your case. Let's walk over to our conference room so we can talk in private."

Ryan furrowed his thick brow. "Sure."

I glanced at David before leaving the lobby. His exuberant chatter of moments before had given way to an uneasy silence. Even he seemed disturbed by Ryan Hunter's presence. I smiled at David and closed the office door behind me.

Veronica led us into a dark wood-paneled conference room. "Can I get you anything, Ryan? Coffee, water, a soda?"

I was reminded of the first time I'd met her—she'd shown up uninvited to a beer bash at my off-campus apartment with a liter of Pepsi, of all things.

Ryan settled into a brown leather chair. "Do you have any bourbon?"

"No, but we have Pepsi."

What is her deal with Pepsi?

Ryan frowned. "I'll skip the drink. I don't have much time anyway."

"Okay, then. Let's get started." Veronica took a seat and opened up her laptop, careful not to break one of her perfectly manicured pink nails. "We have some routine questions that we typically ask our clients. So if you'll just bear with us for a few minutes, we'd appreciate it."

Ryan snorted and stared at her.

Veronica seemed unfazed by his rudeness. "So, from what you told me over the phone, you're the main suspect in the murder of Jessica Evans. Is that correct?"

"I'm the *only* suspect in Jessica's murder."

I leaned forward. "Did you give the police an alibi for the time of the murder?"

He shot me a blank look. "No, because I don't have one."

I couldn't help but notice that he didn't offer any explanation of his whereabouts. "Do you know if the police have any other leads?"

He frowned. "Either they don't have any, or, if they do, they're not interested in investigating them. That's why I'm here."

"Okay. We'll look into that." Veronica typed a reminder on her laptop. But for now, let's talk about Jessica. How long had you been seeing her?"

"About six months." He twisted a paper clip he'd found on the table.

"Did you live together?"

"Yeah, for the last couple months or so. She moved into my place." He glanced out the window, clearly bored.

"Were the two of you close?" Veronica asked, almost hope-fully."Yes and no."

I could see that she was getting nowhere fast, so I took over the questioning. "How would you describe your relationship?" "Jessica and I had our ups and downs. Like other couples."

"What do you mean by 'downs'?"

Ryan snapped the paper clip in half and tossed it onto the table. "We fought."

This guy wasn't going to give an inch, so I pressed the issue. "Can you tell us about the fights?"

He sat up in his chair and cast daggers at me. "What are you getting at, exactly?"It was clear to me that he had something to hide." I mean, was there anything about your relationship that would cause the police to suspect you?"

He snorted and leaned back into his chair. "Apparently."

"Were the fights verbal? Or did they get physical?" I was unfazed by his lack of cooperation.

He looked at me hard and said nothing.

"Look, Ryan," Veronica intervened, probably sensing that I was running out of patience for this guy. "We want to help you, but we can't do that if you don't tell us everything we need to know."

He let out a long sigh. "About a month ago, we had a fight. Things got out of hand, and Jessica called 911."

Veronica's eyes widened. "What did you fight about?"

"Money. Jessica was private about money. Well, about every-thing. I really didn't know anything about her aside from the fact that she worked at LaMarca. And she always had way too much money for someone who managed a retail store. So I asked her about it. She got defensive, and we started fighting." He picked up a pen from the table and started twirling it with his fingers.

"Was it a violent fight?"

"I threw her purse at her. She got pissed and lunged at me

with a bottle of wine. I bent her wrist until she dropped it, and then I hit her. She fell backward, grabbed her cell phone from her purse, and called the cops." He spoke as though describing scenes from a boring TV show.

"So, she was afraid of you," I said, trying only half-heartedly to conceal the contempt I was feeling for him. During my short time as a cop, I'd met enough domestic abusers to last a lifetime.

He laughed and put the pen back on the table. "Let me clarify something. Jessica wasn't afraid of anyone or anything, least of all me. She called 911 because she was a vindictive bitch."

I flinched at the phrase.

A muscle worked in Ryan's square jaw. "She actually had a smile on her face when she made that call."

Veronica cleared her throat. "I'm not sure I understand. Why would she be smiling?"

He paused for a moment and then gave an ironic smile. "It's simple. Jessica liked to see people suffer. She enjoyed watching people squirm. I'd pissed her off, so she was going to make me pay. That's just who she was."

"Then why were you still dating her?" I asked, despite the fact that I was starting to think Jessica and Ryan were made for one another.

"Because she was beautiful, and she was good in bed." His tone was matter of fact, as though those were the only criteria to judge a woman by.

Just like a man. "Well, if Jessica was like you say she was, then it's possible that she had enemies. Do you know of anyone who might've had a reason to kill her?"

"Look, I don't know if she had family or friends, much less enemies. Like I said, she was private. Secretive even."

Veronica looked at me and then nodded. "All right, Ryan. I think that's all we need for now. The first thing we'll do is find out where the police are in the investigation, then we'll start looking into Jessica's background to see if we can come up with other leads in the case. We'll also need to set a time to come by your place to look through Jessica's things for any clues."

He frowned. "I'd rather you didn't. I only recently got the damn police out of my house. And besides, she only had clothes and shoes and stuff. I'll box it all up and bring it to you next week. You can do whatever you want with it."

Veronica licked her lips. "Whatever works for you."

Ryan rose to his feet. "So when can I expect to hear from you?"

"We'll call at least twice a week to update you on the investigation and to ask any follow-up questions."

"I look forward to it." He nodded and walked out the door.

I let out a breath I hadn't realized I was holding. "Wow. That's an oddly enthusiastic comment from such a reluctant client."

"Yeah." Veronica pressed her index finger to her mouth. "What do you make of that guy? He's a real weirdo, right?"

I leaned back in my chair. "Well, judging from his defensive attitude and the nonchalant way he mentioned that he'd hit Jessica, I'd say he's a sociopath."

"We're going to have to do a full background check on this guy before we do anything else. If it turns out that he's a convicted felon or something, I'm not sure we want him as a client. I'll have David start on that." She closed her laptop.

"Good idea. I can call the detective in charge of the case."

Veronica burst out laughing. "You're joking, right? As an ex-cop, you of all people should know that the police don't work with private investigators."

I'd only worked as a beat cop in Austin, so I had no idea how detectives interacted with the public on a case. But I had seen a whole lot of *Murder, She Wrote* episodes where detectives were all too willing to discuss cases with Jessica Fletcher. Not the best example, but still. "You'd think the New Orleans PD would want to help us solve a high-profile murder case."

"No, they're afraid we'll crack the case before they do, which would make them look like fools—and on every news channel in Louisiana."

"Then how do we get police information?"

"Well, there are public records, which we can access like everyone else, but the police usually black out potentially compromising information on cases that are still under investigation. So, that means we either have to luck into a corrupt detective who's willing to trade information, or we use Benjamin."

"Who's Benjamin? An informant?"

Veronica reached into her handbag, pulled out a pink Chanel wallet, and extracted a crisp one-hundred-dollar bill with a flourish. "*This* is Benjamin. And sometimes I have to rely on a whole army of Benjamins to get the information I need from the police."

I smiled. "So, you *do* have an informant."

"Yeah, a police crime analyst who feels it's her duty to ensure that cases get solved—by any means necessary. Especially crimes against women."

"Perfect. Then this is a case she's sure to help with. Murdering a woman who also had the great fortune to manage a LaMarca is a double crime against women." It sounded like I was kidding, but I wasn't.

"Agreed." Veronica looked at the clock. "It's five already. We'd better leave, or traffic will be a nightmare. I'll drop you off at the apartment on my way to run errands."

"All right." But I wasn't particularly eager to go home because I had two big boxes in my kitchen that I was doing my best to avoid unpacking.

Veronica typed a message on her phone. "There. I texted

David and told him to do the background check on Ryan Hunter. Oh yeah, do you want to meet at Thibodeaux's at seven o'clock for a drink? I'll invite Glenda..."

I laughed. "Now there's someone I'd like to see a background check on."

~

AT SEVEN P.M. on the dot, I opened my front door to the grim reality of the cemetery across the street. I had quite the setup in New Orleans. My bordello-style apartment constantly reminded me that I wasn't having sex, and the cemetery constantly reminded me that I was going to die. I definitely needed that drink. I walked the thirty or so steps to Thibodeaux's Tavern and entered.

Veronica hadn't arrived yet, but Glenda was already at the bar contemplating three empty tequila shot glasses with a long *Breakfast at Tiffany's*-style cigarette holder in her hand. To complete her Audrey Hepburn look, she wore a black-sequined jumpsuit à la Cher and red platform stripper shoes à la Lady Gaga. She wasn't wearing a boa, probably because it would've covered the skin she was trying to expose.

I approached the bar, surprised by the sumptuous brown leather furnishings, the stainless steel-covered bar, and the warm glow of candlelight. "Hi, Glenda. *Heeeey*, this place is really sophisticated for a tavern."

"Did Miss Ronnie put you to work yet?"

So much for the formalities. I sat down on a barstool to her right. "Yeah, we got a big case today."

"You lookin' for a runaway, or what?"

I found it interesting that she would ask about a runaway. But then, she must have encountered quite a few of them in her line of work. "No, it's actually a murder case."

Glenda dragged off her unlit cigarette. "It's not that strangled girl, is it?""Yes, it is." I was stunned by her insight.

She exhaled nonexistent smoke into my face. "I heard about that. She worked at Prada, right?"

For some reason, I waved away the smoke she didn't exhale. "No, better. LaMarca."

"Personally, I don't care for their designs. All that fabric they use on their evening dresses is frumpy and confining."

Of course, LaMarca had the most sought-after gowns in all of fashion. But compared to the clothing Glenda wore, their evening dresses—even ones that were strapless, backless, and slit to the pelvis—probably looked like pilgrim apparel to her.

An unkempt Sean Penn doppelganger approached me from behind the bar. "Can I get you something to drink?"

"Um—"

"Another tequila shot," Glenda interrupted.

"I'll have a glass of Prosecco, please."

Veronica slid onto the barstool next to me. "Make that two, Phillip."

I turned toward Veronica. "I didn't see you come in."

"That's because you two ladies were deep in conversation." She smirked. "What were you talking about?"

"We were talkin' about that girl who was strangled with the scarf, Miss Ronnie."

Veronica looked at me quizzically. I shook my head to indicate that I hadn't told Glenda any specifics.

"The case reminds me of a striptease I used to do when I was working at Madame Moiselle's in the Quarter."

"Oh?" I was instantly drawn in. There was something about Glenda that intrigued me.

"It was an artistic rendering of a woman's transformation from victimization to self-empowerment."

Her burst of intellectualism left me at a loss for words.

Veronica hadn't been kidding when she'd said Glenda was smart.

"I dressed entirely in sheer scarves. As I stripped away each one, it signified her metamorphosis. There was a top layer of black scarves, then underneath a layer of gray, beneath that a layer of white and then finally, a single pink scarf."

To my total astonishment—I was moved by her description. "That's really beautiful, Glenda."

Veronica leaned around me. "What did the pink scarf represent? The woman's soul?"

Glenda looked taken aback. "No. Her vagina."

"Ah." I was again speechless—but this time for a different reason.

Phillip the bartender returned with our drinks.

Veronica pressed a finger to her cheek. "So, the woman reclaimed her power by taking back her vagina from her victimizer?"

Oh God. I took several gulps of the drink that I was overjoyed to have at hand.

"Exactly." Glenda looked at her with renewed respect. "And after she took her vagina back, she did whatever the hell she wanted with it." She cackled and elbowed Veronica.

Taking "The Vagina Monologues" as my cue to leave, I stood up and chugged the remainder of my Prosecco. "Well, guys, I hate to drink and run, but I'd better head out. After all, I've got a case to start investigating tomorrow."

Veronica looked up at me. "I haven't had a chance to tell you this, Franki, but I feel so much better now that you're here. I know I can't go wrong with an ex-cop on my team."

Glenda tossed back another shot of tequila. "That's the first time I've ever heard that one."

"Thanks, Veronica." I shot Glenda a haughty look. "It's a nice change to work for someone who has so much confidence in my abilities. See you tomorrow."

I exited the bar into the crisp January night and got an instant chill—but not from the wintery weather. It struck me just how much was riding on this case. It wasn't only about my self-esteem, pride, and career. It was also about Veronica's professional reputation and the success of the business she'd worked so hard to establish, not to mention the family of the woman who'd been killed. And then there was the not-so-insignificant matter of Ryan Hunter, the sinister-seeming accused killer I'd be helping to potentially walk free.

With all of that sitting on my shoulders like a five-hundred-pound barbell, the thirty or so steps back to my apartment seemed like the longest walk of my life.

4

The knocking at my front door grew insistent.

I hopped from my bedroom, pulling on the gray pants I'd bought on clearance at Target, and opened the door.

Veronica entered in a sleek brown Elie Tahari pantsuit with a cream-colored silk blouse. She looked like a gazelle, while I was the spitting image of a hippo.

"Morning." Her tone practically beamed sunshine. "How are you and Napoleon adjusting to your new surroundings?"

"Pretty well, especially Napoleon." I closed the door behind her as she entered the living room. "The bordello chic decor is really bringing out the animal in him. Last night when I came home from the bar, I found him lying on his back sound asleep on the zebra print chaise lounge with his legs splayed wide open."

"Men—of any species—have no shame." She followed me into my bedroom.

"I know, right?" I thought of Vince and his brazen attitude about his infidelity. I entered the adjoining bathroom to put on my makeup and was surprised by the scowling face looking back at me in the oval mirror of the knockoff red Louis XVI vanity. I forced myself to smile. I refused to waste anymore of my precious emotion on that cheat.

Veronica flopped onto the bed next to Napoleon. "Speaking of shame, we're going to church this morning."

My anger toward Vince was replaced by waves of Catholic guilt. I tried to remember the last time I'd been to church. I'd visited the Vatican on my trip to Rome three years ago, but they turned me away at the door for having bare shoulders, so I was pretty sure that didn't count. "Why in the hell would we do that?"

She sighed. "Relax, Franki. We're not going to mass."

I shot her a questioning look from the bathroom doorway, holding my liquid eyeliner brush like a weapon.

"Or confession," she said, interpreting my gaze. "We're going there to meet Betty Friedan."

I gasped, and my Catholic guilt morphed into feminist guilt for putting on my signature Sophia Loren-style cat eyeliner. "The founder of the National Organization for Women?"

"Gah, Franki. Calm down, will you?" Veronica was lying on her side with her head propped up by her arm, indifferent to my issues. "Betty Friedan is our informant's code name."

I was relieved that Betty was just an informant because that meant I could wear blush and lipstick too. "How was I supposed to know that? I mean, why doesn't she have a normal informant name like Deep Throat or Huggy Bear?"

"Because she's not Bob Woodward's Watergate source or a TV character from Starsky and Hutch. She's a feminist crime analyst from the New Orleans PD."

"So, we're going to a church to pay off a corrupt feminist employee of the police department." That seemed like an obvious violation of all that was holy. "What's the occasion?"

"She's going to give us the police report on the Evans murder and photos of the crime scene. I called her and asked for them after David texted me the results of Ryan Hunter's background check. His record is clean, by the way. That is, except for the assault charge on Jessica he told us about and a surprising number of moving violations."

I remembered how angry and aggressive he'd seemed yesterday. "I'm sure he's got a serious case of road rage. People like that are capable of anything."

"That's a big accusation coming from a woman who once intentionally ran her car into her ex-boyfriend's house."

I glared at her. "It wasn't his *house*. It was his *fence*. The little picket fence we'd painted white together when I was still stupid enough to think he was going to marry me. And I can't believe you would bring up Todd Rothman. College was years ago."

She blinked. "That was road rage, wasn't it?"

"No, it was relationship rage after he forgot to tell me he'd found a new girlfriend and was sleeping with her in the house that was supposed to be ours." I rubbed blush on my cheek so vigorously that it turned red on its own. "Besides, knocking down Todd's fence certainly doesn't make me like Ryan Hunter."

"Of course not." She rubbed Napoleon's belly, and he looked at her with love in his eyes. "I'm just trying to point out that road rage doesn't make someone a killer. So, until we find evidence to prove otherwise, we have to proceed on the assumption that Ryan is innocent, no matter how despicable he may be."

"I know, I know." It was so annoying when Veronica was right. I *had* all but convicted Ryan and was fully prepared to throw away the key. "But the jury's still out on that guy. And for the record, I've come a long way since Todd. Just look at how well I've handled Vince's cheating."

"I'm very proud of you for that."

Her admission took the angry wind out of my sails. "So where is this church?"

"On Rampart Street in the Quarter. It's the old Mortuary Chapel."

"A mortuary chapel, Veronica?" She knew how creeped out I was by cemeteries and churches, so I couldn't believe she would take me to a combination of the two. "Really?"

"Really. It's close to the police station where Betty works. And they haven't kept dead bodies there since the yellow fever epidemic of the 1800s, so you'll be fine. You'll like it too because it became an Italian immigrant church."

She'd intentionally used our heritage to persuade me. *Such an attorney.*

"Now let's go." Veronica gave Napoleon a final scratch and jumped off the bed. "I'll drive. You're kind of jumpy today."

"Okay, but we're going out the back door. There is no way in *inferno* that I'm passing by a cemetery on my way to a mortuary chapel."

Veronica stopped the car in front of the chapel. "See? No gothic spires or gargoyles on the outside, and I promise there are no bodies inside."

I stared out the passenger window. "Why did you tell me this was called the Mortuary Chapel? The sign says Our Lady of Guadalupe Catholic Church."

"Because I know you, and if you'd read the historical plaque over there and learned that the original name had the word *mortuary* in it, you would've caused a scene. Possibly even in the church." She turned off the engine and put her keys into her brown Balenciaga bag.

Good point. I exited the car and walked over to the plaque eager to find out if there was anything else about the church she'd failed to mention. "Hey, this doesn't say anything about being an Italian immigrant church. But it does say that it's the official chapel of the New Orleans Police and Fire Departments. Is it really a good idea to meet Betty here?"

Veronica walked up behind me in her dainty Jimmy Choos. "It's the perfect place. No one in the police department would be surprised if an employee came here. Plus, with all these people around, no one would suspect a payoff was going down either."

"I hope you're right. You know my nonna would never live it down if I got busted in a church." My nonna was convinced that my lapsed Catholicism was a major impediment to my ability to attract a suitable husband. If I got excommunicated too, it would surely seal my fate as a lifelong zitella in her eyes.

Veronica looked at her phone, ignoring my concerns. "We're early. Betty might not be here yet. Let's go inside and wait."

"Why not?" I asked—not without a note of bitterness.

When I followed Veronica into the church, I noticed a line of people in front of a statue of a Roman centurion holding a cross and stepping on a bird that, on closer inspection, appeared to be a crow. He looked like one of the modern-day Italian men who hang around the Colosseum in Rome dressed in cheesy centurion and gladiator costumes to pose in pictures with tourists. I watched as each person who approached the statue rubbed its feet, murmured something, and then made the sign of the cross. A few people had deposited flowers at the base of the statue, but others had left slices of what looked like pound cake.

"Man, I wish people would leave me flowers and pound cake. Which saint is that anyhow? The patron saint of florists and bakers?"

"That's Saint Expedite," a strong masculine voice said behind me.

I turned to see an unorthodoxly attractive young priest with thick, wavy brown hair, sensual lips, and a ravishing smile. If he'd lived in Rome he would have been a candidate for the annual priest calendar, which, in my mind, was the bizarre and seemingly sacrilegious Italian equivalent of the fireman's calendar. Of course, I didn't think this priest was good looking or anything—it's just that he wasn't *anything* like the old priests I'd grown up around in Houston.

"I'm Father John." He clasped my hand in his.

The minute his skin touched mine, I itched. Ever since I was a young girl in Sunday school, I'd been allergic to the clergy. It was a psychosomatic reaction to the Catholic guilt I felt about my sporadic visits to church as a child, thanks to my parents' seven-day-per-week work schedule and the fact that my over excitable nonna couldn't be trusted with a car.

I withdrew my hand from his as though it had been burned by the fires of hell and blurted, "Bless me father for I have sinned."

He looked confused. "Did you come for confession?"

"Oh, no." I felt my face turning as red as communion wine. The phrase was the only thing I could remember ever saying to a priest. I forced nonchalance as I scratched a spot on my left elbow. "I'm good. I'm here with a friend. She needs to confess, though." It wasn't true, but it served her right for disappearing.

"Well, we can certainly help her with that." He flashed another gorgeous smile.

"Gr-great." I scratched my side. The icky combination of his handsomeness and his holiness really freaked me out. "I don't remember learning about Saint Expedite in Sunday school."

"You didn't learn about him in Sunday school because he's not officially recognized by the Catholic Church." He cast a doubtful look in Saint Expedite's direction. "But the Church occasionally tolerates the veneration of local saints."

I scanned the church for Veronica and mentally cursed her. Then I felt guilty for thinking profanity in a church. "What's he the patron saint of?"

"Anyone who's looking for a quick solution to a problem, who needs money, or wants to stop procrastinating."

Me, me, and me. The saint had gotten a lot more interesting. "So, why are those people leaving him pound cake? I mean, I can kind of understand the flowers, but cake?"

"Well, in recent years, Expedite has become the patron saint of people who need to win court cases. They leave him a slice of pound cake as an offering so that he'll be more inclined to help them stay out of jail or—"

"Hold on." A pang of guilt jabbed at my gut for cutting off a priest, but I had to get to the bottom of the cake thing. "They leave him pound cake so that he'll keep them out of the slammer?"

"It has its origins in voodoo. In New Orleans, voodoo and the Catholic Church are closely related. The fusion of the French and African cultures in Louisiana resulted in an association of the voodoo spirits with Christian saints. Some people call Saint Expedite the Voodoo Saint because he represents Baron Samedi, the voodoo loa of death."

I was shocked that a saint would be associated with voodoo. "The voodoo loa of death? What's that?"

"A loa is a voodoo deity. And Baron Samedi is a shady voodoo god who wears a top hat and tails. Voodoo legend has it that when people die, he digs their graves, greets their souls, and leads them to the underworld. He's also a sexual loa who loves to swear, smoke, drink rum, tell filthy jokes to the other spirits, and chase women." Father John winked.

Awk-ward. My cheeks were as hot as Hades as I scratched my neck and looked for Veronica from the corners of my eyes. "I still don't understand what Saint Expedite has to do with voodoo."

"It works like this: Followers of New Orleans' legendary voodoo queen Marie Laveau, who died in the late 1800s, visit her tomb in Saint Louis cemetery #1 to ask her for help with a problem. Since the cemetery is right behind the church on Basin Street, afterward they come into the church and leave a slice of pound cake for Saint Expedite so that he'll fast track, or *expedite*, the favors asked of Marie Laveau. It's really a fascinating mixture of religions."

"So, voodoo's a religion." I scratched my head. "I thought it was just like dark magic or something."

He smiled. "That's how pop culture has painted it, but it's centered around religious themes and a desire to do good in the world by channeling saints." He paused. "Hey, do you like James Bond?"

I slowly shook my head, wondering whether God approved of priests watching James Bond movies.

"No?" He sounded shocked. "Too bad, because Baron Samedi is a character in *Live and Let Die* with Roger Moore."

I spotted Veronica beckoning to me like a saving angel from near the altar. She stood next to what could only be described as the anti-Veronica—a young woman with short, dark hair tucked behind her ears, black rectangular glasses, a thin mouth, and no makeup. She resembled a real-life Velma from *Scooby Doo*.

Betty. I thanked heaven that I had finally found an avenue of escape. "Well, thank you for the information, Joh—, er, Father," I faltered. It was hard for me to think of a good-looking young guy as a priest. "I need to join my friend."

"Anytime. I hope you'll join us for mass this Sunday."

"Sure," I said, knowing there wasn't a chance in hell I'd show up. *Great, I just lied to a priest.*

I turned and hurried up the aisle to the altar, almost at a run. Then I turned right and walked to the end of the first pew where Veronica and Betty were sitting. I extended my hand. "You must be Betty."

She opted to pass on the handshake to take a moment to size me up. "Who are *you*?"

Veronica smiled. "Betty, this is Franki, my new partner I was telling you about. She's a super smart ex-cop."

"Right." Betty pulled a large manila envelope from a worn, brown leather bag and handed it to Veronica. "So anyway, here's the information you asked for. You won't find much in the report that hasn't already been leaked to the press, but the pictures should be useful."

Veronica, in turn, produced Betty's payoff, which she had disguised by placing it into a church-offering envelope. "Thank you so much. This is going to make a huge difference in our investigation."

"No problem, V." Betty stuffed the envelope into her briefcase. "I just hope you catch the sorry son of a bitch who committed this crime."

"You know, it might've been committed by a woman," I interjected, playing devil's advocate.

"The odds are against it." Betty spoke with a sneer. "Statistically speaking, this is likely an open-and-shut case of femicide—a man killing a woman just because she's a female—and we women need to come together to prevent this type of thing from happening." She stood and pushed up her glasses. "Let me know if you find the asshole who did this."

I watched her walk away, clutching her leather briefcase to her chest. "Wow, that Betty's a real charmer."

Veronica rose to her feet. "She takes crime very seriously. Now let's get going. I'm dying to look at the police report."

As we walked out of the church, I saw Father John waving goodbye to me. Instead of waving back, I tried to duck all 5' 10" of me behind Veronica's tiny frame. I must have looked like I was having a seizure.

The second we got into the car, Veronica tore open the envelope and studied a photo of Jessica at the crime scene. "Look at this."

It was a gruesome sight. Jessica was lying on her left side in the middle of four scarf racks that were situated in the shape of a square. Her face was directed toward the ceiling, and her eyes were open in a look of shock. She had been strangled with a black-and-white checked scarf with a bright yellow border.

Veronica, who owned a different scarf for every day of the year, was intently focused on the murder weapon. She pulled out the police report and quickly scanned the pages. "I knew it."

"What?"

"The scarf used to strangle Jessica isn't from LaMarca." Her eyes danced with excitement.

"How do you know?""It's a cheap cotton-polyester blend. Everyone knows that LaMarca only sells silk scarves."

I didn't know that, but I did know that LaMarca's signature scarves were the most sought after in the fashion industry. "So, the killer brought a scarf to a store that's famous for selling scarves."

But why?

STANDING on Canal Street in front of Pontchartrain Bank, I leaned into the passenger window of Veronica's Audi. "I'll go straight to LaMarca after I get some cash. Anything in particular you want me to find out?"

Veronica lowered her sunglasses. "I trust your judgement. And if you have to buy something to keep up your cover as a customer, I'll reimburse up to fifty dollars, so hang on to the receipt."

I would. Because after my move to New Orleans, I was pretty sure that there wasn't enough room left on my credit cards to shop at the Dollar Tree, much less LaMarca. Thankfully, my parents had made a deposit to my account as a belated Christmas gift to help cover my moving expenses.

I entered the lobby and rummaged in my knockoff Gucci hobo bag for a pen. I filled out a withdrawal slip and got in line.

"Next," the teller called.

I approached the window. The teller, who couldn't have been more than 4' 10", looked remarkably like Tinker Bell sans bun and wings.

"May I help you?" Her accent was thick.

I glanced at her nameplate—Corinne Mercier—to confirm my suspicion that she was French. New Orleans was a popular city among French immigrants because of its historical ties to France. "I'd like to make a withdrawal, please." I slid my withdrawal slip toward her. "I haven't gotten my ATM card yet."

"Oh, *mademoiselle*, I am so sorry. Are you new to ze bank?" Her big blue eyes were rimmed with red like she'd been crying.

Guessing that she was having man trouble, I sympathized. "Yeah, I just moved here from Austin to take a job as a private investigator. Where are you from?"

"I come here from Toulouse to start a new life. My mother, she is *américaine*, but I was raised in France."

"I moved here to start a new life too. Besides getting a new job, I wanted to get away from my cheating ex-boyfriend."

"Ah. My boyfriend, Thierry, he cheat too. I come home yesterday, and I find him wis a woman." She struggled to enter my transaction into the computer as her eyes welled up with tears.

"I'm really sorry to hear that. The same thing happened to me. I'm Franki, by the way. You're Corinne, right?"

She nodded, wiping her nose with a tissue. "You too? Men! Zey are so...so...*volages, non*?" She blew her nose with a very un-Tinker Bell-like honk, and then handed me my money from the teller cash dispenser.

"Exactly." I put the money into my wallet. I had no idea what she'd just said, but I agreed with the tone of her voice one hundred percent. "All they think about is sex. You know, I really believe the old saying that a man thinks with his penis is true."

Corinne's big blue eyes got even bigger, and she fiddled with her pixie-style blonde hair.

I thought it was because I was coming on a little strong for a stranger and all, but then her eyes darted to something—or someone—over my shoulder. I turned and saw one of the most handsome men I'd ever seen in my life. He had dark brown hair, a chiseled jaw, and a sensuous mouth.

"Is this yours, miss?" He held up my birth control case—with a twinkle in his eye.

I must have dropped it when I was standing in line digging through my bag for the pen I'd used to fill out my withdrawal slip. My whole body burned from embarrassment. Not only had he probably heard my cutting remarks about men, but now he also knew I was having sex with at least one of them.

I realized that I'd been staring at him slack-jawed. I closed my mouth and swallowed hard. "Oh, gosh. Those? They belong to a friend. I'm just holding them for her." I laughed, and it sounded hollow. "While she's out of town."

I'd never been one to stop while I was ahead.

The corners of his mouth curled into a devious smile. "I'd better check the pharmacy label on the back to be sure. It says they were prescribed to—"

"Don't read that." I snatched the package from his hand. "You wouldn't want to violate the HIPAA Privacy Rule."

"Certainly not. My apologies." He gave a mock bow. "To your friend, of course."

Clearly, he enjoyed my unease.

I pretended to check the label. "They're hers, all right." I shoved the pills into my bag. "Thank you, Mr....?"

"Hartmann. Bradley Hartmann," he replied—not unlike James Bond. My Bond-loving priest friend would no doubt be impressed. "I'm the president of the bank." He reached out for a handshake. "Your name is Francesca, right?"

So he did *read the back of my birth control case. Just what my life needed—more men who delighted in humiliating me.* "Franki," I replied through the heat in my cheeks. "Franki Amato."

"I heard you tell Miss Mercier that you haven't received your ATM card yet. Why don't you let me look into that for you?" His devious smile turned dazzling.

To my dismay, my knees grew weak.

Corinne furrowed her brow. "*Mais non*, Mr. Hartmann. I will help Miss Amato."

"That's all right, Corinne." He placed a hand firmly at the small of my back. "I'll take care of Miss Amato."

The way his eyes were twinkling, I couldn't tell if he was flirting or mocking me.

"Call me Franki."

"I'd like that."

Yep, definitely flirting. And based on the way his thick-lashed blue eyes stared at me, I wasn't sure I minded.

I attempted a little flirt-back of my own, doing a spontaneous Veronica-style bat of my eyelashes that promptly dislodged my right contact lens.

"Are you okay?" he asked. "Your eye is tearing up."

"Oh, it's nothing." I tried to look composed as my lens sent little stabs of pain into my eye. "Just something in my contact."

He nodded. "Okay, good. Well then, I'll find out what's going on with your ATM card and give you a call."

"Great." The pain from my contact was shooting straight into my brain. I flashed him a Julia Roberts smile that probably ended up looking more like that of The Joker.

As I turned to leave the bank, I worried that Bradley might

be checking me out from behind. To cover my oversized back-side, I slung my bag behind me and walked serpentine-style toward the door, stopping and turning to one side every so often to feign admiration for a plastic plant or an employee-of-the-month plaque on the wall.

Ironically, however, when I got outside in the bright sunshine and popped my contact lens from my eye, things came more into focus. Bradley was more than likely being friendly to me to get me out of the bank. After all, there probably weren't too many bank presidents who would welcome clients who boomed about men, sex, and penises while leaving a trail of birth control behind them.

5

———————

I walked the short distance down Canal Street from the bank to LaMarca, with its signature Italian white marble sign with the gold logo. Thanks to the police report, I had the name of the salesgirl who'd found Jessica Evans' body—Annabella Stevens. But I knew that if I introduced myself as a private investigator, she wouldn't give me the time of day.

A lot of people wouldn't talk to PIs because they weren't the police, which was ironic considering that a lot of people wouldn't talk to the police either. And, in all probability, LaMarca management had advised its employees not to discuss the crime with its customers. So, the plan was to find out whether Annabella was still working for LaMarca and, if she was, to approach her on the pretense of needing assistance with selecting a scarf for my mom. With any luck, I would glean some information about the crime.

I grasped the handle of LaMarca's tall glass door and discovered that my palms were sweating. This was my first real undercover assignment because rookie cops weren't allowed anywhere near detective work, and I was nervous. So, I did what any female PI would do as I entered the elegant store—I summoned Nancy Drew's cool-headed sleuthing techniques from the dark and murky depths of my adolescent reading memory.

Inside, I spotted the scarf department where Jessica's body had been found. Four, long, shoulder-height scarf racks were positioned in the shape of a square in the center of the room. On all four sides of the racks, there were glass cases displaying jewelry, wallets, and other accessories, and the walls were lined all the way to the ceiling with multiple rows of handbags of varying colors and shades. The ceiling itself was covered with ornate gold decorative elements like those of a Catholic Church. For a moment, I was breathless with emotion—not because I was at the scene of the crime, mind you, but because I was busy worshipping all those glorious LaMarca bags.

"May I help you?"

The blonde Amazonian salesgirl's booming voice startled me out of my fine leather-induced stupor. I glanced at her nametag. "No thanks, Svetlana. I'm just looking."

Without giving her a chance to respond, I scurried to the scarf racks. Nancy Drew would have never acted so nervous. I took a deep breath and tried to focus. I knew I should be looking for clues related to the crime, but I had no idea what those might be.

As I gazed at the beautiful silk scarves, the image of a vibrant young woman with shoulder-length blonde hair lying strangled popped into my mind. Again I wondered why the killer had strangled her with a scarf from another store when there were so many scarves right at his or her fingertips. Maybe Ryan Hunter or another male admirer had brought the scarf to Jessica as a gift and then used it to strangle her during an argument. Or the scarf could have belonged to a woman who'd removed it from her own neck to strangle Jessica.

But was it mere happenstance that she'd been strangled with a cheap polyester scarf in a sea of expensive silk? Or was it some kind of message?

"Can I help you with something?" a chipper voice asked from behind me.

I turned to see a chubby young girl with hazel bug eyes and Shirley Temple curls in a Lucille Ball red straight from the bottle. She wore a white, short-sleeved angora sweater, a black poodle skirt, and a pink scarf knotted around her neck, which was an astonishingly 1950s look for someone who worked in contemporary fashion. Her nametag read Annabella.

It's her.

"Yes, I'm trying to find a scarf for my mom, but I'm overwhelmed by all the options." My words sounded fake and stilted to my ear, but the 1950s pinup girl didn't seem to notice.

"Oh, I can totally help you with that. I just love scarves. What color did you have in mind?"

"Yellow." I waited to see her reaction. Even though Annabella had an airtight alibi—she was in the emergency room with a nasty case of the hives at the time of the murder— my instincts told me that she knew more about the situation than she had shared with the police.

Annabella's bulging eyes opened even wider for an instant, then she regained her composure. "What a lovely choice," she said stiffly. She beckoned me to follow her to another rack.

As she sifted expertly through scarves in hues of amber, gold, and yellow, I came up with a casual segue into the crime. "I'm so glad your scarf area is open. I wasn't sure it would be... after the murder."

"LaMarca is open three hundred sixty-five days per year." Annabella recited the hours like a slogan. Then she looked me in the eyes. "Actually," her voice had lowered, "we were open for business later that same day."

"Now that's customer service." It was the most innocuous

thing I could think of to say. I sensed that she was the gossipy type, so I decided to try winning her trust with flattery. "By the way, I *love* your look. You should be on TV, you know that? You have that glamorous quality about you."

Annabella blushed. "That's what I think, but Svetlana is always telling me I look dowdy."

"I can't believe that," I lied as I looked through the scarves. "So, um, did you know her? The woman who was strangled?"

"She was our manager," she whispered, her eyes darting from side to side to make sure no one was in earshot. "Her name was Jessica Evans." Annabella stopped searching through the scarves and draped her arm casually over one of the racks.

My compliments were taking effect—she was clearly in the mood to talk murder. "What was Jessica like? I mean, was she as stylish as you? I'm asking because I'm obsessed with true crime."

She leaned forward. "Well, she was drop dead gorgeous for one thing. A lot of people said she looked like a young Kim Basinger. And she only wore the latest styles—LaMarca, Hermes, Gucci, Chanel, Armani. You name the brand, she had it. And she *always* accessorized with a scarf."

"You don't say."

"Yeah, she said that a scarf gives your outfit that touch of class, unless it's a cheap one, of course."

One look at Annabella's scarf confirmed that she hadn't internalized that all-important accessory rule. But if Jessica had said that, what had it meant that she'd been strangled with a cheap scarf she would have detested? "Did she really say that? About cheap scarves, I mean?"

"Yeah."

I looked through the scarves. "Was she a good manager?"

"Well, she was cold as ice to her employees." Annabella's happy tone had turned huffy. "I mean, I know you're not supposed to speak ill of the dead. But for her, we were nobodies

—lower than nobodies. But that's the way it is in fashion, and she knew this business like the back of her hand. She actually got to intern at the original LaMarca store in Milan's Via Monte Napoleone fashion district. I don't know how she did it, either, because they never give internships to foreigners."

"How nice for her." I considered the connections Jessica must have had to land that kind of opportunity.

"I was hoping she would mentor me. You know, so I could work my way up? But she thought I was too unfashionable." Her double chin trembled with emotion from the perceived injustice of that last statement.

"Well, that's just *her* opinion." I wanted to reassure her even though I *did* think that the poodle skirt was killing her career chances. "I mean, you look like a 1950s version of Geri Halliwell —you know, Ginger Spice? So how in the *world* could you be unfashionable?"

"I know, right?" She sniffled. "But Jessica was nothing if not brutally honest. Besides, she always said that emotion had no place in the business world and that we should leave our feelings at home—along with our personal lives."

"Speaking of personal lives, the police think her boyfriend did it, right?" I pulled a hideous scarf from the rack and pretended to examine its bizarre horseshoe pattern.

"Yeeeeeah." Annabella's tone was doubtful as she plucked a stray yellow thread from her white sleeve. "But I'm not so sure."

"Why do you say that?" I watched as she twisted the thread around her fingers.

"Well, for starters, fashion is a cutthroat industry. If you've made it in this business, you've got enemies." She gave me an extra wide-eyed and knowing look.

"Gosh, I had no idea the business was like that," I fibbed as I put the ugly scarf back on its hanger. "Do you know if Jessica had any enemies?"

"Maaaaaybe," Annabella said, suddenly vague and evasive. Then she batted her eyelashes. "Oh, I guess I can tell *you*. You're not the police." She glanced from side to side again and even took a look behind her. "There was at least one guy who didn't like her. He came in here one night after we were closed. Jessica didn't know I was here because I'd left for the night, but I came back because I'd forgotten my purse. I went in through the back of the store, so I never saw him, but I heard him yelling at her."

"What did he say?" I turned to look at her, abandoning all attempts to seem like a scarf shopper.

"Well, I couldn't hear all of it, but I know he said she'd broken an agreement they had. And I think he warned her to stay away from New Orleans. He also said something about the London College of Fashion, and it almost sounded like Jessica had gone there. The weird thing is that Jessica never mentioned going to that school. It's not even on her company profile."

I shared her confusion. Leaving a prestigious institution like the London College of Fashion off your famous design house company profile was like intentionally not telling your doctor that you had cancer. It just didn't make sense. "Maybe you misunderstood."

"No." She broke the thread in half. "I'm positive the guy said she was a student. I mean, how could I mistake the London College of Fashion? Jimmy Choo went there."

"Of course." I said it as though I were an expert in Jimmy Choo's pedigree. "Did she say anything back to the guy?"

"Just that LaMarca had offered her amaaaaazing incentives on the condition that she manage the New Orleans store for a year. Sales were down, so they wanted a Louisiana native to try to turn it around. I heard her tell him that she wouldn't be in town for long, but he said he wanted her gone right away."

"Maybe it was an ex-boyfriend. You know how demanding men can be."

"I don't know."

I followed her bulging gaze as she glanced at someone who appeared to be a manager and then resumed the scarf search. "How long ago did this happen?"

"A few months ago, so I doubt there's any connection to her death. Hey, do you like any of these?" Annabella shoved four yellow scarves at me.

"That bright yellow one."

"Great. Should I put this aside for you while you continue shopping, ma'am?"

I could tell by her shift to a more professional tone that the gossip fest had ended. "No, I think that's it for today." I noted the two hundred forty-dollar price tag on the scarf with a sinking feeling. *Well, if I go without food this month, I might finally lose that twenty pounds.*

As Annabella bounced off to the register in her pink bobby socks and dingy white Keds, I pulled my wallet from my bag and accidentally upended my coin purse in the process.

"*Mannaggia.*" I muttered the Italian version of *damn* as my change spilled onto the gold carpet. I bent down to retrieve a quarter that had rolled underneath the base of the first scarf rack on the right, and I dislodged a small, hard object. It was a brownish-white bead the size of a hazelnut, and it was carved from ivory or some type of bone in the form of an eerie-looking skull. *Could it have something to do with Jessica's death?*

I checked to make sure no one was watching as I pocketed the bead and headed to the cash register.

"A SKULL BEAD? THAT'S FREAKIN' awesome," David exclaimed as I pulled the bead from my pocket during an impromptu meeting in Veronica's office. He grabbed the bead with his long, skeletal fingers. "Hey, this looks exactly like one of those beads from Marie Laveau's House of Voodoo."

"Marie Laveau?" I took the bead. "The voodoo queen? Father John told me she was dead."

"She is." Veronica leaned back in her maraschino cherry-colored leather chair. "It's a voodoo store on Bourbon Street that uses her name."

David nodded. "Yeah, my buddy Alex has a bracelet made of those beads hanging from the rearview mirror of his Honda. He said he got them from there."

"Really?" Veronica sat forward. She had always been one to take an interest in jewelry, even of the voodoo variety. "Do you know what these beads signify?"

"Nah, you'd have to ask the kid who works at the store. I'd check it out though, cause that place is rad," David said in college speak. "They have voodoo dolls, chicken feet, gator heads, all kinds of potions. It's badass in there."

It sounded more beastly than badass. "Potions? For what?"

He shrugged. "Lots of stuff, like love potions and ones that'll help you score some cash. There's even one that'll help you beat the law, like in court."

I remembered the pound cake left for Saint Expedite. "There sure is a lot of voodoo that centers around winning court cases. I wonder if they make one that will help you *solve* a case."

"Speaking of solving cases," Veronica stood and removed a pale pink trench coat with a ruffled collar from the coat rack near her desk, "it's getting late, and tomorrow is Saturday. But there are a few things you and I will have to do this weekend, Franki. First, I need you to stop by Marie Laveau's sometime before Monday. If the murderer dropped the skull bead—and that's a big *if*—then we need to find out whether it came from that store."

"No problem." I kind of wanted to take a look at those love

potions David had mentioned while I was there. Not that I believed in that sort of thing, of course—at least, not completely. "Do you want me to call the police too?"

David stared at me, motionless.

Veronica blinked. "What for?"

"To tell them about the skull bead. If it does turn out to be connected to the Evans case, then it's evidence."

"We're not required to share evidence with the police." Veronica spoke slowly, like I was a child. "Just like they're not obligated to turn over any evidence to us."

"Oh, right. I know that." I did my best to sound like I'd simply forgotten that not-so-minor detail.

An awkward silence followed.

I rose and went to the door. "I'll go call the London College of Fashion to verify that Jessica was a student there."

"It's too late to call London now, so I'll take care of that first thing Monday morning." Veronica slipped on her coat. "Anyhow, the other thing you and I have to do tomorrow is scour local shops for that scarf. If we find out where it came from, we might be able to track down who bought it. Besides, all this talk of scarves and London has put me in the mood to do some shopping."

At nine p.m., I slid into a lavender-scented bubble bath in my pink-claw foot tub, and my phone rang. "Figures." I glanced at the display, which was face up on the toilet lid. "Aaaaand it's my parents."

I considered letting it go to voicemail but decided to answer. I would need a relaxing bath after a call from home. And maybe a bottle of Chianti. I took a deep breath and picked up.

"Hello?" I tried to conceal the anxiety in my voice.

"Francesca, I got-a you two." My nonna spoke with the cadence of someone who'd just crossed the finish line of a long, arduous marathon.

"Two what, Nonna?"

"Dates, Franki. Dates. *Mamma mia.*"

"Only two?" The question came out before I could fully think through the ramifications.

"It's-a hard work-a finding a date for a zitella who is-a twenty-nine years of age. Give-a me a break-a! Besides, you been around-a the block a time or two, *eh*? And you don't even go to church. *Dio mio!* I'm-a no Mother Theresa here. I don't work-a no miracles."

There was no point in arguing. Grandmothers in contemporary Sicily had modernized with the times, but those like my nonna, who had immigrated to the United States in the first half of the twentieth century, still mentally lived in Fascist Italy. We granddaughters could try to challenge their dictatorial rule, but we knew it was a futile and even risky endeavor. "So, who are these guys?"

"Bruno and Pio."

Brown and Pius, I translated. With names like those, they had to be the sons, grandsons, or nephews of her Sicilian friends. I just hoped that they didn't have the stereotypical Sicilian-American worldview, which necessarily precluded the best that modernity had to offer women—things like working outside the home, eating pre-made food, and wearing brightly colored clothing.

"Franki, are you still-a there?"

"Yes, Nonna." I tried to come up with a reason that would prevent me from going out with those guys. For lack of a better excuse, I opted for the truth. "Listen, I appreciate you trying to help me, but I don't feel comfortable going on blind dates."

There was a long, frustrated sigh on the other end of the

phone followed by silence—a sure sign that my nonna was summoning her inner matriarch in preparation for battle. And a Sicilian grandma was a formidable opponent, especially if she was your father's *mamma*. In that case, a girl couldn't rely on her dad for support because Sicilian mothers played their sons like finely tuned mandolins, and my dad was no exception.

"Francesca, you go on-a these dates, or I go to my grave-a."

In one savvy maneuver, my nonna had won the battle before it had begun. If I didn't go on the dates, she would tell my father that I was killing her. And my father, like a good Italian son, would tell me that I was being selfish for making my nonna so unhappy and guilt me into complying with her demands. There was nothing left to do but feign acquiescence, and then try to find an alternate method of escape.

"Okay, Nonna." I glanced at Napoleon, who'd entered the bathroom with one ear cocked to listen in. "What can you tell me about these guys?"

"Bruno, he is-a the son of-a my friend Santina. She's-a the one who hurt-a her back in that terrible car accident."

My ear pricked up like Napoleon's. "What car accident?"

"The one where Bruno was-a driving her to mass, and he run-a the red light."

I seized upon Bruno's less-than-ideal driving skills as an excuse to get out of the date. "He doesn't sound like a safe driver. I'm not sure that I should be going anywhere with him."

"Don't-a worry, Franki. He don't have-a the driver license no more. Besides, you gonna meet-a him at-a his house."

Foiled again. "I don't know this guy, so I'd rather meet him at a neutral place like a restaurant," I countered as I extended my hand and stroked the fur on Napoleon's head.

"No, because his *mamma* she gonna cook-a the dinner."

"Nonna, I'm too old to be chaperoned on a date by someone's mother."

"Franki, she's-a no gonna chaperone. Bruno live-a with his *mamma.*"

Of course he does—like all single Italian men.

"And he is a nice-a boy because he take-a good care of his *mamma.*" Her tone reflected her utmost respect. "And he don't have-a no kids."

My nonna was clearly trying to sell me on Bruno, which meant she was hiding something.

"How old is he, and what does he do for a living?" My voice was wary, and Napoleon's eye narrowed as though he were wary too.

"He is-a thirty-nine, and he work-a for the New Orleans Saints-a for twenty years."

My nonna was well aware that as a Texas girl I was a *huge* football fan, and I was already envisioning a date that included box seats at the Superdome with catered Cajun food and a few Hurricanes thrown in. But I wondered if she knew that the Saints were a football team and not an association of Catholic martyrs. "What does he do for the Saints, exactly?"

"He manage a food-a stand at-a the stadium."

So much for the box seats. "What about Pio?"

"Pio, he is-a forty, and he is-a the nephew of Luisa, who is-a the cousin of my cousin, Agatina."

A relative? This is an easy out. "Nonna, I'm not going to date anyone I'm related to, no matter how old I get."

Napoleon must have felt comforted by my strong stance, because he closed his eyes and curled up on the bathroom rug.

"Franki, he don't have-a our blood. And his-a *famiglia* they own-a the funeral parlor in-a my town, Porto Empedocle."

Of course they do, because that sort of thing makes my skin crawl. "Does he live at home with his mother too?"

"No, he live at-a the YN-aCA."

"The YMCA, Nonna. And why does he live *there*?"

Napoleon reopened one eye, backing up my suspicion.

"He can't-a live with his *mamma* because he pay-a for her to live at-a the retirement home, and he also have-a to pay-a the alimonies to his ex-wife and kids."

"He's divorced, *and* he has kids?"

"*Sì*, five. But he has a good-a job, *eh* Franki?"

She threw the job part in, knowing full well that an invalid mother, an ex-wife, and five kids definitely qualified as baggage.

"Nonna, I don't mean to sound like a snob, but I'd rather not date a man who works at a funeral home. You know that sort of thing is disturbing to me."

Napoleon opened both eyes and raised his head. If he could've talked, he would've agreed with me.

"Franki, he work-a for the sanitation department."

So did Tony Soprano. But if Pio lives at the Y, then I can rule out the Mafia. Well, maybe. "I have an idea. Why don't you give me their phone numbers so I can call them?" I asked, knowing that I never would. It was a weak last-ditch attempt, but it was all I had.

"I already gave-a them your number. And your street address and your address for the emails too."

Nonna had covered her bases. Hers was no ordinary act of war—she'd declared a full-on state of emergency.

"I gave-a them-a Veronica's number too. It's-a better to be safe than-a sorry, *no*? And you've been-a sorry for a long-a time."

Okay, that's it. Time to cut the call short, with or without my dating exit strategy. "Nonna, I'll wait for Bruno and Pio to call. Give my love to Mom and Dad. *Ciao ciao!*"

I hung up and did what any self-respecting Italian-American girl would do following a crushing defeat from her nonna—I climbed from the bubble bath and headed straight for the kitchen where I opened the pantry door and grabbed a bottle of Chianti.

As I downed my first glass of the rich, red liquid, I wondered whether my dating prospects were so grim that I needed my grandmother to set me up with reckless mamma's boys who worked in concessions and divorced mobsters who lived at the Y. After all, I wasn't bad looking, and even though I'd gained a few pounds, I was trying to lose weight.

I poured myself another glass of wine and grabbed some fontina cheese from the refrigerator. Plus, I refused to believe that a single woman had to raise the white flag of dating surrender at the age of twenty-nine. To thwart the intentions of my nonna and her army of Sicilian suitors, I needed to find a guy and quick. And I couldn't lie about it because my nonna definitely had her sources.

I took a swig straight from the bottle and resolved to pay another visit to Pontchartrain Bank. If it was between Nonna's picks or Bradley, who may or may not have been flirting with me, I'd give the sexy bank manager a second chance—that is, unless he had a Sicilian mamma or nonna.

6

"Veronica, are you alive?" I crouched beneath her tiny front porch to avoid the pouring rain and knocked on her apartment door for the third time.

"Be right there!"

"Okay." I felt a tinge of apprehension. I'd been in New Orleans for almost a week and still hadn't seen the inside of Veronica's apartment. When we were in college, she had a Cinderella-style dorm room that had always made me uncomfortable. I could deal with the pink—even though I'd always been a purple girl myself—but her delicate princess furniture made me feel like Alice in Wonderland after she'd eaten the cake and grown to the size of a giantess.

Veronica threw open the door, and both she and Hercules were dressed in matching orange rain gear. "Sorry it took me so long. I could *not* get Hercules's galoshes on."

"No worries. Are you ready to go murder scarf shopping?"

"Yeah, I'm just going to run him outside for a sec. To do his business," she whispered and walked Hercules past me and out into the yard.

"I'll wait inside." As I turned to close her door behind me, I caught a glimpse of the living room and did a double take. Instead of the familiar princess furnishings, I saw chunky, animal print-upholstered furniture made of dark wood—the legs, arms, and backs of which had been carved to look like tiki idols. Adding to the bizarre décor were tropical curtains, lamps with fuzzy orange shades, lime green wall-to-wall shag carpeting and enough plants to simulate a rain forest. It looked like our landlady Glenda had bought out the contents of Elvis Presley's Jungle Room at Graceland on one of her antique-shopping trips.

Veronica returned with Hercules and removed her raincoat. "What do you think of my new couch?"

"Th-this is *your* furniture?"

"Yes." She beamed. "Do you like it?"

"Uh, it's wild." I took a seat in an armchair that had what looked like an angry island god perched atop its back.

"I know." Veronica kicked off her galoshes and freed Hercules from his teensy galoshes and itty-bitty raincoat, which looked a lot like a doggie straitjacket. "Franki, I think I've discovered something important about the Evans case."

"What?" My tone was hesitant. I was still trying to come to grips with her Polynesian Primitive style.

"Take a look at this." Veronica retrieved a crime scene photo from her lava rock coffee table and shoved it under my nose. "I don't know how I missed it before." She pointed to the photo, which featured the yellow-trimmed scarf that had apparently been used to strangle Jessica.

I scrutinized the edge of the scarf, which Veronica was jabbing at with a perfect pink nail. "I don't see anything."

"Here, use this." Veronica handed me a magnifying glass in the shape of a hibiscus flower.

As I looked through the lens, I saw something thin and white where she was pointing. "What is that?"

Her eyes glowed as bright as the lampshades. "It's a fine barb."

"Um, okay," I said sarcastically. "I guess you could call the scarf 'fine garb'—if you work at the Renaissance Fair."

Veronica rolled her eyes. "I said 'fine *barb*.' It's the piece of plastic used to attach a price tag to a garment."

I blinked. "You *would* know what that thing is called."

"Yeah, me and the millions of people who work in retail." She took the photo and magnifying glass from my hands.

"So, what do you think that fine barb thingy means?" I leaned over to stroke Hercules's fluffy fur.

She sat in the tiny armchair. "It means that the scarf was new."

"Why do you say that? Someone could have left it there without noticing."

"What kind of person leaves a fine barb on clothing and doesn't notice?"

"Beats me," I said, thinking of all the times I'd unknowingly walked around with stickers from the store still on my clothes, not to mention the occasions when I'd put on my underwear or even my T-shirt inside out. *Come to think of it, had I managed to put everything on the right way today?* I did a quick spot check and then returned my attention to the case. "But, so what if it was new?"

"I'm convinced that someone brought a brand-new scarf there on purpose." She crossed her arms with conviction.

"You mean, as a gift? But remember, Annabella said that Jessica hated cheap scarves. So why would someone bring her a scarf they knew she wouldn't like?" I smoothed Hercules's fur to see what he would look like without his Pomeranian poof.

"Maybe the person who brought it to her didn't know that. If it was a man—well, you know how clueless men can be about clothing."

"And if it was a woman, she would probably know that Jessica wouldn't like the scarf."

"Precisely."

Veronica seemed to understand everything perfectly. I, on the other hand, couldn't figure out how a gift-buying *faux pas* could solve a murder.

"So what do you make of it?" I leaned back and assessed Hercules. With his fur flattened, he looked a lot like a Jorge.

"If you're talking about Hercules's fur, I think it looks awful. But if you mean the scarf, I'm not sure yet. But something tells me that if we find out why someone gave her that particular scarf, we may have our answer."

"Well, the fact that the scarf was new should make it easier for us to track down."

Hercules struggled out of my arms and ran to Veronica.

"Correct." Veronica repoofed his fur and gave him a reassuring pat. "So, I've made a list of local stores and their addresses. We'll have to split up to cover more ground."

"Split up? That's no fun."

"Francesca Lucia Amato." Veronica shook her head. "A day of shopping is *always* fun."

After spending several hours scouring boutiques in the Canal Street area, I decided that it was time to break for a late lunch. The rain had stopped, and it was shaping up to be a sunny and unseasonably warm day. Fortunately, Pontchartrain Bank was open from noon until six on Saturdays. So, I figured I'd stop by before grabbing a bite—to check on the status of my ATM card, of course.

I entered the lobby and scanned the room for Bradley. There was no sign of him, but I did see Corinne. She beckoned to me from her teller window, and she looked pale and despondent, like Tinker Bell without her pixie dust.

I approached her window. "Is everything okay?"

"Franki, you are a private investigator, *non*?"

"Yes. Why?"

Her eyes filled with tears. "Yesterday I come home from work, and my *petite Bijou*, she is missing."

I wasn't entirely sure who or what a *petite Bijou* was, so I hazarded a guess. "Is Bijou your pet?"

"*Oui*, she is my *chien—pardon*, my dog. She was a gift from Thierry." Corinne choked down a sob." She is just a puppy."

"What kind of dog is she?"

"She is a *bichon frise*." She reached for her handbag under the counter and pulled out her phone. She pulled up a picture of Bijou. He looked a lot like a white powder puff with black eyes and a black nose. "Franki, can you please help me find her? I pay whatever you want."

"Of course." I examined the picture. "How did the thief get into your house? Had any of the doors been tampered with? Or a window?"

"*Non*." She blew her nose with a honk. "I live in an *apparte-ment* on ze fours floor."

"Was anything else taken?" I handed the phone back to her.

"Only *Bijou*." She wailed and covered her eyes.

"So, it sounds like someone went there just to steal her. Corinne, the last time I was here, you said that you and Thierry had broken up. Are the two of you back together?"

"*Non*. We are *fini*." She put her head in her hands.

"Do you think he could have taken Bijou?"

"It is possible." She raised her tear-stained face. "He still has ze key, and he is very angry wis me. But he loves *Bijou*, so I don't know if he would do zat to her."

"Does anyone else have a key? Like your parents or a friend?"

"No, but in ze *appartement* office, zey have a key."

I pulled a notepad and pen from my purse. "Where does Thierry live?"

"He stay wis a friend named Brady Reiff who lives near ze *Place d'Armes*. I don't know ze *adresse*."

"Where is the Place Darm?" I asked in my very best Texan-French.

"Ah, *pardon*. It is ze French name for Jackson Square, ze park by ze Mississippi River. You know, when Thierry live wis me, he take *Bijou* zere on Saturday afternoons for a walk."

"Then that will be the first place I look. I need you to text or email me the picture of Bijou and a few pictures of Thierry so that I know what he looks like." I wrote my contact information on a piece of paper for her.

"*Tout de suite*. But Franki, can I help you with somesing? You came to ze bank…"

"No, I just wanted to check on my ATM card." I tore the paper from my pad and handed it to her.

"Ah, *oui*. It came yesterday afternoon. I was going to call you, but Mr. Hartmann say he would do it. I get it for you. *Un moment*."

"*Non*," I shouted in French, not wanting to leave even the slightest bit of room for doubt. Nothing and no one was coming between me and a call from Bradley Hartmann.

Corinne blinked, confused.

"There's no time to lose. I have to get to work on your case right away," I gushed, trying to cover for my outburst. I shoved my notepad and pen into my purse and started to leave. "*Au revoir*."

"Wait."

I turned to look at Corinne.

"*Merci beaucoup*." Her big blue eyes were full of gratitude.

"*Prego*." I thanked her in Italian in keeping with the foreign language theme. "And don't worry, Bijou will be back before you know it."

As I turned and headed for the door, I again scoured the room for Bradley, using my peripheral vision so as not to seem too obvious. But there was no sign of him, which either meant that I was a bad investigator—entirely possible—or that he had the day off.

Outside I glanced at my watch and saw that it was two o'clock. Marie Laveau's was open until one thirty in the morning on Saturdays, so I had plenty of time to stake out Jackson Square before going to investigate the skull bead. But first I would need to let Veronica know that I'd taken a new case. I pulled my phone from my purse and dialed her number.

"Hey, Franki."

Veronica sounded extra upbeat, probably because she was shopping. "Any luck?"

"Well, I've found plenty of things for me, but I haven't found the scarf, if that's what you mean. What about you?"

I leaned against a lamppost. "No scarf, but I did get a case."

"How?"

"A bank teller I met named Corinne wants us to find her stolen dog. I know we're in the middle of the Evans investigation, but I'm thinking maybe her ex-boyfriend took the dog, so it should be a fairly simple case to solve."

"Way to go."

I breathed a sigh of relief. "So you don't mind?"

"Mind?" She giggled. "Private investigators work multiple cases all of the time. Besides, we could use a bank contact."

"What for?"

"At the moment, for the Evans case. Ryan Hunter seems to think that Jessica Evans had more money than she should. Your teller might be able to help us find out if someone was paying her."

"I'll keep that in mind. Corinne is really nice, so she might be willing to help us. Speaking of the Evans case, I'm going to Marie Laveau's later today. Right now I have to follow up on a lead about the dog."

She sighed with mock despair. "I guess I'll have to go it alone in the scarf search, then."

"You're a real trooper, Veronica." I'll call you later with an update." I closed the call and headed toward my car. I had parked at the office, which was just down the street from Jackson Square. But I needed to go home and get Napoleon. He and I were going undercover.

"WE'RE on the clock now, Napoleon." I shot him a somber look as we walked along the sidewalk toward Jackson Square Park in the French Quarter. "And we're Texans, so we've got to go big or go home."

He turned and lifted a paw, confused.

I realized how my words of encouragement must've sounded. "I'm not talking about doing your business—or going back to the apartment. You dogs are so literal."

He resumed walking—his version of a shrug.

I scanned the area. I was fairly certain that Thierry wouldn't bring a stolen dog to the park, but it was as good a place as any to search. First I wanted to case the streets that bordered the square because they were more popular with pet-walking pedestrians than the park itself. Also, I had to keep Napoleon moving as I investigated the area because, as dogs go, he wasn't the ideal park companion. Either he didn't understand the concept of fetch, or he just plain didn't want to play the game. And like the French conqueror after whom he was named, Napoleon was territorial and made darn sure the other dogs knew it. On the plus side, he was the perfect cover for staking out a prospective dog thief.

We arrived at the heavy iron fence that enclosed Jackson Square Park, and I peered through the slats. It was fairly empty and really lovely with its brilliant pink and yellow flowers, perfectly manicured lawns, and gorgeous old oak trees. In the center there was an equestrian statue of Major General Andrew Jackson, commemorating the Battle of New Orleans. Overlooking the park was the Cathedral-Basilica of St. Louis King of France, the oldest Catholic cathedral in continual use in the United States, with its stunning gray and white spires.

Before entering the park, I led Napoleon across the street to Washington Artillery Park on the Mississippi River. A crowd had gathered at the small amphitheater near its replica Civil War cannon to watch a couple of boys tap dance, but there was no sign of Thierry or Bijou.

We walked back toward the Jackson Square Park entrance and turned left onto St. Peter Street, which ran along the park's west side and was home to the famous French Market with the yellow-gold archway. I stopped to window-shop at a cute little jewelry store called Ooh La La. After all, I had to look the part of a local on a Saturday afternoon stroll with her dog.

Next, we took a right onto Chartres Street, on the north side of the park. We were immediately thrust into the throng of tourists who had gathered to see the street musicians, mimes, and open-air artist colony. I enjoyed the work of street musicians and artists, but not the mimes. The appeal of painting oneself monochrome and silently pretending to do something like juggle or cry was lost on me. As I browsed the caricatures, portraits, and landscape paintings displayed on the iron fence that encircled the park, I did my best to ignore a pesky silver-colored mime who pretended to give me what I can only assume was a pretend flower.

After scouring the masses on Chartres, we turned right onto St. Ann Street. Napoleon pulled at the leash and growled at some tarot card readers who'd set up their little tables in front of the shops.

"Hey, Dog Whisperer." A genie wannabe with a hoop earring and a head scarf rose from his tiny card table. "How about you control your deranged mutt?"

I looked him in the blue-eyeshadowed eyes. "Let's go, Napoleon. I don't trust these sham fortune-tellers either."

A tarot reader in a top hat and tails scowled and stood in solidarity with the genie.

Before they could put a curse on us, or whatever tarot card readers did, I dragged Napoleon down the street to the gourmet and kitchen shop Creole Delicacies. I tucked him under my arm and popped inside to buy some pecan pralines—the riverfront streetcar box of twelve, to be precise. I didn't need the calories, but I considered sampling local specialties to be an essential part of my cover.

With pralines in hand—and in mouth—I decided it was time to stake out the park. We took a right onto Decatur Street and entered through the iron gates. We walked down the park's gravel-lined walkways, and I kept my eyes peeled for Thierry and the powder puff.

Napoleon kept his peeled for pigeons and squirrels.

We circled the park a few times, and I sat on a bench near the statue of Andrew Jackson. To pass the time, I pulled out my phone and snapped a few pictures of the statue and the St. Louis Cathedral. Then I reviewed the pictures that Corinne had sent of Bijou and Thierry. The photos of Thierry were blurred, so I wasn't sure if I would be able to identify him if he walked by dog-less. But the plan was to stay put for an hour or so, munching on pralines and watching joggers, people pushing baby strollers, and dog-walkers.

A small, fluffy white puppy appeared from behind a giant oak tree, and I dropped the last praline in the dirt. "*Mannaggia*."

Napoleon grabbed it before I could invoke the five-second rule.

With a sad sigh, I pulled out my phone and studied the photo of Bijou. As I looked from the photo to the dog, a big, strapping man with reddish hair emerged from behind the tree and scooped the tiny puppy into his powerful arms.

"Poo, poo, poo." He snuggled his ruddy red, freckled face into the little white ball of fur. "Poo, poo, poo."

I wasn't sure whether he was cooing or telling the dog to go, but either way it was embarrassing.

He turned the dog in his arms, and I spotted a tattoo on his right bicep. I looked again at the picture of Thierry. He seemed to have light brown hair, not red, and he wore a sweater, so it was impossible to tell whether he had a tattoo.

I dialed Corinne's number while the guy made smooching sounds at the dog. *Whoever this dude is, he sure loves that fluffball.*

"*Allo*, Franki?"

"Hey, Corinne." I spoke in a whisper. "I'm at the park at Jackson Square. There's a white puppy here that could be Bijou—"

"Really? What does it look like?"

"It's definitely a bichon frise, but the photos you sent of Thierry aren't very clear. And the guy who's here with the dog looks, well, Irish."

"Zat is him."

"What? Thierry is just Terry? I thought he was French." I glanced nervously at the guy, but he didn't seem to have heard me.

"No, he is Irish. His surname is O'Callaghan. Oh, Franki, it is him, *non*?"

"There's an easy way to find out. Does Thierry, er, Terry, have a tattoo on his right bicep?"

"*Oui.* It is a leprechaun. From ze *americain* cereal."

"Wait a second. Do you mean Lucky? The Lucky Charms leprechaun?"

"*Voilà.* You know him?"

"I know him well, Corinne." My tone had turned grim. Terry was kind of lame. An Irishman with a Lucky the Leprechaun tattoo was like an Italian with a tattoo of Super Mario. Pitiful. Notre Dame's Fighting Irish mascot would have made a way better stereotypical tattoo, especially for a big, muscular guy like the one romping around before me with the white powder puff.

"Franki, are you still zere?" She sounded panicked.

"Yes, sorry. I got distracted for a moment."

"Zis man, does he have ze lucky leprechaun?"

I turned, and the guy was walking the dog. His right arm was extended from holding the leash, so I had a clear shot of the tattoo.

Lucky.

I would know that leprechaun anywhere. "It's him, all right. Get down here right away."

7

"Corinne might look like Tinker Bell, but she definitely doesn't have her speed," I grumbled to myself. Twenty minutes had passed since I'd called and told her to come to Jackson Square. Terry wasn't going to stay at the park forever, and I didn't want to have to confront him over Bijou. After all, the guy was the size of The Jolly Green Giant.

I sent Corinne a text asking for an ETA. Then I looked up.

Terry and Bijou walked toward the exit.

"Dangit. I could die for what I'm about to do, and I'm not even getting paid for it." I sighed and chased down Corinne's giant ex, stepping in front of him. "Terry O'Callaghan? Stop where you are."

He lowered his eyelids but did as I instructed.

It occurred to me that if his whole body were green like his Lucky the Leprechaun tattoo, he would look a lot like The Incredible Hulk.

"Do I know you?" His voice was soft, but dangerous.

"No. I'm a private investigator, and I know that dog is stolen. So if you leave this park, I'm going to have to make a citizen's arrest."

He blinked. And then he began to cry like a baby—a large Irish baby. He sobbed and blubbered in a mix of English and Gaelic, calling Bijou his "wee *aingeal*" and "little *leanbh*," which I knew were terms of endearment from all the *Murder, She Wrote* episodes set in Ireland.

I took the leash from his boxing glove-sized hand, and I saw Corinne running toward us. Her face was drawn.

"Thierry! What is ze matter? Why you are crying?"

Terry's sobs turned to wails. And oddly enough, he sounded exactly like a howling dog.

Corinne wrapped her tiny Tinker Bell arms around his Hulk-like waist. "Zere, zere. Everysing is okay."

Open-mouthed, I wondered what I was witnessing. Then I left the odd duo to work out their differences.

I headed in the direction of the office to drop off Napoleon before going over to Bourbon Street to Marie Laveau's. Although I was hungry, I was going to skip dinner thanks to the pralines I'd eaten for lunch while staking out the park. Mardi Gras was just around the corner, and Veronica had told me that the average New Orleanian gained six pounds during the season, which meant I was sure to gain twelve. And frankly, I couldn't afford to gain any more weight because I was already bursting from my clothes, and I was in no position to buy a new wardrobe.

Trying to drive thoughts of food from my mind—a hard thing to do in the Quarter near dinnertime—I walked up Decatur Street toward Saint Ann. But after only about five minutes, I stopped dead. Right in front of me at an outdoor table at Market Café sat none other than Bradley Hartmann. This was my chance to work my date-getting magic. I'd always been pretty good at getting a guy—I just had trouble keeping one.

I stood up straight, sucked in my stomach, and sauntered past his table, but he didn't notice me because he was absorbed in *The Times-Picayune*. There were some empty tables near where Bradley sat, so I hurried to the hostess. In my haste, I bumped into a burly waitress with short, electric-blue hair, a sleeve tattoo, and triple-pierced eyebrows, causing her to drop a tray loaded with food.

"You just cost me a tip, lady." Her tone was as tough as her look.

"I'm so sorry." I bent down to help her pick up the dishes.

"Why don't you let me take care of this? I think you've done enough already."

I looked up from the pile of broken dishes and read her nametag—Charity. *Talk about a misnomer.* "Like I said, Charity, I'm sorry." I put another plate shard on the tray. "And I can take care of that tip."

"Like *I* said, lady, I got this." She shot me an aggressive look.

"Well, if you insist." I rose to my feet. "Listen, I'm really pressed for time, and I don't see your hostess. Would you mind if I seated myself?"

Her pierced brows twitched. "A member of the staff has to seat you. Restaurant policy."

"All right. Can you seat me then, please?"

She stared at me for a moment and clenched her teeth. "Let me get you a menu."

By then I was in such a hurry that I didn't want to wait. So I blew right past her and made a beeline for the banker. "Bradley!"

Apparently, he wasn't used to women shouting his name in restaurants, because he jumped and knocked over his beer, spilling gold liquid all over the bulk of his newspaper.

"I'm so sorry." I sounded like a broken record. "I didn't mean to startle you."

He gave an ironic smile as he rose to his feet. "I didn't want any more of that beer, anyway."

Charity, who had been standing with arms crossed by what was supposed to be my table, rolled her eyes and came over to help us clean up the spill with a towel. She wadded up the wet newspaper and pointed to a table far away. "Your menu is on the table *over there*."

"Thanks, Charity," I said none-too-appreciatively and willed her to leave. For reasons I couldn't fathom, she seemed adamant that I was going to sit at the table she'd selected for me, because she wouldn't budge. And I wasn't budging either.

Bradley, who couldn't help but notice the standoff between Charity and me, came to my rescue. "It's Franki, right?"

I nodded.

"Would you like to join me? I ordered a few minutes ago, so I'm sure there's still time to add your order." He winked at Charity to smooth things over.

"I would love to." I cast Charity a triumphant look. "But I'm not hungry," I lied, hoping he couldn't hear the growling—make that the roaring—of the mighty lion who had chosen that moment to take up residence in my stomach. "I was just going to have a glass of Pinot Grigio."

"So, just the wine?" Charity asked.

To my dismay, I remembered that I was still on the clock—and on a diet. "Make that a cup of coffee. Decaf."

She looked me up and down, as though weighing me with her eyes, and went to place my order.

Bradley turned to me. "You've really got a way with the staff, don't you?"

Okay, so maybe he wasn't the best choice for a date. I opted to change the subject to safer ground. "So, what have you been up to today?"

"Errands mostly. And Trixi and I took a walk along the river."

"Trixi?" I felt as though I'd just been kicked in the stomach by that ornery lion.

"Yes, she's my devoted companion." His eyes were twinkling.

"Oh." I was taken aback by my disappointment. After all, I wasn't really interested in the guy. I just needed a date to ward off my nonna.

Bradley looked under the table. "There's my girl."

I followed his gaze and saw a darling cairn terrier with wheaten fur lying at his feet. Of course, cairns were my favorite breed, but I hadn't exactly pegged Bradley as a cute little dog guy. It was definitely a point in his favor.

"She's adorable." I reached down to pet her.

Without raising her head, Trixi lifted one side of her mouth and flashed her teeth at me.

I recoiled in surprise. She wasn't as sweet as she looked. But then again, maybe she was timid and needed a little time to get to know to me. I acted as though nothing had happened with Bradley's beloved canine. "I have a cairn too. His name is Napoleon because he's small in size but big in personality."

"Cairns are great dogs, aren't they? I like them because they're spunky and independent. That's the way I like my women too." He shot me a wicked grin.

Charming. I shifted in my chair. The movement angered Trixi, who snapped at my shoe with the speed of a snake. I yanked my foot away. "You have to be careful with cairns, though."

"Yeah, but not with my Trixi." Bradley reached down to stroke her head. She rolled onto her back exposing her butterball belly. "She's an angel."

I glared under the table. *More like a con artist.* "She's something all right."

Charity the waitress returned and gave Bradley his sandwich, a po' boy filled with oysters that had been battered and deep-fried to a golden brown.

She placed the cup of decaf on the table. "Can I get you guys anything else?" Charity looked straight at me. "Like, for example, a meal instead of a cheap cup of coffee?"

I met her gaze with a hint of a glare. "Nope, we're doing great."

"Awesome." She slammed down a plastic tray with the bill and walked away.

Of course she'd left only one peppermint.

"This sandwich is huge." Bradley picked up half. "Would you like some?"

"No thanks." I devoured the po' boy with my eyes. "I couldn't even *think* of food right now," I fibbed, pouring four Splenda packets into my coffee in hopes of adding some density.

"Well, okay, then." He took a hearty bite.

I was starting to think that Bradley knew I was hungry and was rubbing it in. Trying to avoid watching him chew, I took a big, hungry sip of my decaf. It was much hotter than I'd realized, and it scalded my mouth. "Mmm," I moaned, tightening my lips to avoid spitting blistering hot coffee onto Bradley like an erupting volcano. I opened my mouth a crack to let some steam out. "Aawwhh."

"Are you all right?"

"Ow-huh." I forced the burning liquid down in one fiery gulp. "Iss juss so...goouh," I said, avoiding any contact been my tongue and the roof of my mouth.

"Oh, okay. Listen, I was planning on calling you—"

"You were?" I interrupted, forgetting about my scorched mouth—and my dignity.

He flashed a mischievous smile. "Your ATM card finally arrived."

"Right. My ATM card. That's what I thought you'd be calling about." I feigned an intense interest in stirring my coffee.

"I could mail it to you, if you'd like." He took another bite of po' boy.

"Oh no." I wanted to be sure I got that card in person. "What I mean is, I need it before that. I'll just drop by the bank and pick it up."

"Well, the bank's actually open until six today, so you could make it over there in time if you leave after you finish your coffee."

I detected a hint of teasing in his voice. Bradley seemed to think I was into him, which was utterly ridiculous. My interest was strictly business—family business. "It can wait until Monday. I mean, I have lots to do today."

He looked amused. "Anything fun on the agenda?"

"Well, after this I have to go to the voodoo store."

Bradley stopped in mid-bite. "Mind if I ask why?"

"For a case I'm investigating."

"That's right, Corinne said you were a PI. So tell me," he cocked an eyebrow, "which Charlie's Angel are you most like?"

Resentment boiled in my belly—or maybe it was the coffee. He was obviously insinuating that I was both a dilettante *and* a sex object, but I wasn't play-acting at my job. "Well, if you must know I..."

Bradley reached out and freed a strand of my hair that had gotten stuck on my lipgloss, his fingertips lightly grazing my check and my neck.

A shiver ran down my traitorous spine.

He leaned back and draped an arm over the chair next to him. "You were saying?"

"Um, what?" I didn't remember anything before those fingertips.

He flashed one of his fabulous smiles. "About your work?"

"Oh, yeah. That." I shot him an annoyed look. "Well, not just anyone can be a PI. It's a dangerous job. For instance, I just wrapped up a dicey missing dog case, and now I'm investigating a *murder*."

"Which one?"

"The Jessica Evans murder." I gave a solemn nod for effect.

He massaged his chin. "That was such a terrible thing. She was a client at the bank."

"She was?" I asked, surprised.

"Yeah, but I didn't know her very well. She only came in once a month, and she was pretty reserved."

"Really? Just once a month?"

"To make a deposit."

Charity barged up to the table. "Sorry to interrupt." She looked anything but regretful. "My shift actually ended at five, so I'm, uh, on my way out."

Bradley looked at his watch. "I didn't realize how late it was." He stood and pulled his wallet from his back pocket. "I've got a few more errands to run, so I'd better get going."

"Yeah, I'd better be on my way too. I've got to get over to the voodoo store." I shot a pointed look at Charity.

"Franki, I'd like to hear more about your work sometime." He handed Charity a twenty-dollar bill. "How about dinner?"

A date! I'm saved! my inner voice cheered. But I had to play it cool. "That would be wonderful."

Charity made a disgusted snort and left, no doubt intending to keep the change.

"Great. If you like Cajun food, we could go to one of Emeril Lagasse's restaurants."

"Perrrfect," I purred.

"I'll make reservations this week and call you."

As I stood up from the table, Trixi lunged at my feet. I stumbled and lurched forward into Bradley's arms.

Trixi, who was undoubtedly lying in wait for any misstep on my part, jerked her head down in the direction of my shoe as though prepared to strike again.

I gazed at Bradley, realizing with a shiver just how tall he was.

He gave a rakish grin, oblivious to Trixi's attack stance. "You didn't have to throw yourself at me, Amato. After all, I *did* just ask you out."

"You don't think I did that on purpose?" I was outraged, but I didn't dare move both because I liked being pressed against his muscular body and because I felt Trixi's hot breath on my foot. "I tripped over your d—"

"Shh." He placed a finger on my lips. "I was trying to get a rise out of you." His voice was husky. "You're really hot when you get worked up."

My eyes went into autopilot, closing in anticipation of a kiss. But, inexplicably, Bradley released me.

As he and the Trixinator turned to leave, I stood as straight and still as a statue. I was numb all over, and it wasn't from fear of his killer cairn.

AT SIX P.M. THE throng of partiers on Bourbon Street was already dense, and the sounds of blues and jazz blasted from the doorways of the bars. As I weaved my way through the crowd toward Marie Laveau's House of Voodoo, I was practically floating from the excitement of being asked out. In fact, I was so elated that I didn't even mind when a drunk girl wearing a pink boa, a black mini skirt, and a red-sequined halter top spilled strawberry daiquiri from her elongated plastic fleur-de-lis glass onto my arm. And I actually smiled when a shirtless and unshaven fifty-something-year-old man in a red-white-and-blue top hat looked at me and screamed the Mardi Gras cry, "Show me your tits!"

Yes, life is good.

I spotted the hand-painted black sign for Marie Laveau's at the corner of Bourbon and St. Ann and made my way through the crowd. I climbed the two small steps to the store and stopped short in the doorway, surveying the ghoulish scene. The place was jam-packed with candles, voodoo dolls, severed chicken feet, alligator heads, and a creepy altar to Marie Laveau, which had unidentified dead things on it and signs that said, "DO NOT PHOTOGRAPH" and "DO NOT TOUCH."

Don't worry. I won't.

"Can I help you?" A bored-looking cashier with a severe case of acne stifled a yawn.

"Yeah, do you have any beads like this one?" I pulled the skull bead from my purse and held it up for him.

"In the back next to the shrunken heads." He nodded in the direction of the next room as he picked at a cyst.

"Um, thanks." *I think.*

I walked to the back of the store. Despite the dim lighting, I could see that the smaller, secondary room was for the more serious voodoo practitioner. There were books on voodoo, talismans of various shapes and sizes, and supplies for creating altars and spell kits. As soon as I entered, my eyes were drawn to the "Speak No Evil Kit," which showed users how to drive coffin nails into a tongue to prevent someone from saying bad things about them. I shuddered but told myself that the tongue included with the kit couldn't be real.

"Did you come for a reading?" The deep James-Earl-Jones voice erupted from the semi-darkness.

And I almost erupted from the store.

The source was an older, heavy-set man with an oversized rockabilly pompadour. He sat behind a counter against the back wall of the room, next to a bizarre wooden statue of a seated woman.

I considered getting a reading to see what my future with

Bradley held, but I decided against it. Voodoo wasn't real—at least, I hoped it wasn't. I deposited the skull bead on the counter. "No, I was looking for beads like this one."

He glanced at the bead with bloodshot eyes. "It's from a Tibetan prayer *mala*. We sell them in necklaces and bracelets. They're right over there." He gestured toward the wall on his left, revealing a colorful tattoo of a decorative skull with his same rockabilly hairdo on his bicep.

"What's a *mala*?"

"It means 'garland,' but it refers to prayer beads. Buddhists use them like a rosary to keep track of time while they're meditating with mantras." His eyeballs darted left to look at the wooden statue.

"Oh. I thought this bead was for voodoo since it's made of bone and carved like a skull." *I mean, what else would anyone use a skull carved from bone for? Not decoration, surely.*

"Buddhists use skull beads made of bone or wood in prayer, and they often wear them around their wrists for protection and long life." He pulled a pack of Marlboro reds from his front pocket. "But devotees of Kurukulla, the Buddhist Goddess of witchcraft and enchantment, wear skull beads made from human and animal bone to—"

"Wait a second. This bead isn't made from a *human* bone, is it?"

"I couldn't tell ya." He shot a nervous look in the direction of the wooden statue.

Although I suspected that the guy was a little off, I pressed on. "So what does this Kookarulla do?"

"Kurukulla." He extracted a cigarette from the pack and laid it on the counter. "She's a young goddess who uses her nudity and voluptuousness to seduce and bewitch others to bring them under her control." The subject of sex must have reminded him to groom himself, because he pulled a comb from his back pocket and ran it through his greased-back hair. Then he tucked the cigarette behind his right ear and folded his hands on the counter.

"So, if you wear the beads, you could use them to try to make others do what you want?"

"That's right." He glanced at the statue. "Kurukulla's followers wear them to overpower spirits and humans who get in their way."

I thought about Saint Expedite, the pound cake, and even the potion. "Are these beads used to try to win court cases, by any chance?"

He nodded. "Yeah, we have a lot of customers who buy them for court."

"Dem beads don' madda none to Baron Kriminel," a deep female voice said from the darkness.

I jumped backward at least a foot. The wooden statue wasn't a statue at all—it was a real live woman with graying black dreadlocks, cappuccino-colored skin, and dark brown freckles on sunken cheeks. And she was shuffling toward me.

"He goin' ta git dem who profit from death." The nostrils of her wide, flat nose flared as she spoke.

"A-are y-you talking t-to me?" I stuttered. "I-I'm working a m-murder case, but I'm t-trying to *help*."

The woman's piercing amber eyes looked straight through me. "Ya not from 'round heuh,"

"N-no, I'm new to town." I hoped that my newness to NOLA would release me from the impending clutches of Baron Krim-inel, whoever he was.

"Baron Kriminel come from de grave to seek justice agains' de guilty."

"But I'm not guilty."

She raised a crooked, knobby finger. "Dat girl, she know what dat boy do."

Wait. Who's 'dat girl'? My mind was racing, but in my panicked state all I could think of was the old Marlo Thomas show I'd seen on Nick at Nite. *And 'dat boy'?* "I'm sorry, but I don't understand."

"I cain't tell ya what ya don' see, chile. But Odette see. She see." She had a faraway look in her eyes as she walked past me toward the door.

"Odette?" I watched her leave, more confused than ever.

She stopped and turned in the doorway, her mouth contorted with anger. "Dat boy, he done put a spell on her." Her faced softened. "Ya got a man. A good man. But ya goin' ta have ta work ta keep him."

I've got a man? Is she talking about Bradley? "What do you mean, work?" If she was talking about Bradley, then I wanted an answer.

"But don' let 'im take ya down ta de bayou. Ya bes' stay *far* from de bayou, chile, and everythang in it." She turned and shuffled out.

I stood gaping, trying to decipher her cryptic messages.

The aging rockabilly broke the silence. "That's Odette Malveaux. She's a *mambo*."

I turned to face him. "A what?"

"A voodoo priestess." He pulled the cigarette from behind his ear. "Some say she's a descendent of Marie Laveau, which is why she comes to the store from time to time. To keep an eye on things."

I swallowed my shock. "Do you know who she was talking about?"

"No, but if I were you, lady, I'd figure it out." He pointed the cigarette at me. "Baron Kriminel is an evil voodoo god. If he's after you, you're a goner. And it won't be pretty." He put the cigarette between his teeth and rushed from the room.

As I left the store and exited onto Bourbon Street, I realized that the excitement I'd felt when I first arrived was long gone. Instead, apprehension filled my chest. Because I was pretty sure Odette knew things about the Evans case and about Bradley too. Things that I couldn't see.

I headed down St. Ann Street in the direction of the office to get Napoleon, wondering what in the netherworld The Crescent City had in store for me.

8

Barking awoke me, and my eyes flew open. *Had Bradley's dog, Trixi, come to terminate me?*

From my prone position on the bed, I raised my head and realized that it was my new "Who Let the Dogs Out" ringtone. I'd changed it to something sure to wake me up, which had turned out to be an awful idea.

Collapsing face-down, I reached for my pillow so that I could put it over my head, but I couldn't find it. I reopened my eyes, peered over the side of the mattress, and saw it on the floor. Thankfully, the phone had gone silent, so I prepared to go back to sleep.

Less than a minute later, the barking started again.

I needed a new ringtone. I pulled myself into a sitting position, but my head spun so violently that I lay down. Whoever was calling could wait.

When the barking stopped, I wracked my aching brain to figure out what was wrong with me. *Was it a sinus headache? Or the flu?* Then I remembered. It was the quarter bottle or so of Limoncello that I'd tossed back on an empty stomach after my heebie jeebie-inducing encounter with Odette Malveaux.

The ringtone sounded a third time. Lying flat on my back, I felt for the evil device on the nightstand with my hand. When I finally found it, I picked it up and looked at the display with one eye—*Unknown*.

Who would call so early on a Sunday? Reluctantly, I tapped *Answer.*

"Hello?" There was so much phlegm in my throat that I sounded like Louis Armstrong.

"May I speak to Francesca Amato?" The male voice was high pitched—like Mike Tyson's but without the lisp.

"This is she." I used the flat tone I saved for telemarketers.

"Oh," the voice squeaked.

Silence ensued, and I wondered whether the line had dropped. "Are you still there?"

"Yeah. I thought you were your father."

Embarrassed, I cleared my throat. "Um, who is this?"

"Pio. Pio Principato." His tone was expectant, as though I would know his name.

"Oh, right." I mentally cursed my interfering nonna—in English and Italian—for giving out my phone number. "Listen, Pio, you've kind of caught me at a bad time."

"But your nonna said you'd be expecting my call."

I could tell that Pio and I were going to get along famously. "Well, yes, just not so early in the morning."

"But I was calling to invite you to mass at noon."

Mass? On a first date? "I'm afraid I can't. This is awfully short notice, and I have a lot to do today."

He snorted in frustration. "Well, how about tomorrow then?"

"I'm sorry," I said, even though I wasn't feeling the least bit apologetic in light of his rudeness, "but the truth is that I'm expecting a call from another man." *There. The proper thing to do was to tell him about Bradley and end the call. Honesty is the best policy, right?*

"Wow. I didn't know you were that kind of a woman."

Stunned by his presumptuousness, I had to ask for a clarification. "What kind of a woman is that, exactly?"

"A two-timer."

"A what?" I shouted. To hell with my aching head—my pride was more important.

"Well, apparently you date around."

Who did this guy think he was? I should have ended the call, but I was too mad to let it go. "In the first place, Pio, you and I are not dating. And second, I haven't even gone out with the other guy yet. All I said was that I was expecting his call. I hardly think that makes me a two-timer."

"I'm sorry, but this isn't going to work out."

Un.Be.Lievable. "You don't know how much I agree."

"This is goodbye, then, Francesca." His statement held a warning, as though he was giving me one last chance.

"Before you call another woman," I repressed the urge to yell, "try reading a dating manual." I tapped *End* really hard on my phone. Cell phones were convenient, but sometimes I missed being able to slam down a landline receiver.

I lay in bed, livid, wondering whether Marie Laveau's sold a potion or a spell that could make arrogant men like Pio vanish. Or better yet, one that could make Sicilian grandmothers stop meddling in their granddaughters' love lives. *No, not likely. Not even all the voodoo priestesses in Louisiana could conjure up a spell that powerful.*

Thanks to Pio's call, I was fully awake and far too angry to stay in bed. I got up and headed to the bathroom for some aspirin. And I almost stumbled over Napoleon, who was splayed out on his back on the floor against my pillow with one ear open and the other flopped over. He looked like he'd had a hard night too.

I stepped over him, grabbed three aspirin from the bathroom medicine cabinet, and headed for the kitchen where I found the telltale evidence that I'd tied one on the night before. On the counter, beside the empty bottle of Limoncello, sat a half-eaten jar of Nutella. *So much for skipping dinner to lose weight.*

I poured myself a glass of water and popped the aspirin. It hurt when I leaned my head back to take a drink, and my mouth was so dry it felt like I'd been eating spoonfuls of salt instead of the creamy chocolate-hazelnut spread.

As soon as the aspirin were down my throat, I collapsed into a Bordeaux-and-gold cushioned dining chair and tried to remember what, if anything, I needed to do that day—that is, besides tell my nonna to call off her Sicilian attack dogs.

My phone barked.

I sighed, steeled myself for another suitor call, headed back into the bedroom, and looked at my phone. *Unknown.* I didn't think Pio would call again after we'd ended things so badly, but just in case, I decided to give him one final piece of my mind.

"Hello?" I responded a little too testily.

"Franki Amato?" an equally testy male voice asked.

"Yes?" I tried to remember where I'd heard the angry voice before.

"Ryan Hunter."

Did Mambo Odette put a curse on me? Because not even I could be this unlucky all on my own. "I'm sorry, Ryan, I thought you were—"

"Listen to me." His tone was nasty, like him. "I don't have time to chit chat. I'd like to know why no one has called me with the biweekly update on my case that I was promised."

Yeah, she put a curse on me all right. I could envision the voodoo doll of me, tiny cell phone in hand, with pins jabbed into its head and stomach.

"Franki, are you there? I expect an answer."

"Yes, I'm here, Ryan." Despite my hangover haze, I remembered that we had accepted his case on Thursday afternoon, and it was Sunday. "We just took your case a few days ago, and I can assure you that Veronica is extremely organized when it comes to handling our workload. I'm sure she plans to call you tomorrow or the next day. During *business hours*." I added the last part to make the point that Veronica and I didn't need to be spending our free time on the likes of him.

"Look, I've already wasted fifteen minutes this morning trying to track down your contact information, which I don't appreciate. Luckily, I called your office and that kid Donny was there."

I sat on the edge of the bed. "David."

"David, Donny, whatever. The point is that I've already left two messages on your partner's cell this morning, but she hasn't bothered to call me back. Now, I have a meeting with my attorney first thing tomorrow. So if you've got any information, I need it. *Capish*?"

I stifled a gasp at his inappropriate use of Italian and somehow stopped myself from telling him off for being so rude *and* for calling me on the weekend. After all, Veronica was in charge of the human relations aspect of the business. And, whether I liked it or not, Ryan Hunter *was* paying us to investigate the Evans case. I took a deep breath and tried to recall everything we'd discovered.

"Okay then. We got the photos of the crime scene, and we have reason to believe that whoever killed Jessica intentionally brought an inexpensive scarf to LaMarca to strangle her with. The killer either wore it to the store or may have even brought it as a gift.

He laughed so hard his breath sounded like a storm in the receiver. "Well, that should clear me then, because I knew better than to give Jessica a cheap present."

His repulsive humor left me speechless. I stayed silent to let him know I had no comment.

"So, tell me, Franki," his tone was mocking, "how did you figure out that the killer brought the scarf there on purpose?"

"Because LaMarca is known for its silk scarf collection, but the killer didn't use a scarf from the store."

"Gee, you're a regular Miss Marple. What else you got?"

I flopped backward onto the mattress. The man was exhausting. "I went to LaMarca and spoke with the salesgirl who found Jessica's body. While I was there I found a bead made of bone and carved like a skull, near where Jessica's body was found and—"

"How do you know it's connected to the murder?" he interrupted. Again.

"I don't. Right now it's just a hunch."

"A hunch. Jesus Christ, my life is on the line here, and all you guys have are hunches?"

I rolled my head back and forth on the bed in silent protest, but the room began to tilt so I stopped. "No, that's not all we've got."

"Well then let's hear it, Franki. I don't have all damn day."

Neither do I, and yet I'm spending my day off taking abuse from you. "If you'll just let me speak I'll explain everything."

He stayed silent. Blissfully.

"Thank you. A man went to see Jessica at LaMarca one night after the store had closed, and from the sound of things she knew him, and they were arguing."

"Yeah, well, that's hardly surprising. Jessica had a talent for bringing out the worst in people."

His derogatory remarks about Jessica were getting on my already frayed nerves. "This guy was threatening her, Ryan. He said she'd broken some agreement they had and told her to leave New Orleans. Do you know anything about this?"

"So, you're asking me if I was that guy, right?" He snorted. "Why is it that every time I talk to you, I get the feeling that you're interrogating *me* instead of looking for the *real* killer?"

I bolted upright—and had to lay down again. "I just met you a few days ago. For all I know, you and Jessica had a fight one night at her workplace, and you told her to get out of your life or something."

"Well, that didn't happen because I've never even been to LaMarca."

"Okay, fine. But you need to understand that when I ask you a question, I'm not implicitly accusing you." *Although I certainly wouldn't put anything past you.* "I have to cover my bases to make sure I'm not following up on a dead end."

"Fair enough."

I sat up again, astonished. That was the first time Ryan Hunter and I had seen eye-to-eye on anything. "Apparently, this guy also mentioned the London College of Fashion during the argument. Do you know if Jessica attended this school or had friends there?"

"Like I told you the other day, I don't know anything about her past. She didn't talk about it, and I didn't ask."

"All right. Veronica is going to call—"

"Wait," he interrupted yet again. "I heard her mention London once."

Excitement coursed through my chest, and I rose and began to pace, albeit slowly. *A lead, finally.* "When?"

"On a phone call. A month or two ago."

"Do you know who she was talking to?"

"No, but she said a name. It sounded like a woman's name, but I couldn't say for sure. It was Eye-talian or something."

"Do you remember what it was?" I figured it was unlikely given his inability to recall the proper pronunciation of *Italian.*

"No, it was a weird name. All I know is that it ended in an *a.*"

Well that narrows it down since pretty much all Italian women's names, including my own, end in the letter a. "How did London come up in the conversation?"

"She said something like, 'You don't know what the hell you're talking about. You know I wasn't even in London when it happened.'"

"So, she was angry."

"Oh yeah. At the time, I thought she was having a fight with some Eye-talian girlfriend of hers from London."

I sighed. *Was it really so hard to say the* it *in* Italian? "Did she tell you anything about the call when she hung up?"

"No, she just stared at me. I don't think she even knew I was home. Then she started bitching at me about something." His tone had turned bitter. I think I'd forgotten to take out the trash or pick my clothes up off the floor. Who the hell knows. I could never do anything right in her eyes..."

I sidestepped the toxic topic of his relationship with Jessica. "Okay, well, we're going to follow up on the London angle tomorrow, so I'll have Veronica call you in the afternoon with an update."

"Good, because I'm paying you for information. *Solid* information." He hung up, and he did it from a landline too because I could hear him slam down the receiver.

The jerk.

All that standing was getting to me, so I made my way to the chaise lounge to call Veronica. I tapped her number, closing my eyes as I waited for her to answer.

"Hello?" She sounded breathy.

"Uh, did I interrupt something?"

"Hercules and I are on our Sunday morning jog. What's up?"

Thanks to my hangover, I shuddered at the thought of bouncing up and down. "I just got a call from Ryan Hunter."

"What did he want?"

"His weekly update—and to harass me."

"Ugh. I'm sorry."

"No worries, but only because he told me something important. It's looking more and more like something went down in
London that involved Jessica Evans. Any chance you can meet
today?"

"Of course I can meet." Her cheerful tone megaphoned into
my ear. "How about Thibodeaux's at noon? I could really use a
mimosa. Oh, and some onion rings. *Mm.*"

The mention of alcohol and greasy onions made my
stomach lurch. "Works for me. See you then."

I hung up and pondered the logistics of how I was going to
make it from the chaise lounge to the bathtub.

The phone rang again, interrupting my planning.

Assuming it was Veronica calling back to change the time or
something, I answered. "Hey."

"Franki, we've-a got a *problema.*"

A mental image of Odette plunging a pin into the backside
of my voodoo doll flashed through my aching head. "What is it,
Nonna?"

"I just-a got a call from-a Luisa, the cousin of my cousin,
Agatina. Pio called her, and he told-a her you're a loose-a
woman."

I sighed and spread out on the chaise lounge. In Sicilian-
American circles, it was a cardinal sin for a woman to have questionable virtue, and in terms of gravity it was second only to the
inability to make a good *ragù.* "Nonna, all I told Pio was that I
couldn't go out with him because I have a date with another
man. So—"

"A date? *Dio mio!* "

Her *my God* told me that the slight to my honor was old
news.

"Who-a with-a? Bruno?"

"No, his name is Bradley. He's the president of Pontchartrain Bank here in New Orleans."

She let out a whistle like a sailor seeing a woman after six months at sea. "You did-a *good*."

I basked in her praise. "*Grazie*."

"Is-a he Italian?"

"He's not." I waited for the inevitable comment.

"Well, we can't have-a it all-a, can-a we Franki?" She was so happy she practically crowed. "Now-a when is-a this date?"

"Um..." I didn't want to admit that I didn't know, but I couldn't lie because she would call me immediately after the date—probably even during—to get the details. "I'm not exactly sure."

She gasped. "Not-a sure? You mean-a that you gave up a date with a fine-a man like-a Pio, and you don't even have-a no date with-a Bradley?"

Fine man, my rear. "Bradley said he would call me this week, and he will."

"Francesca Lucia Amato, you *never* turn-a down a date when you don't have-a no date."

"Have some faith, okay?"

"The only-a man I have-a the faith in, Franki, is-a the Pope."

When my nonna mentioned the Pope, it was time to end the call. "I've gotta run, Nonna. I'll call you right after the date. *Ciao ciao!*"

Next, I did what I should have done three phone calls earlier —I pressed the off button on my phone. Then I turned it back on because there was always the possibility that Bradley would call. Although, after talking to my nonna, I wasn't feeling all that hopeful. Maybe I really did "have-a no date." It wasn't like Bradley had set a time and place, or anything. The more I thought about my dating prospects, the better that mimosa Veronica mentioned was sounding. But not the onion rings.

I agreed with my nonna on one point, though—I shouldn't count on a date until I knew for certain that I had one. But I wasn't ready to believe that the Pope was the only man a girl could trust, at least not yet. And I couldn't afford to give in to defeat. Bradley Hartmann was going to call me whether I had to resort to Vulcan mind control, Jedi mind tricks, or even voodoo to make it happen.

9

"Jeez. It's like a giant lightsaber in the sky." I shielded my eyes from the noon sun that glared at me when I opened my front door. I recoiled into my apartment, rummaged in my purse, and pulled out my tortoise-shell sunglasses for the walk across the street to Thibodeaux's. After donning my shades to block the sunlight—and the equally harsh reality of the cemetery—I set off on the one hundred-foot trek. The street was deserted, so I stepped from the yard into the street.

A twelve-year-old kid on a bike appeared from out of nowhere and sped by not two inches in front of me.

I flailed my arms like a tipsy tightrope walker, landed squarely on my rear end, and, voluntarily, lay down in the grass to regroup.

"You're lucky I have extra cushioning, kid," I shouted from my supine position with a raised, clenched fist. If I could've stayed on my feet, it might've gotten ugly between him and me.

After a few minutes of contemplating the clouds, I stood, brushed the dead grass from my clothes, and walked my bruised behind to the bar. At the entrance, I paused to summon the strength needed to endure Veronica's ever-effervescent Sunday afternoon chatter. When I pushed open the door, I spotted her sitting at the bar with her back to me. She was sporting a Madonna ponytail á la The Blond Ambition Tour, a sunny yellow velour tracksuit, and matching yellow tennis shoes.

I slid onto the barstool next to her and caught a revolting whiff of fresh air and sunshine. "Hey."

She gave me the onceover. "What happened to *you*?"

"What do you mean?" I placed my bag on the bar.

"You look a little rough." She smirked and sipped mimosa from a straw. "Been rolling in the hay with anyone I know?"

I looked at her for a few seconds and realized that I must've had grass in my hair. "Give me a break, all right?" I finger-combed my long brown locks. "Within the past twelve hours, I've had run-ins with a voodoo priestess, Ryan Hunter, a Sicilian guy, a crazy kid on a bike, a bottle of Limoncello, and my nonna." I didn't mention the jar of Nutella because it just made me look pathetic.

"Oh wow, your nonna?" Veronica was unfazed by the mention of the voodoo priestess et al. "What did she want?"

"To alert me to the earth-shattering news that my womanly honor was besmirched after I jilted one of her saintly Sicilians." I started to remove my sunglasses but thought better of it. The dimly lit bar seemed excessively bright.

"Your womanly honor." Veronica belly-laughed and slapped the bar. "That's a good one."

The glare I shot her was not unlike that harsh sun.

Phillip the bartender approached. "What can I get ya?"

The thought of alcohol made me feel like crawling back to that spot in the grass to lie down. "A club soda with lime."

Phillip walked away, muttering to himself.

"So what did Ryan say about London?" Veronica fished a

piece of orange out of her mimosa with a toothpick. "I've been dying of curiosity ever since you called."

"He said that he came home one day and found Jessica on the phone with someone he thought was an Italian girlfriend. She was really angry and reminded the caller that she wasn't in London when something or other happened."

"When what happened?"

I gave her a look. "Don't you think I would've mentioned that if I knew?"

She shrugged and popped the orange into her mouth. "So, why does Ryan think she was talking to an Italian woman?"

Phillip passed me my drink, and I nodded my thanks. "Because she said an Italian woman's name."

"That doesn't mean anything. She could have just been gossiping about the woman or mentioning her for some reason."

"True." I nursed my club soda. My brain was in no mood to hypothesize about the case.

"Hey, Phillip," Veronica shouted into my ear. "Can I get an order of onion rings?"

"Sure thing, Ronnie."

"Sometimes, you just need a little greasy food in your diet, right Franki?"

I tilt-nodded, and my stomach also tilted at the mention of grease, but not just because of my hangover. My first impression of Phillip was that he looked a little greasy himself. And since the last time I was in the bar, I'd learned through the neighbor-hood grapevine that he was in an environmentally conscious grunge rock band that didn't believe in showering more than once a week, to save water. Unfortunately, Phillip also did double duty at Thibodeaux's as the cook.

Veronica leaned her arms on the bar. "Normally I'd say that Jessica's phone call was probably nothing. But it *is* interesting that London keeps coming up, and in such negative contexts. By the way, I'm going to call the London College of Fashion first thing in the morning. I hope they have some information for us, because as of right now, we've got nothing on Jessica's past."

"David hasn't been able to find anything?"

"Oh, he's found some things. Too many." She waved her drink toothpick.

Veronica might not have looked Italian, but her habit of talking with her hands gave her heritage away. "What do you mean 'too many'?"

"He googled 'Jessica Evans' and got over three hundred thousand hits, so I told him to not to bother checking the links. With his part-time schedule, it could take him weeks or even months to find one related to our Jessica Evans." She waved the toothpick close to my cheek.

Keeping a watchful eye on the wooden weapon, I asked, "Did he try narrowing down the search with any personal information, like her address?"

"Yeah, but that didn't turn up anything concrete either." She looked down at the bar. "At this point, we really don't have much to go on. We know Ryan doesn't have a clue about Jessica's personal life, and the only information on the police report was her Louisiana driver license number and birth date."

Surprised by the downturn in Veronica's chipper demeanor, I mustered up as much positivity as I could. "Well, that's good, right? Since we have her birth date, we can get her birth certificate and find out her parents' names. Annabella said that Jessica referred to herself as a Louisiana native when she was talking to the man at the store, so the certificate should be easy to find."

She shook her head. "No, it's not good. Louisiana doesn't have a public birth index like Texas. It's a closed record state, so only Jessica or her parents could request her birth certificate, not us."

"Oh. What about Facebook, Twitter, and Instagram? Or wait. I bet she had a LinkedIn page." I hoped that Veronica would perk up soon because being perky on her behalf was exhausting.

"Nope, not even a Pinterest page." Veronica gave a wild thrust of her toothpick.

I scooted my barstool a few inches away from her. "Maybe she's going by her middle name?"

"Could be. It's also possible that she was using an assumed name." She put the toothpick in its rightful place—on the counter.

"Yeah, I was thinking the same thing." I laid my aching head down on my purse. "So what do we do next?"

"We hope the London College of Fashion has some information for us. Because if they don't, we're at a standstill in this case."

Phillip slid a steaming basket of onion rings down the length of the bar.

I raised my head to avoid getting hit in the face and watched as the basket stopped in front of Veronica, who perked right up and clapped. "Nice sliding skills."

She cast an admiring glance at Phillip. "I know. Want one, Franki?"

"Nah." I eyed the basket with revulsion and suspicion.

"Now, tell me about this voodoo priestess." Veronica bit into an onion ring.

"First off, it was one of the craziest experiences of my life! Her name is Odette Malveaux and—"

"Odette Malveaux," a familiar chain-smoker voice exclaimed. "You into voodoo, Miss Franki?"

I turned to see Glenda in all her splendor. She wore what looked like a Kmart knockoff of J Lo's iconic jungle-green Versace dress—the one with the neckline that plunged several inches past the navel—only Glenda's plunged a good two inches lower, almost past something else.

I closed my jaw—with the help of my hand. "I can barely handle the mysticism of yoga, so no voodoo for me."

Glenda cackled as she took a seat beside me.

Veronica touched the sleeve of Glenda's dress. "What a stunning look."

That's one way to describe it.

"Thank you, sugar." Glenda crossed her legs and exposed six-inch-heeled stripper shoes with clear plastic, hollow bases that had writing on them. "So Miss Franki, how do you know Mambo Odette?"

"I met her at Marie Laveau's House of Voodoo last night." I tried to decipher the word on Glenda's shoes. "Do you know her?"

"Sure do. A long time ago, I consulted with her about a man I was seeing."

I lowered my sunglasses, intrigued. "Did you want to get even with him or something?"

"Get even? Real voodoo isn't about hexes and sacrifices and things. But that's a common misconception thanks to the way Hollywood has sensationalized it. Voodoo is about serving others, Miss Franki, especially the poor, the sick, and the lonely. And Odette is one of the finest priestesses in all of Louisiana when it comes to matters of the heart, I guarantee you that."

I wondered how in the world that terrifying woman could have become an expert on love.

"Besides, if I wanted to get even with a man, I wouldn't need any help. Know what I mean, jelly bean?"

I nodded. I had no doubt that Glenda could be a formidable foe. "Hey, before I forget, what do your shoes say?"

"*Tips.* There's a slot for inserting bills right below the word, see?" She spun around on her barstool and kicked a long, skinny leg out in front of her with the ease of a Rockette dancer so that I could examine her shoe, up close and personal.

"Why would clients put the tips in your shoe?"

"Because they're too damn drunk to reach the G-string." Glenda leaned over the counter and waved Phillip over with a dollar bill, like a customer in a strip club.

Veronica gave a tip of her head. "That's good business."

Phillip approached to take Glenda's drink order and flinched as he got a full-frontal of her in the dress. "The usual?"

"No, handsome, I'll take a mint julep with extra powdered sugar." She gave him a cougarish wink. "I'm feeling like a Southern belle today."

A hoop-skirted Glenda flashed through my mind. *Never happen. She'd suffocate in all that clothing.*

"You know, Miss Franki, I also consulted with Mambo Odette about a voodoo dance I used to do. It was inspired by Marie Laveau."

"Really?"

"I modeled the dress after Marie Laveau's own clothes."

Despite my better judgment, I wanted to know more. "Was it made of raffia and seashells like the voodoo priestess costumes I saw on sale for Mardi Gras the other day?"

"Hell no." Glenda wrinkled her mouth in disgust. "I wouldn't be caught dead in a cheap outfit like that."

Veronica shook her head. "Of course you wouldn't."

"It was a long muslin dress with a *tignon* that had seven knots pointing up like a crown."

Phillip appeared with the mint julep, blushing schoolboy style.

"Thank you, handsome." Glenda made eyes at him while licking the sugar from the entire rim of the glass.

My stomach tilted again. I had to get her to put her tongue back into her mouth. "What's a *tignon*?"

Veronica, who was the resident fashion expert of every culture and era, turned to me. "It's the type of headdress Marie Laveau wore." She turned to Glenda. "What color was the dress?"

"White to symbolize inner purity, and I had a boa around my neck."

I chewed my soda straw. "I knew women in New Orleans liked to wear boas during Mardi Gras, but I didn't realize that voodoo queens wore them too."

Glenda stared at me like I'd sprouted another head. "A boa *constrictor*. You know, a *snake*?"

"Oh, of course." My cheeks grew warm.

Veronica's brow creased. "What did the boa symbolize?"

"Well, in voodoo, the snake represents the practitioner's spiritual connection to the otherworld. So, when I wore the snake, it meant that if you connected with me, it'd be outta this world." Glenda laughed and slapped me on the back so hard that it felt like my brain rattled in my skull.

It was time to put me out of my increasing misery. "Hey, Phillip. How about a Bloody Mary?"

His face drooped as though he didn't want to return to our area.

Go figure. I turned to Glenda. "Was the snake real?"

"Of course the snake was real. But this wasn't no Tijuana donkey show, this was a *class act*." She slurped the last of her mint julep and let out a tremendous belch. "The snake was just a live accessory to cover my lady parts, no more no less."

I recoiled. "Wait, you wanted your, um, *lady parts* covered?"

She gaped at my lack of stripper sense. "Well of course, child, until the big reveal."

I considered asking how she got a live snake to cover her privates but decided to quit while I was ahead.

"Here you go." Phillip said placed the Bloody Mary in front of me, averting his eyes.

"Thanks. This should cover my tab." I shoved fifteen dollars under his chin so he could see it.

He took the money and scurried to safety.

Veronica blinked. "Are you leaving already, Franki? You just got your drink."

"I know. I'm going to finish it and head home."

"What are you going to do today?"

I stared at the glass. "This drink. This is all I'm going to do."

"Miss Franki's a real live wire, Miss Ronnie."

"Right?" Veronica's tone was as dry as my club soda.

I ignored them both and tossed back half my drink.

Glenda leaned forward to look at Veronica. "Whaddya say you and I celebrate our inner Southern belles by doing some corset shopping at Trashy Diva?"

Veronica beamed like her yellow tracksuit. "That's a terrific idea."

And the perfect place for this mismatched duo.

"Good. This one's on me, Miss Ronnie." She pulled some crumpled bills from her lacy black bra and dropped them on the bar. "I'll see you later, handsome." She shot a knowing look at Phillip and pulled a short red cigarette holder covered in cubic zirconias from her purse. Placing it between pursed lips, she exited the bar shaking her bony hips.

"See you tomorrow, Franki." Veronica waved and followed Glenda.

I finished my drink in one gulp and headed out. As soon as I got outside, I looked for cars and wayward biker kids before crossing the street. My only goal for the rest of the day was to make it to my bed without incident.

Midway to my apartment, my phone rang instead of barking. *Grazie a dio I changed that ringtone.* I looked at the display and saw the theme of the day—*Unknown. So much for making it home unscathed.*

I continued walking and debated whether to take the call or just go inside and hide. Then I reminded myself that it could've been Bradley and tapped *Answer.*

"Hello?" I used a sultry voice that was only mildly tinged with apprehension.

"Hey Franki, it's Bradley."

"Oh thank God," I exclaimed before I could stop myself.

"What did you say? The phone cut out for a second."

"Just 'hi.'" I uttered silent thanks to my cell phone for preventing me from making a fool of myself. I inserted my key into the lock and opened my front door.

"Listen, I was hoping to take you to dinner next weekend, but I have to leave town Thursday on business, and I won't be back until Sunday."

"Oh, I understand." I closed the door and tossed my purse in frustration on the chaise lounge. *Was he trying to back out of the date?*

"But if you're free on Tuesday night, I'd like to take you to a restaurant in the Quarter."

"Of course I'm free." *Smooth, Franki, real smooth.*

"Great. They serve classic New Orleans cuisine, things like gumbo, jambalaya, and red beans and rice. They even have my absolute favorite, the muffuletta."

The muffuletta? I stopped in my tracks and placed my hand on the wall. Then I drew it back. The fuzzy wallpaper freaked me out. "You're not Sicilian are you?"

"No, why?"

"Just checking." Relieved, I bent down to ruffle the fur on Napoleon's head. "That sounds wonderful, Bradley. I've been dying to eat some good Cajun food."

"Well, if you like Cajun food, they also have crawdads and even alligator for the more adventurous eaters."

I shot up arrowlike and gripped my spinning head. *Crawdads? Alligator? What was it Odette had said about the bayou?* I tried to keep my tone casual. "This place isn't on the bayou is it?"

"No, it's on Bourbon Street, but it's called Le Bayou." He paused. "Have you been there before?"

It was all coming back to me. Odette had told me in no uncertain terms not to let a man take me to the bayou. I was supposed to stay away from the bayou and everything in it, i.e., crawdads and alligators. *Should I suggest another restaurant?*

"Franki, is everything okay?"

I had to hide my fears about Odette's voodoo predictions or risk blowing the date. "Yes, absolutely. I guess my phone is acting up again. So, what time on Tuesday?"

"How about seven o'clock? I'll pick you up your place."

"I'll text you my address."

"Sounds great. I'm looking forward to it." There was a hint of devastatingly sexy in his voice.

"Me too." I tried to match his sexy tone, but it came out suspicious. "Bye, Bradley."

I hung up and went to my bedroom. As I crawled into bed I had a funny feeling in the pit of my stomach, and it wasn't from the Bloody Mary. I was probably overreacting about my encounter with Mambo Odette, but it *was* odd that right after she warned me about a man taking me to the bayou it seemed to be happening. On the other hand, Bradley wasn't taking me to an *actual* bayou. It was a restaurant in the French Quarter. And nothing and no one was going to prevent me from going. All I had to do was avoid the crawdads and the alligator, and everything would be fine.

Wouldn't it?

10

As I drove to work the next morning, I couldn't help but be in a good mood despite the disturbing developments around Odette Malveaux's predictions. My hangover was gone, the sun was shining, and I had a date with Bradley Hartmann. To celebrate, I'd put the top down on my Mustang and popped my "Beauty and the Beat" CD by The Go-Go's into the stereo. Nothing like '80s girl power pop to make you leave your voodoo cares behind.

I pulled up to the office and couldn't believe my luck—as if by magic, there was a parking space right in front. *This day is getting better and better.*

I parallel-parked, opened the car door, and started to get out, but I was knocked back into my seat by the appetizing aroma of marinara sauce from Nizza restaurant. *Yeah, it's going to be a great day.*

I bounded up the stairs to the office singing "Lust to Love" at the top of my lungs. In my mind, I had the same smooth and powerful voice as Belinda Carlisle, but in reality I sounded a lot like a female Neil Young—with a head cold.

I entered the office, and Veronica sashay-ran into the lobby, her forehead creased with worry.

Instead of alarm bells, I heard the barking from my ex-ringtone. "What's the matter?"

"Didn't you hear that?" She exited the office and went to the stairs. "It sounded like a dog yelping in pain."

Maybe I had *heard barking.* I stood still and listened, but I couldn't hear a thing. Then it dawned on me—she was talking about my singing.

I went to the stairwell. "Hey, Veronica?"

She turned to look up at me from the bottom step.

I hated to lie to my best friend, but if she thought my voice sounded like an injured animal, there was no way I was claiming it. "I think that sound you were hearing was the squeaky brakes on a truck that went by."

"Are you sure?"

"Absolutely."

Veronica sighed and climbed the stairs. "Thank goodness."

"You're here early." I changed the subject even though my ego was still smarting from the indirect insult.

She reentered the lobby. "I couldn't sleep. I wanted to call London as soon as possible."

"And?" I followed her to her office.

She took a seat behind her desk. "There's no record of a Jessica Evans at the London College of Fashion."

I dropped into the armchair. "Well, like you said yesterday, she might've been using an assumed name. Maybe that's why the school has no record of her."

"Or she never went there at all. I mean, that salesgirl Annabella could've misunderstood what she overheard at the store that night."

"True, but I think we should check with the police."

Her brow went up. "What for?"

"Because, unlike us, they can get a court order to obtain Jessica's birth certificate. So, if she *was* using an assumed name, they might already know that. Why don't we ask your crime analyst friend for an update on the police's case?"

Veronica shook her head. "No, Betty puts her job on the line every time I ask her for help, so I only use her as an absolute last resort. For now, the best thing we can do is shift gears."

"How so?"

She opened her day planner. "We've got to get back out there and find the store that sold the killer the scarf."

"Sounds logical. Besides," I paused for effect, "I need to buy a new outfit for my date."

She gasped and leaned forward. "Your what?"

"My date." I hid a smile. "Jeez, Veronica, is it really so shocking that someone would ask me out?"

"I didn't mean it like that. It's just that I'm surprised you're going on a date so soon after Vince."

"Why?" I turned away so she wouldn't see me tear up. "It's not like I need time to get over that cheating bastard."

"Well, that's what I mean." Her tone had gone soft. "Are you sure you're ready to trust a man again?"

"Of course." Although, after thinking about it for a split second, I realized I wasn't sure at all.

"If that's the case, then I'm glad." She leaned back in her chair. "I'm just worried about you."

"Relax. Bradley isn't one of those deceptively sincere types I usually go for. He's a genuinely good guy. I can tell. The only thing we have to worry about is what I'm going to wear."

"Where are you going?"

"To Le Bayou restaurant." I sidestepped the probably insignificant matter of the warning I'd received from Mambo Odette about men taking me to the bayou. Veronica had no patience for my Sicilian-inspired superstitions, so she was sure to be annoyed by my voodoo misgivings, even though a healthy respect for the unknown was nothing to scoff at.

"You can always wear a basic LBD. It's perfect first-date material."

I hesitated. "I don't have one."

"What?" Her pitch neared a scream. "We're going to have to take care of that right now. I saw one at Ann Taylor the other day that would look amazing on you." She opened her laptop. "Let me see if I can find it on their website."

For Veronica, the little black dress was a simple, yet fabulous wardrobe item for any occasion. But for me, the LBD looked like what I would wear *underneath* my dress—a Spanx slip. I needed more coverage to feel at ease with a new man, not to mention the new roll that had appeared on my stomach since moving to New Orleans. But Veronica had an excellent eye for fashion, so if she knew of a dress that would be flattering on me, it was worth taking a look.

The lobby bell interrupted our style search.

Veronica was so immersed in online shopping that she didn't react, so I rose and went to the lobby.

Ryan Hunter held a large box and a woman's red crocodile handbag that must have been worth the GDP of a small country.

"Hello." My greeting was intentionally cool. I wanted to comment on his bag, but I didn't dare use sarcasm on this guy for fear of what he would do. "You know, Veronica was going to call you today with your report—"

"I'm not here about that."

His voice reminded me of the barking on my ex-ringtone. "Then what can I help you with?"

He placed the box on a nearby chair. "I found something in Jessica's things that might help my case."

Inexplicably, adrenaline surged in my chest. "Let me get Veronica."

I hurried to her office and poked my head inside. "It's Ryan."

Her eyes rose from the laptop.

"He's found something of Jessica's that he thinks may be important."

She stood and followed me into the lobby.

"Hi Ryan." Veronica's tone was professional, but distant. "Franki said you've found something?"

"Yeah, last night I packed up Jessica's stuff to bring it by today. I dropped one of the boxes as I was putting it into my trunk, and this handbag fell out. When I went to pick it up, I noticed the corner of a white envelope sticking out from between the interior lining of the purse and the exterior leather. Right here." He showed us an area of the bag where the stitching had given way.

Veronica's eyes widened. "What was in it?"

"This old letter." He pulled an envelope from inside his suit jacket and handed it to her. "It's postdated June 27, 1988."

She pulled the letter from the envelope and scanned the page.

My heart thumped so hard I was sure they could hear it. I had a gut feeling that the letter contained a key clue to Jessica's past. Plus, the whole idea of a secret letter made me feel like a sleuth in a mystery novel. "What does it say?"

"It's really short. I'll read it." She cleared her throat. "*Barbara, I got laid off from the refinery last week. I'll send you money for Angelica when I can. But like it or not I got a new wife and kid to take care of now. Sincerely, Bill.*"

"Wait." I looked over Veronica's shoulder. "Who are Bill and Barbara again?"

She examined the envelope. "Well, they have the same last name, Evangelista." She let the arm holding the envelope drop to her side and looked at me. "Are you thinking what I'm thinking?"

"I'm not thinking anything." My mind always went blank whenever people expected me to guess their thoughts.

Ryan shot me a contemptuous look. "Nice intuitive skills."

I pretended not to hear him. "Was Jessica maybe blackmailing these people?"

Veronica folded the letter. "I don't know, but now I'm convinced she was hiding something." She turned to Ryan. "Does any of this make any sense to you? Have you heard these names before?"

He shook his head. "No, never. Maybe this Angelica was one of Jessica's friends or a cousin or something."

The door burst open.

"Hey, party people." David entered the lobby and tossed his backpack on his workstation.

Veronica smacked the letter against her thigh. "David, one of these days we're literally going to die from fright."

He hung his head. "Uh, sorry."

I shot Veronica a drop-it look. There was no reason to embarrass the kid in front of a client. "Don't worry about it, David."

Ryan, true to arrogant form, didn't bother to acknowledge his presence.

Veronica looked at the clock by the door. "I hate to run, Ryan, but I need to call the London School of Fashion before they close to find out whether they have a record of an Angelica Evangelista. I called earlier this morning, and they had no record of Jessica."

"Well, isn't that interesting." Ryan rubbed his chin. "Okay, I'll bring up the other boxes from my car, and then I need to get to the office. But can I count on one of you to actually update me today on what you find out?"

"Of course." Veronica turned to me. "Franki, fill David in on everything and help him do an Internet search on Angelica Evangelista, okay?"

"Sure." I nodded a frosty farewell in Ryan's direction. "David, let's go use my computer."

"Right on."

I went to the hallway, and David followed. I didn't want to have to deal with Ryan when he returned with the remaining boxes, and I was sure David felt the same.

I entered my office and gestured to my desk. "You're the resident research guru. You take my chair. By the way, what time do you have class today?"

"Uh, I have Brazilian Dance at one." He took a seat and opened my laptop.

"Brazilian Dance? I thought you were a computer science major."

His gaze darted from mine to the floor. "Not a lot of girls, like, take comp sci courses."

"Got it." I smiled both at the thought of him taking classes to meet women and at the mental image of his long, lanky frame doing Brazilian dance moves.

His fingers flew over the keyboard, and he pressed the return key. "So, I just googled 'Angelica Evangelista' and got almost eight thousand hits. Let's add 'New Orleans' to narrow the search."

I walked behind him and looked at the screen. "Less than a hundred results. That's more doable."

We were interrupted by the clacking of Veronica's Manolo Blahniks, which were quickly approaching my office.

She burst into the room. "Incredible news. A student named Angelica Evangelista graduated from the London College of Fashion in 2008. Can you believe it?"

I looked at David and back at her. "Did you find out anything else?"

"Yes. Angelica got a bachelor's degree in Fashion Management."

I sat on the corner of my desk. "Which is exactly what Jessica Evans did for a living."

Veronica's eyes sparkled. "Exactly."

"Is that a four-year degree?"

"Yeah, why?"

I did a rapid calculation in my head. "Well, then the year would be about right, because Jessica was twenty-six, and that would make her around twenty-two years old when she graduated."

"Could Angelica be Jessica?" Veronica spoke as though she didn't dare believe it.

"I'm beginning to wonder that myself." I rose and returned to my position behind David. "Try searching 'Angelica Evangelista' and 'London.'"

Veronica joined me to see the search results.

"Whoa," David breathed.

Veronica and I didn't need to ask him why. The first link was a Wikipedia page entitled "Murder of Immacolata Di Salvo."

"What is this?" I said, stunned.

David clicked the link, and we all leaned in to read the screen.

Immacolata Di Salvo, an American exchange student from New Orleans, Louisiana, was murdered on May 1, 2008. Di Salvo, aged twenty-two, was found dead in her dorm room in London, where she attended the London College of Fashion.

I glanced through the rest of the article but didn't see the name Angelica Evangelista. "David, scroll down. I want to see how this Angelica person is connected to the murder."

He searched for "Angelica" and found her name in the middle of the page.

"There." I pointed to the cursor highlighting the name. "I'll read it aloud. *Angelica Evangelista, an American exchange student from New Orleans, Louisiana, and the flat mate of Di Salvo, found Di Salvo's body after returning home from a trip abroad at 3 a.m. There were no signs of forced entry in the dorm room, which led police to believe that Di Salvo knew her killer.*"

"Oh. My. God." I sat on the desk.

Veronica stared at me in shock. "Could this be related to our case?"

"Dude," David exclaimed.

I started and almost fell to the floor. "What?"

"It mentions Stewart Preston. I totally remember hearing about this when I was a kid."

I couldn't help but repress a smile at the notion that David was anything but a kid in the present.

Veronica eyed the screen. "Who's Stewart Preston?"

"His family is rich. I'm talkin' uber rich. His father, Stewart Preston, III, owns, like, half of New Orleans."

"What does he do?"

"I never really knew. One second." David opened a new page and typed "Stewart Preston, III" into the search field. He found a Wikipedia page on Preston and scanned the contents. "Looks like he owns a bunch of textile companies."

I ran my finger down the long list of corporations owned by Preston and his associates. "Make that a textile empire."

Veronica squinted. "Franki, read the part in the murder article about Stewart Preston."

"Sure," I said as David switched back to the other screen. "It says, '*Stewart Preston, IV, an American exchange student from New Orleans, Louisiana, who was attending the London School of Economics, was charged with the sexual assault and murder of Di Salvo in August of 2009.*'"

David nodded. "Right. And he never went to jail either.

Everyone said it was because of his daddy's money and connections."

I leaned on the desk with my forearms. "It says, '*Preston was eventually acquitted and cleared of all charges in January of 2012.*' I wonder why."

Veronica frowned. "Does it say?"

"No, and it doesn't explain how Immacolata was killed either."

She sat on the opposite end of the desk. "David, look for a local article on the murder, maybe one from *The Times-Picayune.*"

He returned to the main search results page.

She tapped her cheek. "It's certainly looking like Jessica Evans and Angelica Evangelista are one and the same person, but I wish there was something more concrete to link the two of them."

David pulled up a *Times-Picayune* article on the Di Salvo murder dated May 4, 2008. The opening line of the article reported, '*On May 1, 2008, Immacolata Di Salvo was found strangled to death in her dorm room at the London College of Fashion.*'

Veronica shot me a questioning look. "Strangled?"

My insides felt twisted, like they were being strangled. "Just like Jessica."

David pointed a bony finger at the second line of the article. "Yeah, and look at this part. '*The murder weapon was a scarf.*'"

"*Tombola,*" I whispered in Italian. Then I remembered that David didn't speak the language. "I mean, *Bingo.*"

11

"A scarf." I shook my head. "I can't believe it."

The three of us stared at the computer screen for a few minutes, dumbstruck.

David swallowed. "So, Angelica and Jessica were, like, the same girl."

Veronica looked like she'd just witnessed the strangulation, "It sure looks that way, doesn't it?"

"Yeah," I breathed. "This case is getting crazy, isn't it?"

David opened his eyes wide. "And dangerous too. Like, you guys could be dealing with a serial scarf strangler. If I were either one of you, man, I wouldn't even *think* of wearing a scarf while I was workin' this case."

Even though I wasn't wearing a scarf, my hand went to my throat. I started to protest but then opted to remain silent. The kid had a point.

Veronica walked to the front of my desk to face us. "Let's not jump to any conclusions, David. Even if these two cases are related," she paused to pace, "there's no guarantee that the same person committed both murders."

"I guess." David stared at his dirty white tennis shoes. He was clearly attached to the idea of a serial scarf strangler.

Veronica stopped and looked at him. "We need to actually prove that Jessica was really Angelica before we spend any time investigating the relationship between these two cases. Otherwise, we could make a critical mistake."

I exhaled a long breath. The plot was getting as thick as the marinara sauce I'd smelled earlier. "So, we need to track down Bill and Barbara Evangelista."

"Yeah, and Immacolata's family. Since Immacolata roomed with Angelica, then one of her relatives or friends must've seen a picture of Angelica at some point."

David's fingers flew over the keyboard. "Uh, here's an obituary for Immacolata Di Salvo. It mentions her family."

I scanned the text on the screen. "Here we go. It says, *'She is survived by her father, Rosario Di Salvo, her mother, Maria Di Salvo, and her sisters Concetta and Domenica.'* Wow, those are some serious Italian Catholic names."

"Huh?" David turned to look at me. "What do you mean?"

"Well, 'Immacolata' is Italian for 'Immaculate,' and the other family members' names mean 'rosary,' 'Mary,' 'conception,' and 'Sunday.' Oh, and the 'Salvo' part of their last name is the nickname for 'Salvatore,' which means 'savior.'"

His head bounced in approval. "Wicked."

Righteous, maybe, but not wicked. "Religious-themed names are super common in Italy, especially in the South, so I'm guessing that the Di Salvos are fairly devout." I returned my gaze to the obituary.

Veronica was behind me again, trying to read over my shoulder. "Does the obituary list a funeral home?"

"Yeah, and it's in Slidell." I looked at David. "Where is that?"

"It's a suburb of New Orleans," His chest swelled with pride.

"It's, like, a forty-minute drive from here, but I can make it in twenty-five."

"That reminds me…" I turned to Veronica. "You never told us the cities that Bill and Barbara Evangelista were living in."

"Oh, right. Let me go get the envelope." She hurried from the room.

I leaned over David's shoulder. "See if you can find an address for the Di Salvos."

"Already got it. There's a Rosario Di Salvo in the white pages on St. Augustine Street. His phone number's listed. But I can't believe people still have landlines, man. That's sooooo last century."

Veronica clacked into the office with an envelope and stopped in front of my desk. "Barbara lived on East Queens Drive in Slidell, but Bill didn't write his return address. It was postmarked in Baton Rouge, though."

"Well, David just found a Slidell address for a Rosario Di Salvo. If it's the right person, then Angelica and Immacolata could've known each other before they went to college."

She put her hands on her hips. "Let's call the Di Salvos and see if we can find that out, shall we?"

"Sure." I looked at the screen to find the number.

She handed David the envelope. "While Franki and I are on this call, I need you to look up the property tax appraisal records for the parish that East Queens Drive is in and find out whether the Evangelistas own that house. Then get me anything you can on Barbara and Bill Evangelista."

He rose from my desk chair and stretched his long limbs. "Yes, ma'am."

Veronica shot him a scowl as she took his seat in front of my computer.

"Uh, I mean, *mademoiselle*." He scurried from the room to his workstation.

She smiled after him and then turned toward me. "Will you dial the number on speakerphone? I don't want to miss any details of the call."

"Okay." I pulled my desk phone closer toward us. "Do you want me to talk, or you?"

"You talk, but if they refuse to meet with us, I'll chime in and ask a few questions."

As I dialed the number, a knot the size of pizza dough formed in the pit of my stomach. It was one thing to chat up a gossipy salesgirl at LaMarca, but it was quite another to call a family whose loved one had been the victim of a brutal murder. I hoped the Di Salvos would be glad to know that someone was looking into their daughter's cold case. I tapped my fingers on the desk and waited through seven or so rings.

"Hello?" a female voice answered.

"Hi, Mrs. Di Salvo?"

"Yes, who's speaking?"

Even though she'd asked who I was, I could tell from her hollow tone that she didn't care about the answer—or anything, for that matter. "My name is Franki Amato, and I'm on the line with my partner, Veronica Maggio." I decided to sidestep the issue of Immacolata's case. "We're investigating a New Orleans murder that we'd like to talk to you about."

There was silence on the other end of the line. "But, we've already talked to the police."

"Oh. Uh..." I side-glanced at Veronica. "About your daughter Immacolata's case, right?"

"No, about Jennifer's murder, or whatever Angelica was calling herself."

Veronica and I exchanged a full-on look.

My heart pounded in my chest. "You mean, Jessica. Jessica Evans."

"Yes, that's it. What is this about?"

I sat speechless, replaying Maria Di Salvo's words in my mind, and Veronica tapped her chest to let me know that she would take over.

"Mrs. Di Salvo, this is Veronica. I know it must be tremendously painful for you to discuss your daughter, but my private investigation firm, Private Chicks, has been contracted by a local individual to investigate Angelica's murder. We're trying to determine whether her death is related to Immacolata's case. Would it be possible for us to meet with you this week?"

Another long silence ensued followed by muffled sobs. "You can come tomorrow morning at ten o'clock."

There was so much sadness in her voice that my eyes welled with tears. I couldn't imagine the nightmare that she and her family had been living.

"Thank you so much." Veronica leaned toward the screen to see the address. "Are you still at the St. Augustine Street address in the phone book?"

"Yes...see you tomorrow."

I hung up. "That was hard, especially when she started crying. She sounded so unhappy, almost haunted."

"I'm sure you know from your police work that when you're interacting with the family of a victim, it can take an emotional toll on you. Even if you solve the case, you can never undo what was done to their loved one. So, you have to try to keep your personal and professional life separate to the extent that you can. And if the case starts to get to you, then you need to do something to deal with the feelings of helplessness."

"Well, I know one thing I can do."

Veronica looked at me. "What's that?"

"Go out and find that scarf."

As I WALKED toward Ann Taylor, I looked at my phone. *Six o'clock? No wonder I'm so hungry.* I'd spent the last seven hours scarf hunting at The Shops at Canal Place and hadn't thought once about lunch. I was pretty sure I'd never forgotten to eat a meal in my entire life, not even when I'd had a stomach virus. I had heard about people who "forgot to eat," but I always assumed that they had some sort of brain deficiency or damage from an accident or aneurism. But it looked like I'd just been going about the whole losing weight thing all wrong. Instead of dieting, I should've been doing some serious shopping. *Why hadn't I thought of that before?*

I arrived at the store and saw a ghastly pale, thin, and bald mannequin rocking the LBD that Veronica had picked out for me. I figured that what I lacked in terms of thinness, I could make up for with my olive skin and long hair. But after questioning the staff, I left Ann Taylor without buying the dress. I wasn't in the mood to dress shop after learning that no one in the store, or in the entire mall for that matter, had ever seen a black-and-white checked scarf with a yellow border. Plus, every time I thought of my conversation with Maria Di Salvo, I felt guilty about shopping for my date when I could've been working on a case that in all probability was related to the horrific murder of her daughter.

Scarf-less and LBD-less, I headed toward the mall exit and passed a jewelry kiosk displaying silver voodoo doll earrings. My mind flashed to Mambo Odette and her bizarre warning about the Evans case. *What was it she'd said?*

I thought for a moment, and it came to me—"Dat girl, she know what dat boy do." No matter how hard I tried, I couldn't understand who "dat boy" was. *Was it Ryan Hunter?* If so, I certainly didn't know anything about that guy or his past. I also didn't get why Odette had called me "dat girl" when she was talking directly to me. *Or was she?*

A light bulb went on in my head as if by voodoo—"dat girl" wasn't me, she was Jessica.

I rushed from the mall and speed-walked down Canal Street —I made it a policy never to run unless my life was in danger. It was less than a mile to Marie Laveau's House of Voodoo, and I wanted to get there fast to talk to Mambo Odette. As creepy and crazy as it seemed, there was a possibility that she knew something about the case. Although I certainly wasn't familiar with the inner workings of the New Orleans voodoo community, I had a sense that it was rooted in a system of informants and spies, much like the criminal underworld. It wasn't that I thought voodoo practitioners were crooks. I just knew that all underground movements—social, political, cultural, and religious—had historically relied on the covert exchange of information.

At Bourbon Street, I hooked a right and slowed my pace to weave through the thick crowd. Even on a Monday, the street was hopping. But I hardly noticed the revelers and the blaring jazz music because I was so focused on deciphering the riddle of Odette's message. *If Jessica was "dat girl," who was "dat boy"?*

My mind kept returning to Ryan. *Did Jessica know something he'd done?* His criminal record was clean, but that didn't mean anything. *Could he have been the one who strangled Immacolata?* It seemed unlikely that a strong-willed type like Jessica would have been living with him if he had. *Or...*

I stopped dead. *Had Jessica been covering for Stewart Preston?*

"Excuse me." I shoved my way through the last two hundred yards that separated me from Marie Laveau's and caused a guy to spill one of the two sixty-four-ounce plastic bottles of Miller Lite he was drinking. "Oops, sorry."

He stumbled and blinked.

The guy didn't need to be drinking that much, anyway. I hurried up the steps to the store and rushed inside, just in case he decided to come after me. Instead of the cashier with the acne, I saw an older woman who looked like she was dressed for a Sunday sermon.

"Hello." I gave a polite smile as I walked toward the back room.

"Mm." She frowned and looked down at me through her gray, horn-rimmed glasses.

I had to wonder why a woman like her would be working at a voodoo store, especially while wearing a pale pink church suit and a strand of pearls. *Was she keeping a watchful eye on the heathen world for her congregation?*

As I entered the dimly lit room, I saw the rockabilly sales clerk in his seat behind the counter. He was smoothing back his pompadour with a small black comb.

"Can I help you with somethin'?"

He seemed much more relaxed than when I was last there. "Yeah." I strained my eyes in the darkness for the wooden-statue woman. "I'm looking for Mambo Odette."

"She doesn't usually come in on a school night." He stood and began playing air upright bass and bouncing his head to the imaginary beat.

I tried to act like his rockabilly air concert was normal. "School night?"

"You know, a week day?" He pretend-strummed.

"So, she only works on weekends?"

"No, it's the other way around. She makes the long green during the week, then she comes in here on the weekends to hang out."

I might speak Italian, but rockabilly was Greek to me. "I'm sorry, the long what?"

He stopped air-strumming. "You know, baby. Bread, grain, money."

"Ah, gotcha." I opted to overlook the "baby" since it was part of his rockabilly culture. "So, being a voodoo priestess is a regular Monday-to-Friday job?"

"The weekend is when all the cheatin' and thuggin' goes down, you dig? So, Odette spends the work week helping the hapless victims."

"Oh. Then I'll come back another time."

"That's cool." He spun his nonexistent bass. "If you need anything else, just let me know. My name's Hep."

"Hip?"

He recoiled as though I were the least "with it" person he'd ever met. "No, darlin', 'Hep,' as in 'Hep Cat'?"

"Oh. Right." I smiled and returned to the main room. Hep was a different person when Mambo Odette wasn't around—*really* different.

As I headed for the door, the gleaming glass vials of potions near the cash register caught my eye. Although I was reluctant to endure the disdainful stare of The Church Lady, I decided to take a look. After all, I *had* kind of hoped to ask Odette about my date with Bradley after I'd discussed the Evans case with her. But since she wasn't around, it wouldn't hurt to see whether a love potion would counteract any voodoo hexes the Le Bayou restaurant had in store for me.

I browsed the assorted potions, wrestling with my ambiguous position on voodoo, superstition, and things of the like. I didn't want to believe in mysticism, but occasionally things happened in the world that made me wonder whether I was wrong. And sometimes, especially on a sad and frustrating day like the one I was experiencing, I needed to believe in magic.

In the end, I settled on the obvious choice—Love Potion #9. *A steal at only fourteen ninety-five*, I thought as I approached the cash register and placed the bottle on the counter.

The church-suited lady rang up the potion. "That'll be sixteen dollars and eighteen cents with tax."

I counted out the exact amount and handed it to her. I waited for her to tell me that there were better uses of my money, like tithing, but instead she grimaced at me as I placed the potion in my handbag and left the store.

As I walked in the direction of the office to get my car, I pulled out my phone and dialed Veronica's number.

"Hey, Franki. Any luck?"

"Nope. And I covered The Shops at Canal Street so thoroughly that I can even recite its motto—'32 names. 3 floors. 1 place.'"

"Impressive. So now that we've covered all the stores in the vicinity of the crime, we'll have to expand our search to the broader New Orleans area."

"I'm starting to feel like we're looking for a needle in a haystack."

"I know, but we have to keep looking." There was a firmness to her tone that left no room for discussion. "Now, tell me about the dress. Did Ann Taylor have it in your size?"

I hesitated for a moment. "I didn't get it."

"What? Why not? Your date is tomorrow night."

"I wasn't in the mood to dress shop."

Veronica sighed. "What did I tell you about keeping your personal and professional lives separate?"

"I know, I know."

"Then go back to Ann Taylor and buy that dress."

"Or what?" I was half kidding, half not.

"Or I'm going to have Glenda dress you for your date."

I got a mental image of me opening the door to Bradley in a black leather bustier, a gold lamé miniskirt, purple stripper shoes, and a green boa, with a long black cigarette holder in my left hand. "I'm on my way."

AT EIGHT FORTY-FIVE P.M., I strolled through Lenton's at Lakeside Shopping Center listening to the loudspeaker message announcing the mall closure in fifteen minutes and carrying the Ann Taylor LBD in a size twelve. The dress fit to perfection, which had done wonders for my mood. I'd even splurged on a pair of black pumps to celebrate the occasion.

Right before the exit, I spotted two large tables piled high with merchandise marked seventy-five percent off. Of course, I'd already maxed out my meager clothes allowance for the next four months with the purchases I'd made, but who could pass up the opportunity to buy clothing at a quarter of the price? It would've been financially irresponsible of me not to try to find *something* at those prices.

I sorted through the piles and saw the sleeve of what looked like a cute mulberry sweater tangled in a mass of clothes. I put my bags on the floor to unravel the knotted items. I set to work and caught sight of fabric with a black-and-white checked pattern in the mix. My heart raced as I worked to free the item from the other clothes.

It was a scarf—and it looked exactly like the one in the crime scene photo, except that it had a mauve border.

With scarf in hand, I picked up my bags and ran to a cash register. A heavyset woman with a nametag that read "Keisha" was busy putting anti-theft devices on a stack of cardigans. "Didya need help findin' somethin'?"

"Yes, I was wondering if this scarf came in any other colors." I placed it on the counter.

"One minute while I check." Keisha snapped another device onto a cardigan. She picked up a scan gun, scanned the barcode on the price tag, and looked at her cash register screen for what seemed like an eternity. She furrowed her brow. "Looks like it came in one other color."

By this time, my heart beat so fast that I thought I might faint. "Can you tell me which color?"

"Is says lye-moan-sell-low," she syllabified.

"What color is that?"

She shrugged. "Beats me. That's all it says."

"Do you mind if I look?"

She stepped to the side and splayed her arms. "Be my guest."

I rushed behind the counter to the screen. After scanning through a series of product names and lengthy codes comprised of letters and numbers, I saw it.

Style: Limoncello.

I threw my arms around Keisha. "It's yellow!"

She pulled away and took a step backward. "O-kaaay."

"Listen, Keisha, does Lenton's keep records of its sales?"

"Of course. But you'd have to talk to the store manager about that."

"Is the manager here now? It's important."

She looked at me for a moment, and her big brown eyes narrowed. "Hey, you're not a detective are you?"

"Yes, more or less." I hoped the slight exaggeration would convince her to help me.

"Is this a cheatin' husband case, or somethin'?"

"It's much more serious than that."

Her eyes bugged from their sockets. "*Murder?*"

I bit my lower lip.

She nodded. "The manager will be here tomorrow morning at nine thirty. Ask for Ed Orlansky."

12

———

"I'm just thrilled that you found the scarf store." Veronica threw her hands into the air as we sped down Interstate 10 East toward Slidell in her Audi the next morning.

"Me too." I watched to make sure she put her hands back on the steering wheel. Luckily, she did.

She veered into the left lane, cutting off a jacked-up pick-up truck with tractor-trailer tires in the process. "What time did you say we could call the manager?"

I looked over my left shoulder at the road-raging truck driver, who hit the gas and swerved into the middle lane. I shrunk into my seat, but not far enough to miss him saluting us with his middle finger as he roared around us. "Keisha told me he would be in at around nine thirty today."

Veronica glanced at the clock on the dashboard, oblivious to what had occurred. "That was ten minutes ago."

"I know. Let's give him another five minutes to get settled in."

"But we're going to be at the Di Salvo's house in fifteen minutes." She stared at me for way too long.

"All right. I'll call him." I straightened in the seat and pulled my phone from my purse. "You just watch where you're going. Eyes back on the road, missy."

She rolled said eyes. "You know I'm a trained racecar driver."

I gave her a look. "A few hours on the Ferrari racetrack in Italy doesn't make you Mario Andretti." I searched my phone contacts for the number for Ed Orlansky that Keisha had given me. "And honestly, when you get on the highway, you drive like you've had one too many skinny margaritas."

"Whatever you say, Nonna."

I ignored her, like my grandmother would do. "Now, what should I say to this guy?"

"Try to get us on his calendar for today or tomorrow, and don't tell him you're a PI if you can help it. Otherwise, he might not agree to meet us."

"Then how, exactly, are we going to convince him to spend hours and hours scrolling through electronic store receipts for all the people who bought that scarf once he finds out we're not with the police?"

"You leave that to me." She tossed her blonde mane.

"Gladly." I tapped the number and put the phone to my ear. Veronica ran a charm offensive that would rival that of even the savviest Washington political strategist. It was based on what I called the "bat-and-twirl effect," an irresistibly seductive combination of batting her eyelashes while twirling her dazzling golden locks around her fingers. The one and only time I'd tried it on a guy, he told me that I shouldn't tug on my hair because it made my eyes twitch.

"Is it ringing?"

I shook my head. "Voicemail."

"Hang up."

I pressed *End*. "Why?"

"He's the manager of a huge department store, so if you leave a message saying that you're investigating a local crime, he'll probably contact the police to verify that you work for them."

"And then he won't call me back when he finds out I'm not a police officer."

"Precisely."

"So, how do you want to handle this?"

"We know he's supposed to be at work today. I think we should drop in unannounced after we meet with the Di Salvos."

We both jumped at the unexpected sound of my new Booty-licious ringtone. It was better than the barking because it made me feel good about my curves, but it was still startling. On the display was the all-too-familiar *Unknown*.

"Maybe this is him." I tapped *Answer*. "Hello?"

"Yes, hello," a male voice exclaimed a little too animatedly. "Is this Francesca?"

I shook my head at Veronica. The caller was definitely not the Lenton's manager, because the only people who called me Francesca were my relatives or my prospective Sicilian dates. And this was no relative. "This is she."

"Fantastic. I'm Bruno Messina, and my mother, Santina, is friends with your nonna."

My heart sank, and I felt myself turning red. I glanced at Veronica and shrank in my seat. I wanted to get this call over with, but he sounded so excited that I actually felt kind of bad about intending to turn him down. "Yes, my nonna told me you'd be calling."

"Great. Listen, I'm calling to invite you to my house for dinner tonight."

What is it with these guys asking me out on the day of the date?

"My mamma is making her Sicilian specialty, *arancini*."

The thought of the deep-fried balls of rice, tomato sauce, meat, and cheese distracted me from the conversation, but I shook myself from my fried-food daydream and got back to the task at hand.

"Thanks for the invitation, Bruno, but I already have plans for this evening." Halfway hoping he'd think I was a loose woman like Pio had, I decided to clarify. "A date."

"Ah." His tone was less enthusiastic. Then he chuckled. "Well, we could meet after your date—for a nightcap."

Seriously? "That would be disrespectful to the man I'm going out with, don't you think?"

"Maybe he wouldn't have to know? After all, what we don't know doesn't hurt us, right Franki?" He chuckled again.

It was time to get down to the business of a brushoff by borrowing Pio's infamous line. "I'm sorry, but I just don't think this is going to work out."

"I see. Mamma will be so disappointed."

My eyes narrowed at the Catholic-guilt-inducing Mamma line. "I'm sorry about that. Goodbye, Bruno."

"Goodbye?"

The second I heard that uncertain "goodbye" I pressed *End* before he could bounce back with an exuberant "What about tomorrow morning?" Then I turned off my phone to be on the safe side.

Veronica raised an eyebrow. "One of Nonna's boys?"

"Yes, and hopefully the last." I sighed. "He just asked me out on a date for tonight at his house with his mother. I mean, how could my nonna think I would want to go out with a guy like that?"

"You know the mentality of our grandmothers." She turned into a neighborhood with small shotgun-style houses and covered porches. "Back in their day in Sicily, unmarried women our age had no expectations whatsoever of getting married. A warm body was more than *zitelle* like us could hope for."

"I know, I know. But what is it with men? I told this guy

about my date tonight, and he actually suggested that I go out with him afterward on the sly."

"That's his problem." She slowed to scan the street addresses.

"You think? If you ask me, cheating is fairly standard male behavior."

Veronica rolled the car to a stop in front of a modest-looking white house, pulled the keys from the ignition, and turned to face me. "You've had some bad luck with men, I agree. But you can't make a blanket generalization like that. Really, Franki, you need to start rethinking your attitude about men, or you could blow it with Bradley before you even get started."

"I'll see what I can do," I snapped, wondering what had gotten into Veronica. Normally when she was right, she was gentler about it.

"Good." She opened the car door. "Now that that's settled, we're here."

I got out of the car and followed her up the sidewalk, noting the particulars of the Di Salvo home. It was small, no more than fifteen hundred square feet, with cracked and peeling white paint. The yard was overgrown with weeds, and a few of the windows were broken. I wondered whether the general state of neglect of the house had anything to do with the tragic events the family had endured.

Veronica turned to me at the front door. "Ready?"

"I suppose so." But I wasn't at all sure I was emotionally prepared for the meeting.

She knocked and took a step back to wait.

After a few seconds, a chubby young woman in heavy Goth makeup opened the door. Her dyed black hair was boyishly short, and her bangs were long and brushed to one side, covering her right eye. She stood staring at us with her exposed left eye.

Veronica cleared her throat. "Hi. We have an appointment at ten with Maria Di Salvo?"

"I know." The young woman used her teeth to flick a silver stud in her tongue.

I looked at her, unsure of whether I should be grossed out, irritated, or empathetic in light of everything she'd been through. "Can we come in?"

She shrugged and turned to walk down the hallway, leaving the door wide open.

Veronica entered first, and I followed, closing the door behind me. The entryway consisted of a hallway lined with family photos, a large white ceramic cross, and a painting of the Virgin Mary. At the end of the hallway was a cluster of photographs of family members in their caskets. Many of my elderly Italian relatives had similar pictures in their homes, so I was familiar with the old-fashioned custom. But there was one photograph in particular that caught my attention. It was of a raven-haired young woman with fair skin and full red lips, who looked more like a sleeping Disney princess than a dead person. It had been taken more recently, and in an unusual twist, there was another individual in the picture—a young, rather homely woman standing beside the coffin. I was certain that the deceased was Immacolata. *But who was the woman standing next to her?*

I turned away from the photograph and saw the Goth girl glowering at me while slowly twisting her tongue stud with her hand.

She let go of the stud and led me into a small living room where Veronica was already seated on a floral-patterned couch encased in plastic.

As I took a seat beside my best friend, I noticed another cross on the wall behind the couch.

"Hang on." The girl disappeared down another hallway.

"I can't say I'm sorry she's gone," I whispered to Veronica. "She kind of gives me the creeps."

"It's just the all-black effect of her hair, makeup, and clothes."

"No, it's the all-black effect of her personality."

I scanned the room for any insights into the family, but aside from the cross, there wasn't much to see. The floor was covered in beige carpeting, and there were two dingy avocado-green armchairs facing the couch. One of the armchairs had a worn footstool in front with some knitting needles and yarn on it. Between the two armchairs was a small table with a lamp and what appeared to be an old photo of the Di Salvo family.

I rose and walked over to the photo to get a closer look. Then I heard the sound of footsteps approaching. I turned and saw a woman in her mid-fifties entering the living room in a worn housecoat and slippers. She had gray hair and a grayish tone to her skin, but it was clear from her high cheekbones and sensual lips that she had been beautiful in her youth.

She looked past Veronica and me, but not at anything in particular. "May I help you?"

"Yes." Veronica rose to her feet. "I'm Veronica Maggio, and this is my partner, Franki Amato."

Maria Di Salvo gave no sign that she recognized our names.

Veronica gestured to me. "We're the private investigators who called you about the Angelica Evangelista case?"

"Oh, yes."

I extended my hand. "Nice to meet you, Mrs. Di Salvo."

She grasped it limply. "Call me Maria."

Veronica and I took our seats on the couch. The noise was so loud when we sat on the plastic that I almost didn't hear Veronica ask, "Was that your daughter who greeted us at the door?"

"Yes, that's Domenica." She let out a sigh as she took a seat in the armchair with the footstool.

Veronica glanced at me, willing me not to comment. "And you have another daughter, right?"

"I have two. The twins, Concetta and Immacolata."

Concetta must've been the woman in the photo who was standing next to Immacolata's casket. "Immacolata had a twin sister?"

"Yes, they're fraternal twins. Concetta wanted to be here today, but she couldn't leave the convent."

"She's a nun?" I don't know why, but I was surprised.

"After Imma's death, Concetta felt she had a calling to become a nun. She wanted to help others to honor Imma's memory."

Veronica gave a sweet smile. "What a selfless, loving gesture."

"Yes, I'm very proud of all my daughters. But I'm especially proud of what Concetta has become, especially after the agony of losing her twin."

"Which high school does Domenica attend?" I resisted the urge to ask why she wasn't at school today.

"Slidell High. She's working toward her diploma and studying cosmetology at the same time."

Veronica licked her lips. "Can you tell us about Imma? We'd like to know more about her life in London."

"You mean, you want to know who murdered her," Domenica interjected from the hallway.

Maria gave a tired sigh. "Domenica..."

"It was that sick son-of-a-bitch Stewart Preston." Domenica was insensitive to the embarrassment, not to mention the pain, she was causing her mother.

"Domenica, please."

Undaunted, she entered the room. "And the bastard killed Angelica too, because she knew he strangled Imma."

Veronica and I exchanged a look.

"That's enough now." Maria's firmness was surprising given her obvious state of depression. "I'd like to speak to these ladies alone."

I looked at Veronica, and then watched Domenica storm out.

Maria turned to us. "I'm sorry about that." She looked down at her lap for a moment. "She's really been through a lot."

It made me feel awful that she felt she had to explain. "We understand."

"First her sister, then her father..."

Veronica's brow shot up. "Her father?"

"Rosario passed away a few days after Stewart Preston was acquitted of Imma's murder." Maria wiped a tear with her index finger. "It was his heart."

I was stunned to hear of the loss of her husband. "I'm so sorry."

"He never really recovered from Imma's death." She suppressed a sob. "None of us did, but Rosario took it especially hard because he felt he should've been there to protect her."

I thought of my own dad and how he would've felt if anything had happened to me. "Fathers are especially protective of their daughters."

"Yes, and he was so upset when Imma started hanging out with Stewart." She pulled a handkerchief from the pocket of her housecoat. "He told her to stay away from him, but she didn't listen."

Veronica leaned forward. "Why did he tell her to stay away from him? Did he know him?"

"No, but he knew of him." She twisted the handkerchief with her hands. "Stewart is the son of a very wealthy New Orleans family. He was always in *The Times-Picayune* society pages with a new woman on his arm. He'd also been in the news after being arrested for several DWI's and possession of the drug Ecstasy."

I was confused. "So, did Imma meet him in New Orleans or London?"

"They met during London Fashion Week in 2007, the year before Imma died. There are fabric tradeshows in London at the same time as fashion week, and Stewart was there representing the family textile business. Imma never missed the fabric shows because she was majoring in fashion textiles. One thing led to another and then..."

Veronica pressed her temple. "Um, we've read about Immacolata's case in the papers, and we've also seen reports of the trial. Do you believe Stewart is responsible for her death?"

"Yes." Her tone was harsh, and she jerked the handkerchief. "They went to a party, and he took her back to her dorm. There were witnesses who testified that they saw him go upstairs with her to her room."

"So there was no chance that she met someone else later that night after he left?" I asked.

"In our opinion, no. But the jury didn't see it that way." Anger had crept into her voice. "They acquitted him due to a lack of evidence."

"What about Angelica? She testified at the trial, right?"

She stiffened. "She did, but she insisted that she didn't know anything."

Veronica and I exchanged a look.

Maria wiped her eyes. "At the time, I believed her. But later, she changed, and then Rosario wasn't so sure anymore. He thought she knew something, but I just thought she felt guilty for not being able to help at the trial."

The change in Angelica could be important. "How did she change?"

"Well, we'd known her since she was a child." She shifted in her seat as she put the handkerchief back into her pocket. "She practically grew up in our house because her mother, Barbara, worked long hours as a seamstress. Angelica's father ran off when she was small. So, we were like her family. But after the trial, she was different. She avoided us, and we eventually lost contact with her."

She could've avoided them to escape the painful memories, but her behavior was curious. "Did you know she'd changed her name to Jessica Evans?"

"Not until the police came and questioned us. We didn't even know she was back in New Orleans. We just assumed she'd gone to work in the fashion industry in some big city somewhere."

"What about her mother?" Veronica asked. "Did you keep in touch with her?"

"She died a week before Imma's death. Breast cancer. In fact, Angelica was returning to London from Barbara's funeral here in Slidell the night Imma was murdered."

So much tragedy. "An article we read indicated that Angelica returned from a trip abroad at three a.m. the morning of the murder. What was the official time of Imma's death?"

Her gaze lowered to her lap. "Around one a.m."

I wondered whether Angelica had actually witnessed the murder. "Do you think it's possible that she returned earlier than she reported?"

Maria looked surprised. "Rosario asked that same question, but the police were able to verify the time she arrived with flight records and the taxi service that took her back to the dorm."

Veronica scooted forward on the couch, causing the plastic to crackle. "Do you have any pictures of Angelica?"

Maria hesitated. "Well, we have the twins' high school yearbooks."

"Could we see one, the most recent?"

"Give me a minute." She rose from the chair and shuffled down the hall.

"Did you get the feeling she was hiding something?" I whispered.

"Yeah."

"I wonder what it could be? I mean, we just asked to see some pictures."

Veronica opened her mouth to reply but stopped.

Domenica and Maria were arguing in a back room.

I strained to listen but couldn't make out a word.

A few minutes later, Maria returned to the living room, flushed. She handed a yearbook to Veronica. "Here you are. Angelica would've been a senior that year, the same as the twins."

Veronica flipped through the pages as I looked on. First she went to the Ds to the class pictures of Concetta and Immacolata. The difference in appearance between the twins was striking. Imma was an exotic beauty with almond-shaped eyes, full lips and high cheekbones, but Concetta was plain with a round face, close-set eyes, and a pencil-thin mouth.

She turned the page to the Es and stopped. It wasn't hard to locate Angelica's picture—not only because she was a dead ringer for Jessica Evans—but also because there was a word scrawled across it in red ink—*puttana*, the Italian word for "whore." Whoever had written the insult had gone over it several times with the pen, tearing the photo.

An uncomfortable silence ensued.

Maria rose from her seat and walked into the adjoining kitchen. "I have another picture of her."

She returned with a brown billfold and opened it to reveal a small, black-and-white photo. "There, that's her." She pointed to a young blonde in a sundress standing beside Immacolata and Concetta. "It was taken at a family barbecue."

Even though Maria suspected Angelica of having information about Imma's death, she carried her picture in her wallet. I realized that instead of losing one daughter the night Imma was strangled, Maria Di Salvo had actually lost two.

"Barbara made that dress for her," she said softly. "She hated it."

I remembered Angelica's penchant for expensive designer clothes. "Why? Because it was homemade?"

"Most of her clothes were homemade, or they were purchased at yard sales. And they were a constant reminder to her that she was poor. She always used to say that she was going to do whatever she had to do to make money when she grew up so that she could buy herself expensive clothes."

I offered a wan smile. "And she did."

"But that's not why she hated the dress."

Veronica looked up. "Oh?"

"She hated it because it was yellow."

My gut gave a little kick. "Yellow?"

"Yes, when she was a little girl, her mother told her that yellow was her father Bill's favorite color. You see, Barbara still loved Bill even though he'd run out on her and Angelica. I know because Barbara used to tell me that Bill would come home to them one day, and when he did, she wanted them to look nice for him. So she made Jessica wear yellow, and often." Maria looked at her lap and grimaced. "But as the years passed and it became obvious that Bill wasn't coming back, Angelica began to despise yellow. She wore it to make her mother happy, but she always said it was the color of cowards."

Yellow is the color of cowards. My mind began to race like a black-and-white checked flag had been waved in front of it—or the black-and-white checked scarf with the Limoncello yellow border that was wrapped around Angelica's neck in that horrible crime scene photo.

Had the killer known of Angelica's hatred for the color yellow?

13

———

"What's Orlansky doing back there?" I knocked the back of my head against the wall of the Lenton's waiting room. "Sleeping, or something?"

Veronica shifted in her seat. "Calm down, Franki. I'm sure he'll meet with us soon."

"You said that thirty minutes ago." I leaned forward in my chair. "Seriously, he had better hurry. Otherwise, I won't have time to get ready for my date. And if that happens, you'll have another murder to investigate."

"You know," she rummaged in her red Fendi bag, "I just can't stop thinking about Domenica's reaction to our visit."

I crossed my arms. "I still say we should've questioned her."

"No, we need to talk to her alone to avoid the mother-daughter dynamic." She opened a compact. "That way we can find out if she meant the things she said, or if she was just trying to get a rise out of her mother."

"I'm not sure I want to be alone with The Dark One. There was something about the way the girl looked at me that made my skin crawl."

"She *is* awfully angry." Veronica powdered her nose. "I'm

going to have David do a background check on all of them. If this business about Jessica hating the color yellow is relevant to the case, then every member of the Di Salvo family is a potential suspect."

I looked at my phone. "It's six o'damn clock." I leapt from my seat and paced the room, and I ran right into a stick-thin fifty-something administrative assistant as she walked through the doorway. "I'm so sorry."

She straightened and pushed up her glasses. "Mr. Orlansky will see you now."

Veronica and I looked at one another before following the woman as she tottered on scuffed beige heels down a long hallway and stopped without a word beside an office doorway marked "Ed Orlansky."

I followed Veronica into a small, windowless room decorated in varying shades of brown. The balding middle-aged man behind the desk was also wearing brown from head to toe, including the cigar in his mouth. I looked at the cigar to see whether it was lit.

His eyes met mine. "Don't worry, I don't smoke this thing." His voice was gruff like his demeanor. "I just like to chew on it."

My stomach lurched at the thought of swallowing tobacco cud. "Oh. Sure."

He rose and pulled up his pants, which sagged below his protruding belly.

"Which one of you ladies is Veronica?"

"That's me." Veronica extended her hand. "Thank you for agreeing to see us about the Jessica Evans case."

"Happy to be of service." He shook her hand and stared into her eyes. "Did you say that you and Miss—"

"Amato," I interjected. "But please call me Franki."

He nodded. "Franki. Are you with the New Orleans PD?"

"Actually," Veronica grasped a lock of her hair and gave it a twirl, "I own a private investigation firm called Private Chicks, Inc." She batted her long eyelashes.

"We don't normally give information to private investigators…" The cigar went limp between his lips.

Veronica's bat-and-twirl offensive was taking effect.

He drew in his breath, as though shaking off a spell. "But, given the seriousness of this case, I suppose I could help you ladies out."

"That's wonderful, Mr. Orlansky." Veronica clapped and leaned closer to his desk.

"Please, call me Ed." He flashed a mouthful of yellow teeth. "Why don't you take a seat?"

I sat in one of the two chairs in front of his desk. I had a date to get ready for, so it was time to get to it. "Were you able to look up the sales information for the Limoncello scarf?"

He started as though he'd forgotten the reason for our visit. "Oh, yes. Well, the scarf belongs to an exclusive Lenton's line that's only sold in this store. And based on our inventory records, we received five in yellow and five in mauve."

Veronica batted and twirled. "Can you tell us who you sold the five yellow scarves to?"

He paused, mesmerized by her charms. "We have an electronic record of all purchases. But those would only tell you who bought the scarf if the customer used a credit card or check to pay."

I glanced at the time on my phone. "Is there any way to find out the identity of a customer who paid with cash?" Ed hesitated, as though debating something, and licked his dry lips. "You could get an image of the customer from the computer."

"Computer?" I met Veronica's baby blues straight on.

"Yeah, we have a camera on every cash register in the store, and the video from the cameras is stored on a computer hard drive. So we can search the electronic receipt files for the ID number of the scarf, and then check the computer video file for the day and time the scarf was sold."

I nodded to encourage him. "Would it be possible to check the video file for all the Limoncello scarves purchased with cash? We'd like to see those first."

"It depends. If the scarf was sold more than thirty days ago, then the video would be backed up to DVD and stored at our headquarters in Baton Rouge."

"You could get the DVD from Baton Rouge, though, right?"

"Well yes, my secretary could have them mail us a copy. But I'm not sure we have the resources to go through all that video right now. We're understaffed at the moment, and that kind of thing could take hours."

Veronica batted and twirled away. "I could help you go through it."

"In that case," he lit up like a cigar, "I'm sure we could work something out."

"Oh, Ed, you're the best." Veronica gave a sensual hair flip.

He blushed. "Thank you, but it's going to take time." He paused to ogle Veronica. "We'll probably be working late for quite a few nights."

Veronica gave another sexy hair flip. "I'm available."

"All righty then." I shot to my feet. "We sure appreciate it, Ed. We'll check in with you in a day or two to see how the research is coming, but right now we're late for another appointment." I headed for the door and gestured to Veronica to follow suit.

"Yes, thank you, Ed." She sprung from her seat and gave a little wave. "I'll call you."

"I'm looking forward to it." He breathed the words as though exhaling smoke.

We rushed from his office, and I turned to Veronica. "You have mad skills."

"Who, me?" She batted her eyelashes and twirled a lock.

"And while we're on the subject of your skills," I looked at the time, "I'm gonna need you to kick that racecar driver thing into high gear. My date with Bradley is in forty-five minutes."

～

"*Madonna santa*," I whispered as Veronica and I pulled up to the fourplex exactly forty-five minutes later thanks to the evening traffic.

She squeezed the steering wheel. "Holy mother of God, indeed."

Not only was Bradley waiting in the driveway in his black BMW, but Glenda was leaning into his driver-side window in one of her lingerie loungewear ensembles—a black teddy and a fuchsia fur-lined robe with matching high-heeled slippers. She wasn't holding her customary cigarette lighter. Instead, she had a bottle of champagne in one hand and two long-stemmed champagne flutes in the other. And she was clearly in the mood to entertain.

Veronica nudged me from my stone state. "You get into the house and get your LBD on ASAP. I'll have Bradley help me walk Hercules and Napoleon around the neighborhood. That'll give you some time to get ready and get Glenda out of the picture. She won't be able to walk the dogs in those heels."

I spun in the seat. "Are you kidding? That woman has been performing in six-inch platform stripper shoes since the age of sixteen. Not only could she walk the neighborhood in those heels, she could run a marathon and then compete in the freakin' high jump."

She chewed her lower lip. "Don't worry. I'll think of something."

"You do that." I threw open the car door and mad-dashed to my front door.

I wasted precious seconds fumbling with the lock, and then I pushed open the door and started to run toward my bedroom. Unfortunately, Napoleon was waiting to greet me on the other side of the door, so I took an impromptu leap to avoid stepping on him. My foot caught the tooth of the bear head on the bearskin rug, and I careened onto the floor, landing on both knees. I jumped up, limped to the bathroom, and threw off my clothes only to discover that both of my knees were bleeding.

"*Mannaggia*," I cursed, rubbing an antibiotic on my wounds. I had about twenty minutes to get ready to avoid making us miss our dinner reservation at Le Bayou. There was no time to wash and dry my hair. Instead, I took a speed-of-light shower.

I started to apply my make-up and heard Veronica and Bradley returning with the dogs. To my dismay, I also heard Glenda's unmistakable smoker's-cough laugh. I willed Veronica to keep her in line, but I knew there was no use. Glenda was a force of nature, and she was more powerful and unpredictable than a hurricane.

My hands shook as I did my eyeliner. When I stood back from the mirror, I saw that my signature Sophia Loren-style cat eye looked more like that of Cleopatra. There was no time to fix it. "It's okay, Franki," I said to my horrified reflection, "Cleopatra was one of the greatest seductresses in history."

I hurried to my closet, pulled my dress off the hanger, and stepped into it. I wrestled with the zipper and slipped on my black slingbacks. I didn't stop to look in the mirror again for fear of what might look back at me.

When I entered the living room, I saw the second most horrifying spectacle of the day—Glenda had propped one of her skinny white spider-veined legs on the chaise lounge and was doing her best to look sexy while extracting a card from her fuchsia garter belt.

"Here you go, sugar," she said to a grinning Bradley as

Veronica looked on in a mix of astonishment and admiration. "My business card."

"Thank you, Miss Glenda." He took the business card and raised her hand to his lips.

"If you ever need anything, darlin', and I *do* mean *anything*, you just call Miss Glenda."

The only thing I could think of to do was clear my throat. But thanks to my mold allergy, I sounded like a cat hacking up a hefty fur ball. The noise startled the unlikely trio, who turned to look at me.

"Oh." Veronica put her hand to her mouth and rushed to the kitchen.

Glenda raised an eyebrow and tossed back an entire glass of champagne.

I felt what must have been a trickle of blood run down my right knee. *So much for my grand entrance.*

Bradley had a gleam in his eyes. "Jaclyn Smith with an Italian twist."

"What?" I didn't have a clue what he was talking about.

"That's which Charlie's Angel you are."

"Thanks." Of course, I would have preferred to be Farrah, but at least he hadn't compared me to Bosley.

He shoved his hands into his pockets. "But..."

But what? Is it the blood? Or did I cough up some phlegm? I felt around my mouth to check.

"Did you get my message?"

"No," I said, confused, as Veronica knelt and dabbed at my knee with a paper towel. "What message?" Then I remembered —I'd turned off my phone after Bruno called, and I hadn't turned it back on.

"There's been a change of plans. A client of the bank, Craig Burns, is having a crawdad boil, so I thought you might like to do that instead."

"Oh." I tried to think of anything I could change into that was both cute *and* clean.

Glenda, seizing upon the momentary lapse in conversation, sidled up to Bradley. "The crawdad boil reminds me of a strip-tease I used to do—"

"You know what?" I practically shouted over her as I walked toward the door. "If it's all right with you, Bradley, I'll just go like this."

I simply could not allow her to subject him to one of her stripping stories, especially one that involved shellfish and boiling water.

"As you wish." Bradley smiled as he followed me from the apartment. "With you in that dress, I'll be the envy of every guy at the party."

I smiled up at him. Despite his obsession with Charlie's Angels, Bradley Hartmann was growing on me.

~

"Here we are." Bradley eased the BMW to a stop in front of a stately Victorian home.

I admired the long white columns that lined the exterior. "What a gorgeous house."

"Yeah, Craig owns a major construction company here in New Orleans, so he's done quite well for himself."

I sighed as I stared at the serene-looking body of water directly across the street.

"It must be wonderful to sit on that veranda and gaze at the river."

"The river?" He turned to look at me. "You mean, Bayou St. John?"

My head spun like Linda Blair's in *The Exorcist*. "Bayou?"

"Yes." He frowned. "Is something wrong?"

"No, no." I couldn't tell him about Mambo Odette's warning, or he'd think I was a flake. "I just thought I knew my bodies of water better than that."

"Well, if you're interested in bodies of water, Craig would be only too happy to tell you all about the history of this bayou. He's always going on about how this particular stretch in front of his house is where Marie Laveau used to practice some of her voodoo rituals."

"What? Right here?" I looked back at the bayou. Upon second examination, that water was definitely murky.

"So local legend would have it." He opened his car door. "One sec, I'll help you out of the car."

"Thanks." I smiled and turned to scrutinize the bayou. *Why did Marie Laveau choose this spot for her rituals?*

He helped me out of the car and pulled me close. "Are you sure you're okay, Franki?"

"I'm terrific." I smiled and returned his sexy gaze. *To hell with superstition.*

We walked up the driveway and entered the backyard through an iron gate. Twenty or so people stood around two long tables in the center of the yard. Each was covered in newspaper and had piles of crawfish that had been boiled with corn on the cob, large chunks of onion, and potato and spice bags full of Cajun seasonings. On the opposite side of the yard was an outdoor bar manned by a bartender.

Bradley took me by the hand. "Let's head over to the bar. Then I'll introduce you to some of the guests."

We stepped off the concrete walkway into the grass, and my three-inch heels sunk into the soft earth. I sighed and walked on the balls of my feet like I'd seen high-heeled Italian women in Rome do on the cobblestone streets. I imagined that I was taking the graceful strides of a runway model, but I suspected that I actually looked more like I was plodding along on a Stairmaster.

We reached the bar, and an elegant blonde with aristocratic features turned and looked at Bradley. "Why, look what the cat dragged in." She threw her arms around him and kissed him on the cheek.

Bradley stiffened as he returned the woman's embrace. "I didn't realize you were in town, Sheilah."

"Oh, you know how dull Boston society is during the winter months, darling." She pulled from the embrace but made no move to back away. "But then again, you haven't been home in so long. Maybe you've forgotten."

Darling? Home? I stepped closer to Bradley to make it clear that we were together.

Sheilah turned to look at me and frowned. "Who's this?"

"This is Franki Amato." Bradley gazed at the ground. "She just moved here from Austin."

I couldn't help but notice that he hadn't introduced me as his date, nor had he mentioned precisely who the woman was. I didn't need to be a PI to know they had a history.

The bartender looked at Bradley. "What can I get you, sir?"

"A white wine and a Sam Adams." Bradley pulled out some bills to tip him.

Sheilah looked me up and down. "What an interesting outfit to wear to a crawdad boil."

I looked at her white Capri pants. "You know what they say. It's better to be overdressed than underdressed."

She scowled and opened her mouth but closed it when Bradley approached with my wine.

"Franki," he handed me the glass, "why don't we go find a quiet table somewhere?"

It was clear that he wanted to keep me from Sheilah, and I intended to find out why.

"Brad the Bad," a male voice boomed behind me.

I started, and my heels sank deep into the dirt. I lurched backward, spilling wine on my chest.

"Damsel in distress!" The man grabbed me from behind, wrapping his arms around my breasts as I fell into his soft belly.

"Let me help you, Franki." Bradley took the glass from my hand and placed it on the bar.

Sheilah snorted. "That's what happens when you wear high heels to a backyard party."

I shot her a look of death. Whoever this woman was, she was no friend of mine.

"I'll hold 'er steady, Brad," the man said, "and you yank her feet from the dirt."

"Oh, I can manage." I tried to extract my heels, but Bradley knelt and helped me step from my shoes. I cringed as I remembered that I hadn't had time to do my toes.

Bradley pulled my shoes one by one from the earth. "Franki, meet Craig."

"You ready to suck some mudbug heads, Franki?" Craig released me from his clutches.

"I'm sorry, what?" I was certain that I'd misunderstood him.

Craig grinned. "That's what we call crawdads in these parts."

"I think I knew that." I took my shoes from Bradley.

Sheilah smirked. "Craig, Franki's new to New Orleans. She probably doesn't know about the local traditions."

"Actually, I know about sucking crawdad—I mean, mudbug —heads. I've just never done it, but I've been dying to," I fibbed and slipped my shoes back on. As much as I wanted to keep them off, I didn't dare give Society Sheilah the opportunity to point out that my unpedigreed feet were unpedicured.

"Let's show her how to eat a mudbug, Brad." Craig led me by the arm to the nearest table and picked up a tiny crawdad with his huge hand. "You grab the little guy by the torso, see, and you yank off his tail. Then you peel off the shell and eat the meat.

Right after that, you suck the head to get the fatty brains and the juice. It's dee-licious."

"Sounds, uh, great."

"Here, try it." He peeled the tail and handed me the meat with his bare hands.

I hesitated before taking it, and then, not wanting to look like a germaphobe, popped the meat into my mouth. "It's good."

He handed me the crawdad head. "Okay now, pucker up and suck."

Reluctantly, I placed my lips around the crawdad head, and as Craig, Bradley and the ever-present Sheilah looked on, I inhaled sharply.

Bradley gave a half smile. "What do you think?"

"It *is* delicious," I said, surprised. "I really like the spicy flavor."

"I told you she'd like 'em." Craig chuckled. "I know a mudbug sucker when I see one." He gave my back a hearty slap.

I jerked forward but managed to maintain my balance and smile, even though I was unsure whether to be flattered or upset by the remark, especially after I saw Sheilah smirk.

Bradley reached for a stack of dishes. "I'll make us a couple of plates."

I felt a serious need for alcohol. "Okay. I'm going to get another glass of wine. Can I get you anything?"

"Sure, I'll take another beer."

"Be right back." I smiled and trudged to the bar.

The bartender looked up from a glass he was drying with a towel. "What can I get you?"

"A glass of Pinot Grigio and a Sam Adams, please." I licked my lips, which were tingling from the spicy Cajun seasoning. I needed to touch up my lip gloss after sucking that crawdad head. I rummaged in the bottom of my bag and felt the cylindrical-shaped object. But it wasn't lip gloss that I'd found. It was the bottle of Love Potion #9.

"Here's the Sam Adams." The bartender placed the beer on the bar. "I need to run into the house to get another bottle of Pinot."

"No problem." I stared at Bradley's open beer and grasped the potion in my hand. *Should I?*

Sheilah's flirtatious laugh cut across the yard.

I turned and saw her sitting next to Bradley at a patio table, practically in his lap. *I must.*

Glancing from side to side, I opened the potion. No one was looking, so I poured the contents into his beer and slipped the empty vial into my bag. *I mean, it's probably just water, right?*

I approached the table, annoyed to see Sheilah and Bradley huddled together in conversation. I slammed the beer onto the table, and they jumped like two necking teens who'd been caught by the cops.

"I've got to go get my wine." I locked my gaze onto Bradley's like a laser. "Don't forget about me while I'm gone."

I ball-footed it back to the bar. I couldn't leave those two alone for a minute.

The bartender extracted the cork from the Pinot Grigio. He poured a glassful and handed it to me.

"Thanks." I pulled a dollar from my wallet and put it in his tip jar.

He looked at me wide-eyed. "Sure."

I wasn't sure why he would look so surprised by a dollar tip, but I assumed that most people didn't tip at backyard parties.

I turned and headed toward the table. My feet ached from the high heels and from walking on the balls of my feet. And my mouth was strangely numb. I wondered what kind of spices were in Cajun seasoning and decided to lay off the mudbug heads and stick to the tails.

Given Bradley and Sheilah's suspicious behavior, I snuck up behind them to do a little eavesdropping.

Bradley sipped his beer and muttered something to Sheilah.

"Now, darling," she gave him a playful shove, "is that any way to talk to your wife?"

Wife? The glass slipped from my hand and shattered on the tiled patio.

Bradley spun around and gave a start, and Sheilah spit out the sip of wine she'd just taken.

Not one for discretion, Craig shot up from a nearby table. "Ho-ly smokes, Franki. Your lips are all fat."

"Bwhat?" I touched my lips. They felt unusually full, which would've been great if it weren't for the speech impediment.

Everyone at the party went silent and gawked.

Bradley turned to Craig. "She's having an allergic reaction. I need to get her to the hospital."

"Let's give her some Benadryl first so her throat doesn't close up," Craig said not-so-soothingly. "I've got some in the bathroom next to the kitchen."

Taking me by the arm, Bradley rushed me into the house with Craig close behind.

I wanted to confront him about Sheilah's stunning revelation, but my tongue had gone numb.

He led me to a small room off the kitchen. "There's the bathroom."

I entered first and switched on the light. As Craig searched a cabinet for the Benadryl, I looked into the mirror. But instead of my regular semi-full lips, I saw inflated pillow lips—almost twice the size of Angelina Jolie's.

14

———

"They're still pretty big." Veronica stood in front of my desk, scrutinizing my lips. " But you can't seriously think this is voodoo."

"Mambo Odette told me to stay away from the bayou. I didn't, and look what happened." I pointed to my mouth. "I ended up on a date with a married man. And to punish me, some loa puffed me up like a blowfish."

She rolled her eyes. "Like I said, I'm sorry about Bradley. But really, you're as superstitious as your nonna. Deep down, you know this whole lip thing has nothing to do with voodoo. It's a coincidence."

"Here's what I know." I snapped the cover of my laptop shut. "I've been eating shrimp from the Gulf of Mexico all my life, and I've never had a problem. I suck the head of one lousy mudbug, or crawdad, or whatever they call the stupid things down here, and my lips plump up like Ball Park Franks."

"So what? Crawfish are more closely related to lobster than shrimp. Just because you can eat one doesn't mean you can eat the other."

"I don't need a lecture in marine biology to know what's

going on here, Veronica. Don't you see? Mambo Odette has some kind of psychic voodoo power. She knew that the bayou and I wouldn't mix. So now I need to find her and ask her about Bradley."

Veronica furrowed her brow. "Why? You're not thinking about seeing him again, are you?"

"Certainly not." I leaned back in my chair and crossed my arms. "It's just that Odette told me he was a 'good man,' and now I want to know why she would say that if she knew he was married."

"Maybe she didn't know."

"Oh, she knows, Veronica. She knows." I gave a grave nod. "In fact, I think we should consult with her on the Evans case."

She shook her head. "Not a chance."

"Odette's omniscient, and my lips are the proof." I puckered the evidence.

The main door of the office slammed, and Veronica jumped and threw up her hands. "David's here."

Footsteps bounded up the hallway, and David popped his head into my office. "G'day, la—" He dropped the faux Australian accent and recoiled like a turtle pulling its head back into its shell. "Whoa, Franki. Did you get into a throw down or somethin'?"

"Yeah, with an overzealous crawfish."

He shot Veronica a questioning look.

"Don't ask," she said under her breath.

"That's cool." He looked at the floor.

Veronica turned to face him. "I'm about to call Ryan Hunter with a case update. Were you able to find out anything about Bill or Barbara Evangelista?"

"Oh." He stood up straight and pulled back his shoulders to assume his professional stance. "So, I couldn't find any record of the Evangelistas owning the house in Slidell, but I did find an obituary for Barbara. The problem is that it doesn't tell us anything we don't already know."

I sighed away my lip frustration and decided to get to work. "What about Bill? Did you find anything on him?"

"Nope, not yet." He stared to my left to avoid my lips.

"Keep digging. And don't forget about his wife and child. They could factor into this case too."

Veronica nodded. "And while you're working on that, I need you to run background checks on the Di Salvos—Maria, Concetta, and Domenica."

I shivered at the mention of Domenica's name, and my phone began to vibrate like it was scared of her too. I looked at the display and saw the number of my parents' deli. "Sorry guys. I need to take this."

Veronica and David filed out of my office, and I answered the phone in speakerphone mode. "Hello?"

"Francesca?" my mother asked shrilly, as though she were unsure whether she was speaking to me or to some random woman who sounded exactly like me and had my same phone number.

"Yes, Mom, it's me. Is something wrong?"

"Why would something be wrong, dear?"

I was already irritated with the call. "Because you normally call me from home."

"Well, your date with Bradley is a special occasion."

I put my face in my hands. This wasn't going to go well.

"Your nonna and I are calling to find out how it went."

"*Nonna*? What's she doing at the deli?" My nonna *never* left the house, not even for mandatory hurricane evacuations.

"Well, your father and I made her promise not to call you to ask about your date until we came home tonight. She refused to keep that promise, dear, so your father made her come to work with us."

Embarrassment paralyzed my brain. "Wait. Dad's in on this call too?"

"Yes, dear, we've all been talking about it this morning. Rosalie Artusi, Larry from the drycleaner's, Mr. Giangiulio from the bakery, Marjorie—"

"Mom," I interrupted through clenched teeth, "I've asked you a thousand times not to discuss my personal life with the customers."

"But you know we've always thought of our customers as family, Francesca, so it wouldn't be right not to share good news about our children. Besides, everyone has been worried about your problem with long-term relationships."

I focused on resisting the overwhelming urge to curl up in the fetal position under my desk. Then I inhaled. "Mom, about that good news..."

"Yes?"

"The date didn't go perfectly."

She slammed the phone receiver onto the counter. "Joe! The date was a disaster."

I gasped. "Mom."

My dad groaned. "Not again, Brenda."

"*Mom!*"

"Yes, dear?"

"I didn't say it was a disaster."

"Well, then what happened, Francesca?"

"Bradley took me to a party, but after we got there my lips began to swell because—"

The phone slammed to the counter again. "Her lips swelled during the date."

"Oh, Lord," a customer half-shouted. "Franki's got herpes."

"Lip swelling's also a sign of hand, foot, and mouth disease," another bellowed.

I cringed as I listened to the customers, who continued to theorize about the source of my unfortunate lip mishap.

My mother returned to the phone. "Francesca, was it herpes? Or foot and mouth? Or something even more terrible?"

I mentally counted to ten. "Mom, I don't have a disease. I went to the hospital, and the doctor said it was an allergic reaction to crawfish."

Down went the receiver. "She's allergic to crawfish, Rosalie." My mother wailed, as though my chances of ever finding another man were now even further diminished in light of my new shellfish affliction. "What are we going to do?"

I put my head on the desk and heard what sounded like the phone hitting the floor followed by a scuffle.

"It's-a not-a the crawfish-a, Franki. It's-a Bradley." Nonna's doom-and-gloom voice boomed through the speaker. "I told-a you that you should-a go out-a with only Italian boys, but don't-a you worry. I find-a you a nice Sicilian."

Oh, sweet Gesù, *no.* I had to discourage a second round of the Sicilian Dating Game. "Nonna, it's not possible to be allergic to a person. And besides, I don't have time to go out with anyone right now. After all, I've got a killer to track down."

"If-a you got-a the time to find a killer, you got-a the time to find a husband."

The line went dead.

In a shocking tactical maneuver, my *nonna* had hung up on *me.*

To keep my mind off the whole Bradley affair—or rather, marriage—I buried myself in work. After spending several hours sifting through British and American websites for details about the Di Salvo murder trial, I pondered a disturbing picture of Stewart Preston. It was taken on the steps of the courthouse after he'd been acquitted for murder. He sneered with his fist raised in a sign of victory. Everything about the guy oozed sleaze, from his distasteful gesture to the gold chain link necklace and dark chunky watchband he'd selected to accessorize his designer suit. And that was how he looked and behaved after his attorneys had undoubtedly worked overtime to get him to clean up his image.

The image of an arrogant Stewart did nothing to calm my already upset stomach. I pulled the seventh or eighth Tums tablet from the roll in my desk drawer and put it between my back-to-normal lips.

What is wrong *with me?* I pressed my hand to my burning belly. Of course, my heartburn could've had something to do with the four slices of sausage and garlic pizza I'd eaten for lunch at Nizza. It also might've been caused by the threat of a renewed surge of Sicilian suitors looming on the horizon. But the most likely culprit was the fact that I'd fallen yet again for a cheater, and a married one to boot.

The lobby bell interrupted my personal pity party.

I rose from my desk and headed down the hallway.

A young, dark-haired woman stood in the middle of the lobby with her hand on a large crucifix hanging from her neck. She wore sensible black shoes and a plain white cotton shirt with a full, ankle-length gray skirt, which accentuated her thick waist and chubby thighs. "May I help you?"

"Yes." Her voice was soft, soothing. "I'm here about the Jessica Evans case. I'm Concetta Di Salvo."

I realized that I recognized her from the photos I'd seen at her mother's house.

"I'm Franki Amato. My partner, Veronica Maggio, and I spoke with your mother and sister yesterday."

She grasped my hand rather than shaking it. "That's why I'm here. May I sit down?"

"Of course. Let me show you to our conference room, and then I'll have Veronica join us."

"That would be nice." She gave a pleasant smile. "Thank you."

After I'd settled her at our conference table with a glass of water, I closed the door and ran from the room to Veronica's office. And I understood why she hadn't responded to the bell.

She stared at her computer with her hot pink headphones on, which could only mean one thing—she was communing with the goddesses—The Spice Girls.

I waved my arms SOS-style in front of her desk. "Concetta Di Salvo is here."

"She is?" Her lips went into yikes-mode as she rose to her feet. "But I haven't prepared any questions for her yet."

"We'll have to wing it." I waited for her to gather her laptop and pushed her toward the conference room.

We entered, and I let Veronica take the lead.

"Thank you for the unexpected visit, Concetta."

She squeezed a rosary. "I loved Angie like a sister, so I want to help with the investigation in any way I can."

She had a calming presence about her. *No wonder she'd become a nun.*

Veronica opened her laptop. "Your mother told us that Angelica was like one of the family."

"Oh, absolutely. In fact, Imma, Angie, and I used to joke that we were actually triplets."

I glanced at the rosary. "But your mom also said that your family lost touch with Angelica after Imma died."

"Yeah. Things were never the same after we lost Imma." She took a sip of her water. "My whole family was in mourning, of course, and then there was the emotion and stress of the investigation and later the trial. After it was all finally over, we never heard from Angie again. But I'm sure she felt uncomfortable after everything that happened."

"Why do you say that?"

"Well, because my family was in ruins, for one thing. We weren't the same big happy family that Angie had known before." She paused and looked at her rosary. "You see, Imma was the beautiful, extroverted one. And she had so much energy and enthusiasm for life. Without her we all just...fell apart. But I also think Angie cut off contact with us because she felt bad that she didn't help us at the trial."

Veronica furrowed her brow. "Your mother told us she testified."

"Well, she took the stand, but she said she didn't know anything about Stewart or his relationship with Imma."

I pursed my lips. "And you didn't believe her."

"I wanted to." Her eyes were earnest, like her tone. "It's just that Imma died so *violently*. I felt that Angie must have noticed something, like some sort of abusive behavior. And..."

I leaned in. "What?"

"Well, I'm sure Imma told me that Angie had been the one to introduce her to Stewart when they met at London Fashion Week."

Veronica straightened in her chair. "So Angie knew Stewart before Imma did?"

"Yes, I'm positive that Imma said Angie had met Stewart at Mardi Gras before she and Imma ever went to the London College of Fashion. I remember because she said that Stewart had pulled Angie from the crowd onto his float in the Krewe de Eros parade."

My eyes went wide. "He had his own parade float?"

Concetta nodded. "Yes, he's very active in Mardi Gras."

Veronica typed a note on her laptop. "Why do you think Angie would have lied in court about knowing him?"

"I don't know. Maybe because she was scared?"

I glanced at Veronica. "Of what? Stewart?"

Concetta harrumphed. "Angie wasn't the type to be intimidated by anyone. If anything, she was worried about her reputation. She was very driven to succeed. In fact, Imma said that as soon as Angie got to London, she would only associate with people who could help her career in some way."

That certainly jives with the way Ryan and Annabella described her.

Veronica resumed typing. "Did you see Angie again after the trial?"

"No, never." She sighed. "The last we knew she was in London. We had no idea that she'd come back to New Orleans, and we certainly didn't know she'd changed her name."

Veronica tapped a finger to her cheek. "Do you have any idea why she would've used the name Jessica Evans?"

Concetta looked at her hands. "The name specifically? No. But my guess is that she wanted to disassociate herself from Imma's murder."

I scratched my head. "Why would she want to do that? Do you think she had something to do with your sister's murder?"

"No, not at all." Concetta's eyes filled with tears. "Angie could never have killed Imma. I'm sure of that."

Not wanting to upset her further, I changed the subject. "You joined the convent after the trial, right?"

"No, I entered aspirancy about six months after Imma died, before the trial. God called me to service after I lost her." Her voice was soft, distant. "It's funny, when Imma was thousands of miles away in London, I still felt like she was with me. But then when she was really gone...well...let's just say that I could never have gone back to the life I led before."

I felt terrible for her, and I hoped that her decision to become a nun was truly the right one, and not a choice made solely based on her loss.

Veronica placed a hand on Concetta's back. "I've always heard that the bond between twins is so powerful."

"It is," she whispered. Then she cleared her throat. "And I'm sure my mother told you about my father."

I nodded. "Yes, we were so sorry to learn of his passing, especially under the circumstances."

Concetta's lips tightened, and she touched the crucifix at her neck. "Imma's death killed my father. And it killed my mother too, even though she's physically still with us. The person she used to be died a long time ago."

I thought of her Goth sister. "What about Domenica? How has all of this affected her?"

She inhaled. "Domenica was only thirteen when Imma died. Then she lost her father—and her mother, for all intents and purposes. She's had an awful time coping."

Veronica closed her laptop. "That's certainly understandable."

"Yes, and even though I haven't always agreed with the way she's handled her grief, I know she still has faith in God, so she'll be all right."

I wondered whether she was referring to Domenica's dark look and demeanor. "What haven't you agreed with?"

"Well, her dropping out of school, mainly. But I also disapprove of her Goth makeup and clothes."

"So, she became a Goth after Imma's death?"

"Yes, I think she felt isolated, but she also wanted to be left alone. The Goth persona was like a mask for her to hide behind."

Veronica's lips thinned. "I'm sure it's just a phase."

"I think so too."

I wasn't so sure I agreed with them, but I knew I shouldn't press the issue. "What about Stewart Preston? Did you or anyone in your family ever have any interaction with him before Imma died?"

"No. My family doesn't have much money, so we weren't able to visit Imma in London while she was seeing Stewart."

"And she never came back to New Orleans with him after they began seeing each other?"

Concetta looked at her rosary. "Like I said, we didn't have the money. The annual tuition at the London College of Fashion was around sixteen thousand dollars, not including the cost of living. So Imma took out student and private loans, got scholarships, and worked to pay her way through school. My parents helped as much as they could, but I can tell you for sure that she had *nothing* left over for an international plane flight."

My mind wandered to Angelica's flight home for her mother's funeral. *If Imma couldn't afford a plane ticket with her parents' assistance, then how had Angelica managed to pay for one?* "Do you know anything about Angie's finances during school?"

She shrugged. "In the beginning, she had a harder time paying for school than Imma did because she didn't have any help from her parents. But then she came into some money at the end of her senior year."

Veronica's chin lowered. "You mean, when her mother died."

Concetta reached for her crucifix. "Yes, but she didn't inherit any money from her mother, if that's what you mean. Angie always said that she and her mom lived paycheck to paycheck. She also told me that her father had stopped sending child support when she was only two or three."

I sat up, intrigued. "Then, where do you think the money came from?"

"We never knew, but my mother thought it must have been an advance from a company. You know, like a signing bonus."

"Do you know whether it was a large sum of money?"

"I have no idea. I just know that around the time of the investigation, money no longer seemed to be an issue. Plus, she started wearing the occasional piece of pricey jewelry or an expensive blouse. She would tell people that these things had belonged to her mother, but I knew better."

Veronica and I exchanged a look.

"Let's go back to Stewart," Veronica said. "Did you talk to him during the investigation or at the trial?"

"Definitely not." Her hand went to her crucifix. "The police warned us that if we had any contact with him, we could jeopardize the case. And of course, our attorneys wouldn't let us speak to him during the trial, either." The corners of her mouth tightened. "But he wouldn't have talked to us anyway, even if we'd tried. In fact, he never so much as looked at any of us at the trial. Not even after he was acquitted."

Veronica licked her lips. "Are you convinced that he's guilty of Imma's murder?"

Concetta looked her in the eyes. "I am, yes."

I leaned forward. "And what about Angie's murder?"

"What about it?" she asked, surprised.

"Well, you know that Imma and Angie were murdered the same way, right?"

Concetta winced. "Yes, they were both strangled."

I met and held her teary gaze. "With scarves."

She nodded, seemingly unable to speak.

"So, do you think it's possible that Stewart had anything to do with Angie's murder?"

"I couldn't possibly speculate on something like that." She spoke as though winded. "It wouldn't be right."

Veronica put a hand on her shoulder. "Of course not."

Concetta placed her rosary on the table. "I pray for Stewart every day, and I've forgiven him for what he did to Imma. I hope that one day he confesses his sin and asks the Lord for forgiveness, but I don't think he will."

I would've expected a nun to hold out hope that a sinner would repent.

"Why do you say that?"

"Well, if what I've seen in the society pages is true, then it seems unlikely. He was known around New Orleans to be a partying playboy when he met Imma, and it appears he still is."

Veronica opened her laptop.

"Plus..." Concetta pressed her lips together. "I doubt he would seek counsel from the Church since I've heard he practices voodoo."

My brow shot up. "Voodoo?"

I barely heard her when she replied, "Of course, that could just be a rumor." I was too preoccupied with thoughts of the skull bead I'd found at the murder scene.

15

___

"Can you believe the bomb Concetta dropped?" I asked after I'd watched her exit the building from the conference room window. "Stewart was involved in *voodoo*."

"She also said that might not be true." Veronica picked up her laptop and headed out the door to her office.

I followed close on her heels. "But even *you* have to admit that the skull bead I found takes on a whole new meaning in light of this news."

"It *is* intriguing." She spoke over her shoulder as we walked down the hall. "But we need proof of Stewart's association with voodoo. And then we have to connect that bead to him, which could be next to impossible considering that this town is full of people who buy that stuff."

"That's where Odette Malveaux comes in. If Stewart *does* practice voodoo, then she might know him. That would explain how she knew about this case."

"Talk to Odette." Veronica entered her office and took a seat behind the desk. "But take whatever she says with a grain of salt."

"Sure." I leaned casually against the doorjamb, even though I was cheering inside. "Apparently, she only goes to Marie Laveau's on weekends, but I'd be willing to go there on my day off if it meant getting a lead on this case." *And asking her about Bradley.* "But first I'll do some research on Stewart to see if I can find anything connecting him to voodoo."

Veronica gave a dismissive wave. "Enough of this voodoo nonsense. What did you think about the revelation that Jessica came into money right around the time of Imma's murder?"

I took a seat in front of her desk. "Honestly, it made me wonder if someone was paying her off."

"I thought the same thing." She tapped a pen on her chin.

"I mean, even Ryan Hunter said Jessica had a suspiciously large amount of money, which is odd for a woman who, by all accounts, didn't inherit anything from her mother and should've been strapped with student loan debt."

"Good point." Veronica leaned back in her chair and propped a resplendent pair of beige and gold Louis Vuitton pumps on her desk.

"So, I have this theory." I held up my hands. "Suppose Concetta was right, and Jessica *did* know something about Imma and Stewart's relationship, or maybe even about—"

"Imma's murder," she interrupted with a flourish of her pen.

"Precisely."

"Then Stewart could have been paying her to keep quiet."

I nodded and crossed my arms. "That would also explain Jessica's reluctance to testify at the trial. Of course, it's pure supposition at this point, but this could be the link between the cases that we've been looking for."

"True." Veronica pressed the pen to her lips.

"That reminds me. Have you looked at the picture of Stewart at the courthouse after his acquittal?"

"I have. And judging from his demeanor, I wouldn't put bribery past him."

The mention of bribery jogged my memory. "Oh my gosh. I just remembered something."

"What?"

"That day I ran into Bradley at Market Café, he told me that Jessica came to the bank to make a deposit every month. Do you think it could've been a payoff?"

"Well, it might've been her paycheck. But we definitely need to look into that."

"I'll text Corinne and ask if she'll help." I pulled my phone from the pocket of my jacket. "After all, I did find her dog."

"Great idea. I also think it's time we paid Stewart Preston a visit."

"I doubt he'd talk to us." I typed a message to Corinne. "I mean, it's not like he's going to want to associate himself with Jessica's murder, especially not after he was lucky enough to get off for Immacolata's."

"Oh, I know he won't talk to us. We'll have to go undercover."

I placed my phone on her desk. "What do you have in mind?"

"Well, what do we know about Stewart?" Veronica had a mischievous gleam in her eyes.

I shifted in my chair. I'd seen that look before, and it always spelled trouble—for me. "Besides the fact that he's an acquitted murderer, you mean?"

She cocked her head. "Yes, Franki. Besides that."

"He loves Mardi Gras and women?"

Veronica picked up my phone. "Right. The Mardi Gras parades have started, but according to this year's schedule, the Krewe de Eros parade isn't until a week from tomorrow. So, we'll have to go with women." She gave me the once-over.

"Oh no." I jumped to my feet in alarm. "*You're* the bat-and-twirl girl. And I already went undercover at LaMarca, so it's your turn."

"If Immacolata is any indication, Stewart has a weakness for busty, dark-haired Italian girls. That would be you." She nodded in the direction of my breasts.

I shot her a look. It really was true that blondes had more fun, mainly because they left all the crap to us brunettes. "All right." I sighed and flopped into my chair. "What do I have to do?"

She grinned, triumphant. "First we have to contact Stewart. I've been doing some searching, but I can't find a phone number or email address for him. His parents are listed in the phone book, though, so we'll start with them."

"Do you just want me to pretend to be interested in him, or something?"

"If you get one of his parents on the phone, yes. But if by some chance Stewart actually answers, then tell him you're an old friend of Jessica's and that you need to talk to him, urgently."

I again leapt from my seat. "Are you crazy? If he *did* have anything to do with Jessica's murder that'll make him think I want to blackmail him. You could get me strangled."

"You'll be fine." She leaned back and crossed her legs. "Besides, you know we're going to have to play hardball to get a guy like Stewart's attention. If you just pretend to be some floozy who wants to sleep with him, he'll figure out that you're a fraud the minute you ask a question about Jessica. This way, he'll know you're looking for information about her from the start."

"Yeah, and he'll be suspicious of me from the start, too." I rubbed my neck. "Maybe he'll even bring a scarf to our meeting."

"We can worry about the meeting later. Right now, all you

have to do is call him. I've already signed you up for a Google Voice number to conceal your identity."

"Veronica, a guy with Stewart's financial means could find out the identity of the most protected person in the federal witness protection program. He's not going to have any trouble figuring out who owns a Google phone number."

She leaned forward. "There's a chance a master hacker could trace it, but it would take some time because I registered the number from a public computer. And besides, I used an old email address that can only be traced to me."

"I see that you've been thinking about this." I glared at her as I returned to my seat. "Have you picked out a fake name for me too?"

She repressed a smile. "I have."

"What is it?"

"Gina Mazzucco."

"That sounds like one of the freakin' Pink Ladies." Veronica had always gotten to play Sandy in our college dorm *Grease* sing-alongs, while I'd been forced to play Rizzo. I had the sneaking suspicion that she was rubbing that in yet again.

"I know." She chuckled and dialed a number on my phone and then shoved it into my hand. "Here you go, Rizzo—I mean, Gina."

Suspicion confirmed. I scowled at her and gripped the device.

"Preston residence," an older woman's velvety voice replied on speakerphone.

Nerves pricked at my belly. "Uh, hi. May I speak to Stewart, please?"

"The third or the fourth?" she drawled.

"Pardon?"

The woman gave a sigh that sounded more like a huff. "Are you looking for my son or his father?"

"Oh." My face grew warm. "Your son."

"He lives in New York."

Even though Stewart's mom clearly wasn't in the vicinity, she was pretty darn intimidating. "Um, would you mind giving me his number?"

"Yes, I would mind." Her tone had turned to steel. "Who *is* this?"

"Gina Mazzucco." I glared at Veronica. "I'm an old friend."

"Stewart has asked me not to give out his private number. Good day."

"Wait—"

She hung up, and it was definitely a landline receiver because the sound punched my ears. "Nice manners."

Veronica shrugged. "She *did* say 'Good day.'"

I sigh-huffed like Stewart's mother. "What now?"

She drummed her manicured fingernails on her desk. "We'll try again tomorrow. Maybe someone else will answer."

"And if not?"

"Then we'll just have to wait and pay a visit to the Krewe de Eros parade."

"Do you really think Stewart will come home for Mardi Gras? He might want to steer clear now that Jessica has turned up dead."

"Franki," she gave a knowing tilt to her head, "it's one of the biggest parties in the world, and one of the few where women flash their breasts unprompted."

I folded my arms across my chest to send her a don't-look-at-me message. "You're right. A scumbag like Stewart won't be able to resist a powerful combination like that, not even under the threat of a murder investigation."

∽

I LOOKED at my phone—eight p.m.—and shoved it back into my bag. I'd been waiting for Odette Malveaux for two hours, but I was determined to stay at Marie Laveau's until it closed. I'd been unable to find any link between Stewart Preston and voodoo on the Internet, so Mambo Odette was my best chance to establish a connection.

I walked to the store entrance and looked out at the bawdy crowd on Bourbon Street. Then I turned and leaned against the cashier counter. Thankfully, the kid with the acne was back, so I didn't have to endure the disapproving gaze of The Church Lady.

To kill time, I glanced around the room at the merchandise, starting with the vials of potion right next to me on the counter. Heartburn crept up my throat. *So much for Love Potion #9.*

My gaze moved to the necklaces on the other side of the cash register. I inspected the various charms, and a woman shoved her way into the store, thrusting me into the cash register.

I turned to say something and stopped dead.

Mambo Odette.

With her graying black dreadlocks hidden by a crisp white *tignon* and matching dress, she seemed more approachable than the last time I'd seen her, despite the fact that she'd shoved me. So, I summoned up the courage to walk over to her. She was grabbing handfuls of chicken feet from a bin and throwing them into a burlap sack.

I was so stressed that my heart did a voodoo dance. "I don't know if you remember me, but you gave me some advice when I was here a few days ago."

Mambo Odette didn't respond. She kept her head down as she continued to put chicken feet into the sack.

Nevertheless, I was undeterred. "I'm investigating the murder of Jessica Evans, and I'd like to ask you a few questions. I'm willing to pay you for your time."

She moved from the chicken feet to the alligator teeth without a word.

I decided on the direct approach. "Do you know anything about Jessica Evans?"

"I know she didn' make no offerin' ta Baron Samedi."

I jumped but tried to act cool. "Offering?"

"He don' have ta dig de grave fo' Baron Kriminel if he don' wan' ta. But ya got to give 'im rum soaked in twenty-one hot peppas an' Pall Mall cigarettes."

"I-I'm sorry?" I got distracted by the mention of grave digging.

Mambo Odette didn't reply. She sifted through the alligator teeth as though looking for a specific one.

Looks like I need to try another tack. "Can you tell me anything else about Jessica?"

Again no response. Instead, she counted the items in her bag.

Okay, I'll take that as a no. "What about Stewart Preston, IV?"

"Don' know 'im. But Erzulie D'en Tort do. And she goin' ta deal wit 'im."

I wondered whether this Erzulie was associated with Jessica or Imma. "Who?"

She moved to another bin full of some shriveled items.

I shrunk from the bin in case they were body parts or heads. "Can you tell me if Stewart Preston practices voodoo?"

Mambo Odette stopped sifting and looked me in the eyes. "I tol' ya, chile, I don' know him."

I took a step back before I pressed on. "Can you tell me anything else about this case?"

She looked down. "Watch out fo' dem who take magic."

"Take magic? Do you mean drugs or something?"

Without a word, she began selecting dried up items from the bin, sniffing them, and placing them into her bag.

The conversation was going nowhere, and I was starting to think I'd been wrong about consulting Mambo Odette. So, I shifted the focus to Bradley.

"You told me to stay away from the bayou—"

"And ya didn' do it," she interrupted.

I was struck yet again by the scope of her knowledge. "No, and now I've found out that the man I'm crazy about, the one you said was a 'good man,' is married."

"Thangs ain't always the way they seem, chile." Odette turned to a small display of gris-gris bags that promised everything from love to prosperity to the bearer. She selected a red bag and untied the yarn at the top. Then she rummaged around in the pocket of her white cotton dress and pulled out a dried root. She put it into the bag, retied the yarn, and pressed it into my palm. "Ya need ta go *home*."

I wasn't sure what I was supposed to do with the gris-gris bag, but there was no point in asking. I pulled a twenty-dollar bill from my wallet and handed it to her. She slipped it into her pocket and returned to selecting items for her sack.

I went to the kid at the cash register to pay for the gris-gris bag. "So, do you know who Erzulie Dentor is?"

"*D'en Tort*. It's French for 'of the wrongs.'" He rung up the gris gris bag. "She's a voodoo loa who protects women and children and takes revenge on people who do bad things to them." He scratched his neck. "Five dollars and forty cents."

"You've been a big help." I handed him the exact change, deposited the gris-gris bag in my purse, and exited the store.

And I wondered whether Erzulie of The Wrongs should've been protecting me.

～

ON THE DRIVE HOME, I tried to crack Odette Malveaux's enigmatic words. I had to figure out what she'd meant when she said that Erzulie was after Stewart. Based on Erzulie's role in the voodoo world, it seemed like Mambo Odette was implying that Stewart had harmed a woman. *But if so, who? Imma? Jessica too?* I also needed to know if she was trying to tell me that Stewart wasn't involved in voodoo when she said that she didn't know him. As for the crazy warning about people who take magic, if she was referring to drugs, then it was possible that she was talking about Stewart.

Of course, I knew it seemed insane to put so much stock in the bizarre ramblings of a voodoo queen, but New Orleans was like nowhere else in the world. If something was going down in The Big Easy, the voodoo world knew about it before anyone else. It was just a matter of figuring out how to speak their language.

The worst part of all was that I was out twenty bucks plus the five for the gris-gris bag, and I hadn't found out a thing about Bradley. I couldn't imagine what Odette had meant when she'd said that things weren't always the way they seemed, because it was painfully clear to me that Sheilah was Bradley's wife. It was also glaringly apparent that he hadn't tried to call me, maybe because he'd figured out that I'd overheard what Sheilah had said.

I pulled up to my house and walked to my front door, debating whether to text Bradley and confront him about Sheilah. I inserted the key into the front door lock and froze.

Someone was at my back.

My police academy training kicked in—literally. I gave a few swift kicks to the genitals and a mighty karate chop on the back of the neck, and the perpetrator was in the grass, rolling in pain.

As soon as I had a chance to look at his face, my body went cold. "Bradley!" I knelt. "I didn't realize it was you."

"Yeah." The word sounded like a grimace looked. "I got that."

"I'm so sorry," I said, although a swift kick to the groin seemed appropriate for a cheater like him. "Can you stand up?"

"Just...give me a minute." He rolled onto his back and inhaled sharply.

I waited at his side with a heavy feeling in my stomach. The heartburn was gone, but I had a lead weight in my gut. Seeing Bradley again made me realize how much I didn't want him to be married.

After a few minutes, he stood and brushed himself off. Then he bent over, still favoring his privates, to retrieve the dozen yellow roses he'd brought me. "I shouldn't have come up behind you like that, Franki. I'm sorry."

"You're right, you shouldn't have." My tone was more hostile than accusatory. "What are you doing here, anyway?"

He scrutinized my face and handed me the bouquet. "I came in hopes of giving you the goodnight kiss I wanted to give you last night."

I lowered my gaze. Bradley had no idea that I'd overheard him and Sheilah. Telling him to get lost was going to be so much harder than I'd thought.

"Franki." His voice was soft, sinuous, seductive.

I looked up, and his fingers slid to the nape of my neck and wove into my hair. His other hand pressed the base of my back. He pulled me close, and his lips covered mine. He kissed me gently at first, and for a second I went rag doll. When he parted my lips with his tongue and kissed me more deeply, energy—not to mention heat—spread through my limbs.

As I wrapped my arms tightly around his neck, I wondered whether the magic between us was the work of Love Potion #9, the gris-gris bag, or something more primal than voodoo. Then Bradley pressed his body hard against mine, and I decided that I really didn't give a damn what it was.

When he released me, I gazed into his beautiful blue eyes. And I gave him a right hook to the cheek.

Without so much as a glance back, I entered my apartment and closed the door. *Serves him right for kissing me when he's married.*

16

"Thank you for meeting me at seven a.m., Corinne."

She took a seat in front of my desk. "You have been so kind to me and Bijou. I am happy to do it."

I wasn't happy. I hadn't slept a wink after punching Bradley, and my insomnia had nothing to do with the fact that he'd pounded on my door for twenty minutes demanding to know what was going on. It was because I'd wanted so badly to open the door and throw myself into his arms, even though I knew he was a cheating rat. "So, how *is* the little powder puff?"

"She is growing so fast. She look more like a little pillow now." Corinne laughed, and then her face grew serious. "By ze way, I did not receive ze bill for your services."

I shook my head. "I can't accept your money, especially not now that you've agreed to help us with the Evans case."

She hesitated. "*Bien*. If you insist."

"I do." Catholic guilt panged my chest. "But are you sure you want to do this? I mean, you could lose your job for giving us client information."

She blinked her big blue eyes. "I did not know Jessica, but I sink it is so awful ze way she died. If I can help find who killed her, zen it is wors ze risk."

"That's incredibly generous of you." I double-clicked the Evans file on my laptop. "And just so you know, I'm going to do everything in my power to make sure that no one finds out you helped with the case."

She smiled. "What do you need for me to do?"

I glanced at the file notes. "Well, we know that Jessica came to the bank to make monthly deposits. We need to find out whether she was depositing her paycheck from LaMarca. And if not, we'd like to know who the deposits were from."

She shrugged her shoulders. "Zat is easy to discover."

"I'm not so sure." I closed my laptop. "I'm assuming that she made the monthly deposits in cash."

"Why do you say zat?"

"Because we have reason to believe that the deposits were a payoff."

Corinne crinkled her Tinker Bell nose in confusion. "What is zis 'payoff'?"

"A bribe."

"Ah." She nodded. "Well, I don't remember her bringing cash. I sink she always deposit a check, but I will find out." She looked at her watch. "I must go. I have to be at ze bank before eight."

"Okay. Thanks." I rose to see her out. "And remember, if you change your mind about helping, I'll understand."

"I know." She grasped the doorknob and turned to face me. "But I will not change my mind."

After she left, I thanked my lucky stars that I'd met a nice woman like Corinne.

My thoughts turned to Bradley, but I was no longer thinking about the night before. Instead, I wondered how he'd react if he found out that I'd asked one of his employees to provide me with confidential bank information. But whatever. It served him right.

AT TEN A.M., I rose from my desk to stretch and glimpsed something yellow outside the window.

Across the street from our building stood a plump, sixty-something woman in a yellow sack dress with a white scarf tied over coiffed silver hair. She looked like a giant lemon with bright pink lipstick.

The she-lemon glanced from side to side through huge white Jackie O-style sunglasses, as though she were afraid she was being followed. She lowered her shades, looked up, and made eye contact with me. She dipped her head, shielded her face, and hurried toward the entrance to our building.

"Looks like we have a reluctant visitor," I called to Veronica as I walked into the hallway. I entered the lobby.

The woman's white-scarfed head emerged from the other side of the door. "Pardon the intrusion," she said in a Southern drawl. "Are you with Private Chicks, Incorporated?"

"Yes ma'am," I said in Southern kind.

The rest of her body entered. "Well, hiii. My name is Twyyyla. Twyla Upton." She extended a hand with yellow-lacquered fingernails. "I'm the wife of *the* Harold Upton?"

I shook her chubby, bejeweled hand. I had no idea who "*the* Harold Upton" was, but I could tell by the exquisite rings she wore that he was a wealthy man. "I'm Franki Amato."

Veronica clicked into the lobby. "Mrs. Upton, I'm Veronica Maggio. What a pleasure to meet you."

"Likewise."

Veronica turned to me. "Mrs. Upton is something of a local

celebrity here in New Orleans because of her fabulous rose garden."

Mrs. Upton removed her sunglasses and untied her scarf. "I have eighty-nine species of hybrid teas, miniatures, climbing roses, and floribundas. And please call me Twyla."

"Wow," was all I could think of to say. I wondered whether she'd tried to conceal her identity when entering our office to protect her rose-gardener reputation.

Veronica gestured toward the door. "Why don't we chat in our private conference room across the hall?"

"That would be luuuvely." Twyla smiled and followed Veronica out. "I *do* love to chat."

We sat at the table, and Twyla sniffled. She retrieved a lace handkerchief, also lemon yellow, from her vintage white beaded handbag and dabbed her eyes. "It may surprise you young ladies to know that I'm not here on a social call."

I feigned surprise. "No?"

"I was out shopping, and I saw your sign out front. I came in because I simply have nowhere else to turn." Her sniffles turned into sobs. She reached into her bag and pulled out a glass vial, which she placed in front of me on the table.

Panic leapt into my chest. *Was it Love Potion #9? Was she here to expose me for dosing Bradley?*

She looked me in the eye. "Those are my smelling salts. I'm prone to fainting spells."

"Good to know." Relieved I hadn't been outed, I accepted the responsibility of reviving her from a future faint.

She gave a sniffle. "I'm here because my Harry has been working late for the past several weeks, which is very unlike him. In the forty-eight years we've been married, why, he's never missed a dinner at home. That is," she dabbed her eyes, "until recently."

"I see." Veronica opened her laptop. "Have you asked him why he's been working late?"

"Y-es," she said—in two syllables. She gave a dismissive wave. "He says he's working on a big legal project. He's a highly respected patent attorney, you know."

I smiled. "Well, if he's an attorney, it wouldn't be unusual for him to work late, right?"

"It is unusual because my Harry doesn't work. That's what his employees are for."

The smile slipped from my face. As an employee myself, I resented that. "So, what do you think he's doing?"

"Oooh!" Her tear-stained eyes squinted with anger. "He's in the clutches of a brazen hussy."

Veronica began typing. "Is this a woman you know?"

"Oh, yes." Her drawn-on eyebrows furrowed. "Her name is Patsy Harrington, and we've been rivals since our debutante ball in 1963."

"Rivals?" I loved cotillion catfight stories.

"I met my Harry at that ball. Patsy had her eye on him because he was the most eligible bachelor in New Orleans, so she purposefully spilled punch on my dress. But that didn't matter one whit to Harry. He danced with me the whole night, and Patsy has been after him ever since. She's not one to be outdone."

I was skeptical. "That's a long time to chase after a man. Are you sure about this?"

"I'm sure." She wiped away a tear. "Even after all these years, my Harry is still a catch. And that Jezebel Patsy is shameless. She'll go to any lengths to get him."

Veronica looked up from her laptop. "So, how can we help you?"

"I need for you girls to follow Harry and get pictures of him with Patsy so that I can confront them." She raised her chin, and with it her pride. "He's going to be working late tomorrow and Saturday night."

Veronica put a finger to her cheek. "We have a big case right now, but it sounds like we could take care of this in an evening or two. What do you think, Franki? Are you willing to work some overtime?"

Twyla looked at me and turned up the sniffling, sobbing, and dabbing a notch.

I didn't mind giving up a weekend if it meant catching a cheater in the act. I, of all people, knew the pain and self-doubt that came with betrayal, and it infuriated me to think that a husband would cheat on his wife. Especially if that husband had been dating me. "I'm game."

"Maaahvelous!" Twyla turned off the tears as quickly as she'd turned them on. She reached into her purse and pulled out an envelope that she handed to Veronica. "Here is a recent picture of Harry, his business card, the make, model, and license plate of his car, and my contact information."

Twyla was well prepared for a woman who'd happened upon our office by chance.

Veronica examined the picture and passed it to me.

Her "catch" of a husband looked exactly like Alfred Hitchcock with a Hitler mustache and a bad toupee. *If Patsy's been chasing this guy for fifty years, she's either blind or senile. Or both.*

Veronica rose. "We'll be in touch Sunday morning with a report."

"Thank you, ladies." Twyla tied her scarf around her hair. "When this dreadful mess is all over, I *do* hope you'll stop by for some tea in the rose garden. In the springtime, of course."

Veronica beamed. "We'd love to."

Slipping on her Jackie-O glasses, she wiggled her chubby fingers at us. "Toodle-loo."

She slunk out the door.

VERONICA LEANED over the steering wheel of the Audi and squinted at the students exiting the Slidell School of Beauty. "They must be coming out for lunch or a break."

I sunk low in the passenger seat. "It's not going to be easy to deal with the Babe of Blackness so soon after that sunnily clad Southern belle, Twyla Upton."

"I'm sure you'll manage."

"Don't be too sure of that." I glanced out the window. To my dismay, I spotted Domenica smoking a cigarette with some other students. I pointed in her direction. "There she is. At the picnic table."

Veronica lifted her Chanel sunglasses. "Where?"

"How can you miss her? She's the only one wearing all black."

"I see her now." She placed her sunglasses into her handbag. "It was hard to make her out with that black SUV behind her."

I snorted. "So, how do you want to handle this?"

"We'll go over there and tell her we'd like to talk to her."

"In front of the other students?" I asked, surprised. "Do you think she'll agree to that?"

"She won't let the presence of the students stop her. If she's got something to say, she'll say it."

I remembered the no-holds-barred comments Domenica had made in front of her mother. "You're probably right about that." I opened the passenger-side door. "Let's get this over with."

We walked across the campus, and Domenica shot up from the picnic table, her face dark with fury—and a lot of Goth makeup. She threw her cigarette to the ground, stubbing it out with her foot, and strode toward us.

Veronica forced a smile. "Hello, Domenica."

"What are you doing here?" She looked from Veronica to me. "Why are you harassing me at school?"

I was already over her attitude. "Looks like you're on a smoke break to me."

Veronica shot me a silence-it look. "We'd like to ask you a few questions. This will only take a few minutes."

"My mother and I already told you everything we know." She flipped her bangs. "Stewart killed Imma and got away with it. Then he obviously killed Angelica too. End of story."

I struggled to control my temper. "That's what we wanted to talk to you about. Is there somewhere we can sit down?"

Domenica stared at me blankly, refusing to make a suggestion.

"Okay then." I abandoned all attempts to hide my frustration. "Let's just do this right here. I'll start. Why are you so sure Stewart killed Angelica?"

Domenica took a step toward me and raised her chin in defiance. "Who the hell else would have done it?"

"I don't know. But she could've had other enemies. From what we've been told, she was a difficult person to deal with."

"That's for *damn* sure." She flicked her tongue piercing. "But do you really think anyone else hated her enough to kill her?"

"Domenica," Veronica said in a soothing tone, "that's what we want to find out. But we need your help."

She shook her head. "The only person who had a reason to kill Angelica was Stewart."

"But why? He'd already been acquitted of your sister's murder, so what did he stand to gain by going out and killing someone else?"

"You're the PIs." She curled her lips. "Why don't you two go figure that out and leave me alone?"

I rolled my eyes. "Come on. If you know something, you need to tell us. Do it for your sister."

She assumed her hostile, sociopathic stare. "Here's what I think happened. Stewart got sick of paying her to keep her mouth shut, so he told her he wasn't going to do it anymore. She threatened to go to the cops, and he strangled her—with a scarf, just like he did my sister."

Veronica met her gaze. "Why do you think he was paying her?"

"Well, someone certainly was. All of a sudden she started buying fancy clothes and jewelry and stuff, and she didn't have a job. Even my dad thought Stewart was paying her off."

I licked my lips. "Did your dad have any proof?"

"He didn't need any. It was painfully obvious."

Veronica shifted her handbag. "Okay, but what do you think Angelica knew about Stewart? According to your mother and Concetta—"

"Wait," she interrupted, stunned. "You talked to Concetta?"

"Yes."

"Well, that's interesting, because my Mom and I haven't seen her for months."

Despite her acidic disposition, I felt kind of sorry for Domenica. One by one, her family members had all abandoned her, and some had apparently done so of their own volition.

"I'm sorry to hear that," Veronica said. "But as I was saying, Angelica testified that she didn't know anything about Stewart or his relationship with Imma, so I'm not sure whether she really did have any evidence against him."

She crossed her arms. "That's hilarious, because Angelica made it her number one priority to know other people's business. That's how she got ahead in life. So I'm sure she was keeping an eye on Stewart, if for no other reason than his connections."

I pursed my lips. "In the fashion industry, you mean."

"Yeah, what else? I'm sure you've heard all about Jessica's

ambition by now. It was legendary." She turned to look at the other students, some of whom were returning inside the school. "Are we done here? Because I've gotta get back to class."

Veronica touched her arm. "Just a few more questions."

She pulled back. "Like what?"

"Your sister told us that you became a Goth after Imma's death."

"Oh, God. Of course my sister, the saintly nun, would bring that up."

I shrugged. "She's worried about you."

"Only because she thinks I belong to a Satanic cult." She crossed her arms. "But black clothes, makeup, and death rock don't make me a devil worshipper."

"True," I said, although I had my doubts, particularly in light of what appeared to be the points of a pentagram tattoo protruding from the low-cut neckline of her black cotton shirt. "So, what you're saying is that Goth is basically a fashion statement for you."

"No, I'm not saying that. For me, Goth is a way of life. But having a fascination with death doesn't make me a disciple of Satan."

"O-kaaay." I was unsure what to make of the "fascination with death" revelation.

"I'm glad we're clear on that." She looked behind her and saw that the other students had gone inside. "Now I've *really* got to go."

I took a step toward her. "One more question. Were you close to Angelica, like Imma and Concetta were?"

"Let's see, Angelica always told me I was fat and ugly when I was a kid, and she betrayed my sister's memory for money. So, what do you think?"

Veronica exhaled. "It sounds like you didn't like her very much."

"Honestly, lady, I hated the bitch, and I'm not the least bit sorry she's dead." Domenica stormed toward the school.

I waited until she was out of earshot and turned to Veronica. "So, do you still think she's just going through a phase?"

She didn't reply, and she didn't need to. Like me, she was wondering whether Domenica could've killed Jessica.

I was also wondering how long our list of suspects would grow.

"Concetta left an interesting message while we were out." Veronica stood in her office with the phone to her ear and her hand on her hip.

"What did she say?" I returned the growing Evans case file to its place on her desk.

She hung up. "She remembered something she'd forgotten to tell us. She's coming in."

"I wonder if it's about her psycho sister."

"No clue." She glanced at the time on the phone display. "But she'll be here any minute."

"Intriguing. Any other messages?"

"Mr. Orlansky's assistant." Veronica took a seat at her desk. "Apparently, three of the five scarves were purchased with cash. They have the video file for one of the scarf purchases, but they had to request the DVD for the other two from Baton Rouge. Mr. Orlansky wants to go through the first file with me tonight."

"Looks like someone's in a hurry to watch videos with you." I sat down on the edge of her desk and shot her a knowing grin.

Veronica's smile was wry as she turned on her laptop. "Maybe I should bring some popcorn and Raisinettes."

"That should keep his hands and mouth busy. For a while, anyhow."

"Cute, Franki." She looked at her agenda. "Right now I've got a scheduling problem to work out."

"What do you mean?"

"Well, we've got the Upton stakeout tomorrow and probably even Saturday night. So, if the DVD for the other two purchases arrives in the next day or two, we won't be able to look at it until Sunday at the earliest. And I can't let the Upton case jeopardize the Evans investigation."

"Do both of us need to do the stakeout?"

"It's my company policy to have backup in a situation like that. It's one thing to go undercover to talk to a sales girl at LaMarca, but it's another thing altogether to try to entrap a man committing a crime. For all we know, Harry Upton could be dangerous."

"I'm sure Mr. Orlansky would be only too willing to work some really late nights with you." I winked, but I hoped she wouldn't ask me to go with her. Although I'd been doing my best to keep my chin up in the workplace, I was really down about Bradley. All I wanted to do was go home and curl up in my bed.

"I don't want to be there alone with him after the store closes." She chewed her lip for a moment. "Maybe David could go through the tape with him?"

As much as it pained me, I had to give her my honest two cents. "Veronica, you know as well as I do that Mr. Orlansky isn't going to work late with the likes of David."

"You're right. So..."

Here it comes.

"Any chance you could go with me after the stakeout? If it comes to that, of course."

"Yeah." I looked at the floor. "I don't have any plans for the weekend."

"How are you feeling about the whole Bradley situation?"

"Bummed." I sighed. "But my main worry right now is my nonna. She's been too quiet after hanging up on me."

"You think she's up to something?"

"Of course she is." I gesticulated Veronica style. "She's busy scaring up some more Sicilian suitors. And based on the ones I've encountered so far, Harry Upton *is* a 'catch' by comparison. So is Ed Orlansky, for that matter."

The lobby bell sounded.

Veronica rose. "That must be Concetta."

I followed her into the waiting area, where Concetta stood looking uncertain. She was dressed almost exactly as she had been the day before, in the same sensible shoes and white shirt, only her ankle-length skirt was a muted brown instead of gray.

"I hope I'm not interrupting." Her close-set eyes had a worried look about them, and she was fingering the cross at her neck.

Veronica patted her arm. "No, not at all."

"Oh, good. This case is so personal to me. I'd really rather not talk about it over the phone."

"I understand." Veronica gestured to the door. "Why don't we go over to our conference room?"

Concetta shook her head. "This won't take long. I remembered something about Angie and Stewart, but I'm not sure it's important."

Veronica retrieved a pad of paper and pen from David's desk. "We appreciate all the information you can provide."

She tugged at the crucifix. "Well, not too long after Imma's murder, the police called and told us we could come and get Imma's things. So, my father and I flew to London a few weeks later, um, under the radar, so to speak."

I flopped onto a couch. "Under the radar?"

"We didn't tell Angie we were coming." She sounded

remorseful. "My father didn't want to give her time to prepare for our visit."

Veronica's head snapped up from her notepad. "Why not? Did he think Angelica had something to do with Imma's death?"

"It's not that he believed Angie killed her, but he *did* think she knew something about her murder. And after I told him what I'd seen, he was convinced of it."

My curiosity was more than piqued. "What did you see?"

"Well, I went into Angie and Imma's room first, while my father was downstairs talking to the dorm manager. The manager had given me a key so that I could get in. When I walked into the room, Angie was there with Stewart."

I was shocked that Stewart would be bold enough to return to the scene of the crime when he was under suspicion for the murder. "Really?"

"Yeah, and I could tell that they'd been deep in conversation." Her eyes opened wide. "In fact, when Angie saw me, she jumped up and started babbling, as though she felt nervous. Or guilty."

Veronica scribbled a note. "Did you hear anything they said?"

"Nothing."

I scooted forward on the sofa, eager to hear more. "And what did they say to you?"

"Stewart never said a word. He lowered his head and then walked past me and left. But Angie said the usual things. You know, like 'What a surprise!' and 'Why didn't you tell me you were coming?'"

I noticed that Concetta was gripping the crucifix so tightly her knuckles were white. "Did you ask her what Stewart was doing there?"

"Of course." She jerked her necklace. "But she never answered because my father walked in."

Veronica looked up from the pad. "And you didn't tell him what was going on."

"Not until we got back to New Orleans." She looked at the floor.

I massaged my neck. "Did you ask Angelica again later what Stewart was doing there?"

"I never got a chance to. She refused to speak to me after that trip."

"So," I said, confused, "why didn't you tell your father that Stewart had been there?"

She looked at Veronica and me. "My father was a stereotypical, hot-blooded Italian male. I was afraid that if I'd told him what I'd just witnessed, he would have done something awful. To Angie or Stewart or both. I'd already lost my sister, and my mother was ill...I couldn't lose my father too."

"Of course not," Veronica soothed.

Concetta's eyes filled with tears, and she studied Veronica's face as though searching for something. "But I lost him anyway."

Veronica placed her hand on Concetta's back. "I think we have all the information we need. Can I get you a glass of water? Or maybe some chamomile tea?"

She shook her head as though coming out of a stupor. "I need to get back to the church." She headed for the door. "I'll let you know if I remember anything else."

After she left, I turned to Veronica. "What do you make of that?"

"I think it confirms what we already suspect—that Jessica and Stewart had some sort of illicit relationship."

"It also confirms that Stewart is every bit as arrogant as he looks in that picture of him after he'd been acquitted."

"That reminds me," Veronica tapped her pen on the pad, "have you tried calling his parents again?"

"No. I'll do that now."

I went to my office and dialed the Preston number. I waited for a couple of rings.

"Preston's rezidens," a husky female voice responded.

"Mrs. Preston?" I wasn't sure whether it was her, but I thought whoever it was might be drunk. Or Hungarian.

"No, I maid."

"Oh, hello. May I please speak to Stewart Preston, IV?"

"He not here."

"Okay, well—"

"Who zis?" she interrupted. "Zsuzsanna?"

I hesitated, unsure how to respond.

"Vat you vant?"

I couldn't tell whether she was being harsh or just foreign. "Um, his cell phone number?"

"I say you before," she whispered, "I sink he bad man. But, you vant number, I give. You vait."

"Thank you." I was shocked at my unexpected success. I grabbed a scrap of paper on my desk—a receipt for tampons, gelato, and wine—and prepared to jot down the number.

The maid returned to the phone and recited Stewart's contact information.

I repeated it to her.

"Good. You no call again."

I shook my head, marveling at the less-than-stellar phone manners of the Preston household.

My message tone sounded. It was my dad reminding me to check the oil on my car. I rolled my eyes. And I got another text. My heart skipped when I saw that it was from Bradley.

In back-to-back meetings. But we need to talk. Call you later, B.

Veronica entered my office. "Did you call the Prestons?"

I jumped as though I'd been caught cheating on a test. "You're not going to believe this, but I actually got his cell number."

"Have you called him?"

"I was just about to." I fired off an angry one-word reply in Italian to Bradley. Even though he didn't speak the language, I was certain he'd know what it meant.

"Let's put it on speaker." Veronica pulled up a chair.

"Sure." I typed Stewart's number on the keypad and tapped *Call*.

The phone rang three times and went to voicemail. There was no recorded message, only a beep.

"Hello, Stewart. My name is Gina Mazzucco." I shot Veronica a nasty look as she flashed a wicked smile. "I'm calling about an urgent matter regarding Angelica Evangelista. Please call me back at your earliest convenience." I recited my number and hung up.

Veronica crossed her arms. "Now we sit back and let him stew."

"I hope he takes the bait."

My phone vibrated.

Veronica and I exchanged a look.

With my heart pounding, I read the display. "Oh. It's my parents. They know better than to call me while I'm at work."

"You should take it. It could be important."

"I suppose." I tapped *Answer*. "Hello?"

"Francesca?" My mother's voice was unusually shrill. "This is your mother."

"Mom, I'm in a meeting, so I don't have much time. What's up?"

"Well, your father says he texted you about your car, and you replied '*vaffanculo*.' We're just wondering what in the heck is going on down there."

I swallowed—hard. I'd told my *dad* to go screw himself, albeit in slightly more scathing terms, instead of *Bradley*. The only thing to do was take the easy way out. "Mom, like I said, I can't talk now."

"Now Francesca, your father is waiting for an explanation."

"Tell him I meant to send that message to Bradley, okay?"

"I don't think that's going to make him feel any better, dear. You know we didn't raise you to use language like that. Not in Italian or English."

"Mom, I've *got* to go." I hung up and dropped the phone on my desk, as though it had scalded my hand.

Veronica raised an eyebrow.

"Don't ask." I massaged my temples. That text message wasn't going to help the already tense situation with my parents. On the positive side, I figured it would put a stop to the annoying car reminders from my dad.

"You got a minute?" David's usually bright eyes were dark.

Veronica had warned me that he was lovesick for a girl in his Brazilian dance class who only had eyes for the Samba instructor. "I was about to head home for the day, but I've always got time for you." I threw that last part in to try to lift his spirits. "What's up?"

"I've got to get to the library to study for an exam, but Veronica's on the phone. Can I fill you in on my research real fast?"

"Absolutely. What've you got?"

He sat in front of my desk and leaned over with his elbows on his knees and his hands clasped in front of him. "Not much." He looked even more defeated than he had moments before. "I ran the background checks on the Di Salvos, and they're all clean."

"Even the Diva of Darkness?" I was kind of expecting some

sort of run-in with the law to surface—a public menace charge, at the very least.

"Yeah, her too." He looked down at his hands.

"What about Bill Evangelista?"

David sighed. "Nothing. It's like the dude dropped off the face of the earth."

"That's so odd. You know, I just keep wondering whether he or his family could be connected to this case in some way."

"You mean, like his daughter, right?"

I nodded.

"Yeah, she definitely could've been jealous of Jessica, and maybe she wanted to eliminate the competition, you know? Women are ruthless like that." His face turned as red as an apple, and he held up a spindly fingered hand. "But not you or Veronica, or anything."

I smiled. "I knew what you meant. Anything else you want to talk to me about?"

He opened his mouth, but Veronica burst into the room. "Come to my office. Quick."

David and I followed the order.

Veronica's face was somber. "I just got off the phone with Betty at the police station. Domenica Di Salvo has been arrested."

David and I looked at each other, stunned.

"For Jessica's murder," I breathed. "I *knew* it."

"Not for Jessica's murder." She frowned. "For grave dancing."

David yelled "Holy crap!" as I shouted, "Say what?"

"According to Betty, Domenica was arrested two hours ago, at around four forty-five . Apparently, she belongs to a group that dances on graves, and they've been charged with defacing a tombstone."

I closed my shocked mouth. "I *told* you that girl was creepy.

What normal person would *ever* want to hang out in a cemetery, much less freakin' dance a jig there?"

David's head bobbed. "I know, right?"

"And where, exactly, have they been doing this?" I held up a hand. "No, don't tell me. Let me guess—where Marie Laveau is buried."

Veronica cocked her head. "Wrong. In Slidell. In the cemetery where *Immacolata* is buried."

I stared at her, speechless. "No. Way."

"Yes way. From what I've been told, it's the only place they've been doing this. And that's not even all there is to the story."

I wasn't sure how much more of the story I could take.

"The police are also investigating whether this group had any involvement in the murder of a man named Henry Withers." Veronica placed her hands flat on her desk. "He was the cemetery's caretaker, and he was hacked to death with an ax in the cemetery last Halloween night."

David stood openmouthed as I gasped and collapsed into a chair. I'd been suspicious of Domenica and her deviant demeanor, but I hadn't expected a hacking murder.

She reached for her day planner. "So, we're going to have to pay Domenica yet another visit."

I ran my fingers through my hair. "How are we going to do that if she's in jail? You know her mother isn't going to have the money to bail her out."

"I'm a criminal attorney, Franki. I have a right to speak with my client."

"Veronica, you're not seriously thinking of representing her, are you?"

"Definitely not." She raised her chin like my nonna. "But that'll be our little secret, now won't it?"

18

———————

It seemed perfectly normal that I would be at an Elvis Presley concert. But something in the back of my mind told me that The King wasn't singing "Burning Love" to me in person. It was the sexy, black leather-clad Elvis from the '68 Comeback Special, not the sparkly cape-wearing, bell-bottomed Vegas version, and I was pretty sure he hadn't gotten back in shape since he was dead.

Then it hit me—I'd been listening to my "Burning Love" ringtone in my sleep. *I really need to get an old-school alarm.*

I opened my eyes and shrunk from the daylight. Elvis was singing below me, so I peered over the edge of the chaise lounge where I'd spent the night. Nothing could have prepared me for what I saw. On the floor next to my phone were a bag of potato chips, a tub of sour cream and chive dip, a container of Ben & Jerry's Dublin Mudslide, a box of chocolate-covered cherries, and a bottle of red wine, all of which were empty. I whispered a silent prayer that Napoleon had eaten all the food while I'd been sleeping, because it was clear that I'd been the one to drink the wine. But given that he was sitting beside the empty containers with his plastic food bowl in his mouth, the chances of that were slim.

I rooted out my phone from underneath the potato chip bag and saw that Corinne was calling—at seven a.m. "Hello?"

"*Bonjour*. It is Corinne. Is zis Franki?"

I couldn't blame her for not recognizing me. I sounded like my mouth was full of gravel. Or chips. "Yes, hi. It's me."

"I have some information for you." Her tone was hushed. "But I am at ze bank, so I must hurry before ze osers come to work."

I flopped onto my back. "Is it about Jessica's monthly deposits?"

"*Oui*. Ze deposits she make each mons were checks."

"Her LaMarca paychecks?" I held my breath in anticipation.

"*Non*, for her paychecks she have ze direct deposit. Zese checks were from a life insurance company."

I exhaled. They weren't payoffs from the Prestons, after all. "A life insurance company? Is there any way to tell who the policy holder was?

"*Non*, but ze policy is from an oil company in Baton Rouge."

"Really?" That was weird. "How big were the checks?"

"Zey were small. One hundred dollars."

It was looking like the bank lead was a bust. "I guess the policy was from a relative or family friend. It's obviously not a bribe."

"Wait, Franki. I save ze best for last."

Hope filled my chest. "What?"

"Jessica receive other PPD deposits, besides her paycheck."

"What do you mean by 'PPD deposits'?"

Napoleon put his food bowl down and gave a high-pitched bark.

I put my finger over my lips as though he could understand.

"Ah, 'PPD' is an SEC code, so it tell ze bank ze transaction type. A code of PPD means 'Prearranged Payment and Deposit.' It is a repeat deposit, like for a paycheck or pension or somesing."

"How much were these deposits for?" I switched the phone to my left ear so that I could pet Napoleon with my right hand to keep him from barking.

"Ten sousand dollars."

I sat straight up on the chaise lounge. "Ten *thousand* dollars?"

"*Oui.*"

"How often did she receive them?" I was reeling from the amount of those deposits.

"Every mons."

It looked like I'd hit pay dirt—as, apparently, had Jessica. "Is there any way to tell who these direct deposits were from?"

"Ze registry shows zey are from ze Vautier Group."

"Could you spell that?" I ran and grabbed a pen from the kitchen counter. For me, French might as well have been Sanskrit. Using the box of chocolate-covered cherries as a note pad, I jotted down what she said. "Do you have any idea what this company does?"

"*Non,* I never hear of it."

"Corinne, this is very important. Can you tell me how long Jessica has been receiving these deposits?"

"Since she open ze account with us in 2012. I do not know if she receive ze money before zat."

If only she'd been with the same bank since Immacolata's murder. "Did you see any other activity in her account that looked unusual?"

"*Non,* zat is all."

"Well, if these payments are what I think they are, this could be a *huge* break in the case. I can't thank you enough for your help."

"It is my pleasure. But now I must go. *Au revoir.*""

"*Ciao*, Corinne."

I hung up and saw the second awful sight of the day—Bradley had called the night before. And I needed to talk to him—to tell him to stop calling me, of course.

I flopped onto the chaise lounge in a funk. I'd fallen asleep early because of the wine, which I'd only drunk because I'd been disturbed by Domenica, a.k.a. the Dame of Demise, and her deathly antics. That girl was getting on my last nerve. Or maybe I should say she was dancing on it. And I had to be ready in half an hour to go to the police station with Veronica to question her.

I sent a text to David asking him to find out the names of the owners and board of directors of The Vautier Group. Then I walked and fed a testy Napoleon before heading to my closet to pick out something attorney-like.

THE SLIDELL CITY JAIL came into view, and my stomach tensed. I didn't relish the idea of going into a police station on false pretenses. "So, what am I supposed to do when we get inside?"

Veronica turned into the parking lot. "I'm going to introduce you as my paralegal. That way, the police will direct all the questions to me."

"That's good." I glanced at her smart gray suit and raspberry silk blouse. In comparison, the Forever 21 black blazer and leopard-print dress I'd thrown together made me look more like I was ready for a night of fist pumping at the Jersey Shore than a day of representing incarcerated clients.

She maneuvered the Audi into a parking space right next to an old pink Toyota that was covered with Barbie parts.

I was mesmerized by the dismembered dolls. "I wonder if

the driver of that car is in the slammer. If so, it's got to be for Barbiecide."

"Killing Barbies isn't a crime, but bad taste in car décor should be." She put her sunglasses into her bag. "We'd better get going. Domenica will go before a judge first thing this morning, and we have to talk to her before that happens."

"Why?" I reached for my purse. "Aren't we allowed to talk to her after that?"

"No, the judge is going to ask her who's representing her. So we need to meet with her before she names her attorney or before the court appoints one to her. Otherwise, it'll be too late for me to pose as her legal counsel."

"Burning Love" blared from my purse. "Why didn't I change that thing?" I muttered as I pulled out my phone. "It's Bradley."

"Are you going to answer?"

The tension in my stomach crawled to my chest. "I have to talk to him sooner or later."

"Okay, but try to be cool."

I nodded and tapped *Answer*. "H-hello?"

"Franki, it's Bradley."

"Oh?" I feigned a surprise that I regretted. In the smartphone era, it was obvious who was calling.

"I'm sorry to call you so early, but I've got back-to-back meetings again today, and I wanted to catch you before they got underway. Do you have a minute?"

"I suppose." This time I feigned an indifference I didn't feel. Even after finding out about his wife, my mind couldn't help replaying the kiss-to-end-all-kisses.

"I tried to call you last night, but I guess you were out?"

"Uh-huh." I *had been* out, just not the kind of out he was thinking.

"Listen, I've been thinking about what happened the other

night, and I realized that I came on a little strong with that kiss. So I want to apologize if I was, uh, forward."

I bit my lip. If only it were as simple as a kiss.

"Anyway, I know it's short notice, but I have two tickets to the opening of *Jersey Boys* tonight. I was hoping you'd do me the honor of going with me. I promise I'll behave like a gentleman."

There were no words to express how much I did *not* want to turn down a date with Bradley, especially when he was being surprisingly sweet and respectful—and when I was already wearing the perfect Jersey-style outfit for the occasion. But after everything I'd been through with Todd and Vince, I couldn't go from being cheated on to being a cheater. I didn't want to hurt another woman, not even Sheilah. I had to draw the line firmly in the sand—or maybe quicksand because I felt like I was sinking. "I'm sorry, Bradley, but I don't date married men."

There was a deafening silence on the other end of the line followed by what sounded like a sharp intake of breath.

"I was planning on talking to you about that after we—"

"So it's true?" I interrupted.

He paused. "I can explain..."

That was exactly what Vince had said. Tears filled my eyes and anger surged in my stomach. "I don't need your explanation, Bradley. It's all quite clear, thank you very much."

"Franki, it's complicated..."

I gave a bitter laugh. "Another tried and true cliché."

He let out a long sigh. "Will you please hear me out?"

"No, because there's nothing more to say except that I don't ever want to see you again." I ended the call and then stared at the phone before throwing it into my purse.

Veronica looked at me. "This guy really got to you, didn't he?"

I nodded.

"I'll take you home." She pulled her keys from her purse.

"No." I placed my hand on her arm to prevent her from starting the ignition. "I came here this morning to do a job, and I'm going to do it."

"I know, but I can handle this one on my own."

I shook my head. "I can't keep getting sidelined by unfaithful men. The plan was to start over in New Orleans, and that's what I'm going to do. Life is just going to be a little different than I thought."

She cocked an eyebrow. "How so?"

"Well," I opened my car door, "instead of getting a guy, I'm going to get...cats."

Veronica smirked. "I think Napoleon will fiercely object to you becoming a cat lady."

"True." I glanced at the Barbie car. "Maybe I'll start a dismembered doll collection."

"THIS IS TAKING WAY TOO LONG," I said for at least the tenth time since we'd entered the jail. After going through a rigorous security screening and a meticulous administrative process complete with a semi-interrogation about the purpose of our visit and a stack of paperwork almost as high as my Jessica Simpson heels, we'd finally been taken to a small room to wait for Domenica.

Veronica didn't look up from her notepad. "Welcome to the life of a criminal attorney. It shouldn't be much longer now."

"I hope not. I can actually feel myself rotting away in this jail."

"It's not like you're locked up in a cell. Besides, be glad you're not at the police department in New Orleans. This place is a palace in comparison."

"Well, it's better than I expected." I surveyed the room. Everything about the Slidell jail was surprisingly clean and well kept, from the mowed lawn out front to the sparkling tile floors inside. It looked nothing like the seedy pictures of the New Orleans jailhouse that I'd seen in the tabloids following the much-publicized arrests of Nicholas Cage and Russell Brand.

The door opened, and Veronica stood. Domenica entered followed by a tall brunette police officer with a Miss America smile. Instead of her customary basic black, the Darling of the Dead was outfitted entirely in tangerine courtesy of the Slidell PD.

"I'll be back for her in fifteen or so." The officer flashed her pearly whites and closed the door behind her.

"To what do I owe the pleasure?" Domenica spoke in a bored monotone as she took a seat at the table.

I bared my teeth. "We're here to ask you some follow-up questions. You know, in light of your recent arrest?"

"Is this even legal? I mean, I'm in *jail*. So how is it, exactly, that the two of you can just cruise in here and interrogate me?"

Veronica folded her hands. "I'm a criminal defense attorney."

Domenica scrutinized her for a moment. "So, are you here to defend me, or something?"

She looked at the table. "No, I'm not." Then she looked Domenica in the eyes. "But I've been informed of the charges against you, so I can provide you with free legal advice in exchange for your answers to a few questions."

Domenica looked from Veronica to me. "You people are incredible." A silence ensued that included several pensive flicks of her tongue piercing. "So, what is it you're so desperate to ask me?"

I draped my arm on the table. "For starters, we'd like to know if you had anything to do with the murder of the cemetery caretaker."

Her eyes cast daggers—or tongue spikes. "I had nothing to do with that, understand? I've never even seen that guy before."

"But you admit that you were a frequent visitor to the Slidell cemetery, right?"

"Sure."

I smirked. She acted as though hanging out in cemeteries was as natural as hanging out at the mall.

Veronica stared at Domenica. "You know, I actually don't believe that you had anything to do with Henry Withers' death, but I may be in the minority on that count. So if you know something, even if it's just secondhand gossip, then I'd advise you to tell the police with your attorney present."

Domenica returned her stare but remained silent.

"Because if you don't," Veronica said, undaunted, "there's a strong chance based on your Goth appearance, your defiant attitude, and this grave-defacing charge that you'll go down with your friends for first degree murder, a charge that carries the death penalty in the state of Louisiana."

"That's profiling."

I leaned forward. "Is it? Or is it just reality? Because I'm an ex-cop, so I can tell you from experience that the police will be a *whole* lot more inclined to believe that someone like you murdered a cemetery caretaker than someone like my partner here."

She shot me a look of pure hate. Then she studied her hands and began picking the black nail polish off one of her fingernails.

Veronica crossed her arms. "Now, why don't you tell us about this grave dancing business?"

"What about it?"

I snort-laughed and shook my head. "You *do* understand that most people find the notion of dancing on a grave to be bizarre?"

"That's their problem."

Veronica sighed. "Can you tell us why you do it?"

"It's not a big deal, all right?" Domenica's devil-may-care demeanor had turned defensive. "My friends and I think death is cool. It's a part of life, you know? So we dance on graves to celebrate it."

I shuddered. I could think of *plenty* of ways to celebrate life, and none of them included cemeteries.

She smoothed her black bangs over her eye. "And it's not like we're doing anything bad."

Veronica held up a finger "But you *did* do something illegal. The arresting officer said that you spray-painted a word on a gravestone, but he wasn't sure if it was foreign or just misspelled."

I remembered the insult Domenica had scrawled on Jessica's yearbook picture. "What did you write?"

She hesitated. "*Vendicata.*"

I straightened in my chair. "The Italian word?"

She nodded and looked at her nails.

Veronica and I exchanged a look. *Vendicata* meant *avenged*, and the *a* ending indicated that the avenged person was a woman.

I instantly thought of Immacolata. "Whose tombstone did you write this on?"

"Imma's," she said, deadpan.

Veronica and I stared at each other, trying to process the revelation.

I cleared my throat. "Can you explain what you meant when you used the word?"

"I think it's self-explanatory."

"Actually, it's not. Here's why—It doesn't indicate who did the avenging."

The door opened, and the brunette officer flashed another pageant-winning smile. "It's time to go."

Domenica stood, and a smirk formed at the corners of her mouth. "Well, I guess that's what you two hotshot PIs have been hired to find out, now isn't it?"

As I watched her leave, I pondered the ramifications of her use of the word *vendicata*. And I wondered whether someone with such a positive view of death would find it easy to take a human life.

19

———

"You're off the hook, Franki." Veronica stood in my office doorway.

I looked up from my mid-afternoon bag of beignets, consumed by Catholic guilt for whatever I'd done wrong. "For..." I inhaled a mouthful—make that a throat full—of powdered sugar and coughed. "...what?"

"I just got off the phone with Ed Orlansky, and he agreed to let me screen the video this afternoon."

"Huh?" Powdered sugar puffed from my mouth. "And miss a chance to work late with you tonight?"

"I told him about the stakeout and said that if I couldn't come within the next hour, I was going to have to cancel."

"That explains it." I turned back to my beignets. Like a good Italian-American girl, I'd decided to drown my dating sorrows in dough products.

"I also talked to Ryan."

I yawned. That guy made me tired. "What did the charming Mr. Hunter have to say?"

She smiled like a cat who'd caught a canary *and* a cockatoo. "He's pleased with our progress."

"*Pleased?*"

Her smile turned Cheshire. "Apparently, the police hadn't figured out the *vendicata* clue."

"I *told* you Italian was a useful language." I felt vindicated. During our sophomore year, I'd persuaded her not to switch from Italian to Swedish when she was in the throes of a burst of Nordic pride. "But how did Ryan know what the police had or hadn't found?"

"Simple. His attorney went to the police station after Domenica was arrested and demanded to know what was going on."

"Smart move." I nodded and noticed I had powdered sugar on my chest. I was going to have to switch to something less messy, like raw cookie dough.

"He also found out that the police questioned Stewart Preston." She crossed her arms. "Two days ago."

I steepled my powdered fingers. "So he's probably in town and hasn't returned my call, which means I'm going to have to get insistent."

"Or even demanding."

"While you're at Lenton's today, I'll go through *The Times-Picayune* society pages and make a list of the restaurants and bars where he's been spotted in the past. That way, if he doesn't return my call, we can try to track him down at one of his favorite hangouts."

"That's a great idea." Her lips thinned. "Stewart Preston is no match for two Private Chicks."

The slamming of the lobby door announced the arrival of David.

I grinned at Veronica, who massaged her forehead.

"Ladies." David bowed and entered my office. "May I?"

"You may." I wondered whether I should've been concerned about his uncharacteristic formality.

He bounded into my office and plopped into a chair. "Prepare to be amazed." He pulled his laptop from his backpack with a flourish. "I had some time to kill between classes this morning, so I did some research on corporate affiliations." He paused for dramatic effect. "Turns out that The Vautier Group is the parent company of Preston Textiles, Inc."

"So the Prestons *were* paying Jessica." I pounded my fist on my desk. Then I looked at Veronica, anticipating one of her voice-of-reason-style responses.

"Now hold on, Franki," she said, not disappointing me. "I know it looks suspicious, but Jessica *was* in the fashion business, as is Preston Textiles. There's always the possibility that they were paying her for a legitimate service."

"But Preston Textiles wasn't paying her. The Vautier Group was."

Veronica turned to David. "What does The Vautier Group do?"

"Uh, basically, they just buy and control other companies through majority stock ownership. And by the way, Stewart Preston, III, is on the current board."

"Well," she met my gaze, "it's certainly beginning to look like those deposits could've been payoffs."

"Which would explain the weird conversation Concetta witnessed between Stewart and Jessica *and* the extravagant purchases Jessica started making right after Immacolata's death."

She chewed a pinky nail. "We've got to find Stewart ASAP."

"Don't worry. As soon as you leave, I'll start calling him. Every hour if I have to."

David cleared his throat. "Um, before you go, I've got some more information."

Veronica lowered her hand. "What is it?

"So, I've been going through the Google hits for 'Bill Evangelista' and 'William Evangelista,' and I found one that says a guy named Bill Evangelista died in a car accident in Gulfport, Mississippi in 1989."

"That's close to here, right?" I asked.

"Yeah, a little over an hour away." He broke into a boyish grin. "My buddies and I went there for spring break last year because it's got some freakin' *awesome* beaches. Even though it *is* an oil town."

I thought of the life insurance payments Jessica had been receiving from the oil company.

Veronica looked at me. "Sounds like our Bill Evangelista. The age of the daughter would also be about right, since Bill referred to her as a baby in his letter."

"Dude—" David looked up from his lashes. "I mean, mademoiselle—it's totally him."

I leaned forward. "What makes you so sure?"

"Because the obituary I found said his daughter was named Jessica. And she and her mother, Wanda, died in the accident too."

VERONICA SLOWED the Audi's speed to ensure that we were following Harry Upton's blue Mercedes at a safe distance.

I looked out the passenger window at the gorgeous nineteenth-century architecture of the historic New Orleans neighborhood of Uptown and sighed.

"What is it?"

"I spent all day calling Stewart Preston, and I haven't heard a peep out of him. Not even a text telling me to go to hell. I feel like the chances of questioning him are getting slimmer by the minute."

"Give it a little more time. I think he'll call, either out of concern or just plain curiosity."

"Maybe." I turned toward her. "Anyway, you haven't told me what happened at Lenton's today."

"It must have slipped my mind."

"I take it you didn't find anything?"

Veronica shook her head. "The scarf buyer was an African-American male."

I flashed a lascivious smile. "How was Ed?"

"He wasn't there. He's got the devil's grip."

"Do I even want to know what that is?"

She smirked. "It's a disease that causes severe chest pain that lasts for up to a week."

I had to goad her a little. "Are you sure he wasn't just overexcited about spending the day with you?"

Veronica stared eagle-eyed out the windshield. "Harry just pulled into Pascal's Manale."

"Hey, I read about this restaurant today."

She slowed the car to a stop outside the parking lot. "It's kind of a New Orleans tradition. Everyone eats here sooner or later."

"Including Stewart Preston. According to *The Times-Picayune*, he comes here fairly often."

"Really?" Veronica gave a well-what-do-you know frown. "That would be amazing if we saw him here too."

"Yeah, well, don't get your hopes up." I watched Harry park in the back of the lot. "Coincidences like that only happen in books."

She pulled into the lot and parked in the row in front of Harry's car, and we slouched in our seats.

I peered over the dashboard and watched Harry open his car door and struggle beneath the weight of his Hitchcockian belly before exiting. He buttoned his over-sized sport coat, patted his toupee, and smoothed his mustache with his index finger and thumb. Then, he gave a little skip and a hop and set off for the restaurant entrance.

I gasped, outraged. "Did you see that? He's so jazzed about his affair that he did a little dance."

"Oh, that reminds me." Veronica rummaged in her pink Prada handbag. "Twyla emailed me a picture of Patsy." She handed me her phone.

I flinched when I saw the photo of the alleged cotillion coquette. Patsy had the white beehive hairdo and sharp features of the late Texas Governor Ann Richards, but the teeth of Alvin the Chipmunk.

"She won't be hard to spot in a crowd." I gave the phone to Veronica. "So, what do we do now?"

"We need to go inside. If we wait out here, we run the risk of Harry and his date leaving the restaurant separately. Then we'd miss the photo op."

"We're not going to let that happen." I leapt from the car, slung my hobo bag over my shoulder, and assumed a vigilante posture. "Let's do this."

I entered the restaurant followed by Veronica and did a double take. The place teemed with men in full-on cowboy gear, from cowboy hats and neckerchiefs to chaps and boots.

I leaned over to Veronica. "The newspaper said this was an Italian restaurant, but based on the clientele, it looks more like a Wild West saloon. Minus the showgirls."

Veronica tightened the belt of her Burberry trench coat.

We made our way through the crowded lobby, avoiding any spurs, to the empty hostess stand.

While we waited for someone to arrive, a lonesome-looking cowpoke with a toothpick between his teeth tried to take a gander down the front of my dress. I narrowed my eyes like Clint Eastwood in a spaghetti western. "Giddy on, little doggie."

The toothpick fell from his lips. Then he adjusted his hat and moseyed away.

A harried-looking hostess rushed up to us. She had a partially untucked shirt and a run in her stocking, and I wondered whether an overzealous broncobuster had tried to lasso and hogtie her. "I hope you're not waiting for a table."

Veronica peered at the waitlist. "Actually, we are."

"Well, then," she said in a grim tone, "you're looking at a two-hour wait."

I counted ten total cowhands in the waiting area. "It doesn't look like that many people are waiting."

The harassed hostess gripped the edges of the stand, bowed her head, and took a deep breath before looking me straight in the eye. "There aren't. But the good folks who decided to organize a cowboy convention in New Orleans thought our famous barbecued shrimp were cooked on a grill instead of a stovetop. So, the cowboys have all sent their orders back to the kitchen and are threatening to quote 'rustle up a passel of wood and cook the dad-gum shrimps in the dad-blamed parking lot.' As you might imagine, it's going to take us a while to settle what the cowboys are describing as 'this here sitchiation.'"

I sensing that it wasn't the time to insist. "You know, I think we'll just head on over to the bar."

I led Veronica to an oyster-shucking area. "I don't know about you, but I think we need to leave before these crazy cattlemen decide to brawl or stampede or something."

"I agree, but we have to figure out a way to get a few pictures of Harry first."

I thought for a moment. "I know. I'll pretend like I'm one of those people who go around taking courtesy pictures of the guests."

"That's perfect. What do you need me to do?"

"Help me find Harry at the O.K. Corral here."

"On it." She took off, weaving through the tables.

I followed close on her heels and got an idea of what it must've been like to have been a pioneering woman in the Old West. The lewd whistling, suggestive winking, and flat-out leering—a girl could get used to that.

I spotted Harry at a table in the back corner of the restaurant. His back was to me, and he was blocking my view of his date.

I grabbed Veronica's arm. "There he is."

"Okay, give me your purse."

I pulled out my phone and handed the bag to Veronica. "Here goes nothing."

I walked to the table where I was shocked to discover that Harry's date wasn't Patsy at all but rather an attractive forty-something brunette in a white Chanel suit with black trim.

How does *he do it?* I approached the double-crossing duo. "Good evening."

Harry jumped in his seat, and the brunette hung her head.

"How would you two like a picture as a memento of your dinner at Pascal's Manale?"

The bashful brunette looked at Harry.

His cheeks puffed like Alfred Hitchcock's. "Oh, no. No. That won't be necessary."

"Don't be silly." I gave Harry a not-so-playful shove. "This'll just take a sec."

He shielded his face with his hand. "We'd really prefer not to have our picture taken."

"Nonsense." My teeth were clenched as I placed my hand on Harry's back and pushed him toward the brunette. "Now you two lean in and say *cheat*. Wait, did I say *cheat*? Oopsy, I meant *cheese*."

"Please leave us alone." Harry waved his arm and knocked

his wallet, which he had placed beside his silverware, onto the ground. He leaned down to retrieve the wallet.

"Franki!"

I turned and saw Veronica pointing at a manager-type who stormed in my direction. I had to take the picture, and fast.

I spun around, aimed, and snapped. When I pulled the phone away from my eyes, a red-faced, toupee-less Harry with little pieces of pink tape on his head made a grasping motion toward my chest.

"Whoa, there, partner." *Was Harry trying to take a swing at me?*

He grabbed at me again, and I looked down and saw it—his toupee was caught on the top button of my blazer. *Eww.* I struggled to remove the rebellious rug from my button.

The manager-type arrived at the table. "What's going on here?"

"She...my...we..." Harry sputtered.

"I'm helping this gentleman with his toupee." As proof, I slapped the offending item on Harry's hairless head. "There. That toupee tape ought to stick now, sir." I turned and hightailed it outta there faster 'n a polecat in a perfume shop, followed by Veronica.

Outside, we jumped in the car and peeled out of the parking lot.

Veronica glanced in the rearview mirror. "I wonder who that woman was with Harry."

"Who knows. A 'catch' like that could get any woman in the city."

~

"WHAT THE...?" I stared out the window of Veronica's Audi.

In our yard stood a five-foot-five body builder with gel-styled hair and a thick gold chain with a huge cross and a *cornicello*, a twisted horn-shaped charm for warding off the evil eye. Even in the dim porch light, I could see the Italian pride-themed tattoos on his bulging biceps and the orange glow of his spray tan.

Veronica gripped the steering wheel. "Do you know that guy?"

I squinted to get a better look. Although I had no idea who he was, I didn't have to look beneath his wife beater to know that he'd spent far too much time at the gym. "No, but he looks like he would have been a shoo-in for the cast of *Jerseylicious.*"

The steroid stud's eyes caught mine. He puffed out his chest like a toad expanding its throat and revealed a mouthful of teeth as florescent white as his velour track pants. Then he bent over to pick up something.

"Get down." I ducked into my seat. "He's got a gun."

"Actually, it looks like a small guitar."

I peered out the window and saw the offending instrument —a mandolin.

"*Mamma mia,*" I wailed, sinking into my seat. "I'm about to get a Sicilian serenade—Jersey style."

No sooner had I spoken the words than I heard my nonna's favorite song, *E vui durmiti ancora,*" which meant *"And you're still sleeping."*

Veronica looked thoughtful. "Say what you want about your nonna, but I really admire her determination."

I didn't bother to comment. I sat in my seat waiting for my ripped Romeo to finish his serenade and leave.

"Well?" Veronica nudged me. "Aren't you going to get out of the car?"

"No." I crossed my arms like a stubborn child.

"Come on, Franki. You've got to deal with this."

I turned to face her. "Or what? He'll wake the dead across the street with all that romantic racket?"

Veronica rolled her eyes. "So you can ask him to leave."

"Good point." I started to get out of the car, but then a disturbing thought occurred to me. "Oh no."

"What?"

"I'm wearing leopard print."

Veronica blinked. "So?"

"He's from New Jersey. They go *crazy* for leopard print there."

Veronica shook her head. "That's stereotyping, Franki."

"Can you not *see* him, Veronica?" I gestured toward my serenader. "He's pretty much a walking stereotype, I'd say."

"Well, at least he's not singing 'O Sole Mio.'"

"Ain't that the truth."

Veronica and I exited the car and started up the sidewalk, and Glenda flung open her front door. She was wearing what looked like Borat's mankini in shocking pink underneath a sheer baby doll robe. Of course, because it was cold out, she'd put on matching faux fur leg warmers over her high-heeled slippers. To keep her calves warm, naturally.

"Loooord almighty," Glenda breathed as she gave the buff bodybuilder a once-over that would make a seasoned gigolo blush. "What *do* we have here?"

I shot her a wry look. "We have what's known in New Jersey as a juicehead."

Glenda took a drag off her foot-long pink cigarette holder and blew an alarming smoke signal—a perfectly formed heart-shaped smoke ring. "Well in that case, sugar, I'd like to take a long, slow drink of that nectar."

My stomach churned. I had to put a stop to the serenade-slash-stripper circus, and *pronto*. I turned to the strapping Sicilian. "Stop singing."

He ceased, mid-word, and stared at me.

I walked up to him and looked down (I was a good seven-to-eight inches taller than him in my heels). "Listen, uh…"

"Guido."

Seriously? "I'm sorry, Guido, but you went to all this trouble for nothing. I'm not interested in dating right now. Or in men, for that matter."

"Yo, if you're into chicks," his lips spread into a leer, "I'm down wit' that."

My lips went Mr. Grinch. "How incredibly generous of you."

Glenda took another drag off her cigarette. "Speaking of men…"

I turned and followed her gaze toward the street. Bradley had just walked out of Thibodeaux's. My stomach dropped. I didn't want to see him. Well, I did, but I didn't.

Bradley crossed the street. He narrowed his eyes as he walked up the sidewalk. "Evening ladies." He nodded stiffly at Guido.

I feigned a look of surprise. "I thought you'd be at *Jersey Boys*—with your wife."

Guido jutted out his lower lip. "That's a great show, bro."

I turned and shot Guido a piercing look, and his chest deflated like a popped balloon.

Bradley put his hands in his pockets. "I guess I deserved that." His brow rose. "Am I interrupting something?"

Glenda sidled up to Bradley like a stripper to a pole. "Miss Franki's getting a serenade from a juicehead. Isn't it delicious?"

Bradley's lips tightened into a line. "I see."

I moved to stand beside Guido, who reinflated his chest, and an uncomfortable silence descended upon the yard.

Bradley sought my gaze. "I guess that's my cue to leave."

I wanted to ask him to stay, but I couldn't.

He turned and headed for his car.

Glenda dragged off her cigarette. "A crying shame, sugar."

"Stay strong, Franki." Veronica slipped her arm around my shoulders as I stared after him.

"I'm trying. But this time it's really hard."

She gave me a squeeze. "You're a tough girl, though."

I nodded and heard the reprise of the mandolin. I spun around to give Guido a piece of my mind and stopped, horrified.

He was no longer serenading me—he was serenading Glenda. And she was doing what she did best—a striptease.

I saw the first faux fur leg warmer fly, and I fled to the sanctuary of my bordello, er, house.

20

The morning sunshine streamed into the CC's Community Coffee House on Royal Street. The bright, warm room and smell of coffee made me kind of glad that I'd had to wake up early to get my laptop from the office. After the events of the previous night, I'd intended to wallow in self-pity in my house—actually, in my bed—all day. But an early Saturday trip to the French Quarter had turned out to be what I'd needed to lift my spirits.

"What can I get you?" a teenaged cashier with charming braids and freckles asked.

"A double soy latte to go."

"Anything else?"

"Now that you mention it, I could use a little something to eat." I rested a hand on my bloated belly. *How could something so empty feel so big?* "I'll take a lemon pastry."

"The iced lemon pound cake or the lemon square?"

"Both. And make that three of each."

She placed the pastries into a bag and rang up my order. I swiped my credit card through the reader, dropped fifty cents into the tip jar, and headed toward the coffee bar.

While I waited, I looked around the rectangular-shaped room at all the people enjoying a lazy morning reading newspapers, studying, and surfing the Internet on their laptops. An older man at the table closest to me edited what looked like a play or a screenplay with a red pen, and I was reminded of some of the cool movies that had been filmed in New Orleans—*A Streetcar Named Desire*, *Interview with a Vampire*, *The Curious Case of Benjamin Button*, and the all-time classic *Big Momma's House 2*.

I admired the architectural features of the old building, starting with elliptical transom window over the entrance. My gaze lowered to the glass pane of the door below.

And I jumped.

Concetta peered inside wearing a scowl that clashed with her nun's habit.

I wondered what she was doing in the area, and then I remembered that there was a Catholic Center up the street. I held out hope that she wasn't looking for me. Maybe she was mad because she hadn't had her morning coffee.

Her eyes zeroed in on me like a heat seeking missile.

No such luck.

She shoved open the door and marched to me. "I heard you and Veronica paid Domenica a visit in jail yesterday."

I shifted in my purple Ugg boots. Gone was the charitable nun—she'd been replaced by an overprotective big sister. "Yes, that's right."

She leaned close. "Do you mind telling me what that little charade was all about?"

"It wasn't all a charade, Concetta." I guiltily watched the cross on her necklace swing from side to side rather than look her in the eyes. "Veronica *did* give her some legal advice."

She put her hands on her hips and snorted in disbelief. "You call telling her to be frank with her attorney 'legal advice'?"

"Listen, I can understand why you're upset, but Domenica

needed to hear what Veronica had to say." I glanced around to make sure that no one was watching me argue with a nun. "She's not exactly forthcoming, you know."

She rolled her eyes. "Well *of course* she doesn't feel like talking, much less being interrogated after losing half her family. Tell me, just *how* do you expect a teenager in her situation to behave?"

"I don't know. But I certainly *don't* expect her to dance on graves and deface her own sister's tombstone, and especially not in a cemetery where an unsolved murder took place."

Concetta's face contorted in anger, and her right eyelid twitched. "I told you and your partner before—I don't approve of Domenica's Goth look. But that's all it is, *a look*. My sister is *not* a Satanist, if that's what you're insinuating. And she's definitely not a *murderer*."

From the corner of my eye, I saw the cashier conferring with a pasty-faced twenty-year-old guy who appeared to be the manager. They were whispering and casting concerned looks in our direction.

"We're disturbing the customers. I think it would be best if we continued this conversation with Veronica at our office."

"That won't be necessary. But you guys gave Domenica advice, so let me give you some—If you really want to solve this case, you'll leave my sister alone and start interrogating Stewart Preston. Unlike her, he's a known voodoo practitioner *and* a killer." She spun on her heels and left the store.

"Double soy latte," the barista shouted.

Ignoring my coffee call, I reflected on what had happened with Concetta. I was frustrated by her inability to understand that we had to re-question Domenica after her unexpected arrest. But I did think she'd been right about one thing—If Veronica and I were ever going to solve this case, Stewart Preston was the key.

I walked over to the counter to get my latte and resolved to step up my phone call assault on Stewart, right after I called Veronica about my run-in with the nun.

I PULLED in front of my house twenty minutes later and scanned the yard for Sicilians before getting out of the car. I hadn't heard a word from my nonna since the serenade, so the Sicilian coast was by no means clear. As soon as I was certain the area was suitor-free, I grabbed my bag of lemon goodies and bounded up the sidewalk to my apartment. It was my first lazy Saturday morning in ages, and I was determined to enjoy it—boyfriend or no boyfriend.

I opened the door expecting to find Napoleon waiting for me to take him on a walk, but he was nowhere to be seen. Dogs were supposed to greet their masters when they came home, but Napoleon occasionally opted to continue napping because his life was so exhausting and all. No matter—it meant that I could get right to the important business of the morning—eating and shopping online. In between calls to Stewart Preston, of course.

After grabbing a plate from the kitchen, I headed to the living room and sat cross-legged on the chaise lounge. I opened my laptop, placed it in front of me, and laid out my pastry picnic. I picked up a slice of the pound cake and was preparing to take my first delicious bite when I heard a whimper coming from the floor below. Napoleon was staring at me, begging.

"You know sugar isn't good for you. Go lie down."

Napoleon knew the phrase "go lie down" as well as he knew the words "bath" and "treat," but he chose to ignore me and whimpered again.

I looked him in the eyes. "Trust me, boy. I'm doing you a favor."

He stared at me with the intensity of a hypnotist, willing me to give him the pound cake.

I sighed and put down the pastry. "Come on." I went into the kitchen to get him a dog treat. I took a biscuit from a box in the pantry and held it to his mouth. "Here you go. Now scram."

He took the treat with his teeth and ran to the living room to eat it, presumably so that he could punish me by leaving crumbs on the bearskin rug.

I flopped onto the chaise lounge and picked up the pound cake.

Someone knocked on my front door.

I bowed my head. "Who is it?"

"Veronica. Open up."

I rose and opened the door to find Veronica dressed in a faux shearling coat, jeans, and boots. "Howdy, partner," I drawled in Texan. "Are you on your way to the cowboy convention?"

"Don't be silly." She blew past me into the room. "The whole cowboy incident reminded that I hadn't worn this outfit in a while."

I closed the door and returned yet again to the chaise lounge, doing an eye roll on the way.

"Anyway, I got your message about Concetta." She spotted my mini banquet and squealed. "Yummy. Thanks for getting me some too."

My heart was as heavy as the pastry bag. I wasn't going to admit that all six of those lemony treats were for me. "No problem."

Veronica bit into the slice of pound cake that I'd been trying to eat for the past ten minutes. "So, you don't think Concetta was following you, do you? I mean, from what you told me, it sounds like she just happened to see you as you were going into CC's."

"That's what I think too." I snatched a piece of the cake for myself. "I guess I was just taken aback by how angry she was."

"Well, I can see how she'd think we were targeting Domenica, so it's really not surprising that she would get upset. Nuns are people too, you know."

"I suppose so." Although, based on my Sunday school experiences, I was half convinced that nuns were actually a special race of super humans who had x-ray vision that they used exclusively for the purpose of seeing right through those with guilty consciences.

"I wouldn't worry about it." Veronica waved what was left of her pound cake. "She's such a nice person. She'll probably call you to apologize."

"Maybe." But I wasn't so sure about that. Concetta had seemed pretty darned mad.

She finished the last of her pound cake. "So, are you ready for round two of the Harry Upton stakeout tonight?"

I watched with a growing sense of panic as she moved on to a lemon square, and I seized one for myself. "As long as we don't have to go back to the rodeo restaurant."

"Definitely wear a dress again in case we have to follow him into someplace nice."

"Ugh, I don't want to be in a dress while we're looking at video at Lenton's. I'd rather be in my comfy jeans."

"We're not going to Lenton's."

"Why not? Is Ed still in the grip of the devil?"

She shrugged and took a bite of lemon square. "I don't know, but his assistant called me this morning and said that the DVD of the other two purchases hasn't arrived yet."

"That doesn't sound promising."

"Don't worry. It should be here in a day or so. She said it was sent via FedEx." Veronica looked at her phone. "Oh, crap. I have a mani-pedi in thirty minutes. I've got to go."

I looked at the plate and was relieved to see that I still had one of each of the pastries left.

Veronica grabbed the last piece of pound cake to go.

"Well, I'll see you later." I rushed her from the apartment before she could do any more damage to my dessert, er, breakfast. Then I locked the door behind her.

Alone with one lousy lemon square, I picked up my laptop and clicked my Internet browser. On a whim, I pulled up *The Times-Picayune* picture of Stewart Preston waving on the courthouse steps. There was something about the photograph that wasn't right, but I couldn't figure out what it was.

I studied the image for a few more minutes. As my eyes roved the picture, it hit me—There was no clasp on Stewart's watchband. I stared at the watch trying to determine whether it was the slip-on kind, and then I decided that it wasn't a watch at all. But to be sure, I needed a high-resolution version of the photo. I scrolled to the bottom of the page and clicked "Times-Picayune Store." After a quick search, I discovered that the picture wasn't readily available, so I filled out a web-form request for a copy.

If the watch was actually a bracelet, it could blow the Evans case wide open.

BRADLEY LICKED MY FACE, and I turned over on my left side with a giggle.

Wait. That doesn't sound right.

I sat up with a start. Napoleon stood on his hind legs with his front paws perched on the chaise lounge, his tongue lolling from his mouth. I put my hand on my right cheek and touched something wet and sticky. Dog saliva mixed with lemon square.

Nice.

I looked at my phone to check the time. *Three o'clock?* I

must've crashed and burned from my caffeine-sugar high, which meant that it had been a successful lazy Saturday, after all.

There was also a voice mail from my parents' number. It had to be my nonna wanting to find out the results of her serenade scheme. I gave silent thanks to the universe for allowing me to miss that call. I tapped the message and steeled myself for what was to come.

"Franki, I talk-a to Guido, and a wow-a." My nonna had never sounded so happy. "He tell-a me that-a you two had a date last-a night. And he say that-a you're gonna have another one again-a tonight. I *told-a* him that-a song would do the trick-a. Now, he did-a say that you were *a lot older* than-a he thought-a you was gonna be, but that-a was because-a I tell-a him that-a you were twenty-one and not-a twenty-nine." A smack ensued. "Ha!"

I imagined her slapping the kitchen table in a fit of self-induced hilarity and paused the message.

What is she talking about? Guido and I did not *have a date last night. And just where did he get off saying that I looked "a lot older" than he'd anticipated? I could pass for twenty-one or so.*

A disturbing realization dawned on me—He was talking about Glenda. *Guido thought I was Glenda.*

I lay back on the chaise lounge slightly nauseated, and it wasn't because of the pastries and coffee. I toyed with notion of deleting the rest of the message—I wasn't sure I wanted to hear anymore. *Who knows what Guido had told my nonna about what he and Glenda did on their date?*

Then I remembered something I was always hearing on TV or wherever—Knowledge is power. And power was something I needed to take on my nonna.

I tapped the play arrow.

"So make-a sure you don't-a tell-a him your real age. Remember, a zitella like-a you—"

I tapped the trash can.

For a moment, I wondered whether I should tell my nonna the truth about what had happened. But I realized that I must've been delusional from low blood sugar. Because if Guido was dating Glenda and thought she was me, then I was finally off the hook. No more nonna in my love life. I just had to hope—or, rather, pray—that Guido wasn't the type to kiss and tell. The mere thought of the stories he could divulge made me cringe.

My phone vibrated.

I looked at the display and sat up with a jolt.

Stewart Preston.

My hand shook as I tapped *Answer.* "Hello?"

"Who the hell *are* you," he practically growled, "and why have you been calling me and my family?"

Stewart was ready to play hardball, so I needed to stay cool. "Like I said in my messages, I'm an old high school friend of Angelica Evangelista."

"What's that got to do with me?" His voice was thick with suspicion.

"I need to talk to you about her murder."

"You must not have heard my last question," he said in a slow, threatening tone. "I repeat, what's that got to do with me?"

"Well, I know you and Angelica go way back—"

Stewart cut me off with a loud, raucous laugh. "Darlin', Angelica goes way back with a lot of men."

The conversation was harder than I'd expected, so I spoke to him in the only language he seemed to know. "First of all, don't call me 'darling.' And second, I know your father's company was bribing Angelica to keep her quiet, and I can prove it."

A stony silence followed on the other end of the line.

Fueled by a surge of confidence, I summoned my inner TV detective. "So if you know what's good for you, you'll meet me tomorrow night."

"Where?"

I gulped down my surprise at his blasé reaction. "The Carousel Bar and Lounge at five o'clock. Don't be late." I ended the call.

My palms were sweating, and I was breathing hard. I'd tracked down the elusive Stewart Preston, but there was a voice inside my head reminding me of the obvious. All indications were that he was a cruel, callous killer—and I'd just put myself squarely into his murderous hands.

21

———

"You're bringing a *gun* to the Carousel Bar when I meet Stewart Preston?" I turned in the driver seat of my Mustang.

"Just as a security measure." Veronica kept her binoculars trained on Harry Upton's office building on the Garden District's swanky St. Charles Avenue.

I didn't even know she *had* a gun. And while I was confident in my own ability to handle a firearm, thanks to my police training, I had less faith in Veronica. "But I'm meeting him in a public place in broad daylight."

"Franki, you and I both know that Stewart Preston could be dangerous."

I swallowed hard and glanced across the street as Harry emerged, pants drooping well below his massive belly, from the rotating glass doors of his office building.

"Heeere's Harry!" Veronica sounded like Jack Nicholson's character in *The Shining*. "Precisely at six, just like last night."

"He's nothing if not punctual."

Harry stopped and pulled up his pants, and a gust of wind blew his toupee into an upright position on his head. Seemingly unfazed, he tamped down the unruly rug and climbed into his Mercedes.

"Jeez." I started the engine. "You'd think a guy with all that dough would have a better hair piece."

"I know. It's amazing what men are able to get away with in terms of their appearance."

I pulled onto southbound St. Charles, staying a few cars back from Harry's Mercedes. I followed him for about a mile and a half, trying to focus on his car and not on the spectacular multi-million-dollar mansions that lined the avenue.

"So, what kind of gun do you have?" I asked, more out of concern than curiosity. Guns weren't one size fits all, particularly when you had tiny hands like Veronica.

"A Smith & Wesson."

"A LadySmith?"

"No, it's the nine-millimeter Pink Breast Cancer Awareness model."

"Interesting marketing choice."

Veronica leaned forward. "His turn signal is on. It looks like he's turning onto Seventh Street."

"On it." I slowed down and turned onto Seventh just in time to see Harry turning onto Prytania Street. I followed suit, careful to hang back.

He drove a few hundred yards and pulled to a stop in front of a stunning pink two-story Greek Revival mansion with a columned porch and wrought iron balcony. The house was shrouded in privacy hedges and majestic oaks and magnolias. I pulled to the curb, and Veronica and I slouched in our seats.

Harry carried out his now familiar car-exiting routine—battling his belly to get out of his seat, tamping down his toupee, buttoning his sport coat, and smoothing his Hitleresque mustache.

Veronica pulled her camera from its bag. "Okay, now drive

slowly by the house. I'll get shots of him with whoever comes to the door."

I straightened in my seat, pulled away from the curb, and drove at a crawl. When I reached the mansion, an elegant brunette opened the front door. It only took me a second to recognize her. "That's the woman from last night."

"It sure is." Veronica was slouched in her seat, snapping pictures.

As we drove past, the brunette glanced at my car. She ushered Harry into the house and closed the door.

I hit the gas. "I think she saw us, but I'm not sure."

"Let's hope she didn't." Veronica straightened in her seat.

"It doesn't matter because we've got what we need. Let's go back to the office so we can download the pictures and send them to Twyla."

"What?" Veronica looked at me. "We can't leave now. We still need more pictures."

"Why?" I braked at a stop sign. "Twyla hired us to take pictures of Harry with Patsy so that she could use them to confront him. Now we just need to show her proof that he's spent the last two evenings with another woman. It's up to her to decide whether she still wants to confront him or have us find out the brunette's identity first."

"But the pictures we have don't prove that Harry is actually cheating on Twyla." We need to try to get some photos of Harry and the brunette in a compromising position."

I turned to look at her. "How do you propose we do that?"

"Easy. We could snap some photos through one of the windows."

"But what if they're on the second floor?"

"Well, in that case, we might be out of luck."

I tapped her arm. "I know. We could climb ones of those trees."

Veronica crossed her arms. "I don't know, Franki. We're in dresses and high heels."

"So? Charlie's Angels wore dresses and heels all the time." The reference reminded me of Bradley, and my gut gave a pang.

"No. One of us could fall out of a tree and get hurt."

"C'mon, Veronica. Where's your sense of investigative duty?" I appealed to her scrupulous, workaholic side. "This guy is cheating on his wife of forty-eight years. We've got to prove it and nail him."

She scrutinized my face. "Do you think you might be taking this case a little personally, Franki?"

I feigned a look of disbelief, both for her benefit and my own. "What are you talking about?"

"I can't help but think that your zeal to nail Harry, as you put it, might have something to do with Bradley."

"Don't be ridiculous." My voice was a telltale octave too high. "This case is purely business."

She shrugged. "If you say so. Anyway, for now let's just plan on doing a quick round of the house to see if they're in one of the rooms on the main floor."

"Sure." I turned onto Sixth Street and shivered. It bordered Lafayette Cemetery No. 1, the oldest and creepiest city-owned cemetery in New Orleans. I parked the car in front of the cemetery and stuffed the car keys into my bra for safekeeping.

Veronica grabbed her camera from the floor. "So, how do you suggest we do this?"

"Because the backyard is fenced, we're going to have to approach the house from the side. And we need to do this fast in case the brunette did see us. If she called the police, we could get arrested for trespassing."

She nodded.

We exited the car and set off down the street. When we reached the house, we dashed into the yard and peeped in the windows—the living room, family room, den, parlor, and study.

I couldn't believe the luxury. "What does a single family *do* with all these living spaces?"

"Shh!" Veronica looked into the kitchen and adjoining dining room. "Empty," she whispered. "They must be upstairs. Let's get going."

"No," I whisper-shouted. "We've come this far. We've got to get some pictures."

"Franki, we can't climb these trees. I can't take the chance of one of us getting injured."

Unwilling to accept defeat, I scanned the side of the house and saw a metal trellis. "But I can."

I rushed to the ladder-like structure, kicked off my beige pumps, and climbed the twenty-or-so feet to the second floor.

"Get down," Veronica whisper-shouted. "That thing can't possibly hold your weight."

"Just what are you trying to say, Veronica?" I scowled down at her.

She scowled back. "It's made of flimsy pressboard."

Ignoring her warning, I climbed until I reached a window. I peered over the windowsill into a spacious office and spotted Harry and the brunette sitting close on a sofa. She was curled up with her arm stretched out behind him on the back of the couch, and they were looking at what appeared to be a photo album.

"I see them." I realized that I had no way to photograph them. "I need the camera."

"I'm not climbing up that thing," Veronica whisper-protested. "It'll break."

"Fine," I whisper-huffed. "I'll come down."

I lowered myself slightly more than halfway. Gripping the trellis with one hand, I leaned and extended my arm.

Veronica rose on her tiptoes. "I can't reach you."

"One sec." I took a step down and leaned a little farther.

The top half of the trellis cracked and pulled from the wall.

I heard Veronica gasp and fabric tear as I fell. I landed rear-end first on an immaculately groomed shrub as the trellis smacked loudly against the side of the house, like a rubber band that had been stretched too far and then released.

Veronica ran to the shrub. "Are you okay?"

"I think so." I checked my limbs to make sure they were all intact.

Veronica gasped again. "The brunette just looked out the window. We've got to get out of here."

I tried to move, but my bottom was stuck in the shrub. "Pull me out."

She grabbed my hand and tugged with all her petite might. While she pulled, I leveraged myself on a branch with my other hand and broke free of the stubborn bush. I rolled onto my stomach, hopped down, and grabbed my pumps.

The front door opened.

Veronica and I exchanged a look of panic before hoofing it down the street. We reached the cemetery, and I ripped the car keys from my bra. Then we jumped into the Mustang and burned rubber.

Veronica patted her camera as I drove back to the office. "I wonder how Twyla is going to react to these photographs. After all, she's expecting to see Patsy, not a beautiful young brunette."

"Give me...a sec." I gasped between breaths. A few minutes had elapsed since we'd left the brunette's mansion, and I still hadn't recovered from the two-hundred-yard sprint to my car.

"Maybe we should deliver them to her in person. She *is*

prone to fainting spells, and I'd hate for something bad to happen."

"Me too," I wheezed.

"Okay, then it's settled. We'll bring them to her tomorrow."

I slowed to a stop at the intersection of Governor Nicholls and Bourbon. It was a residential district, so the streets were quiet. I looked both ways and did a double take.

Bradley walked down the street with a masked young woman in a Mardi Gras queen costume—make that a teeny bikini with a few sequins and feathers.

I recovered the full force of my lungs. "Is that Bradley with that hot blonde?"

Veronica looked out the passenger window. "Didn't you say his wife was a blonde?"

"Yeah, but that's not her. She doesn't have waist-length hair."

"Well, it's impossible to tell who that man is. He's walking away from us, and it's dark."

"Oh, it's not impossible." I speed-turned onto Bourbon.

"What are you going to do?" Her tone was panicked. "Run them down?"

"No. We're going to follow them."

"But there's a barricade up ahead. You can't drive through there."

I pulled into a rare Bourbon Street parking space and shut off the ignition. "That's why we're going to follow them on foot."

Veronica put her hand on my arm. "Franki, this is *not* a good idea. If it *is* Bradley, what are you going to do?"

"I'm not going to do anything," I said, although I wasn't sure I was being entirely honest. "I just need to know if it's him or not."

"You might want to look at your dress first. It's torn."

"Veronica." I threw my hands in the air. "This is hardly the time to worry about a little rip in my dress."

Before she could reply, I blew out of the car and rushed down Bourbon. I could still see the man and the blonde a couple of intersections ahead. I had to catch up to them before they passed the barricade at St. Ann Street that separated the homes from the bar district. My high heels were slowing me down, but there was no way I was taking them off. It was one thing to run barefoot down a residential street in the wealthy Garden District, but it was quite another to do it on Bourbon.

I arrived at the intersection and spotted the guy and the blonde near the barricade. He turned to her and said something that made her laugh. The minute I saw his profile, I recognized the outline of Bradley's Roman nose and strong jaw.

Veronica caught up to me. "Well?"

"It's Bradley, all right." I was so angry that I was sure flames shot from my eyes. "He's already found a new woman to cheat on his wife with."

"Okay. Now that you know it's him, let's go back to the car."

I clenched my teeth. "Not before I get a better look at that blonde."

I ran to St. Ann and pushed my way through the partiers, keeping my eyes glued to the back of Bradley's head.

"Franki, wait," Veronica called. "I'm trapped."

I saw that she was stuck behind a group of tall men dressed as Catholic cardinals.

"Push 'em the hell out of the way," I yelled and turned back around.

Bradley and the blonde had disappeared.

I scanned the crowd for any sign of them.

"Hey, catch," a sexy male voice shouted from a balcony above.

I looked up and a bead necklace hit me in the face.

The man who had thrown the necklace winked and raised

his glass in a silent toast. A group of his friends gathered around him and smiled at me.

"Here ya go, beautiful." One of them tossed a handful of necklaces in my direction.

I stood there, surprised. I'd been to Bourbon Street several times before, once even in my pre-cellulite days, and I'd never seen that kind of action.

"Are you supposed to be Poison Ivy or Eve in The Garden of Eden?" a drunken male voice asked.

I looked away from the balcony and saw a Humpty Dumpty-shaped guy in a Court Jester outfit standing in front of me. "Huh?"

He took a sip from his long, neon green, hand grenade-shaped cup. "Those leaves on your hooters and your hoo ha."

I looked down. At some point during my fall from the trellis and the ensuing struggle with the shrub, my three-quarter-sleeve, beige knit dress had acquired leafy accessories in the nether regions. It had also gained a ten-inch plunging neckline that could only be described as Glenda-worthy. *That explains the beads.*

"Because if you're Eve," he said, "then you really should've worn a bikini instead of that big dress."

That from a Court Jester whose only exposed body parts on the chilly January night were his face and hands. "Speaking of big," I leaned in close to the egg-shaped joker, "if you don't shut your big mouth, I'm going to take your big cup and shove it up your big—"

"Franki," Veronica interrupted after she'd broken free from her Catholic-costumed captors. Then she clasped her hands to her face and stared at me. "Your dress."

"Believe me, I *know* about my dress." I glared at the Court Jester, who took that as his cue to beat it. I bent over, collected my beads, and put them around my neck to cover my fully displayed cleavage. Then I plucked some leaves from the area below my waist. "Now let's get going. But first I need a drink."

"I think I do too."

I saw a young woman in black shorts, a bright green tube top, and white go-go boots selling Jell-O shots outside the Funky 544 club. "Perfect." I pointed to the woman. "Let's go over there."

"A Jell-O shot?" Veronica crinkled her face. "Those are so disgusting."

"I haven't eaten dinner yet, so this way I can get something in my stomach while I drink. Otherwise, you're going to have to drive home."

Veronica gave me a look. "I don't think Everclear-infused Jell-O qualifies as solid food."

I walked up to the shot seller. She shivered in the cool night air and chewed gum a mile a minute. "How much?"

She popped a gum bubble. "Three bucks for the test tubes, seven for the syringes."

"You have them in *syringes*?"

The girl smacked her gum and nodded. "You can inject 'em."

"Even better. I'll take two."

The girl handed me two syringes the size of toothpaste tubes.

"If you want, I can inject them into your mouth." She pocketed my fifteen dollars in cash and then adjusted her sagging tube top.

I looked at her hands. "Thanks, but I can handle it from here." I squirted them one by one into my mouth.

Veronica looked annoyed. "Can we go to the office now? I'd really like to get these pictures printed."

"Let's go." I said it as though I'd fully intended to go to the office after drink-eating Jell-O shots.

The mob on Bourbon seemed to grow by the minute, so it took a while to make our way back to the car. At around the halfway point, we were forced to stop behind a huge crowd that had gathered in the middle of the street to listen to a traveling jazz band that was playing "Shake It and Break It."

"Let's wait until the song ends and then forge ahead," I shouted over the music.

Veronica nodded.

We stood at the edge of the crowd, and I got the creeped-out feeling that someone was watching me. I looked over my left shoulder but didn't see anyone out of the ordinary. Then I glanced to my right.

There, down a side street, was Domenica with a group of Goth teens. The others were absorbed in conversation, but she was watching me, her face so full of loathing that I took a step backward.

I tapped Veronica on the arm. "You'll never believe who's standing down the street over there."

She turned and huffed. "Domenica? She's not drinking is she? All she needs right now is a minor-in-possession charge."

"I don't see a drink. She's just glaring at me. Maybe she thinks we're following her."

"Who knows." She turned to watch the jazz band. "But it would be best to stay away from her right now."

"Fine with me." The farther I stayed from Domenica, the better.

The song ended, and the crowd dispersed.

I looked in Domenica's direction, but she'd vanished.

Veronica and I resumed our trek to the car. My high-heeled feet moved slowly, but my mind raced.

If Domenica was Jessica's strangler, would she be desperate enough to try to kill me or Veronica to silence us? And what about Stewart Preston? He'd already killed once. What would he do if he found out I wasn't a friend of Jessica's at all but a private investigator working her murder case?

As I contemplated the questions, not even the warm glow of my syringe-shot buzz could eliminate the chill that had spread through my body.

22

———————

I took a bite of my boudin and tossed my fork onto the plate. Even though I'd lost my appetite after seeing Bradley with the blonde bimbo the night before, I'd ordered Thibodeaux's breakfast special—Cajun-style eggs Benedict with boudin patties and home fries, a side of *pain perdu*, otherwise known as French toast, and unlimited juice refills. But I asked for carbonated water to cut calories.

"Cheer up, Franki." Veronica sat across from me with a half-eaten Creole omelet and a few remaining mini baguette slices.

I swallowed a mouthful of oozing eggs and Tasso ham Hollandaise sauce. "How, exactly, am I supposed to do that? I mean, it's bad enough that Bradley turned out to be married, but then I have to see him with a beautiful blonde on his arm."

Veronica picked up her *café au lait*. "You're an attractive woman too, you know. Have you forgotten that men were throwing beads at you left and right on Bourbon Street last night?"

I shot her a look. "Maybe that had something to do with the fact that my boobs were bursting out of my dress and my vajayjay was framed in leaves."

"That wasn't the only reason."

"Whatever. Looks aren't the issue here. His marriage certificate is the problem."

She buttered a slice of baguette. "Have you considered the possibility that he might have a logical explanation for all of this?"

"You mean, for going out with a barely dressed Mardi Gras queen instead of his wife?" I stuffed a cluster of fries into my mouth.

She rolled her eyes. "Well, that and the fact that he's married. You never really let him explain."

My look was pointed—like a dagger. "What's there to explain?"

She shrugged. "For one thing, why his wife lives in Boston while he lives here. Maybe the marriage is over."

"Or maybe they're living apart while he spends a year at a New Orleans bank." I cut into my boudin with a little too much zeal.

"Maybe. But that's the kind of thing you should find out. Because it's real obvious that you still care about Bradley."

I put down my knife and fork, in case I got the urge to stab myself. "It doesn't matter how I feel about him. I'm tired of sharing my boyfriends with other women. I want a man all to myself. So, as long as Bradley's married, he's off limits."

"That banker man got you down, sugar?" Glenda stood at our table.

She was in all her glory. Her top was nothing special by her standards, just a red spandex jog bra, heavy on the cleavage. It was her matching red spandex pants that were so spectacular. They were essentially crotchless, but it wasn't only the crotch that was missing. It was all the fabric below the waistband. So her red G-string was prominently exposed, from hip to hip and on down, so to speak. *And to think I was worried about a few lousy leaves.*

"Oh, Glenda." Veronica put a hand to her chest. "You look sensational in red."

She batted her two-inch false eyelashes. "It's scarlet."

Veronica stared expectantly at me.

I spit out the first compliment that came to mind. "Nice biceps." I chose to focus on Glenda's upper body. "Have you been going to the gym?"

"No, it's from years of swinging on poles."

"Uh-huh," I said, since my mouth was hanging open. I hoped that she would either sit or leave. Having that G-string right next to my face was killing my urge to emotional eat. Then again, maybe that was a good thing—diet by disgust.

Veronica looked up at Glenda. "Would you like to join us?"

"No, I phoned in a to-go order." She paused and shot me a guilty look. "I have a gentleman caller at the house."

I knew she was talking about Guido. For a split second I felt something akin to jealousy—certainly not of Glenda having the Jersey juicehead in her bed, but of her ability to attract men so easily. But ultimately I was happy. I needed their relationship to continue to keep my nonna off my back. "If you mean Guido, I'm totally fine with the two of you seeing each other."

"Well, if you need a man to replace that banker, sugar, I'm willing to share." Glenda gave a Vanna White-like flourish of her arm. "A body like this can't be wasted on only one gentleman, even if he is a strong man in the circus."

"A strong man?" Veronica clapped. "Tell me more."

I, on the other hand, had already heard all I wanted to hear. I picked up my phone and stared at the time. "Gosh. It's almost ten thirty. We'd better get going if we're meeting Twyla at the office at eleven."

Veronica frowned. "Duty calls." She pulled two twenties

from her wallet. "Let me get this since you're having to work on a Sunday."

"Thanks." I grabbed my purse and fled the bar.

~

"Good afternoon, ladies." Twyla's tone was somber as she entered the office lobby. Her vibrant pinkish-yellow sack dress made her look a lot like a giant grapefruit.

"Hi, Twyla." I scooped up the photos of Harry and the brunette that Veronica and I had been reviewing on the coffee table.

She took a seat on the couch across from us, clutching a vintage wooden decoupage purse to her chest as though it were a shield she could use to protect herself from the news she was about to receive. "I'd like to thank you girls for so kindly agreeing to meet me at your office on a Sunday." Her ruby red lips set in a thin line. "I would have dearly luuuved to invite you to tea, but Harry is at home right now playing with his train set."

A train set? Harry was the opposite of a catch—he was a release.

Veronica rose and sat beside Twyla. "It's not a problem. It's probably better if you look at the pictures here, anyway."

A muscle twitched in Twyla's cheek. "What did you find out, Veronica?"

"We—"

Twyla raised her right hand. "Don't tell me yet." She opened the clasp of her purse with pinkish-yellow-lacquered fingernails and took out her smelling salts. She placed the bottle on the coffee table and pulled her purse back to her bosom. "Okay. I'm ready now."

Veronica cleared her throat. "As you know, we've followed Harry for the last two nights. On Friday, he went to Pascal's

Manale restaurant in Uptown, and on Saturday he went to a private residence in the Garden District."

Twyla's eyes grew wide at the mention of a home. "Was this house on Magazine Street, by any chance?"

I shook my head. "Prytania."

She blinked.

I pushed the photos of Harry and the brunette across the table to Twyla. "He met this woman on both occasions."

She peered down at the photo on the top of the pile with one eye closed. With a sharp intake of breath she jerked her head up in alarm. "That's not Patsy."

Veronica glanced at me. "No. We haven't been able to identify the woman yet. The house where Harry met her is listed in a man's name."

Twyla stiffened, her eyes rolled back in her head, and she fell back against the couch, her head hanging over the back.

She was out cold.

Veronica fanned her with a photo. "Grab her smelling salts."

I snatched the vial off the table and snapped it open. Veronica lifted Twyla's head, and I waved the vial under Twyla's nose.

She jerked. Her eyelids fluttered, and she opened her eyes. She blinked a few times. "Am I in heaven?"

I half-smiled. "No."

She raised a brow. "The ICU?"

"You're at Private Chicks," Veronica said. "You hired us to investigate your husband, Harry."

Twyla furrowed her brow as though deep in thought and went straight to despondent mode. "Haaaarry." She choked back a sob. "How could he *do* this to me? And after almost fifty years of wedded bliss."

Veronica handed her a box of tissues. "Twyla, we don't know

if Harry has done anything to you. All we know is that he met with this woman two nights in a row."

Twyla's tears shut off as quickly as water from a closed faucet. "You mean you don't actually *know* whether he's been unfaithful to me?"

I shook my head. "No."

She dabbed her tear-stained eyes with a tissue. "Well, Harry's quite fatherly, you know. Maybe that was the daughter of one of his clients, and he was just trying to be of assistance in some way?"

I looked at Veronica, and my gaze said *Unlikely.*

Twyla patted my knee. "You don't have to answer that, darling. It was just a rhetorical question."

Veronica looked concerned. "We apologize if there was any confusion about our findings."

"Not at all, dear." Twyla rose to her feet. "I want to thank you girls for all your trouble. I'll let you know if I need you to investigate this unseemly matter any further, after I've talked to Harry." She walked to the door and then turned to face us. "Whatever you girls do, don't make the tragic mistake of choosing a dashing man like my Harry to be your groom. Because if you do, you'll have to protect him from shameless trollops for your entire marriage."

"BAD BOY, NAPOLEON." I scolded him for the second time since carrying him into the house. I'd taken him out for a walk, and he'd pulled the leash from my hand to chase a cat through the cemetery. Nothing like a romp through a graveyard hours before a meeting with an alleged murderer to lift your spirits, so to speak.

I hung the leash on a hook by the front door and looked

around the living room. It was three o'clock, so I still had a good hour and a half before I had to leave to meet Stewart Preston at the Carousel Bar. I needed to find something to do to keep my mind occupied because I was nervous.

Dust the furniture?

I was never that desperate.

Read?

I wouldn't be able to focus on the page.

Have a snack and watch mindless TV?

Sounded like a plan.

After grabbing a bag of Mint Milanos and the Nutella from the pantry, I headed for my bedroom. I swung open the doors of my hot pink and black armoire and switched on the tiny TV set I'd received as a hand-me-down from my parents. I flopped onto the bed and flipped through the channels with the remote. The first movie I came across was *The Silence of the Lambs*.

FBI trainee meets cannibalistic serial killer?

Definitely not. I shuddered and changed the channel.

Unsolved Mysteries?

Not that either. There was every possibility that I would become an unsolved mystery myself.

I switched off the TV.

Now what? Eating the entire bag of Mint Milanos—dipped in Nutella—would while away some time. I pulled out the first cookie and heard a whimper coming from the floor.

I narrowed my eyes. "Not a chance, Napoleon, especially not after that cemetery caper."

My phone rang—a nice old-fashioned phone ring.

Talking on the phone was always a good distraction. I checked the display, and my heart thudded.

Bradley.

I wanted to answer with every fiber of my being and ask him what the hell he'd been doing with a bikinied bimbo when he was married. But I couldn't. Bradley's wandering ways were no concern of mine. But I *did* wish I knew what it was about me that attracted cheaters. *Was I not interesting or attractive enough to keep a guy? Or did I give off a cheat-on-me vibe?*

The ringing stopped, and I waited with to see whether he had left a voicemail. At least two minutes passed. I checked the voicemail box—nothing.

Inconsiderate jerk.

I had to find a way to take my mind off him. I decided to check my email. I grabbed my laptop from the bedside table and logged in. Some of the messages were spam—an ad for Viagra, news I'd won an overseas lottery, and an offer of marriage from a Russian bride. But then I saw "photo request" in the subject line of one of the messages.

It was the picture I'd requested from *The Times-Picayune* of Stewart Preston waving on the courthouse steps.

I opened the message and double-clicked the attachment. It wouldn't open. I tried two more times and discovered that the file was corrupt. I started to reply to the email but changed my mind. I was meeting Stewart in less than two hours, and I needed to know whether my hunch about his watchband was right. I checked the email for a signature and saw the name Dmitriy and a phone number. I entered the number into my phone and waited.

"Times-Picayune," a youthful male voice responded.

"Hi, could I please speak to Dmitriy?"

"You got him. How can I help you?"

"My name is Franki Amato, and I just got an email from you with a corrupt .jpg file."

"Was it the photo of Stewart Preston?"

I was surprised that he'd remembered the picture. "Yes."

"What is the *deal* with that image?" he muttered under his breath.

"Pardon?"

"Oh, I wasn't asking *you*. It's just that when I originally went to retrieve the photo, it wasn't on our server. Luckily, my friend Norm was the photographer assigned to that story, so I was able to get the picture for you from his personal archives. It's just weird that now there's a problem with the file."

My heart sped up. "So, the photo was deleted from your server?"

"Yeah, because it was used in an article, it should've been in our process file, but it wasn't there. It wasn't in our stock file either. But hey, when your staff consists of mainly unpaid interns, these things happen. Someone probably deleted the image by mistake."

I doubted that an intern would've accidentally deleted the picture from two separate files. "Are you still able to open it?"

"Yeah, it opens right up for me. It's a pretty big file, though. It could be that the picture didn't completely download from our server."

"Could you email it to me again?"

"I hit *Send* a second ago."

Holding my breath, I refreshed my inbox. The message was there. I clicked the attached file, and it opened without incident. "Got it. Thank you so much for your help, Dmitriy."

I closed the call and laid back on my bed, stunned. *Who would've deleted the file from not one but two places on the newspaper's server? Could it really have been a careless intern? Or was it someone connected to Stewart Preston?* If it was the latter, then it could mean only one thing—there was incriminating evidence in that photo that Stewart and his family didn't want anyone to see. Like I'd suspected.

I picked up my laptop and scrutinized Stewart's raised hand and wrist in the photo. The watchband protruded about a half an inch from the cuff of his suit coat. I enlarged the area click by click until it consumed the screen. On the fifth click, my body stiffened. Stewart wasn't wearing a chunky watchband.

Hidden beneath the sleeve of his suit coat, he wore a bracelet of skull beads—exactly like the one I'd found lodged underneath the scarf rack at the crime scene.

My mind flashed to the night of Jessica's murder. *Had Stewart gone to LaMarca wearing the bracelet?* If he had, then it was possible that the bracelet had been broken during a struggle. Jessica could've ripped the bracelet from Stewart's wrist and lodged one of the beads under the rack to implicate him as he strangled her.

Unfortunately, the only person who could've confirmed my theory was Jessica. There was only one thing I could do—find out whether Stewart still had the bracelet. It seemed an impossible task, but it was a matter of life and death.

Specifically, my own.

23

"I just can't get over it." Veronica stood at her kitchen sink wringing water from a cashmere sweater. "I've looked at that picture of Stewart a dozen times, and I never noticed anything unusual."

"That's because you don't like watches." I'd paced back and forth on Veronica's green shag carpet so many times in the past five minutes that I was wearing a path into it.

"True, but I still don't get it. What made you suspect that Stewart wasn't wearing a watch?"

"First of all, I've never seen a watchband with big bumps on it like that. Even the Gucci bamboo watch that I've been lusting over has a smooth silver link bracelet for a band. Plus, in the photo there's no buckle or clasp showing on the underside of Stewart's wrist. So I thought it might be some kind of bracelet."

"Well, I'm impressed." She placed the sweater on a drying rack near the sink.

"Thanks, but now we have to figure out what happened to that bracelet. If Stewart wore it to the murder scene, then he must've picked up the beads after it broke, except for the one that rolled under the rack."

Veronica entered the living room and took a seat on the couch next to a bowtie-adorned Hercules, who had been watching me pace with a worried gaze. "In that case, I seriously doubt he would've kept the beads. He would've gotten rid of them right away."

I stopped in my tracks. "So what do I do? I can't just say, 'Hey, Stewart, did you ever happen to own a skull bead bracelet from Marie Laveau's?'"

She stroked Hercules's fur. "Actually, you could ask him that and see what kind of a reaction you get."

"Unless his reaction is to lunge for my throat, that won't tell me anything definitive." I resumed pacing. "I'll have to think of some other way. Maybe I could work voodoo into the conversation somehow."

"Whatever you do, don't mention Odette Malveaux. I don't believe for a minute that Stewart Preston is the Hollywood movie-style voodoo worshipper that Concetta made him out to be."

"Maybe not." I pointed at her. "But he did wear a skull bead bracelet to court. That has to mean something."

"It just makes me think that he's one of the countless people in New Orleans who are superstitious enough to turn to voodoo trinkets in moments of crisis."

I threw up my hands. "I guess that makes sense. It's just so unsettling to find out about the bracelet and then the whole missing photo thing right before I meet the guy."

Veronica furrowed her brow. "Yeah, the fact that the photo disappeared from *The Times-Picayune* archives looks bad for Stewart, doesn't it?"

I put my hand on my neck. "I've had heartburn ever since I found that out."

Her face softened. "I know you're scared. To be honest, I'm worried too."

"Well *that* doesn't make me feel any better."

"Remember what you told me—you'll be meeting Stewart in a public place during the daytime. And don't forget that I'll be there to back you up."

I wrung my hands. "Ah, yes, with the pink breast cancer special."

Veronica blinked, as though offended by my jab at her girly gun. "It's a nine-millimeter handgun, Franki. Its color won't affect its performance, I assure you."

"You're right. I'm just on edge." I collapsed into the armchair. Ten minutes of pacing was an intense workout.

"Can I get you something? A nice hot cup of tea might help."

I looked at the angry island god perched on the back of my chair. "I think it would take a couple of shots of tequila."

She frowned. "This is definitely not the time for a drink."

"I know, I know." I sighed. "Let's just go back over the plan."

"Okay." Veronica leaned forward. "We're going to rent a car for you so that Stewart can't trace the license plates. Then I'll follow you from the rental lot to the Carousel Bar in my car. We'll both park at the Hotel Monteleone."

"Do they have a parking lot?"

"Yeah, it's beneath the hotel. You pull into the garage, and a valet takes your car and parks it underground for you."

"All right. After we park, I'll go to the bar and—"

She shook her head. "It rotates like an actual carousel. You know how dizzy you get on merry-go-rounds."

"True." It was a well-known fact that I'd never gotten my carousel legs. Within seconds of stepping foot on one, I was on my knees, puking.

"Besides, there's no way you'd be able to have a private conversation with Stewart at that bar. It's always crowded, and the seats are too close together. You'll have to meet him at one of the seating areas in the lounge. It's down a small flight of stairs, which is great because that way I can sit up at the bar and have a clear view of the two of you."

"So, if he's at the bar when I get there, I'll ask him to move downstairs."

"Right, and then if you leave before he does, I'll stay and keep an eye on Stewart. I'll text you when I leave. Will that work?"

I nodded.

"Okay then. Go get ready." Veronica adjusted the bow on Hercules's head. "We leave in thirty minutes."

I PULLED my rented Chrysler convertible around the back of the Hotel Monteleone and encountered a line of cars waiting to get into the parking garage. I looked in my rearview mirror and was relieved to see Veronica waiting three cars back.

So far, so good.

As I waited to park, I leaned my head on the headrest and looked at the sky. Usually, when I put the convertible top down and let the wind blow my hair and the sun shine on my face, it was a stress reliever. But not at that moment. All I could think about was meeting a murderer. Well, someone I was fairly sure was a murderer, anyhow. And unlike my cop days, I had no uniform, no badge and, worst of all, no gun since I'd turned in my service pistol. But the Evans case had made it clear that I needed to get one—nothing pink or disease-related like Veronica, just a plain purple Ruger.

The car in front of me pulled ahead, and I inched the Chrysler forward. A flash of bright red caught my eye. It was a guy dressed like a giant crawdad—complete with red tights, torso and tail, and a headpiece with eyes and antennae—leaning against the wall smoking. He'd had to remove one of his pinchers to hold the cigarette. While I was taking in his costume, our eyes met. He narrowed his gaze as he took a drag and nodded appreciatively in my direction. I looked away. After my last experience with a crawdad, I didn't want any more trouble.

Finally, I pulled up to the valet. I was so nervous that I practically jumped from my car and jogged the few steps from the garage entrance to the hotel. As I crossed the busy lobby, I had the unshakable sensation that I was walking toward my doom. Nevertheless, I forged ahead. I was so close to solving Jessica's murder that there was no way I could turn back. I took a deep breath and entered the Carousel Bar and Lounge.

With Mardi Gras season in full swing, the place was packed and buzzing with an electric energy. I scoured the patrons for Stewart Preston and tried not to look at the brightly lit merry-go-round-style bar as it rotated beside me. I was already nauseated from fear. I didn't want to add motion sickness to my existing stomach woes.

When I didn't see him, I scanned the customers in the adjoining lounge. I spotted Stewart immediately. He sat on a couch in the middle of the room with a drink in his hand. I looked at him from the top of the steps, and he stared at me and then lowered his gaze to my breasts.

My fear turned to anger.

I balled my fists and marched down the stairs. As I approached him, I was struck by how bloated his face was. *Could that be from drug use?* I thought of Odette Malveaux's mysterious warning to "Watch out fo' dem who take magic." And I took a deep breath. "Stewart Preston?"

He took a sip of his drink and, with bloodshot eyes, gave me a slow, insolent once-over.

"I'll take that as a yes." I sat on the couch opposite him, my back to the bar.

"So, what is it that you're calling yourself?" He raised his cleft chin. "Tina, was it?"

He hadn't bought my cover. "Gina. Gina Mazzucco."

Stewart narrowed his eyes. "Why don't you drop this little charade and tell me who you really are?"

I swallowed hard. "I don't know what you're talking about."

"Lady, you and I both know that Angelica Evangelista didn't have any girlfriends. And if she did, they sure as hell wouldn't be investigating her murder."

The jig was up. I had to stop playing games. Otherwise, he might walk. I calculated my risk and went for broke. "That's not true. Immacolata Di Salvo was her friend."

Stewart showed no sign of emotion at the mention of Immacolata's name. "What would make you think I care about Immacolata Di Salvo?"

"I know you were charged with her murder."

A muscle worked in his jaw. "And I was acquitted."

"I know that too."

For some reason, he relaxed. Then he grabbed a handful of mixed nuts, leaned back against the couch, and propped his foot on the coffee table between us. "So, you're a private investigator."

I didn't respond.

"I'll take that as a yes." He sneered and popped a few nuts into his mouth.

I seized the moment to look at his jewelry. He wasn't wearing a voodoo bracelet, just a top-of-the-line gold Rolex.

He took another sip of his drink. "So what is it you want to know?"

"I want to know if you killed Angelica Evangelista."

Again, no reaction from Stewart. He turned and flagged a passing waitress. As she approached us, I glanced over my shoulder at the bar. Veronica was there with a strawberry daiquiri looking right at me.

"I'll take another Maker's Mark, darlin'. Get this lady here whatever she wants."

I turned and looked at the waitress. "Nothing for me, thanks."

She nodded and headed to the bar.

I looked Stewart in the eyes. "You haven't answered my question."

He drained the whiskey from his glass and placed it on the coffee table. "Oh yeah. I did not kill Angelica."

"Then why was your father's company putting ten thousand dollars a month into Angelica's account, under the assumed name of Jessica Evans?"

"She was working for my dad as a textile consultant."

I snorted. "I don't believe you."

He yawned. "That's not my problem."

Time to shift tactics. "Where were you the night Jessica was killed?"

"What business is it of yours?"

He was playing games with me. It was time to get real. "You can drop the act, Preston. I know you strangled Immacolata in her dorm room. Angelica knew it too, so your father paid her to keep her mouth shut and sent her packing to Milan. But she defied your daddy's orders and returned to New Orleans, so you went to LaMarca and told her to leave town. When she didn't comply, you went back to LaMarca and killed her the same way you killed Immacolata. You strangled her with a scarf."

Stewart leaned forward. "You be careful who you tell that story to, understand? Because I'll sue you for slander, and I'll win." He sat back and crossed his leg over his knee. "Do you really think I, or anyone in my family, was worried about a lousy hundred and twenty grand a year? With all the money we're worth?"

"Maybe it wasn't about the money." I was pretty sure I'd

struck a chord. "I'll bet Angelica had information that proved you killed Immacolata, and you needed to shut her up once and for all before she went to the police."

"What reason would I have had? I can't be tried for the same crime twice." He grinned. "That's what they call double jeopardy, darlin', and it's illegal."

"No, but the Di Salvos could've brought a civil suit against you, which would've put a nice dent in the family fortune."

"Nah. The only gold digger in that family was Immacolata. And she's dead, isn't she?"

A chill ran down my spine, and my courage wavered.

The waitress returned with his drink, giving me a moment to regain my composure.

Stewart took a sip from his glass. "What's the matter? Didn't you know about Immacolata's fortune-hunting ways?"

I stared at him coldly.

"I'm surprised, you being a private investigator and all."

"I don't see what her wanting to marry into money has to do with her murder."

"Oh, but it has everything to do with it. For the record, Angelica was sexy and savvy. She didn't need to blackmail anyone for money." He swirled the brown liquid in his glass. "But poor little Immacolata didn't have Angelica's business sense. The only thing she knew was men and money. And she was willing to do anything to catch her a rich husband. When she died, she was sleeping with half the men on campus. But I was the one she'd told her parents about. So when she turned up dead, I was the obvious target."

I pursed my lips. "You're saying that you had nothing to do with Immacolata's death?"

"That's right, and a jury of twelve of my peers agreed with me." He took a long drink and wiped his mouth with the back of his sleeve. "I rue the day I met her and that crazy twin of hers."

I blinked. Concetta had told Veronica and me that she didn't know Stewart. "You know Concetta?"

He burst out laughing. "Indeed I do. In the biblical sense."

My jaw practically hit the floor. "You had *sex* with her?"

"Before I knew Immacolata was better in bed."

I ignored his crude comment. "How did you meet her?"

"We met at a happy hour at the Columns Hotel. Then I met Immacolata by chance at Mardi Gras a couple of months later, and Concetta flipped out. She was jealous of her sister, big time. After I started sleeping with Immacolata, Concetta kept showing up in the middle of the night at my apartment, acting all psycho. I still can't shake her."

I was stunned. "What do you mean you can't shake her?"

"I mean that the freak stalks me to this day. She even broke into my apartment once, right after I was acquitted."

I scrutinized his face for signs that he might be lying, but it was impossible to tell. "How do you know it was her?"

"I had a security camera installed. It was definitely Concetta on that tape."

The more Stewart spoke, the more I felt that he might be telling the truth. "What did she take?"

He laughed. "That's the funny part. I have a wooden chest on my dresser that I keep my cufflinks and watches in. I guess she was trying to save me from the devil or some religious BS like that, because she took a fifteen-dollar bracelet I bought at a voodoo shop and left all of my Rolexes."

My blood ran cold. "A v-voodoo bracelet?"

He waved his hand. "Yeah, you know, one of those kitschy bead things they're always selling to tourists."

"With little skulls." I said it more to myself than to him. *But a nun couldn't have planted a skull bead at the scene of a crime just to implicate someone who'd spurned her, right?*

"Yup." He grabbed another handful of nuts. "What a friggin' whacko."

The lounge seemed to close in on me. I had to take my leave and tell Veronica. If Concetta was stalking Stewart, then she could be in the area. And that meant we could all be in danger. I shot to my feet.

Stewart cocked an eyebrow. "You leaving already?"

"Yeah, I have all the information I need."

"And this was starting to get fun." He downed his whiskey.

I turned and walked up the steps to the bar, avoiding eye contact with Veronica. I stepped into the hotel lobby and pulled my phone from my bag. As I headed for the parking garage, I sent a text to Veronica telling her that Concetta could be in the vicinity and might be dangerous.

And then Mambo Odette's warning came to me, and it finally made sense—Concetta had taken magic when she'd stolen Stewart's voodoo bracelet.

24

___

"Where are you, Veronica?" I talked to myself as I pulled into the empty Lenton's parking lot to feel less alone—and less scared.

I parked near the employee entrance and left the engine running. I looked in my rearview mirror for about the thirtieth time since I'd left the Carousel to make sure that neither Stewart nor a crazed Concetta had followed me. I grabbed my phone and called Veronica.

She answered on the first ring. "Hey. I'm almost there."

I could hear traffic in the background. "Why did you text me to meet you here? This place is deserted, and creepy."

"Ed Orlansky's secretary called me right before I left the Carousel and said that the DVD had arrived from Baton Rouge. He's waiting for us inside."

I breathed a sigh of relief. Given the circumstances, I felt like I had a giant target on my back. "So what happened when you left the bar?" I glanced out the window. "Was Stewart still there?"

"Yeah, he was putting the moves on that waitress."

"Oh, no. I wonder if she knew he was an alleged murderer."

"I made sure she did before I left."

"Good." We women had to look out for one another. "So what do you think about this business with Concetta?"

Veronica was silent. "It's a pretty far-fetched story."

"I think so too. But I'm still freaked out that Stewart brought the bracelet up like that, without me even asking him about it." I glanced at the chipped violet fingernail polish on my left hand.

"That could have been a calculated move on his part. I mean, if he knew you were a PI, he may have also known that you'd found the skull bead at the crime scene. After all, you did tell Ryan Hunter about the bead—"

"And he told his attorney who probably told the police." My heart sunk, and I sunk further into my seat.

"Right. And you know darned well that Stewart is keeping a close eye on the police investigation into Jessica's murder."

"Oh yeah, I'm sure of that."

"Anyway, I'm pulling into the parking lot right now. See you in a sec."

I hung up and scanned the area for lurkers. I no longer knew what to think about Stewart, Concetta, or anyone else connected to the case, so I had to stay on my guard.

Ed Orlansky leaned forward to adjust the brightness of an old PC monitor in an armoire in his office. The combined scent of his Old Spice aftershave and the pomade he'd used to slick back his hair overwhelmed the tiny space.

He leered at Veronica—make that her breasts. "Is that better?"

"Yeah." She frowned.

Since we had the DVD of the last two scarf purchases in the bag, Veronica had dispensed with the bat-and-twirl. I scrutinized the grainy image of the teenaged girl standing in front of the sales counter. "I think we can move on to the next one."

Ed used the mouse to click and drag the video progress bar to the start of the next purchase.

The video played for thirty seconds before a young man with a Lenton's nametag approached the cash register. He held the Limoncello scarf in one hand as he scanned the price tag in the other.

I held my breath as a woman with waist-length brown hair and long bangs stepped to the register holding a billfold. She avoided eye contact with the employee. "This may be our suspect."

Veronica nodded. "It's hard to tell with the quilted down coat she's wearing, but her body type could be similar to Domenica's."

"Or Concetta's. It would help if we could tell how tall she is."

The employee asked the woman a question, and she shook her head, keeping her gaze lowered.

Veronica looked at Ed. "Too bad there's no sound on this video."

"We'll have sound soon now that corporate has finally approved our new digital system. It's got all the bells and whistles." He beamed, trying to impress her with the equipment upgrade.

I turned to Veronica. "Can you make out her face?"

"Not really. I wish she would look up."

"Then we could at least see the shape of her face and mouth. With those bangs, I can't see her eyes at all."

The woman opened her wallet and handed cash to the employee, who placed it in the register drawer. As he handed her a few bills and some coins, she raised her face.

I sat forward and turned to Ed. "Could you rewind that?"

"Sure." He spoke to Veronica instead of me. He rewound the video and paused on the woman's uplifted face.

I touched the screen. "Look at her lips. Doesn't that look like it could be either Domenica or Concetta's mouth?"

Veronica cocked her head. "I don't know. Maybe."

I slouched in my seat. "Okay, Ed, you can hit play."

"You got it." He again replied to Veronica as he clicked the button.

While the employee placed the scarf into a bag, the woman put the bills into her wallet but dropped the change. She bent to retrieve the coins and shook her hair from her eyes as she stood.

"Freeze it right there," I shouted.

Ed had been so busy gazing at Veronica's chest that he started in his seat. "What? What happened?"

Veronica rolled her eyes. "There's something we need to see. You know, on the video?"

"Oh. I knew that."

"Here, let me do it." I batted away Ed's outstretched arm. I grabbed the mouse and rewound the tape to the shot of the woman's face. I clicked pause and immediately recognized the close-set eyes.

Veronica gasped. "That's Concetta."

"Let's see what happens next." I clicked play again.

The woman put the coins into her wallet, took the bag from the employee, and walked away.

Veronica turned to me. "I think it's time we take the video and the skull bead to the police."

"Hey." Ed's eyes opened wide. "What about our dinner tonight?"

Veronica glared at him, and I stood, crossed my arms, and followed suit.

Ed's eyes darted from Veronica to me, and he licked his chapped lips. "I'll take a rain check?"

I INSERTED the key into my front door lock.

Veronica sighed. "Next time, promise me you'll keep any evidence you find at the office."

"I said I was sorry." I pushed the door open. "It's just that so many people pass through there. I thought the bead would be safer here."

Veronica followed me into the dark apartment. "Napoleon doesn't come to greet you?"

"Not unless he has to tinkle." I laughed. "Nine o'clock is past his bedtime." I flipped the light switch by the front door, but the light didn't come on. "Shoot. The light bulb's burned out. Will you turn on the kitchen light?"

"Sure." She headed toward the kitchen, and I bolted the door behind us.

The light came on, and Veronica let out a bloodcurdling scream.

I ran to the kitchen doorway and stopped short.

Concetta stood in the middle of the room wearing a full habit and surgical gloves, and she held a butcher knife to Veronica's throat.

I put my hands to my mouth.

"Nice décor, Franki." She smirked. "What are you, a PI by day and a prostitute by night?"

"Let her go."

"I don't think you're in any position to call the shots." Her voice was eerily calm. "Now, why don't you come over here and sit at the kitchen table?"

I nodded and did as I was told. I knew from my police training that I needed to establish a rapport with a hostage-taker so that he or she wouldn't see me as a threat. But there was one glaring problem with that tactic. Veronica and I *were* threats to

Concetta because we were the only ones standing in the way of her freedom. I took a seat and hoped that Veronica was still armed.

Then I saw the rope on the table.

Concetta walked Veronica behind me. "Okay, take a piece of rope and start tying the big one up."

The big one? It wasn't enough that she was going to kill me, she had to insult me too?

"And don't try any tricks, either. If you don't tie those knots nice and tight, you're a goner."

Veronica tied my hands behind my back, and I glared at Concetta over my shoulder. "What did you do with my dog?"

She looked at me like I was an idiot. "I let him out. I'm allergic."

I prayed she was telling the truth. If she'd hurt Napoleon, I wouldn't be able to live with myself. That is, *if* I lived.

Veronica tightened the rope around my wrists. "Why don't you let us go, Concetta? You're in enough trouble, as it is."

She let out a hysterical laugh. "I'm not in any trouble. You'd think that would be pretty clear by now to you two crackerjack PIs."

I had to keep her talking in hopes that she would get distracted and slip up somehow. "We know you killed Angelica, and the police know it too. Veronica brought them the video file that shows you bought the murder weapon."

"You're bluffing. If she'd stopped to drop off the video, she wouldn't be here with you now, would she?"

She had me there.

Concetta pushed Veronica to the floor and threw a rope at her head. "Tie her feet."

Veronica threaded the rope around my ankles, and I glared at Concetta again. "We have proof that you did it."

She smiled to herself. "*You* do. But the police don't."

My stomach felt like it had been ripped from my body. That last comment didn't bode well.

"You're right, though." Concetta's tone was strangely chatty. "I did kill Angie."

Veronica tightened the rope.

"Get up," Concetta said through clenched teeth. She pulled Veronica by the hair, causing her to cry out.

I bit my lip to keep from screaming at her.

Concetta put the knife to Veronica's neck with her right hand as she checked the knots with her left. She stood and shoved her into the table. "Take a seat."

Veronica stumbled and fell into a chair, and we exchanged a frightened look across the table. If Concetta tied up Veronica, we were goners.

After selecting a length of rope, Concetta held the knife as she tied Veronica's wrists behind her back.

I worked my hands and wrists, trying to loosen the rope. Under threat of death from Concetta, Veronica had tied the knots tightly, so I could move each wrist only a fraction of an inch. To make matters worse, the rope cut into my flesh.

Concetta finished tying Veronica's hands and took a step back. "I had to do it. Angie knew Stewart had strangled Imma, but she wouldn't testify against him. She let those horrible people buy her silence so she could get herself a degree, designer clothes, and a career in the fashion industry, all courtesy of the Preston family. But that wasn't the only reason I killed her."

Veronica looked over her shoulder. "What other reason would you have?"

Concetta grabbed another piece of rope from the table and knelt to tie Veronica's feet. "You're both Italian, so you should know about the concept of vendetta. It's a question of honor."

As soon as she said vendetta, I thought of the word *vendicata* that Domenica had spray-painted on Immacolata's tombstone. "Did Domenica know you killed Angelica?"

"Of course not." She tugged at a knot. "In case you haven't noticed, my little sister's not the brightest bulb on the Christmas tree."

"Then why did she spray paint that Immacolata had been avenged on her tombstone?"

Concetta stood. "She was celebrating the fact that Angie was strangled with a scarf the same way that Stewart strangled Imma."

I continued working my wrists, but I didn't seem to be making any headway. I hoped that Veronica was making more progress. "Angelica hated cheap scarves and the color yellow. Is that why you chose the yellow-bordered polyester scarf?"

Concetta smirked. "I wanted her to see yellow and feel cheap fabric on her skin as she was dying. I had to make sure that the last thought she ever had in her wretched life was that she was nothing but a two-bit coward, like her dad."

Veronica looked up. "What do you mean?"

Concetta's eyes opened wide. "Isn't it obvious? Angie ran out on her best friend for money. Instead of paying her own way through school and trying to work her way up from the bottom, she did it all the easy way. She kept her mouth shut at the trial so she could get her education and her career bought and paid for."

I met her gaze. "And to get even with Stewart, you planted the bead from his bracelet at the scene of the crime."

Her eyes twinkled. "Yeah, and by the way, he was telling you the truth tonight when he said I'd stolen that bracelet from his apartment."

Veronica gasped. "You were at the Carousel Bar? But we would've seen you in your habit."

I stared at Concetta, openmouthed. So Stewart had been telling the truth about the stalking too.

She gave Veronica a mock sad look, as though she were nothing but a pathetic fool. "I've been following the two of you since you took the case, genius. And I definitely know how to dress for the occasion. I was sitting on the couch behind Stewart, with my back to him, and not a one of you was astute enough to see me."

So she *had* been following me the day I saw her at CC's Community Coffee, and who knew where else. "But I don't understand why you'd frame Stewart. Why didn't you kill him like you killed Angelica?"

She rolled her eyes. "Because Stewart is different than Angie. For him, there's a fate worse than death—rotting day after day, year after year in prison, cut off from his money and privilege and, most importantly, from women and partying. And since those imbeciles on the jury acquitted him of Imma's murder, I had to make sure there was another murder he'd be found guilty of."

Veronica shook her head. "How could you, an ordained nun, take another human life?"

Concetta curled her lips at Veronica. "You have no idea what it's like to lose a twin. After Imma was gone I felt lost without her, empty. At first I thought the Lord would fill me up. But one day I realized that I couldn't serve a god who'd allowed my sister to be murdered by a lowlife like Stewart Preston."

Any shred of hope I'd had that she might spare Veronica and me was lost with that statement.

"Plus, if you'd known Angie, you probably would've killed her too. She was something else, that one. Take the night I strangled her. When I showed up at LaMarca with that scarf, I presented it to her as a gift. Being the bitch that she was, she ripped open the package, took one look at the scarf, and said it was ugly and tacky, just like me."

Concetta stared at the floor and chuckled. "If you could have seen the horrified look on her face when she realized that I'd come there to strangle her with that scarf." The chuckle turned cackle, and tears streamed from her eyes. "Priceless."

I couldn't bear to listen to her laugh about the last moments of Jessica's life, particularly while Veronica and I faced the last moments of our own. "So what are you going to do to us?"

"Well, the first thing I'm going to do is search your cars for the video you got at Lenton's." She looked at me. "Yes, Franki, I followed you there too. Then I'll dispose of the disc and the skull bead, which I found in your nightstand. And tsk tsk." She waved the knife. "Such an obvious hiding place.

I shot her a go-to-hell look.

"After that, I'm going to go call the police and say that when I was driving through the area, I saw a masked intruder leaving your apartment. In theory, he would've exited through your bedroom window, Franki. The same one I broke to get in to your little bordello here."

Veronica glared at her. "What excuse are you going to give them for being in the neighborhood?"

"I'll tell them I was coming to talk to the two of you since you were investigating the murder of my twin and her best friend." She gave a wicked grin. "And I can tell you this. The New Orleans PD doesn't usually question the motives of a nun. And if they did, thanks to my gloves here and this handy coif on my head, they certainly won't find my fingerprints or DNA in this whorehouse."

Her gloating made me so angry and so frustrated that I alternated between wanting to cry and wanting to scream bloody murder. And it was more apparent by the second that I was powerless to stop her. My hands were numb, and I was no closer to freeing them. And judging from the sick look on Veronica's face, she wasn't faring any better. The situation looked grim, so I had to buy more time. "You still haven't said what you're going to do with us."

"Oh, that's because I like drama." She giggled.

I held my breath.

Concetta put her finger to her cheek. "One night I asked myself, 'What would be a fitting end for two busybody PIs who kept sticking their necks out to help that awful Ryan Hunter and that scumbag Stewart Preston?' Of course, whatever it was had to be symbolic." She gave a dry laugh. "I mean, once a Catholic, always a Catholic, right?"

Veronica snorted.

The smile faded from Concetta's face, and she studied Veronica. "The answer actually came to me in prayer." She placed the butcher knife on the counter, reached into the pocket of her habit and pulled out a dark red scarf. "Strangulation."

25

Concetta wound the red scarf around each of her gloved hands and walked toward Veronica. A devilish smile spread across her face. "You first, Miss Private Chicks, Incorporated."

"Wait," I shouted, desperate to stall. "Don't you want to tell us what the red scarf means? Otherwise, the symbolism will be lost on us."

Her eyes rolled to the heavens. "Well, if you read the bible, Franki, you'd know what it meant. But judging from this den of iniquity, it's pretty clear that you don't spend your leisure time perusing the word of the Lord."

"I just haven't unpacked my bible yet." I made a quick promise to God that I'd redecorate if he let me live.

"Red is the color of Christ's blood." Concetta's tone was patronizing. "It symbolizes atonement for one's sins, so as you can see—"

"How have *we* sinned?" Veronica's eyes blazed with anger.

"Oh, don't act so innocent. You've been aiding a murderer. Last time I checked, honey, that qualified as a sin."

From the corner of my eye, I saw movement in the kitchen

doorway. To my astonishment, there stood Glenda. Although her thin, lined face was red with rage, and she was wearing an S&M outfit replete with a silver boa, she looked nothing short of a saving angel.

I turned and saw to my horror that Concetta had wrapped the scarf around Veronica's neck, and my best friend thrashed in her chair.

With the stealth of a ninja, Glenda snuck up behind Concetta and clubbed her with the tallest stripper shoe I'd ever seen.

A dull thud echoed, and Concetta collapsed to the floor in a pool of black fabric like the Wicked Witch of the West.

"Glenda?" Veronica croaked wide-eyed, no doubt from the lack of oxygen. "Is it really you?"

Despite the fact that she'd just knocked out a homicidal maniac with the shoe in her hand, Glenda nevertheless held her signature cigarette holder in the other. "In the flesh, sugar."

Judging from her S&M outfit, I assumed she'd meant that literally.

Glenda slipped the shoe back on her foot and turned to me. "I called the cops right before I let myself in. You girls all right?"

"I think so. Thank God you're here."

"You can say that again, Miss Franki. Now give me a minute while I take care of some unpleasant landlady business."

I watched in a mixture of awe and amazement as Glenda made quick work of Concetta. She put her cigarette holder in her mouth and removed her black leather garter belt, which was attached to partial black leather pant legs. First she detached the pant legs, and then she used the belt to tie Concetta's hands behind her back. Next, she used the garter straps to bind her feet to her hands. When she was done, Concetta looked like she was doing the yoga bow pose.

Glenda stood up, adjusted her short, zippered black leather

vest, and took a long drag from her cigarette. Then she put her cigarette holder on the counter and picked up the butcher knife. She walked over to Veronica and began cutting the ropes binding her hands.

I was still in shock. "How did you know we were in trouble?"

"Well, I was entertaining Guido, and he happened to glance out the window and see a nun pass by. Naturally, I got suspicious."

"Makes sense to me." With a Visitor Policy that allowed women to have two men stay the night, the fourplex was no convent.

"I would've come to check on you two sooner, but Guido was all in a panic. He started crossing himself and saying Hail Marys and Our Fathers like he was possessed."

I stared at her, speechless.

Veronica rubbed her wrists as Glenda freed her feet.

When Glenda was done, she walked over to the counter and took another drag off her cigarette. "And then Guido started going on about how what we were doing was a sin." She exhaled a frustrated puff of smoke. "So, I had to kick him out." She walked over to cut my binding and gave Veronica and me a knowing look. "I don't think I need to tell either of you ladies that a man who doesn't sin isn't sexy."

Veronica shook her head. "Of course not."

"Around that time I heard a scream, and that's when I knew the nosy nun was up to no good. So I came downstairs and found Napoleon outside—"

"Is he all right?" I interrupted.

"He's fine, sugar." She freed my hands. "He's in the pleasure palace."

I had no idea what she meant, but I hoped she was talking about her apartment.

As she knelt and cut the rope from my ankles, I looked at

Concetta and saw that her head moved from side to side. "She's coming to."

Concetta raised her head and swore. "What the—?" She rocked back and forth on her belly trying to break free. "Who did this to me?"

Glenda sighed and put down the knife. Her eyes narrowed to slits and, in a move that undoubtedly came from one of her stripteases, she crawled to Concetta and leaned low so she could look her in the eyes. "I did. Now, until the cops come and haul your unholy heinie away, you keep your trap shut, sister, or I'll be forced to club you again. And while you're lying there all nice and quiet, you'd best pray you didn't scratch my Ginsu knife."

She sat up, removed her boa, and stuffed one end into Concetta's mouth.

Concetta's eye twitched, and she went limp.

Because Glenda prided herself on her stripper clothes, I decided to pay her a costume compliment. "You and your S&M outfit saved our lives."

"Miss Franki, this is my biker stripper costume. I don't dress S&M. That's not ladylike."

I heard the wail of police sirens in the distance.

Glenda rose. "Well it's about damn time the cops got here. I've got a reputation to protect, and I sure as hell don't want people to think I'm running a home for wayward nuns."

I TOOK a sip of my double soy latte and leaned back in my desk chair, relishing the early morning silence of the empty office. I hadn't slept a wink after the events of the previous night. All I could think about was my family and how they were going to react to the news that I'd solved my first murder case. I half expected my parents to insist that I come home and fulfill my pre-ordained destiny to work in the deli. Of course, my nonna was going to tell me that I needed to use my newly honed investigative skills to get serious about finding a husband. I wondered what she would say if she knew that I'd actually found a husband—one who belonged to someone else.

The lobby bell sounded.

I stood and peered out my doorway.

Veronica walked up the hallway.

"Good morning." My words sounded strange after everything that had happened.

"How do you feel today?" Veronica asked as I followed her into her office.

I took a seat in front of her desk and noticed that she looked as tired as I did. "Other than rope burn on my wrists, I'm fine. How about you?"

"Same. It kind of seems like it was all just a crazy, bad dream."

"I wish it were."

She toyed with a pen on her desk. "You know, I wouldn't blame you if you wanted to resign after almost getting killed."

I looked her straight in the eyes. "I'm not going anywhere. I knew that being a PI could be every bit as dangerous as being a cop. Besides, I've learned more after two weeks of working for you than I did the whole time I was on the force, and I've figured out something really important about myself too."

"Oh?"

I shifted in my seat. "This may sound kind of weird, but it has to do with what Concetta said when the police were taking her away."

"You mean, when she kept screaming, 'What did I do to deserve losing my twin?'"

"Exactly. Last night I was thinking about how she was looking at Immacolata's death from the wrong perspective. She thought she'd done something to bring about Immacolata's death, when it's so obvious that it had nothing to do with her. I mean, she's not responsible for Stewart Preston's actions."

Veronica raised her brow. "And so?"

"It just got me thinking about myself and how I've been taking it for granted that the way men have treated me was my fault."

She stared at me, expressionless. "I'm not following."

I straightened. "The cheating. I've been driving myself crazy trying to figure out what it is about me that leads my boyfriends to cheat. But, like Concetta, I had it all wrong. It's not about me. It's about them and their own weaknesses. And you know something else?"

"What?"

"I'm done taking responsibility for other people's bad decisions."

Veronica leaned back, crossed her arms, and smiled. "I'm so lucky to have you working for me."

"Why do you say that?"

"Because you're one smart cookie. And you're resilient too."

I laughed off the compliment, but inside I was glowing. "Just the same, after last night I'm hoping we get nothing but a steady stream of insurance fraud and cheating spouse cases. That reminds me, did we ever hear back from Twyla Upton?"

"Not a word. But I did talk to Ryan Hunter. He was very grateful, and he apologized when he heard we were almost killed."

"That's nice of him and everything, but I'm glad to be done with that guy and with the whole Evans case."

"I know. I just feel so bad for the Di Salvo family, especially Maria."

I wrinkled my lips and looked at the floor. "Me too. Can you even imagine what she's going through? First Imma, then her husband, and now Concetta, the one who was supposed to be so good."

"It's just awful."

"And all she has left now is Domenica. You can bet that one is going to give her more trouble."

Veronica sighed. "I really hope not."

The front office door slammed.

I grinned. "David's here."

He rushed into the room. "Are you guys—uh, ladies—okay?"

I smiled. "I guess you heard what happened?"

"Did I? Private Chicks is all over the morning news."

Veronica's face lit up. "Franki, turn on the TV."

I stood and switched on a small television set on top of a file cabinet. The first image I saw was Glenda sidling up way too close to a local news reporter.

Veronica gasped. "What in the world is she doing?"

David rubbed his nose. "A lot of interviews. I can't believe you didn't know. Everyone's talking about how a gutsy stripper saved two PIs from an evil nun."

She groaned and put her face in her hands. "Turn the sound down. I don't want to hear it."

I did as she asked. "Come on, Veronica, it's not as bad as all that. You know the old saying, 'There's no such thing as bad publicity.' Plus," I glanced at the TV, "at least Glenda's dressed somewhat chastely for her interviews." And she was because the TV station had blurred out her royal blue velvet Prince pants, the ones with holes that fully exposed the butt cheeks. There was also the little matter of a three-inch rhinestone choker around her neck that spelled VIXEN.

"Uh..." David nudged me. "Is that your phone?"

"Oh, yeah, thanks." I'd been so absorbed in the details of Glenda's outfit that I hadn't heard it ringing. I walked into the hallway to take the call.

"Hello?"

"Francesca?" My mother's voice was crazy shrill, even for her. "This is your mother, dear."

"Yeah, hi, Mom." The familiar tension rose in my chest.

"Your nonna called your father and me at the deli and said that you and a stripper had a nun arrested. I know you haven't been comfortable with your Catholicism, but this is taking things too far, don't you think?"

I sighed. "Mom, that nun almost strangled Veronica and me. She was the one who murdered Jessica Evans."

"What?" Her shrill had turned shriek. "Almost getting killed by a nun is big news, Francesca. Why didn't you call us?"

"I wasn't exactly in the mood to chat after it happened. And I had no idea it would be on the news, especially in Texas. I was going to call you guys tonight to tell you about it. But how come nonna called you and not me?"

"She wanted to let us know that she was going straight to Saint Mary's."

"Why did she go to church?"

"To pray for your salvation, dear. She says it's a very serious sin to have a nun sent to jail."

Naturally. Wait until she hears that I've broken up with Guido. "Listen, I'm at work, so I'll call you tonight, okay?"

"Wait a second. Your father has something he wants to say to you."

A knot the size of the ones in Concetta's rope formed in my stomach.

"Franki," he sounded surprised, "Mr. Giangiulio told me you solved that murder case."

"I had some help from Veronica and David."

"Well, I'm glad that you're okay."

I held my breath and waited for the *but*.

"And I wanted you to know that I'm proud of you," he said in a soft, almost embarrassed tone. "Real proud."

My eyes opened wide, and a rush of warmth filled my chest. "Thanks, Dad," I breathed. "That means a lot."

"Now you be careful out there." He'd switched to his usual gruff tone. "And come home for a visit soon."

I smiled. "I will, Dad. I promise."

I closed the call and returned to Veronica's office.

She looked up from her notepad. "Is everything okay?"

"My Dad just told me he's proud of me."

"Do you think he's starting to see the light?"

I flashed a sardonic smile. "I wouldn't go *that* far. But it's a start."

The office phone rang.

"Private Chicks, Incorporated," Veronica answered in her professional voice. "If you give us the time, we'll solve your crime. What can I help you with?"

I watched as she scribbled some notes on a scrap of paper.

"We can definitely handle that. How did you hear about us? On TV this morning." She glanced at me. "How about today at two o'clock? Perfect." She hung up.

"I hate to say I told you so..."

She smirked. "No you don't."

The office phone rang again at the same time the bell in the lobby sounded. Veronica and I exchanged a look.

"It looks like Private Chicks, Inc. is on the map." I rose and went into the lobby.

Twyla Upton, staying faithful to the citrus family, stood by the door in a lime-green sack dress. "Oh, Franki." She clasped her hands in front of her face. "The case is solved."

"Wait, you're not talking about the Evans case, are you?"

She gasped and put lime green-lacquered fingers to her

orange-painted mouth. "Did poor Mrs. Evans think her husband was cheating too?"

I smiled. "No, Twyla. I was just confused."

"Oh good." She was visibly relieved. "I just came to tell you that my Harry wasn't betraying my honor with that delightful woman in your pictures."

I would have bet all the toupees in Hollywood that Harry had been unfaithful. "Really?"

"Ye-es," she said in two distinct syllables. "That woman is one of the best interior designers in all of Louisiana, and she's been helping Harry with the plans to redecorate a *charming* little mansion he's bought me for our upcoming anniversary."

"Well, that's terrific news."

"So, I came to invite you all to Brennan's for a celebratory brunch. The head chef has agreed to open the restaurant early today just for us."

I imagined a meal of bananas foster and more bananas foster. "We would love to, Twyla. Let me go and get Veronica off the phone."

"You take your time. I'll meet you all there when you're ready. Toodles." She waved and slipped out the door.

I entered Veronica's office.

She hung up the phone. "That was another client. We have three new cases."

I leaned against the doorjamb. "All thanks to TV?"

"Yes, every one of them mentioned Glenda."

"Then maybe you should hire her," I joked. "Apparently, she's a natural-born marketer, and she's got some mean self-defense skills. While you're at it, you might want to put Mambo Odette on the payroll. I mean, she had the answers to the Evans case all along."

Veronica smirked. "I wouldn't go that far. Who was in the lobby?"

"Twyla. She's taking us all to brunch."

"What? I can't leave now. I might miss a call from a new client."

"Whoever calls will leave a message. I mean, who would hire a regular PI when they could hire two PIs who were saved from a nun by a stripper?"

Veronica shot me a look. "What's the occasion for the brunch?"

"Turns out we were wrong about Harry. He wasn't cheating with the brunette, after all."

"Well, that's good news."

"It is. And Twyla's waiting for us, so we've got to get going."

Her brows furrowed.

"Don't worry, we're going to have plenty of business after this case."

Veronica looked at me, a smile spreading across her face. "We are, aren't we?"

"Um, *yeah*. So let's take the time to celebrate the end of our first big case before we dive into all these new ones."

"Great idea." She smiled and rose to her feet.

Veronica and I entered the lobby, and I looked at David. "Come on. You're going to that brunch too."

He spun in his desk chair. "Aaaawwwesome."

My phone rang, and I whispered a prayer that it wasn't my nonna before looking at the display. "It's Bradley." I bit my lower lip. "Hang on, I'm going to take this in my office." I hurried down the hall. "Hello?"

"Franki, this is Bradley."

"I know." I used my telemarketer tone.

"I'm calling on business. Do you have a minute?"

"Business?" I repeated, taken aback. "Did you see us on TV this morning?"

"You were on TV?"

"In a way," I hedged. "So what's this about?"

"I need to hire you to investigate an important case. It's about a woman I met."

I recoiled, outraged. "If this is about that scantily dressed Mardi Gras queen I saw you with on Bourbon Street, then you can take your business somewhere else."

"You mean, Sheilah."

"*That* was Sheilah?" I disliked her even more.

"Yes." He sighed. "She came by the bank after hours. Because it was dark out, I offered to walk her to a party she was attending that evening."

My stomach clenched, annoyed. "What does this have to do with me?"

He paused. "You have the wrong impression of me."

"I doubt that," I muttered, remembering my earlier revelation about cheating.

"Look, it's true that Sheilah and I are married—"

"No kidding."

"—and will be for about three more weeks."

I blinked. "Come again?"

"That's how long it'll take the divorce papers Sheila signed at the bank the other night to go through the courts."

"Oh." My jaw shut with an audible click. The word *divorce* had never sounded so sweet.

"I swear I wanted to tell you, but I was under a gag order until now. Sheilah and I got married too young, mainly because our families were close. We wanted to end it almost immediately, but her mother got sick, and after that her father's business fell apart. So, we waited. In the meantime, I left Boston to kickstart my career, so the divorce delays weren't a huge issue. All of that changed, though, when I met the woman I mentioned."

I pulled up a chair. The case was starting to pique my interest. "This woman...what can you tell me about her?"

"She's a knockout private investigator with a mean right hook. I'm crazy about her, but she's not talking to me. I need you to do some investigating to find out whether I still have a chance with her."

My smile was as big as Julia Roberts' in *Pretty Woman*. "Sounds like an exciting assignment. Too bad Veronica and I are booked for the next month."

"The whole month, huh?"

"Yeah, but since the situation is obviously urgent, I suppose I could have you over for dinner tonight at, say, sevenish to discuss the details?"

"I'll be there." The playfulness had left his tone.

"I look forward to it," I said. And boy did I.

BOOK BACKSTORY

Limoncello Yellow came to be because of five random events in my life:

1) A car trip from Texas to New Orleans that I took with my parents in the early nineties so that my father could stock up on Italian deli meat at Central Grocery (Italians will go to great lengths for their food);

2) An accidental encounter on Bourbon Street in my twenties with half-dressed day-shift strippers and a bucket of Popeye's fried chicken;

3) An unexpected introduction to limoncello on my honeymoon thanks to Serbian waiters in Rome;

4) A superb and inspiring online writing class I took from Internationally Bestselling Author Kristin Harmel;

5) The amazing "Femme Fatale" contest I entered on *New York Times* Bestselling Author Gemma Halliday's website (the grand prize was a Kindle and month of mentoring, and yet I ended up with a two-book deal!).

If I could go back and thank each and every one of the above individuals—especially the strippers and the bouncer that let me into Big Daddy's when it was closed for an emergency bathroom stop—I totally would. It's funny how random events can all add up to a big, life-changing thing like writing a book.

While I'm thanking people, there is no way I could have finished this book without the help of my husband, my parents, and my parents-in-law. My guilt for taking precious time away from my young son, was lessened by the knowledge that he was in their loving hands. I owe them a huge debt of gratitude that I will never be able to repay (and no, Dad, I'm not giving you any of the royalties).

Speaking of my son, I'd like to thank him for putting up with all the writing. D, you will always be my boy.

I would also like to thank the fabulous Barbara Marking Steiner (ex-cop-turned-elementary-school-principal who owns a pink handgun, y'all!) for being available on a moment's notice to advise me on police matters.

Words cannot express how grateful I am to Linda O'Krent for pushing me (forcefully) down the writing path and to Chelsea Drescher for telling me that I didn't want to write academic texts anymore. I should have known that I didn't want to be a professor when I chose Italian mystery writer Andrea Camilleri as the subject of my dissertation. (Incidentally, *giallo*, the Italian word for "yellow," also means "mystery novel" because the covers of the first mysteries published in Italy were yellow. Of course, this is why the color yellow simply *had* to be in the title of the first book in the Franki Amato Mystery series.)

On the subject of symbolism, I need to say *grazie mille* to Matthew Amato, Marissa Maggio, Benji Orlansky, Mike Reiff, and Bill Savoie for letting me use their last names, which are every bit as vibrant as they are, and to Brady Harris for unknowingly lending me his appropriately individualistic first name. It bears noting that I chose the Italian surname "Amato" for Franki because it sounds tough but means "loved" and because Matthew Amato, who was one of my Italian students at the

University of Texas, is one of the finest young men I know. I selected the name "Francesca," a.k.a. "Franki," in memory of my parents' cairn terrier—one of the most inquisitive, determined and flat out adorable dogs who ever lived.

Last but not least, I would like to extend my appreciation to The Flight Path Coffee House in Austin, Texas, for being my local source of inspiration and to the city of New Orleans for being the weird, wild, and wonderful place that it is. My plan was to write a mystery with a colorful title and colorful characters, and from the moment I came up with that goal, I knew that The Big Easy was the *only* possible setting for *Limoncello Yellow*.

Cin cin (Cheers)!

Traci

COCKTAILS

Franki Amato appreciates a good cocktail every so often—okay, maybe more often than not. After all, it's hard work fighting crime in New Orleans. In general, her motto is "When life gives you lemons, make Limoncello." But in extreme cases she revises it to "When life gives you lemons, skip the 'making Limoncello' part and go straight to drinking it."

LIMONCELLO

Here is Franki's recipe for three bottles of pure lemon heaven.

Ingredients
>   10 medium (or 15 small) Meyer lemons
>   1 quart Everclear (a brand of grain alcohol)
>   1 and 1/2 quarts water
>   2 and 3/4 pounds of sugar

Wash and peel the lemons. Soak the lemon peels in three quarters of the Everclear for one-to-two months, storing the mixture in an airtight container in a cool, dark place.

When the peels are infused with the Everclear, boil the sugar and water until it makes syrup (about five minutes). After the syrup has cooled, pour it into the lemon-peel mixture along with the remaining Everclear.

Store the Limoncello mixture in a cool, dark place for forty days. Then strain it with cheesecloth to remove the lemon peels before bottling the Limoncello. Serve chilled. *Cin cin!*

LIMONCELLO MARGARITA

Because Franki is originally from Texas, she occasionally enjoys her Limoncello with a Tex-Mex twist.

Ingredients

  2 ounces tequila
  1 ounce Grand Marnier
  1 ounce Limoncello
  1/2 ounce fresh lemon juice
  1/2 ounce fresh lime juice
  1/2 teaspoon sugarsalt for the glass rim

Prosecco pink

A Franki Amato Mystery

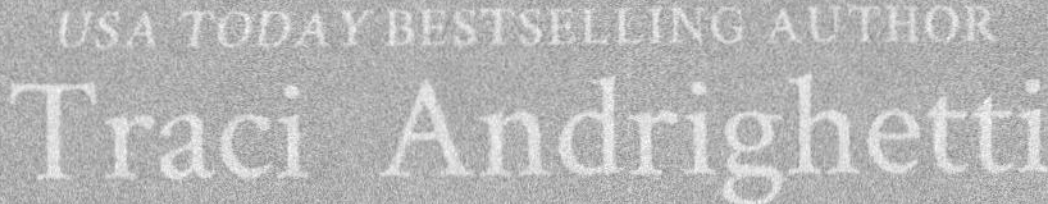

USA TODAY BESTSELLING AUTHOR

Traci Andrighetti

PROSECCO PINK

by

TRACI ANDRIGHETTI

***

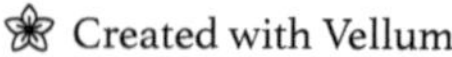 Created with Vellum

1

"Who takes their secretary to a working dinner at a freaking bed and breakfast?" I asked aloud as I sped down Great Mississippi River Road in Louisiana plantation country. I didn't usually talk to myself, but the stress of the situation more than justified it.

"I mean, what's wrong with a restaurant in the French Quarter? People travel from all over the world to eat there."

I steered my 1965 cherry-red Mustang convertible out from behind the 18-wheeler to make sure the black BMW was still up ahead. As soon as I'd spotted it, I dropped back behind the hulking truck. I couldn't let Bradley know I was following him.

Bradley Hartmann was the president of Pontchartrain Bank on Canal Street in New Orleans. With his shocking blue eyes, full lips, and chiseled jaw, he was without a doubt the sexiest bank executive this side of the Mason-Dixon line. And he was mine. We'd been seeing each other for the past three months, ever since his divorce was finalized. Okay, maybe we started seeing each other a bit before then, but that was an accident. I promise.

The problem was, now that his ex-wife was out of the way, his sexy new Chinese-French secretary was in the way. All six feet of her. And at five feet ten inches myself, I wasn't used to looking up to a woman, especially not one as lowdown as Pauline Violette. She did everything she could to keep me away from Bradley— including scheduling these weekend working dinners at bed and breakfasts outside of town. And judging from the way she batted her violet, almond-shaped eyes at him, it was clear why.

"How is it even possible that her eye color matches her last name?" I asked as I hit the gas. "Her boobs are clearly manmade, so those eyes have to be too."

I glanced out the passenger window to try to catch another glimpse of Bradley's BMW, and a flash of pink caught my eye. But it wasn't the coral-pink hue of the thousands of oleanders that framed a stunning, three-story, columned plantation home. It was the pink crinoline skirt of the woman standing on the balcony. It was a hauntingly beautiful image, like something you'd see in an old oil painting.

Unfortunately, the road started to curve sharply, but I was too busy staring at the Southern belle to notice. My tires hit the soft shoulder, and I jerked the steering wheel hard to the left. But it was too late. My car slid sideways right into a swamp.

"*Mamma mia!*" I exclaimed as I realized what had happened. And I did want my mother. Because when I restarted the engine and tried to drive to land, I discovered that I was stuck in the filthy swamp mud.

I threw open my car door, mentally whispered a farewell to my new boots, and stepped into the black swamp water. I trudged around to the back of the car and saw that the rear passenger tire was the problem. I needed to find some wood or stones to put beneath it to try to gain traction. Just as I was about to turn around and head for shore, I made a horrifying discovery. The water was moving.

That's when a bumpy black reptile lifted its moss-covered head above the surface of the murky swamp water, and I came face-to-face with an alligator.

The unsightly beast opened its toothy, cavernous mouth and made a loud hissing sound.

Make that an angry alligator.

"G-good gator," I stammered, frozen with fear.

The alligator lowered its head back into the water and began swimming in a circle, its large cat-like eyes trained on me like the sight of a gun.

"Nice b-boy, Al," I said as I began inching backward through the watery, foul-smelling mud. In case the alligator decided to charge at me, I needed to make it to the driver's side taillight to have a clear shot at the open car door. "Or, maybe you're an Alli?"

As though confirming my suspicion, she slapped her tail hard against the surface of the water.

I estimated her to be around six feet in length—precisely Pauline's height. Then I promptly reminded myself that during my rookie cop days in Austin, Texas, I'd once tackled a male ostrich that was getting frisky with some mothers at a petting zoo. Plus, I'd seen the Gator Boys *and* the Swamp Men wrestle alligators on TV, so I figured that I could take her if push came to shove, er, thrust came to lunge.

Alli stopped near the stump of a bald cypress tree and opened her mouth, revealing eighty or so two-inch-long yellow teeth.

Okay, maybe not.

I took another step backward, and she resumed circling.

"That's right, girl. Just keep swimming," I whispered, advancing another inch or two. "It's good for your waistline." I took another step, and my right foot sunk into what felt like a muddy mass of tree roots. I tried to pull it out, but it was stuck solid. Just like the rear tire of my Mustang.

I felt a fresh wave of fear wash over me, but I knew I had to keep calm. I took a deep breath of the putrid swamp air and tried again to free my foot.

"Franki?" a male voice called.

"Bradley," I breathed. "Oh thank God." My relief quickly gave way to dismay, however, when I realized that he must have seen me following him and Pauline before I ran my car off the road. But surely he would overlook that minor detail now that I was standing in filthy, mosquito-infested swamp water *and* being stalked by an alligator.

"Don't move," he said in a calm, even tone. "You don't want to startle him."

No, I most certainly don't, I thought.

"As soon as he turns to swim away, make a dash for the other side of the car."

"Don't you think I would've done that by now if I could?" I asked, trying to control my increasing hysteria.

"Why can't you? What's wrong?"

"Let me see... Where should I start?"

"Franki," he began, a note of tension creeping into his voice, "why can't you get to the car door?"

"My shoe is caught on something." Should I add that my new boots were the knee-high lace-up kind—with triple buckles?

"Okay, then slip your foot out of your shoe," he said through clenched teeth.

No, now was clearly not the time to tell him. "Um, it's not exactly the slip-your-foot-out-of-your-shoe kind of shoe."

There was a heavy silence.

"Then we're going to have to wait him out," he said.

I gasped. Was he seriously not going to come into the water and pull me out? I mean, saving me from an alligator was the least he could do after planning to take his secretary to a B&B, right?

"If I move, he could attack," Bradley explained. "And you're his closest target."

Before I could protest, I heard an ear-splitting bellow behind me. I jerked my head to the left and saw the largest alligator I'd ever seen. At roughly fifteen feet in length, he was practically a dinosaur.

Terror shot through my body like a white-hot flash of lightening. But I fought to keep my wits about me because the gargantuan gator was standing near Bradley. And as mad as I was about Pauline and the whole leaving-me-to-the-gator thing, I could hardly let Bradley be eaten by a Tyrannosaurus alligator on my account. I had to do something. And fast.

I started jerking my trapped foot as hard as I could. But each time I did, I sunk deeper and deeper into the gooey swamp bottom. The water level was now above my knees, and my panic level was considerably higher.

"You've got to stay still," Bradley warned. "He's extremely dangerous."

"No kidding."

"April is mating season. I think he's looking for a mate."

"Well, tell him Alli isn't interested. And neither am I," I added, just in case.

The big gator bellowed again, causing the hair to stand up on my arms.

Had my refusal offended him or something?

"He's headed toward the water now," Bradley said. "Stay calm."

"Easy for you to say," I muttered under my breath.

I heard a splash as the alligator entered the swamp. At that same moment, Alli dipped beneath the surface of the water. Now there were two of them. Lurking.

Oh God, oh God, oh God. I promise I'll never lust after an alligator handbag or shoes again for as long as I live if you let me survive this, I thought. Then I held my breath and waited.

The swamp was deadly silent, except for the croaking of some green tree frogs.

I started when I heard the sound of a car door opening.

"Bradley, get back in the car!" Pauline called. "It's not safe."

No need to worry about me, *Pauline,* I thought. Not only was the sultry secretary trying to steal my boyfriend, now she was also trying to convince him to leave me for gator food.

"I need you to stay in the car, Pauline," he replied. "I can't have anything happen to you."

Wait a minute. He can't have anything happen to her? *What about* me? I felt a sudden surge of anger-induced adrenaline course through my body. With a steely calm, I crouched down, unbuckled and unlaced my boot and pulled my foot free. Then I yanked the boot out of the tangled roots and rushed around to the driver's seat. I'd paid three hundred bucks for those boots, so there was no way I was leaving one of them in the swamp— gators or no gators.

The second I got into the car, I pulled my 9mm purple Ruger from the glove compartment box. I looked out my driver's side window and saw Bradley kneel down to examine my rear tire.

"Start the engine and press the accelerator," he called.

I did as I was told and watched through the rearview mirror as mud flew from the spinning tire.

He motioned for me to stop. "Let me find something to put under the tire, and then I'll have you try again."

"Be careful," I said.

With my gun in hand, I surveyed the area for hungry—or horny—alligators while Bradley gathered a few small cypress branches.

He arranged the branches beneath my tire and stood up, wiping his hands. "Okay, now."

I hit the gas full throttle and felt my tire gain traction. The car started forward and then spun out to the right, just as something struck the side of my car. I had a terrifying thought. *One of the alligators had lunged for Bradley and hit my car instead!* I threw the car into park and leapt out with my gun drawn.

"Are you crazy?" Pauline screamed. "You could kill him!"

Oh, so now she was worried about the alligator too? Ignoring her protests, I scoured the scene for the offending creature, and that's when I saw him. Bradley, that is. Covered in mud and propped up on his elbows in three-inch-deep swamp water. That was no gator I'd hit, it was my boyfriend. At least, I really, really hoped he was still my boyfriend.

I rushed into the water and knelt at his side. "Are you okay?"

He spit something brown and slimy into the water. "Fine," he replied, a tad tersely.

"Let me help you."

"Now there's an offer you can refuse," Pauline said.

I shot her a look. Was that a Mafia jab?

Bradley stood up in silence and did a quick body check before walking to the shore.

"Let me see if I have a towel or something in the car," I said. I ran to the Mustang, but all I could find was a travel-sized package of Kleenex.

I hurried back to Bradley and began dabbing at the mud on his shirt with a tissue. "I'm so sorry about your suit."

He pulled away.

I blinked, surprised. "I said I was sorry."

"It's not about my damned suit, Franki."

"Oh?" I asked, doing my darnedest to feign innocence. But I knew exactly what this was about.

"What were you doing out here on River Road, miles from New Orleans?" he demanded.

Pauline sauntered over and folded her arms across her chest. "Yes, what *were* you doing? Shopping for a plantation home?"

I met her arrogant gaze straight on but avoided her question. "Nice of you to finally get out of the car."

Bradley looked from Pauline to me and sighed. "Never mind, Franki. We'll talk about this later."

Pauline glanced at her smartphone and turned to Bradley, instantly dismissing me. "We still have twenty minutes before your meeting with Mr. Stafford, and according to Google we're only about twenty-five miles from the bed and breakfast. We can still make it if we hurry."

Bradley looked down at his wet, mud-stained clothes. "I can't go looking like this."

"Well, you have that extra shirt and your suit coat in the car, and I have a bottle of Perrier in my purse. If you slip off your pants, I can have some of the more visible stains out before we get there."

Bradley nodded and started for his car.

I gasped. "You're not actually going to take your pants off for her, are you?"

He turned to look at me. "Franki, it's business. This meeting is critical to the future of the bank, and it's my job to do whatever I can to make sure it's a success. I've got to go."

As Bradley climbed into his car, Pauline spun around to face me. She was standing so close that her long, black hair lashed across my face like a silken whip, and her heavy perfume stung my nostrils. "Well, I hope you're satisfied," she said. "Thanks to your little spy game, you've not only ruined Bradley's thousand-dollar suit, you've also potentially cost him a multi-million dollar business deal."

I stared at her open-mouthed. When Bradley told me that he couldn't come over because he and Pauline were having a working dinner at a B&B outside of town, I'd assumed it was just the two of them. I had no idea that they were meeting a client there, not to mention such an important one.

"Now close your mouth and go get cleaned up," Pauline continued. She narrowed her undoubtedly fake violet eyes and looked me up and down. "You're a hot mess."

She did a runway-model turn and strutted to the car.

Oh, I was hot all right. With shame and blinding rage.

STILL SMARTING from Pauline's smackdown an hour later, I kicked open my front door and threw my mud-caked boots onto the floor.

"Well, look what the cat dragged in," my landlady, Glenda O'Brien, said from a backbend position on the bearskin rug on my living room floor. For a sixty-something-year-old woman, she was startlingly flexible, no doubt due to her forty-something-year career as a stripper.

My best friend and employer, Veronica Maggio, was on the floor beside Glenda, looking exactly as she had when I first met her in our freshman dorm at The University of Texas at Austin. She had her tongue sticking out one side of her mouth as she put the final strokes of Raspberry Fields Forever nail polish on her pinky toe. When she finished, she gave me the once-over. "What happened to *you*?"

I sighed and tossed my purse onto the velvet zebra print rococo chaise lounge. I'd forgotten that Sunday was movie night, or "ladies' night" as Glenda had christened it, and that it was my turn to host. "Oh, not much. I spied on Bradley and Pauline, I nearly got us all killed by a couple of alligators in heat, and then I hit Bradley with my car and pulled a gun on him."

"Oh, sugar," Glenda said, kicking her skinny, veined legs forward out of her backbend and coming to a standing position. "That sounds sexy."

I rolled my eyes. "I'm dead serious."

A coy smile formed at the corners of her mouth, and then she took a long, sensuous drag off her signature Mae West-style cigarette holder. "So am I, child. So. Am. I."

I didn't bother asking her not to smoke since she owned the fourplex that all of us lived in as well as the rather unique bordello-style furnishings in my not-so-humble abode. But I did make a mental note to ask her to stop letting herself in to my apartment.

"Why would you spy on Bradley?" Veronica asked, her brow furrowed. "You said you trusted him."

She never ceased to amaze me. "So, the trust thing is what you're worried about? Not the part about the gator or the gun?"

Veronica screwed the cap on the bottle of nail polish. "Well, you're in one piece, and you're not in jail, so I assumed that those other things got worked out somehow."

"Well, you could at least *act* concerned, you know."

"I'm sorry," she said, fidgeting with the ribbon on her pink baby doll pajamas. "It's just that I thought you were finally over your trust issue with men. That's all."

"I was. I mean, I am," I hurried to add. "I trust Bradley, but I don't trust Pauline around Bradley."

Veronica cocked her head to one side. "Well, isn't that the same thing?"

"No, it isn't. You have no idea how manipulative she is. Plus, she's always so perfect and prepared. I mean, the woman carries a bottle of Perrier water around with her just in case she needs to remove a stain."

"Perrier?" Glenda asked, wrinkling her mouth. "I don't get women who drink bubbly water when they could be drinking champagne. This Pauline sounds suspect, if you ask me."

I cast Veronica a triumphant look. "See? Glenda doesn't trust her either."

Veronica shook her head. "Trusting Pauline isn't the issue. The problem is that you're underestimating Bradley, and it's not like he's stupid."

"No, but he's a man, and she's drop-dead gorgeous. She's built like a model, and she looks like Lucy Liu. To top it all off, she has violet eyes, just like Elizabeth Taylor. And you know how good Liz was at stealing other women's men."

Glenda batted her inch-long, blue false eyelashes. "You know, Ronnie, I think Miss Franki's right. If there's one thing I learned while I was stripping, it's that even the smartest man is no match for a cunning woman."

I nodded, vindicated, although I wasn't entirely sure that you could compare my Harvard-educated, bank president boyfriend to the average strip club patron. But then again, maybe you could.

"You know what I think, sugar?" Glenda continued after taking a long, thoughtful drag off her cigarette.

"What?" I asked, eager to hear her opinion. Glenda was a little rough around the edges, but she often had sage advice.

"You need to make sure that she doesn't put nothin' over on you," she replied, exhaling a cloud of smoke. "So you're gonna have to stick to this Pauline like a pastie on a titty."

Veronica cleared her throat. "Franki, will you let the dogs in? My toes are still wet."

"I'll do it," Glenda said, hopping to her five-inch-high-heeled, slipper-clad feet. "I need to freshen up my glass of champagne, anyway."

As Glenda paraded past me to the kitchen, I noticed that she too was wearing baby doll pajamas—in tight black fishnet with large holes cut from beneath her armpits all the way down to below the hip. It was quite possibly the most clothing I'd ever seen her wear.

Glenda opened the back door, and my brindle cairn Terrier, Napoleon, bounded over to me, his tail wagging.

"There's my good boy," I said, bending over to greet him.

Napoleon skidded to an abrupt stop, gave a quick sniff of my feet, and took a giant leap backward.

"So much for the unconditional love of pets," I said. "I guess I'll take that as my cue to go shower the swamp off me."

Veronica adjusted the bowtie on her cream Pomeranian, Hercules. "Hurry up so we can start the movie."

"What did you get?" I asked, even though it really didn't matter what the movie was. The only thing I'd be watching were the images of Bradley's hurt face and Pauline's haughty one that kept replaying in my head.

"*Zombie Strippers*," Glenda called from the kitchen.

Obviously her turn to pick the movie, I thought.

"By the way," Veronica began, "I made sugar cookies, and Glenda brought an extra bottle of champagne. Isn't this going to be fun?"

I gave her a blank stare. "Yeah. Tons."

Veronica placed a reassuring hand on my arm. "I know you're worried about Bradley, but try to relax and enjoy the evening."

"I can't. On top of everything else, I might have cost him an important business deal. Do you think I should call and ask how it went?"

"No," she replied. "Let him have tonight to cool off. Then tomorrow you can apologize and explain how you feel about Pauline. I'm sure he'll understand."

I nodded, but I wasn't so sure about the understanding part, especially after my jealousy had almost gotten him killed—first by the alligators and then by me. I set off for the shower thinking that it was going to take a lot more than champagne, sugar cookies, and strippers to get me through the night.

2

I parked in front of the old brown brick building at 1200 Decatur Street in the French Quarter and glanced up at the bright green, shuttered windows of Private Chicks, Inc. It was the fifth time in two weeks that I'd been late to work, so I was hoping that Veronica hadn't made it to the office yet. There was no sign of her White Audi, but just in case she'd parked on one of the side streets, I tiptoed up the three flights of stairs. As I pushed open the main door, the lobby bell blared like a foghorn.

"You're late!" Veronica shouted from another room.

I walked into her office, my head hung low. "I know. I'm sorry."

"Sorry?" she hissed, sounding remarkably like a Parselmouth from a Harry Potter movie.

I raised my eyes and was surprised to see that in place of her usual designer business attire, Veronica was wearing a dress that looked like something straight out of Glenda's stripper costume closet. She was also really pale—gray, actually. "Are you feeling okay?"

In reply, she stood up from her fuchsia leather chair, threw back her head, and let out a blood-curdling howl.

Wait. A howl? I opened my eyes and realized that a) I was still and bed, and b) Napoleon was the one doing the howling.

I lifted my head to scold him, and it felt like a hatchet had just been buried deep into my skull. "Bad boy, Napoleon," I whispered.

He cocked his head to the side, probably confused by my unusually soft tone.

I settled back into the pillow and wondered whether my dream was some sort of sign that I shouldn't be working for my best friend. But then I quickly decided it was more likely an indication that I needed to lay off the Limoncello. And the zombie strippers.

Rather than lift my head again, I felt around on the nightstand until I found my phone. I glanced at the display—seven a.m., no missed calls, and no texts. The realization that Bradley hadn't tried to contact me hit me like a sledgehammer.

I tossed the phone back onto the nightstand, and, as if on cue, it began to ring.

Certain it was Bradley, I sat up—through the pain—and grabbed the phone. It was my parents. If they were calling on a Monday before they went to work at our family deli, it spelled bad news. I laid down in preparation for the undoubtedly deflating conversation to come.

"Hello?" I replied, trying to hide my concern.

"Francesca? It's your mother, dear." Her shrill voice bore into my head like a drill, as did her habit of stating the obvious.

"Yeah, I know that, Mom."

"You didn't call us last night. Is everything okay?"

I thought about the alligator almost eating me and me almost killing Bradley. "Everything's fine, Mom."

I heard the sound of the receiver slamming down on what I knew to be the kitchen counter.

"Joe!" she shouted. "Francesca's fine!"

I waited for the inevitable grumbled response of my father.

"Tell her that just because she's in New Orleans now doesn't mean she can forget about her family here in Houston," he said.

And there it was.

"Did you hear your father, dear?"

"Yes, but why do you guys get so worried when I miss one phone call?" I asked, even though I already knew the answer. Worrying was my parents' favorite pastime, after Yahtzee.

"Because you usually call us on Sunday, dear."

"I know that, but I was watching a movie with Veronica and Glenda, and it ran late."

"How nice. What did you see?"

This was one of those times when honesty was not the best policy, so I threw out the first innocuous movie that came to mind. "*Gone with the Wind.*"

My mother let out a dreamy sigh. "I've always loved that movie! My favorite part is when Rhett looks at Scarlett and says, 'Frankly, my dear, I don't give a damn.'"

"I'm pretty sure that's everyone's favorite part, Mom."

"Did you know that Clark Gable was bisexual, Francesca?"

This conversation was taking an alarming turn. "Listen, Mom, I need to start getting ready for work. Were you calling to tell me something?"

"Oh yes, dear. Do you remember your cousin Giovanna? The one who's only twenty-four and is already an attorney?"

I put the back of my arm over my eyes. The fact that my mother was bringing up my cousin's age and profession meant one of two things. Either she was calling to tell me that Giovanna was engaged or that she'd been promoted. I was betting on the former. "Of course I remember her. She's my cousin."

"Well, you're not going to believe this, but she's engaged to a judge!"

"*Tombola*," I said aloud.

"Are you playing Italian bingo, dear?"

I sighed. "It's seven o'clock in the morning, Mom."

"Well, I distinctly heard you say '*tombola*.'"

"I know, I just... Never mind. When's the wedding?"

There was a long pause, and then I heard muffled voices and the sound of a scuffle. I knew from years of experience that my eighty-three-year-old Sicilian grandmother, Carmela, was trying to wrest the receiver from my mother's hands.

"First she's gonna have-a the *festa del fidanzamento*," my nonna announced, breathless from the struggle.

I should've predicted that my nonna would be listening in to a conversation about a wedding. She'd been trying to get me married for the last thirteen years, since I was sixteen.

"She found a nice-a Sicilian boy," Nonna continued, "so they gonna get married in a church in-a *Sicilia*."

I couldn't help but feel a tinge of resentment toward Giovanna. By announcing her plans to get married in a Sicilian church, of all damned places, she'd opened up a world of grandma hurt for me. My nonna had already accepted the fact that Bradley wasn't Sicilian, reasoning that a twenty-nine-year-old *zitella* like me couldn't "have-a it all-a." But I wasn't sure how she was going to react to the news that a church wedding to Bradley—provided that he ever proposed to me, that is—was out of the question in light of his divorce. Of course, I avoided the issue and muttered a polite, "That's nice."

Nonna gave a bitter laugh. "'That's-a nice,' she says. Well, if-a you think it's-a so nice, then why you no wanna date those-a Sicilian boys I find-a for you?"

I thought of the string of Sicilian-American chauvinists and mammas' boys she'd given my phone number to a few months before. "Uh, they weren't exactly my type."

"No? And-a what's-a your type, Franki? This I want-a to hear."

I was treading on dangerous ground. If I wavered in my response, she would sic her army of Sicilian suitor-soldiers on me again. "My boyfriend, Bradley Hartmann," I replied in no uncertain terms.

"Okay, and-a when is-a this-a Bradley gonna come-a to meet-a your mamma?"

"Nonna, we've only been dating for a few months."

"That's-a plenty of time. I got-a engaged to your *nonnu*, God rest-a his soul, after two-a weeks.

"But that was in Sicily during Fascism. This is the United States, a democracy, sixty years later."

"And-a you see where all-a this-a freedom has-a gotten you, eh? Twenty-nine years old without-a no husband. *Una tragedia*."

These calls from home were always so uplifting. "Nonna, I've really got to go. I have a list of things to do before I go to work this morning."

"Well, you add-a this to your list. Tell-a Bradley to meet-a your mamma. Because I'm-a hearing the tick-a tock-a tick-a tock-a of-a your clock all-a the way here in-a Houston."

If I stayed on this call a minute longer, my brain—and my biological clock—were going to explode. "I'll do that," I gushed. "*Ciao Ciao!*"

Happy Monday, I thought as I threw the phone onto the nightstand. I kicked off my hot pink velvet duvet and climbed out of the French bordello-style bed. Thanks to my family, I was now painfully aware that I was old, husbandless, and quickly closing in on barren. So I figured that there was no time like the present to drop by Pontchartrain Bank to find out whether I was boyfriendless too.

~

An HOUR AND A HALF LATER, I was strolling down Canal Street toward Pontchartrain Bank, taking in the sights and smells of the busy thoroughfare. Unlike the narrow, shop-and-bar-lined streets of the adjacent French Quarter, Canal was one of the main arteries of the city. In the colonial era, it was the dividing line between the French and Spanish portion of the city and the newer American Sector, which is now the Central Business District. Four lanes across with a two-way trolley line in the center, Canal looked more like something you would see in an urban metropolis such as Los Angeles than in a small Southern city like New Orleans. And the same could be said about its hordes of tourists and bums.

As I approached the foreboding black slate walls of the bank, I felt a growing sense of anxiety. I wondered whether Bradley was still mad about the alligator-accident-gun thing. But then I reasoned that the fact that he hadn't called me didn't necessarily mean anything. After all, it was entirely possible that he hadn't been able to call because his meeting ran late. And, looking back on the whole swamp incident now, the only real harm done was a little muddy water on his suit and possibly a lost business deal. But life was about so much more than work. Surely he could see that.

Feeling a surge of newfound confidence, I pushed open the heavy glass door and glanced toward the teller area on the right. Despite her petite 4' 10" frame, I immediately spotted Corinne Mercier, a teller who had helped Veronica and me solve a homicide case at the nearby LaMarca luxury goods store a few months before. She was just finishing up with a client, so I started in her direction to say hello.

"Why, Franki," Pauline's pompous voice boomed from behind me as I was enveloped by a cloud of her perfume. "I'm surprised to see you here."

I turned around and saw Pauline sitting at her desk in front of the row of offices on the left side of the room. "I hardly think it's surprising that I would drop by my bank," I said. Then I added, with emphasis, "And my boyfriend's place of work."

She blinked. "I couldn't agree more. It's just that I thought you'd be hard at work wrestling alligators or gunning down innocent people."

I sighed and slung my hobo bag over my left shoulder to free up my right arm. You know, for gesturing. "Listen, Pauline. I don't have time for this."

She rested her chin on her folded hands and looked me straight in the eye. "Neither do I."

I shifted in my slingbacks. This woman had a lot of nerve. "Could you buzz Bradley and let him know I'm here?"

"He's in a meeting," she replied. And, as though dismissing me, she picked up a jar of opaque white glitter and began sprinkling it into a stuffed envelope.

I gave an impatient toss of my hair. "Okay, what time will it end?"

"No clue." She picked up another envelope and added the white flakes.

"Can you at least tell me how the meeting went with Mr. Stafford last night?" I asked through quasi-clenched teeth.

She ceased sprinkling and glared up at me. "I'm not at liberty to discuss confidential bank business."

I'd set myself up for that one. "All right, then. Just tell Bradley I stopped by."

"That'll be number one on my to-do list." She flashed a false smile.

Somehow, I doubted that. I started to walk away, but my curiosity got the better of me. "What are you doing, anyway?"

Pauline turned up her nose with a self-important air. "Not that it's any of your business, but I'm putting together the invitations for the 'Shoot for the Moon' charity event I'm organizing for the bank. It's to raise scholarship funds for kids who were victims of Hurricane Katrina."

"So, what's the white stuff?"

"It's supposed to be moon dust," she replied, rolling her eyes.

"You sure it's not anthrax?"

She smirked and shook her head in disgust. "Everything's a crime to you, isn't it? And we saw where that got you last night."

I felt a wave of anger rise in my chest, but I fought to maintain my composure. I couldn't cause a scene at Bradley's bank, especially not after the events of last night. "Think what you want, but a lot of people are going to open those envelopes and panic when they see white powder."

"Oh, and I see you're also a cynic," she said, raising her eyebrows in mock surprise. "How charming."

I narrowed my eyes. "Coming from someone like you, I'll take that as a compliment."

She fluttered her eyelashes and faked a mournful frown.

My hands balled into fists. I needed to leave before my free right arm did something I would regret. I spun on my heels and stomped toward the teller area.

"See ya later, *alligator*," Pauline intoned.

I froze in my tracks but didn't turn around. I had no intention of giving her the satisfaction. Instead, I headed straight for Corinne's friendly face.

"*Bonjour*, Franki," Corinne said in her thick French accent. "I see you meet Pauline."

I took a deep, calming breath. "Yeah," I said, casting a hostile glance in her direction, "I had the great pleasure of meeting her a few weeks ago when you were on vacation."

"Ah." Corinne looked down. With her pixie haircut and big blue eyes, she looked like a sad Tinker Bell.

I rested my arms on the counter. "What's the matter?"

She looked up. "I sink she does not like me very much."

Even though I was convinced that Pauline was evil incarnate, I was surprised that she'd take issue with a sweet person like Corinne. "Honestly, I don't think she likes anyone very much, so I wouldn't take it too hard if I were you."

"*Peut-être*," she said, her chin quivering.

"Did something happen between the two of you?"

She wiped away a tear. "I suppose I can tell you. But please, do not tell Bradley."

"Of course not," I said, leaning forward.

She took a deep breath. "On Friday, zere was money missing from my teller drawer. Pauline say I took ze money. But I did not."

Now I was shocked. I didn't know Corinne very well, but I knew she wasn't the type to steal money from her place of work. "How much was missing?"

"Five hundred dollars."

I gasped. "What happened? Do you think you made some kind of mistake?"

"I don't know, but I repay ze money."

"Out of your own pocket?" That was a sizeable chunk of change on a bank teller's salary. And on mine, for that matter.

She nodded. "But now Mr. Hartmann sinks I steal."

"I doubt very seriously he sinks—I mean, *thinks*—that. He knows what an honest, loyal employee you are."

She shook her head. "No, he does not. Pauline say she *saw* me take ze money."

"Oh, Corinne. I'm so sorry." I couldn't imagine why Pauline would go so far as to accuse Corinne of theft. I didn't think it likely that she was after Corinne's job since she struck me as the type who would set her career sights much higher. But what other reason would she have had for saying Corinne took the money? And what had happened to that five hundred dollars, anyway?

"Franki," Corinne said, shaking me from my thoughts.

"Yes?"

"Be careful. Zis Pauline, she is not a nice person."

I thought of her potential influence on Bradley, and my jaw tightened. "I will. And you do the same. Keep your eyes on your teller drawer at all times, and let me know if anything else happens."

As I HEADED down Canal Street toward the Mississippi River, I couldn't stop thinking about that missing money. I really hoped that Bradley was looking into the situation. Because even though I had no idea what was going on at Pontchartrain Bank, my gut was telling me that something wasn't right.

My gut was also telling me, loud and clear, that it was time for breakfast. And for me, breakfast in the French Quarter, and often lunch and dinner, meant only one thing, beignets. But it was already nine, so the world-famous Café du Monde was out of the question. By this time, the line to get in usually stretched all the way down to the Civil War era, model cannon in neighboring Washington Artillery Park. I took a left on Decatur Street and stopped instead at the less renowned but optimistically named New Orleans Famous Beignets and Coffee Café and ordered a dozen of the powdered-sugar pastries. To share with everyone at the office, naturally.

Ten minutes later, I exited the restaurant cradling a bag of piping hot beignets. When I looked down to grab my sunglasses from my purse, I ran straight into a little woman with the body type of the Pillsbury Doughboy and a Chanel handbag the size of a sixth grader. The impact was so strong that we bounced off one another.

"Oooh!" the woman exclaimed. She straightened her purple

knit poncho and then smoothed her platinum-highlighted, bouffant brown bob. Her stubby fingers were tipped with white, paddle-shaped acrylic fingernails decorated with tiny replicas of the same silver and gold moons and stars that adorned her charm bracelet, necklace, and earrings.

"I'm so sorry," I gushed. "Are you okay?"

She stared at me with green eyes as big as saucers and raised her pudgy hand to her small mouth. "I'm fine," she said in a honeyed voice. "But you're obviously not."

I felt my face and did a quick check of my limbs. Everything seemed in order, that is, except for that twenty extra pounds in my mid-section and backside. "Um, I'm not sure I understand."

Her round face grew serious. "I wasn't referring to your earthly body. I meant your *aura*. It's black."

That explains the moons and stars, I thought. "Yeah, I've had kind of a rough morning."

She shook her head, causing her jewelry to jingle like Santa's sleigh bells. "It's not about your morning. And I know, because I talk to spirits."

My first inclination was to tell her that the only spirits I wanted to know about were those of the alcohol variety. But in the short time I'd been in New Orleans, I'd learned to treat the drunks and the crazies in the Quarter courteously—and then flee. "How interesting," I said with a polite nod. "But, I'm late for work, so I'd better be on my way."

"Wait!" she shouted. "This could be a matter of life and death."

At that precise moment thunder rumbled overhead.

I glanced up and saw that dark clouds were quickly obscuring the sunny sky of moments before. I looked back at the woman, and an uneasy feeling came over me. I didn't like the turn the weather was taking, not to mention the turn of this conversation.

"Stay still." She grabbed my left arm, and then her eyes rolled back into her head.

My jaw dropped. I couldn't tell whether she was about to commune with spirits or have a seizure.

As I was pondering what to do, the woman's left arm shot into the air, and her charm bracelet began to vibrate.

Definitely a seizure. I pulled out my phone to call 9-1-1.

"It's worse than I thought," the woman wailed. "Much worse."

"What is?" I asked, alarmed. "Are you going to faint?"

She opened her eyes and dropped my arm. "No," she said in a surprisingly wail-less tone. "I told you, I'm fine. But the spirit I'm talking to isn't. She's in complete hysterics."

The spirit's not the only one, I thought as I slipped my phone back into my purse.

The woman began wringing her hands and pacing back and forth in her denim mini miniskirt and four-inch-heeled, leopard-print boots. "The spirit wants you to know that she did something bad for a family member, and it got her *killed*." She stopped and grabbed hold of my arms. "She was *murdered*."

"O-kaaay." I contemplated shaking free of her grip and making a break for it, but then I opted for a more rational approach. "Well, tell her that I just happen to investigate murders for a living, but only for clients who are alive."

She let go of me. "The spirit knows *thaaat*. Why do you think she's trying to warn you?"

"Warn me? Why on earth—I mean, why in heaven—would she need to do that?"

"What she did has put you and possibly even your friend Valerie or Vicki—no, Veronica—in grave danger."

Veronica? I got goose bumps on my arms. This wasn't crazy anymore; it was downright creepy.

"And the worst part of it is," she continued, "that there's nothing she can do to help you now. You're on your own."

I stared at the ground, trying to process what I'd just heard. I didn't believe in psychics, but where the supernatural was concerned, I made it my policy to be safe rather than sorry. And since I didn't know how this woman knew about Veronica, I decided to err on the side of caution and consider her warning. Now, even though the "you're on your own" part of her message was troubling, it hardly came as a surprise. My solitary state had been the theme of the day, starting with the reminder of my *zitella*-hood from my nonna and ending with Pauline's refusal to let me anywhere near Bradley. But was I really in some kind of danger?

As though in reply from the spirit herself, a bolt of lightening flashed as thunder cracked in the blackened sky. Then a hard rain began to fall.

3

Seizing upon the downpour as my opportunity to escape the whole psycho situation with the psychic, I shrugged and said, "Gotta run!"

As I dashed beneath the green-and-white striped awning of the café's covered patio, the strap of my hobo bag caught on the back of a wrought iron chair. I lurched forward, narrowly missing a table of Japanese tourists who started screaming as though they were witnessing a real-life version of *The Return of Godzilla*. When I regained my balance, I turned to free my purse strap. And then *I* let out a scream. The odd little woman was standing right in front of me, rooting around in her colossal Chanel bag.

"I wish I would have known it was going to rain," she whined, pulling out an entire box of tissues.

"Yeah," I muttered. Apparently, her metaphysical abilities didn't extend to meteorological phenomena.

"I *just* had my hair done this morning," she added as she began dabbing at her Texas-sized tease.

"That's a bummer," I said, staring fascinated at her huge hair-style. It had a peculiar sheen to it, like it was gleaming. Not in a rain-spattered or even an otherworldly way, but in a freshly applied varnish one.

She sighed and reached into her bra. "Anyway, take this," she said, pulling out a business card. "You're going to need it."

I took the moon-embossed card—using only my fingernails —and read aloud, "Chandra Toccato, Crescent City Medium."

"'Chandra' is Hindi for 'shining moon.'"

And your last name is Italian for "touched," I thought.

"Well," she prodded. "Do you get it?"

I glanced up at her. "What?"

"Chandra? Crescent City Medium? They both refer to the moon!" she said, beaming. "So, becoming a psychic was literally in the stars for me. Or in the cards—as in, tarot cards?" She put her chubby fingers to her lips and giggled, exactly like the Pillsbury Doughboy does. "And you're not going to believe this, but I'm also a Cancer. You know, a moon child?"

I nodded and then scrutinized her moon-pie face, yet another aspect of her lunar life theme, looking for signs of insanity.

"I need to be honest with you, though," she continued, touching my arm. "I'm originally from Boston. But after Katrina, I felt called to the Crescent City, which is only natural given my celestial essence and all. So I convinced my husband Lou—we were high school sweethearts—that we had to move to New Orleans because the people here were in desperate need of our services."

"He's a psychic too?" I wasn't really interested—just coerced into conversational compliance by her incessant chatter.

"No," she said, furrowing her brow. "A plumber."

"Oh."

Chandra reached into her purse and pulled out a compact. "I was talking about the living *and* the dead," she explained as she examined her hair in the mirror. "Hurricanes are murder on plumbing, and they're terribly stressful for spirits, what with the atmospheric changes and high winds."

The high winds? I had a mental image of a gaggle of Caspar the Friendly Ghosts clutching their heads and screaming in fear of their non-lives while getting tossed around by a hurricane. Clearly, it was time to shake myself out of my Chandra-induced stupor. "So...about that warning. Can you give me some specifics?"

She snapped the compact shut. "Not right now."

"Why not?"

"The spirit's just too upset to speak," she said, depositing the compact into her bag.

"Oh, she is, is she?" I asked, annoyed. This spirit, provided she was real, of course, was something else.

"Try to understand her point of view," Chandra said, putting her hand on her hip and gesturing with her free hand. "She just had to fess up to some pretty rough stuff, so naturally she's embarrassed."

I frowned. I should have been biting into a beignet by now, but instead I was bickering with a selfish spirit via her mad medium. "Tell her that I'm kind of upset *myself* now that I know she's put me in danger."

She pursed her lips. "That wouldn't help. Spirits are really temperamental beings, so I don't want to push her. And, between you and me," she whispered, shielding her mouth with the back of her hand, "spirits kind of freak me out."

Now I was really taken aback. "You're a psychic, and spirits make you uncomfortable?"

Chandra glared at me. "It's not like I chose this profession. It was preordained. Besides, how would you react if a spirit was yelling at you?"

I wanted to tell her that I'd probably see a psychologist, but to be polite I went with, "I'd run like hell."

"You see?" she said, raising her brow. "So, we'll just have to wait until she feels like talking again."

"Whenever that is, please let me know." I handed her my card.

"I most certainly will." She took the card and looked at the front and back. "Franki Amato, Private Investigator. Private Chicks, Inc.," she read. "I don't get it."

Now it was my turn to get defensive. "You know, there's the two references to 'private,' and 'chicks' rhymes with 'dicks'—as in, 'detectives?'"

"Hm." She sniffed and dropped the card into her purse. "Well, it's stopped raining, so I really should be going."

As I watched Chandra walk serenely down Decatur Street, I pulled the bag of now lukewarm beignets closer to my chest. Even though I had my doubts about her psychic abilities, I couldn't help but feel concerned about my personal safety—and my conspicuous lack of business card symmetry.

I SLUNK into Veronica's office a good hour late and silently deposited the bag of beignets on her desk. I saw it as a kind of peace offering, albeit a cold and soggy one.

Veronica eyed the bag and then looked up at me. "What's the matter with you?"

"Huh?" I asked, startled by her unusually harsh tone. I felt like I was dreaming about zombie-stripper Veronica again. But one look at her healthy glow and crisp pink Donna Karan suit confirmed that she wasn't undead.

"You look like you've seen a ghost," she replied, leaning back in her chair.

"Oh, it's probably powdered sugar," I explained, wiping my mouth. "I ate a couple of beignets on my way in to the office."

Okay, so I really had five or six. But who could blame me after my anxiety-inducing encounter with that psychic?

"No, you're pasty," Veronica said. "Are you feeling okay?"

"I think so," I whispered as I felt the lymph glands in my neck.

"Now don't go all hypochondriac on me," she warned. "It was just an observation."

"I'm not," I fibbed, casually moving my hand to my earring. It was a well-established fact that where contracting illnesses was concerned, I was open to suggestions. And now that she'd mentioned it, I *was* feeling kind of sick to my stomach. Not that it had anything to do with those half-dozen beignets.

"Wait. This is about Bradley, isn't it? Have you talked to him yet?"

I flopped down into a chair in front of her desk and let out a deep sigh. "No, I went by the bank, but he was in a meeting. Or, at least, that's what his protector, Pauline, claimed."

"Ah," Veronica said, crossing her arms. "That explains it."

"What?" I asked.

She smirked. "You're still feeling threatened by her."

"I am not," I snapped. "Pauline is hardly threatening. Controlling and deceitful, yes, but nothing I can't handle."

"Well, I've known you long enough to be able to tell when something's wrong. So, what is it?"

I debated whether to tell her about Chandra and the spirit. In keeping with her incredibly disciplined, workaholic nature, Veronica had a strictly practical, non-mystical approach to life. But on the positive side, you could always count on her for down-to-earth advice. Plus, I was terrible at keeping secrets. So I blurted out, "Something really freaky happened at New Orleans Famous Beignets and Coffee this morning."

"What? The cashier predicted you'd order a dozen beignets without you even telling her?" She snickered.

I shifted uncomfortably in my seat. How did Veronica know I'd ordered twelve beignets? "No," I replied, refusing to confirm or deny the specifics of my order. "I met a psychic who said a spirit told her I was in danger."

She rolled her eyes. "Well I hope you did the *scongiuri* because if a psychic said it, you know it's true."

Scongiuri was an Italian hand gesture used to ward off the evil eye. It looks like The University of Texas' hook 'em horns sign, but with the index and pinky fingers pointed toward the ground. My nonna taught it to me when I was little, and Veronica never missed an opportunity to make fun of me for doing it. The thing was, I didn't think I'd made the gesture after Chandra told me I was in danger, so I immediately dropped my hands to my side, out of view of Veronica's judgmental eyes, and did so. Then I gave her a pointed look and said, "I wouldn't be so blasé about this if I were you, because that spirit knew your name."

"Come on, Franki. Psychics make it their business to know people's personal information. That's how they reel them in."

I resented the implication that I was a sucker, so I retaliated with a sure-fire comeback. "Okay then, explain to me how she would've known that I had a friend named Veronica."

"Hm, let me see." She pressed her index finger to her temple in mock concentration. "Our Private Chicks television commercial?"

"Oh. Right." I'd completely forgotten that our first-ever commercial was airing this week. In all likelihood, Chandra had seen us on TV, which meant that the Crescent City Medium was nothing but a Crescent City Con Artist.

No sooner had I reached that conclusion than thunder boomed in the sky so violently it shook our building. I jumped in my seat and told myself that those eerily timed thunderbolts couldn't possibly be messages from the spirit. Could they?

Veronica stood up and looked out the window just as the lobby door slammed hard.

I instantly recognized the exuberant slam as that of David Savoie, our nineteen-year-old, part-time employee.

"Will David ever learn to close the door like a normal person?" Veronica asked.

"Not until he gives up those Red Bulls and his testosterone stops surging," I replied.

A drenched David burst into the room holding a dripping wet Tulane backpack. "*Dude*, what's up with the *rain*?"

Veronica frowned at the water pooling around him on the hardwood floor. "Let me get you something to dry off with."

David moved aside to let her pass and turned to face me. "Like, the rain totally came out of nowhere. When I was parking my car, it was sunny and clear. But then when I got out, it was instant downpour."

"It happened to me too," I said. "It's kind of weird, isn't it?"

"I'll say," he said with a brisk nod.

Veronica returned with two towels and handed one to David. "Well, it *is* the rainy season. You know the old adage about April showers."

"I dunno," David said, as he began to towel dry his hair. "I've lived here all my life, and I've never seen anything like it."

I shifted in my chair. So, I wasn't wrong in assuming that the weather was bizarre, even for New Orleans. There was something unusual in the air today. But was it even remotely possible that it was a spirit?

"Hey, speaking of weird," he continued, "are you guys expecting a client?"

I looked at Veronica, who was crouching in the doorway and sopping up the water.

"There's nothing on the books," she replied. "Why?"

"Because there's this really creepy lady out front in a black Cadillac DeVille," he replied.

I felt my stomach lurch as I thought of Chandra. "She's not, by any chance, a doughy little woman with a Dallas-style do, is she?"

"Nah," David replied. "From what I could tell, she's way skinny, and her hair is black and white and spiky. Oh, and she's got a crapload of dogs."

Veronica stood up and walked to the window overlooking Decatur Street. "I see the car, but I don't see her."

"That's because I'm right here," a deep feminine voice drawled from the doorway. "I've been waiting in the lobby for the past five minutes."

We all turned, and I stared open-mouthed at the woman. Not because she'd startled me with her brash manner of speaking but because of her imposing appearance. She was sixty-ish and rail thin with skin as pale as the pearls around her neck. But her high cheekbones and prominent chin, not to mention her blood-red lips and fingernails, made it clear that she was anything but delicate.

"I'm sorry about the wait," Veronica said as she walked over to greet the woman. "We didn't hear you come in. I'm Veronica Maggio and—"

"Delta Dupré," she interrupted, extending her hand like she was expecting it to be kissed rather than shook.

Veronica took her hand and awkwardly shook-raised it up and down. "What can we do for you, Ms. Dupré?"

Delta cocked an eyebrow à la Cruella De Vil. "That's 'Mrs.' And the first thing you can do is have your boy take my coat."

"Uh, yes, Mrs.—I mean, uh, ma'am," a red-faced David stammered as he took her white floor-length fur and scurried away.

Delta frowned. "I hate to be cliché, but it's just so hard to find good help these days."

I was fuming at her rudeness. "Actually, David isn't our servant."

She turned and looked me up and down. "And you are?"

"Franki Amato."

"Interesting name," she said in a decidedly disinterested tone. Rather than extending her hand, as she had for Veronica, she began toying with a Gothic black cameo brooch that was pinned to the bodice of her red silk dress. It was framed in diamonds and depicted a skull in a top hat against a backdrop of guns and roses.

I glanced at Veronica and realized that she was oblivious to Delta's arrogance. Whenever jewelry was in the vicinity, she zoned out on her surroundings and zoomed in on the sparkly object.

"What an unusual brooch!" Veronica exclaimed. "Who is that supposed to be on the cameo?"

"It's Baron Samedi, a degenerate voodoo god who leads depraved souls to the underworld. I wear it because it reminds me of my late husband, Jackson Dupré."

Must have been some guy, I thought. *Much like his wife.*

Veronica cocked her head to one side. "That name sounds familiar. Was your husband in local politics?"

"He was the chief of police for twenty-five years. And now that I need him, the SOB isn't around. That's why I'm here."

"Please, have a seat," Veronica said, ignoring Delta's jab at her not-so-dearly departed. "I'm sure we can help you."

"I think you can too," Delta said, taking a seat in one of the two chairs facing Veronica's desk. "I saw that skinny old prostitute on the evening news a few months ago—the one who did all the interviews after you girls solved the murder of that shop girl?"

"Her name is Glenda, and she's an ex-stripper," I said as I reluctantly sat down beside her.

Delta waved her hand. "Prostitute...stripper... Same damn difference. Anyhow, I have an unusual case on my hands, so I need investigators who can think outside the box, unlike the ones currently employed by our police department. And since you two outsmarted the cops on the shop girl strangling, you're perfect for my predicament."

"Can you tell us more about your, uh, predicament?" I asked.

"I'm the executive director of Oleander Place, the antebellum plantation on River Road?" She looked at Veronica and me for signs of recognition.

I recognized it all right. It was the very plantation home that had distracted me and caused me to swerve into the swamp. "I just drove past it yesterday. You've got a really eye-catching place there."

"Yes, well, I'm afraid its beauty has been marred by a rather unfortunate incident," she said, fiddling with her brooch. "You see, three days ago, a twenty-eight-year-old woman named Ivanna Jones was murdered there. I found the body when I opened the plantation at eight o'clock the next morning."

"I heard something about that on the radio last night," Veronica said.

"Unfortunately, it's all over the news," Delta replied. "As you can imagine, the cancelations have already begun—weddings, craft fairs, even a TV show. And the problem is that Oleander Place isn't just my livelihood—it's my heritage. I'm a descendent of the original owner, General Knox Patterson. So, I'll do whatever it takes to protect my income and my family name."

I had no doubt she was telling the truth. She was no sweet Southern belle. She was a surly Southern beast. "Do you know how the victim got to the plantation?"

"She drove. Her car was in the parking lot, unlocked, with her purse on the front seat." Delta reached into her black Louis

Vuitton and pulled out a manila envelope. "This is a copy of the police report and photos from the scene."

I looked at her in surprise. "How did you get those?"

"Thanks to my Jackson, I still have important connections on the police force."

Veronica took the envelope and began to examine its contents. "This will be a tremendous help to us."

I turned to Delta. "Did you know the victim?"

"No, but she took one of our plantation tours a few weeks ago. I'm sure it was her, but I can't prove it because she didn't pay with a credit card or sign the guest registry."

"Was anyone with her?" I asked.

"I don't know. Our tour groups are often fairly large, and I wasn't really paying attention."

I looked at Veronica. "Anything interesting in the report?"

She scanned the information on the first page and then looked at Delta. "The cause of death is listed as 'undetermined.'"

"Which is why I need your help," Delta said. "The police are dilly-dallying around with this investigation because they think the woman committed suicide. And as a business owner, I don't have time to waste. Every day this crime goes unsolved is a day I lose money."

By now it was clear where Delta's priorities lay. This woman was a real steel magnolia. "What makes you think it wasn't suicide?"

"It has to do with the placement of the body and the plantation's history," she replied.

"Take a look," Veronica said, handing me a photo.

It was a shot of a beautiful young woman with long, golden-blonde hair and rose-red lips. If I didn't know better, I would have said she was asleep. "Wow," I breathed, "she looks just like Sleeping Beauty."

Delta shook her head. "No, she's the spitting image of Evangeline Lacour."

"Who's that?" I asked.

"She was Knox's second wife. He spent a fortune building Oleander Place for her, and then the tramp went and cheated on him. You know how those French women are," she said with a knowing look.

I couldn't resist asking, "Are you related to her, as well?"

"Certainly not!" Delta replied, her eyes wide with alarm. "I'm descended from Knox and his first wife, Caroline Landry. He and Evangeline had no children, thank heaven."

Veronica cleared her throat. "Why do you say the victim looks like Evangeline?"

"Well, for one thing, she's the spitting image of the oil painting Knox commissioned of Evangeline when they were married. And for another, she was found lying in Evangeline's bed in the exact same position Evangeline was in when she died in 1837, and she was wearing her pink crinoline dress."

I immediately thought of the woman I'd seen on the balcony of Oleander Place. But I knew that it couldn't have been Ivanna Jones, because she was killed the day before.

"You mean, the dress Evangeline was wearing when she died?" Veronica asked.

Delta nodded. "We have it in storage at Oleander Place. It's the one we always see Evangeline wearing when she appears."

Now *my* eyes opened wide in alarm. "Come again?"

"Evangeline's spirit still resides in the house," she replied.

I swallowed hard. "The plantation is haunted?"

Delta raised her chin and gave a smug smile. "As haunted as they come. Oleander Place ranks among America's top ten most haunted buildings."

To say that my mind was reeling would be putting it mildly. I simply couldn't process the possibility that I'd seen the ghost of

Evangeline Lacour on the balcony of Oleander Place yesterday. Surely it was one of the plantation tour guides, right? And then I thought of Chandra. Despite my better judgment, I wondered whether there was any connection between the spirit she'd claimed she was talking to and Evangeline. Or was it just one big transcendental coincidence that two people had approached me about incidents involving spirits on the same day? Either way, I was starting to get the distinctly ominous feeling that the inhabitants of the netherworld—or their earthly representatives—were trying to tell me something. And I didn't like it. Not one bit.

4

———

I cocked my head to the side. "When you say 'as haunted as they come,' what do you mean, exactly?"

"What do you think I mean?" Delta snapped. "I mean we have a lot of ghosts floating around Oleander Place."

"Whoa!" David exclaimed—from a safe distance in the hallway.

"You can say that again," I muttered. I was starting to feel like I was in a speeding "doom buggy" on Disneyland's Haunted Mansion ride, and I wanted it to slow the hell down.

"Besides Evangeline," Delta continued, "Knox and Beauregard are the main spirits on the plantation."

"Who's Beauregard?" Veronica asked as she began typing notes.

"He's Knox's brother, and he was a decorated army colonel," Delta said with pride. "But then when Knox made general before him, he turned pirate."

"Pirate?" I squirmed in my seat. Of course, I'd never met a pirate, alive or dead. But if I were a betting girl, I'd wager that a pirate ghost was not the friendliest of souls.

"They called him 'Beau the Black,' and he was notorious for

his ruthlessness." Delta touched her pearls, and the corners of her mouth turned upward into a Joker-like smile. "I'm assuming you girls have heard of him?"

I looked questioningly at Veronica.

"I'm sure he's very infamous," she began politely, "but I'm afraid we're not well versed in pirate lore."

Delta frowned. "He was one of the pirate Jean Lafitte's right-hand men. In fact, Beau and Lafitte helped General Andrew Jackson defeat the British at the Battle of New Orleans. You *have* heard of Lafitte, I presume?"

"Oh, sure," I replied as I grabbed the stack of photos from Veronica's desk. "When I went to that bar 'Jean Lafitte's Black-smith Shop' in the French Quarter a month or so ago. And if he was anything like that purple voodoo drink they serve there, then he must have been a real swashbuckler."

The room fell silent. I looked up from the pictures and saw both Delta and Veronica staring at me. I felt my face flush, probably similar in color to that drink. "So...how was Evangeline killed?"

Delta raised her brow. "She was poisoned."

Veronica's fingers began flying over her keyboard. "How do you know? Are there any records?"

"Yes, the *Times-Picayune* reported on her death. And we also have Knox's journal in our plantation archives. Both sources indicate that Evangeline was found with an oleander flower in her hands. At first, everyone thought it was because she loved oleanders. It was well known at the time that she was the one who had them planted on the grounds." She looked hard at Veronica. "And for the record, she just insisted on that coral pink. Had it been me, I would have selected a less vulgar shade."

Veronica nodded. She'd always turned up her nose at coral jewelry because she didn't approve of orange in her pink.

"But then they discovered oleander in a half-empty cup of

tea on the table beside Evangeline's bed." Delta paused and curled her lips. "As far as I'm concerned, that flower was a message that Evangeline was as toxic as the oleander plant."

Talk about the pot calling the kettle black, I thought as I flipped through the pictures.

"Who did they think poisoned her?" Veronica asked.

Delta exhaled deeply. "Knox blamed Antoinette, the house slave who'd served her the tea, and the police agreed. Of course, she fled the plantation, and the case was closed. Nevertheless, a rumor persisted that Knox had done it."

I looked up at Delta. "Why would anyone suspect Knox?"

"Because the day before the French tart was killed, he found out that she was planning to run off with his brother," she explained with a pointed look. "Apparently, he came across a letter she was writing to Beau that detailed their sordid affair. And everyone knew about it, too, because Knox woke the whole plantation that night."

"What for?" I asked.

Delta snorted. "He was tearing the place apart looking for a pink diamond Beau had given Evangeline."

Veronica leaned forward, her eyes sparkling like a precious gem. "There was a pink diamond?"

"Yes. In the letter Evangeline mentions an emerald-cut diamond that Beau had secretly given her as a promise of his intent to marry her. Like her beloved oleanders, it was that tacky coral pink," she said with a dramatic eye roll. "He told her he would come for her as soon as he'd made enough money from smuggling to buy some land and build her a house."

Veronica sighed. "That's so romantic!"

Delta threw her head back and gave a raucous laugh, revealing a row of yellow teeth that clashed with her alabaster skin. "Foolish, if anything. But men are blind when it comes to a beautiful woman."

I instantly thought of Bradley and Pauline and grudgingly found myself agreeing with her. "What ever happened to the diamond?"

"No one knows," Delta replied. "The only record we have of it is what Evangeline wrote in the letter. She said that she would sit on the balcony holding the stone in her hand while she waited for Beau's ship to come down river. And that's where we usually see her, on the balcony."

I shuddered. *Was that what I had seen? The spirit of Evangeline waiting for her buccaneer beau, Beau?*

"What happened to Knox and Beau after Evangeline's death?" Veronica asked as she resumed typing.

Delta picked a white hair off her blouse. "Knox died in 1838, presumably of a broken heart." She straightened in her chair and raised her chin. "But Beau died valiantly in 1862 in the capture of New Orleans, trying to defend our beloved city from those dreadful Union forces during the Civil War."

I got the distinct feeling that Delta was prouder of the pirate than the general.

"Today, Beau's spirit roams the grounds of Oleander Place looking for Evangeline—Knox had the trollop buried in an unmarked grave, naturally. And Knox storms the halls looking for Beau."

Great. A ruthless pirate and *an angry general,* I thought as I studied a photograph of Ivanna's body. *Can't wait.*

"Do you know where Evangeline was buried?" Veronica asked.

"I don't, nor do I care to," she replied, crossing her arms.

The more I looked at Ivanna's body, the more something seemed off about the picture. And then it hit me. "You said that Ivanna was found in the exact same position as Evangeline, but I don't see an oleander flower."

Delta clutched her creepy cameo. "Oh yes. That's because she was holding a bottle of lip gloss."

Veronica began turning the pages of the police report. "That's mentioned here, but it says the bottle was unmarked. Do you know who made it?"

She shrugged. "Who knows?"

"Wait a second," Veronica said, returning to the first page. "The report has a business listed as Ivanna's personal address. Lickalicious Lips. I wonder if it was one of their brands."

I sat up straight in my chair. "Hey! They make that flavored lip gloss I used to wear in college, remember? The one I had to stop buying because I couldn't stop licking my lips?"

"Yeah." Veronica grinned. "That was the semester you sprained your tongue on Baileys Irish Cream Brown."

Delta curled her lips in disgust. "The victim made liquor-flavored lip gloss? No wonder someone up and killed her."

Veronica and I exchanged a look.

"Anyway," Delta continued, "that lip gloss is one of the things that makes me think this wasn't a suicide. If this Ivanna woman was just some nutcase who wanted to recreate Evangeline's deathbed look, then why in the world would she be holding a bottle of lip gloss instead of an oleander flower?""

I held up the picture of Ivanna. "Did the bottle match the shade of red she was wearing?"

"No, it was coral pink. Just like her dress."

I bit my lip. "That's odd."

"Indeed," Delta conceded.

"What about the cup of tea?" Veronica asked.

"There was no tea. But since there was no obvious cause of death, the coroner's office is testing for poison among other things."

Veronica flipped through the police report. "I don't see any interrogation records. Have the police questioned your employees?"

"They haven't bothered because they think it was suicide and because the plantation was closed at the time of death. But that's another thing that makes me think this was a murder. We have an alarm system at the plantation, and it was on the night this happened. Yet this woman got inside without setting it off."

I had to agree with Delta. Unless Ivanna had somehow managed to get a key to the plantation and the code to the alarm, then someone had let her in.

"Has anyone from Ivanna's family contacted you?" Veronica asked.

"Not so far. I don't even think the police have talked to them yet. From what I understand, her father is overseas."

"We'll need to talk to your employees," Veronica said. "When would be a good time for us to come to Oleander Place?"

"It'll have to be tomorrow." She glanced at a diamond-encrusted silver watch. "In about an hour we have to start setting up for a dinner. Fortunately, the charity hosting the event didn't cancel on us, but they did demand a discount, the cheap bastards. Anyhow, it's getting late, so I'd best be on my way."

As if on cue, David popped around the doorjamb with her fur coat.

She scowled at him as she rose to her feet and snatched the coat from his hand.

Seeing Delta's fur reminded me of something we'd forgotten to ask. "Wait. I have one more question."

"Make it quick," she snapped as she slipped on her coat.

"Did you find Ivanna's clothes at the scene?"

She blinked. "No, just her purse. Like I told you before."

"Thanks," I said, puzzled. That implied that Ivanna had arrived at Oleander Place already wearing the dress, which raised a lot more questions than it answered.

"Now, you girls can come to the plantation at one o'clock tomorrow," she said. Then she narrowed her eyes and pointed a bony finger at Veronica and me. "But come alone. And don't even *think* about talking to the press."

I watched in a mixture of awe and fear as she spun on her heels and exited the room, her fur flying behind her. The second I heard the lobby door slam shut I turned to David. "So, those dogs you saw in Delta's car...they weren't Dalmatians, were they?"

I TUGGED at the handle of my front door to make sure it was locked and then headed across the street to Thibodeaux's Tavern. As I walked, I averted my gaze to avoid seeing the spooky cemetery that was next to the bar. It might sound childish, but living by tombs, sarcophagi, obelisks, and gothic statues didn't exactly raise your spirits. In fact, some days it damn near drove me to drink. But for reasons I simply couldn't fathom, Veronica had no problem with it, which is why she arranged for me to live next door to her in Glenda's fourplex. If I'd known about the burial ground before I'd signed the lease, I would have told her to go straight to hell.

The sounds of Amy Winehouse's "Rehab" greeted me as I arrived at the bar and pulled open the heavy wooden door. Once inside, I scanned the dimly lit room for Veronica, but there was no sign of her. It was ten after six, and we'd agreed to meet at six o'clock for dinner. Unlike me, Veronica made it a habit to show up at least fifteen minutes early to an appointment. But for the past week or so, she'd been showing up late, and I was starting to wonder why.

"What can I get you, Franki?" the bartender, Phillip, asked in a monotone voice as he ran a wet dishrag over the stainless steel bar.

I slid onto a bar stool and placed my Gucci knockoff bag on the counter. "How about an Italian margarita?"

He nodded and reached across several rows of bottles for the Amaretto.

I studied his face as he poured the amber liqueur into a shaker. Veronica said he resembled a young Kurt Cobain, probably because he was in a grunge rock band, albeit an environmentally conscious one. But I thought he looked and sounded exactly like the stoner Jeff Spicoli in *Fast Times at Ridgemont High*.

"How's your music coming along?" I asked, tapping my knuckles on the bar to the beat.

Phillip shook his stringy dishwater blond bangs out of his eyes. "Aw, I quit Saving Pumpkins. Making it in the industry these days is such a long shot, man. I decided it was time to focus on something more secure."

"Smart move," I said, impressed. "What are you working on now?"

"My skateboarding career," he replied, wiping his nose on his sleeve. "I think it's finally gonna be an Olympic sport."

I stopped tapping. "Yeah, the Olympics are always a good fallback plan," I replied. But the irony was lost on him.

Philip handed me the margarita just as Veronica rushed into the bar.

"Sorry I'm late," she said, slipping her powder blue Prada bag off her shoulder. "How'd the research go today?"

"Well, I spent some time online going over the media accounts and some articles on the history of the plantation. I didn't find anything we don't already know, but I'm starting to think this case has something to do with obsession."

Veronica took a seat and grabbed the drink menu. "Why do you say that?"

"When I was at the police academy, we studied something called Obsessive Love Disorder. People who have it usually start out by idealizing someone. But then they feel jealousy and resentment when the object of their affection can't live up to their unrealistic expectations. That's when their so-called love can turn violent."

"Okay, but I don't see the connection between this disorder and Ivanna's death."

"Think about the way her body was neatly laid out on that bed. If she swallowed a bunch of sleeping pills, I think her arm or her head or something would have shifted. But instead it's like someone carefully arranged her hair, her dress, even her hands to make her look as beautiful as possible. Someone who put her on a pedestal."

"Or someone who wanted to make her look like Evangeline."

"Could be," I said, stirring my drink. "But why?"

"I don't know. That's what you're going to have to find out."

I froze in mid-stir. "Wait. *Me?*"

She smiled. "Yeah, I've decided to make you the lead on the case."

I stared at her, stunned. Veronica was so type A that even her blood type was A, so it was shocking to say the least that she was assigning me the case when I was still new to the company.

"I'm going to help you, of course," she continued. "But, I think you're ready. Plus, we've gotten busier, so I'm going to have to handle some of our smaller cases."

Phillip slid a bar napkin in front of Veronica. "What'll it be, Ronnie?"

She looked at the drink list. "Hm. One of the Italian sparkling wines..."

While Veronica pondered the Proseccos, I pondered my

promotion. It just didn't make sense that she was turning down the lead on a case that involved a legendary diamond, and a pink one at that. If there was such a thing as Obsessive Love Disorder for diamonds, then Veronica had it. Her favorite song was "Diamonds are a Girl's Best Friend," and one of the last vacations she took was to Crater of Diamonds State Park in Arkansas to dig for the dazzling gems.

"I'll have a glass of the Riondo, please."

Phillip nodded and turned to get her drink.

I took a long sip of my margarita. "Hey, so, is there anything you want to tell me?"

She twisted a lock of hair around her finger. "Why would you ask?"

"Because you've been really distracted lately. And because you've decided to let me handle a case that potentially involves a pink diamond."

"What's this about a pink diamond?" Glenda asked from behind me.

I turned to reply but stopped short. I wasn't prepared to find her wearing an ensemble that vaguely resembled exercise attire. Nor was I ready to discover that her red shorts were so short they were practically panties. Ignoring her question, I asked, "Have you started exercising?"

"Hell no, child," she said with a red cigarette holder between her teeth as she unzipped a sporty red hoodie—cropped directly beneath the breasts—to reveal a matching jog bra that was more like a sweatband. "I'm teaching a boot camp for strippers."

"How fun!" Veronica said, clapping her hands together. "I want to Strippercise."

Glenda placed the cigarette holder on the bar beside Veronica. "This is no strip aerobics class, Miss Ronnie. My old manager down at Madame Moiselle's on Bourbon Street asked me to whip some of his girls into shape. And it's a good thing he did, because I never saw a sadder bunch of strippers. Today one of the sorry fools went and slathered herself with lotion right before pole practice. So, when she cartwheeled into an upside down leg hold, she slid right down the pole and popped a damn breast implant on the stage."

I crossed my arms over my chest even though my boobs were real and, I sincerely hoped, unpoppable.

Phillip placed the Prosecco in front of Veronica and turned to Glenda, keeping his eyes downcast. "What would you like, Miss Glenda?"

"A tall drink of water," she replied with a sultry wink.

A shade of red that matched Glenda's jog bra spread from his cheeks down to his neck.

Glenda leaned over the counter and looked at me. "Now tell me about this diamond."

"We've been contracted to investigate a suspicious death at Oleander Place," I replied.

"So you girls are talking about the Lacour diamond," Glenda said.

"How'd you know that?" I asked, surprised. Although I shouldn't have been. Where local legends were concerned, Glenda was a walking encyclopedia, probably because she was one herself. In the sixties and seventies, under the stage name Lorraine Lamour, she'd stripped for the biggest names in politics, show business, and organized crime.

"I make it my business to know about jewelry, sugar. And I'm sure the same was true for that woman they found at that plantation."

Veronica took a sip of her Prosecco. "What do you mean?"

"I mean I'll guaran-damn-tee you that pink diamond is why she was there. Diamonds are to women what hookers are to men."

I took a swig of my margarita. Glenda's analogies, while impressive, always left me speechless.

"What woman can resist a pink diamond?" she continued. Then she licked her lips with gusto. "And especially one from a lusty pirate."

I wrinkled my nose. Whenever I thought of pirates, *lusty* was not a word that came to mind. *Crusty,* yes.

"Like that pirate on TV," Glenda said.

"You mean, Captain Feathersword from The Wiggles?" I asked.

Glenda batted her red eyelashes. "What in heaven would I do with a pirate whose sword is made of a feather, sugar?"

"I think she means Captain Jack Sparrow," Veronica explained.

Glenda looked at Veronica. "Is he the one who wears the sexy black guyliner?"

She nodded.

"Well, he can shiver me timbers any day of the week," she said with a flip of her long platinum Cher hair. "Ooh, now I have a hankering for a pirate something awful." Balancing the six-inch heels of her stripper-style tennis shoes on the rungs of her bar stool, she rose up and waved her arm at Phillip. "Bring me a Salty Dog, sugar."

Phillip went from red around the collar to green in the gills.

"Speaking of manly marauders," Glenda said, "isn't that your banker beau, Miss Franki?"

I followed her gaze out the window and saw Bradley walking toward Thibodeaux's. My stomach did a little flip, not because I was happy to see him, but because I could see the frown on his face from inside the bar. "I'd better go talk to him."

"Need any help, Miss Franki?" Glenda asked with a tinge of hopefulness in her voice.

I shot her a look. Then I downed the rest of my drink and pulled my wallet from my purse.

Veronica put her hand on mine. "I've got this. You go."

"Thanks," I said as I rushed outside.

"Hi," Bradley said coolly as the tavern door closed behind me.

I flashed him a smile. "I wasn't expecting you."

He put his hands into his pockets. "I thought I'd swing by on my way to the airport."

I blinked. "You're going out of town?"

"Yes."

I gathered from his curt one-word reply that it was time to apologize. "Listen, I can understand why you're mad and—"

"Can you?" he interrupted. "First you follow me, then you almost get yourself and me killed. And all because I was going to a meeting with my assistant."

"Well, in my defense, the location of that meeting was a little suspect."

"The place isn't the point, Franki."

"Actually, I think it is," I huffed. "What was I supposed to think when you took Pauline to a bed and breakfast?"

"You were supposed to think exactly what I told you—that it was a business meeting," he said, throwing his hands into the air. "Franki, Pauline is my assistant, and she's a damn good one. She worked on Wall Street. Now, there's a lot riding on these meetings, including my job. So I can't have the two of you at each other's throats. I need you to find some way to tolerate her."

I looked at the ground and desperately tried to think of something nice to say about Pauline—for Bradley's sake, not hers. I managed to choke out, "Well, she did do me one favor."

His face softened. "What's that?"

"She told you I dropped by the bank this morning."

Bradley stared at me blankly.

I felt tension rising in my chest. "Pauline did tell you I came by, right?"

He looked away. "She must have forgotten."

My hands balled into fists, one finger at a time. "Oh, I'm sure that's what happened," I said in a convincing tone. But I thought it in a sarcastic one.

"Anyway," Bradley said, glancing at his watch. "I'd better get going. I'll be out of reach off and on. But if you need me, call Pauline. You know her number."

He bent down and gave me a quick and completely unsatisfying peck on the cheek before crossing the street and climbing into his car.

Oh, I've got her number all right, I thought as I watched him drive away. *And before long, she'll have mine.* I was going to prove to Bradley that Pauline was a snake if it was the last thing I did.

5

———

At ten a.m. the next morning, I strode through the French Quarter filled with a new resolve to get a handle on the out-of-control events of the past few days, starting with the out-of-this-world experiences. My first order of business was to question Chandra about the suspicious spiritual goings-on before Veronica and I went to Oleander Place to begin our investigation of Ivanna Jones' death. My second and most immediate objective was to navigate Bourbon Street, where Chandra's office was located, without incident.

As I turned onto the famous party street, I buried my nose in my scarf to escape the unpleasant odors produced by the bacchanalia of the previous night. I also made it a point to walk down the middle of Bourbon despite the crunch of Mardi Gras beads and broken plastic drink cups beneath my feet. That way I was able to dodge the restaurant, bar, strip club, and souvenir shop employees who were spraying the sidewalks and surrounding street with much-needed disinfectant as well as the lingerie- and bikini-clad strippers and waitresses who were already stationed outside their respective establishments selling sex and neon-colored test-tube drinks.

After I'd walked a couple of blocks, I began scanning the addresses of the balcony-lined, two-story structures until I spotted the one listed on Chandra's business card—626 Bourbon Street. It was a cute little building painted terra cotta with a large, white-trimmed twelve-pane window. There were bright red steps with black wrought-iron railings leading to a small covered porch, and fronds of potted ferns hung charmingly from the balcony above.

I bounded up the steps and pushed open the glass door to my left. As I entered, I was greeted by a wall of T-shirts, boas, shot glasses, voodoo dolls, and countless other New Orleans souvenirs. I thought I had the wrong address.

"Can I help you?" a male voice asked.

I turned and saw a forty-something-year-old with a tremendous Afro and a goatee hanging a hand-painted Mardi Gras mask on the wall behind the cash register. Based on the sheer height of his hair, I had a feeling he was Chandra's colleague. "I'm looking for the Crescent City Medium."

"In the back," he said, gesturing with his head.

I nodded and set off for the rear of the shotgun-style shop, wondering whether the "Just Deux It" T-shirt he was wearing was available in the store.

I arrived at two doors, one of which said *Restroom* and the other *Cartomancy and Crystallomancy.* Although I had no idea what the latter terms meant, I didn't have to be a private investigator to know they had something to do with the paranormal.

"Come in, Franki," Chandra's sugary voice called from inside —before I knocked.

She probably heard me talking to the cashier, I rationalized as I entered the closet-sized room.

Apart from a crystal ball, nothing in Chandra's office was what I'd expected. The walls were bare and painted a dull ivory color, and the furniture consisted of an ordinary gray card table and three folding chairs. Instead of patchouli, the aura of Chanel weighed heavily in the air, thanks to Chandra's Chanel No. 5 perfume and her suitcase-sized handbag.

"I haven't had time to decorate," Chandra announced from her seat behind the table. She was wearing the occult version of the ugly Christmas sweater. It had all the planets of the solar system in brightly colored sequins. In place of the stereotypical psychic turban, she had her huge hairdo.

"That's cool," I said, really wishing she'd stop reading my mind and anticipating my presence.

"How can I be of service?"

Wish granted, I thought with relief. "It's about that spirit you were talking to yesterday. Can you tell me her name?"

"I have no earthly idea."

I cast her a blank stare. "Do you have a heavenly idea?"

She shook her head, causing her moon and star earrings to swing like pendulums. "People who've crossed over don't always identify themselves. Besides, I'm not good with names, and it's hard work keeping up with all these spirits."

"Right." The more I talked to Chandra, the more surprised I was that she actually managed to earn money as a medium. "Is there any chance the woman was an older spirit, like from the early 1800s?"

She cocked an eyebrow. "Do you really think that a female spirit who doesn't want to tell me her name would reveal her *age*?"

I sighed. These spirits were driving me crazy with their vanity. "How about this," I said, folding my arms on the table. "Could you look in your crystal ball there and tell me if you see a female spirit at the Oleander Place plantation on River Road?"

"That's going to cost you twenty dollars." She placed her hands in her lap and looked at me expectantly.

"Fine," I muttered, as I pulled a twenty from my wallet.

In a move reminiscent of Glenda, Chandra took the money and shoved it down the neck of her sweater into her ample bra. Then she began waving her plump hands over the ball. As she moved, her charm bracelet jingled so loudly that it sounded like a wind chime.

"Well?" I asked, after several minutes had passed.

"I see a woman."

"Interesting," I said, thinking that I could *so* do her job for a living. "What's she doing?"

"She's pulling at the handle of a French door."

"I guess she wants out," I theorized. "What does she look like?"

Chandra squinted and leaned closer to the crystal ball. "She's blonde."

I rolled my eyes. I'd heard that psychics conned their customers by speaking in vague generalities, but this was ridiculous.

"Oh, and she's wearing a pink crinoline dress," Chandra continued.

I sat up straight in my chair. That was no generic detail. "What else can you tell me?"

"Nothing. Everything went black."

"Would it help if I took you to the plantation?" I offered. "I'm going out there in a couple of hours."

She frowned and leaned back in her chair. "I don't do onsite readings. I told you before, ghosts scare me."

I put my head down for a moment, and then I looked her straight in the eyes. "No offense or anything, but you need to get over your fear of ghosts if you're going to work in this profession."

She jerked her head backward an inch. "I've done very well for myself, thank you."

"Okay, but will you please think about it? This is really

important. I've been assigned a case at Oleander Place, and it's looking like it involves a murder."

Chandra gasped as she drew her paddle-shaped fingernails to her mouth. "Murder? Oh, no. I couldn't!"

The spiritual angle was looking like a dead end. But since she'd hit on the color of Evangeline's dress, I did have one more pressing question for her. "Just for curiosity's sake, could you look into your crystal ball and tell me what my boyfriend Bradley's new secretary is up to?"

"You need a tarot card reading for that," she explained, folding her hands back into her lap. "That's an extra twenty bucks."

"Of course," I grumbled, reaching back into my nearly empty wallet. I handed her the cash.

She stuffed the money into her bra and then handed me the cards. "Shuffle and cut the deck."

I followed her instructions and then watched as she laid out three cards. I felt instant anxiety when I noticed that one of them was upside down. "What does that card mean?"

Chandra's lips tightened into a thin line. "It's the Three of Cups. As the middle card, it represents your present. When it's upright it means that friendships and relationships with loved ones are in harmony. But when it's reversed, it usually indicates that you've had a falling out with your friends or that there's a third person in your relationship."

Everything was fine with Veronica, so that could only mean one thing. Pauline was trying to turn my circle of love with Bradley into a love triangle. *I knew it!* I jumped up and threw my hobo bag over my right shoulder.

Chandra looked up at me with wide eyes. "Don't you want me to read the other two cards? They're your past and future."

"Uh-uh. I definitely don't want to revisit my past, and I

already know that I'm woefully unprepared for the future." I turned and opened the door. "I'll be in touch."

I left Chandra's office feeling a weight in the pit of my stomach. It was one thing to suspect Pauline of trying to steal my boyfriend, but it was quite another to have my worst fear confirmed, even if it was by a pseudo psychic.

As I rushed past the merchandise, I bumped into the cashier, who was on his knees putting black and gold "Geaux Saints!" scarves onto a low-hanging rack.

"Hey, now," he said. "Watch where you're goin'."

I turned and read his nametag. "Sorry, Xavier. I just got some surprising news during my reading, and I was trying to figure out what to do about it."

He rose to his feet and began to break down the empty scarf box. "Well, whatever you decide, remember one thang. This ain't Disneyland, this is Noo Awlins. And it's a war zone out there."

"I'll keep that in mind." I pushed open the door and headed out onto Bourbon Street, steeling myself for the battle to come.

"You still haven't told me what you found out from the Psychic Friends Network," Veronica said as she steered her Audi onto River Road.

I snorted. "You know, Chandra's not part of any clairvoyant company. She's just an ordinary woman working from an office."

"Precisely. You remember that before you get all worked up about something she says."

"It's not like I'm buying in to this whole psychic thing,'" I said, scratching my nose and visualizing Pinocchio. "But I *am* paying attention to the fact that she knows things about me and this case."

"Okay, but this is the information age," Veronica said with a pointed look. "She can go online and find out pretty much anything she wants to know, starting by looking at your meticulously maintained Facebook page."

My text message tone chimed.

Saved by the bell, I thought as I reached into my bag for my phone. When I read the display, I got a fluttery feeling in my chest.

Back in town tomorrow. Dinner at 7? Missing you, Bradley.

I smiled. Maybe I'd overreacted to my tarot card reading just a smidge. After all, Bradley *did* tell me in no uncertain terms that Pauline was just his secretary. And one person didn't make a love triangle, right? I texted him an enthusiastic "It's a date!" and tossed the phone into my bag. "Speaking of information, do we have background checks on the Oleander Place employees?"

"David finished them late yesterday. Everyone was clean except for one of the tour guides, Scarlett Heinz. Last year she was charged with assaulting a woman."

"I wonder if it was because the woman teased her about her name," I said. "I mean, it's essentially 'Red Ketchup.'"

Veronica shot me a look. "I seriously doubt it."

I looked out the passenger window and mused, "So Miss Scarlett has a colored past..."

"If you're thinking about moving on to Clue jokes, don't," Veronica said, leaning menacingly toward me.

I moved closer to the passenger door, just to be safe. "Did you have David run a check on Delta too?"

"Yeah. Nothing."

"So, assuming Ivanna was murdered, do you think there's any chance that Delta's involved? She seems kind of proud of the fact that her plantation has a murderous history."

Veronica shook her head. "When your business is weddings, charity dinners, and craft fairs, you don't want this kind of publicity. You heard Delta say that the media coverage is costing her clients, and she practically threatened us if we went to the press."

"True," I said, again glancing out the window. We were approaching Oleander Place, and the view was spectacular. Oleander bushes dotted the grounds like pink flamingos, and there were two rows of centuries-old Southern live oak trees that dutifully lined the walkway leading to the plantation like soldiers standing at attention. Now that I was focusing on the house instead of the back of Bradley's BMW, I realized that it was painted the palest shade of pink, as was the colonnade that wrapped around the three-story home. I shifted my gaze uneasily to the balcony, and to my relief there was no sign of Evangeline.

Veronica pulled into a long driveway and parked in a lot in the back of the house that was conveniently located next to a ticket booth. Directly in front of the parking lot were the slaves' quarters and a gift shop with a restaurant. Beyond the gift shop were two old sugar mills and the sugar cane fields.

"Any special instructions, *capo*?" Veronica asked.

I got a little thrill from being called "boss," but I acted casual. "Yeah, look for any evidence that Ivanna's death was actually a murder."

"On it."

As I stepped out of the car, I saw Delta and an older Southern gentleman in a seersucker suit standing on the back porch beside a magnolia tree. I felt like I was on the set of the *Murder, She Wrote* episode where Seth Hazlitt's plantation-owner cousin is battling a perfume company over the scent of the flowers from his secret magnolia tree. But I was quickly reminded that Delta was no Jessica Fletcher when I saw her shake her fist at the man, who cowered and held up his straw hat like a shield.

"You leave this property at once, Floyd Buford!" she shouted. "I don't want to see your face around here again."

"I'm sorry you feel that way, Delta," he said with a slight warble in his voice. He placed his hat on his head. "But if that's what you want, then good-day."

Veronica and I ambled toward the porch as Delta watched the man hurry away.

"Is everything okay?" I asked.

"That was the president of the Antebellum Plantation Historical and Preservation Society," Delta replied. "He just canceled a luncheon they'd scheduled here for next week."

"I'm sorry," Veronica said.

"I'm not," she snapped. "Believe you me, it's no picnic catering to a bunch of snobbish geriatrics with digestive issues."

Veronica and I exchanged a look.

Delta turned and opened the door. "You girls come on in. I'll show you around."

"I'd love to," Veronica said as we entered a wide hallway with gleaming hardwood floors.

I was less enthusiastic about seeing the house. It was beautiful, but the tarnished history of plantation homes—specifically the fact that they were operated on slave labor—made me uncomfortable.

"This place is gorgeous!" Veronica exclaimed.

Delta stopped and turned to face her. "It is *now*. Knox designed the home in the Greek Revival style to make that nitwit Evangeline happy. But thankfully one of his descendants had the good sense to strip the house of the garish cornices, crown moldings, and ceiling medallions to bring it in line with the Federal style."

"What happened to those things?" I asked.

"They're stored in the little mill," she said with a dismissive wave of her hand. "Now, my office is here on the left. And on the right is the kitchen, which used to be the house-slaves' quarters. The original kitchen was located in a separate building to keep the odors and the heat to a minimum."

I nodded and followed Delta to the front of the house.

"This is the parlor," she said, gesturing to the left. "And across the hall is the dining room."

Veronica and I peered into the parlor, which was protected by a cordon. A gold-plated crystal chandelier, a large gilt mirror, and several bronze candelabra gave the room a sumptuous look. In front of the fireplace was a courting area with Empire-period seating covered in blue velvet. Above the black marble mantel was an enormous oil painting of a beautiful blonde woman with delicate features. She was dressed in coral pink and painted against a dark background of bluish black.

"Is that Evangeline?" Veronica asked, as though reading my mind.

"Yes," Delta said drily, clutching her pearls.

"She was lovely," I enthused. "Like a real-life Disney princess."

Delta scowled. "I'll take you up to her room."

We climbed a tall wooden staircase to the second floor.

"On either side of the hallway are the guest bedrooms," Delta said, "and the children's bedroom is in the middle. In keeping with the custom of the era, Evangeline and Knox had separate bedrooms in the front of the house." She turned to Veronica and me. "I don't know why we ever did away with that tradition."

I flashed a wry smile at Veronica as we followed Delta the length of the hallway to the master bedrooms.

"Those French doors lead to the front balcony," she explained, pulling a set of keys from her pocket. She unlocked the door to the left. "And this is Evangeline's bedroom, otherwise known as 'the pink room.'"

Veronica, a connoisseur of pink décor, gasped and covered her mouth with her hand. "It's pink perfection."

I had to agree that it was a beautiful room, but I'd always been partial to purple. "Can we go past the cordon?"

Delta raised an eyebrow. "Just don't touch anything."

I smirked and entered the spacious bedroom with Veronica in tow. On the right was a seating area with a pink armchair and matching chaise lounge. Between the windows was an imposing armoire with decorative wood inlay and a white marble bust on the top. But the most impressive piece of furniture in the room was a canopied bed covered with pink pillows and draped in sheer pink netting.

"Is this the original furniture?" Veronica asked.

Delta nodded. "Evangeline died in that bed."

"It's awfully small," I remarked. It reminded me of the dainty Princess furniture Veronica used to have before she redecorated her apartment like Elvis Presley's Jungle Room at Graceland.

"People were smaller back then," Delta said, eyeing my 5' 10" frame with evident disapproval.

I made a point of turning my back to her and began inspecting the area to the right of the bed, next to the windows, while Veronica searched the area to the left. On a white marble–covered night table beside the bed sat a stunning bronze snuff box adorned with a picture of Marie Antoinette.

"Is this box an original too?" I asked.

"Yes, it's from France. So is the trio of perfume bottles."

I looked at the delicate pink glass bottles with gold filigree. "I only see two."

Delta frowned and rushed to my side. "I don't understand," she muttered. "Where's the other bottle?"

"Could someone have moved it?" Veronica asked.

"That's impossible. I have the only key to this room, and no one has been allowed in here since the body was found." She knelt and looked under the bed.

I stared at the night table, deep in thought. "Are you sure the bottle was here that night?"

Delta stood up and brushed some dust off her navy blue dress. "I think so."

"Hold on," Veronica said, reaching into her beige and leopard-print Furla tote. "I have the police photos with me. There's one of the nightstand, remember?"

"That's right!" I said.

Veronica began flipping through the pictures with Delta looking on.

Meanwhile, I glanced beneath the table but didn't see anything. Then I pulled back one of the heavy, pink silk damask drapes and noticed a two-inch tear in the white sheer curtain underneath.

"It's not in the picture," Veronica said. "There are only two bottles on the nightstand."

"Wait a second!" Delta said, snapping her fingers. "That bottle was here on the day of the murder. I know it for a fact."

"How?" I asked.

"Because a French antique dealer on the same tour as Miss Jones made a comment about the trio. He said he'd never seen the full set intact."

I chewed my lip. I was starting to think there was a connection between Ivanna's death and the missing perfume bottle. "What about this?" I asked, pulling aside the drape to reveal the tear in the sheer curtain. "Did you know it was torn?"

"No, I didn't," Delta replied, her eyes smoldering with anger.

I stepped aside as she stomped up to the drapes and jerked them away from the window, causing a small object to propel across the floor.

Veronica bent down and retrieved the item. "It's a piece of pink glass!"

"That's part of the perfume bottle," Delta said, her pale skin blanching as white as the curtain.

"Was the room cleaned after the tour?" Veronica asked.

"No, the cleaning crew came the morning after I found the body, but the police had me send them away." Delta lowered her head. "I suppose it's possible that a member of my staff could have broken it, but I don't know what reason they would have had to go into the room after a tour, and especially to go behind the cordon."

I thought about the torn curtain and the broken bottle, and in my mind they added up to one thing. "I don't think that's what happened," I said. "There was a struggle in this room the night Ivanna Jones died, which means that your hunch about this being a murder is probably right."

6

———————

Delta crossed her arms and curled her lips. "Of course I'm right. Like I told you, that girl was murdered in this house. The only thing you two need to worry about is finding out who did it."

"We're just covering our bases," Veronica explained.

"This isn't a damn baseball game," she snapped. "This is my business, and I'm paying you to find the killer. No more no less."

I narrowed my eyes and opened my mouth to reply, but Veronica silenced me with a shut-it look.

"And you'll do it soon," Delta added. "I'm losing money by the minute thanks to this disaster."

I'd had enough of Delta and her demanding demeanor. Mentally repeating *the customer is always right* with the intensity of Dorothy when she was trying to will herself and Toto back to Kansas, I exited the room and opened one of the French doors to take in some desperately needed fresh air. As I stepped onto the balcony, I saw an old rocking chair to my right. I took a seat and let my gaze follow the striking tree-lined walkway straight to the waters of the mighty Mississippi River. I wondered how many times Evangeline had done the same as she held her pink diamond and waited for Beau.

The door flung open giving me a start, and Delta popped her head around the side. "Sorry to intrude on your quiet time, but we have a tour starting in half an hour. So, if you're going to question my tour guide, you'd better get started."

I bit my lip to keep from saying something I would only partially regret and rose from my chair. Once inside, I glanced at the narrow flight of stairs leading to the third floor. "What's upstairs?"

"Storage. It was a walk-in attic even when the plantation was functional. Now it houses our document archives as well as some antique furniture and vintage clothes."

I was about to ask whether I had time to take a quick peek when we heard a dull thud followed by a woman's scream. It sounded like it had come from the end of the hall.

"What in the *hell*?" Delta exclaimed as she rushed toward one of the guest bedrooms.

I followed her with Veronica hot on my heels. When I entered the room, I saw a petite young woman in a waist-pinching corset and an old-fashioned white petticoat. She was kneeling and examining a large bronze pineapple.

"I'm sorry, Miss Delta," she said with a distinct Southern twang. "I dropped it on accident."

"Scarlett, you fool! That's a priceless antique!"

"I know, but I didn't realize how heavy it was." She pushed a lock of frizzy, dishwater-blonde hair behind her ear and started to lift the bulky bronze fruit.

"Leave it be!" Delta shouted as she scooped up the pineapple with a single hand. "Aren't you supposed to be getting dressed for a tour?"

"Yes ma'am," Scarlett said, rising to her feet and taking a step backward. "But I remembered that I hadn't dusted the stuff on the bed."

"Never mind that now," Delta said as she deposited the pineapple at the end of the bed next to a gray feather duster. "Where's your hoop skirt?"

"On the back of the door."

Delta stormed over to the door and pulled it back. She stiffened suddenly and turned to Scarlett with a look of pure rage. "What did I tell you about hanging up vintage clothing?"

"That I shouldn't use no wire hangers?" Scarlett ventured.

I felt my body tense in preparation for a Mommie Dearest moment.

"That's right," she said through clenched teeth. "No. Wire. Hangers!"

I halfway expected Delta to pull a Joan Crawford and start beating Scarlett with the hanger. Or with the pineapple.

Instead, she inhaled deeply and looked at Veronica and me. "Scarlett earns extra money doing some light cleaning here at the plantation," she explained. Then she turned to her and gave her an icy stare. "But if she continues to drop two-hundred-year-old artifacts, I'll have to relieve her of her duties, both as a maid and as a tour guide."

Scarlett lowered her head and began biting the fingernail on her middle finger.

I wondered whether she was discreetly flipping Delta off and smiled inwardly at the notion.

"At least nothing was broken," Veronica said.

"Not yet, anyway," Delta remarked, putting her hands on her hips. "Now, I've got to get downstairs to see that everything is ready for the tour. Scarlett, Ms. Maggio and Ms. Amato need to ask you some questions about the murder. You make sure you cooperate, you hear?"

"Yes, Miss Delta."

Delta frowned at her and left the room.

I looked at Scarlett and noted that her hands were trembling. I couldn't tell whether it was because of what had just transpired or because she was afraid to talk to us. Either way, I knew I had to try to calm her down to have a chance at getting any information she may have. "Scarlett is the perfect name for a plantation tour guide." I smiled. "I'll bet you hear a lot of Tara jokes."

She stared at me, expressionless.

Time to try another tactic. "What's up with the pineapple?"

"It's a symbol of Southern hospitality, isn't it?" Veronica chimed in.

Scarlett nodded. "Yes ma'am. But in the old South, if you were a guest in someone's home and you woke up and found one at the foot of your bed, it meant you'd overstayed your welcome."

"Awk-ward." I laughed.

She pressed her lips into a thin line. "Miss Delta said you had some questions about that woman that was killed?"

Clearly, Scarlett was in no mood for jokes. "Uh, yeah," I said. "Were you here between five p.m. last Friday and eight a.m. the next morning?"

"I came in at eight thirty on Saturday for the nine a.m. tour," she said, her eyes narrowing. "Why?"

"We're not accusing you of anything," Veronica began, "we're just trying to find out if you know anything that could help us."

"I don't," she said hotly.

It appeared that Scarlett had a scrappy side, like her *Gone-with-the-Wind* namesake. "Did you see the body after it was found?" I asked.

She nodded. "Miss Delta told me what happened when I came to work. I went into the room to see for myself."

"Did you recognize the victim, Ivanna Jones?" Veronica asked.

Scarlett glanced at the floor. "I seen her here before."

I felt my heart skip a beat. "When?"

"A week or so ago."

I remembered that Delta said she'd seen Ivanna two weeks before. I wondered whether Ivanna had returned to the plantation a week later. "Can you give us a more precise date?"

She tugged at the top of her corset. "Uh, actually, I think it was two weeks ago."

Veronica furrowed her brow. "You're sure?"

"You think I'm lying?" she asked, raising her chin.

"I want to make sure we have the correct information, that's all," Veronica replied.

Scarlett stared at Veronica and said nothing.

Changing the subject, I asked, "Was Ivanna on one of your tours?"

"Yeah." She paused and played with the fabric of her petticoat. "And..." Her voice trailed off as she looked out the window. Then her face clouded over. "I'd better go." She grabbed the feather duster from the bed and pulled her hoop skirt and a red dress from the back of the door. "It's almost time for my tour."

"Okay, but let us know if you think of anything else," I said.

Scarlett left the room without a word.

"Did you see that?" I asked as I hurried over to the window. "She was about to tell us something, but she changed her mind."

"Yeah," Veronica replied with a toss of her hair. "And from the way she kept messing with her clothes, I'd say she was lying about when she saw Ivanna."

I stared out onto the grounds below and immediately locked eyes with a stocky, thirty-something male standing near the back porch. He turned away and headed in the direction of the sugar mills. "I just saw a man looking up at this window. Let's go find out who he is."

I rushed downstairs with Veronica close behind. When I opened the back door, seven miniature pinschers rushed in and circled me with their teeth bared like tiny land sharks preparing for a foot-feeding frenzy. I immediately froze in my tracks and feared for my Dolce Vita wedges and my toes.

Veronica sprung into action. "Bad dogs!" she shouted, clapping her hands. "Shoo! Shoo!"

But the mini mongrels stood their battleground.

Using my best Southern canine speak, I yelled, "Go on, now! *Git!*"

Delta emerged from her office wearing her standard scowl. "What's all the damn fuss about?" she asked, waving an antique candlestick like a club. "We have a tour going on, you know."

"This pack of wild Dobermans!" I said, desperately wanting to gesticulate but holding my body mummy-style still.

Delta looked down as though she hadn't realized the dogs were there. Then she dropped to her knees and drew the dogs into a collective embrace. "Mamma's sweet babies!" she cooed in a manly maternal tone as she kissed each dog on the mouth.

I felt my jaw drop from the shock of Delta's unexpected display of affection.

She looked up, beaming with pride. "These are the seven dwarfs."

More like the seven deadly sins, I thought.

Veronica walked around me. "Delta, we need to identify a man who was staring up at the window when we were questioning Scarlett a few minutes ago."

She used her right knee to hoist herself back to her feet. "It was probably that good-for-nothing Miles McCarthy, our groundskeeper. He's always poking around in the bushes and whatnot, sticking his blasted nose where it doesn't belong."

I noted that Delta had made a quick recovery from her bout with maternal warmth. "Does anyone else help with property maintenance?"

"No, but our historian, Troy Wilson, gives tours of the grounds. He's not here today, though."

Veronica pressed a finger to her cheek. "Hm. We'd planned on questioning everyone while we were here."

"I told him that," Delta said as she began twisting the candle in its spiral-shaped metal holder. "But he said he had some business to attend to at Tulane, something to do with his PhD dissertation. You should ask him about his research, by the way. It's fascinating."

"When can we talk to him?" I asked, glancing down at the Disney-named demon dogs.

"The day after tomorrow," she replied. Then she unceremoniously deposited the candlestick in my hands. "Here. Hold the base while I pull this candle out."

"That's a funky-looking candlestick," I said.

"It's a courter's candle." Flexing the muscle she'd exhibited earlier with the bronze pineapple, Delta gave a hearty tug and the candle slipped free from the metal spiral.

"What's that?" Veronica asked as I handed the candlestick to Delta.

"A courting timer. When a gentleman came calling for one of the eligible young ladies of the plantation, her father would light the candle. When the wax burned down to the top of the metal spiral, it was time for the young man to leave. If the plantation lord felt he was a good prospect he would turn the handle to raise the candle before he lit it to give the couple more time together. But if he didn't, he would lower it."

"Talk about getting the short end of the stick," I joked.

Delta raised an eyebrow and stared at me. She might have a secret human side, but she had no sense of humor.

Veronica peered around Delta's shoulder. "Why are you replacing the candle?"

"One of my staff lit the damn thing, and the wax dripped all over the holder. Probably Scarlett," she added, shaking her head.

"Speaking of Scarlett," I said, "what time does her tour end?"

"In about thirty minutes. There are only six people—foreigners who are blissfully ignorant of the murder, I'm sure."

"Okay, thanks," Veronica said, walking to the door.

I held back until Delta and all seven of the devil dwarfs had retreated into her office. Then I rushed out after Veronica.

"Let's go to the larger mill first," I said.

"Yeah, the smaller one is probably the storage shed."

Veronica and I walked past the slave quarters and the gift shop and veered left in the direction of the big sugar mill. As we approached the rickety old wooden structure, we saw four huge cast iron kettles arranged in order from largest to smallest in front of the building. The tallest kettle was at least five feet high and seven feet across, and the smallest was only about two feet high.

I walked up to the weather-beaten door and knocked. After a minute or so passed, I pressed my ear to the thin wood. "It sounds like a fan or something is running. Maybe he didn't hear me."

"Is the door locked?"

I pushed the door, and its rusty hinges creaked as it opened about a foot. "I'm going in."

Veronica nodded.

"Hello, Miles?" I called as I slipped inside. I followed the loud whirring, which seemed to be coming from somewhere in the back. I passed through a room equipped with several anti-quated-looking machines with grooved rollers and arrived in an adjoining room with wooden worktables and shelving.

Miles was standing at a table with his back to me and using

an industrial-sized Shop-Vac to remove some pink powder from a clear plastic Tupperware container. When the last of the powder was gone, he turned to switch off the machine.

I couldn't see his mouth because he was wearing a white surgical mask, but I thought his brown eyes widened when he noticed me. "Sorry, I didn't mean to startle you. My name is Franki, and I'm a PI investigating the suspicious death here at Oleander Place."

He removed his mask and began stripping off his elbow-length rubber gloves. "Where y'at?" he asked in a Brooklynesque accent.

I started to say, "Right here." But then I remembered that *Y'at* is a white, working-class dialect peculiar to the area around New Orleans' Irish Channel neighborhood, meaning *How are you?*, and I cleared my throat. "Fine. And you?"

"Awrite," he replied. "I was jus' cleanin' up some rat poison. Maybe we should step outside?"

I was all too happy to leave the mill. I could almost feel airborne rat poison entering my lungs, and I was a little leery of Miles. With his bushy reddish-brown brow, flattened boxer nose, and hulking frame, he looked like he could have been an Irish Mafia extra for the cast of *The Departed*.

When we got outside, Veronica was leaning over the next to largest of the kettles.

"Careful, now," Miles said. "You don' wanna fall into de *flambeau*."

Veronica blinked. "The what?"

"All dese kettles have a name. Dis big one here is de *grande*, den come de *flambeau*, de *sirop* an' de *batterie*."

"So they were used in sugar production?" I asked, running my hand over the smooth black surface of the *grande*.

"Yeah, to boil de sugar cane juice down 'til it crystalized. But dey also used 'em to make de meals for de plantation hands.

And during de harvesting season, dey took de boiled cane juice from de *flambeau* and mixed it wit' French brandy to make hot punch." He rubbed his belly. "It's dee-licious."

I felt my mouth watering. Naturally, I'd been craving a mint julep since I stepped onto the plantation. But some condensed sugar juice and European brandy would do just fine. "Listen, my partner Veronica and I would like to ask you a few questions about the murder. Is now a good time?"

"F'sure," he said, crossing his arms against his solid chest.

"Great," I said, pulling a note pad and pen from my purse. "What time did you leave work last Friday?"

"I went home early dat day, at tree p.m."

Veronica crinkled her nose. "At three?"

He nodded. "Tha's right."

I jotted down the time. "Can anyone vouch for you?"

"How ya mean?"

"I mean, do you have an alibi?"

He looked down. "I stay by myself, and I was dere all night. Pahdon my French, but I had de *fois*."

I had a hard enough time deciphering proper French, so there was no way I could do Cajun. "The *fwas*?"

"I was in de battroom," he said, raising his eyebrows.

I looked at him blankly.

He gave a sheepish grin. "I ate a bad batch o' gumbo?"

"Got it," I said, holding up my hand in a stopping motion. I didn't need any of the gory gastric details. "What about Saturday? Did you come to work?"

"I got heuh at eight."

Veronica pulled a crime scene photo from her Furla tote. "Did you view the victim's body?"

"No ma'am. No one was allowed in de house dat day."

"Do you recognize this woman?" she asked, showing him a photo of Ivanna's body.

Miles stroked his unshaven chin and looked to one side. "Nevah seen her before."

I noted that he didn't flinch at the sight of her corpse. "Her name is Ivanna Jones. Does that ring a bell?"

He looked down at his worn brown work boots. "Cain't say it does."

"Thanks, Miles," I said slipping the pad and pen back into my bag. "That's it for me. Veronica?"

She shook her head.

"Looks like we're done for now," I said, extending my hand. "If we need anything else, we'll be in touch."

He grasped my hand in a powerful grip. "Y'all have a blessed day."

As Veronica and I headed back toward the plantation, I whispered, "Miles never once looked us in the eye when we asked him about Ivanna."

"I noticed that. Suspicious, huh?"

I was about to reply when I saw something move by the magnolia tree next to the back porch. I squinted and saw Scarlett peeking out from behind the massive trunk. "True to her Clue counterpart, Miss Scarlett is a spy."

"Interesting," Veronica said. "Let's go to talk to her and find out what's going on."

I cupped my hands around my mouth. "Scarlett!"

She glanced in our direction, and then she put her head down and hurried toward the parking lot.

Veronica looked at me. "What's she doing?"

Scarlett climbed into a beat up, red Ford pickup and started the engine.

"Leaving," I replied as I watched her back up and speed away.

"That's the second time today she's run away from us," Veronica said.

"And both times it was right after she'd seen Miles." Now I

was positive that Miles was hiding something, but what? And what about Scarlett? It seemed like she was afraid of Miles. If she was, I had no idea whether it was because of something he knew about her or because of something she knew he'd done. Either way, I needed to talk to Scarlett. And soon.

7

"Okay, message delivered." I pressed end on my phone and dropped it in the cup holder beside the passenger seat of Veronica's Audi. "Now we just have to hope Scarlett calls us back."

"She will," Veronica said, frowning at the old tan Lincoln Town Car puttering along in front of us on the single-lane highway. "Otherwise, she'll have Delta breathing down her neck."

"Surely she'd want to avoid that," I replied. Although I wasn't convinced she'd call. Scarlett had seemed scared, and fear was a powerful motivator to keep your mouth shut, even when you were mouthy by nature.

Veronica fidgeted in her seat and tightened her grip on the steering wheel. "How could anyone stand to drive so slowly? They're doing 40 miles per hour."

"I think it's an older couple," I said in an attempt to stave off any impending reckless driving on Veronica's part. Ever since she'd driven the Ferrari racetrack in Italy, she thought she was a Formula One driver. And trust me when I say she wasn't. For starters, she could barely see over the steering wheel, and she had to drive in high heels so she could reach the pedals.

"Sunday drivers," she muttered as she craned her neck looking for oncoming traffic. "Don't they know it's Tuesday?"

"You can't pass here," I said. "There's a double yellow line."

Flagrantly ignoring both my comment and the law, she flipped on her turn signal and floored the gas pedal as she steered into the next lane.

I braced myself against the seat and pressed my feet on the floorboard as though that would protect me in the event of a fiery crash. When we'd safely made it around the startled-looking elderly driver and his equally startled-looking passenger, I relaxed a little and glanced at the odometer—85 mph. "Okay, we've passed them. Do you think maybe you could slow down now?"

She gave me a sideways look. "You're such a backseat driver."

"Actually, I'm in the front seat, so I can see that you're speeding. And it's not like we have to be back at the office. It's almost six o'clock."

"I have something I need to do," she said as she eased off the gas.

I wondered whether this "something" was why she'd been acting so weird lately. "What? A date?"

"Just...an errand," she said, tilting her head to the side and running her fingers through her hair.

I recognized that head-hair gesture. Veronica only did it when she was lying.

"Hey," she began in a suspiciously perky tone, "what time did you want to make our surprise appearance at Lickalicious Lips tomorrow?"

A clear diversion tactic. I narrowed my eyes and replied, "First thing in the morning, I guess."

She nodded and looked out the driver side window.

Before I could start systematically prying into her personal life, I was interrupted by the sound of my phone. I looked at the display and saw the main number of Pontchartrain Bank. My heart skipped a beat as I pressed answer. "Hey, babe."

"Do you always answer the phone that way?" the voice of Pauline asked with an audible sneer.

I felt a slow burn ignite in my gut. But I reminded myself that Bradley had asked me to try to get along with her, so I kept my cool. "Only when I think it's my boyfriend calling."

"Classy," she hissed.

Okay, to hell with Bradley's request. "How'd you get this number, Pauline?" I asked with attitude. "My office phone is the only one I have on file at the bank."

"Ancient Chinese secret," she intoned.

"I think you mean 'ancient Chinese snooping through Bradley's personal contact information,'" I snapped.

She gave a haughty laugh. "I don't need to resort to your little tricks. He doesn't keep anything from me."

The slow burn burst into a full-blown flame.

"But while we're on the subject of secrets," Pauline continued, "I thought you'd be interested to know that I just got a call from a fascinating woman named Carmela Montalbano?"

Nonna. The angry fire in my stomach was abruptly extinguished by anxious fear. I started mentally running through all the possible ammunition she could have provided to Pauline.

"She said she was your nonna, and she was calling to talk to Bradley about the *pranzo ufficiale*."

I cringed at her perfect Italian pronunciation and whispered a silent prayer that she'd only dabbled in the language, say, in high school or in preparation for a trip. "Yeah, that's an Italian family thing where the parents meet the boyfriend."

"A fine attempt at understatement," she said in a snide tone. "But my maternal grandmother is from Italy, so I know the score."

Wait. Chinese-French Pauline had a nonna? How multiethnic could her freakin' family be? I swallowed hard and squeaked, "Sicilian?"

"No, *calabrese*."

O. mio. Dio. Calabria is the region right next to Sicily at the toe of the Italian boot, which meant that Pauline, for all intents and purposes, had a Sicilian grandmother too.

"So, just out of curiosity," she said, "does Bradley have any idea that you and your nonna are planning his engagement to you?"

Beads of sweat began sprouting on my upper lip like mustache hairs on an old Italian woman. If Bradley found out what my nonna was doing, he might think I was in on her scheme. And even if he didn't suspect my involvement, it was way too early for him to find out how crazy-invasive my nonna was. I mean, he'd barely had enough time to get used to my teensy little idiosyncrasies, much less the masterful meddling methods of my nonna. As distasteful as it was, I was going to have to try to reason with Pauline.

"Um, *hello*?" she pressed.

I took a deep breath and said, "Look, you have an Italian grandma, so you know how incredibly intrusive they can be. I assure you that I had nothing whatsoever to do with this."

"Riiiight. Just like you didn't have anything to do with spying on Bradley and me last Sunday."

Okay, screw reasoning—it was time to beg. "Pauline, I'm asking you woman-to-woman not to give that message to Bradley."

I could practically hear her lips curling into a satisfied smile.

"Why, Franki," she exclaimed in mock outrage, "I'm his exec-utive assistant. It wouldn't be right not to give my boss his messages."

"Oh, really?" I huffed. "Because you didn't give him *my* message the other day."

"Did you call?" she asked innocently.

"No. I came—"

"Precisely," she said, and she slammed down the receiver.

I stared at the phone in shock. And then in a fit of rage clearly influenced by my recent plantation visit, I raised my phone in my fist and vowed, "As God is my witness, as God is my witness, she's not going to lick me."

"Wow," Veronica said. "Did you just lose everything but Tara in the Civil War?"

I looked at her, expressionless. "Pauline's going to tell Bradley that nonna is already planning our engagement party."

"She's *what*?" she shouted as the Audi swerved to the right. "Franki, you're going to have to find a way to rein your nonna in."

After checking to make sure my seat belt was still fastened, I shot her an annoyed look. "Can you really put a harness on a tornado, a hurricane, or a tsunami? Because that's the kind of force I'm dealing with here."

She sighed. "I know, but what about your dad? She's his mother. Can't he help you get her under control?"

"Are you kidding? You know my family's like a bad 1950s sitcom. Only, instead of *Father Knows Best* it's more like *Nonna Knows Best*. Whenever I complain about her to my dad, he says she's looking out for my best interests, which would be true if I had dreams of being a stay-at-home mom of ten in Fascist Italy."

"Well, you're going to have to do something. Otherwise, you'll end up a *zitella*, which is exactly what your nonna doesn't want.

I put my head in my hands and tried to think. Veronica was right. If I wanted to save my relationship with Bradley, I was going to have to take on my nonna. But she was a formidable foe, so I needed backup. I grabbed my phone from the floor where it had landed during the near accident and pressed my parents' number.

"Hello?" my mother responded shrilly on the first ring.

"Hi, Mom."

"Is that you, Francesca?"

I sighed. "Mom, you have two sons and one daughter. What other woman would be calling you 'Mom?'"

"Well, I see *you're* in a mood," she replied.

"Yes, I am. Nonna is up to her usual antics, and she's gone too far this time. She actually called Bradley at the bank to talk about having a *pranzo ufficiale*."

"I know she comes on a little strong, dear, but she just wants to see you settled down."

"A *little* strong, Mom? *Seriously?* To quote an Italian expression, she's like an elephant in a glass shop—after it's had a few gallons of espresso. It's bad enough that she's always trying to run my life, but now she's orchestrating Bradley's too. We have to—"

"Rosemary and I were just talking about the two of you at the deli today," she interrupted in a cheerful tone.

I instantly felt my hackles rise. I'd asked my parents not to talk about my personal life with the deli customers at least a thousand times, but they recognized that request about as often as my Mom recognized me when I called.

"And she wanted me to be sure to tell you the main benefit of marrying early," she continued.

"Oh?" I asked, making sure to sound as disinterested as possible.

"Yes, dear. You have your kids while you're young so that they're out of the house before you go through 'The Change.' That way, you and your hubby have time to recharge your sex life before the hot flashes hit."

"Mm," I said noncommittally. Where my Mom was concerned, I made it a point never to encourage womanly conversations that centered on changing or recharging.

"Take your father and me."

Dear God, no, I thought.

"When you left for college, we made love on the kitchen table for the first time in twenty-five years."

My stomach crawled into my throat, no doubt remembering with horror all the times it had eaten at that table. "Mom, can you please put Dad on the phone?" I asked, before she could drop any other sex bombs. "This is important."

"Well, all right, dear," she said, her voice dripping with disappointment from the sex-talk shut down. "Let me see if I can find him."

I heard the receiver crash onto the kitchen counter.

"Joe!" she shouted. "It's Francesca calling from New Orleans! Get on the phone!"

I looked at Veronica and shook my head in frustration.

She smirk-smiled at me and then shifted her gaze back to the road.

"How's the job going, Franki?" my father's voice boomed. "Are you chasing any cheating spouses?"

"Not right now," I replied, holding the phone away from my ear. "We're working on a murder case."

"Again? This PI business is starting to sound just as dangerous as your work on the police force," he said with a note of irritated worry. "I thought you wanted to get away from all that."

My dad and I had been around and around about my suitability, both as a woman and as an individual, for fighting crime. And even though we'd made some progress on that front, the battle was far from won. "Dad, being a PI is a lot less dangerous than being a cop. Besides, I've told you before that it wasn't the job I wanted to get away from as much as the partner requirement. I mean, my ex-partner, Stan, was about as nurturing as an absentee father."

Veronica glanced at me, her brow furrowed.

"Well, if you're sure about that..." he said.

"I am, Dad," I asserted firmly. "Anyway, that's not why I'm calling. I need to talk to you about nonna."

"Nonna? What's she got to do with your job?"

"Not my job. My life."

He gave an exasperated sigh. "How many times are we going to have to go over this? Your nonna loves you, and she wants to see you happy. That's all."

"Well, if *that's* what she wants, then all she has to do is stop meddling in my relationships, and I'll be ecstatic."

"Franki," he began in a gruff tone, "your nonna is a lonely old woman who just wants to be involved in your life."

I felt my guilt level shoot straight from five—the amount Catholic girls, good or bad, were taught to carry at all times— to ten.

"Maybe if you shared things with her from time to time," he said, "she wouldn't feel like she had to meddle."

Now my guilt was at eleven. He had a point. I hadn't confided in my nonna in years, but it wasn't entirely my fault. I mean, the minute I reached the dating age she went from a gracious grandmother to a Machiavellian matchmaker.

"Are we clear on that?" he asked in a tone that indicated this call was over.

"Yeah, Dad," I said, resigned. "Talk to you soon."

"Well?" Veronica asked.

I pressed end and shoved the phone into my bag. "A complete waste of time."

"He's not going to help?"

"Nope. He just gave me the usual speech about how she's doing this because she loves me, which is beside the point. It really bothers me that neither one of my parents gets how serious this is. But you know what really gets me?"

"No, what?"

"My nonna never once got on the phone."

She shrugged. "So?"

"So?" I repeated, surprised by her lack of insight. "Her whole M.O. is to get on the phone every time I call and try to pressure me into whatever the scheme *du jour* is. The fact that she didn't can only mean one thing. She's up to something, Veronica. Something bigger than the *pranzo ufficiale*."

"What could be bigger than that?"

"I don't know," I said, looking out the passenger window. "But the prospects are terrifying."

WHEN I OPENED the door of my apartment at six thirty, I half expected to find Napoleon lying on the floor with a burst bladder. Instead, he was in his now customary position, flat on his back on the zebra chaise lounge with his legs splayed wide open. Ever since we'd moved into the bordello-themed apartment, he'd been exhibiting a newfound animal virility. Lately, he'd taken to humping the leg of the lilac velour armchair. It had long gold fringe—to match the drapery—that clearly brought out his inner lion.

"You look like you need to lay off that chair leg, buddy," I said.

He gazed at me through half-lidded eyes.

I smiled and entered the kitchen, tossing my bag onto one of the Bordeaux-and-gold Dauphine chairs arranged around the rococo dining table. I hadn't eaten since lunch and, to cite Duran Duran, I was "Hungry Like the Wolf." I pulled open the refrigerator door and peered inside. Celery and a pan of re-hardened Zip Wax. I slammed the door and rummaged around in the pantry where I found some rock-hard raisins and a jar of

Nutella. Of course, I made the healthy choice—the milk-choco-late hazelnut spread. There was calcium in the milk, cancer-fighting antioxidants in the chocolate, and protein in the hazel-nuts. Sure there was no fruit or vegetable, but let's not forget that nuts contain nutritious oils not unlike those of the olive and the avocado.

After grabbing a spoon from the drawer, I flopped onto the chaise lounge next to Napoleon. From his upside down position, he kept one now fully-opened eye trained on the spoon as I raised and lowered it from the jar to my mouth a couple or twenty times.

"I've told you before, Napoleon, chocolate is good for people but poisonous for dogs."

His ear flopped closed as though refusing to listen to any more of my excuses.

I spooned another gob of the silky-smooth ambrosia into my mouth and heard the phone ring from inside my purse.

"*Sonamabiccia*," I cursed in Italianized English as I jumped up and ran to the kitchen. I placed the Nutella on the counter and threw the spoon into the sink. Then I grabbed the phone from my bag and saw "Bradley" on the display. Instead of the usual chest-fluttering happiness I felt when he called, now I felt nothing but gut-wrenching anxiety. By this time, Pauline had probably given him an earful about me, my nonna, and the *pranzo ufficiale*.

"H-hello?" I stammered, bracing myself for the worst as I carried the phone into the living room.

"Hey, babe," Bradley's sexy voice replied without a trace of animosity.

For a split second, his greeting reminded me of my infuri-ating exchange with Pauline hours earlier, but I was too relieved to think about the venomous vixen now. I curled up on the chaise lounge and purred, "Hey you."

"When you sound like that," he growled, "you make me want to drive straight to your house and break the door down."

My pulse began to quicken, and I said in a husky voice, "Then it's too bad you're out of town."

"Actually, I just got back. One of my meetings got postponed, so I caught a flight out a day early."

"Oh?" Now my pulse was racing. "Where are you now?"

"I'm getting some takeout on my way to the office. I've been craving Chinese."

Chinese? My blood stopped cold. But then I reminded myself that he was talking about food, not scheming secretaries who were after their bosses.

"Sometime I need to bring you to this place," he continued. "It's a dive, but the food is amazing. It's called 'Oriental Triangle Chinese.'"

I sat straight up. Did he say *triangle* and *Chinese?* My mind flashed to my tarot card reading. Was this a sign that Chandra was right about that Three of Cups card?

"They have some French food too," he added.

The minute he said the word *French* I had my answer. "And a bit of Italian, I'm sure," I muttered.

"Sorry, Franki. The cell signal is weak in here. What'd you say?"

I cleared my throat and replied in a frosty tone, "I said, I *prefer* Italian."

He gave a low, sexy laugh that warmed my chilled blood—and some other parts of me too. "I do too."

"Well, in that case," I began, nestling back into the chaise lounge, "you'd better get right over here so I can serve you my specialty." The second the words came out of my mouth I hoped he understood the euphemism. Because if not, the only thing I could offer him to eat was "ants on a log" with hair removal wax in place of peanut butter.

"I wish I could," he said wistfully. "But something came up at the bank today that I have to take care of ASAP."

I swallowed my disappointment, along with a glob of Nutella that had gathered around one of my molars, and resumed my seductive tone. "I guess you'll just have to wait to sample my specialty on our date tomorrow night."

"About that," he began, "Pauline rescheduled the meeting that got postponed as a video conference for tomorrow night. I'm sorry."

I leapt to my feet and bit the inside of my cheek to keep from blurting out something I would regret. I had no doubt that she'd scheduled that meeting to keep Bradley away from me, but I couldn't tell him that. I needed him to think that I was trying to get along with her, even if I had no such intention. So, through clenched teeth, I uttered a normal-sounding "Thursday, then?"

"I'll try, babe, but I can't guarantee anything. Between the merger and some other things going on at the bank, I've been working nonstop. Even Pauline is working overtime to help me put out fires."

Yes, she is, I thought. *Yours and mine.*

I heard my phone beep. I pulled the phone from my ear and looked at the display—Scarlett Heinz. "Bradley, I have to take this call. It's really important."

"Okay—"

I pressed answer before he could finish speaking. It served him right for letting Pauline cancel our dates. "Hello?"

There was silence on the other end.

"Scarlett?"

"Don't call me again," she said in a low, unsteady voice.

"I'm sorry if I'm bothering you. Delta said it would be all right to call—"

"Well, it's not," she interrupted.

"All I want is justice for Ivanna Jones," I said firmly.

"It's too late for her," she gushed. "But it ain't for the rest of us."

"What do you mean?"

"I mean, you don't know what you're messing with," she replied in a frightened tone. "If you're smart, you'll let it lie."

"What's going on, Scarlett? Please tell me what you know." I waited for her to respond, but I heard dead air on the other end of the line. I looked at my phone and realized she'd ended the call.

I lay back on the chaise lounge, stunned. It had been clear from the start that Scarlett had information about the case. But judging from her warning to me just now, something was going on at Oleander Place—something far more sinister than Ivanna's death. And that was a possibility I hadn't foreseen.

As I stroked Napoleon's belly, I wondered what, exactly, was I "messing with" and whether Miles McCarthy was involved in some way. The bigger question, though, was whether other lives were at stake. Like Scarlett's.

Or mine.

8

—————

"So what do you want to do about Scarlett?" Veronica asked the next morning as I exited Interstate 10 in the direction of the French Quarter.

"I guess I'm going to have to go to Oleander Place to try to talk to her after her shift. Depending on how long it takes us to question everyone at Lickalicious Lips this morning, I might be able to do it today."

"That reminds me." She pulled a tube of pale pink Chanel lip gloss from her hot pink Dolce & Gabbana Miss Sicily bag and applied a fresh layer.

I turned onto Canal Street. "Where'd you say this place was again?"

She smacked her lips. "On St. Peter."

I nodded and glanced in the direction of Pontchartrain Bank —which we were passing purely by chance, of course. I immediately spotted Corinne's fairy-like figure walking toward the main door with her handbag clutched to her chest and her head lowered. She looked despondent, like a Tinker Bell with drooping wings.

"That's Corinne Mercier," I said, pointing in her direction. "It looks like something's wrong."

"Why don't you pull over?"

"I think I will." I steered my Mustang into a thirty-minute customer service zone in front of a tourist shop.

Veronica rolled down her window, and I leaned across her lap and shouted, "Everything okay, Corinne?"

She turned toward my car and glanced uncertainly at Veronica. "*Bonjour.*"

"Bone-jure," Veronica replied with a polite nod. Like me, she spoke an unofficial Texas dialect of French.

I cleared my throat. "This is my partner, Veronica Maggio."

"I am 'appy to meet you," Corinne said, approaching the window. She was so small that she barely had to bend over to see inside the car. "After yesterday, I am in desperate need of Private Chicks' services."

I killed the engine. "Why? What happened?"

"Zere was more money missing from my teller drawer." Her big blue eyes welled with tears. "Anozer five hundred dollars."

"This has happened before?" Veronica asked.

I nodded. "Did you have to pay back the money again?"

"*Non.* Mr. Hartmann and I were here until midnight. We did not find ze money, but zis time he tell me not to pay."

So that's the bank business he had to take care of ASAP. I pressed my fingers to my lips. "Could one of your customers be a short change artist?"

"I don't sink so. Ze bank train us to recognize such tricks."

"Does anyone else have access to your drawer?" I asked.

"I don't see how, but I suppose it is possible."

"Well, if someone did steal money without you noticing," I said, "then the security cameras would have captured it."

"Yeah," Veronica agreed. "Has anyone checked the surveillance tape?"

"*Oui*, we review ze tape last night wis Pauline."

"Pauline?" I repeated, surprised. And incredibly annoyed. "What's she got to do with this?"

"She is in charge of ze computer wis ze security files."

"That's odd," Veronica said. "You'd think that an IT person or at the very least a manager would handle that sort of thing."

"And not an executive secretary," I muttered. For the life of me, I couldn't fathom how an intelligent man like Bradley could trust a conniving piece of work like Pauline so implicitly. Whatever the reason, I sincerely hoped it didn't have anything to do with her violet, almond-shaped eyes.

"You know Pauline," Corinne said. "She has her hand in everysing."

"Yes," I said dryly, thinking of Bradley's pants. Then a thought occurred to me. Did she also have her hand in Corinne's teller drawer? She certainly seemed to be around every time cash came up missing. But it didn't make sense unless she needed money or had some ulterior motive for wanting Corinne fired.

"It is almost nine o'clock," Corinne said. "I must go in. But I am serious about hiring your firm."

"We can discuss the details another time," Veronica said.

"Yeah, don't worry about that now," I added. "I'll come by the bank this afternoon to see what I can find out. We'll have to keep this arrangement strictly confidential—for your sake and mine. If Bradley finds out I'm poking around in bank matters, he'll ban me from the premises." *And possibly from his life.*

"But of course," she said. "*Au revoir.*"

As soon as Corinne had entered the bank, Veronica turned to me. "What do you think is going on?"

"I don't know, but I'd be willing to bet my eye teeth that it has something to do with Pauline."

Veronica frowned. "I know you don't trust her, but that's a pretty serious accusation."

I sighed. "I know what you're thinking, and you're wrong. This is business—it's not personal." Okay, so maybe it was. But just a little.

She arched an eyebrow and crossed her arms. "Oh, really?"

"Yes, really," I said, mentally crossing my fingers. "Everything was fine until Pauline showed up on the scene. But ever since then, bad things have been happening. At first I thought she was just after Bradley, but now I'm starting to think she wants more than that."

She smirked. "Like total bank domination?"

"Go ahead and laugh, Veronica. But when I prove that she had something to do with the missing money, I'll be the one to laugh last," I said with a pointed look. Then I started the V-8 engine and revved it—for dramatic effect.

"Okay, but are you sure you want to take this case? You've got a conflict of interest here. And if you're wrong about her, it could ruin your relationship with Bradley."

"I don't really have a choice, do I?" I asked, shifting in my seat to face her. "Corinne is my friend, and I want to help her. And Pauline is already trying to ruin my relationship with Bradley. Any minute now, she's going to lay the news of the *pranzo ufficiale* on him and blame it squarely on me. So if I have a chance to show him her true colors, which are black and blacker, I have to take it."

"All right," Veronica said. "Just be careful."

"Around the perilous Pauline? Count on it," I said as I sped away from the curb and tried to figure out how in the hell I was going to investigate Pauline without her or Bradley realizing it.

After an impromptu stop by the office to retrieve Veronica's laptop, we pulled in front of Lickalicious Lips at nine thirty a.m.

I made a quick U-turn in the middle of St. Peter to grab an unlikely parking spot in front of the Gumbo Shop two doors down. The minute I stepped out of the car, my nostrils were filled with the tantalizing aroma of *roux*, a thickener made of bacon fat and flour used as a base in Cajun and Creole cooking. I fervently hoped that the questioning of the Lickalicious staff would last until lunchtime so that I could have a hearty bowl of chicken Andouille gumbo—and a heaping helping of warm bread pudding with whiskey sauce.

"Look, Franki!" Veronica slammed the car door. "Lickalicious Lips is next door to Fleurty Girl, that darling boutique I was telling you about."

I snorted. It figured that she would focus on fashion while I fixated on food. "Maybe we can check it out later," I said as I headed for the cosmetics company. "*After* lunch."

Veronica stopped to admire a tutu on a mannequin outside the shop entryway while I tried the handle of the worn white door to Lickalicious Lips.

"It's locked." I glanced at the windows for signs of life. "I hope they haven't shut down."

"Try the doorbell," Veronica said, arriving at my side.

I pressed the buzzer and took a step back. As I waited, I scrutinized the exterior of the building. I had expected to see brightly painted brick with a cute lip-themed sign. Instead, it was an unmarked stuccoed structure with faded beige paint and the white-trimmed windows and green shutters typical of the French Quarter. I was about to ring the bell again, when the door opened to reveal a tall male in his mid-thirties wearing a wrinkled, white lab coat and khaki pants.

He blinked as though unaccustomed to sunlight. "Can I help you?"

"Yes." I handed him my card. "I'm Franki Amato, and this is Veronica Maggio. We're investigating the death of Ivanna Jones."

He blinked again, this time from surprise. After reading my card front to back, he narrowed his small steel-blue eyes. "Who hired you?"

Veronica stepped forward. "We're representing Oleander Place."

"We'd like to come in and ask you a few questions, if you have a moment," I added.

"I don't know." His brow furrowed. "I've already talked to the police."

"I understand," I said in a gentle tone. "But our client is dissatisfied with the progress of the police's investigation, so we're retracing their steps to make sure all evidence has been uncovered. For Ivanna."

He hesitated and then gestured for us to come inside. "I'm Dr. Adam Geyer. Call me Adam."

"What do you do for Lickalicious Lips?" I asked as Veronica and I entered.

"I'm their cosmetic chemist or, at least, I was. I have no idea what's going to happen with the company now." He exhaled and ran a hand through his short blond hair. "Please, have a seat."

Following Veronica's lead, I sat in one of two black leather armchairs facing the wooden table that served as a desk. The place looked more like an IKEA showroom than a cosmetics firm. "Is this your office?"

"No," he replied, taking a seat behind the desk. "I work in the next room, in the lab. This was where Ruth Walker sat. She was our administrative assistant, but she resigned on Monday."

I wondered whether Ruth had merely jumped from the proverbial sinking ship or whether there was something more to her resignation. "Would it be possible to speak to her?"

Adam paused and then scribbled something on a piece of paper. "Here's her cell, but I can't guarantee she'll talk to you. She wants nothing to do with this company now."

"Thanks." I took the number and shoved it in my bag.

"Had Ruth been working here long?" Veronica asked, opening her laptop on her knees.

"About three years."

Veronica began typing notes. "What about the other employees?"

"There aren't any. I make the prototypes in house, and then we send them to an outside firm for production and distribution."

That explains the lack of testers here in the lobby, I thought—not without a pang of regret. "How long have you been with Lickalicious Lips?"

"Ivanna recruited me to help her open the company ten years ago. She was working on her Masters in Cosmetic Science at Farleigh Dickinson while I was finishing up my PhD there. She was a student in a class I was teaching, and one day she came to my office hours and said she was going to start Lickalicious when she graduated. I didn't think anything of it at the time, but then a year later she called and offered me a salary I couldn't refuse."

Veronica stopped typing. "She must have had some impressive financial backing."

"She did. From her father, Liam Jones. He's a doctor, and she was his only child. So he could afford to back her."

"Rumor has it that he's been hard to locate," I said. "Have you spoken to him since her death?"

Adam leaned back and crossed his leg over his knee. "No, but I've been trying to reach him. He's works for Doctors Without Borders, so he's often out of contact. Last I heard he was in Syria."

"What about her mother?" I asked.

"She died when Ivanna was a teenager."

"I see." I paused for a moment. "I'm sure the police told you the details of Ivanna's death."

He clenched his jaw and nodded.

I looked him straight in the eyes. "Do you know of anyone who might have done this to her?"

"She didn't have any enemies that I know of." He rubbed his days-old beard. "She was a nice person, and she kept to herself."

"Forgive me for prying," I began, "but was everything okay between the two of you?"

His eyes flashed with anger. "Of course it was," he snapped. "We argued about business from time to time, but that's hardly unusual."

Intrigued by his defensive reaction, I pressed on. "Where were you last Friday night?"

Adam gripped the arms of his chair. "Wait a second," he said rising to his feet. "Do you think I killed Ivanna?"

"We don't think anything," Veronica soothed. "We're just being thorough."

His face relaxed. "Sorry about that," he said, sitting down. "As you can imagine, I've been under a lot of stress."

"Of course," I said. But I was now convinced there had been tension between him and Ivanna. The question was, had it been enough to lead to murder?

"I was here at the lab until midnight on Friday," he explained, "working on the formula for a green lip gloss called Midori Melon."

I licked my lips and told myself that this was not the time to ask for a trial run. "Which shade was Ivanna found holding?"

"That was a pink lip gloss we'd been working on." He began bouncing his right leg. "I can't imagine why she had it with her."

I glanced at his bobbing knee and wondered what had brought on the apparent case of nerves. "What was that shade called?"

"No idea. I just know that it was going to be part of our drink line. But we were having trouble producing the right shade."

Veronica scratched her temple. "How could you mix a specific shade without knowing the drink you wanted to model it after?"

He leaned forward in his chair. "Ivanna was an artist. And like most creative types, she didn't always do things in a way that made sense. Sometimes she would come to me with a color in mind, and then she would wait until I had created just the right shade to announce the flavor."

As he spoke, I tried to think of a brand of liquor that was pink. All I could come up with was a cheap wine I'd found (and may or may not have sampled) in my parents' liquor cabinet when I was thirteen called Boone's Farm Tickle Pink, and I seriously hoped that Ivanna hadn't planned on making a lip gloss version of that. "Could we take a quick look around the lab?"

His eyes widened. "Sure. But there's not much of interest in there."

"That's fine," Veronica said. "We just want to see how the business works."

Adam rose to his feet and opened a door to the right of the desk. "After you."

I entered the lab followed by Veronica. Like the lobby, it was something of a letdown. I thought there would be test tubes, beakers, and maybe even a Bunsen Burner, but instead it was just a kitchen, and a very small one at that. On the left side of the room, there was a sink with cabinets and a small counter on one side and a stove on the other. Next to the stove was a small table with two chairs. And there was still no sign of any testers. "Where do you keep your supplies?"

"In here," he said, opening the wooden cabinet above the counter.

I scanned the contents. Although I was certainly no scientist,

I recognized the ingredients from my years of experience as a grocery store makeup buyer (for myself, that is): lanolin, beeswax, hydrogenated soy glycerides, and assorted bottles of coloring and natural flavors. "There's not much here."

"It doesn't take much to make lip gloss," he said, closing the cabinet door. "You can do it with as little as Vaseline and some powdered or cream blush."

"Or eye shadow or lipstick," Veronica added with a nod.

"Neat," I said, feigning interest. I couldn't be bothered to make myself a sandwich, much less a tube of freaking lip gloss. "What do you keep in the cabinet below?"

He opened the door. "Just kitchen utensils."

"What does that door lead to?" Veronica asked, pointing to the back wall.

Adam walked to the door and opened it. "Ivanna's office and the bathroom. You can look around, if you like."

I followed Veronica into the room, which was decorated with an adorable pink couch and a glass desk with a red leather chair. *Now this is more like it*, I thought.

"The police took Ivanna's computer and her filing cabinets," he said. "So the furniture is all that's left."

"That's too bad," I said, although I'd anticipated as much. I began walking around her office, surveying the scene.

"They also cleaned out her place upstairs."

Veronica turned to Adam. "She lived upstairs?"

He nodded. "She owned this whole building."

"That explains why her business address was listed as her personal address on the police report," Veronica said.

I walked over to the shelving behind Ivanna's desk. There was nothing but a few books and some knickknacks. "Did the police have a key, or did they have the fire department 'spread the door?'"

"Pardon?"

"Sorry." I smiled. "That's police jargon for removing a door without damaging the frame."

"Oh," he slipped his hands into the pockets of his lab coat. "They used her key. Apparently, she'd left it in her car."

"You don't have access to a spare, do you?" I asked.

"I don't know of anyone who does."

I looked around Ivanna's office once more. "One last question, did Ivanna ever talk to you about a pink diamond?"

He rubbed the back of his neck. "Never. Why?"

"Just curious," I said. "Would it be all right if we contacted you with any follow-up questions?"

"Sure," he replied.

I wasn't positive, but I thought I'd seen a look of disappointment in his eyes.

Adam pulled his billfold from his back pocket and extracted a business card. "Call my cell. I'm not sure how much longer Lickalicious will be open."

"Thanks." I took the card. "We'll be in touch."

Veronica and I walked outside into the spring sunshine.

"That was disappointing," I said.

"How so?" Veronica asked, making a hard left toward the boutique.

"Well," I began, close at her heels, "Adam didn't tell us much, and it looks like the police beat us to any evidence."

"Maybe. But you are making progress in the case."

"I suppose." I sighed. "The décor left a lot to be desired too."

She laughed. "You're just upset that they didn't have any free samples."

"Maybe," I said. "I *was* kind of looking forward to a reunion with Baileys Irish Cream Brown. It's been a long time."

Veronica stopped in front of Fleurty Girl. "Mind if I pop in for a sec?"

I looked at my phone. It was only ten o'clock, which meant

that I could kiss my gumbo goodbye. "Nah, we're ahead of schedule. I'm going to stay out here and call Ruth."

"K," she said as she dashed through the doors.

I dialed Ruth's number and started pacing up and down the sidewalk. After several rings, I heard someone pick up.

"Hello?" a matronly voice replied.

"Ruth Walker?"

"Yes. Who's this?"

"I'm Franki Amato. I've been hired to investigate the Ivanna Jones murder."

"Well thank goodness you called," she said in an its-about-time tone.

I stopped in my tracks. "I just got your number from Dr. Adam Geyer. Did he already tell you I'd be calling?"

"No, but I've been waiting for someone besides the police to get involved in this case."

"How come?"

"Because there were some suspicious goings on at Lickali-cious Lips between Ivanna and Dr. Geyer right before she was found murdered, and the detective I spoke to doesn't seem too concerned about it."

I spotted a group of oncoming tourists and moved to stand beside the mannequin. "Can you tell me about it?"

"Not on the phone. But I will say that it has something to do with that coral-pink lip gloss Ivanna was found with at the plantation house."

My breath caught in my throat. "Did you say *coral* pink?"

"Mm-hm. It's a shade Ivanna wanted Dr. Geyer to make before she died."

"Yes." *And it was Evangeline Lacour's favorite color too*, I thought. "Any chance we could meet today?"

"Do you know Napoleon House on Chartres Street?"

"No, but I'll find it."

"Can you be there in an hour?"

"See you at eleven thirty." I closed the call.

A million questions were running through my mind, but there was one thing I was certain of. If Ruth knew the shade of pink that Ivanna wanted Adam to produce, then he must have known it too. What I didn't know was why he would lie about it. I mean, I was certain that the lip gloss had something to do with the case, but I hadn't really thought too much about the color. Now I had good reason to believe that Ivanna was trying to match the shade of pink near and dear to Evangeline Lacour's heart. But was it the oleander flowers or her dress that Ivanna was trying to match? And why would she want to match the shade of one of these items for her drink line instead of the liquor itself?

I leaned the back of my head against the facade of Fleurty Girl. The deeper I got into this case, the less I understood what was going on.

9

When Veronica and I entered Napoleon House an hour later, I was immediately struck by its old-world charm. The music of Beethoven filled the air, and the main room had a high, wood-beamed ceiling with a hanging light that looked like Thomas Edison had designed it for his newly invented light bulb. There were quaint arched doorways set in distressed plastered walls covered with oil paintings and drawings of various historical figures. Overall, the place had a real colonial vibe—apart from the odor of meatballs and marinara sauce coming from the kitchen.

While we waited for the hostess, my eyes were drawn to a white bust of Napoleon sitting unimperially atop the cash register in the center of the hand-carved wooden bar. He seemed to be looking down his nose at the patrons, as though disgusted that his likeness wasn't somewhere more befitting of an emperor. "Why is this place called Napoleon House, anyway?"

"Because this used to be a house, and the original owner invited Napoleon to live here during his exile," Veronica replied, scanning the clientele. "But he wasn't able to escape from the island of Saint Helena."

"Why would he even want to?" I loved New Orleans and all, but if I had to be exiled, I'd root for the beach over the swamp or the banks of the Mississippi any damn day.

Ignoring my question, Veronica nodded toward a fifty-something female sitting alone in the corner. "Do you think that's her?"

"Let's go find out."

As we weaved our way through the rustic tables and chairs, the woman's head snapped up from her menu. Her tight, graying brown bun didn't move a millimeter, but the chains on either side of her black horn-rimmed reading glasses swung back and forth like jump ropes. "I'm glad you two showed up."

"Of course," I said as Veronica and I sat down. Ruth's familiarity was becoming a little off-putting, to put it mildly.

"I got here a little early, so I ordered us some appetizers and waters." She removed her glasses and let them hang from the chain around her long neck. "They make a good gumbo, and if you're in the mood for a cocktail, this place is famous for its Pimm's cup."

I uttered a silent thank you to the gumbo gods but looked with longing at the bottles lining the bar. "We don't drink on the clock."

"Personally, I never touch the stuff," she said as a waiter arrived with our waters and what looked like an iced tea garnished with cucumber for Ruth.

I had to question why a woman who didn't drink would ask Veronica and me to meet her at one of the most famous bars in America, not to mention work in a place that produced liquor-flavored lip gloss.

"But given what I've been through at Lickalicious Lips," Ruth continued, "I thought a nip of Pimm's would do me good." She took the glass from the waiter and lifted it in a salute. "It's made from herbs, you know."

Question answered, I thought.

The waiter pulled out a pad of paper and a pen. "You all ready to order?"

"Oh, we don't have time to eat," Veronica announced to my utter shock and disappointment. She glanced in my direction. "I just remembered that I have to meet a client at a restaurant near the office at twelve fifteen."

I narrowed my eyes. Veronica never forgot an appointment, especially when it came to business. I was starting to get annoyed with her secrecy—and with the fact that it was the second time that day I'd had to give up gumbo. And now meatballs too.

Ruth waved her hand at the waiter. "I'm good with the appetizers." Then she tapped her glass with a neatly trimmed nail. "But I'll be needing another one of these."

He shoved the pad and pen into his apron, took our menus, and stalked away.

Veronica turned to Ruth. "What can you tell us about the relationship between Ivanna and Adam?"

She pressed her thin lips into an even thinner line. "Well, to start with, they were having an affair."

Veronica and I exchanged a look.

I was surprised Adam had neglected to mention that not-so-insignificant detail. "Are you sure about that?"

"I'd say so, after catching them in the act on the table in the lab."

What was up with sex on the table? I thought, my mind flashing regrettably to my parents.

"Plus, some mornings when I got to work early, I'd see him slinking down the stairs from her apartment." She gave us a knowing look. "In the same clothes he'd worn the day before."

I nodded. It sounded like the walk of shame—not that I had

any personal experience with that or anything. "Was he in love with her?"

Ruth sat back in her chair and crossed her arms. "I'm not sure the man knows what love is. But he worshipped the ground she walked on. He used to follow her around like a puppy dog, until they started fighting, that is."

Veronica leaned forward. "Did you ever witness any of their arguments?"

She snorted and reached for her drink. "They were hard to miss. In the two weeks before she died they fought every day."

"Did the fights ever become physical?" Veronica pressed.

"Not that I saw. But it wouldn't surprise me if they had."

"What did they fight about?" I asked.

Ruth sucked down half of her Pimm's cup. "Adam had a taste for gin. He'd been coming into work hung over more and more often, and she confronted him every time. The day before she died, she told him to sober up or get out."

I thought about Adam's disheveled appearance. I'd attributed it to grief, but now that Ruth mentioned it, he could have had a hangover.

"Did he stop drinking?" Veronica asked.

"Nope." She tossed back the rest of her drink and raised her glass to the waiter, signaling the second round.

All Ruth's imbibing was making me thirsty, so I took an unsatisfying sip of my water. "Do you think Ivanna would've fired him?"

She laughed. "That and have him blacklisted too. She made it clear that he was replaceable. And Ivanna was tough. You messed with her business, and she let everyone who mattered know about it. She would've ruined him in the cosmetics industry, and he knew that."

"What can you tell us about the coral-pink lip gloss?" I asked, toying with my table knife.

"Well, I don't know what Ivanna was doing with it at the plantation, if that's what you mean. But I wasn't surprised to hear she had it with her."

I looked up. "Why not?"

The age lines around Ruth's mouth deepened. "There was something weird going on with that lip gloss. I know Ivanna was mad that Adam couldn't get the color right, but it was like she was obsessed with it or something." She stared off into the distance and then shook her head. "All I can tell you was that there was a tension between the two of them over that lip gloss, and it was so thick you could have cut it with a knife."

I dropped the offending utensil. "Do you believe he could have killed her?"

Ruth smirked. "I think all humans are capable of murder, don't you?"

"I don't know," I said with a shrug. "There's a big difference between being capable and actually carrying it out."

"Maybe." She stirred her ice cubes with her straw, searching for one last sip. "But given Adam's recent downward spiral, I wouldn't put it past him."

The waiter returned with Ruth's drink.

"It's getting late," Veronica said. "Is there anything else you can tell us?"

"Yes." She grabbed the Pimm's cup from the waiter's hand. "Keep an eye on Adam Geyer. He's involved in this somehow. You mark my words."

"We'll do that." Veronica rose to her feet. "We really appreciate the information, Ruth."

"And the appetizers we didn't get to have," I said as I stood up and cast a hungry, hateful look in Veronica's direction.

"You let me know if you need anything else," Ruth said before she set to work draining her second drink.

"There is one more thing," I said. "Did Ivanna ever mention a pink diamond?"

Ruth stopped in mid sip. "I can't say she ever did."

As I followed Veronica to the exit, I thought about how Ruth had described Ivanna as *obsessed* with the lip gloss. Why was this particular shade so important to her? And what about Adam? Was his so-called *worship* of Ivanna an obsession? If so, then her criticism could have been a catalyst for violence. Of course, this was all supposition. But Adam's lies and omissions were raising lots of red flags where his innocence was concerned.

I DROPPED Veronica off in front of our office at five after twelve. I briefly considered following her to the alleged client meeting to see what I would find out. But then I decided to go straight to Oleander Place. I didn't need a repeat of what happened the last time I fancied myself a spy.

The subject of spying reminded me that I hadn't seen Bradley since he'd returned from his trip. I thought about stopping by the bank to see if he was free for a quick bite, and then I got an idea. If he'd already gone to lunch, that meant I had a forty-five-minute window of opportunity to do some investigating at the bank. I took a left turn and headed toward Canal Street. The plantation could wait another hour.

As I drove, I ran through my plan of attack. I needed to find out two things—Pauline's employment history, so I could do a little digging into her past, and the location of the security room. I didn't know how I was going to do it, but I had to get my hands on a copy of the video files for the days the money went missing from Corinne's drawer.

When I pulled up in front of the bank, I backed into a thirty-minute customer service zone and turned on my hazard lights. I rationalized that I was a) a bank customer in need of service, and b) in an extremely hazardous situation—especially if Bradley or Pauline learned what I was up to.

I exited the car and strolled casually into the lobby, where I saw Pauline hard at work on one of her essential bank tasks—writing on a poster board with a glitter pen. I took a deep breath and approached her desk.

"He's at lunch," she proclaimed without even looking up at me.

"Thanks." I needed to get her talking, so I asked, "What are you making?"

Pauline looked up at me, her gold earrings swaying. "A poster for the children's fundraiser. Now if you'll excuse me, I need to get back to work."

My eyes zeroed in on her earlobes. Those dangles were triangles! *Damn you and that Three of Cups card*, I fumed. But I kept it together and said, "I've been meaning to ask you about the perfume you're always wearing. What kind is it?"

"Pure Poison by Dior," she replied, resuming her drawing.

If ever there was a scent that captured Pauline's essence that was the one, I thought. "Well, I just love it."

She put her glitter pen down and leaned back in her chair. "What do you want?"

"Nothing. Just trying to be nice." I had to bite the tip of my tongue to stop myself from adding, *You should try it sometime.*

"Uh-huh. Well, I'm busy right now, okay?"

I noticed that she had several rows of pictures of herself on her desk (not that she was self-absorbed or anything). This was my chance to bring up her work. "Wow! Is that you?" I gushed, picking up a photo. "You look like a model."

She sighed. "That's because I *was* a model. In New York."

"Oh, I thought Bradley said you worked at a bank there. What was it called?" I asked, trying to conjure up a fake bank name in hopes that she would correct me. All I could think of was the unfortunately named, "Brokeman Bank."

"Brehman," she grunted as she added more glitter to the poster.

I felt a little rush. It wasn't her complete job history, but it was a start.

Pauline stared up at me with a scowl. "Listen, I don't have time chit chat. I've got to finish this before lunch."

"Yeah, that's an important poster," I said, unable to resist one tiny jab. "I've got to go make a deposit, anyway."

She rolled her eyes. "Thanks for sharing."

I smiled as sweetly as my tense facial muscles would allow and then headed over to Corinne's teller window. As I waited in line behind a customer, I took a deposit slip and pen from a nearby table and wrote, *Pretend like I'm making a deposit in case Pauline is watching.*

"Next," Corinne called.

I walked up to the window and slid the deposit slip toward her to make it look legitimate.

Corinne read the slip and nodded.

Looking down at the counter, I asked in a low voice, "Are employee resumes kept on file here at the bank?"

She typed something on her keyboard. "If zey are, zey would be in ze employee files in ze left-hand drawer of Mr. Hartmann's desk."

"Last question, where is the computer with the security video files?"

Corinne tore off my copy of the deposit slip. As she handed it to me, she pointed over my shoulder.

I turned and followed her finger to an unmarked door next to Bradley's office—just in time to see Pauline pull her keys from her purse and head to the exit. "Thanks," I said brightly. "See you next time."

She flashed a nervous smile. "You're welcome. Have a nice day."

I put the deposit slip in my bag and glanced at a clock in the lobby. It was twelve thirty, which meant that I had at least twenty minutes before Bradley returned. With my heart in my throat, I walked to his office. When I reached the door, I entered as though I belonged there. I *was* his girlfriend, after all.

Once inside I hurried to his desk and pulled open the left-hand drawer. Sure enough, there were files with the names of employees on them. In the back of the drawer was a label that read "Pauline Violette." I pulled the papers from inside the file and began flipping through them. Insurance information, an annual review, confirmation of a raise (that I was sure she didn't deserve). Then I found it. Pauline's resume.

I shoved the other papers back into the file and sat in Bradley's chair. His desk pad calendar caught my eye. Out of curiosity, I checked to see whether he wrote down our dates. I saw red—both literally and figuratively—when I realized that "Date with Franki," which he'd penciled in for yesterday, had been scratched out with red ink and replaced with "Video Conference" in a decidedly feminine handwriting.

"One of these days I'll cross you out, Pauline," I muttered as I began scanning the list of her previous employers with renewed determination. If her résumé was accurate, which was questionable, she'd worked for two banks from 2010 to 2011 and then from 2011 to 2012. For 2013, she had listed her freelance modeling work. *Because that's so pertinent to the world of banking*, I thought.

"I'll be right with you, Rich," Bradley's voice boomed from outside the door.

I froze in my seat—correction, Bradley's seat—as sheer panic coursed through my body.

"I need to grab my laptop," he continued.

Luckily, adrenaline followed the panic. I leapt up from the chair, kicked the file drawer shut, and stuffed the résumé up my shirt. I had just enough time to tuck the bottom of the sheet into the waistband of my jeans and sit on the corner of his desk before the door opened.

Bradley saw me and started. "Franki! What are you doing here?"

"Uh," I began, pushing a lock of hair out of my eyes, "before Pauline went to lunch, she said I could wait in your office."

He cocked his head to the side for a fraction of a second before removing his suit coat and hanging it on a coat rack. It must have sounded strange even to him that Pauline would be so accommodating.

I fervently hoped that he didn't mention this to her. Otherwise, she'd make good on her threat to out me about the *pranzo ufficiale.*

"It's great to see you, babe," he said as he crossed the room. He put his arms around my waist and pulled me in for a kiss.

For a second, I was seduced into an oblivious state by his touch. Then, remembering the resume, I arched my back like a cat so that his stomach wouldn't press against mine. As a result, his lips landed squarely on my nose.

Bradley pulled away and looked into my eyes. "Is everything okay?"

"Fine, fine," I said, thinking how ironic it was that even Pauline's résumé managed to drive a wedge between us.

Before I realized what was happening, he pulled me toward him again. As his body pressed against mine, there was a loud paper-crumpling sound.

He took a step back, his right arm still encircling my waist. "What was *that*?"

"Um," I said, racking my brains to think of a paper product I would have a logical reason for wearing around my mid-section —besides Depends. "It's a...new...maxi-maxi pad."

He stared at my stomach and blinked.

"It goes up to the abdomen," I explained, feeling my cheeks flush. "For when you need that extra super protection."

"Oh," he said, as embarrassed as I was.

I glanced at my wrist—where a watch would have been if I'd been wearing one—and said, "Gosh! I need to go." And then using Veronica's lie as I rushed to the door, I added, "I just remembered that I was supposed to meet a client near the office at twelve fifteen."

"Wait a minute, Franki," he said in a stern tone.

I felt my stomach sink. He knew I was up to something. I turned to face him—and the consequences.

"Have dinner with me tomorrow night," he said softly with that familiar gleam in his eyes.

My knees went weak. I wanted to throw myself into his arms, but instead I smiled and nodded. Then I ran from the room, crinkling all the way.

THREE HOURS and a wasted trip to Oleander Place later, I stomped up the three flights of stairs to Private Chicks and pushed open the door.

"Hey Franki," David said. He was sitting at his desk in the corner. "That package on the coffee table is for you."

"Awesome." I flopped down on the couch and picked up the cardboard box. "Hopefully someone sent me a rope to hang Delta with."

Veronica walked into the lobby from her office. "Why? What happened?"

"I just went to Oleander Place to talk to Scarlett, but when I got there I found a note saying the plantation had closed early.

So I just blew three hours of my afternoon for nothing, and now I have to go back out there again tomorrow."

"That's weird." Veronica put her hand on her hip. "Delta called a few minutes ago, but she didn't mention that."

I narrowed my eyes. "She wasn't at the plantation, was she?"

"She didn't say. She was calling to let us know that the medical examiner said Ivanna died from respiratory failure."

"Do we know the cause?" I asked.

"Well, here's where it gets interesting. Ivanna didn't have any health conditions or injuries, which means that we're looking at a possible drug overdose. Or poisoning."

"Wow." I shook my head. "Then there's a possibility that Ivanna was poisoned—like Evangeline."

David spun around in his chair to face me. "Dude, that would be insane."

"That's one way to describe it," I said, staring at the box in my lap. "I hope they're testing for oleander."

"I would imagine they are at this point," Veronica replied, handing me a letter opener from David's desk.

I started slicing through the tape on the box. "This is just a thought, but Adam would know how to extract the poison from oleander."

Veronica took a seat beside me. "Yeah, but you don't have to be a scientist to poison someone with oleander. Evangeline is a perfect example of that. Whoever poisoned her just boiled oleander leaves in her tea."

I opened the box and stared inside. Then I turned to Veronica, my eyes wide with disbelief.

"What is it?" she asked.

"A pineapple."

"What?"

"In the package. It's a whole pineapple."

Veronica leaned over and looked inside. "Who sent it?"

I pointed to the outside of the box. "There's no sender name or address."

"David, who delivered this?" Veronica asked, visibly upset.

He shrugged. "It was by the front door when I got here."

I removed the pineapple and saw a typed note at the bottom of the box. I picked it up and read aloud, *You've worn out your welcome, Miss Franki.*

"Huh?" David said. "I don't get it."

"Actually, it's pretty clear," I replied in a surprisingly calm tone considering that my heart was hammering my rib cage. "It's a Southern-style threat to stay away from the Ivanna Jones case."

10

———

I arrived at Private Chicks at ten the next morning, exhausted and on edge. Following the shock of the package, I barely slept a wink. It seemed like I'd had the same nightmare all night long. I'd been pushed into a vat of fruit cocktail at the Dole pineapple plantation and was about to be canned alive.

Given the uncertainty of the situation, I kept an eye out for suspicious items as I climbed the stairs. Then I scoured every inch of the office. I felt kind of silly about being wigged out over a pineapple, but after yesterday, I was never going to look at the spiny fruit the same way again.

I'd just pressed start on my laptop when, out of nowhere, Veronica popped her head around the doorjamb.

"You okay?" she asked.

After prying myself off the ceiling, I replied, "How would you feel if you'd received the Southern equivalent of a severed horse head in your bed?"

She pursed her lips and took a seat in front of my desk. "I know you're upset. Believe me, I am too. But a pineapple isn't exactly a *Godfather*-caliber threat."

"Then I should feel good about the fact that I was threatened by an old-school Southerner rather than a mobster?"

"I'm just saying that I think it was a scare tactic. You should definitely be careful, but I don't believe you're in any real danger."

I cast her a sideways look. "All I know is that the next time I get a pineapple, it had better be on top of a piña colada."

Veronica gave a half smile. "So, who do you think sent it?"

"Scarlett comes to mind." I hugged my knees to my chest. "She's the one who told me what the pineapple symbolized in the Old South."

"She wouldn't set herself up like that."

"I'm not so sure. She didn't strike me as the brightest bustle dress on the plantation. But I do think Miles is also a possible culprit."

Veronica examined a fingernail. "Have you considered Adam?"

"If it was Adam, then he's connected to someone at Oleander Place. Whoever sent it had to know about the incident between Delta and Scarlett."

"Not necessarily. Remember, I told him that Oleander Place is our client. And Louisiana is plantation country, so the pineapple custom is well known here. In fact, you can buy pineapple merchandise at kitchen and gift shops all over the state."

"I don't know." I rested my chin on my knee. "It would be quite a coincidence for Adam to send a pineapple without knowing what went down."

"Mornin', miladies!" David exclaimed in a British accent as he appeared in the doorway.

I jumped out of my seat and almost out of my skin.

His face wrinkled in confusion. "Did I scare you, Franki?"

"Nah," I scoffed, picking up my overturned chair.

"We didn't hear your signature door slam," Veronica said.

"Oh! I get it now." He laughed, his head bobbing with each "ha." "I didn't close the door. My vassal did."

Veronica smirked. "Whatever your vassal is, I like it."

"It's a he." David puffed out his chest. "He's, like, my servant."

A short young man with hair slicked to one side and round, coke-bottle glasses stepped from behind David's lanky frame. "'Vassal' is a medieval term for a type of servant."

"Silence, vassal!" David commanded. Then he turned to Veronica. "My fraternity gave him to me. He's a freshman pledge, so he has to do my bidding for the day."

"What kind of fraternity is this?" I asked. "A feudal one?"

"Uh, that would be fairly ridiculous," David replied. "It's, like, a comp sci frat."

The vassal leaned forward. "I wanted to major in Radio, Television, and Film, but my parents wouldn't let me."

David stared open-mouthed at the young man. "Vassal, must I flog thee?"

"David!" Veronica rose to her feet and put her hands on her hips. "There will be no flogging in this office, do you understand?"

"Yes, ma'am. I mean, mademoiselle." He bowed his head. "But I wasn't really going to flog him. Honest."

I held up my hand. "Okay, enough about fraternities, feudalism, and flogging. I need you to do a background check for me ASAP on a woman named Pauline Violette."

David's head shot up. "Yo, she sounds *hot*."

The vassal nodded vigorously, careful to keep his lips sealed.

"Well, she's not," I snapped.

"Right," David said, bowing his head again. "I'll get to work on that now."

"You do that," I said.

David scurried from the room, but the vassal stood there looking at me, slack-jawed.

I realized that he was probably waiting for his orders, so I used a language I knew he would understand, Shakespearean English. "Be off with thyself, vassal!"

He turned and fled.

Veronica stared after him, shaking her head. Then she turned to me. "I see you've stepped up your investigation of Pauline."

"I have, starting with the résumé I snagged from Bradley's desk yesterday."

"Nice work," she said with an appreciative nod. "What's the plan?"

"I'm going to contact her previous employers to see what I can find out."

"Most Human Resources offices won't tell you anything without a signed release from Pauline."

"I know, but I'm hoping I'll get lucky and talk to an unprofessional ex-boss. Most bosses are jerks, you know."

Veronica lowered her eyelids.

"Not you, of course," I hurried to add. "Anyway, there are a few things about her résumé that are interesting." I pulled the document from a file in my desk. "For example, she worked at two different banks in New York in a short period of time, and then she did some freelance modeling."

"So?"

"Well," I began, frustrated that she couldn't see the gaping issues, "why'd she leave the two banks so fast?"

"From the sound of it, because she wanted to be a model."

"Sure, but was that really lucrative enough for her to be able to live in New York for a year? Probably not, because she's not doing it anymore."

She shrugged. "Maybe her family helped support her."

"Okay, then why, after she quit modeling, would she take a bank job in New Orleans and not in New York? That's where all her contacts were."

"Because she wanted to get out of the city, more than likely. New York is famous for burning people out."

I frowned. Maybe there were logical explanations for my questions, but my instinct was telling me that there was more to the résumé than met the eye. "Well, I still say it's worth looking into. I'm going to start by calling..." I scanned the page for the bank Pauline had mentioned. "That's weird."

"What?"

"The bank she told me she worked for in New York isn't listed."

Veronica smiled, her eyes sparkling. "Now that *is* interesting."

I HUNG up the phone and looked out my office window. Rain clouds had moved in and turned the sky an ominous black. Just like my mood.

I shivered and zipped up my hoodie. Then I went into the kitchen and poured myself some much-needed French roast. I'm pretty sure my Italian cappuccino mug was offended.

"How's the investigation going?" Veronica asked as she entered and pulled a container of chopped vegetables from the refrigerator.

"Well, it took me half an hour to figure out that Brehman Bank is spelled with an *h*. Then I spent another forty-five minutes on hold with HR only to be told that I needed the signed release form."

"That's what I was afraid of." She took a bite out of a radish.

I grimaced. I was convinced that radishes were as poisonous

as the oleander flower. Then I began spooning my customary five tablespoons of sugar—unrefined, of course—into my coffee.

She popped the rest of the radish into her mouth. "Did you call the two banks that were on the résumé?"

I nodded. "Same thing. I need Pauline's signature to get any info."

The lobby bell buzzed.

"Is David still here?" I asked, stirring my coffee sugar sludge.

"He made the vassal drive him to class."

"At least the vassal went with him this time." I picked up my mug. "I'll go see who it is."

I walked into the lobby and saw Chandra. She was standing by the door in a white plastic rain poncho that did nothing for her dough-ish figure. "Hey, Chandra. What brings you to Private Chicks?"

Her jewelry jingled as she pulled the poncho over her head and smoothed her over-styled do. "That spirit came to me again."

"She did?" I sat down on the couch, cradling my coffee cup. I hated to admit it, but I was excited.

"Uh-huh, and she was calm this time," Chandra said, flopping down beside me. "Maybe it was because Lou and I were in our yard, enjoying nature. It's planting season, you know, and he just installed a sprinkler system in my flowerbeds." She stared at her chubby flip-flopped feet, which were dangling over the edge of the sofa. "Being married to a plumber certainly has its advantages."

"I'm sure." There was something to be said for a lifetime of good water pressure and unclogged toilets. "But what about the spirit?"

"Well, this year I wanted to plant moonflowers and starflowers, but they're both white. So Lou insisted we add a touch of color. He just loves bright things, that one. He picks out all my outfits," she said, gesturing toward her yellow sunburst-themed T-shirt and bright orange short shorts.

"How romantic," I said, picturing a stocky, balding man with a closet full of Hawaiian shirts. "But what does any of this have to do with the spirit?"

She put a hand on my arm. "I'm getting there. Be patient."

Patient? I thought. *Who has time for that?*

"Anyway, Lou went to the nursery to get the plants. And I had him get some extra mulch and fertilizer too."

I was seriously starting to worry that planting season would be over by the time she finished this story.

"And do you know what he came back with?"

"Um, the stuff you asked for?"

"Impatiens."

Go figure. "I still don't see what this has to do with the spirit."

Chandra sighed. "They were pink, exactly like the flowers at Oleander Place."

I placed my mug on the coffee table. *Now we were getting somewhere.*

"I didn't notice the similarity of the pink, but the spirit sure did. She came to me on the spot and told me to warn you about Oleander Place. She said that it may seem like a welcoming place, but it's downright inhospitable. Dangerous even."

"Yeah, I've gotten that message," I said, thinking of the pineapple package.

Thunder rumbled in the sky, as though underscoring my precarious position.

"She also said not to be fooled by the oleander flowers."

I leaned forward. "What did she mean by that?"

"How should I know?" Chandra pulled a family-sized bag of Zapp's New Orleans Kettle-Style Voodoo chips from her Chanel bag.

"Um, because you're the medium who talked to her?" I

suggested, observing the bag with a certain interest—the Zapp's, not the Chanel.

"It's not my job to interpret messages. I'm only supposed to relay them. That's what 'medium' means."

She had me there. It was up to me to decipher the meaning. But was the spirit telling me that oleander had nothing to do with the case? There was only one way to find out. "Listen, I wish you would reconsider coming out to the plantation."

Chandra nibbled on a chip. "I have."

"Really?" My stomach rumbled as I watched her chew. I wanted some chips. With a ham po' boy. And a slice of bourbon pecan pie. Or just the bourbon.

"After the spirit came to me in the flowerbed I said to myself, 'Now Chandra, it's just plain silly to be scared of spirits. You came to The Crescent City to serve them. They're your cosmic clients.'" She bit into another chip.

I licked my lips. "That's so true."

"Then I said, 'Chandra, the spirits will keep you safe. The only one in danger here is Franki.' And that made me feel better about everything."

Gee, me too. "So, can you go to Oleander Place with me later this afternoon?"

"With the lunar eclipse coming, I've got clients practically beating down my door."

I imagined a pack of half-men, half-werewolves trying to claw their way into her tiny office.

"But I suppose I can make some time tomorrow before noon." She rose to her feet and gathered her bags. "I never do business during lunchtime."

"That's a good policy," I said, consulting the lobby clock. I had just enough time to run over to Tracey's bar in the Irish Channel for that po' boy. And some gravy cheese fries. I ushered her to the door and said, "I'll pick you up at your office at ten."

"Okay." She stepped into the stairwell. "But make sure you bring a hundred bucks. Cash."

As the door closed behind her, lightening lit up the room like a kind of meteorological exclamation point.

I collapsed onto the couch, certain that the weather—or maybe the spirit—was mocking me. One hundred dollars was a lot to pay for something as unscientific as a psychic reading. But I told myself it was worth the price to see what Chandra would discover at the plantation—provided that she wasn't a fraud, of course. I wanted to find out the identity of the spirit that was contacting her and that of the blonde in the pink crinoline dress she'd seen in her crystal ball. It had to be either Evangeline or Ivanna, and I needed to know which.

First, however, I needed lunch. I hurried to my office to grab my bag, hoping that Veronica would let me bill Delta for Chandra's services. Otherwise, after today, there would be no more po' boys for me.

The lobby bell sounded.

"*Porca miseria*," I cursed in Italian. And I was in "pig misery" because something or someone out there didn't want me to have my pork po' boy.

When I returned to the lobby, I gave a start. I saw what looked like a werewolf in transition—human flesh and patches of gray fur with two ears and a long tail—holding a cardboard box about the size of the pineapple package. But then I saw the cigarette holder between its teeth and realized that it was just Glenda.

"That wasn't left outside the door, was it?" I asked, eyeing the box with concern.

Glenda placed the container on the coffee table and removed the cigarette holder from her mouth. "Nah, these are a little something I made for you girls."

"How nice," Veronica said as she entered the lobby.

I relaxed and went back to my spot on the couch.

"I just finished teaching my stripper boot camp class, so I thought I'd run them by."

"How's that going?" Veronica asked.

Glenda sighed and sat down beside me, crossing her fur-leg-warmer-clad calves and adjusting her matching loincloth. "I tell you, those girls are gonna drive me to drinkin'. Today they had to present a three-minute routine in costume. I went first to show them how it's done."

"What are you supposed to be?" I asked, scrutinizing her fur wrist warmers.

Glenda batted her inch-long orange eyelashes. "Why, I'm sexy Big Bad Wolf."

"Gah, Franki," Veronica chided, as though sexy Big Bad Wolf costumes were as common as blue jeans.

"Sorry," I muttered. "But why not sexy Little Red Riding Hood?"

Glenda exhaled two lungsful of smoke. "Sugar, do I look like a sexual victim to you? No self-respecting woman would play the part of that red-hooded idiot."

"Definitely not," Veronica huffed.

"Wow," I said, reeling from the red-riding-hood revelation. "I just thought it was a children's story about stranger danger."

Veronica and Glenda stared at me like I was the red-hooded idiot, even though my hoodie was purple.

"Anyway," Glenda said with a flip of her platinum hair, "this one girl put together a sexy maid routine. Not very original, but hey, she's a beginner so I kept an open mind."

"Good for you," Veronica said.

"But then what does the fool go and do? She sashays onto the stage in three-inch heels."

Veronica gasped and put her hand on her heart.

I looked from Veronica to Glenda, unsure of "the fool's" faux pas.

"Once I recovered from the shock," Glenda continued, "I said, 'Sugar, are those tap dancing shoes?' To which she replied, 'They're my strippin' shoes.' So I went, 'Child, anything less than six inches is just plain sad. And that goes for the boudoir too."

Veronica nodded.

"And do you know what she proceeded to inform me?" Glenda asked, waving her cigarette dangerously close to my cheek. "That platform heels hurt her feet, so she needed a *sensible* stripper shoe. Can you imagine such a thing?"

I shook my head. In all honesty, I really couldn't.

"So, I told her, 'Well, if you want to sell sensible, sugar, go get yourself a job at the Naturalizer store, because here we sell sex.'"

Veronica patted Glenda's bare thigh. "Those girls are so lucky to have you as their teacher."

"Thank you, Miss Ronnie." Glenda stood up and took another drag off her cigarette. "But this younger generation just isn't willing to suffer for their art. And if that doesn't change, I'm afraid they're going to cheapen the whole stripping profession."

"We can't have that," I said.

"Speaking of stripper shoes," Glenda began, reaching into the box, "I made this for you, Miss Franki." She handed me a white, ceramic stripper-shoe planter with a prickly pear.

I stared speechless at the item. *Was everyone in New Orleans planting but me?*

"And this is for you, Miss Ronnie." She handed Veronica a cute little pink handbag planter with sweet-smelling white jasmine.

Veronica squealed. "It's adorable!"

I looked at her planter with envy. Why did she get the precious purse while I got the slut shoe? With a cactus, to boot.

"Anyway, girls," Glenda said, picking up the box, "I don't want to keep you from your work, especially since it involves a pink diamond."

As Veronica walked Glenda to the door, I thought about Glenda's comment. Could the diamond be the key to this case and not the oleander? That would certainly fit with the spirit's warning not to be fooled by the flowers—that is, *if* I wasn't being duped by Chandra.

"Bye Miss Franki," Glenda said, snapping me out of my thoughts.

I turned as she opened the door and saw Delta standing on the other side in a dramatic floor-length black mink. If there were ever two personalities destined to clash it was the proper southerner and the promiscuous stripper. I held my breath and watched the standoff with a mixture of fascination and fear.

Glenda made the first move. She narrowed her eyes and took a deep drag off her cigarette.

In reply, Delta grasped her pearls and raised her chin.

Given their attire, I felt like I was watching a Louisiana-style territory-marking ritual on Animal Planet.

Glenda exhaled. "Nice fur."

"Likewise," Delta said, jerking her head backward to avoid the fumes.

Seizing upon Delta's submissive posture, Glenda nodded and—with her cigarette holder in one hand and her tail draped over the other—made a triumphant exit.

Breathing a sigh of relief, I thanked heaven for their mutual fur fetishes.

"Hello, Delta," Veronica said, closing the door behind her.

I rose to my feet. "I didn't realize we had a meeting."

"I didn't realize I had to set up a meeting to talk to you," she said, waltzing into the room and taking a seat on the couch.

"Oh, you don't," Veronica hurried to add.

I really wished Veronica hadn't said that. Something told me that being at Delta's beck and call could be brutal. I sunk down onto the couch beside her. "So what brings you away from the plantation again?"

"Again?" she repeated.

"Yeah, yesterday I went out there to talk to Scarlett, but it was closed."

She touched her Baron Samedi brooch. "Why would you need to talk to her? Is something wrong?"

"That's what we're hoping Scarlett can tell us," Veronica said.

"We think she has information about the case," I explained. "She was acting strange when we were at the plantation."

"Strange?" Delta threw her head back and laughed. "That's because the girl's as dumb as a stump. But if you think it's worth your time to question her again, her last tour ends at three o'clock today."

Sidestepping the stump issue, I asked, "So, the plantation is open?"

"Yes, I closed early yesterday because we didn't have a single tour booked for the afternoon, and I had to meet with my informant about the coroner's report. Naturally, he can't discuss the investigation over the phone."

I nodded.

"Anyway, there's been a development in the case. The test results came back on the lip gloss. It contains a significant amount of oleander."

Veronica gasped. "So, Ivanna might have been poisoned just like Evangeline?"

"It looks that way," Delta replied.

I was almost inclined to agree. But I reflected on the spirit's warning, and a thought occurred to me. Ivanna wasn't wearing the pink lip gloss—she was wearing red. So, unless she ingested the lip gloss as a taste test or something, it couldn't have caused her death. If that was the case, then why was the lip gloss poisoned? And what killed Ivanna?

11

"Anyhow," Delta said as she rose and made her way to the door, "I've got to get over to Arnaud's for a luncheon." She flashed her yellowed teeth in something that resembled a smile. "I just adore their Filet Mignon Charlemond."

My stomach growled at the mention of meat. "Before you go, has your informant said anything about the results of the mass spectrometry?"

"The mass what?" she asked, drawling the word *what* for a good three syllables.

"It's a type of test done in forensic toxicology for cases of possible drug overdose or poisoning."

"Those must be the results we're still waiting for," she said, pulling her Cadillac keys from her Louis Vuitton. "I assume they'll show that Miss Jones died of oleander poisoning."

"Yeah," I said despite my doubts. "I'd like to see them, just the same."

As Delta reached for the doorknob, the vassal entered with two carryout bags.

My stomach instantly recognized the Johnny's Po-Boys logo on the bags and let out a mighty roar—more from outrage than hunger.

"Well, excuse you, young man," Delta huffed.

The vassal looked at her with his coke-bottle-lens-enlarged eyes and stepped to the side, leaning against the door to hold it open.

"Greetings, good ladies," David bellowed as he strode big-man-on-campus-style into the room. His strut went straight to slump when he caught sight of Delta.

She wrinkled her nose in disgust and looked from David to the vassal. "What *is* that ghastly odor?"

The vassal blinked but maintained his fraternity-imposed silence.

David stood at attention, more like a common footman than a feudal lord. "Uh, it's three french fry po' boys with gravy and two hot dog po' boys with chili, ma'am."

"Well, it smells like road kill," she snarled.

The vassal pushed up his glasses with his index finger and proceeded to stare at Delta in his mouth-breather manner.

She gathered her mink around her neck and scowled at him as though he were a vulgar voyeur. Then she turned to Veronica and me, her lips thinning into a straight line. "I don't know how you two can work in these appalling conditions."

The second she went out the door, Veronica shot me a wry smile.

David relaxed and resumed his fraternal-feudal air. "Vassal, I'm ready to be served."

I watched with envy as the vassal pulled the sandwiches from the bag and laid out a po' boy picnic on David's desk.

"What are you thinking, Franki?" Veronica asked.

"That I would kill to have the metabolism of a college male."

"Well, that goes without saying," she said, glancing at David as he licked brown gravy from his fingers. "I meant about the oleander in the lip gloss."

I sighed. "I don't know what to think. Nothing makes any sense."

"Let's go talk it out in my office." Veronica turned to David. "When you're finished feasting, could you research the effects of oleander poisoning on the body?"

David nodded with french fries protruding from his mouth like cigarettes.

I took one last longing look at the boys' po' boys and then followed Veronica down the hallway. I was starting to worry that I would never get to eat again.

"All right," she said, taking a seat behind her desk, "what do we know?"

I flopped into my usual chair. "That Ivanna was holding poisoned lip gloss she wasn't wearing. And unless she had some sort of lip protectors like Gilligan wore in his spy dream when Ginger kissed him on *Gilligan's Island,* then I seriously doubt that she was planning to wear it to kiss an enemy."

Veronica smirked and turned on her laptop.

"So, the way I see it," I said, kicking my legs over the side of the chair, "we have three possible scenarios. First, Ivanna was planning to poison someone with the lip gloss, but it backfired."

"How?" she asked as she twisted her hair into a knot.

"Maybe the person figured out what she was up to and killed her instead by making her swallow some of the lip gloss."

Veronica worked a pencil into her bun to hold it in place. "That's possible, I suppose."

I crossed my arms and sunk deeper into the chair. "The only problem with that is we don't know how much oleander it would take to kill a woman Ivanna's size. A little bit in some lip gloss may not be enough."

"Good point. I'll send David an email right now asking him to add that to his to-do list," she said, clicking the keys on her keyboard.

As she typed, I casually swiped a lone peppermint from the corner of her desk. I felt it was owed to me since she was delaying my lunch. "We also need to figure out where the poison came from."

Veronica looked up. "You don't think it came from Oleander Place?"

"It depends," I said, quietly unwrapping the peppermint out of view. "We know Ivanna was at the plantation before she was murdered, so maybe she took some oleander leaves. But—and this is my second theory—Adam could have added the oleander to the lip gloss with or without her knowledge. And if that's the case, it could've come from anywhere."

"Why would Adam poison the lip gloss?" she asked, cocking her head.

I discreetly popped the peppermint into my mouth and replied, "Either he was in on Ivanna's poisoning plan, or he wanted to poison Ivanna."

She folded her hands beneath her chin. "It sounds like it's time to have another face-to-face chat with Dr. Geyer."

I nodded, savoring the yummy peppermint flavor.

Veronica resumed typing. "What's your third theory?"

"That whoever killed Ivanna put the lip gloss in her hand to make a statement."

"Such as?" she asked, raising an eyebrow.

I shrugged. "Maybe it's like Delta said about the flower Evangeline was holding. You know, that she was toxic or something."

"Or that her products were."

"I'm not so sure." I blatantly chewed the peppermint and wished it were a po' boy. "Remember, I looked at the ingredients

Adam uses, and they're all harmless. Plus, the lip gloss tube didn't have the Lickalicious Lips label."

"So, what are you planning to do?"

"I'm finally going to track down Scarlett," I said, neglecting to mention that I'd be lunching at length first. "Then I'll pay a visit to Adam."

David cleared his throat in the doorway.

"Yes?" Veronica asked.

"The mail just came," he said, depositing several envelopes on her desk. "And I found out that acute oleander poisoning causes cardiac arrest."

I sat up in my chair. "What about respiratory failure?"

"Nope." He consulted the printout he was holding. "It affects the heart, the gastrointestinal system, and the nervous system."

Veronica and I exchanged a look.

"So," he continued, "it could make you puke, give you the runs—"

Veronica held up her hand. "Thank you, David."

"But it wouldn't cause the lungs to fail," I muttered.

"This is getting more and more interesting," Veronica said.

"You mean, confusing." I stared at the pink Post-It notes on Veronica's desk and thought of the diamond. "David, have you ever heard of a nineteenth-century pirate called Beau the Black?"

He scratched his forehead. "I think we studied him in, like, the seventh grade, but I don't remember anything about him."

"His real name was Beauregard Patterson, and he used to be a confederate army soldier. I need you to try to locate any of his descendants. Do you think you can do that?"

"Aye aye, captain," he said with a salute and then limped away like he had a peg leg.

I had to smile at his pirate persona.

Veronica tore open an envelope. "Why do you want to find Beau's relatives?"

"It's time to look into the legend of the pink diamond. Something is off about this case, starting with the cause of death."

"I think you're right." She pulled a card from the envelope and put her hand to her mouth. Then she looked up at me with fear in her eyes.

I glanced at the envelope lying on her desk. Noting the shiny purple of its interior flap, I froze in my chair. I had only one question, "What did Nonna do?"

"Now, stay calm," Veronica said, gripping the sides of the card as though hanging on for dear life. "It's a little thing, really."

I ripped the card from her hand. It was an invitation to a cocktail party celebrating my engagement to "Bradli Artman," the Italian phonetic spelling of "Bradley Hartmann" minus the *h* (which is always silent in the Italian language and never begins a word). My first thought was that maybe the name looked just different enough to convince Bradley that it wasn't actually him I was getting engaged to. But then it occurred to me that another man wouldn't make the outcome any better.

Fueled by a burst of rage that would rival that of Rocky Balboa on steroids, I marched into my office and grabbed my purse and cell phone. Then I pressed my parents' number and headed for the lobby.

"Franki!" Veronica called, her high heels clicking behind me. "What are you going to do?"

"What I do best—fight with my nonna and then stress-eat," I shouted as I stormed from the office. I ran down the stairs two at a time while the phone was ringing. When I got to the parking lot, the answering machine switched on. Certain that Nonna was dodging my call, I climbed into my car and pressed my parents' work number. I was about to start the engine when someone picked up.

"Amato's Deli," my mother responded in a shrill, singsong tone.

To avoid the delay of our usual name game, I blurted out, "Mom, this is Francesca."

"Well, of course it is," she said in an offended tone. "Are you suggesting that I don't know my own daughter's voice?"

So much for saving time. "Mom, I—"

"Well, what else am I supposed to think when you tell me your name, Francesca?"

I sighed and leaned my head against the window. I couldn't win where my family was concerned. "You're right. That was silly of me. Now, can I talk to Dad?"

"He's making Italian sausage, and he's up to his elbows in ground pork."

And I'm knee-deep in poop, I thought. "I need to talk to him about Nonna. It's urgent."

"It's not a good time, dear. Your nonna is here."

My radar went up. There were only three reasons my nonna would ever leave the house: Sunday mass, a papal visit, or a secret mission related to one of her meddling schemes. "What's she doing at the deli?"

"She said she wanted to help your father make the sausage," my mother whispered. "But between you and me, I think she really wanted to get out of the house. Right now she's holding court with Rosalie Artusi, Crispino DiRuggiero from the ceramics store, Agostino Fossati from that new chocolate shop—"

"Okay, Mom?" I interrupted. "I don't need the whole list. Just let me talk to Nonna."

"She's talking to Father Will and Father Roman. I'd hate to disturb them."

"Wait." I paused to collect my thoughts. "Did you say 'Father?'"

"Twice, dear. They're new priests at Holy Rosary Church, and they've become regulars at the deli. They said they've been assigned to teach the marriage preparation classes. Isn't that nice?"

I felt a stabbing sensation in my chest as the reality of what was going on came crashing down on me. *Holy mother of God, Nonna's arranging my wedding.*

"Francesca, are you all right? You sound like you're choking."

"Mom," I said through clenched teeth, "why the hell didn't you tell me Nonna was communing with clergy?"

"You said you didn't want the whole list," she replied, clueless to my priestly plight.

My heart was pounding out the rhythm of *the tarantella.* "Never mind that. Just put her on the phone."

I heard the receiver crash down onto the counter.

"Carmela!" she shouted, even though the tables were all of five feet from the deli's phone. "It's Francesca!"

Next came the usual murmur of the customers, who, upon hearing my name, began asking what I knew to be prying questions about my personal life—questions to which my mother would respond in lavish detail.

"*Pronto,*" Nonna responded with the customary Italian *ready.* And I could tell from her tone that she was indeed ready—for battle.

"Nonna," I rasped, breathless from stress, "I saw the invitation. How could you do this?"

"What's-a the big-a problem?"

I gasped. "The 'big-a problem' is that Bradley hasn't asked me to marry him. And if he sees that invitation, he never will."

"He will-a, he will-a," she reassured. "You leave everything-a to me."

I laughed in disbelief. "If I do that, I'll end up a *zitella* for sure. Now please tell me that you did *not* send him that invitation."

"*Calmati*, Franki," she reassured. "I only send it-a to Veronica."

I bowed my head on the steering wheel and silently thanked God, Jesus, Mary, and Joseph for their divine intervention. But then curiosity got the best of me. "Why did you only send it to her?"

"Because it's-a just a sample, and I want-a her opinion."

"Why *her* opinion?" I asked, admittedly a little put out. After all, it was an invitation to *my* engagement party.

"It's-a simple," she said matter-of-factly. "Veronica's got-a class."

The woman sends out clandestine purple invitations to my non-engagement with the name of my non-fiancé misspelled, and she implies that I'm the one who's unrefined? "Class or no class," I hissed, "there is no engagement. So do not send out any more invitations, *capito*?"

"I can't-a make-a you no guarantees," she replied without missing a beat.

I wanted to scream, but I remained calm because I knew I had Catholicism on my side, er, sort of. "Nonna, even if Bradley and I do decide to get married one day, we can't have a church wedding because he's divorced. If you have any questions about that, I'm sure Father Will and Father Roman would be more than happy to explain the Church's policy regarding divorcees."

She chuckled softly. "It's a like-a we say in Italy, Franki, 'rules are just-a suggestions.'" Then the line went dead.

"As God is my witness, I'll never be hungry again," I vowed à la Scarlett O'Hara before I popped the last bite of po' boy into my mouth and pulled into the parking lot of Oleander Place. I cut the engine and climbed out of my car, slamming the door as I mentally cursed my nonna. Thanks to her Machiavellian machinations, I'd eaten not one but two po' boys and a whole bag of Spicy Cajun Crawtators—the family size, not the individual serving. But what did it matter? It wasn't like I was watching my figure because that was a full-time job, and I was far too busy for that. And besides, with Nonna in my life, I was destined to grow old alone, anyway.

Speaking of being a zitella, I thought as I walked up the path to the back porch, *I could really go for some baked ziti.* I climbed the steps to the porch and pulled my second-hand Burberry scarf tightly around my neck. The sky was still overcast, and the temperature had dropped by at least twenty degrees. I approached the back door, and the magnolia tree quaked violently in the wind as though warning me not to enter. Shaken from my nonna ruminations, I suddenly realized that the plantation appeared to be deserted. I glanced at the time on my phone. It was only two thirty. But since there was no "closed" sign on the door, I turned the handle and went inside.

"Delta?" I called. I peered into her office, but it was empty.

A pall of silence hung in the air. And for the first time, it occurred to me that the plantation home was actually kind of spooky. Because of the cloudy day, it was particularly gloomy inside. The house smelled of must and decay, and the antique furniture and old family portraits seemed to cast dark, deathly shadows on those who entered, i.e., me.

As I crept down the hallway toward the parlor, I considered going back to the car to retrieve my gun. After all, someone had warned me to stay away from Oleander Place, and that someone might be a plantation employee. But then I told myself to get a grip. I was fairly certain that the noises I was hearing had something to do with Delta or Scarlett, and I definitely didn't believe that the infamous plantation ghosts were responsible. And even if I did, my gun certainly wouldn't stop them.

When I entered the parlor, I gave a start. Beneath the painting of Evangeline, the courter's candle was flickering. *Was this a sign that Evangeline was alive and waiting for her flame?* I shook the thought from my head. No, a spirit hadn't lit that candle, a real live person had. And it looked like they'd done so recently because it was barely burned.

Now that I thought about it, Delta had complained that Scarlett was always lighting the candle. So I assumed that she was in the house somewhere, avoiding me. "Scarlett? It's me, Franki. I have a quick question for you."

I waited for her to reply and heard a loud thump from above. Something had fallen, like a piece of furniture—or a body. Thinking that Scarlett might be hurt, I rushed up the stairs to the second floor. "Scarlett? Are you okay?"

When I reached the landing, there was another thump followed by a scraping noise. It sounded like something was being dragged across the floor above. *Or was it "someone?"* I swallowed nervously as I tried to decide whether to proceed without my weapon. But then I remembered that the third floor was a storage area. Relief flooded through my body when I realized that Delta was probably up there moving things around.

"Delta. I'm here to question Scarlett," I called as I climbed the stairs.

It was noticeably darker on the top floor, but there was a light shining from the doorway on my right. As I approached, I caught a glimpse of a shadow on the wall to my left. It took a moment for my eyes to make out the shape, but when they did, my heart skipped a beat—or several. The shape was that of a man wearing a long coat and a tricorne, the triangular-shaped hat worn by eighteenth-century soldiers and pirates. My mind flashed, terrified, to Beau the Black.

This time, instead of thumping or dragging, I heard the unmistakable metallic sound of a sword being drawn from its sheath.

I took a step backward. *Was it? Could it be?*

"Avast!" a craggy male voice cried. "Or I'll cleave ye to the brisket, I will!"

As a Texas girl, I knew darn good and well what a brisket was. I shielded my chest with my arms and screamed bloody murder.

12

———

The sword clattered to the floor as the pirate ghost let out a distinctly unpirate-like—and unghost-like—shriek. I cut my screaming short and peered through the crack between the door and the doorjamb. I saw a nice-looking guy, around twenty-six or so, with sandy blond hair and twinkling blue eyes. Beau the Black he was not.

He stepped into the hallway with his hat in his hands. "Sorry about all of that. I was goofing around with the clothes, and I didn't realize anyone else was in the house." He grinned sheepishly. "We're all kind of jumpy around here these days."

I laughed. "I can understand why. I'm Franki Amato, the PI Delta hired to investigate the murder of Ivanna Jones."

"Troy Wilson," he said as we shook hands. "I'm the Oleander Place historian."

"Great! You're the last staff member I need to interview."

He looked thoughtfully at me. "You know, Delta said she'd hired a private investigator, but..."

"Is something wrong?" I asked.

His face flushed with embarrassment. "It's just that she described you a little differently."

Now my face flushed—with anger. I was sure that Delta's description of me had been less than flattering. "Oh she did, did she? Care to elaborate?"

He shoved his hands into the pockets of his khaki-colored Dockers. "Uh, she made it sound like you were a lot taller." He paused. "And dark."

My lips curled. I was fair-skinned, but because I was Italian, Delta was stereotyping me. "You mean swarthy?"

He smiled. "Delta isn't all bad. She's just a little high strung, as we say down here in the South."

"That's one way to describe her," I said through gritted teeth.

"Do you mind if I put these clothes away?" he asked, gesturing toward the storage room.

"Not at all," I replied. I followed him to the doorway and shivered when I looked inside. It was straight out of a haunted house, with dusty antiques, boxes, clothing dress forms, and porcelain dolls strewn about.

Troy knelt and placed the tricorne into a hatbox inside an old trunk. "So, are you Italian on both sides of your family?"

"Yeah, my mom's maiden name was Pavan."

He rose to his feet and dusted off his pants. "That's from the Veneto region, right?"

I nodded, impressed. Unlike other Italian surnames, those from the Veneto were often missing a final vowel. "How'd you know?"

"I specialized in the Italian Renaissance for my Masters, so I had to study the Venetian Republic. But then I switched to American history."

"What made you change from the Venetian Republic to the Early American Republic?"

He smirked. "The language requirement. To study European History, you have to know two foreign languages, and I only know Greek."

"Greek?" I repeated, surprised. "I thought you'd say Italian."

"My mother is from Greece. Can't you tell?" he asked, shaking his blond hair.

"Honestly, I would have said you were a California beach boy, except for your pirate clothes. Do you always wear a waistcoat?"

"This old thing?" Troy joked as he removed the coat. "It's just a little something I threw on."

I laughed. It was nice to finally meet someone at Oleander Place I could relate to—except for the part about the graduate degree in history, of course.

He wrapped the waistcoat in tissue paper and placed it into the trunk with the hat. "Seriously, though," he continued, "I was doing research for my dissertation."

"Delta said I should ask you about that." I leaned against the doorjamb and crossed my arms. "What are you studying?"

He smiled. "Plantation chic."

I blinked. "You mean, plantation fashion?"

"That's right. What we wear influences the way we perceive ourselves, so it says a lot about who we are and what we value. You know the old saying "Clothes make the man"? And Oleander Place is a veritable treasure trove of information. Or should I say 'treasure chest'?"

I smiled. "Definitely the latter."

Troy locked the trunk and dragged it to the back wall. Then he hoisted it onto another trunk.

That explains the thump and the dragging sounds, I thought.

"Shall we go downstairs?" he asked as he brushed off his shirt.

"Please," I replied. "It's creepy up here."

"This whole place is creepy," he began with an exaggerated shudder, "especially now that there's been a murder in the pink room."

I followed Troy downstairs to the first floor.

"Let's go into the dining room," he said, ushering me into an elegant, marble-floored space. "Would you like something to drink?"

What I wanted was a shot of Pepto-Bismol to counteract the effects of those po' boys. But instead I said, "A glass of water would be nice."

I took a seat at the mahogany table. While I waited, I counted fourteen place settings with polished silverware, cornflower blue and white china, and fluted crystal goblets. On one side of the table, a rope was hanging. I looked up and saw that it was connected to a contraption that was shaped like an upside down lyre and had a panel of rich red velvet trimmed in gold fringe attached.

"That's a fan," Troy said, handing me my water. "While the family and guests dined, a slave would pull the cord to make the fan sway back and forth for the duration of the dinner. Wretched life, eh?"

I nodded. "Speaking of wretched lives, what can you tell me about the murder victim, Ivanna Jones?"

"Not much," he replied, taking a seat beside me. "I was at a graduate student conference in Nashville that day."

I took a sip of water. "When did you get back?"

"I drove home on Saturday night, and I got in around ten thirty. So I missed all the drama. But Delta showed me her photos of the crime scene when I came to work on Monday."

"Had you ever seen Ivanna before?"

"Based on the photos, it's hard to say." He straightened the silverware at his place setting. "She might have taken one of my tours of the grounds, but I can't be sure. Up until the time of the murder, we had as many as three hundred visitors per day."

I thought about Troy's expertise as a historian and wondered whether he had any special insight about the crime scene. "Did anything about the pictures strike you?"

"There were so many similarities to the death of Evangeline Lacour, the room, the dress, the bed, the position of the body. Even Ivanna's hair was the arranged the same way. The only thing we don't know is whether she was poisoned by oleander."

I couldn't disclose the presence of the oleander in the lip gloss because the police hadn't released that information. But I needed to know whether the poison had come from the plantation. "During your ground tours, did you happen to notice whether any of the oleander bushes had been tampered with?"

He shook his head. "I only focus on the lives of the slaves, so I don't really pay attention to the plants. Our groundskeeper, Miles McCarthy, would be the one to ask about that, but he's already left for the day."

"That reminds me, do you know where Scarlett is? Delta said that her last tour would end at three o'clock."

Troy furrowed his brow. "That's weird. Scarlett told me her last tour ended at noon."

"*Cavolo*," I muttered.

"Pardon?"

"Oh, it means 'cabbage.'" I gave a wry smile. "Italians use it like we use 'crap' or 'dang.'"

"If it's any consolation," he began, leaning back in his chair, "I don't think you would have gotten much out of Scarlett today. She was really upset about something."

I leaned forward. "Do you know why?"

"I asked, but she wouldn't say." He shrugged. "She was on edge the whole morning, though. It was like she couldn't wait to get out of here. But who can blame her after everything that's happened?"

I nodded, but I wondered whether her behavior had anything to do with Miles or her warning to me.

Troy glanced at his watch. "Listen, if you don't have any other questions, I need to get back to my research." He sighed. "Unfortunately, that dissertation isn't going to write itself."

I smiled. "Thanks for your help. I'll let you know if I need anything else."

After Troy left, I debated whether to phone Scarlett. But I decided she would be more likely to cooperate if I respected her request not to call her. I would just have to try to talk to her the following morning when I returned with Chandra.

As I stood up to leave, I remembered the courter's candle. I went into the parlor and saw that it had been extinguished. I assumed that Troy had put it out moments before, but something prompted me to touch the wick. It was cold, as was the wax. Someone had put out the flame while we were upstairs. But who?

I RECLINED on the chaise lounge in my living room and counted the shiny gold *fleurs-de-lis* on my fuzzy, blood-red wallpaper while I waited for Adam to answer the phone. It was the second time I'd tried to call since leaving Oleander Place an hour and a half before, but not even his voice mail was responding. I pressed *end* and tossed my phone to my side, narrowly missing Napoleon.

He leapt to the floor as though I'd thrown it straight at him.

"Napoleon, I did *not* try to hit you with my phone," I chided. "I'm the one who just came home early to let you out, remember?"

He shot me a "whatever" look before settling on the bearskin rug and resting his chin on his front paws. That was his pensive pose.

"So that's the thanks I get? For the record, I should be on my way to Lickalicious Lips right now trying to locate a possible lip gloss poisoner."

Napoleon sighed through his nose.

"And you're not the only one who feels like they're under attack, you know. A psycho-killer sent me a death threat yesterday—okay, so they didn't threaten to *kill* me, but that's beside the point. Meanwhile, Nonna is threatening to send invitations to my non-engagement to Bradley, and Pauline is threatening to tell him about it so she can steal him from me."

Wait. Bradley! I bolted upright. *Was tonight the night we were having dinner?*

I sent a quick text to his cell and then stared at my jagged fingernails and hairy legs. With Pauline lurking in the periphery, I had to go big—not broken and bushy—or go home.

My text tone sounded. *Late meeting. See you at Antoine's in the Quarter at 7? xoxo, B*

I looked at the time—five o'clock. I fired off a confirmation reply and fled to my bathroom in a panic.

Two hours and a flurry of plucking, polishing, painting, preening, and perfuming later, I exited my apartment in a fitted (read *unintentionally tight*) red dress and turned to lock the front door.

"Va-va-voom!" Glenda shouted from behind me. "That's some get-up you've got on there, Miss Franki."

I turned and saw Glenda and Veronica walking up the sidewalk. "Speaking of get-ups," I began, noticing that they were both wearing yellow, "you two look like twins." *Albeit in a Danny DeVito-Arnold Schwarzenegger way.*

Veronica was beaming with a post-shopping-spree glow. "To celebrate spring, we bought matching sundresses."

"Um, yeah," I said as I tried but failed to see the similarities between the two dresses beyond their color. Veronica's was a sleeveless Diane von Fürstenberg, while Glenda's was more like a crotchless Dita Von Teese. And there was no way to compare the plunging neckline of Glenda's dress to Veronica's V-neck, unless the *v* stood for "vagina."

"How did it go today?" Veronica asked.

"Well, I'm pretty sure Scarlett and Adam are avoiding me, but I finally managed to question Troy, the historian tour guide."

Upon hearing the word *historian,* Glenda yawned in mock boredom and began admiring the live yellow roses inside the clear plastic soles of her stripper shoes.

"What was he like?" Veronica asked, brushing a lock of hair from her eyes.

I raised my hands like a director framing a scene. "Think smart California surfer."

Veronica nodded, but Glenda's foot popped like Mia's did when she kissed Michael in *The Princess Diaries.* It was like a divining rod, only instead of water, it sensed men.

"If I'm right in thinking that this case involves Obsessive Love Disorder, then Troy might be able to help us understand Ivanna's appearance."

Veronica twisted her mouth to one side. "But he's a historian, not a psychologist."

"Yes, but he studies the social meaning of clothing from the plantation era. In fact, he was wearing a pirate outfit when I met him."

"There's a surfer pirate at that plantation?" Glenda whispered to no one in particular.

"Oh, wow," Veronica said. "So he might be able to shed some light on Evangeline's pink dress."

I gave a satisfied smile. "And why Ivanna was found wearing it."

Glenda took a drag from her yellow cigarette holder and exhaled slowly. "I just might have to take a tour of Oleander

Place. I've got a yearning for some California-flavored pirate booty."

"Speaking of booty," I said with a wink, "I need to get going, or I'll be late for my date."

AT SIX FORTY, I was driving down Canal Street on my way to the French Quarter when I noticed that the lights were on in Pontchartrain Bank. Because the bank closes at six, I assumed that Bradley was still inside. Thinking that we could go to the restaurant in one car, I pulled into a parking space and headed for the main door.

"Bradley?" I called as I entered the lobby.

There was no answer. I walked to his office to see whether he was still in his meeting. I was surprised to find that the lights were out and it was locked. Bewildered, I looked around at the other offices, but they were dark too. The only explanation I could think of was that the last employee to leave had forgotten to lock up.

I was about to call Bradley to inform him of the situation when an Italian expression popped into my head. *Prima il dovere, poi il piacere,* which means "Duty before pleasure." I needed to get my hands on the bank security tapes for Corinne's case, and what better opportunity than this?

I turned and looked at the unmarked metal door next to Bradley's office. As I debated what to do, the strains of Elvis Presley's "It's Now or Never" infiltrated my brain. It was as though the King was guiding me. With a trembling hand, I reached for the handle and turned. The door was unlocked.

I felt a rush of excitement as I entered the room and closed the door behind me. Not only was the computer screen lit up, but a folder with the video files for April was open. Someone had recently been working with the files.

With my heart in my throat, I quickly scanned the files for April 12th and 16th, the days that Corinne was missing money from her drawer. They were right where they should be, by order of date.

I rummaged around in a desk drawer and found a flash drive. I plugged it into the USB port and copied the two files. Then I glanced at the clock. It was ten to seven, which meant I had just enough time to get to Antoine's.

"It's like it was meant to be," I whispered as I ejected the flash drive and put it in my silver clutch.

I stood up to leave and heard a key being inserted into the lock. I froze as the realization of what had just occurred struck me like a club. Someone had locked me into the security room.

I tried the doorknob—it didn't budge. My first instinct was to beat on the door, but I held back. If Bradley had been the one to lock the door, I certainly didn't want him to unlock it and find me on the other side. But when I thought about missing our dinner and spending the night in the bank, I began pounding on the door. "Bradley! It's me, Franki! Let me out!"

He didn't come. *Surely he heard me,* I thought. *Why isn't he letting me out? To teach me a lesson?*

As I was contemplating my next move, the scent of Pure Poison wafted into the room—like a noxious gas. *Pauline!* She was in charge of the security room, and she'd probably been working with the files when I came into the bank. I smacked myself in the forehead with the butt of my hand. The Italian word *scema*, or *fool*, came to mind, and then I smacked myself again because Italian is what had gotten me into this mess in the first place. "Duty before pleasure!" I scoffed. "Why would anyone in their right mind live by that credo?"

I mentally ran through the techniques I'd learned at the

police academy for escaping from a locked room, but none of them applied. I didn't have the strength to break down a metal security door, and I couldn't pick the lock thanks to the protection plate covering the latch. And there was no point in calling Veronica because I was convinced that Pauline had left and locked the main door good and tight behind her. "Oh, God," I whined. "What am I going to do?"

But deep down I knew there was only one thing I could do—call Bradley.

While I pondered what to tell him, I tried to calm my nerves with a breathing method I'd learned the time I took yoga. I inhaled for three counts and exhaled for six, but my heart was still racing like I'd just run a marathon. *Okay, forget yoga breathing*, I thought. *This is going to take Lamaze.*

I pulled my phone from my clutch. But before I could dial the number, I heard a sound I knew all too well, a police siren.

"Oh no, she didn't," I breathed.

The siren stopped in front of the bank.

"Oh yes she did." I started the Lamaze breathing.

Within a matter of seconds, there were excited voices in the lobby. They were coming toward the security room.

"New Orleans Police!" a gruff male voice cried.

Following police procedure, I shouted, "I'm unarmed, and I'm an ex-cop." Then I held my hands in the air.

"Franki?" Bradley asked in an incredulous tone.

I stopped breathing.

The door opened.

I gave a wan smile and a little wave—and tried to look incredibly hot in my red dress. "Yeah, it's me."

Bradley's jaw contracted as his mouth drew into a thin line, and his eyes narrowed into slits.

The ruddy-faced officer scrutinized me through gold, wire-rimmed glasses and then turned to Bradley. "Do you know this woman?"

"I'm afraid I do, John," he ground out through clenched teeth. "Can I talk to you in my office for a minute?"

"Sure," the officer replied.

Bradley turned to me. "Don't move a muscle," he said, pointing his finger at my chest. "Not even to blink. Do you understand?"

I nodded and watched as Bradley and the officer went into his office and shut the door.

I'd never seen Bradley this angry before, not even after I'd punched him in the face and kicked him in the *coglioni* (that's Italian for...well, you know), which I still say was perfectly justified given that he'd kissed me while he was married to his ex. I simply had to think of some way to justify my presence at the bank both to Bradley and the police without betraying Corinne's confidence.

Bradley marched out of his office and right up to my face. "As a personal favor to me," he said in a dangerously low tone, "Officer Quincy is going to forget he saw you here."

"Oh, thank God," I gushed. "Why don't we just go to Antoine's, and I'll explain..."

"We're not going to Antoine's, and you're not going to explain because I don't want to hear it. Now, I don't know where you're going when you leave here tonight, but I can tell you this—you'll stay far from this bank."

"But—"

"No buts," he said, raising his hand.

I took a step backward, just in case.

"Officer Quincy may be willing to forget you were here," he continued, "but I still have to deal with the anonymous tip to the police. Management will expect a detailed explanation as to why someone saw an intruder in the bank after hours. So if I were you, I would get going before I change my mind about asking Officer Quincy not to arrest you."

I looked searchingly in his eyes and then stalked out of the bank. I was angry with him for not letting me explain, but I was also mad at myself for being so careless. Oh, and at Pauline for being so evil. I didn't know what was going to happen between Bradley and me, but I knew one thing for sure. The fact that Pauline had made an anonymous call to the police told me that she had something serious to hide. And I was going to make it my duty to expose her. Make that my pleasure.

13

I placed my "Italians Drink It Better" cappuccino mug on the kitchen counter and glanced at the microwave clock. It was nine a.m., which meant Veronica would be expecting me at the office any minute. But the last way I wanted to start my day was by telling my employer that I'd almost gotten arrested for burglary of a bank. So instead, I flopped down at the kitchen table and opened the bakery box in front of me.

Bradley might not have known where I would go when I left the bank last night, but I sure did—to Bittersweet Confections on Magazine Street. It was closed by the time I got there, but luckily the night baker let me in when she saw my frantic face and fancy attire. Naturally, I bought the peanut butter–banana Elvis cupcake to wolf down in the car and the decadently chocolate Bittersweet Cake to scarf up at home. The King was indirectly responsible for me entering that security room, after all, and a cake eaten following a fight with one's boyfriend can only be bittersweet.

I picked up a knife and scraped the sludgy remains of the cake bottom from the box. As I slid the yummy goo into my mouth, I remembered how angry Bradley had been. I definitely had some 'splainin' to do, but I couldn't figure out what I was going to say. As far as he was concerned, Pauline was a dedicated professional, and I was just a jealous girlfriend. (Okay, the last part was true, but only partially.) To add insult to injury, I'd promised to get along with her—the mere thought of which almost made the cake come back up—so I could hardly tell him my suspicions. No, I needed hard, cold evidence before I talked to Bradley, and I planned to get it.

I polished off the last of the cake sludge and dialed the office. While the line was ringing, something bumped against the back door. Napoleon was out like a light on the chaise lounge, so I knew it wasn't him trying to get in. Worried that it might be my aggressor coming to peel me like a pineapple, I opened the gold velour curtains of the window beside my kitchen table and peered into the backyard. Fortunately, I didn't see anyone.

"Private Chicks, Incorporated," David answered in a clipped, professional voice. "If you give us the time, we'll solve your crime."

"I'm so glad you're there," I breathed. "Have you been able to do that background check on Pauline?"

"I just finished it. She's clean."

I don't know how when she's so dirty, I thought. "Listen, if I bring in some video files from a security camera, will you be able to tell whether they've been tampered with?"

"Uh, it kinda depends on what they did to the file. My vassal could for sure do it, though. He's a total video pro."

I vaguely remembered the vassal saying something about wanting to study film. "That's fine with me, but I thought he only had to serve you for one day."

"For that one entire day," David clarified. "But he *gets* to do whatever my fraternity brothers and I tell him all year long. It's one of the privileges of rushing a frat."

"Uh-huh," I agreed skeptically. "So, if I bring the files to the office this morning, could you take them to him?"

"Sure. I'll see him in algorithms class this afternoon."

I shuddered. I couldn't think of a more boring way to spend my time. "How fast do you think he could analyze the video?"

"I dunno, but he's throwing a party for his comp sci buddies at his dorm tomorrow. He could do it then, I bet. Wanna come?"

Now I could think of a more boring way to spend my time. For me, computer science parties conjured up mental images of Lord of the Rings posters, Star Wars action figures, comic books, and unwashed males unfamiliar with the female gender. But I was willing to do whatever it took to out Pauline to Bradley, even if that meant spending my Saturday night with a bunch of leering freshman nerds playing video games. "Count me in."

"Solid," he said in college-ese. "I'll pick you up tomorrow at two."

"In the morning?" I asked, shocked.

"No, the afternoon. The vassal likes to be in bed by nine," he explained in a matter-of-fact tone.

That vassal is a real party animal. "Okay. Is Veronica there?"

"Yeah. One sec."

As I waited for Veronica to pick up, I saw something move in the backyard. I jumped up and stood to one side of the window. When I peeked out, I spotted Glenda watering her plants in nothing but six-inch heels and a smile (her robe was so sheer it couldn't be considered clothing). I pulled down the blind *and* closed the curtains.

"Hey!" Veronica answered. "How'd your date go last night? I'll bet you really wowed Bradley with that racy red dress."

"I wowed him, all right," I said, collapsing back into my chair. "But it had nothing to do with my dress."

She paused. "Uh-oh."

"Look, I'll spare you the undignified details, but last night I snuck into the security room at the bank, and Pauline tipped off the police anonymously."

An awkward silence followed, and I knew that the attorney in Veronica was running down a mental list of Private Chicks' potential liabilities.

"Everything is fine," I added to ease her concern. "And I think I've figured out why Pauline didn't seize the opportunity to rat me out personally to Bradley."

"Why's that?"

"I can't prove it yet," I began, as I picked up the cake knife and scrutinized it for more sludge, "but I think she's stealing from Pontchartrain Bank."

"You're talking about the money from Corinne's teller drawer, right?"

I snorted. "Trust me, Pauline's not the type to content herself with a lousy thousand dollars. I have a hunch she's planning to steal a lot more than that, if she hasn't already. And by taking money from Corinne's drawer, she's setting her up to look like the thief."

"So, what are you going to do?" she asked, her liability anxiety no doubt approaching a critical level.

"I'm going to research everything I can about the New York branch of Brehman Bank until I find the name of a manager who knew her." I scratched a speck of sludge from the knife and popped it into my mouth. "I'm telling you, there's a reason she left that bank off her resume."

Veronica let out a long slow exhale. "Just be careful, Franki. If she *is* stealing from the bank, it sounds like she could be dangerous if you back her into a corner."

"Don't worry. I won't fall into one of her traps again," I said, and I meant it. Now that I had an idea of how far Pauline would go to get me out of the picture, I would be sure to keep my guard up. "Speaking of being trapped, I'm taking Chandra to the plantation today, and I could use a buffer during the car ride. In addition to her psychic ability, that woman's also got the gift of gab."

"Sorry. I have a packed schedule."

"Oh." I swallowed my disappointment. As much as I loved being the lead on a case, I missed having my best friend fighting crime by my side.

"I have an idea," she exclaimed. "Since tomorrow's Saturday, why don't we have brunch at Atchafalaya and stuff our faces? My treat."

I put the knife back into the empty cake box. Between last night and this morning, I'd consumed enough calories to keep a platoon of soldiers alive during a weeklong survival-training course. "I don't know..."

"They have a make-your-own-bloody-mary bar," she intoned.

"I'm in," I gushed. After all, empty calories weren't as bad as full ones, right?

"Good. Then it's a date."

"Yeah, and let's drop by Lickalicious Lips afterward. Adam won't be expecting us on a weekend."

She cleared her throat. "I can't. I need to be somewhere at noon."

"I guess I'll see you tomorrow then," I said and closed the call. I wondered whether Veronica was avoiding me, but I dismissed the idea since she'd just invited me out to eat. Whatever was going on, I intended to get to the bottom of it at brunch.

I SWITCHED the windshield wipers to high and strained to see the turnoff to River Road. Even though it was only eleven a.m., the sky was as black as night, and the torrential downpour wasn't helping visibility. I glanced at Chandra snoozing in the passenger seat. Her head was pressed against the window, and drool was dripping from her open mouth.

As it turns out, I hadn't needed a buffer from her babbling but rather from her snoring. She'd nodded off before we even got to Private Chicks to drop off the flash drive. And she'd snored the entire way to the plantation. In fact, sometimes it was hard to tell whether thunder was rumbling or Chandra was sawing logs.

Now that I thought about it, I realized that the weather turned every time I was around her. I debated whether this was proof that she really was cosmically connected to the universe. If it was, I decided that it might not be such a swell sign that storms followed her wherever she went. But then it occurred to me that the bad weather might not be a reflection on Chandra but on me. *Was I living under a dark cloud—literally and figuratively?*

I was mulling over this possibility as I pulled into the Oleander Place parking lot. The second I shut off the engine, Chandra shot up in her seat.

"Oh God, are we at the plantation?" she shouted, already in the clutches of her phasmophobia. Then she grabbed her head. "Owww. I shouldn't have let Lou talk me into that third beer sampler last night at the Crescent City Brewhouse."

My first thought was, *Does Chandra ever go anywhere or do anything that doesn't have a moon-related theme?* Next I wondered whether bringing a hungover psychic with a fear of ghosts to a haunted plantation was a good idea. I was about to suggest that she stay in the car when I saw Miles heading toward the parking lot from the direction of the little mill. "I need to talk to this guy real quick," I said, motioning toward him. "I'll be right back."

Chandra followed my gesture and perked right up when she saw Miles. "I'll come with you," she offered as she smoothed her hair, which was shaped like a cone after being pressed against the window. "I need to stretch my legs."

I gave her a sidelong glance. It figured that a Boston native would be attracted to a big Irishman. When I turned to exit the car, I found Miles looking into my window. I rolled it down a crack. "Hi, Miles."

"Mornin', Miss Franki," he said.

Chandra practically threw herself across my lap. "I'm Chandra Toccato, the Crescent City Medium."

I gripped the steering wheel and moved forward in my seat in an effort to block her from his view. "Do you have a minute?"

"I was fixin' to run to de hardware store, but I always have time to talk to two beautiful ladies," he said staring at Chandra, who was batting her eyelashes so fast she looked like a crazed cupie doll.

"Great," I said in a flat tone, trying to discourage any further flattery. "Listen, have you noticed anything unusual on the grounds in recent weeks? Like, any changes in the plants?"

"De plants?" he repeated, scratching his head.

"Well, the oleander bushes," I clarified.

Chandra sighed. "I just *adore* oleanders."

I spun around and shot her a cool-it look.

"All de oleanders are doin' jus' fine, Miss Franki." He looked at the sky. "Dey're sure lovin' dis rain."

"I wasn't talking about their health. What I need to know is whether any of the bushes have been altered. You know, like maybe someone picked a bunch of flowers or cut off some branches?"

His nostrils flared, and I knew that something about my question had angered him.

He forced a smile. "I can't say as dey have."

I looked into his eyes to see whether he would avoid my gaze, but he met it straight on. I knew there was no point in pressing him further. "Interesting," I said in an intentionally suspicious tone. "Have you seen Scarlett today?"

His face relaxed. "I saw her goin' into de main house dis mornin', but I haven't seen her since."

"Thanks," I said, still scrutinizing his face.

"Anytime, Miss Franki." He nodded at Chandra. "You ladies have a lovely day at Oleander Place."

"Oh, we will," Chandra replied before kicking off another round of eyelash batting. "I've just been *dying* to see the house."

I rolled my eyes and rolled up the window before their coquetry could continue. Then I watched in my rearview mirror as Miles got into his car. He was looking in our direction, which meant that either Chandra had made an impression on him or my question had. Something told me it was the latter. I was positive he was hiding something. What I didn't know was whether it concerned only the oleanders or Ivanna's murder too.

Chandra sighed. "It looks like the rain is letting up. I guess it's time to get this reading over with."

"Yeah, let's make a run for it," I said, grabbing my keys.

As we ran to the back entrance, I outpaced her three-to-one —not so much because of the difference in our strides but because of the difference in our shoes. Ever since Delta's dog-sharks had feasted on my feet, I'd worn riding boots to the plantation. But Chandra was in four-inch platform stilettos with lace ankle socks. *Definitely not standard Ghostbusters issue*, I thought as I watched her hop like a bumbling bunny across the soaked lawn.

When she reached the porch, she followed me inside with eyes as big as, well, two moons.

"First, I'll introduce you to Delta," I said in an effort to steady her nerves. "Then while I'm questioning the tour guide, Scarlett, I'd like for you to do readings in the pink room and on the balcony."

She didn't respond.

I turned and saw that she looked kind of green, or maybe

lunar blue. Either way, I wasn't sure if it was because of the Oleander Place spirits or those three samplers. "Are you okay?"

She bobbed her head up and down and began what sounded like a series of sighs.

"Um, is that a psychic technique?" I asked, more than a little concerned about her mental state.

"It's a stress-reliever," she replied, staring at me like *I* was the crazy one.

I shrugged and tried the handle of the office door. It was locked. "Delta must have stepped out. I'll take you to see the painting of Evangeline before we go upstairs."

We'd just started down the hallway when Chandra began making suction noises.

I stopped and stared at her. "*What* are you doing *now*?"

"Nothing," she said defensively. "My socks got wet."

I took a deep breath and headed for the parlor as she sighed and squished along behind me. Apart from the racket she was making and the intermittent rumbling of thunder, the house was ominously silent. And dark.

"Sweet Jesus!" Chandra shrieked as her hands clamped onto my triceps like lobster pinschers. "Is that a ghost?"

I clenched my teeth and wrenched free of her grip. Then I looked down the hallway and saw a flickering light coming from the parlor. *The courter's candle!*

I rushed into the room with Chandra practically attached to my back. The entire parlor had been turned into a shrine to Evangeline. Coral-pink tulle was draped over her painting, and dozens of oleander bouquets filled the room. The courter's candle, which was once again alight on the mantle, cast an eerie glow over the scene. Even more haunting, all the windows were open, causing the white sheers to flail like frenzied spirits in the storm winds.

I stood there open-mouthed until a crash of thunder shook

me from my stupor. I went to close the windows, and as I latched the last one, the door shut behind me.

"Someone locked us in!" Chandra shrieked. Then she leapt on me, piggyback-style.

"Get off me," I ground out as I pried her legs one-by-one from my waist.

"We've got to get out of this place," she wailed.

"You've got to stay calm," I snapped as I walked to the door. I grasped the doorknob, and it fell into my hand. The part of the knob that attached to the door had a round opening, and the knob itself was hollow inside. I got down on my knees and inspected the doorplate. There was a rod protruding that was connected to the doorknob on the opposite side. After I'd reinserted the rod into the knob, the door opened on its own. "See?" I turned to Chandra, who was standing all of two inches from me. "No one locked us in."

"Do you think the wind closed it?" she whispered.

"Maybe," I replied. Although I wasn't convinced since the door opened into the hallway. The more likely scenario was that Scarlett had closed the door so that she could slip past me.

I walked to the window. Her truck was in the parking lot, so I knew she was around somewhere.

"What's the matter?" Chandra asked, raising her hands to her mouth.

"Scarlett's avoiding me, but I have to question her before she leaves today," I explained. "Do you want to go wait in the car while I look for her?"

She scowled and put her hands on her hips. "Oh, no. You're not leaving me alone on this ghost trap of a plantation!"

Things psychics should never say, I thought.

We searched the first floor, but Scarlett was nowhere to be seen. Chandra stuck to me like glue until I headed up the stairs, and then she started to drop back. She was no longer sighing and squishing, just huffing and puffing. As I approached the second-floor landing, she'd only made it halfway up the staircase. I looked back at her. "Are you sensing any spirit activity yet?"

She shook her head. "They're (huff) laying (puff) like (huff) broccoli (puff)."

"You mean, being still like vegetables?" I joked, paraphrasing from *Pretty Woman*.

She didn't laugh.

She's probably saving her breath, I thought. *Because that was funny.*

When I reached the second floor and looked in the direction of the pink room, I jumped from fright. There was a tall figure looming in front of the French doors. I couldn't make out who it was in the semi-darkness, but I could see the outline of a crinoline dress. It was a woman, and she was moving slightly—actually, floating. *Like a ghost.*

"H-hello?" I stammered. I felt my knees start to buckle and grabbed the stair rail for support. *Was I seeing the spirit of Evangeline Lacour?*

Chandra arrived at the top of the stairs. "Did (huff) you (puff) find (huff) Scarlett (puff)?"

A flash of lightening illuminated the figure, and I immediately recognized the red fabric of the dress.

"Yes, I did," I whispered as Chandra let out a hair-raising scream and fell to the floor.

I knelt down and checked her pulse. Then I looked up at Scarlett.

And I wondered how long she'd been hanging.

14

———————

I sat on one of the canopied beds in the children's room and put my head between my legs. Six hours had passed since I'd found Scarlett's lifeless body, but I still felt dizzy and nauseated. I was convinced that she hadn't committed suicide, because there was nothing on the floor below that she could have used to reach the noose. Someone had hanged her like she was a worthless rag doll, and I couldn't stop wondering whether there was something I could've done to save her. Maybe I should have insisted that she go to the authorities or at least tell me what she knew.

Overwhelmed by a wave of guilt, I sat up and looked enviously at Chandra dozing on the opposite bed. When she'd regained consciousness and learned that the looming figure in front of the French doors hadn't been a ghoulish ghost but rather a mundane murder victim, she'd returned to her serene, sleepy self. In fact, after the St. James Parish PD had asked us to wait in the children's bedroom while they completed their preliminary investigation, she'd flopped onto the two-hundred-something-year-old bed and started snoring.

Footsteps pounded up the stairs as the responding officers

returned from the makeshift command post they'd set up outside.

The sound awoke Chandra, who sat up and stretched. "I'm sheets!"

"Where'd you find liquor?" I asked. Now I was really envious.

She fluffed her bed-head hair with her fingernails. "Who said anything about alcohol?"

"You said you were 'sheets.' You know, as in 'three sheets to the wind?'" I mimicked a drunk chugging a drink.

She gave an exasperated sigh. "'I'm sheets' is a Boston expression for 'I'm tired.'"

"Too bad." I walked over to the window. "I could use a drink."

"Right?" She stood up and tugged at her miniskirt. "We've already told the police everything we know. When are they going to let us go?"

I pulled the curtain to one side and saw the CSI unit van in the parking lot. "After they've secured the crime scene and questioned the staff."

The door opened and Delta entered. Her hair was spikier than usual, and with her black jeans, smudged white work shirt, and red neckerchief, she looked like a cowgirl Cruella. She furrowed her brow and gave Chandra the once over. "Are you one of those police psychics?"

Chandra put her hand to her chest. "I *am* a medium. How did you know?"

"Just a lucky guess," Delta drawled.

I repressed a laugh. It didn't take a psychic to figure out that Chandra was a psychic. She was covered in stars and moons, and her T-shirt said, "I talk to dead people." I cleared my throat. "Sorry, Delta. I didn't even think to introduce you after what happened. This is Chandra Toccato."

"Charmed, I'm sure," Delta replied dryly.

Chandra's face beamed like a full moon. "I believe you are."

"Well, apparently you're not, because you didn't look into your crystal ball and see this disaster coming," Delta snapped.

The glow on Chandra's face waned as Delta's dubious charm wore off.

"For that matter," Delta continued, "neither did you, Miss PI."

I sighed. "No one saw this coming, not even the police."

"Well, that's why I hired you, isn't it?" she asked, pointing her finger at my chest like a gun. "To figure out the things the police couldn't?"

I held up my hands in surrender. "Scarlett refused to cooperate with me, so there was nothing I could do. But speaking of doing my job, I have a few questions for you, starting with where you, Miles, and Troy were when Scarlett was killed."

Delta glared at me and began pacing, as though agitated by the mention of Scarlett's death. "We were in the little mill pulling artifacts for a photo shoot. *Southern Living* magazine contacted me last month about doing a feature on plantation life in the Old South. It's scheduled for tomorrow—that is, if it's still going to happen."

Out of the corner of my eye, I saw Chandra handling items in a curio cabinet. I moved to block her from Delta's view. "How long had you been there?"

"Since eight this morning," she said, massaging the back of her neck as she paced.

"Did any of you leave the mill?"

She stopped and put her hand on her cheek. "Just Miles, when I sent him to the hardware store for rust remover. That was around ten forty-five or eleven."

Fifteen minutes could have been enough time for Miles to go to the house and kill Scarlet before I saw him in the parking lot at eleven. But he'd been coming from the little mill, and I wasn't sure that he could have committed a murder and then returned to the mill in that time frame. Also, I couldn't understand why he wouldn't have gone straight from the house to the hardware store. "Did Miles come back to the mill for any reason before he left?"

Delta shrugged. "He may have, but Troy and I didn't see him. We were in the back of the mill."

I chewed my thumbnail. I couldn't rule Miles out as Scarlett's killer. But if he wasn't the culprit, then the only other suspect I knew of was Adam. The problem was that I had no way to connect him to her. "Do you know what Scarlett was doing in the house?"

"She had a tour booked for one o'clock, but she came early to do her cleaning," she replied, twisting the tips of her neckerchief. "Miles saw her arrive at around nine thirty."

"Wait." I scratched my head. "How did he see her if none of you left the mill?"

She wrinkled her mouth into a smirk. "One of the mill windows overlooks the parking lot. That Miles is always watching the goings-on at the plantation."

"Oh, right." I remembered her mentioning that before. I was also reminded of the day Scarlett had seen him looking in the window when she was cleaning in her corset and petticoat, and then a thought occurred to me. "Did Scarlett usually clean in her costume?"

"Of course not," she said with a wave of her hand. "Corsets and crinoline dresses are uncomfortable as hell, and they're expensive too. Even if she'd wanted to wear her costume to clean, I wouldn't have allowed it."

"And yet she was hanged in her red crinoline dress," I observed.

"Odd, isn't it?" she asked. "You might want to talk to Troy about those dresses. He's spent a lot of time studying them, from what I understand."

I nodded. Delta had a point. It was possible that the killer attached some sort of significance to Scarlett's red dress, as with Ivanna's pink one, and Troy's historical knowledge of plantation chic might offer some clues.

Chandra gave a sonorous yawn and plopped down on the bed.

Delta spun around to face her. "What do you think you're doing? That bed is almost three hundred years old."

"Someone has a brown aura," Chandra muttered. Then she shielded her lips from Delta's eyes and mouthed the word *greedy* to me.

Delta grabbed a giant rolling pin from the foot of the other bed. "Well, someone is going to have a black and blue aura if they don't get off my antique furniture."

"There's no need for violence," I said, extending my hand to stop her. "Why don't you give that to me, and I'll take it down to the kitchen?"

"It doesn't belong there," she snapped. "In the Old South, it was used for smoothing moss mattresses." She looked pointedly at Chandra. "But nowadays it's used for smacking mouthy mediums."

Chandra slid her "aura" off the bed and rushed to my side, just in case.

There was a knock at the door.

Delta threw the rolling pin onto the mattress. "Come in."

I stifled a gasp when the policeman entered. It was Officer Quincy from the bank.

"Oh, John. Thank God you're here!" Delta exclaimed. "It's so nice to have a friend from the New Orleans PD by my side at a time like this."

"I came as soon as I heard," he said, smoothing his gray-blond comb over.

At the sound of his voice, Delta forgot all about her furniture and collapsed onto a pink cushioned armchair near an antique crib. "I'm ruined, John!" She buried her face in her hands. "Over two centuries of my family's legacy down the drain."

"Now calm down, Delta." He placed a hand on her shoulder.

"How can I?" she wailed. "I was planning to turn the plantation into a bed and breakfast, but no one will stay here now."

"You're right about that," Chandra agreed, taking cover behind my back.

I turned and gave her a dirty look. "You never know," I said, feigning an optimism I didn't feel. "The guests may return in time."

Officer Quincy lowered his glasses on his hawk-like nose and narrowed his piercing blue eyes at me. Then he looked down at Delta. "Do you know this woman?"

She looked at me and frowned. "This is Franki Amato, the private investigator I hired to look into the Jones murder. A lot of damn good it did."

"Oh, I know Miss Amato." He sneered. "I had the pleasure of making her acquaintance the night before last."

"At my boyfriend's bank," I hurried to add. Then I shot him a pleading look. If Delta found out I'd burgled a bank, I could kiss this case *arrivederci*.

He opened his mouth to speak, but my phone began to ring.

I answered before he could say a word. "Hello?"

"Franki," Nonna began, "we need-a to talk."

Surrounded by the enemy, I thought. "Just a minute, Nonna."

I looked at Officer Quincy. "It's my grandmother—a family emergency," I said, which was never a lie where my nonna was concerned. "Can I take this in the hall?"

"Don't you contaminate that crime scene, you hear?" he growled. "You stay just outside that door."

I gave him a blank stare before escaping into the hallway, careful to shield my eyes from Scarlett's body. "Okay, Nonna." I sighed. "I'm at work, so please make this quick."

"Your mamma told-a me that-a your new-a case is at a *piantagione*."

"Plantation," I corrected. "And yes, I'm there now. Working."

"Is it a big-a place?"

I nodded in greeting at a crime scene investigator as he passed by with a camera. "It's three stories, maybe forty thousand square feet. Why?"

"The Internet-a say it's-a fifty-five-a thousand."

I leaned against the door in shock. The last time I was home, my nonna couldn't turn on a TV, much less surf the net. "You know how to use a computer?"

"I'm-a chock-a full of surprises," she replied, dead-pan.

Don't I know it. I heard the clicking of the crime scene investigator's camera behind me, and then something clicked in my head. "So, why are you looking up information on Oleander Place?"

"It's-a really interesting," she said with no enthusiasm whatsoever. "We don't have-a no plantations in *Sicilia*."

The only things my nonna had ever expressed an interest in were *ragù*, babies, and my marital prospects, so now I knew she was up to something. But I decided to play dumb. "Sicily might not have plantations, but it does have noble palaces that are older and far more luxurious, like the one you took me to in Palermo when I was little."

"You mean-a *Palazzo Ajutamicristo*?"

The palazzo was named after a sixteenth-century baron whose surname meant *Help me Christ*, which is exactly what I was thinking in that moment. "That's the one."

"It's-a too far away."

Here we go, I thought. "Too far away for what?"

"I'm-a thinking about-a having a *festa*."

I clenched my teeth and started to respond, but the door behind me opened without warning, and I had to grab the doorjamb to keep from falling flat on my rear end. Officer Quincy escorted Delta out, scowling over his shoulder at me as they descended the stairs. "What kind of party would that be?"

"Eh, for the *famiglia*."

Chandra popped her head into the hallway.

I turned my back to her. I wasn't equipped to deal with the medium and the meddler at the same time. "Nonna, you and I both know that this is for me and Bradley. But since we're not engaged, drop the party plan, and *pronto*."

"Maybe if-a he knows you can-a get a discount on the plantation, he'll ask-a you to marry him."

I laughed incredulously. "Why? Because I'm frugal?"

"*Sì*. It's a fine-a quality in a woman."

I closed my eyes and ground out, "I'm not going to book the plantation for my engagement party. Not now, not ever."

"Why-a not?" she asked in a perplexed tone. "Now that there's-a been a murder, you can get a real-a deal-a."

I felt my whole body tense. I didn't dare tell her that there'd been two murders, otherwise she'd want me to reserve the plantation for my wedding reception too.

"Your grandmother's right, you know," Chandra whispered from behind me. "After today, you could rent this place for a song."

I turned and pushed Chandra by the forehead back into the children's room and pulled the door closed. "Nonna, I'm only going to tell you this once. Stop trying to marry me off to Bradley because we're not getting married." I should've stopped there, but my anger got the best of me. "We're just going to live in sin."

She let out a combined gasp-gag—the kind of sound you'd expect from an elderly Sicilian woman who believes that her only granddaughter has just been possessed by the devil.

"*Ciao ciao*," I intoned and closed the call.

I leaned the back of my head against the door. A wedding-planning call from my nonna was the last thing I'd needed today. Not only were Bradley and I not getting married, we weren't going to live together either. And after he'd found me in the bank security room, I was pretty sure we weren't going to be doing anymore sinning. But I couldn't think about that now. I had another murder to solve, and this one was personal.

Chandra knocked on the other side of the door.

"Come out," I called.

She pulled open the door. "I think they forgot about us. And if I don't feed Lou dinner soon, he's likely to pass out."

And if I don't let Napoleon out soon, he's likely to p—. "Um, I'll find the detective in charge and ask if we're free to go."

Her saucer-sized eyes grew to the size of plates. "And leave me alone in here?"

"This place is crawling with cops," I said, putting my hand on my hip. "The killer won't come after anyone now."

Chandra folded her hands in front of her mouth. "It's not the killer I'm afraid of."

"Ghosts are afraid of cops too," I said as I patted her on the shoulder and pushed her back into the room. "I know because they never show up at crime scenes."

"If you say so," she said uncertainly.

"I do." I closed the door and hurried downstairs. As I made my way outside, I put in a call to Adam to find out whether he had an alibi for that morning, but I got his voice mail. I hung up and headed for the command post, which had been set up in one of the cabins in the slave quarters. When I approached the doorway, Troy stepped out, looking pale and slightly dazed. "How are you holding up?"

"It's rough," he began, running his hand through his hair, "but I'll deal."

I nodded. "Listen, have you seen Detective Sims?"

Troy shoved his hands into his pockets. "You just missed him. The district attorney and the medical examiner pulled up a few minutes ago, so he went to meet them."

I would kill to be a fly on the wall during that conversation, I thought. "Do you have a minute?"

"Sure." He gestured toward the doorway. "Let's sit inside."

I entered the cabin and sat at the crude wooden table. "I wanted to ask you about crinoline."

He looked surprised. "You mean, the historical significance?"

I crossed my arms on the table. "That and whether you think it has a connection to the murders."

Troy furrowed his brow and stared at the table. "I guess it's possible. Crinoline has certainly been controversial among historians, so I suppose it could evoke some sort of emotion in the killer."

I leaned forward, intrigued. "How so?"

"Well, according to feminist historiography, the crinoline dress functioned as a female prison, which turned women of the Victorian era into quote 'exquisite slaves,'" he said, making quotation marks with his fingers.

"That's ironic considering the plantation context," I remarked.

"Right, but the opposing view maintains that women who wore crinoline weren't slaves at all. They were actually asserting their independence."

I blinked. "How does wearing a huge dress qualify as asserting your independence?"

He smiled. "That's the point. The dresses were so big that they emphasized women's presence in the patriarchal society. Women were no longer content to be wallflowers. Instead, they were literally filling rooms with their crinoline dresses, and in the process they were violating social norms by taking center stage."

I thought about how Scarlett O'Hara's dresses had been considered scandalous in *Gone with the Wind* and how she'd used her clothing to flout social expectations to get what she wanted—and then I made a mental note to get myself a poofy dress. "So, women derived power from wearing crinoline."

"And narcissistic pleasure," he added. "But of course, the feminists say that it's inappropriate to speak of female pleasure since men used the dresses to domestically enslave women."

I glanced out the window and saw the detective and two men entering the house. "There's Detective Sims. Sorry to run, but I need to ask him something."

"No problem," he said, rising to his feet.

I sprinted across the lawn to the house and crept up the stairs with the stealth of a ninja, er, nonna. Silence had never been my thing.

Before stepping onto the landing, I peeked through the railing and saw Detective Sims flanked by a man in a three-piece suit, who I presumed to be the district attorney, and the medical examiner. They were looking up at the noose around Scarlett's neck, so I seized the moment to slip into the children's room unobserved.

"Well?" Chandra huffed, hands on hips. "Can we go, or what?"

"Shhh!" I waved my arms to quiet her and then peered around the doorjamb.

Detective Sims turned to the medical examiner. "Any chance poisoning could be at work here?"

"The discoloration and swelling is consistent with hanging," the medical examiner replied, pointing to Scarlett's face. "I'll have to run a Mass spec. to tell whether any poison was involved."

"Can you hear anything?" Chandra whisper-shouted into my ear.

I glowered at her, and she took a step backwards.

"The previous victim died from oleander poisoning, right?" the D.A. asked.

"That's what we thought initially," Detective Sims replied. "But this morning there was a toxicology hit for belladonna."

Belladonna? I thought, stunned. Was this what the spirit had meant when she'd said not to trust the oleander flowers? The hair stood up on my arms, and I glanced back at Chandra. Maybe she was better at this psychic stuff than I'd thought.

The D.A. stroked his chin. "Was it ingested or injected?"

The medical examiner put his hands on his hips. "Probably ingested. There were no needle marks on the body, but there was no food in her stomach, either."

"Adding eavesdropping to your criminal repertoire, Miss Amato?" Officer Quincy snarled.

I leapt at least a foot in the air and then acted like I was just doing a combined ballet-yoga stretch. "Actually, I was waiting to ask Detective Sims if we could leave."

He removed his glasses and rubbed his forehead. "This is a complicated and dangerous case that's best left to police professionals."

"I think he's right," Chandra said softly.

I allowed myself a moment to fantasize about beating her with the bed roller, and then I said, "I used to be a police officer, so I can handle this case just fine."

He narrowed his watery blue eyes. "I want you to listen and listen good," he said in a menacing tone. "If I catch you interfering in this investigation again, I'll have the two of you locked up before you can say 'hard time.'"

I clenched my fists. "On what grounds?"

"I'll make some up," he said, raising his chin. "Now beat it before I make good on my threat."

Chandra, despite her platform stilettos, ran down the stairs and to the car like Florence Griffith Joyner on speed.

For the sake of my dignity, I exited the house with my head held high, but inside I was anything but poised. Scarlett was dead, and I felt semi-responsible. And now I knew I'd been dead wrong about the poison that had killed Ivanna Jones.

No matter how hard I tried, I couldn't understand why Ivanna would have been killed with belladonna when she had oleander-laced lip gloss in her hand. But I was starting to think that she'd known about the poison in the lip gloss. And if she had, I figured that she'd been coming to the plantation either to get the oleander or to give the lip gloss to an enemy. Of course, she could have been making trips to Oleander Place for some other reason. But what?

Once again my thoughts drifted to the pink diamond.

15

———————

The busty blonde waitress literally bounced up to the table with a pot of coffee in hand. "Can I get y'all anything else this mornin'?"

"I'm good," I said from beneath her bulky breasts. Then I realized how that sounded under the, um, circumstances. "I mean, nothing for me thanks."

Veronica gave a wan smile and shook her head.

The waitress flashed a toothy grin. "Be right back with your check."

"Sorry if I've been a boring brunch date," Veronica said, staring at her mimosa glass as she twisted it in circles on the wooden table. "I just can't believe Scarlett's dead."

"I know." I looked at my half-eaten plate of Eggs Louisianne. "I woke up this morning thinking that it had all been a nightmare, but then reality hit me like a baseball bat. I can't help but feel partly responsible."

She glanced up at me. "You shouldn't, Franki. Scarlett was either involved in the murder or she knew who did it, and it was her responsibility to do the right thing. You reached out to her, but she made it clear she didn't want your help."

"I guess," I said, picking at my poached eggs with my fork.

"Do you think she was poisoned too?" she asked and then tossed a popcorn crawfish into her mouth.

"I doubt it." I rested my elbows on the table and clasped my hands. "This wasn't like Ivanna's murder. Whoever killed Scarlett did it to shut her up."

"Are you sure it wasn't some sort of ritualistic thing? After all, you did see that shrine."

"Yeah," I began, shifting in my chair, "but because the shrine was to Evangeline, it tells me that Obsessive Love Disorder was a factor in Ivanna's killing. My guess is that when Scarlett went to work early yesterday, she surprised the killer while he was worshipping Evangeline."

"That's so disturbing." She drained the last of her drink. "Who do you think did it?"

"Well, Miles might have had time to kill her before he left for the hardware store." I glanced at the wall of old wooden window frames that separated the dining area of Atchafalaya from the lobby. "But if I'm right about my altar theory, he couldn't have been inside the house when Scarlett came to work because he was looking out a window in the sugar mill when she arrived. And now that we know about the belladonna, I think Adam is a possibility. As a chemist, he'd have access to all kinds of poison."

She drummed her fingers on the table. "I still don't get why the killer would've put Scarlett in her crinoline."

"Remember, we don't know why she was wearing that dress." I popped the last of my crab cake into my mouth and licked creole hollandaise sauce from my fingers. "She could have put it on herself for some reason."

"But if she didn't?" She took a bite of her Eggs Treme.

"Then I might know why she was wearing it," I said, wiping my hands. "Ivanna too, for that matter."

"Why?" she pressed, leaning forward in anticipation.

"Troy said that crinoline literally gave women a larger presence in Victorian society and that it had an erotic aspect. And if you think about it, all of that fits with Obsessive Love Disorder. The killer transferred his obsession for Evangeline and her pink crinoline dress to Ivanna. But at some point, Ivanna crossed a line, so he put her in her place. As for Scarlett, she overstepped her bounds, so she got her comeuppance too."

Veronica nodded. "It makes sense, I suppose. But why the belladonna?"

I shrugged. "That's the part I don't get."

"Do you think the name is significant?" She cut into a boudin cake. "It does mean 'beautiful woman.'"

"I thought about that," I replied, stirring my green tomato bloody mary with the pickled green bean garnish. "My laptop is at the office, but I used my phone to look up belladonna on a poison control website. It didn't mention anything about the origin or history of the drug, but it listed some fascinating symptoms."

"Such as?" Veronica smiled at the waitress as she placed the check on our table.

I took a sip of my drink. "Well, it causes respiratory failure, for one thing. But it also causes blurred vision, blindness, and hallucinations."

"Well, aside from the respiratory failure, we don't have any evidence that Ivanna experienced those other symptoms," she said as she examined the bill.

"No, but if she was going blind or hallucinating, she might have been thrashing around the room, and that could account for the torn curtain and the broken perfume bottle." I sucked down the last of my bloody mary. "But then again, maybe she was in a fight for her life with the killer."

Veronica shuddered. "Let's change the subject. Have you heard from Bradley?"

At the mention of Bradley's name, I was filled with longing for another make-your-own-bloody-mary. "I texted him this morning, but he hasn't answered."

"It's only been a couple of days," she said, reaching for her billfold. "Give him a little more time."

"And let Pauline move in for the kill? Uh-uh, no way." I bit angrily into my alligator sausage as I flashed back to that dark day at the swamp. As far as I was concerned, those gators were partially responsible for my current relationship predicament.

Veronica rolled her eyes. "You don't have any proof that Pauline is after Bradley."

I started to tell her about the Three of Cups card, but I bit my tongue. Even I knew that a tarot card didn't exactly constitute hard evidence.

"Besides," she continued, "deep down you know she's not his type."

"I never underestimate the power of an enemy, Veronica, especially not one as pernicious as Pauline." I glanced at my watch and realized that it was almost eleven a.m. "I'm going to call him later, but first I need to find an elusive chemist, and after that I've got a frat party to attend."

"I'll go with you," she said. Then she held up her hand. "But only to Lickalicious Lips."

I looked at her in surprise. "I thought you had something to do."

"It can wait," she said, laying four twenties on the tip tray. "I don't think you should be alone when you question Adam about the belladonna."

I smiled. I was glad to have my partner back. As we left Atchafalaya, I joked, "I can't believe you'd miss the vassal's party. I mean, besides the Rex Ball at Mardi Gras, it's the social event of the season."

By the time Veronica and I drove from Uptown to the French Quarter, located a parking spot, and made our way through the throngs of Saturday tourists, it was almost noon when we arrived at Lickalicious Lips. As I'd suspected, Adam was there. In fact, he was in the process of locking the front door as he balanced a large cardboard box on his hip.

Given that he'd never bothered to return any of my calls, I dispensed with the friendly greeting and went straight to the point. "Did you resign or something?"

Adam stiffened and then threw his head back and sighed. "If you must know, I've been relieved of my services."

"I'm sorry to hear that," I said. "Does that mean Ivanna's father is in town?"

"Not yet," he said pulling the key from the door and turning to face us. "But his secretary called to let me know that he'll be arriving in New Orleans tomorrow to make funeral arrangements and put the business up for sale."

"Could you please let him know that we'd like to speak with him?" Veronica asked.

He gave a caustic laugh. "His secretary also let me know that the good Dr. Jones would rather not see me—since I'm a suspect in his daughter's death and all."

I could see that Adam was in no mood for questions. But he'd been avoiding me, and I wanted to know why. I also felt now might be my only opportunity to get some answers. So I decided to press. "Speaking of the investigation, I'm sure the police have contacted you about the death of Scarlett Heinz."

"They have indeed," he said as he stepped around Veronica and me and opened the trunk of an orange Corvette parked on the street.

I crossed my arms and shifted my weight to my hip. "Do you mind if I ask whether you have an alibi for yesterday morning?"

"Actually, I do mind." He loaded the box into the trunk and slammed the hood. "But if it'll get you to stop calling me," he began, dusting his hands on his faded jeans, "then I'll gladly tell you that I don't have an alibi because I was here yesterday morning packing up my things."

"No one can vouch for you?" Veronica asked. "You didn't see anyone or make any calls?"

"Look, I said I don't have an alibi, all right?" he yelled.

Adam was starting to try my patience. "Listen, we're just trying to get to the bottom of this case before anyone else is killed. Obviously, you don't have to talk to us because we're not the police. But I can tell you that refusal to cooperate only makes you look like a more appealing suspect."

"That's odd," he said in mock bemusement. "Because I have been cooperating, and yet I seem to be everyone's prime suspect." He yanked open his car door.

"Wait," Veronica said, making a clicking sound as she ran around his car in her heels.

He rested his arm on the car door. "I'm kind of in a hurry."

Using her signature manipulation move that I'd nicknamed the *bat and twirl,* Veronica immediately began batting her eyelashes and twisting a lock of her golden hair around her index finger. "Could we please just ask you one more question?" She stepped closer to him, opened her cornflower-blue eyes extra wide, and gave one last bat. "Pretty please?"

Adam softened like butter on a sweltering summer day. "What do you want to know?"

"Whether you've ever used oleander or belladonna in your products," she replied sweetly.

"Or elsewhere," I hurried to add.

He shook his head in frustration as he looked up at the sky.

"They're highly toxic plants that have no use in cosmetics. Now, if you'll excuse me, I have somewhere to be."

Before Veronica or I could respond, Adam got into his Corvette and hit the gas. The car spun toward the curb and ran up on the sidewalk—narrowly missing a bodybuilder with a blond brush cut who was carrying a giant frozen margarita and wearing a wife beater that read "Keep Calm and Carry a Go-Cup"—before righting itself and speeding down St. Peter. The bodybuilder kept on walking, either too drunk or too calm to react.

Veronica removed her Gucci sunglasses. "What do you make of that exit?"

"Well, a) the Corvette is too much car for the chemist, and b) he didn't answer the question."

"He didn't, did he?" She rested the tip of her sunglasses on her lower lip. "Do you think he really had somewhere he needed to go?"

"He just wanted to get away from us," I said, as we began walking up St. Peter. "The question is why."

I LOOKED at David out of the corner of my eye and smirked. He had a swagger in his step as he strutted down the musty corridor of Monroe Hall, presumably because he was a sophomore in a freshman dorm and because he had an older woman, i.e., me, at his side.

"Yo, Shor-tay!" David cried as he high-fived a skinny, five-foot-tall kid wearing orthodontic headgear.

I held my bag against my chest as we continued down the hall. "Is this the vassal's floor?"

"Someone's ready to party," he observed with a wink.

"Actually, I'm ready to have some answers about Corinne's

case," I replied. But that was only partially true. The fact was that walking past the hormonal teenaged males milling in the hallway made me uneasy. Although I was modestly dressed in white Capri pants and a sleeveless turquoise shirt, you'd have thought I was wearing one of Glenda's stripper costumes. Every time I passed a boy, his beady, sex-starved eyes bore into my exposed flesh like lasers, or, given the context, like Star Trek phasers.

David stopped at an open doorway and gave a chivalrous bow. "After you, Ms. Amato."

When I entered the vassal's room, I expected to see a dorm-sized version of the set of "The Big Bang Theory." But the small space was so jam-packed with electronics that it looked more like the inside of a Best Buy, and it had that same plastic, new technology smell too. I glanced at a group of gamers gathered around a video console. "Where's the vassal?"

No sooner had I asked than the bathroom door opened and the vassal emerged. He was in full party mode—the top button of his plaid shirt was undone, and his bangs were hanging loose on his forehead. "Welcome," he said with a casual nod. "Can I get you a drink from the cooler?"

I eyed a nearby ice chest full of Mountain Dew Game Fuel. "Um, I really don't have much time. I'd rather just get to the video, if you don't mind."

"Not at all." He took a seat in the replica of Emperor Palpatine's throne that was facing his computer. "Give me a minute to pull it up."

While the vassal searched for the file, I studied a silver, crystal-studded sword mounted on the brick wall above his computer. "Is that from *Game of Thrones*?"

David's jaw dropped.

"Harry Potter," the vassal corrected in a hushed tone. "It's an authentic recreation of Godric Gryffindor's sword."

I rested my hand on his shoulder. "You *do* know that there was no Godric Gryffindor, don't you?"

The vassal scrutinized me with his slack-jawed stare. Then he turned away and cleared his throat. "So, both of the video files were altered."

I felt like I'd just won the lottery. "How do you know?"

He pointed to the bottom right on the screen. "You can tell by looking at the time stamp." He clicked the play arrow. "But first, just watch this clip from April 12th."

I leaned in and saw Corinne standing at her teller station. She handed a customer some cash and a receipt and then turned to look at the female teller at the next station, which was about three feet to her right. The teller said something, and Corinne walked over to her.

"Is there audio?" David asked.

The vassal shook his head. "But I think the woman is saying that something's wrong with her computer."

I watched as Corinne and the woman knelt down and pulled a tower computer from beneath the counter. Corinne jiggled one of the computer cables, and then she stood up and smiled before returning to her own station.

The vassal clicked pause.

I frowned. "I didn't see anything unusual in that clip."

"That's because whoever edited the video made clean cuts," he explained. "Now I'm going to slow it down, and I want you to watch the last two digits on the time stamp. They represent the seconds."

I nodded. The time stamp read 11:32:01 AM when the vassal clicked play. I kept my eyes glued to the *seconds* column.

"There!" David shouted. "Dude, it jumped by like thirty seconds."

"I saw it too," I said, struggling to contain my excitement. "At

11:32:19 AM, when Corinne was checking the cable, the time jumped to 11:32:49 AM."

"Right," the vassal said. "So your friend was probably at the woman's computer for another thirty seconds before she got up and walked back to her station."

"Which was enough time for someone to grab some cash from her drawer," I concluded. "What about the video from April 16th?"

"Same thing," the vassal replied. He opened the file and clicked play. "Someone edited out twenty-five seconds."

In the next clip, Corinne again went over to the teller station on her right, this time to see a customer's baby. I watched as she, the other teller, and the proud mother smiled and cooed at the infant. And then I saw another woman appear briefly in the bottom left corner of the screen. "Stop the video!"

The vassal jumped so high that his head hit the curved roof of his throne.

"What did you see?" David asked.

I motioned for him to wait. "Replay that, please, and slowly."

The vassal rubbed his head as he restarted the video.

I held my breath as I squinted at the screen. About thirty seconds into the clip, I saw Pauline's long, silky hair obscuring her face as she straightened some magazines in a waiting area near the teller stations. She glanced furtively through her hair toward Corinne and the others and then disappeared from view. "Did you see that woman?"

Both David and the vassal nodded, their tongues practically hanging out of their mouths.

"Never mind," I said with an eye roll. There was no point in discussing what I'd seen with the boys. I had what I needed, sort of. I could now go to Corinne and show her when the money was taken from her drawer, I just couldn't identify who did it.

Of course, I knew that Pauline was the culprit, especially

after seeing her pretending to tidy up the waiting area in the second clip—something I was quite sure she would never lower herself to do without an ulterior motive. But there was no way I could prove it to anyone, and especially not to Bradley. He didn't want anything to do with me, much less with video I'd stolen from his bank. And even if I did summon up the courage to show him the clips, I wouldn't put it past Pauline to accuse Corinne of altering them to eliminate herself as a suspect.

The time had come to get someone at Brehman Bank to talk to me about Pauline, and by any means necessary. Because I was no longer dealing with a hard-hearted hussy—I had a cold-blooded criminal on my hands.

16

At four o'clock on the dot, I pushed open the door to Private Chicks and marched into my office. It was bad enough that I was working on a Saturday, but because David had driven me to the party, I'd lost precious Pauline investigation time while I waited for him and the vassal to finish a very un-rousing game of Scrabble—played entirely in Klingon, I might add. To add insult to injury, Bradley still hadn't returned my text. So, I was probably going to be working a lot more Saturdays unless I could prove that his super secretary was a stellar stealer, which is precisely what I was going to do.

I woke up my computer and set about tracking down a Brehman Bank manager. I couldn't find the name of a single employee on the website. Then I did a Google search and found several of the managers' profiles on LinkedIn. I wanted to send them an InMail, but I could hardly tell them that I was a PI investigating a possible embezzler. I tapped my Leaning Tower of Pisa necklace charm on my teeth as I pondered how to proceed.

My best option, I reasoned, was to make myself look like an enticing client. Because PIs were notoriously cash poor, I changed my LinkedIn job profile to *finance entrepreneur*. It wasn't a total lie since I was always trying to come up with creative ways to manage my money (around two hundred dollars) and my credit (ahem, debt). Then I sent each of the managers a message saying that I had questions about investment funds, omitting the minor detail that I wanted to know whether one of their former employees had ever stolen said funds.

Feeling rather pleased with my progress, I texted Corinne and asked her to call me when she had a minute.

Next, I switched gears and googled belladonna. A Wikipedia reference popped up first, but I wanted something academic. I scanned the search results and was surprised to see belladonna listed on a botany site, since the name had a synthetic ring to it, like *ecstasy* or *spice.* I clicked the link and saw an image of a plant with purple bell-shaped flowers and blueberry-like berries that was labeled *atropa belladonna.* According to the article, this plant was one of the most toxic in the world.

"Just like oleander," I observed.

I resumed reading and learned that belladonna was a shade plant native to parts of Europe, North Africa, and Asia, but it was naturalized to moist climates in North America.

"New Orleans is nothing if not moist," I muttered. And then I bolted upright in my chair. What if belladonna was being grown at Oleander Place? If so, that would point the finger away from Adam and squarely at Miles.

I was going to have to pay an early evening visit to the plantation to look for the plant away from Miles' prying eyes. But even if I did find it on the grounds, that wouldn't tell me why it was used to kill Ivanna. Oleander made a kind of sick sense given the killer's obvious obsession with Evangeline. But belladonna?

I looked back at the article, and a sentence got my attention.

Belladonna has a long history of use as a medicine, cosmetic, and poison.

"A cosmetic," I breathed. The medical examiner had reported that Ivanna was healthy at the time of her death, so I could rule out the medicinal use of belladonna. And given Ivanna's education and line of work, I knew she wouldn't be caught dead—pardon the expression—using makeup that would kill her. But what if the killer had used a cosmetic to kill the cosmetics CEO? It would make sense, and it would also point the finger right at Adam.

Or maybe at Ruth? No, she was so blunt she would've called me and told me she'd murdered Ivanna. And then she would've called the police and demanded to know why they were taking so long to arrest her.

I rested my elbows on the desk and massaged my temples. Until I found the source of the belladonna, I was at a standstill in this case.

My "Baby Got Back" ringtone sounded from inside my bag. Hoping it was Bradley, I grabbed my phone and looked at the display. "Hey, Corinne," I answered, deflated. "Thanks for calling."

"But of course," she said. "I am on a break at work, so I do not have much time. Is everysing okay? I haven't seen you at ze bank in a few days."

I couldn't tell her I'd been banned from the premises, because I knew she'd feel responsible when she found out why. "Bradley and I had an argument," I fibbed. And then I added a flat out lie. "I'd rather not see him right now."

"I am sorry, Franki. But if you need to come in, he is not here at ze moment. He just left to take Pauline home."

I felt a pang of jealousy. "What happened to her car?"

"Oh, zey came to work togezer zis morning."

That pang turned into a stab.

"Because zey went to New York yesterday for a meeting," she hurried to add.

And spent the night, I thought as *Psycho*-style stabs pierced my gut. I unclenched my teeth and asked in a forced casual tone, "So, where does Pauline live? I'm just curious."

"In Faubourg Marigny."

"That's the artsy neighborhood below the French Quarter, right?"

"*Oui*, ze locals call it ze Marigny Triangle."

The whooping of a battleship attack alarm sounded as the word *triangle* echoed in my brain. Whether it had anything to do with the Three of Cups card or not, that was one too many triangles for my liking. Pauline was clearly on the offensive. I needed to counterattack, and quick.

"Listen, I'll make this fast," I said, pulling my keys from my bag. "I watched the security tape for the days money was taken from your drawer, and it was definitely tampered with."

She gasped.

"Both times, someone took money when you went to talk to the teller next to you," I continued, "and I have reason to believe it was Pauline."

"I kill her wis my bare hands," Corinne rasped.

I was startled by the Clint Eastwood quality to her typically fairy-like voice. But then I remembered that even the Disney Tinker Bell was vindictive. "Don't do anything rash," I warned, "because I can't prove it yet. Just hold tight, and I'll be in touch."

"Okay," she said. "I wait for your news."

I closed the call and headed for the door. I had a triangle defense to plan before I went to the plantation, and I knew exactly with whom I was going to consult.

～

I CRAMMED the last bite of Lucky Dog into my mouth and entered Chandra's office. I started to say hello but began to cough as "Slap Ya Mama" Cajun seasoning stung my throat.

"Would you like some of my Tab?" Chandra asked, holding up a hot pink soft drink can with purple lipstick stains.

I gagged a little, and then I choked out, "I'm fine. I just need your advice."

She wrinkled her mouth. "Okay. Don't eat food from Bourbon Street vendors."

I tossed my purse on the floor and straddled a chair. "I see your psychic powers have returned."

"That has nothing to do with it." She pulled out a box of Sandalwood incense. "You smell like a cheap hot dog."

"Better than smelling like a cheap whore," I quipped.

"No, it isn't." She lit the incense. "Are you here on business?"

"I wanted to ask you about Bradley."

"It's going to—"

"Will forty dollars cover it?" I interrupted, shoving a couple of twenties in her face. Two could play this psychic game.

She tucked the money into her bra. "It depends on the seriousness of the issue."

"It's about that Three of Cups card." I waved a stream of smoke away from my face. "Ever since you told me about it, everything's coming up triangles."

"Triangles?" she echoed.

"You said the upside down card meant that I was in a love triangle, remember?" I huffed.

"Oh." She leaned over and began rummaging around in her giant Chanel bag. "Well that's just one interpretation."

I looked at her from beneath my brow, wavering between hatred and hope.

"It could also represent a separation," she continued, pulling out a rag.

"You mean, like spending time apart?"

Chandra shrugged. "Yeah, or that Bradley's indulging in threesomes."

I hung my head as I tried to maintain my composure. "Meaning aside," I ground out, "is there anything that can undo the Three of Cups card?" I thought of Odette Malveaux, the mambo who'd helped me solve my last case. "Like voodoo?"

"Voodoo?" She scoffed as she dusted her crystal ball. "Don't tell me you believe in that hocus pocus."

About as much as I believe in clairvoyance, I thought.

"There's no easy way out," she said, shaking her dust rag at me. "You're going to have to tackle this problem head on."

So much for that triangle defense, I thought. "I'm already working on it," I said, resting my chin on the back of my chair. "Listen, I also wanted to talk to you about Oleander Place."

She turned up her nose and began wiping incense ashes from the card table. "I'm not going back to that haunted house of horrors, if that's what you want to know."

"I wouldn't ask you to go back after what happened," I said. "I just want to know if you can summon the spirit of Ivanna or Scarlett here in your office."

Her lips thinned. "I don't think so."

I looked her in the eyes. "Because you can't, or because you won't?"

Chandra fingered a charm on her star and moon bracelet. "I don't want anything to do with that place. Those spirits are scary."

I suppressed an eye roll. "Look, I wouldn't ask if it wasn't important. There's been a surprising development in the case," I said, wishing I could tell her about the belladonna. "And I need to make sense of it if I'm going to find the killer. He could strike again, you know."

She sighed. "Even if I wanted to help, I couldn't. Lou has

forbidden me from having any more to do with the investigation. I'm sorry." She began dusting a crystal.

Chandra didn't strike me as the type to go against her
beloved Lou, so I knew there was no point in pressing further. I
picked up my bag and rose to leave.

"Wait. There's something I need to tell you." She put down
the crystal. "You know the French doors where we found
Scarlett?"

I nodded.

"Something about the door on the right is off."

I sat down and crossed my arms on the back of the chair.
"What is it?"

"I'm not sure."

"Is it stuck or something? I mean, maybe that's why you had
a vision of the spirit tugging at it."

She shook her head. "That's not it. But I'm positive something about it isn't right."

The door opened and hit me in the behind. I turned and
glared at a bug-eyed male in his mid-thirties poking his head
into the room.

"I'll be right with you," Chandra said.

Somehow his eyes opened even wider, and then he closed
the door.

"Don't your clients knock?" I asked, annoyed.

"It's the lunar eclipse," she said under her breath.

"Ah," I said, instantly visualizing half-men, half-werewolves.
"Well, I've got to get out to the plantation, anyway. Let me know
if you figure out what's wrong with that door."

"I will," she said in a soft voice. "Be careful out there,
Franki."

"You be careful in *here*," I said, thinking of the lunar eclipse
loonies. Speaking of which, when I opened the door, Chandra's
client was standing to one side gnawing his nails. Noting tufts of

black hair protruding from his collar, I gave him a wide birth as I headed for the exit.

Just before the main door a voodoo doll with long black hair caught my eye. I picked it up and considered buying it. If nothing else, it would feel good to stick a pin in Pauline. Now that I thought about it, I wished I could get a voodoo replica of Oleander Place too. Between Pauline and the plantation, I was nearing my wits' end. As of this moment, I could no more prove that she was a thief—of money and men—than I could identify the killer. And I was starting to question whether I was cut out to be an investigator, lead or otherwise.

Xavier appeared from below the counter. "You git better news this time?"

I looked at him, startled. "Uh, about what?"

He crossed his arms and leaned against the wall. "From your readin'."

"Oh, well, like you said last time, it's a war zone out there." I put the doll back on the stand. "And I'm engaged in more than one battle."

He nodded toward the voodoo doll display. "Black magic ain't gonna do ya no good."

"What about this Pat O'Brien's Hurricane cocktail mix?" I joked, holding up a package.

He jutted out his bottom lip. "Spirits neither. You just need to remember that the situation ain't never as bad as you think it is. Nine times out o' ten, the solution's starin' ya right in the face."

"Thanks. I really hope you're right," I said and then headed out onto Bourbon Street.

As I began weaving through the throngs of tanked tourists, I wondered whether there was some truth to what Xavier had said. I mean, I did have a tendency to exaggerate—but just the teensiest, weensiest little bit. Maybe it was time to consider the possibility that I'd been overthinking one or both of my cases.

I PULLED into the Oleander Place parking lot at six thirty and switched off the engine. As I'd anticipated, the plantation was deserted, and there was still plenty of light for a plant hunt.

I started to get out of the car but then stopped. Chandra was right. It was time to take the bull by the horns, or the boyfriend by the hairs, as it were, and confront Bradley. Otherwise, I was going to stay in this miserable state of limbo.

I dialed Bradley's number and waited with baited breath.

"Hello," he answered flatly.

Following his lead, I kept it emotionless—that is, on the surface. "We need to talk about what happened at the bank. Can you meet me later?"

There was an awkward pause. "I'm sorry, but I can't. I'm in the middle of some critical negotiations here at the office."

My heart sank. "You can't spare fifteen minutes to talk about us?"

He sighed. "Franki, please understand. Some big changes are underway for the bank, and all of us in management are working twenty-four seven. We're meeting literally throughout the night. I can't just leave."

"So, what does this mean?"

"It means I need some time."

Tears stung my eyes. "I can give you all the time you need."

Without another word, I hung up and leaned my head against the headrest. I wasn't sure what was happening with Bradley and me, but I knew it wasn't good. I could understand that he was upset about finding me locked in the security room, but he was more distant every time I talked to him. I wondered whether Pauline had finally told him that my nonna was planning our engagement.

I shook my head to rid my mind of the thought. I couldn't go there, not now. Just like my pride, daylight was burning. I had to look for the belladonna plant.

I dragged myself from the car and headed for the back porch. Because the plantation had grown sugar cane, there were few opportunities for shade on the grounds. I started by making a round of the house and then searching a pecan grove behind the slave quarters. Next, I checked the area around the restaurant and headed for the little sugar mill.

When I rounded the back of the building, I noticed that sod grass had been laid out in a two-foot area against the wall. I crouched and lifted one of the squares and saw that the ground had been tilled. Of course, it was difficult to grow grass in shade. But because grass was growing along the remainder of the wall, I had to question whether something else had been planted previously in that spot. Like belladonna.

"Evenin', Miss Franki."

My head jerked up as my heart jumped in my throat. "Miles!" I exclaimed, dropping the sod square. "Wh-what are you doing here so late?"

"I'm gettin' de big mill ready for a photo shoot," he replied. He was holding what appeared to be two giant soup ladles, and he looked like he had a bad taste in his mouth.

I glanced up at the ladles from my crouched position, suddenly painfully aware that I was alone on the plantation with a potential killer. I rose to my feet and casually took a step backward, trying my best to remain calm. "I didn't see your car in the parking lot."

"Dat's because I parked 'round back o' de big mill." He swung the ladles over his shoulder.

"Ah," I said, struck by the effortlessness with which he'd swung the heavy-looking objects.

Miles narrowed his eyes. "What was you doin' wit' dat patch o' grass?"

"Oh, that." I forced a laugh. "I've never seen grass planted like that before," I replied, realizing how suspicious that must have sounded. I couldn't let him know I suspected him of anything, so I had to keep talking to put him at ease. "Whatcha got there?"

"Dese are old cane syrup ladles for de kettles. We store all de old artifacts in de little mill."

"Delta said something about that," I remarked, stalling for time. I had to figure out how to ask about the belladonna, because the police still hadn't released that information. "She also said that's where you keep the Greek Revival accents that were stripped from the exterior of the house."

"And some things from inside de house, like de original windows and French doors. Dey was gettin' ruint on account o' de humidity from de rivah."

"Yeah, with the Mississippi right in front of the property, the plantation feels like a tropical rain forest." This was a perfect segue into belladonna, so I decided to go for broke. "Do you ever try to grow any exotic plants out here?"

Miles scratched his head. "Such as?"

"I don't know, like belladonna or...venus flytraps." I mentally cursed myself for that last one, but it was the only other exotic plant I knew. Could I help it if I wasn't a botanist?

He furrowed his brow and frowned. "Nevah heard of 'em."

"Too bad. I mean, okay," I fumbled. "Anyway, I really should get going," I said. Then, as a safety precaution, I lied, "My boyfriend's waiting for me."

He nodded, stonefaced. "Have a nice evenin'."

I smiled and headed for the parking lot, half-convinced that Miles was going to launch a ladle at the back of my head. I glanced over my shoulder, and of course he was staring right at me. He looked angry too. The second I rounded the corner of the mill, I hoofed it to my car and hightailed it home.

WHEN I PULLED into my driveway an hour later, I gave a sigh of relief. After my unsettling encounter with Miles, all I wanted was to spend the night curled up safely in my apartment with Napoleon. But as I walked up the sidewalk, my stomach fell. There was a brown cardboard box beside my front door, and it was just like the one that had contained the portentous pineapple.

I took a step back and debated whether to open it. After all, it could have been a bomb or a severed head. But on the off chance it was an apology gift from Bradley, I wanted it—and how.

I grabbed a stick from the yard and pried the flaps open. Then I peered into the box. As I'd feared, this was no gift. It was a courter's candle that had been burned down to a stump. And just like last time, there was a note. But I knew what this one said before I'd even read it.

Your time is up, Miss Franki.

17

A loud blast rang out, like a gunshot.

In one fluid motion, I leapt from a supine sleeping position into a combat shooting stance with my knees bent and my gun drawn. Actually, after I'd had a second to wake up, I realized I was gripping my phone. Napoleon had assumed my same crouch only he'd drawn his lips.

I took a step backwards to retrieve my Ruger from beneath my pillow when another bang sounded. Then my whole body went slack. It was just Glenda slamming doors in her apartment upstairs.

I looked at the ceiling and gave a long exhale. "All clear, little buddy."

Napoleon relaxed and jumped onto the bed.

"Good idea," I said, nestling back into my pillows. But there was no way I was going to let myself fall sleep again with a death threat hanging over my head. I glanced at my phone display and was shocked to see that it was almost one o'clock. I'd been awake until sunrise, and then I must have drifted off.

"I need a double espresso to deal with my double threat," I muttered as I checked my voice mail. David had tried to call me, but there was nothing from Veronica. And given that I'd knocked on her door and texted her at least ten times since finding that creepy candle, I was starting to get worried. Then a sickening thought occurred to me—w*hat if my aggressor had done something to Veronica?*

I held my breath as I dialed David's number.

"Yo," he answered.

"Hey, have you seen Veronica this morning?" I gushed in a single breath.

"Yup."

"Yay," I snarked in keeping with the one-word *y*-theme. "Where the hell has she been? I've been trying to get hold of her since yesterday to tell her I got another death threat."

A paper bag crinkled on the other end of the line.

"Oh wow," he said, chewing what sounded like a mighty mouthful. "Like, are you all right?"

"Yes," I muttered, unintentionally continuing the theme. "But do you know why Veronica hasn't called me back?"

"Uh-huh." He swallowed loudly. "She lost her phone while we were staking out this lady's cheating husband at The Roosevelt Hotel. We were there until like eleven this morning, and then she had to meet the lady for brunch at The Veranda."

I was glad I'd escaped that lengthy assignment. But still, I was kind of offended that Veronica had asked David to be her partner and not me. "What are you eating, anyway?"

"Uh, Veronica bought me a bag of beignets."

Another knife to the gut, I thought as my hand drifted to my empty belly. She never bought me any beignets after a stakeout. "So, what are you doing working on a Sunday if you've been up all night? You need to get some rest."

"Can't." He made finger-licking noises. "I have to make up some hours. Besides, I'm all right. After I dropped you off yesterday, I went back to the vassal's and *shut that party doooown.*"

Of course, for most college students, staying until the end of a party would mean that they were hung over. But I knew David was jacked up on that hyper-caffeinated gamer drink. "Dude, you need to lay off The Dew. Otherwise, you seriously might not sleep again until you graduate from college. Now, why did you call me earlier?"

There was another telltale crinkle of the beignet bag.

"I tracked down a descendent of Beau Patterson on ancestry.com. Her name is Kristy Patterson, and luckily for us, she hasn't set many of her privacy settings on Facebook."

"What did you find out?"

"On Thursday she posted that she's in town this week for Shore Leave."

"That's fantastic," I enthused, referring both to Kristy and to the notion of thousands of muscle-bound sailors in uniform flooding the streets of New Orleans. "I guess she's with the Navy?"

"Uh," he began through a bite of beignet, "her profile says she's a jeweler in New York City."

"A jeweler? Then what's she doing on shore leave? Trying to find herself a sailor?" *Not that there was anything wrong with that.*

He cleared his throat. "Oh, it's not for sailors. Shore Leave is, like, a four-day pirate festival in the French Quarter. It's run by this group of women called the NOLA Wenches."

Well that stood to reason. Any women who would invite thousands of men in velvet and feathers with fake pirate accents to flood the streets where I worked were wenches in my book. "When does it end?"

"Today's the last day."

"Hm." I wrinkled my mouth. "That doesn't give me much time to find her, but I'll see what I can do. If all else fails, I'll Facebook her."

"I tried that. But if you're not her friend, the message goes to her 'Other' folder. So I doubt she'll get it."

"Okay. Is there a good picture of her on the page, at least?"

"Lots of them. She looks like she's really short, maybe in her thirties. And she's wearing something you'll be interested to see."

I sighed. "Please tell me it's not pirate garb."

"Nope," he said with a lip smack. "It's an emerald-cut pink diamond ring."

I bolted upright in bed. That *was* something I wanted to see.

AFTER A DOUBLE ESPRESSO, a double-decker sandwich, and some Double Stuf Oreos—I was big into themes today—I peeked out the front window and spotted Veronica's car in the driveway. I dialed her number in case she'd found her phone, but the call went to voice mail.

I chewed on my pinky nail. It was two o'clock, so I figured that Veronica was out like a light after her all-night stakeout. But I had to warn her about the threat. I scribbled a quick note about my ordeal and slipped out front, keeping my eyes peeled for a killer. I pounded on Veronica's door and waited.

The door of Glenda's apartment flew open, and I caught sight of black thigh-high boots descending the stairs. Once I saw the rest of Glenda, I averted my eyes. Aside from the boots, she had a black patch on her eye, a stuffed parrot on her shoulder, and not much else.

"*What* is all the racket about, Miss Franki?" she asked.

"I need to talk to Veronica," I said, pretending to be engrossed in my phone. "Besides, I could ask you the same thing. Your door slamming woke me up."

"Well, I couldn't find my skull and crossbones pasties."

"I see you found them," I said, keeping my eyes glued to my

phone. "You wouldn't, by any chance, be going to Shore Leave, would you?"

"When the Quarter is filled with pirates, sugar, I plunder."

I looked up—and winced. "I'm on my way there now for that case I've been working on."

Glenda eye's lit up like a lighthouse. "Oh, a treasure hunt," she squealed, wiggling her hips. "Can I help you look for the pink diamond?"

My initial thought was that I'd rather be in Davie Jones' locker than at a pirate party with Glenda. But I had to admit that it made sense to go with her. She'd know the popular pirate hangouts, which could narrow down my search. "Okay, but let's take my car."

"Not until we get you a costume," she said, tightening the knot on the transparent scarf that served as her skirt. "I've got a reputation to protect. I don't want pirates to think I rent to a landlubber." She pointed her cigarette holder at me. "Come."

I slid the note under Veronica's door and followed Glenda upstairs with a mixture of dread and anticipation. I was anything but eager to let her dress me, but I was excited to finally see her apartment. Judging from the Red Light District décor of my place, I figured hers would look something like the set of the film *Moulin Rouge* or maybe the Louisiana version of *The Best Little Whorehouse in Texas*. But when I entered the all-white fur, feather, and leather living room, I didn't see any stripper poles or sex swings. In fact, there wasn't even a sofa. Just a six-foot tall champagne glass. "Wow," I remarked, impressed. "Is that one of those champagne Jacuzzis like they have at that resort in the Poconos?"

"Bite your tongue, sugar," Glenda spat. "Under no circumstances do you fill a champagne glass with *water*." She grabbed a key from a hook on the wall. "Now let's go find you something suitable to wear."

We went to the apartment next door to hers, which held her infamous stripper costume collection. I'd expected to see racks overflowing with gowns, but instead they were thick with thongs, packets of pasties, tiny strips of cloth and various, um, accessories.

"Of course, none of my pirate corsets will fit you," she said, exhaling a cloud of smoke. "But I have a Southern belle costume that should work." She began rummaging in a closet and emerged with a dome-shaped metal contraption the size of a children's playscape.

Before I could protest—after all, I wasn't *that* much bigger than Glenda—she'd stripped me down and dressed me up faster than a wardrobe changer at a fashion show. After a few twists of a curling iron, she led me to a standing mirror. "What do you think, Miss Franki? It's a replica of Scarlett O'Hara's white ruffled prayer dress from the opening scene of *Gone with the Wind.*"

I stared at my ringleted reflection in shock. Troy had been right about crinoline dresses. In fact, I was larger than "larger than life." Only, unlike Scarlett O'Hara, there was no chance in hell I was going to church in Glenda's version of the getup since it had a tear-away bodice and peepholes beneath the ruffles. "Frankly, I think it gives a whole new meaning to the phrase *tent dress.* You could put an entire pack of Boy Scouts under here."

"Not the Boy Scouts, sugar, the Scoutmasters," she said with a saucy wink. "Speaking of the opposite sex, the dress has a pull-cord."

I had no idea what she was talking about, but it didn't sound good.

"It's here on your right," she continued, grasping a silk cord at my waist. "If you pull it down, it'll raise the skirt so you can flash your man."

I stared at her, open-mouthed.

"What did you expect?" she asked with a shrug. "It's a stripper costume."

Out of curiosity, I gave a slight tug on the cord. The force of the metal cage beneath the dress was so powerful that it knocked the mirror against the wall.

"Whoa!" Glenda shouted as she stood the mirror upright. "This dress wasn't made for the boxing ring—it was designed for the stripping stage. You've got to make sure the object of your affection is standing at a distance before you raise that thing."

I looked at my reflection again. My skirt might be the size of the Superdome, but now that I knew it could take down a persistent pirate—or a potential perpetrator—it was really starting to grow on me.

I BENT over and examined the huge hole that Glenda's cigarette had burned into my skirt. "I told you that you shouldn't smoke in a convertible! Now there's an extra peephole in this dress, and it's right at crotch level."

Glenda took a drag off the offending instrument and narrowed her eyes. "Personally, I think it's an improvement on the design."

"Maybe if I was in a strip club, but I'm on Bourbon Street," I huffed as I did my best to arrange the sash to cover the hole.

"Same difference, sugar," she said, stubbing out her cigarette with her boot toe. "Now, who or what are we looking for?"

"Kristy Patterson." I showed Glenda a picture of the petite brunette from my phone. "She's a descendent of Beau the Black, and she may be wearing a pink diamond ring."

Glenda blinked. "*The* pink diamond?"

"That's one of the things I need to find out," I replied, stuffing my phone in my bodice.

"Well, if she's descended from a pirate, then we need to check Jean Lafitte's."

"Sounds good to me," I said. "I could go for a purple voodoo." I didn't usually drink on the job, but I could use a little relief from driving this dress.

"Not the Blacksmith Shop, sugar," she said with a frustrated flip of her hair. "I mean Jean Lafitte's Old Absinthe House. All the real pirates go there to partake of the so-called green fairy."

"A little green voodoo will work too."

As we set off down the center of the street, the crowd parted like the Red Sea did for Moses. But it wasn't to make room for my dress—it was to make way for Glenda. She was in stripper-strut mode, and with her dyed platinum hair swaying in rhythm with her breasts, she was quite the sight.

"Begad!" a pirate cried. "It be Gunpowder Glenda!"

"Good ol' Gunpowder!" another yelled.

Glenda gave a satisfied smirk and kept strutting.

I kicked my Keds into gear and maneuvered myself to her side. "Why are they calling you 'gunpowder'?"

She gave a throaty laugh. "Because when you load my cannon, Miss Franki, it goes off with a bang!"

I dropped back behind, sorry I'd asked.

When we arrived at the Old Absinthe House, I navigated the entryway with a shove from behind from Glenda.

I flailed my arms to regain my balance. Once I was steady on my feet, I couldn't believe my eyes. Drunken swashbucklers and their women, er, wenches, were singing the predictable "Fifteen Men on a Dead Man's Chest" shanty as they sloshed mugs of beer and grog. It was like a tavern scene straight out of *Pirates of the Caribbean.* The only thing missing was Johnny Depp, and trust me when I say that his absence was felt.

My impromptu Depp daydream was rudely interrupted

when a doppelganger for Peter Ustinov in *Blackbeard's Ghost* approached us.

"Gunpowder Glenda?" he asked, wide-eyed. "Well blow me down!" And then he gave a hearty laugh and slapped his knee. "Or just blow me!"

Glenda put a hand on her hip. "You old scallywag!" she exclaimed with a bat of her eyelashes. "Is that a hornpipe in your pocket? Or are you just happy to see me?"

I rolled my eyes. If this went on much longer, I was going to find a plank and walk it.

I left Glenda to cavort with her pirate and began scanning the room for Kristy Patterson. After only a few minutes, I was starting to get discouraged. I didn't think she was at the bar, and I was overwhelmed at the thought of searching the entire French Quarter.

On a hunch, I pulled my phone from my bodice and checked Kristy's Facebook page. I was relieved to see that she'd updated her location at two forty-five. According to her post, she was going to be sampling rum for an hour or so at Pirate's Alley Café and Olde Absinthe House, which was located on a narrow street known as Pirate's Alley about a half mile away. It was three thirty now, so that gave me fifteen minutes, give or take, to walk there.

I shoved my phone into my bra and realized that Captain Hook's real-life twin was checking me out, or rather, the burn in my skirt.

He gave me a lusty wink. "Mind if I fire me cannon through yer porthole?"

I arched a brow and considered pulling the cord. But instead I heaved my hulking skirt to one side, stepped around him, and then let it rip, so to speak. Next I heard the sounds of shattering glass and a table overturning. *Time to set sail.*

I scoured the motley crew for Glenda.

"Put me down!" Glenda mock-protested.

I looked up and saw her grinning from ear to ear as a brawny buccaneer hoisted her onto his shoulder. "Hey Glenda, we need to leave," I shouted. "Kristy's at another bar, and I might have just maimed a guy with your dress."

"Oh, sugar," she whined as she slid languidly down the length of the buccaneer's body to the floor. "It's just starting to get fun."

"Why don't you stay here?" I asked with a little too much hope in my voice. "I'll be back in an hour or so."

Glenda looked not-so-coyly at her boisterous buccaneer. "Wanna drop anchor in my lagoon?"

On that sour note, I hiked up my hoop skirt and fled. I took the exit at a run, so I was able to get out of Jean Lafitte's unassisted. Once outside, I tried to jog—okay, speed walk—the distance to Pirate's Alley, but my dress was literally dragging me down.

When I got to the café fifteen minutes later, I was out of steam and, I feared, out of time.

Grasping either side of the entrance doorjamb, I catapulted myself inside, knocking a woman flat on her back in the process. "Hey! Why don't you watch where you're going in that thing?"

"I'm so sorry," I said, reaching over my skirt to help her up. "This costume should be a registered weapon."

She picked up her tricorne and brushed her long brown hair from her eyes.

I recognized her face immediately—that and the coral-pink, emerald-cut diamond ring on her right hand. "Kristy Patterson?"

She jutted out her chin. "Who wants to know?"

Spoken like a true rogue, I thought. *Or a New Yorker*. "I'm Franki Amato," I said, extracting a business card from my bra à la Chandra. "I'm investigating two murders that took place at the Oleander Place plantation, and I'd like to ask you some questions, if you don't mind."

"Dammit!" she yelled, kicking the wall. "I knew I shouldn't have come back to NOLA."

A thirty-something male in a velvet waistcoat and foppish feather hat walked up behind her. "What happened?"

Her face hardened. "Delta Dupré gave my name to the cops. You *know* she told them that I single-handedly killed those women."

"No," I objected, stunned to learn that Delta and Kristy had a history. "You're not a police suspect in the murders as far as I know. I just want to talk to you about the pink diamond that your ancestor Beau gave to Evangeline Lacour. I think it might be key to the investigation."

"All right," she began as she put her pirate hat on her head, "but let's grab a seat at the bar. I'm going to need another drink to rehash this sordid story."

18

"We need a round of absinthe over here," Kristy called, waving at a bartender.

My eyes zeroed in on the pink diamond as it reflected the lights that adorned the miniature pirate ship above the bar. "First I have to ask the obvious question—is that the Lacour diamond?"

She looked at her ring. "Don't I wish. Beau bought this to remember Evangeline by after she died."

That was quite a romantic gesture for a ruthless pirate. Maybe I had the swashbuckling types figured all wrong. "What do you think happened to the original?"

Kristy placed her tricorne on the counter. "My family and I are positive that it's still in Evangeline's hiding place, wherever that is."

I glanced at a skull perched on a wine rack. "What makes you so sure? A hundred seventy-seven years is a long time for a precious gem to stay hidden."

"Well," she began, crossing her black leather–clad legs, "we have Evangeline's last letter to Beau. She told him that she'd hidden the diamond in the house and that no one knew the location but her."

"I don't know," I said, rubbing my eye. "It just seems like someone would have found it by now, maybe even on accident."

"Some days, I'm inclined to agree with you. But if someone did find the diamond, I really think that we would have heard about it by now."

I wasn't convinced. There were too many cases of famous jewels and paintings that had been "missing" for decades, even centuries, only to turn up in the hands of private collectors.

"Here ye go, me hearties," the bartender boomed as he put two glasses of absinthe in front of Kristy and me.

I watched, fascinated as he placed a slotted spoon with a sugar cube on top over the mouth of each glass, set the cubes on fire, and opened the spigots of an antique water fountain that dripped water on the cubes until they dissolved into the green liquid below. "You know, I probably shouldn't drink on an empty stomach," I said, eyeing the now murky yellow contents of the glass with concern. "Could I get some rum cake to go with that?"

"Aye, aye." He brushed my cheek with his finger. "A wench after me own heart."

I blushed as red as the scarf knotted around his head and turned away to face Kristy. "Did your family ever try to look for the diamond?"

She took a long drink. "To my knowledge, not a one of Beau's descendants has ever made it past the front door of Oleander Place, except for my dad and me."

"Why not?" I asked, stirring the sugar granules in my drink.

She crossed her arms in a defensive posture. "Beau wasn't just the black sheep of his and Knox's family. He's the black sheep of the entire Patterson ancestral line. Knox's people didn't and don't want Beau's people to have anything to do with the plantation or its contents."

"So, how did you and your dad get in?"

"About five years ago, we went out to the plantation to ask Delta if we could help search for the diamond. We made it clear to her that we weren't trying to claim it. We just wanted it to be found for historical record."

"How did Delta react?" I took a swig of the absinthe and grimaced at the taste of anise.

"In a surprise move, she let us search the house. And then the next thing we knew, the police had arrived, and she fabricated this whole story saying that we'd stolen items from the house."

My eyes opened wide. That was a bold move, even for Delta.

"Then, out of nowhere, a cop produced a warrant to search my purse. And surprise, surprise, there were plantation knick knacks in there that I'd never even seen before, much less stolen."

I gasped. Until that moment I had no idea just how far Delta would go to protect her beloved Oleander Place.

"Just wait," Kristy said, touching my arm. "It gets worse."

I couldn't imagine how.

"Delta also claimed that my dad and I had threatened to hurt her if she reported us to the police for stealing. So, on top of two years of probation, we got restraining orders slapped on us."

"And the police never questioned any of it."

"Of course not." Kristy arched an eyebrow. "You know she has police connections through her late husband, right?"

"All too well." I took another sip of my drink, this time grimacing at the memory of Officer Quincy rather than the anise. "So, that's what you meant when you said you knew you shouldn't have come back here."

"Exactly." She tipped her head back and drank all but one sip of her absinthe.

The bartender placed my rum cake in front of me with a saucy wink.

I averted my eyes and cut into my dessert. "What's the Lacour family's involvement in all this? If anyone can claim ownership of that diamond, it's them."

"Well, Evangeline was an only child, and she never had children. So, she doesn't have any direct descendants. To my knowledge, no one from her family has ever come forward."

I swallowed a glob of gooey cake and cut myself another bite. "I wonder how many times Delta has searched the plantation for that diamond."

"Honestly, I wouldn't be surprised if she never has. Delta doesn't want the diamond to be found."

I stopped in mid-chew. "Why do you say that?"

Kristy shrugged. "Because it adds mystique to the plantation, and where there's mystique, there's money." She took the last gulp of her drink and wiped her lips with the back of her hand. "Delta herself said that a lot of tourists go out there hoping to find the diamond."

"That's interesting," I said, drumming my fingers on the bar. "She never mentioned that to me." I thought about Ivanna and wondered if she were one of those very tourists. "Did Delta happen to mention whether she'd ever caught a tourist looking for it?"

"Not to me, she didn't." She placed her tricorne on her head. "But I can tell you this—I wouldn't want to be that poor bastard."

"Neither would I." I drained the last of my drink. Maybe it was my conversation with Xavier the day before, or maybe it was the alleged mind-altering effect of the absinthe, but whatever it was, I realized that I needed to shift my focus. Instead of trying to verify that Ivanna was after the diamond, I started to consider how Delta would have reacted if she'd perceived Ivanna as a threat to her plantation's main attraction.

WHEN I LEFT Pirate's Alley Café for Jean Lafitte's, I decided to walk up Chartres Street to avoid the partying pirates on Bourbon. Even though it was only five o'clock, I was hoping to convince Glenda to leave soon. I wanted to get out of the Quarter before the marauding turned to mutiny.

After a couple of blocks, I ran into Blackbeard's Ghost and his pirate posse.

"Why look, mateys!" he exclaimed. "It's Gunpowder Glenda's fair friend, the plantation owner's daughter."

Jeez, these pirates are pests, I thought as I gave a wan smile and walked past them. *If only I had some Britney Spears music to drive them away.*

"Would ye like to join me for a glass of rum, me beauty?" he boomed. "I'll show ye why me Roger is so Jolly!"

Resisting the urge to dust him with my dress, I shot him a shut-your-bung-hole look and crossed to the opposite side of the street.

There was a buzz inside my bodice. I pulled out my phone and looked at the display. Veronica.

"I see you found your phone," I answered. "Have you been sleeping all this time?"

Veronica yawned. "You make it sound like I've been asleep for hours."

"Well, I've been trying to get hold of you for forever," I said accusatorially.

"Um, we had brunch together yesterday."

"Well, a lot has happened since then," I chided.

"Are you actually mad at me for not calling you last night?" she asked in a bewildered tone.

I sniffed. "Kind of. I did get another death threat, after all."

"I can't believe this," she muttered under her breath. "How could I have known about the threat when I didn't have my cell?"

"This isn't just about last night," I snapped. "You've been late, distracted, or MIA for weeks."

Veronica said something, but I didn't hear her because a steaming plate of shrimp pistolettes was beckoning to me from a window at the Original Pierre Maspero's.

"Franki, are you even listening to me?" she demanded.

"I'm sorry, what?" I asked, tearing myself away from the savory beignets.

"I said," she began tersely, "you haven't been around much either, you know."

"Me?" I was taken aback. "I can't believe you would say that when I've been slaving away on the Jones case."

She snorted. "You mean, when you've been slaving away on the Pauline case."

I gasped. "Veronica, you know Corinne hired me to investigate the thefts at the bank."

"And I also know you've seized on that as an excuse to investigate the personal life of your romantic rival."

"Wait," I said, screeching to a halt in my skirt. "So, now you think that Pauline really is my competition?"

"Gah! You see?" she marveled. "In the middle of an argument, your insecurity about Pauline rears its ugly head. It's like you're obsessed with her or something."

"That's not true." *Somewhat preoccupied, maybe, but not obsessed.*

"If you're not going to be honest about this, Franki, then I don't see how we can work through it."

I was stunned by that last remark. Was Veronica talking about our friendship or work or both?

As I stormed down the street searching for the right thing to say, the door of K-Paul's Louisiana Kitchen swung closed and caught the back of my dress. I turned to free my skirt and saw Bradley sitting at a table. I couldn't make out who he was with, but I could see that he was gazing at his companion from beneath his brow. And he had a playful smile on his lips that I recognized all too well. I hurried to a window and peered inside. He was dining with Pauline.

I clenched my jaw, my fists, and anything else that would clench. *Working "twenty-four seven" at the bank, eh? "Can't just leave"' you say?*

"Veronica, something's come up," I said, fuming like a downed ship. "I need to let you go."

"Hold on," she ordered. "I know that voice. What happened?"

Against my better judgment, I decided to tell her. I mean, Veronica is my best friend, right? I took a deep breath. "I'm at K-Paul's, and Bradley is here having dinner with Pauline."

She let out an incredulous laugh. "You're kidding me, right? I'm trying to talk to you about your problem with Pauline, and you tell me you've got to go because of Pauline."

I tried to put my hand on my hip, but I couldn't find it because of my skirt. I settled for my waist. "Do I need to remind you that I have a responsibility toward my client to investigate this situation?"

"Of course not," she replied, her voice dripping with sarcasm. "Because what Bradley is eating and who he's eating it with are completely relevant to Corinne's missing money."

"That was a low blow, Veronica," I said as I glanced into the window and saw Bradley hand the check to the waiter.

"You're right. I'm sorry. But I'd like you to remember that while you're working your two cases, I'm juggling six."

"Oh, so are you implying that I'm lazy now? Because if you are, then I'd like *you* to remember that I'm working seven days a week."

She sighed. "I wasn't implying anything. All I was trying to say is that I'm drowning in work, and I could use a little under-standing and support from you too."

"Okay, okay," I said. "We'll talk about this later. I really have to go."

I closed the call and shoved my phone into my bodice. I felt bad cutting Veronica off like that, but I had a full-fledged crisis on my hands, and I needed to concentrate.

I zoomed in on Bradley and Pauline's table, looking for clues that this dinner was strictly business. There was nothing to indicate otherwise, unless you counted the candles, the empty bottle of Dom Perignon, and the crème brûlée they were sharing.

Bradley raised a spoonful of the creamy mixture to Pauline's lips, and she licked the spoon with her tongue.

I stood back and blinked hard, just in case the absinthe had caused me to hallucinate that little scene.

"Hey, can I bum a cigarette?" a guy standing next to me asked.

When I turned and saw that he was wearing a swamp crea-ture costume for Shore Leave, I knew I hadn't hallucinated Bradley's romantic gesture. This was just an average day in New Orleans. "Sorry, I don't smoke," I replied. Then I gave Pauline a hard stare. *At least not inanimate objects.*

I began pacing in a circle—I couldn't go back and forth because my dress would get ahead of me. I only had a few minutes to decide whether to confront them or leave. But that only took a second since I'm hardly the go-quietly type. The real issue was *how* to confront them. Let them see my pain and hurt? Or inflict pain and hurt on them?

"Blimey! Who do we have here?" the exact voice of *Sponge-bob's* Patchy the Pirate exclaimed. He pointed his fake hook hand at the hole in my skirt. "Little Bo-Peep?"

Arrgh! Not another perverted pirate, I thought. "Well, you got the 'peep' part right, Patchy. Now beat it."

"Come again?" he asked, dropping the pirate parley.

"You heard me—scram, *smamma*, as they say in Italy. Or I'll sick my dress on you." I tugged just enough on the cord to raise the dress by a foot.

He looked at me like I was the swamp creature and split.

I turned back to the window and saw Bradley place his hand on Pauline's bare back as he pulled out her chair. *The inflict-pain-and-hurt option it is*, I muttered.

Bradley, oblivious to my presence, opened the restaurant door for Pauline as she made a triumphant exit.

She took one look at me and burst out laughing.

Bradley stepped away from the door and stopped dead in his tracks. I wasn't sure whether it was from the shock of seeing me or my dress.

"I've always questioned your taste in clothing, Franki," Pauline sneered. "But super-sized Shirley Temple? Really?"

Ignoring her taunt, I searched Bradley's face for a reaction. I saw nothing but surprise.

"What are you doing here?" he asked, still frozen in place.

"Actually, that's what I was going to ask you," I said, my voice barely above a whisper. "I thought you had to work all weekend long."

"We *are* working," he insisted. "Pauline and I were just taking a break from the office."

I glanced at Pauline, who was staring stone-faced at Bradley. Apparently, she didn't view their dinner as a break from the office but rather as a break from me. "Some break," I said, "especially considering that you couldn't even spare fifteen minutes for me."

Bradley held out his hand. "Look, Franki—"

"I wonder," I interrupted, putting my hand to my cheek in mock reflection, "were the two of you discussing business when you spoon fed each other that crème brûlée?"

He looked at me with a blank stare. "Can I call you later so we can talk?"

Pauline shot daggers at Bradley and crossed her arms. "What are you waiting for?" she hissed. "Tell her!"

"Tell me what?" I asked, looking from Pauline to Bradley. Although I had a feeling I already knew the answer.

Bradley opened his mouth to speak, but nothing came out.

"For crying out loud!" Pauline exclaimed, turning to face me. "You might as well know. I mean, it had to come out sooner or later." She put her hands on her hips. "Bradley and I have feelings for one another."

Bradley stood as still as a statue.

"Is that true, Bradley?" I asked softly. "Do you have feelings for her?"

He exhaled a long, slow breath and looked at the ground. "Yes."

I felt like a cannon ball had just been fired through my stomach, and I wanted to drop to my knees from the pain. But I stood firm. "And this is how I find out?" I demanded, my voice no longer anything even approaching soft. "You didn't have the decency to tell me in private?"

A couple stepped out of the restaurant and briefly looked at us before walking away.

"Oh, stop your sniveling," Pauline snapped. "You're causing a scene."

"Pauline," Bradley intervened, putting a hand on her arm.

She shrugged him off. "From the moment I met you, you've done nothing but drag Bradley down with your jealous antics—spying on him, breaking into his bank."

When she put it that way, even I had to admit that I sounded like a less-than-ideal girlfriend.

"It's time for you to face it," she continued, getting right in my face. "A man in his position needs to be with a woman of class and distinction, and not with—"

"That's enough, Pauline," Bradley interrupted, grabbing her roughly by both arms. "It's time to go."

"No, let her finish," I said with surprising calm. My eyes narrowed. "Go on, Pauline. And not with what?"

She sneered. "And not with a trashy Texan guidette like you."

The definition of *guidette* flashed before my eyes: n. (derived from 'Guido') *A loud, promiscuous, overly made up Italian-American party girl from the North with a fake tan, a fake rack, and an all-too-real nose.* And that's when I finally pulled the cord.

I DRAGGED myself out of Jean Lafitte's and leaned against the wall. Glenda was nowhere to be found, and I was sorely tempted to drive home—to Houston, that is. Bradley and I were over, Veronica and I were on the outs, and my cases were at a standstill. Suddenly, living and working in New Orleans didn't seem like such a good idea anymore. But I knew what my mom would say to me if I showed up on her doorstep. "Francesca Lucia Amato, I did not raise you to be a quitter."

I sighed and dialed Glenda's number. As I waited for her to answer, I watched a parade float, designed to look like The Black Pearl, making its way down Bourbon Street.

"Ahoy thar, Miss Franki!" Glenda called.

I squinted at the float and saw her. She was standing up top in the crow's nest waving a spyglass.

"Wanna party on the poop deck?" she shouted.

I considered the prospect of going back to my apartment and spending the evening sulking about Bradley while being stalked by a killer. It didn't sound at all appealing.

I walked over to the massive float.

"Need a lift, lassie?" a pirate with a fake peg leg asked as he clung to a rope, extending his hand. "Long John Silver, at your service."

Why not? I thought as I let Long John lift me onto the ship. For tonight, at least, it was a pirate's life for me.

19

———

My eyes popped open. It was dark, and I wasn't in my bed. I was curled up in a fetal position inside a cramped space, and I felt like I'd been hit over the head. I held out my hand and touched the cool, slick side of my enclosure with a rising sense of panic. *Had the killer knocked me out and dumped me in his bathtub?*

No, wait. There was something furry beneath me, and the ceiling was way too close to my face. I sat up and looked around. And then I held out my arms for balance. I was inside Glenda's giant champagne glass.

It was bad enough to wake up with a hangover, but waking up in a glass was a new low.

I massaged my temples as the events of the previous night came flooding back to me. After weighing anchor with Glenda's merry band of men, we went to John Lafitte's Blacksmith Shop where I followed up my green fairy with a purple voodoo, courtesy of the swamp creature. Then I discovered that when you mix green and purple you get brown, so Glenda and the pirates took me home—by car, not by ship. When I drunkenly babbled that I was afraid to go inside because a killer was after me,

Glenda hid me in her champagne glass while the pirates raided my apartment for my necessities—pajamas, a toothbrush, a jar of Nutella, and Napoleon.

Napoleon! I peered over the edge of the glass.

He was staring up at me with narrowed eyes. Clearly he hadn't enjoyed his stay in the pirate den.

"I'll be right down, boy," I fibbed. I didn't know how I'd gotten into the glass, much less how I was going to get out. And I didn't want to disturb Glenda, because if I recalled correctly, she had a gentleman pirate caller—or two. Best to let sleeping sea dogs lie.

Realizing that the only way to get out of the glass was to jump, I stood up with the precision of a surfer on a surfboard and threw myself onto a pile of pillows below. When I landed, the whole house shook. And then it kept shaking. I was well aware that I was no petite flower, but this was just insulting.

"Bury your treasure deeper, Quartermaster!" Glenda shouted from her boudoir.

Oh, I thought wryly. *So that's the cause of the quake.*

I scooped up my belongings and dashed downstairs with Napoleon. I cautiously entered the apartment, and we checked each room—me with my Ruger, Napoleon with his food bowl.

"All clear," I said, removing the bowl from his mouth. "Let's get some grub."

I grabbed my laptop from the living room and headed for the kitchen where I was relieved to discover that it was only eight a.m. I needed time to pull myself together before facing Veronica at the office.

I fed Napoleon and then looked in the pantry. I was craving Cap'n Crunch but had to settle for cold pizza from the fridge. As I chewed my pepperoni and sausage slice, I wondered whether Pauline had been right about me being a guidette. In less than twenty-four hours, I'd gotten into a cat fight (or, at least my dress had), partied with pirates, and woken up in a champagne glass. And now I was eating Italian food for breakfast.

"Better a guidette than a thief," I muttered as I opened my computer. I checked my LinkedIn page, but none of the Brehman Bank managers had responded to my InMail. Of course, it was just after nine in New York, but I couldn't wait any longer. Pauline had already stolen Bradley—I would be damned if I was going to let her steal more money from Corinne.

I went to the bank's home page and dialed the main number, setting the call to speaker.

"Brehman Bank," a youthful-sounding male answered. "How may I direct your call?"

Reading the first name from the LinkedIn list, I replied, "Steve MacDonell, please."

"One moment."

I picked at my purple nail polish as I waited for Mr. MacDonell's secretary to answer.

"This is Steve," a tired voice replied.

I wasn't prepared to get him on the first try. "Uh, my name is Franki Amato."

"How can I help you, Ms. Amato?"

Now what? For lack of a better plan, I went with honesty. "I'm calling about a woman who used to work for your bank. Her name is Pauline Violette."

There was silence on the other end of the line, which told me that he recognized the name.

"If this is regarding a reference check," he began in a stiff tone, "you'll have to contact our Human Resources department."

"It has nothing to do with a reference," I said. "I'm a private investigator, and I've been contracted to look into whether she's embezzling money from a bank in Louisiana."

He snorted. "I can't—"

"She may be stealing from a charity for children," I interrupted. "So if you know anything that could help—"

"Good day, Ms. Amato."

The line went dead.

"Mannaggia," I cursed. *"Damn" indeed.* I was sure he knew something about Pauline, and now I was going to have to call all the managers on LinkedIn.

I decided to target the women first since they might be more empathetic to a case involving theft from children. As I was scanning the list, my phone rang. I didn't recognize the number, but I knew the 212 area code was from New York. "Hello?"

"Franki, this is Steve MacDonell," he said in a low voice. "I'm calling from my personal cell. I could lose my job for this, so I need to make it quick."

My stomach was in knots. "I'm listening."

"The woman you mentioned, Pauline Violette? Well, her full name is Pauline Violette Malaspina, and she was terminated in December of 2012."

I was stunned. That explained why she had a nonna and why she'd been such a pain in my behind—her last name was Italian for *bad thorn.* "Why was she fired?"

"She was the assistant of a manager who's serving time for embezzling from a charity our bank was representing. She was in on his scheme, but she got total immunity in exchange for information. I can't tell you any more."

"I really appreciate you sticking your neck out to help me."

"Yeah, well, I've got kids, so it's the least I could do," he grumbled. "Don't call again, though."

"I won't," I said. But he'd already hung up.

So, I was right. Pauline had a past and probably a present. Of course, embezzling from a Brehman Bank charity didn't prove that she was stealing from Corinne, but it sure made her a suspect. It also raised serious concerns about her involvement in the Shoot for the Moon charity event. The only problem was that I didn't know what to do with the information. I couldn't go to the police because I didn't have any evidence against her. The main person this news would be of interest to would be the president of Pontchartrain Bank. One Bradley Hartmann. But chances weren't good that he'd listen to me, not now that he was Pauline's prey. Nevertheless, I had to tell him. Somehow.

As I CLIMBED the stairs to Private Chicks an hour and a half later, I felt like I had a marching band in my head and a majorette in my stomach. The four aspirin I'd taken had done nothing for my hangover, and I was nervous about facing Veronica after our fight. I knew she'd be upset that I'd cut her off on the phone, so I had no idea what she'd do when I asked her for advice on how to handle the latest Pauline bombshell.

I entered the lobby and stopped short.

Veronica was sitting on the couch across from an elegant older male with a full head of gray hair and an expensive-looking black suit. She rose to her feet. "Franki Amato, this is Dr. Liam Jones, Ivanna's father.

My stomach felt like the majorette had just dropped her baton. "Pleased to meet you." I reached over the coffee table to shake his hand as he rose. "I guess Dr. Geyer told you we wanted to talk to you?"

"No, that was Mrs. Dupré," he replied, settling back in his seat. "I went to the plantation yesterday to speak with her and see the crime scene."

I noticed that he avoided referring to the plantation as the site of Ivanna's death. And despite his serene demeanor, the sadness in his deep blue eyes told me that he was grieving.

Veronica cleared her throat. "Liam was just saying that the police have given him permission to bury Ivanna."

I was so surprised to find him at the office that I'd forgotten my manners. "I'm sorry for your loss. You must have been so proud of your daughter. She was obviously a smart, successful, and beautiful woman."

He smiled. "I like to think that she got her mother's good looks and my head for business," he said. Then he looked down at his hands. "Unfortunately, it wasn't enough for her."

I cocked my head. "What do you mean?"

"Ivanna lost her mother, Rosa, when she was sixteen. And she was never the same after that."

"That's terrible," Veronica said. "How did Rosa die?"

"Heart failure," he replied in a quiet tone. "But Ivanna was convinced that she'd died of a broken heart, and she blamed me."

Veronica and I remained silent.

He sighed. "You see, because of the nature of my work I was away for long periods. And I worked very closely with another doctor. A woman," he stressed as his neck flushed from embarrassment. "Rosa found out about us. She didn't want a divorce because of her Catholic faith, but she returned to her hometown in Italy and took Ivanna with her. She died a short time later."

His story left a bad taste in my mouth. And I couldn't help but wonder whether this woman had seduced him like Pauline had Bradley.

Veronica glanced at me, no doubt sensing my discomfort. "Where was Rosa from?"

"Treviso, in the Veneto region."

The same region my mother is from, I thought. "How did Ivanna change after Rosa died?"

"I was getting to that." He grimaced. "Her opinion of me and all men, I'm afraid, changed."

Understandable, I almost said under my breath.

"From that point on, men were just a means to an end for Ivanna. And I played along by trying to buy back her affection. So when she approached me about starting her cosmetics company, I was all too happy to fund it. She'd always been obsessed with makeup." He looked down and laughed. "When she was a little girl, she used to crush up berries and flowers from our yard and make her own. Rosa and I were afraid she was going to poison herself."

A heavy silence fell over the room.

"Do you think she did?" Veronica ventured. "Poison herself, I mean?"

"Impossible," he said with a wave of his hand. "I don't know how the belladonna got into her system, but I can assure you she wasn't responsible. Ivanna loved life, and she knew all about the potential hazards of cosmetics. She wouldn't have poisoned herself on purpose or by accident."

"But there was oleander in the lip gloss she was holding," I said. "So, either she was making poison lip gloss or someone gave it to her."

"I don't know anything about that lip gloss," he said. "But I know it wasn't the reason she was at Oleander Place."

I glanced at Veronica. "Go on."

He closed his eyes and squeezed the bridge of his nose. "As I said, she changed after her mother's death, but it wasn't just in her attitude about men." His eyes opened. "She also became more focused, driven. But not for the right reasons. She was determined to right past wrongs, particularly those that pertained to her mother. And as far as she was concerned, Oleander Place had wronged Rosa."

I leaned forward in my seat. "What did her mother have to do with the plantation?"

"Well, Rosa must have sensed her health was failing, because right before she died she started telling Ivanna her family history. And, she told her that she was a descendent of Danielle Benazet."

Veronica wrinkled her brow. "I'm sorry, but I don't recognize the name."

"Right, forgive me," he said, holding up his hand. "Benazet was Danielle's married name. Her maiden name was Lacour, and she was Evangeline Lacour's paternal aunt."

The silence was so thick that you could have heard a pink diamond drop.

"So, she *was* looking for the diamond," I said.

He nodded. "I'm sure of it. She would've wanted to find the diamond to honor her mother's memory. Apparently, Rosa had written to Mrs. Dupré some years before, asserting a claim to the diamond if it were ever found."

I flashed back to my conversation with Kristy Patterson about Delta's protectiveness of her plantation. "How did Delta respond?"

"She didn't. When I spoke to her about it yesterday, she said she'd never received the letter."

A convenient excuse, I thought. "Then, Delta didn't know that Ivanna was related to Evangeline?"

"She said she had no idea."

I had my doubts about that. Delta was too shrewd not to suspect a link between Evangeline and a modern-day look-alike who was poking around her plantation.

Liam rubbed his forehead and rose to stand. "Please don't think I'm being rude, but it was a long, difficult trip, and I still have to make arrangements for Ivanna's burial."

"Of course," Veronica said as she escorted him to the door.

He handed her his card. "If you have more questions, please call. I'm so grateful for your efforts on behalf of my daughter."

"Thank you," Veronica said, putting a hand on his arm. "We'll do everything in our power to find the killer." She closed the door behind him and turned to me. "Can you believe Ivanna is a Lacour?"

"No, and yet it was staring us right in the face." I crossed my arms and kicked my feet up on the coffee table. "How crazy is it that she looked just like Evangeline after who knows how many generations?"

"It's pretty bizarre," Veronica said, sitting on the arm of the couch. "But at least one mystery is solved."

"Yeah, but so many remain."

She patted my shoulder and stood up. "You'll figure it all out. I know it."

"I hope so," I muttered as she headed back to her office. But I wasn't too confident. Because I had the funny feeling that there was something about Liam's conversation that I was missing— some detail, some connection. I just couldn't put my finger on what that was.

I ADDED the last of Liam's information to the Jones case file and leaned back in my desk chair. I kept thinking about his recollection of a young Ivanna mixing makeup with plants from their yard. If she'd used flowers to produce makeup before, then there was every reason to believe she'd done it again with flowers from Oleander Place.

I quickly formulated a plan and then located Adam Geyer in my phone contact list. I pressed his name and waited.

"Yes," he answered.

He sounded annoyed. And based on our previous phone history, I was surprised he bothered to answer at all. "I met with Ivanna's father today."

"Oh?" His voice oozed sarcasm. "And how is the good doctor?"

I could tell he'd been drinking for a while, and it was only ten thirty in the morning. "As well as can be expected under the circumstances. He did lose his only child."

"I'm well aware of that, thank you," he growled.

I sighed. "Listen, I didn't call to upset you. I have a cosmetics question related to something Dr. Jones said."

"All right," he said warily.

"Would crushed pink oleander flowers turn a clear lip gloss solution pink?"

He paused. "It would turn the color of the flowers, yes."

Time to go in for the kill, I thought. "So, when you made the lip gloss Ivanna was holding, you used crushed flowers from Oleander Place."

"I don't know what you're talking about," he spat.

"Actually, you do," I insisted. "And it would behoove you to tell me where you got those flowers. Because if I tell the police that you got them from Oleander Place, then that puts you at the plantation, and hence, at the scene of the crime."

It was silent on the line except for the sound of his jagged breathing.

"It's time to tell the truth, Adam," I pressed. "It will help you in the long run, trust me."

"Ivanna gave me powdered oleander," he said.

I bowed my head into my hand.

"But I didn't think anything of it. The plan was to use the flowers to produce a prototype. We would have never sold a toxic lip gloss to the public. You have to believe me."

"I do," I said, moved by the desperation in his voice. "I just wish you would've told me this sooner."

"I didn't kill her, Franki." He choked back a sob. "I loved Ivanna, and I'm going to find out who did this to her."

I started to reply, but the line went dead.

I stared at the phone as I tried to sort through my muddled thoughts. This was a side of Adam I hadn't seen before. There was so much conviction in his voice. I wanted to believe him, but he'd lied on so many occasions. I couldn't be sure he was telling the truth now.

"Did I hear you talking to Adam?" Veronica asked, appearing in the doorway. She was balancing her compact mirror and blush in one hand as she stroked her blush brush across her cheek with the other.

"He just admitted that he and Ivanna made the lip gloss with flowers from Oleander Place."

Veronica's head jerked up from her compact. "He did?" she asked as her blush fell to the floor. She knelt down. "Oh, darn it."

I looked at the pile of pink powder on my floor and said, "I'll go get the vacuum." I headed for the door and stopped. "Oh my God. Miles!"

"What about him?" she asked, rising to her feet.

"That day we went to question him," I gushed. "He was vacuuming up pink powder in the sugar mill!"

"So?"

"He told me it was rat poison, but it wasn't. Adam said Ivanna gave him powdered oleander. Don't you see? Miles was in on it! He dried the flowers and ground them into a powder for Ivanna."

Veronica put her hand to her mouth. "Oh, Franki. Are you sure?"

"Yes! It explains why he was so nervous that day, and why he was so upset when I asked whether any of the oleander bushes had been tampered with." I grabbed my phone from my desk and dialed the plantation. "Plus, it fits with Liam's remark that Ivanna used men for her own purposes."

She took a seat in front of my desk. "Are you calling him now?"

I shook my head. "Delta."

The phone went to voice mail, but I hung up and tried again. I certainly couldn't leave this kind of information in a message.

"Oleander Place," Delta answered.

"Delta, this is Franki," I replied. "I just figured out that Miles knew Ivanna."

"We just figured that out too," she snapped.

Something was wrong—I could feel it. I collapsed into my desk chair. "You knew he was helping her make that lip gloss?"

"All I know is that this morning Troy found Miles inside one of the sugar cane kettles." She paused. "He's been murdered."

20

———

Hoping to stay below Delta's radar, I drove past the plantation and parked at the swamp. The second I got out of the car, the sight and smell of the fetid water brought me back to that fateful day with Bradley and Pauline. *If I'd known then what I know now*, I thought, kicking my car door closed, *I might've let those gators gobble them up.*

I still couldn't believe Bradley had left me for Pauline. It seemed so out of character for him, and yet I'd seen them together with my own two eyes. He was a lying cheat like all the other men I'd dated, a true *truffatore*.

I shook my head in an attempt to force him from my thoughts. Now wasn't the time to lament another lousy love. I had to keep my mind on the Jones case. My life literally depended on it.

As I made my way along the shore to Oleander Place, I almost wished a gator would pull a Jaws and swallow *me* whole. At least then I could be sure that I wouldn't run into Delta. Because, at this point, I figured she was either going to fire me or kill me. And the latter option seemed particularly likely given that the suspects in the Jones case were dropping like characters in an Agatha Christie novel—specifically, *And Then There Were None.*

All jokes aside, my gut told me that Delta was more than capable of murder. But I didn't think she was the killer. Oleander Place wasn't just her livelihood, it was her legacy, and she'd demonstrated in more ways than one that she was fiercely proud and protective of it. Even if her business was in trouble, I couldn't imagine her sullying the name of her beloved plantation—not on purpose, anyway. Besides, if she'd known who Ivanna was and what she was after, she would've slapped a restraining order on her like she'd done to Kristy Patterson and her father. Problem solved.

No, Delta didn't fit the profile, but Adam was a different story. He had a motive to kill. According to Ruth, he was an alcoholic on the edge who'd worshipped Ivanna, and she'd repaid his devotion by threatening to ruin him. Then she turned to a plantation groundskeeper for help making her lip gloss. So, Adam could have viewed Miles as a threat to his job or even his relationship with Ivanna and killed them both for their betrayal.

Another possible scenario was that Adam murdered Miles, believing him to be responsible for Ivanna's death. After all, he *had* vowed to find the person responsible for her murder.

But Scarlett? As hard as I tried, I couldn't come up with a reason for Adam or Miles to kill her. Yet I knew her horrific hanging had everything to do with whatever it was she'd warned me I was "messing with."

As I crept along behind the hedge separating the border of the property from the swamp, I wondered for the thousandth time just what the hell I'd gotten myself into. And I wished Veronica were here with me, helping me get to the bottom of these awful crimes. When this was all over, I intended to talk to her about the way we work our cases—that is, if the killer didn't do me in first.

Halfway down the hedge, I arrived at the back of the slave quarters. I assumed that the police were keeping Troy there or at the big mill where he'd found Miles' body. I dashed to the command post window and peered inside. Troy was sitting at the table with a blanket around his shoulders. His face looked ashen, like a man who'd just seen a ghost. Or a corpse.

An officer passed by the window, so I ducked down. I heard him say something to Troy, and then he exited the building.

I waited until I saw the officer enter the house and then slipped inside the command post. "Troy! Are you okay?"

He blinked a few times as though struggling to recognize me. "I guess."

I glanced back toward the door. "Listen, where's Delta?"

"She's with Officer Quincy in her office." His voice was monotone, like he'd been sedated.

Hopefully they stay there, I thought. I had neither the time nor the inclination to get thrown in jail by Officer Quincy. "Good. I was hoping to talk to you alone. I'm trying to make sense of what happened to Miles."

Troy met my gaze, and his blue eyes looked as though their usual sparkle had been extinguished. "I got a call from Delta Sunday morning. She was in a panic because Miles hadn't shown up for the photo shoot, so she asked me to sub for him."

"I take it he never came."

He shook his head. "But during the shoot, I found his car parked behind the big mill. Delta was worried that he might be injured somewhere on the grounds, so we started searching."

"Whose idea was it to look in the kettles?" I asked. It was well known in police circles that the person who found the body was often the prime suspect.

"No one's." His speech had dropped to almost a whisper. "After we'd looked everywhere we could think of, we were on the back porch trying to figure out what to do next when we saw Delta's dogs circling the *grande* kettle."

Like little vultures moving in for the kill, I thought.

"So I offered to go take a look," Troy continued. "He was hit over the head with a cane syrup ladle, maybe more than once." He swallowed and averted his eyes. "The ladle was in the kettle with him, covered in blood."

I grimaced and put my hand on his forearm. "Who do you think is behind these murders?"

He stared at his coffee. His face was as blank as the plain white mug he held between his trembling hands. "When I was little, my *ya-ya* told me that the three Fates determined life and death. Clotho spun the thread of life on her spindle, Lachesis measured its length, and Atropos cut it short with her horrible shears."

Now was clearly not the time to press Troy for details. He was in shock. "You've been through a traumatic event. Have you thought about seeing a doctor?"

"I can't." He placed his mug on the table, taking care to center it on the coaster. "I have to help Delta tomorrow."

I recoiled at his comment. "You're going to keep working here after everything that's happened?"

"I couldn't even if I wanted to. Delta's closing Oleander Place tomorrow."

Now that was news. "Permanently?"

"Until they catch the killer," he replied.

That was a good plan. If she'd shut down the plantation earlier, Scarlett and Miles might still be alive. "Are you planning to come back to work when it reopens?"

He looked away. "It's a great job for a grad student."

It was hard for me to believe that anyone would describe

working for Delta as *great*, but I kept my feelings to myself. "I guess you have to do what you think is best," I said, rising to my feet. "Anyway, I need to get going before Officer Quincy catches me here. Take care, Troy. And be careful."

I dashed from the room.

"Franki?" he called.

I ran back to the doorway, and I was struck by the intensity in his eyes.

"Stay away from Oleander Place," he said in his strange, flat tone. "It's not safe."

The understatement of the century, I thought as I darted for cover in the hedge.

I WALKED across the street to Thibodeaux's, shielding my eyes from the cemetery. I'd had enough death for one day. I pushed open the door and saw Veronica and Glenda sitting at the bar and watching the evening news on a flat screen TV.

"Hey." I tossed my bag on the barstool next to Veronica and began digging for my wallet. Despite a persistent hangover, I was ready for happy hour.

"I ordered you an absinthe," Veronica said.

My head shot up.

She pressed her fingers to her lips, repressing a smile. "Glenda told me about your escapades at Shore Leave, so I thought I'd order you a cocktail worthy of a corsair."

I sealed my lips tight. I wasn't going to say a word in case there was something about last night I didn't know and didn't want everyone at the tavern to know either.

Phillip approached and placed a fluted glass on the bar napkin in front of me. "Here's your Prosecco."

I smirked at Veronica and slid onto my stool.

Glenda lowered her metallic gold bifocals, which matched her one-legged catsuit to a T. "Miss Ronnie hornswaggled you, sugar."

I took a long sip of my drink. "If the two of you don't mind, I'd like to put my pirating days behind me. Besides, I'm not really in the mood for jokes."

The smile faded from Veronica's lips. "We know you're taking this case really hard, Franki. We were only trying to cheer you up."

"That's nice of you, but I'm past that point." I looked at Glenda. "I suppose you told her about Bradley and Pauline too?"

Glenda tossed back a shot of tequila. "Just the lowlights, sugar."

Veronica put her hand on mine. "I'm so sorry this happened."

I sighed. "Honestly, with all the murders and the death threat, my relationship with Bradley doesn't seem that important right now."

Veronica nodded and tucked her hair behind her ear. "What did you find out at the plantation?"

I crossed my elbows on the bar. "Basically, that I'm a failure as a PI."

Glenda slammed her second shot glass onto the bar. "Now why in heaven's name would you think that?"

"Because my suspects are dropping like flies, and I don't have a clue who's killing them," I replied, waving my arms like an orchestra conductor.

Veronica gave a frustrated flip of her hair. "Franki, you were a cop, so you of all people should know that there are countless homicide cases that even the best detectives can't solve."

"Take me, for example," Glenda said. "Back in the day, I was the hottest strip act in the South, and I do mean hot." She put a finger to her lone, nude butt cheek and made a sizzling sound. "And yet I can't whip a bunch of newbie dancers into shape."

"What do you mean?" I asked, failing to see the connection between me, her behind, and her stripper students.

"After almost two weeks, my boot camp is still nothing but a booty camp. Thanks to rap music, girls these days think the only thing to stripping is butt work, and the ones I'm training can't even do that well. Yesterday one of them was supposed to twerk, but she booty popped instead."

"So?" I was more bewildered than before. "What difference does it make?"

Glenda pointed a gold-gloved finger at me. "I'll tell you what difference it makes. The popper knocked her unsuspecting partner off the damn stage and dislocated the girl's shoulder."

"That's a serious mistake," Veronica said, her eyes wide.

"You're telling me." Glenda shook her head. "Try as I might, I do *not* understand why we can't attract quality girls to the stripping profession."

Try as *I* might, I couldn't understand what Glenda's booty-camp misadventures had to do with my misinvestigation. But I appreciated that she was trying to help.

Veronica patted my thigh. "You see? Sometimes even the best in the business have no control over a situation."

"I guess," I replied, grabbing my glass. "But I feel like there's something I'm missing. Like if I had this one piece of information, the puzzle would be complete." I took a sip of my Prosecco and watched as Phillip put whipped cream on a strawberry daiquiri. "And I still want to know what flavor of alcohol is pink."

Glenda looked at my glass. "The nectar of the Gods comes in pink."

"Ambrosia?" I asked, confused.

"*Champagne*, sugar," she replied in a bite-your-tongue tone. "Your Prosecco comes in pink too."

I felt a jolt go through my body. Ivanna's mother, Rosa, was from the region where Prosecco was made, and her name was

Italian for "pink." And now that I thought about it, the Lacour diamond was alleged to be the very same shade as the Prosecco —coral pink. That's why Ivanna was so obsessed with getting the color of the lip gloss just right! It wasn't just her perfectionism at play—it was her desire to memorialize her mother.

I hopped off my barstool and grabbed my phone. "Glenda, you might've just solved one of the mysteries of this case. I'll be right back."

"Where are you going?" Veronica asked, her brows knitted in concern.

"Outside to call Ivanna's father. I can't hear over the TV." I rushed out the door and held my breath as I dialed the number.

"Hello?" Liam's tone was pleasant but tinged with sadness.

"This is Franki Amato," I said. "Do you have a moment to talk?"

"Yes," he replied. "How can I help you?"

I sat on the curb, resting my elbows on my knees. "I've been thinking about the lip gloss Ivanna was holding, and I was wondering if you knew whether Rosa liked pink Prosecco."

"It was her favorite drink," he replied with a note of surprise in his voice. "It's made in the town of Monteforte d'Alpone where she grew up."

I was so excited I did a fist pump. "Did Ivanna know that?"

"Oh, yes. From the time she was eight or nine years old, Rosa would let her have a small glass—mixed with water, of course. You know how Europeans are about alcohol." He chuckled. "Ivanna would complain every time Rosa added the water."

"Because it diluted the alcohol?" I mean, I would have been disappointed too.

"Because it changed the color," he replied. "Ivanna was always particular about her colors."

Indeed she was, I thought. *So much so that she was willing to use poisonous oleander flowers to get the right shade for her lip gloss.* "Liam, I think that lip gloss was for Rosa. I can't prove it, but I'd be willing to bet that Ivanna was planning to call it 'Prosecco Pink.'"

"That sounds like a product she would've had in her line," he said. "And I know she wanted to honor her mother."

"I'm sure she would have, too, if she'd had the chance."

Liam was silent for a moment. "Do you have any news about the death of the groundskeeper?"

I sighed. "Not yet. But you'll be the first person I call when I do."

"I would appreciate that. And thank you for telling me about the lip gloss. It's good to have at least one answer in this case."

"I couldn't agree more. Bye now."

I closed the call and immediately thought of Chandra. The day I met her, she said that the ghost who'd gotten me in this mess had done something bad, and it involved a relative. If Chandra was for real, then that spirit was Ivanna, not Evangeline. Did that mean Ivanna was the spirit pulling the handle of the French door? If so, why? Was she in danger and trying to get out? Or was there some other reason?

"Pff!" I exclaimed as I stood up. The ghost angle was too absurd to even think about. I brushed off the seat of my jeans and went back inside Thibodeaux's.

Glenda and Veronica were again fixated on the TV. But so was everyone else in the bar.

I slid onto my barstool and gazed at the screen. "What's going on?"

Veronica's mouth was set in a grim line. "Adam was arrested for the murders a little while ago."

I felt like I'd turned to stone. But on the inside, emotions were coursing through my body like liquid fire. Sadness, guilt, and relief flooded through me at the same time. Yet for some reason, I was anxious too. I could tell that Veronica was waiting for me to react, so I blurted out, "Then the case is solved."

"It looks that way." She put her hand on my back. "Franki, an entire police team was working the case, but there was only one of you. So, don't beat yourself up about this. Okay?"

"Yeah, just look at the positive side," Glenda said, jumping off her barstool. "You don't need pirate protection anymore."

"Right!" Veronica nodded with way too much enthusiasm.

"But now that I think about it, sugar," Glenda added, pulling her catsuit out of her crotch, "that's the *negative* side." She cackled and slapped her bare leg.

I said nothing and turned my attention to the news coverage. As I watched a ragged-looking Adam being lead into the police station in handcuffs, I felt a growing sense of apprehension. I'd suspected him of the killings as recently as this morning, and yet his arrest didn't sit right with me.

My phone began to vibrate in my hand, startling me from my stupor. Ruth Walker's name was on the display.

I stood up and headed for the door. "This is Franki."

"I thought you'd have called me by now," she barked.

"I just saw the news a few seconds ago," I protested as I exited the bar. I don't know why Ruth persisted in thinking that I should report to her.

"Well, I, for one, am not buying this arrest nonsense."

I stopped short. "What? You were so sure that Adam was involved in Ivanna's murder."

"Yes, but the police are saying that he had belladonna at the lab. And that's utter hogwash."

"How can you be sure? Adam *is* a chemist."

"Because I drove by Lickalicious Lips this morning and found Ivanna's father there. He was kind enough to let me help myself to anything in the office since he's shutting down the business. So, I went through the place with a fine-tooth comb, and there was no poison there."

Although I was quite sure that Ruth had impeccable strip-the-office-clean skills, I had my doubts about the absence of the poison. "Maybe he hid it in the ceiling or something."

She snorted. "Trust me, I know all the places the man stashed his liquor, and they were empty."

This from a woman who claimed not to drink.

"Now I know I said he was capable of killing Ivanna," she continued, "but something is rotten in the state of Denmark."

"Are you suggesting that the police planted the belladonna?"

There was a pause, and I heard what sounded like the tinkling of ice in a rocks glass followed by a loud slurping sound.

"Not necessarily," she replied a bit out of breath.

"Then who do you think did?"

Ruth harrumphed. "That's your problem."

"Thanks," I said under my breath.

"You're welcome," she was quick to reply. "I'll thank *you* the day you find the killer," she added, crunching an ice cube. "I'm on pins and needles here wondering if I'm his next victim."

"I know the feeling," I muttered. "But now that there's been an arrest in the case, my client's going to terminate my contract."

"Then you'll have to go it alone," she said. "I'll talk to you soon."

As I shoved my phone into my back pocket, Ruth's words weighed on my mind. I already felt like I *was* going it alone, but at least I was getting paid. I wondered whether I could afford to continue investigating the case for free, even though I already knew I had no choice. If Adam wasn't guilty, I had to keep looking for the killer—for my own safety and everyone else's.

The real question was whether there was a chance that Adam was guilty. I flashed back to the day Veronica and I had seen him packing the trunk of his Corvette. He was upset, and I was positive he'd been drinking. And while it was certainly possible that he'd left evidence behind, I didn't think it likely. Careless, forgetful types didn't earn PhDs in chemistry.

But if he didn't leave the belladonna in the lab, then who put it there? Delta?

Or was it Dr. Jones?

21

After what seemed like an eternity, the toaster finally popped. I grabbed the hot waffles with the tips of my fingers and tossed them into a bowl. Yes, a bowl. My plan was to drown my sorrows in waffles drowning in syrup because nothing had turned out like I'd hoped—not the Jones case, not the Pauline case, not my job with Veronica, and certainly not my relationship with Bradley.

"Breakfast is ready!" I called.

Napoleon jumped off the chaise lounge and sped into the kitchen.

I broke off a piece of waffle for him and added a dash of syrup. He was the one constant in my life right now, so he deserved a special treat. I ruffled the fur on his head and handed him the bite. "There you go, boy."

Next, I squeezed a cup or two of syrup onto my waffles and grabbed a spoon. Yes, a spoon. It's the only way to eat waffles swimming in syrup. Then I flopped down at the kitchen table.

As I spooned the waffle-syrup soup into my mouth, I expected the warm gooey sweetness to soothe the ache in my soul. But it didn't. And I knew it had nothing to do with feeling sorry for myself—it was because there was something important I still had to do.

I grabbed my phone and pressed Bradley's number, taking deep breaths between rings. My stomach lurched when I heard him pick up.

"Franki." His voice was soft but practically screamed surprise.

Drawing courage from his docile demeanor, I announced, "This is a business call, so I'd appreciate it if you kept our personal affairs out of this." Oh, and I made sure to stress the word *affairs,* the lousy cheat.

"Listen," he began in a remorseful tone, "if this about me banning you from the bank—"

"It's not," I interrupted. I wished I could tell him that I was working for Corinne. But Bradley wasn't the man I'd thought he was, so I couldn't take the chance that he'd fire her for hiring me.

"Okay." He paused. "What's this about?"

"I can't go into the details of why I have this information, but Pauline omitted her real last name from the résumé she submitted to you, not to mention a bank she worked for in New York."

"How'd you get her resume?" he asked, bewildered.

"That's beside the point," I snapped. "What matters is that Ms. Pauline Violette Malaspina got off scot-free after embezzling from a charity managed by Brehman Bank, and you've put her in charge of a charity for children."

A stony silence ensued.

"Now, I expect you to put your, uh, *feelings* for Pauline aside and look into the probability that she's stealing from your bank. Because if you don't, I'll have to take the evidence I've acquired to the police," I bluffed.

"Franki, what goes on at Pontchartrain Bank is none of your concern," he said through clenched teeth. "Stay out of this."

I was taken aback by his command. "You lost the right to have a say in my life when you hooked up with the embezzler."

He let out a long sigh. "Look, I can't get into the specifics right now, but things aren't what they seem. You've got to trust me on this."

I gave a laugh that was somewhere between incredulous and outraged. "You've got some nerve, Bradley Hartmann."

I hung up and angrily wiped a tear from my cheek. I refused to cry over a bum like that.

My phone rang, and I was positive it was Bradley calling me back. I responded with a resounding, "Go to hell!"

"I'd really rather not," a surprised-sounding male replied.

I gasped. "I'm *so* sorry! I thought you were someone else."

"Well, that's a relief." He chuckled. "The clergy are often unpopular, but that was a little harsh."

Oh God, did I just tell a priest to go to hell? I gulped. "Um, you're with the Church?"

"Yes, my name is Father Roman," he boomed. "I'm a neophyte at Holy Rosary Church."

Did he just say nymphet? I wondered as I nervously scratched my neck and ran down a mental list of the sins I'd committed since the last time I'd set foot in a church. "The name of your church sounds familiar, but I can't place it."

"We're located in downtown Houston."

Now I knew where I'd heard the name before—my mother. "Does this have anything to do with marriage classes, Father?"

"Actually, I've been asked to speak to you about another matter—your plans to cohabitate with your boyfriend?"

"Nonna!" I exclaimed Seinfeld-style.

"Your grandmother's not the only one who's worried about you," he clarified.

"Oh, I'm quite sure my parents are in on this too," I said, squirming with embarrassment.

"And some of the regulars here at the deli," he added. "You have a whole community of people here who love you, Francesca."

I rested my forehead on the kitchen table. From the sound of things, my nonna had told everyone at Amato's Deli that I was planning to shack up in sin. "I appreciate your concern, Father. But I only told my nonna that I was going to live with a man to get her to stop pre-planning my wedding. And the fact is, my boyfriend has started seeing another woman."

"*Madonna santa!*" my nonna exclaimed from out of nowhere.

I bolted from my chair. "Father, is my nonna on this call too?"

"I'm afraid she leaned in to the receiver just now," he replied. "Excuse me for a moment."

He covered the phone with his hand, and then I heard the muffled sounds of his speech and my nonna's shrieks. I was sure he was trying to calm her down from a conniption fit she was having over the news that I was single again.

Father Roman uncovered the receiver. "I'm afraid we have a little misunderstanding here about your living situation."

"What is it?" I asked. But I didn't have to wait for an answer.

"Franki's-a living with-a Bradley and another woman!" my nonna shouted *a squarciagola*, an Italian phrase which is often translated as "at the top of one's lungs" but actually means that someone is screaming so loudly that it's ripping their throat.

"Are you saying Franki's a polygamist, Carmela?" a scandalized-sounding customer asked.

"Well it sure sounds like an episode of *Sister Wives* to me!" another exclaimed.

"But don't you worry, Francesca," Father Roman continued in a harried tone, "I'll set everyone straight."

"Thank you, Father," I whispered. Then I hung up and took a much-needed swig of syrup.

WHEN I LET the door to Private Chicks slam shut behind me, David's head shot up from his desk.

"Whoa!" He wiped drool from the corner of his mouth with his sleeve. "I can't believe I fell asleep."

I smirked. "I guess you're finally coming down from all that game fuel you drank at the vassal's."

Veronica entered the lobby in a smart-looking navy blazer and white skirt. "I was hoping that was you, Franki. Delta is on her way here to settle up what she owes us. Can you give me the total number of hours you've worked?"

"Actually, I wanted to talk to you about that," I said, shoving my sunglasses into my purse. "What time's she coming?"

"Ten o'clock." She looked at her watch. "And it's five till, so you'd better make it quick."

"Okay," I said with a nod. "Will you come with me while I grab a cup of coffee?"

"Sure," she replied as she followed me down the hallway.

When I entered the kitchen, I was thrilled to see a fresh pot of French Press. I pulled my mug from the cabinet and got straight to the point. "Veronica, I don't believe that Adam committed the murders."

She leaned against the counter and crossed her arms. "Well, the police certainly do. Why don't you think he's guilty?"

I grabbed the carafe and poured some coffee into my cup. "Because I know he wouldn't have been stupid enough to leave belladonna in his lab."

She frowned. "That's hardly proof of innocence."

"There's more," I said, pulling my Baileys Sweet Italian Biscotti Coffee Creamer from the fridge. "Ruth Walker told me that Liam was at Lickalicious Lips right before the police came and searched the premises."

"So?"

"So," I began, pouring a cup of the creamer into my mug, "he could have planted the belladonna on the premises to frame Adam."

"Hold on a second," she said, holding up her hand. "You can't possibly think that a nice man like Liam Jones killed his own daughter."

"His daughter, no. But I can't rule out the others." I said, stirring my cookie-creamer coffee. "Think about it. We don't know for certain that he was out of the country when they were murdered. I mean, we haven't checked the flight records."

"True." She twirled a lock of blonde hair around her finger. "But what motive would he have had to kill Scarlett and Miles?"

I shrugged and took a sip of my coffee. "Maybe he thought they killed Ivanna."

"And then he framed Adam for his crimes?" She tossed the lock of hair over her shoulder. "This is too far-fetched."

"Just hear me out, okay?" I took a seat at the table. "I don't believe that Liam killed anyone either. But I have this nagging feeling that he's behind Adam's arrest. I mean, Adam told us himself that Liam doesn't like him, so much so that he had his secretary tell Adam to clear out before he came to town. Remember?"

She nodded, staring down at her shoes.

"So obviously there's bad blood there, and it has to have something to do with Adam's belligerent relationship with Ivanna."

She pursed her lips. "Apparently, he does have some harsh feelings toward Adam, but that's a far cry from framing him for murder."

"It gives him a motive, though," I said, raising my index finger. "And if Liam thinks that Adam killed Ivanna, he could have planted the belladonna to make sure that he went to prison for the crime."

Veronica pulled out a chair and took a seat. "You know this is all highly speculative. Without any evidence, I can't ask Delta to let you continue investigating the case."

"Yes, you can!" I pressed my hands together in a pleading gesture. "All I need is a few more days."

She shook her head. "Based on my conversation with her this morning, she's convinced that the police have the right person in custody. So as of right now, the case is closed."

The lobby bell sounded before I could say another word.

"That must be Delta," Veronica said as she stood up and adjusted the white belt around her blazer. "I'm sorry, Franki."

I hung my head as she headed for the lobby. I was disappointed, but I understood her point. She couldn't ask clients to pay us without proof.

David popped his head into the doorway. "Uh, mind if I hide out in your office?"

"Be my guest." I was tempted to hide out with him and avoid the inevitable dressing-down from Delta, but I knew that Veronica expected me to be professional, regardless of how unprofessional the client. I took a gulp from my mug, fervently wishing that the Baileys' creamer line wasn't non-alcoholic. Then I dragged myself down the hallway to my doom.

Despite the fact that it was seventy-five degrees outside, Delta was sitting on the couch in a full-length red fox coat. She tore a check from her checkbook and handed it to Veronica. "This should more than cover Ms. Amaro's investigative *efforts*."

I suppressed a snort—not because of her emphasis on my so-called "efforts," but because of the particular way she butchered my last name. *Amaro* was Italian for "bitter," and I was definitely that.

"Hello, Delta," I said as I made my entrance.

She sniffed and looked down her nose. "Nice of you to say hello considering that you couldn't be bothered when you came to the plantation yesterday. But then I guess you had investigating to do, what with a third murder and all."

"Now, Delta," Veronica intervened, "Franki did her best to find the culprit. And don't forget that the police were on the case too."

"Thank goodness they were!" she exclaimed with her hand on her chest. "Otherwise, that belladonna might not have been found, and I could've been next on Adam's list."

I rolled my eyes. She hadn't been at all pleased with the police the day she'd come to Private Chicks looking for a PI. "Actually, I have a few questions about Adam's arrest."

Delta stared at me through half-lidded eyes. "Don't you think it's a little late for questions? The case is solved."

"I'm not so sure," I said as I eased onto the couch across from her.

Delta's eyes widened—then she turned to Veronica. "What's going on here?"

Veronica angled an annoyed glance in my direction. "Well, Franki was just telling me that she thinks the police may have rushed to judgment where Adam is concerned."

"That's preposterous," she declared with a shooing motion of her hand. "The police found the murder weapon in his laboratory."

I leveled a glare at Delta. "Someone could have planted it there."

She clutched her pearls and began to laugh. "My, you're quite the sleuth, aren't you?"

My Italian blood was getting hot, but I couldn't let it reach the boiling point. If I did, it could cost Veronica that check she was holding, and we needed to get paid. "One thing I am is cautious," I replied with a pointed look. "Because I know that if the wrong man is behind bars, someone else could be killed. And since I'm the only one who's received a bona fide death threat in this case, that someone would most likely be me."

Delta sighed. "What do you want to know?"

I repressed a satisfied smile. "Has Adam actually confessed to the murders?"

"He's lawyered up, which says to me he's guilty."

"It says to me he's smart," I retorted. "Especially if he's being set up, which brings me to my next question. Do you know where, exactly, the police found the belladonna?"

Delta crossed her arms. "I'm not privy to that information."

I found that hard to believe since she'd been privy to every detail of the case until now. She was either really eager to see an end to this case, or she was hiding something. "Did they ever determine how the belladonna got in Ivanna's system?"

"No idea," she said with a shrug. "Maybe the killer made her drink it or put it in her eyes or something."

"Put it in her eyes?" I repeated. That was an awfully specific answer from someone who claimed to have no inside knowledge of the manner of death. "Why would you say that?"

"I must've read it somewhere," she said, grabbing the handle of her Louis Vuitton. "Now, are you almost through? Because I have an appointment with a public relations firm in less than an hour."

I glanced at Veronica, who was willing me to put a lid on it with her eyes. "Just one more question," I replied, since I'd never been good at keeping my mouth shut, not even when explicitly asked to do so. "Were you aware that Ivanna was descended from the Lacour family?"

She narrowed her eyes and fingered her Baron Samedi

brooch. "Like I said to her father," she began in a soft but defiant tone, "I didn't have the faintest idea."

I could tell that I'd upset her, and I didn't think it was because I'd offended her Southern honor.

"If you don't mind, I'll be on my way." Delta rose to her feet. "I've got a company to rebuild."

"Thank you for so much doing business with us," Veronica said, following her to the door.

Delta grasped the doorknob and locked eyes with me. "I'd like to say it was a pleasure," she drawled, "but it wasn't."

I leapt off the couch as she exited in a swirl of red fur.

Veronica blocked the doorway, extending her arms to either side of the frame. "No you don't, Franki."

"Just give me one minute in the parking lot with her," I breathed. "That's all I need."

"Sit," she ordered, pointing to the couch. "You know she'd have you arrested if you so much as looked at her the wrong way."

I slunk back to my seat with Veronica running defense behind me. "I'm so sick of her hateful attitude that it would almost be worth a trip to the slammer."

"Well, you don't have to deal with her ever again," she said, hands on hips. "Now why don't you take the rest of the day off? I can handle things around here."

Some time to decompress did sound nice. "Are you sure? I know you need help with your caseload."

"I am." She patted my arm. "Now scram."

I looked up at her. "I'm sorry about the way this case turned out."

"Don't be. There are going to be lots of other cases we can't solve. It's the nature of the business." She smiled. "See you tomorrow."

I watched her walk down the hallway and noticed David poking his head out of my office.

"Is the coast clear?" he asked.

Even though I was miserable, I had to laugh. "Yes, the pestilence has passed."

He wrapped his arms around his chest and shuddered. "That lady freaks me out, man."

"Don't I know it," I muttered. "But thankfully, we've seen the last of her."

"Yeah," he said, returning to his workstation, "Veronica said that Adam guy had belladonna at his lab."

The mention of belladonna reminded me of Delta's bizarre comment. "David, I'm curious about something. Would you do me a favor and google *belladonna* and *eyes*"?

He nodded and keyed in the search. "Okay, so that pulled up *atropa belladonna.* Is that right?"

"I guess that's the scientific name," I replied, thinking it sounded familiar. "Do you see anything about using it in the eyes?"

He scanned the page. "Well, ophthalmologists dilate eyes with it."

I chewed my fingernail. "Anything else?"

"Hang on." He paused. "It says the ladies of the Venetian Court, whatever that is, used a tincture of belladonna eye drops because they thought dilated pupils made them look seductive."

My stomach contracted like someone had attached a vice grip to it. I rushed to his computer. "Where did you read that?"

"It's toward the end of the second paragraph," he said, pointing to the text on the screen.

The second I looked at the passage, one sentence jumped out at me as though it had been highlighted in boldface.

The genus name Atropa *comes from Atropos, one of the three Fates in Greek mythology.*

Finally, all the pieces fell into place—the belladonna, the Venetian Court, the three Fates. And the whole horrible reality of what had happened at Oleander Place came crashing down on me like a *grande* sugar cane kettle.

"Oh my God." I whispered, putting my hand on David's shoulder for support.

"Troy!"

22

David looked up at me, his forehead wrinkled with concern. "What about Troy?"

"Oh, I just remembered that I promised to read his master's thesis," I fibbed. I hated lying to David, but Veronica had taken me off the Jones case in no uncertain terms. If I was going to go rogue, I couldn't drag him into it. "That reminds me, do you know whether Tulane publishes its students' theses online?"

He tapped his fingers on his mouth. "Let me check the library catalog."

While David clicked away on his keyboard, I thought back to my various interactions with Troy. Things I hadn't thought about at the time took on new meaning for me now. In some ways, he fit the obsessive profile. There weren't many people who loved plantation clothes so much that they planned to devote their entire careers to them. Plus, I'd noticed that he was extremely meticulous—in the careful way he'd wrapped the pirate clothes, straightened the silverware in the dining room, placed his mug in the exact center of the coaster—a quality that would lend itself well to the staging of a dead body. But on the other hand, he was a personable, down-to-earth guy, and I hadn't seen any signs of mental instability.

"So, the theses and the dissertations are online," David said, disrupting my thoughts. "Want me to email you the link?"

"That would be great," I said as I headed for the hallway. "I'll go pull it up now."

To avoid arousing Veronica's suspicions, I tiptoed into my office and sunk quietly into my chair. Then I opened David's email and clicked the link. Within a second of entering Troy's name in the advanced search field, his thesis title popped up on the screen. *Poison and Poisoning in the Venetian Republic.* And I gave myself a good, swift, mental kick for not looking up his research sooner.

It didn't take long to find what I was looking for. As I'd suspected, there was a section in the paper that described the cosmetic use of belladonna among Venetian courtesans—and its fatal effects from misuse.

I chewed my thumbnail while I pondered the ramifications of Troy's thesis. The focus on belladonna looked bad, but it didn't prove anything. I had to have more evidence. Specifically, I needed to find out whether he had a history of mental illness. Of course, if he did have any mental health records on file, they wouldn't be available to the public. So I had to find someone who knew him well, someone other than Delta. The only other person I could think of was his dissertation advisor, but Troy had never mentioned his name.

"I thought you were leaving for the day!" Veronica exclaimed.

I jumped at least a foot—the guilty kind of jump, not the startled one.

"I didn't mean to scare you," she said, sashaying up to my desk. "I came for the Jones file. I want to get this case wrapped up ASAP."

"Sure," I replied, feigning nonchalance. I reached into my lower right drawer and pulled out a manila folder.

Veronica took the file from my hand and sat in front of my desk. "You know, we really haven't had a chance to talk about Bradley."

"What's there to say?" I asked, unprepared for this line of questioning.

"Oh, I don't know," she replied as she straightened a bent corner of the file. "I just thought you might want to vent."

Of course, I wasn't one to be short on opinions. But the shock of Bradley's betrayal had left me kind of numb. And now wasn't the time to try to open that wound, not when I had a killer to catch. "Honestly, I haven't had time to process what happened. But even if I had, I don't think I'd have much to say about it."

She tilted her head. "Why's that?"

"Because it was so unexpected and yet so utterly predictable," I retorted. "Even though I didn't trust Pauline, I never really believed that Bradley would leave me for her. But then, I have such a dismal history where men are concerned, so why should I be surprised?"

"Has he ever given you an explanation for why he did this?"

"Well, when I called him about Corinne's case this morning, he tried to tell me that things weren't what they seemed."

She flinched. "Did he explain what he meant by that?"

"No, and I didn't ask," I replied, picking at my chipped purple nail polish.

"Aren't you the least bit curious?" she pressed. "That's a pretty provocative statement under the circumstances."

"I saw them spoon-feeding each other over candle light, Veronica. Do you think I'm going to believe a word he says?" I shook my head. "Uh-uh. I'm through with that guy."

"I suppose you know what's best," she replied, rising to her feet.

That was highly debatable, but I kept my mouth shut. This conversation needed to end—because I was through discussing Bradley and because I had to track down Troy's dissertation advisor before it was too late.

"Anyway, you'd better get going," she ordered, shaking the folder at me, "or I might change my mind and put you to work."

I managed a weak smile. "Then I'm leaving now."

As soon as I heard Veronica enter her office, I googled the Tulane Department of History and scanned the list of faculty members. Only one specialized in the Antebellum Era, a Professor Claude Miller, and his office hours were from two until five. Since it was only eleven, I had plenty of time to run some errands and grab lunch before heading to Tulane.

On my way out of my office, I saw a photo from the case file on the floor. It was the close up of Ivanna on her deathbed.

I picked up the picture and stared at Ivanna's image, marveling once again at her fairy-tale-like beauty—her rose-red lips, her porcelain skin, the fair hair that framed her face like a golden fleece. And I was reminded of something Troy had said the first day I met him, that Ivanna's hair had been arranged exactly like Evangeline's. It occurred to me that since there were no known photographs of Evangeline in life or in death, the only way he could have known what her hair had looked like on the day of her murder was if he'd scoured over the historical records of the crime scene. Like a man obsessed.

I laid the photo on my desk. I'd return it to the Jones file tomorrow. Right now I had the rest of the day off—to find Troy's dissertation advisor.

As I WALKED through the first floor of Tulane's Hebert Hall, I hoped that the twenty or so students sitting cross-legged at the end of the corridor weren't camped outside Professor Miller's office. But no such luck.

I approached a geeky-looking kid at the end of the line. His pasty, acne-spotted skin practically exuded panic, along with copious amounts of oil. "Are all of you waiting to see Dr. Miller?"

He nodded. "We've got an essay exam tomorrow on colonization," he replied, glancing at the professor's door. "It's worth forty percent of our grade."

I slid my back down the wall as I eased onto the tile floor beside him. Thinking of the lengthy wait that lay ahead of me and not the lopsided grade breakdown, I said, "That sucks."

"Right?" he commiserated, clutching a notebook to his "I know H.T.M.L. (How to Meet Ladies)" T-shirt. "Especially since we lost our teaching assistant like a month after class started."

I told myself not to take the bait because I didn't want to spend the next hour or so listening to history department gossip. But I'd just polished off a huge plate of chicken Tchoupitoulas at Coop's Place and was in serious danger of falling asleep. "So, why'd you lose your TA?"

"He dropped out of school," he muttered. "I guess he finally realized there was no future in a PhD in plantation chic."

The bottom dropped out of my stomach. Even though I knew who he was talking about, I had to ask. "Was his name Troy Wilson, by any chance?"

The geek's jaw dropped. "How'd you know?"

"I met him around once or twice."

"Well, if you see him again," he began, cocking a brow high on his greasy forehead, "tell him Cody Putfark said 'thanks for nothing.'"

"I will," I promised in an appropriately solemn tone. Then I leaned my head against the wall and thought back to all the times Troy—and Delta, for that matter—had mentioned that he was actively pursuing a PhD. Now that I knew he'd been lying, my anxiety level was starting to rise. In the back of my mind I'd been hoping that I was wrong about what was going on at Oleander Place. But it looked like Chandra's colleague, Xavier, was right—the solution had been right in front of me all along.

My "Baby Got Back" ringtone sounded, and a couple of students snickered. I looked at the display and wondered what they would do if they knew my psychic sidekick was calling.

"Hi, Chandra," I answered.

"Hey girl," she replied with an unexpected show of intimacy. "Lou and I were watching the news this morning, and we saw that the Oleander Place murders have been solved."

"Yeah, the police got their man," I said, careful not to emphasize the word *their.*

"You must be so relieved," she said, pronouncing *relieved* with an ear-splitting squeal. "Now you won't have to go to that awful plantation anymore or deal with that horrible woman. And you'll have more time to work on your relationship with your honeykins."

I cringed at the reference to Bradley (and at the word *honeykins*). I had no idea why everyone suddenly wanted to talk to me about him, but I wanted it to stop. "Um, we're not together anymore."

"No!" she cried with such emotion that it set her jewelry to jingling. "What happened?"

Chandra was starting to stress me out. I mean, she of all people could use her psychic skills to get the scoop and spare me the painful rehash. "Turns out that Three of Cups card you dealt me was right on the money. There *was* a third person in our relationship—his secretary."

"I'm surprised to hear that," she said in a faraway tone. "I didn't get the impression that the third wheel was a love interest."

Now I was really getting annoyed. I'd paid her for that tarot card reading, and now she was admitting that she'd held out on me? "Well, I don't know what made you think that, but I hope it wasn't your psychic intuition."

She sniffed. "I'll have you know that I'm never wrong about these things."

"Whatever," I said, standing up to relieve my aching behind. I'd originally thought the floor was causing the pain, but I was starting to think it was this conversation. "Listen, did you need to talk to me about anything else? Because if not—"

"Evangeline or Ivanna is back," she interrupted. "With a vengeance."

"You mean, that spirit's getting aggressive with you?"

The geek eyeballed me and then pretended to be absorbed in his notes.

"In the sense that I can't get her out of my head, yes," Chandra whined. "Ever since that Dr. Geyer got arrested, she's been pulling at that French door like crazy. I see her night and day, awake and in my sleep. I wish she'd just open the damn thing already!"

I thought the timing of the spiritual activity was odd given the new developments in the case. "What do you think is going on?"

"That's what I was going to ask you."

"Me? I'm not the medium here."

"Clearly," she scoffed. "But I've never had a spirit harass me like this. So something must be happening with the case."

If there was a spirit harassing her, it was probably because it knew that the killer was still on the loose. But I couldn't say that to Chandra or anyone else until I could prove it. "You'd have to ask the police."

"They're not going to talk to me."

"I don't know what else to tell you," I said, glancing up as two students entered Dr. Miller's office.

She sighed. "Then I guess I'm going to have to go out to the plantation and find out what the spirit wants."

I had to stop her. If my fears were correct, the murder spree hadn't ended at Oleander Place. "I wouldn't go now if I were you. Even though the case is solved, the police are probably still trying to find evidence to connect Adam Geyer to the scene."

"But I have to do this, Franki. That spirit's trying to tell me something, and it's my duty to figure out what that is."

"What about all those scary ghosts?" I asked.

Angling a wide-eyed glance at me, the geek scooted closer to the student in line in front of him.

"I've been thinking about that," she said. "And you were right. If I'm going to be in this business, I need to overcome my fear of ethereal beings."

This was not the time for personal growth. I had to try another tactic. "But what about Officer Quincy? If he hears you've gone back out there, he'll have you thrown in jail."

"I told Lou all about him," she huffed. "And he said that if that crooked copper lays so much as a finger on me, he'll have his badge."

Damn Lou, I thought. "Wait. Didn't Lou say that you weren't allowed to go to the plantation?"

"That was before the case was solved. Now, why are you so dead set against me going out there?" she asked, her voice thick with suspicion.

If she only knew that *dead* was the operative word. "Look, I can't go into the details, but right now is a bad time to go to Oleander Place."

"Why?"

"I just said that I couldn't get into that!" I exclaimed.

The geek shielded his mouth as he whispered something to a group of students staring at me.

I lowered my voice. "Can't you just trust me on this?"

She hesitated. "I guess."

Thanks for the vote of confidence, I thought. "Good. Then just sit tight, and I'll be in touch soon."

I hung up and breathed a sigh of relief. At least Chandra was out of harm's way. Now I just had to get in to see Dr. Miller so that I could be sure about the others.

It was ten after five when the geek emerged from the professor's office. To avoid eye contact with me, he held his head so high that he was basically staring at the ceiling.

I stood up and dusted myself off. When I stepped into the doorway, I was met by a bookshelf filled with what looked like rare and expensive books. There was another shelf to my right, forcing me to turn left to enter the tiny room.

An elderly man behind an old wooden desk looked up from a paper he'd been reading. "Are you a student in one of my courses, young lady?"

"No Sir. I mean, Dr. Miller," I stammered. Something about the professor and his antique books made me feel like I was in the principal's office. But since I was pushing thirty, I was thrilled with the *young lady* line.

"Then how can I help you?" he asked, removing his reading glasses.

"I came to talk to you about Troy Wilson," I replied, handing him my business card. "I'm a private investigator."

The already deep lines on his forehead deepened further. "Is Mr. Wilson in some kind of trouble?"

I nodded. "He is."

"Well, I don't understand why you would come to me," he blustered in a burst of impatience. "Shouldn't you go to the police?"

I held up my hand in an attempt to calm him. "I plan to do that, Dr. Miller, but I need some information first. I was hoping you could tell me whether Troy had any history of mental instability."

He rested his elbows on his desk and clasped his hands in front of his mouth. "I think you can appreciate that I'm not at liberty to discuss my students' personal affairs."

I took that as a *yes*. "Certainly."

"It's odd that you would come to see me today," he said, staring into my eyes.

I squirmed like a schoolgirl in my seat. "Why do you say that?"

"I haven't seen Mr. Wilson for several months," he began, leaning back in his chair, "and then he called me out of the blue about an hour ago."

"Oh?" I was anxious to know where this was going, but I was afraid to prod for fear that he would refuse to answer.

"He wanted to say good-bye," he said, looking into my eyes again.

I swallowed hard. "Good-bye?"

"Yes. He said he was going away."

My anxiety level set off on a steady climb. I didn't like the sound of this. "Did he say where?"

"He was deliberately vague." He looked down at his desk. "Of course, I realized that he wanted me to think he was moving somewhere, but I assumed he meant that he was going to some sort of facility."

From the pointed way Dr. Miller was looking at me, I knew *facility* meant mental hospital.

"But now," he continued, "it appears as though he may be going to jail. May I ask what for?"

At this point, my anxiety had reached its peak. I knew I had to leave, and soon. "Like you, I'm not at liberty to say. But thank you, Dr. Miller," I said, rising from my seat. "You've been a huge help."

I exited the maze of books and jogged down the hallway. When I reached the main door, I shoved it open and broke into a run. Then I pulled out my phone and dialed 9-1-1.

Because I knew where Troy was going, and it wasn't to a mental hospital or jail. He was going to Oleander Place.

One last time.

23

When I pulled onto River Road, it was after seven o'clock. Rush hour traffic had turned the easy forty-five minute drive into an hour-and-a-half ordeal. Although the delay had me frantic with worry, I took some comfort in knowing that the police would arrive at Oleander Place before me.

But as I approached the plantation, I didn't hear any sirens or see flashing lights. To be on the safe side, I pulled over just before the house and shut off the engine. There was an eerie silence in the air that caused the hair to stand up on my arms. Something wasn't right.

I tapped the first number on my call list.

"9-1-1," a woman responded. "What's your emergency?"

"My name is Franki Amato. I'm a PI, and I called in a possible code 30 in progress at Oleander Place on River Road an hour and a half ago."

The woman fell silent as she searched for the record of my call. "The St. James Parish police have already been out there, ma'am. The officers on the scene saw no signs of a homicide."

"Listen, this is urgent. Three people have been killed at the plantation in the past two weeks. And I know another murder is about to happen, if it hasn't already."

"We'll send someone out."

"Thanks." I hung up and shoved the phone into my front pants pocket, praying that the officers would hurry. But I knew from experience that even though I'd called in a possible homicide, the police were hard pressed to find time to deal with possibilities.

As I exited the car, I glanced at the full moon and hoped that the lunar eclipse wasn't happening tonight. Based on what I'd learned from Chandra's wannabe werewolf clients, people did some pretty crazy things during an eclipse. And the killer I was hunting was already plenty crazy enough.

With my gun in hand, I ran the hundred yards to the hedge and peered through the branches. What I saw took my breath away. The entire house was aglow in a flickering orange candlelight, like a giant jack-o-lantern. And the Southern live oaks that lined the walkway like camouflage-clad soldiers during the day now resembled a platoon of grim reapers forming a pathway to doom.

Doing my damnedest to repress my fear, I made my way along the hedge to the side of the house. Then I ran across the lawn to the first parlor window and ducked down. My breathing was so ragged that I was afraid it would give me away. When I peeked inside, I saw the shrine to Evangeline. It was alive with lighted candles and fresh oleander flowers and draped with pink netting—exactly like the day Scarlett was hanged.

My heart pounded in my chest as I scaled the rest of the house and tiptoed across the back porch to the door. It was unlocked. Pausing to collect myself, I leaned against the wall and glanced at the parking lot. Troy's white car gleamed in the moonlight.

Police backup or no, I had to go in. I pulled back the hammer of my gun and entered the house.

The hallway looked as though it had been prepared for my arrival. It was lined with white candles and oleander petals, creating a glowing, coral-pink carpet to the shrine. Gripping my gun with both hands, I crept toward the parlor. Just before the door, I stopped. Then I turned into the doorway and took aim.

Troy was right where I expected him to be—standing in the courting area and staring at Evangeline's portrait.

"I'm sorry you came here, Franki," he said in a hollow voice, his eyes fixed on the painting. "Now you have to die too."

The second he said the word *too,* I shifted my gun to the left and stepped into the room to greet my target. "Good evening, Delta."

She curled her lips into a cruel smile and pointed an antique double-barreled Derringer right between my eyes with an aim as sharp as the spikes in her hair. "I knew you were too damn stupid to heed my death threats."

"Apparently not stupid enough to believe Adam or Troy were responsible for the murders," I retorted.

She smirked. "I guess I underestimated you. Because you had to be bailed out of your last murder investigation by that old whore—"

"I told you before, she's a stripper," I said through gritted teeth. "And a far better person than you could ever be."

Delta tightened her grip on her gun, and I noticed that she'd pulled back the hammer. That meant it was too risky for me to try to take a shot at her. I knew from my police training that if I fired off a round when her hammer was drawn, she'd have time to shoot back.

"As I was saying," she drawled, "because you weren't smart enough to figure out your last investigation, I thought for sure you'd fall for my Troy trap."

I wanted to look at Troy to see his reaction, but I didn't dare take my eyes off Delta. "Impossible," I spat. "Unlike you, he's too nice a person to harm a fly, much less murder three innocent people."

"I'd say that's a matter for debate," she countered, raising her chin. "After all, he's a mental case with an intense personal interest in poison, which makes him the obvious candidate for the killer."

I grimaced. "He was never anything but a scapegoat to you, was he?"

Delta put a hand to her chest. "In my defense, he handed me the murder plot on a platter. That love-struck loon was obsessed with everything Evangeline—her painting, her personal papers, the records of her death." She laughed. "He was practically begging to be set up."

Out of the corner of my eye, I saw Troy hang his head. I willed him to get angry, to find his strength, because we were going to need it to escape this house of horrors.

"But then one day a real, live Lacour showed up on our doorstep," Delta jeered. "And the little harlot was a carbon copy of Troy's beloved Evangeline."

"Then you did know that Ivanna was a descendent of the Lacour family," I said.

"Of course I did," she snapped. "Her mother mentioned a daughter in her letter, and Ivanna looked just like Evangeline. I'd have to be a buffoon not to put two and two together, especially when Ivanna came back to the plantation on the pretense of taking several tours of the grounds."

"But you figured out that what she was really doing was seducing Troy to get him to help her find the Lacour diamond," I said.

"That imbecile took one look at her and fell hook, line, and sinker," she said, her voice thick with contempt. "He didn't give a damn about what that would mean to me or to my plantation."

I could see Delta's anger rising. If I could get her to look at Troy, I could shoot before she had time to react. I had to keep her talking and her temper flaring. "Then what happened?"

"Troy succumbed to Ivanna's charms, because she was as close as he was ever going to get to living out his fantasy of sleeping with Evangeline." Her brow furrowed. "They started having Friday night trysts—in Evangeline's bed. Ivanna would dress up in Evangeline's pink crinoline dress, and Troy wore pirate clothes, trying to be her Beau."

"So, you caught them in the act," I said, trying to stoke the fire.

Her eyes narrowed to little slits. "If I had, I would have killed them on the spot. Scarlett was the one who saw them when she came up here after hours to do her cleaning." Delta sneered. "I caught her washing the soiled bed linens the next morning. The filthy pigs didn't even bother to clean up after themselves."

Troy's shoulders slumped.

Look at Troy, Delta. Look at him, I thought. My arms were aching from holding the shooting position, and I didn't know how much longer I could keep my gun level.

"At first I thought Scarlett had dirtied the sheets with some white trash boyfriend of hers. But when I confronted her, she told me the whole sordid tale. I assured her that I'd take care of it."

Now I understood why Delta had killed Scarlett. "So when Ivanna was found dead, Scarlett figured out that you'd 'taken care of it' by killing her."

"Yes, and she said she'd go to the police if I didn't pay her off." She frowned. "Can you imagine the nerve of that girl, accusing me of committing a crime and then trying to bilk me out of my money? Why, just for that, even if I hadn't killed Ivanna, I would have wrung her impudent little neck."

I shivered at the callous way she'd referenced Scarlett's hanging. And my mind started to drift to a bad place—thoughts of what she might have in store for Troy and me. But I couldn't go there now. I had to focus on a plan. "What about Miles?" I asked. "Did he try to blackmail you too?"

She snorted. "You bet he did. That good-for-nothing bum demanded fifty thousand dollars to keep his mouth shut."

"What did he have on you? The belladonna you made him grow behind the little mill?"

"He was too stupid to know what that was," she said with a wave of her hand. "The morning Scarlett was killed, when we were pulling artifacts for the photo shoot in the little mill, he looked out the window and saw me entering the house." She shook her head. "That was his problem—sticking his nose where it didn't belong. Just like that Adam Geyer character."

The mention of Adam surprised me so much that I almost jerked my gun. "He came out here?"

"A couple of times. He wanted access to the plantation for himself and his attorney. When I denied his request, he came out after hours, smashed a window, and let himself in."

I was stunned to hear that Adam had broken in to Oleander Place. I guess he'd meant what he said when he vowed to find Ivanna's killer. "How did you know it was him?"

"He set off the alarm. I'd left a few minutes before, so I rushed back in time to see a car speeding away. I had Officer Quincy run a check on his plates. I was about to press charges, but then he left belladonna in his lab and got himself arrested." She gave an incredulous laugh. "Men are such idiots."

So I was right—Delta hadn't framed Adam. Liam had.

"Speaking of idiots," she continued. "How did you manage to figure out it was me?"

I returned her insult with one of my own. "Well, besides your deplorable character, it was your reference to the belladonna. The medical examiner concluded that Ivanna had ingested it. You were the only one who suggested that it might have been put in her eyes."

She smiled. "Thanks to Troy's exceptional thesis, I knew exactly what to do."

I stole a glance at Troy. He was once again staring enrapt at Evangeline's portrait, oblivious to our predicament. Meanwhile, my arms were growing weaker. "But how did you pull it off?"

"It was easy," she said with a shrug. "The day before Ivanna's death, I sent Troy on a wild goose chase to a conference in Nashville. I told him that I'd made an appointment for the following morning for him to meet with one of the attendees, a history professor who'd discovered a letter from an ex-slave detailing Evangeline's death. When Troy heard the news, he was only too happy to go."

So he'd told the truth about attending the graduate student conference on the day Ivanna died, but he'd lied to me about the date of his return.

"Obviously, there was no such professor," she continued. "And poor Troy had no idea that John would be waiting to pull him over on false charges when he tried to come back for his rendezvous with Ivanna."

My jaw dropped to the floor, but luckily my gun didn't. "Officer Quincy is in on this too?"

"I should say so," she said in a haughty tone. "He's my lover. We tell each other everything."

My already shaky arms got even shakier as the skin practically crawled off my body. "What happened when Ivanna arrived?"

"I'd planned to knock her out with chloroform and then douse her eyes with the belladonna. But when she saw me here instead of Troy, she fainted." She giggled. "I couldn't have planned it any better myself."

Bile rose into my throat, but I had to keep my stomach—and my arms—in check. I took a deep breath and said, "So, you put the poison into her eyes and then you positioned her on the bed, just like Evangeline."

Delta pursed her lips. "Not exactly. As I'm sure you know from Troy's thesis, belladonna causes a violent death—confusion, hallucinations, seizures. So, I had to wait that out and try to minimize the damage Ivanna did to the pink room. The torn sheer was no big deal, but I'm still upset about that priceless perfume bottle."

I was sickened by her account of Ivanna's death. I couldn't imagine the terror and the pain Ivanna had experienced, and it was particularly appalling to hear that Delta's only regret was the loss of an antique. "There's one thing I don't understand about all of this."

She lowered her eyelids, as though bored by my curiosity. "Oh?"

"Why would you intentionally drive your family legacy and your business into the ground with these murders?"

"Isn't it obvious?" she asked, surprised by my question. "Haunted plantations are passé. There are lots of us in Louisiana, and we're all struggling to keep the tourists coming. In the meantime, we're competing with haunted houses that spend tens of thousands of dollars every year to create new themes and props, while we're stuck showing the same old things. And those places aren't just for Halloween anymore—they're becoming trendy year around, especially for Valentine's Day."

I looked at her open-mouthed as I tried to comprehend how the murders of Ivanna, Scarlett, and Miles would bring big bucks to Oleander Place.

"There's a haunted house near here that made twelve thousand dollars in one day with their "My Bloody Valentine" attraction. Do you know how much alligator jerky I'd need to sell down at the gift shop to make that kind of money?"

I shook my head.

"Three *years'* worth."

I was starting to think that Delta was more unstable than Troy because none of this was making sense. "But you've lost all your customers thanks to these grisly crimes. How do you expect to attract them now?"

She smiled like a Cheshire cat. "With the big finale."

I didn't want to ask, but I had to. Because I had the distinct feeling that Troy's life—if not mine too—depended on it. "What does that involve?"

Delta's face seemed to light up with excitement. "Troy poisoning himself at Evangeline's shrine. Can't you just see it?" she asked. "A handsome young man becomes obsessed with the portrait of Evangeline, a beautiful plantation owner's wife who was poisoned with a cup of oleander tea. He transfers his obsession onto her gorgeous lookalike relative, but then he kills her when he realizes that she can never live up to his beloved. In despair, he drinks a cup of oleander tea to join his unrequited love." Her eyes flashed. "Now that's what I call a Greek tragedy."

More like a horror story, I thought. I glanced at Troy hoping that her gruesome plan had snapped him out of his trance, but he continued his adoration of Evangeline.

"Of course, those fools Scarlett and Miles got in the way, but I did what I could to minimize the damage. I put Scarlett in her red crinoline dress to make for a more striking image, and then John and I threw Miles into the sugar kettle to sweeten the pot." She let out a raucous laugh. "Get it? To sweeten the sugar cane pot?"

I got it, all right, and it nauseated me.

"But once the dust has settled, people will only remember Evangeline, Ivanna, and Troy. Business will boom, and everyone in the country will know about Oleander Place."

I shook my head. "They'll know it as a place where unspeakable things happened. No one will come here."

"What do you know?" she shouted. "Contemporary murders have a mystique about them. They draw huge crowds year around."

She had me there. I could think of lots of places where people gathered to seek pleasure from others' tragedies. It was a vile business—one that a vile person like Delta was perfectly suited for. There was no point in arguing further, and I knew I couldn't hold up my arms much longer. I sighed and said, "We can't keep this up all night. It's time for you to surrender."

"Surrender?" she asked, taken aback. "Why would I want to do that?

"Because I called the police before I came. They'll be here any minute."

"Oh, I know that," she said with a gleeful twinkle in her eye. "John got an automated phone message about your 9-1-1 call."

My heart sank, and my stomach fell. Some police departments had a system that enabled officers to receive phone alerts about 9-1-1 calls regarding specific locations. Apparently, the New Orleans PD was one of them.

"In fact, he's on his way right now to help me stage the poisoning. But I told him to take his time." She smiled. "I said that you and I had a lot of catching up to do."

By this point, I wasn't sure whether my arms were trembling from exhaustion or fear. "Don't do this, Delta. You'll never get away with this many murders."

"You're forgetting that I have police connections," she said. "Besides, you won't have to watch, if that's what you're worried about. Because Troy's going to kill you first."

I stared at her as I processed the news that I was part of the Oleander Place murder plot.

She frowned. "It's a shame you're not blonde, because everyone knows that dead blondes make for a better story. But that can't be helped." She squinted as she sized me up. "The real issue is what to dress you in. Not even a hoop skirt will fit over those hips."

I promised myself that if I survived, I'd make her pay for that last crack. But at the moment, I had bigger problems than my hips to deal with. I'd been following standard police procedure for standoffs—talking the perpetrator down. But that had gotten me nowhere fast. Trying to buy time, I said, "Then I guess you'll have to let me go."

"Sorry, but I warned you." She smirked. "Twice."

As I desperately tried to think of something to say or do, I saw the glow of headlights through the window—but no flashing lights. That could only mean one thing.

Officer Quincy.

Risky or not, I had to take the shot before he entered the house. Otherwise, Troy and I could kiss this world goodbye.

"Too bad I don't respond well to threats," I said. Then I pulled the trigger.

24

Instead of gunfire there was silence.

I broke out in a cold sweat as the reality of what had happened dawned on me like a nuclear bomb. My gun had jammed.

I looked from the barrel to Delta.

Her face was as black as her Baron Samedi brooch. "I should blow you away for that stunt," she seethed. "But I'm not going to let the likes of you ruin my plan."

I swallowed hard, trying to choke down the growing fear that I was destined to become part of the plantation's lurid lore.

"Now drop the gun and walk over to Troy," she said, motioning with her pearl-handled pistol.

I let my Ruger fall to the floor and went to his side.

"Go on upstairs." She looked at Troy. "Both of you."

Troy exited the parlor first, and I followed with Delta at my back. As we climbed the stairs, I inched close to him and whispered, "Why didn't you tell me?"

"I couldn't lose Evangeline."

"Silence!" Delta commanded, jabbing the gun between my shoulders.

Troy was worse off than I'd thought. If there was any chance of us making it out alive, it was going to have to come from me. The only thing I could think of was to try to push Delta down the stairs when I reached the second floor.

A door slammed below.

"Delta?" Officer Quincy called.

A fresh wave of fear coursed through my veins. There was no escape now. He'd shoot me if I so much as blinked.

"Up here, John," she replied in a lackadaisical tone. "Franki and I just finished with our girl talk."

I followed Troy onto the landing, fighting the urge to faint. There was no need to ask where we were going. I lowered my head and entered the pink room.

"Franki, sit on the bed," Delta said. "But for heaven's sake, be careful. Antique beds weren't made for people your size."

Too numb to react to her jab, I did as I was told.

Officer Quincy burst into the room. "We need to get this over with quick," he said, handing Delta a pair of latex gloves. "I've been monitoring the St. James Parish PD on my police radio, and our little friend here made a second 9-1-1 call."

Delta sneered. "It's not going to do her any good. I've got the belladonna ready. All I need is for you to hold her arms."

Officer Quincy shoved me backward onto the bed and pinned my torso with his arms and chest.

"Wait!" I shouted, stalling. "Why belladonna?"

She put her hand on her hip. "Because you're Italian like Ivanna. Of course, the *beautiful woman* meaning doesn't apply in your case, but no one will question it when they learn your heritage," she said, slipping on the gloves. "Plus, I want you to die a horrible death."

I was seriously considering bum-rushing her for that first comment, but the *horrible death* one took the wind out of my sails.

"Hurry, Delta," Officer Quincy said. "If they're not dead before the police get here, we'll have a hard time proving Troy acted alone."

"Give me a minute," she snapped, reaching into her Louis Vuitton. She pulled out a small bottle and unscrewed the cap. As she leaned in toward me with the poison, I squeezed my eyes shut and started thrashing.

"Hold her still, John!" Delta yelled.

"I'm trying," he rasped, his voice tense from the struggle. "But she's as strong as a horse."

"The size of one too," she observed.

After hearing their horse comments, I started bucking like a bronco.

"It's no use," he ground out. "I've gotta knock her out."

I kept my eyes closed, waiting for the blow. I heard a thwack, a dull thud, and another thwack. But I felt no pain. In fact, the only thing I felt was Officer Quincy's weight sliding off my body. Then I heard another dull thud.

I opened one eye and saw Chandra high-fiving a balding, beer-bellied man in an island shirt.

"Boston strong!" she cried as they each raised a copper pipe in triumph.

I shot up from the bed and saw Delta and Officer Quincy unconscious on the floor. Woozy from shock, I asked, "What are you doing here, Chandra? I told you not to come!"

"I said I'd trust you, but I didn't say I'd listen to you," she explained as she pulled down her zodiac-themed miniskirt.

I glanced at Troy standing motionless in the corner. "I'm glad you didn't."

"By the way," Chandra began, "this is my husband, Luigi Toccato."

"Call me 'Lou,'" he said, giving my hand—actually, my entire arm—a hearty shake.

"So nice to meet you," I breathed. "You two saved our lives. But how did you do it?"

"Ah, we drove out in my plumber's van," Lou said, kicking Delta's gun out of her reach with his toe shoes. "Then Chandra got one of her visions. She said you were in danger, so we grabbed a couple of pipes from my supplies and came in around back."

I stared at Chandra in awe, remembering how scared she was the last time she came to the plantation. "How did you get up the courage to do this?"

She gazed at her husband. "When Lou's by my side, I can do anything."

"Aw, you," he said, turning as red as a tomato. He leaned over and gave her a smooch.

"Besides," she added, her tone now as hard as the pipe in her hand, "I'm afraid of ghosts, not bitches."

Police sirens screamed up the drive.

Chandra took that as her cue to slip her and Lou's pipes into her super Chanel bag. "Now if you three will excuse me," she began, fluffing her big bouffant bob, "I have a psychic matter to attend to."

Lou and I watched from the back porch as the police led Delta and Officer Quincy in handcuffs to the parking lot.

"Take your hands off me, you ingrate!" Delta shouted at the twenty-something male officer trying to help her into the back of the squad car. "I'm the widow of the late Chief of Police, Jackson Dupré."

"We know who you are, ma'am," the officer replied in a tired voice.

"Then you will treat me with respect, or you'll answer to my attorney," she snarled. "Do you understand me?"

Lou yawned and scratched his belly. "Why doesn't he just shove her into the car already?"

"My thoughts exactly," I replied.

The back door opened and Chandra stepped onto the porch. "Where's Troy?"

"They took him to the station," I replied. "He'll undergo a psychiatric evaluation and get the treatment he needs."

Chandra frowned at the sight of Delta and crossed her arms.

"What's the matter?" I asked. "Aren't you happy to see the diabolical one get her due?"

"It's not that." She sighed. "That spirit's turning the doorknob again."

"Maybe she wants to come outside to see Delta being taken to jail," I joked. "You know having her around the plantation had to be a living hell for those ghosts."

"That's the problem," Chandra said. "The spirit's standing in front of French doors, but she's not in the house."

My smile faded. "How do you know?"

"Because there's a vase on the floor to the left of her. But when I stood in the corner between the French doors and the pink room a few minutes ago, I realized that there was no vase there."

I rubbed the back of my neck. "I don't think I've ever seen a vase by the French doors. But maybe one used to be there."

Chandra shook her head, jingling her jewelry. "This isn't a vision from the past. The spirit's turning the handle in the present."

"Then maybe she's not at Oleander Place," I suggested.

"Or, maybe she is," Chandra countered, "but she's turning the handle of a different French door."

As soon as she'd spoken the words, I knew where that door was. "The little mill!" I exclaimed. "Miles told me that the windows and French doors were replaced, and the originals are stored there."

"What are we waiting for?" Chandra yelled.

The three of us ran across the grounds. I arrived at the mill first, for obvious reasons.

It didn't take long to find the French doors. They were propped up against a wall in the back corner—beside a large blue vase.

I grasped the knob of the door on the right. It was exactly like the one I'd repaired the day Chandra and I got trapped inside the parlor. "We need to remove the handle."

"I (huff) got (puff) this," Lou said, pulling a pipe wrench from the pocket of his cargo shorts. He bent down in front of the handle.

I fixed my gaze on the back of his head to avoid seeing his... Well, he's a plumber.

Lou stuck out his tongue, gave a couple of tugs with the wrench, and the handle fell into his hand. Battling his belly, he rose to his feet. "Here (huff) you (puff) go."

Like Lou, I was breathless—but with excitement. I shook the base of the handle over my palm, and out tumbled the Lacour diamond.

Chandra gasped and clasped her face. "All this time the spirit was trying to show us where the diamond was!"

"Exactly." I stared with wonder at the coral-pink gem.

She put a hand on my arm. "That means the spirit was probably Evangeline, not Ivanna."

I bit my lip. "I have a feeling it was both of them."

"Well, it sure is a beaut," Lou said, pulling up his sagging shorts. "What're you gonna do with it?"

"Oh, I can't keep it," I said. "It belongs to the plantation."

Chandra's lips formed a tiny pout. "But Delta's going to prison. Surely you don't plan to give it to her?"

"I'm giving it to the police," I announced in a steadfast tone. Although, let's be honest, I really wanted to keep it for myself. "We'd better head out."

When we arrived at the parking lot, I approached the policeman who'd loaded Delta into the back of his patrol car. "Officer, we found something in the little mill that's pertinent to the case. It's the legendary Lacour diamond."

Delta's head turned so sharply I thought it was going to spin all the way around like Linda Blair's in *The Exorcist*. "That diamond is mine!" she shouted at the closed window. "Do you hear me, Franki Amato? Mine!"

The officer shined his flashlight on the stone. "That's some diamond."

"And it's my property!" she yelled. "Give it to me this instant!"

"I can't do that, ma'am," he said, turning to the window. "This diamond is evidence."

Seeing Delta's reaction, a thought occurred to me. "Officer, do you mind if we take a few pictures with the diamond, since we found it, and all?"

"Make it quick," he replied, depositing the gem into my palm.

Delta shot daggers at me with her eyes. "Get your filthy hands off my heirloom!"

Chandra and I snapped several selfies with the diamond as Delta raged.

That'll teach her for making cracks about my size, I thought as I returned the diamond to the officer with a huge grin on my face.

By the time he drove away, Delta's fury had given way to tears, and she was wailing and blubbering about her "precious pink baby."

"What a wuss," Chandra said.

"Yeah," Lou agreed. "Southern steel, my *culo*."

I smiled at his use of the uncouth Italian term for derriere. "Once again, Lou, you took the words right out of my mouth."

WHEN I ENTERED my office the next morning, there were beignets and a soy latte on my desk. I turned to find Veronica in the doorway. "What's this?"

"A small thank you for your amazing work on the case."

"Are you sure you're not mad that I continued working the investigation?"

"I can't tell you what to do with your day off, but I am upset that you put yourself in danger." She crossed her arms. "Promise me that you'll give me a heads-up the next time you plan to confront a ruthless killer."

"I promise," I said, taking a seat behind my desk. "But honestly, I thought I was covered after calling the police. And besides, you've been so busy lately that I thought you wanted me to handle the case on my own."

"I have been busy," she said as she eased into the armchair. "And the truth is that after I helped you get the investigation underway, I did take a step back."

"I noticed," I said, reaching for a beignet. "I just don't understand why."

She sighed. "Because PIs don't work with partners like the police do. And even though I'd love for us to collaborate on cases, the budget doesn't allow for that yet. So, I needed for you to gain confidence in your ability to work a case on your own." She smiled. "And after bringing down Delta Dupré, you should be able to handle anyone."

I swallowed a big bite of beignet. "I see what you're saying," I began, dusting powdered sugar from my hands, "and I have to admit that in some ways it was pretty great to call the shots. But you're overlooking the fact that I did have a partner on this case."

"Who? David?"

I took a sip of latte. "Chandra."

Veronica rolled her eyes. "Now, I'll admit that she and her husband saved your life, and for that I'll be forever grateful, but—"

"No *buts* about it," I interrupted. "Like you, I have my doubts about her psychic abilities, but no one can deny that her vision of the spirit and the doorknob led to the discovery of the Lacour diamond. And while we're on the subject, I have some sparkly selfies to show you."

Veronica clapped her hands as I handed her my phone. She was swiping through the photos when my Sir Mix-a-Lot ring tone sounded. She looked up. "It's Ivanna's father."

I grabbed the phone and pressed answer. "Hi, Liam."

"I'm calling to congratulate you on your stupendous work on the case," he said. "You should be proud to know that it's a lead story in the Italian news."

"You're in Italy?"

Veronica looked as surprised as I was.

"I had Ivanna buried beside her mother," he said, the pain evident in his tone.

"I'm glad." I wanted to ask him about the belladonna, but I didn't feel right about doing it after he'd mentioned the burial.

"I also wanted you to know that the police called me this morning." He paused. "They've released Adam."

Liam had just presented me with the opening I needed. "Did they ask if you'd planted the belladonna in his lab?"

There was silence on the line. "As far as they're concerned, the case is closed," he said in a cautious tone. "And as for Adam, the arrest gave him the opportunity to sober up and think about his actions, past and future. So, all things considered, there was no harm done."

I was silent as I wrestled with my conscience. Liam had committed a crime, but what good would it do to turn him in? Adam was already free, but Liam might go to jail—that is, if he came back to the United States. And if he was imprisoned, he could never work for Doctors Without Borders again.

There was a muffled voice over a loudspeaker.

Liam cleared his throat. "That's my boarding call."

I wasn't surprised he was at the airport. "Are you going back to Syria?"

"Afghanistan."

The call came over the loudspeaker again.

This was it—my last chance to insist that he turn himself in. "Liam..."

"Yes?"

But then I thought of all the lives he would save. "Have a safe flight."

"Thank you, Franki," he said softly. "So very much."

I tossed my phone on the desk and looked into Veronica's eyes. We both knew there was nothing to say.

The main door slammed.

"David's here," we said in unison—happy for the distraction.

"Franki!" he yelled, entering the room like a tornado. "You're a hero!"

I grinned. "Chandra and Lou are heroes too."

He curled his upper lip. "They didn't look like it on the news."

"Why not?" Veronica asked. "What do heroes look like?"

"I dunno, but not like cosmic plumbers."

I burst out laughing, imagining them decked out in moons, stars, and plumbing supplies. "I'm sure they looked better than

Glenda did when she was on TV after our last murder investigation."

David turned pink and said nothing.

"So, how are you going to celebrate your success?" Veronica asked.

"Work, I guess," I replied.

"No, ma'am," she said, wagging her index finger at me. "You're taking the day off."

"Dude!" David exclaimed. "The Jazz and Heritage Festival starts today. You should totally go."

"I don't want to go to a concert alone," I said. Then I saw Veronica's brows lower with concern, so I added, "I think I'll spend the day with my man."

Her brows shot up. "Bradley?"

I stiffened, and then shook my head. "Napoleon."

I PULLED into my Uptown neighborhood, wishing I could avoid the cemetery. The realization that I had no one to celebrate with except for my dog had really gotten me down. The last thing I needed right now was a bunch of graves reminding me that I was going to die alone too.

It didn't help that Veronica had mentioned Bradley. I knew I shouldn't miss him, but I did. I even found myself wondering whether Chandra had been right about Pauline not being the third person in my relationship. Because there was one other candidate I could think of—my nonna. She was nothing if not a third wheel. And not your ordinary car wheel, either.

I was trying to figure out what the biggest wheel in the world was when my phone rang. I looked at the display before responding, "*Bonjour*, Corinne."

"Have you seen ze news?" she whisper-shouted.

Oh no, I thought. *What have Chandra and Lou done now?* I envisioned Chandra going into one of her vibrating spirit trances while Lou performed some sort of plumbing demonstration. "About my case, right?"

"*Oui!*" she whisper-exclaimed. "Ze FBI took her away in ze handcuffs."

"Ze FBI?" I echoed. I'd suspected Chandra of faking a vision or two, but I had no idea the feds were involved.

Oui, ze FBI," she repeated. "And Bradley helped!"

When she said his name, I finally understood. And I had to pull over to recover from the shock. "Bradley was working with the FBI?"

"He was undercover! He prove zat Pauline embezzle from ze bank and ze children," Corinne gushed. "Now I must go before my manager see me. *A bientôt!*"

I hung up my phone and hung my head. Bradley had said that things weren't what they seemed, and I'd laughed. Even worse, he'd asked me to trust him, and I hadn't. I doubted that he would ever forgive me.

The final scene from *Gone with the Wind* popped into my head. Scarlett was crying on the staircase after Rhett had walked out on her for the last time. Then she looked off into the distance and vowed to get him back because, after all, tomorrow was another day.

"Southern belle bimbo," I said as I shifted the car back into gear and headed for home.

A few minutes later, I pulled in front of my house and slammed on the brakes.

Bradley was in the driveway in a sleek Armani suit and dark sunglasses. He looked like a male model—with a bouquet of yellow roses in his hand.

Because I had my convertible top down, I almost leapt over

the side of my car to get to him. But I decided that the occasion called for a more ladylike route, i.e., the door.

He took off his sunglasses, and our eyes locked as I walked up the driveway.

"Franki, I—"

"Sh." I put my finger on his lips. "I already know."

Then I replaced my finger with my mouth.

When we came up for air, I narrowed my eyes and said, "But I do have one question."

He ran a hand through his hair. "What is it?"

"How in the hell did you end up working with the FBI?"

He grimaced. "Well, the investigation is still pending so I can't go into details. But what I can say is that I contacted the FBI after a major donor to the 'Shoot for the Moon' fundraiser called about a tax receipt for his donation, and I couldn't find any record of it."

"That's terrible." I looked down. I felt really bad for Bradley, and I was still so angry at Pauline for trying to take advantage of him.

"Hey," Bradley said as he gently lifted my chin with his finger and looked into my eyes. With his free hand he reached into his jacket pocket and pulled out an envelope. "This is for you."

Thinking it was a letter or card, I shivered when I realized that it was an airline itinerary for two from New Orleans to... "Houston?"

He cleared his throat. "Yeah, I got a really, uh, interesting and persuasive call from Father Roman and Carmela about making things right with your mamma."

I put my finger back on his lips. "And you still came here today?"

He took my hand in his and kissed my palm. "Actually, I thought it was charming."

I blinked. Poor man, how could he know? The reality of Nonna was just too unreal for anyone to fathom. He would have to learn for himself. Until then, I thought it best to change the subject. I snuggled up to him and asked, "Do you have to go back to work?"

He sighed. "For a few hours. The bank merger was due to go through this week, but now that Pauline is in the news, I have to do damage control."

I rested my forehead on his. "I'm so sorry."

"I'm not," he breathed and then kissed my eyelids. "Not now that I have you back."

I felt my body go limp and was grateful his strong arms were around me.

"How about dinner tonight?" He kissed the tip of my nose and flashed a devilish smile. "We could go to Nonna Mia."

I instantly regained my strength and punched him in the arm. "When hell freezes over."

He laughed and pulled me closer. "Okay, then. Galatoire's?"

"That's really fancy," I said as he kissed my cheeks. "I'm not sure I have anything appropriate to wear."

He moved his lips a fraction away from mine. "What about that knockout skirt?"

BOOK BACKSTORY

Prosecco Pink is the result of three trips I took to Oak Alley Plantation. With its canopied path of southern live oak trees leading to the Mississippi River, the place is marvelous—and creepy. Cases in point: Bette Davis filmed parts of *Hush, Hush Sweet Charlotte* there, and it was also used in several scenes in *Interview with a Vampire*.

Creepiness aside, my favorite memory of Oak Alley is of my dad buying me my first-ever mint julep. For a few minutes, I sat on the plantation porch sipping my drink and pretending that it was the antebellum era, and I learned why so many women fainted. It wasn't just the corsets beneath their hot, hoop-skirted dresses, it was the Louisiana heat and all the bourbon in those drinks!

Speaking of my dad, I'd like to thank him for making me fall in love with New Orleans. And while I'm thanking family, a very special thank you goes to my son for being as patient as he could while I wrote; to my mother for being my biggest fan and for catching my mistakes (She has *always* had a special talent for that, btw.); and to my husband for reading various passages and listening to me drone on—and on and on and on—about plot issues.

In terms of the plot, I owe a huge debt of gratitude to Detective Ruben Vasquez and Wally Lind, both of whom graciously spend their free time answering the questions of writers like me, and to my friend Gregg Charalambous for inspiring the character of Troy. (He knows why.)

Last but not least, I'd like to thank all my friends who lent me their names for *Prosecco Pink*. You know who you are, and if you don't, you'll have to read the book to find out!

Cin cin (Cheers)!

Traci

COCKTAILS

PINK PROSECCO LEMONADE

Franki Amato loves her Limoncello, but she's also rather fond of pink Prosecco. In the spirit of excess (I mean, where's the spirit in moderation?), she has found a way to combine them in this pink lemony drink.

Ingredients
    Pink Prosecco
    Limoncello
    Pink lemonade
    Strawberry for garnish

In a fluted glass, mix two parts pink Prosecco, one part Limoncello, and one part pink lemonade. Garnish with a strawberry.

PINK PROSECCO WITH RASPBERRY SORBET

Veronica's favorite "ladies' night" drink also involves Prosecco—but with a scoop of yummy raspberry sorbet. It goes without saying that Glenda substitutes pink Champagne—and skips the sorbet).

Ingredients
   Pink Prosecco
   Raspberry sorbet

Place one scoop of raspberry sorbet in a fluted glass. Fill with pink Prosecco and serve immediately.

Amaretto amber

USA TODAY BESTSELLING AUTHOR

Traci Andrighetti

AMARETTO AMBER

by

TRACI ANDRIGHETTI

***

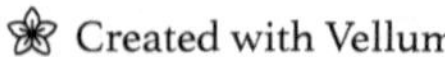 Created with Vellum

1

"It could be the angel of death," I whispered to my cairn terrier, Napoleon, as I peered from the peephole at the black feather-winged figure on my front porch. "I mean, today *is* my thirtieth birthday."

The dark form shifted, and a bony wrist and hand came into view. The palm was extended upward, and the skin was shriveled and ghostly white.

As my eyes traveled the length of the long, curled fingers, the hand lowered slightly, and I saw a sickening sight.

A Mae West-style cigarette holder.

I sighed and rested my head against the door. "No such luck, buddy," I breathed. "It's Glenda."

"Open up, Miss Franki," Glenda O'Brien, my sixty-something landlady, called in her sultry, Southern voice. "The birthday fairy is here, and she's got a surprise for you."

At only nine-thirty a.m. on the Saturday I'd turned thirty I was in no mood for surprises. And judging from the way Napoleon was rubbing his eye with his paw, he wasn't up for any of Glenda's shenanigans either.

"Like it or not, sugar, you're no spring chicken anymore," she bellowed for the whole neighborhood to hear. "So let Miss Glenda in. She'll make it all better."

I was quite sure that she wouldn't, but I opened the door anyway. Along with the cigarette holder and the set of black wings, Glenda was clad in a studded black leather micro triangle top, a tiny tutu, and thigh-high boots. I couldn't decide whether she looked like a winged Hell's Angel or a geriatric Victoria's Secret model whose wings had been clipped. "Um, is that supposed to be your fairy costume?"

"I just made that crap up so you'd open the damn door," she said as she shoved a Bloody Mary into my hand.

I eyed the drink suspiciously. "What's this for?"

She batted her inch-long crimson eyelashes. "Aren't you hung over?"

"No, but I might as well be."

She put her hand on her tutued hip. "The night before I turned thirty, I drowned my sorrows in champagne, and I soaked in it too. A bubbly bath does wonders for a lady's soul and her skin, you know."

On my private investigator's salary, I couldn't afford a glass of champagne, much less a bathtub full. But Glenda was an ex-stripper who'd invested her money in real estate and antiques, including the fourplex we lived in and the not-so-chic seventies brothel pieces in my furnished apartment, so she could afford to bathe in booze. In fact, she had a six-foot-tall champagne glass in her living room for precisely that purpose. "Actually, I wouldn't know."

"Well, don't you fret about that, sugar," she said, waving a bony finger. "Because this year your birthday's gonna be full of fun surprises."

An alarm siren sounded in my head as she took a drag off her cigarette. "What exactly do you mean by 'full of fun surprises'?"

"I can't tell you that, now can I?" she exclaimed, exhaling smoke into my face as she spoke.

I sucked down half the spicy Bloody Mary to calm my nerves. Despite her age, Glenda was as wild as a sorority girl at a Mardi Gras-themed mixer, so one of her surprises could pack a real punch (and not of the delicious rum variety).

She tucked the cigarette holder behind her ear and stepped toward me. "Hold still, sugar."

I eyeballed the lit cigarette, which was dangerously close to my long, brown hair. "What for?"

"You'll see." She pulled a crisp dollar bill from the waistband of her tutu and removed a pin from the teensy triangle of leather tasked with covering her nipple and areola.

I, in turn, uttered a silent prayer to the wardrobe fairy that there would be no malfunction.

"Now stick out your chest."

"No way." I shielded my breasts from both the pin and the ash that was now dangling from the cigarette. We lived in New Orleans, so for all I knew she was about to perform some kind of stripper voodoo ritual to ward off the evil spirits of sagging and wrinkling. "Not until you tell me what you're going to do."

"Oh, quit your bellyachin'," she scolded as she shoved her hand down the V-neckline of my beige sweater and pinned the dollar above my left boob.

"What's that for?" I asked, feeling flustered and felt up. After all, she was the stripper, not me.

Glenda removed the cigarette holder from behind her ear. "It's a local tradition, Miss Franki. Someone pins a dollar to your shirt on your birthday, and then all day long people add money. Sometimes, fives, tens, even twenties."

I drained the other half of my drink as I pondered this possibility. Free money would definitely qualify as a "fun surprise."

My cell phone began to ring.

"You go on and get that, Miss Franki. I'm late for practice."

"Practice for what?" It was none of my business, but I had to know what kind of organized activity would require such a ghastly getup.

Her eyes lit up like a stripper stage. "In honor of St. Patrick's Day and St. Joseph's Day, my old manager at Madame Moiselle's has invited some of us more seasoned dancers to do a show called 'The Saints, Sinners, and Sluts Revue.'"

Madame Moiselle's was the Bourbon Street strip club where Glenda, dancing as "Lorraine Lamour," had made quite a name for herself in the sixties and seventies. She'd also been courted by a slew of prominent suitors, including a wealthy sheikh who asked her to join his harem after he'd watched her "1001 A-labian Nights" routine. Ever since she'd retired she'd been helping out at the club, teaching the new girls the tricks of the trade, but I knew that her real passion lay in performing.

"What are you supposed to be, like, a sinner-saint?" I asked, nodding toward her black wings.

Her face fell. "No, sugar," she replied. "I'm a slut. Isn't it obvious?"

"Of course," I reassured. "I don't know what I was thinking."

"No worries," she said with a flip of her long, platinum hair. The corners of her mouth formed a lewd grin. "You have a stimulating day, now."

Her wings flapped as she turned and strutted toward a waiting taxi.

I closed the door and wondered what she'd meant by "stimulating" as I searched for my now silent phone. I found it on the end table beneath a half-eaten bag of Hampton's Cajun Creole Hot Nuts. When I looked at the display, I breathed a sigh of relief—that is, until the phone started ringing again. I gave a sigh of resignation and stretched out on the chaise lounge before pressing answer. "Hi, Mom."

"Happy birthday, Francesca," she said, her usually shrill voice descending with every syllable until it was so low and lugubrious that it sounded like it wanted to jump off a ledge.

"Thanks," I replied, already trying to figure out a way to get her off the phone. These calls from home were typically a downer, but judging from the way this one had started, we were destined to sink to new depths of despair. "Is Dad there?"

"He's at the deli, dear," she said in a dejected tone. "The city shut off the water this morning with no warning, so he had to run some jugs of water over for the kitchen staff."

My parents, Brenda and Joe Amato, had owned Amato's Deli in Houston's Rice Village since before I was born. And if you were thinking that the water issue was the reason for my mother's depression, you were dead wrong. From the moment I graduated from the University of Texas when I was twenty-two, she'd been upset that I wasn't married. The thing was that both of my parents were first generation Italian-Americans, and they believed in the "old country" values. But they didn't hold a candle to my dad's eighty-three-year-old Sicilian mother, Carmela Montalbano. She declared me a *zitella*, which is Italian for old maid, at the advanced age of sixteen—almost half my life ago.

I suddenly realized that my mother had fallen silent, no doubt wallowing in maternal misery. So I said, "That's a bummer about the water, Mom, but I'm sure they'll turn it back on soon." Then I made the fatal mistake of asking, "Everything else okay?"

The silence continued, which was the signal that she was about to segue into the really bad news. "Well, I might as well tell you, Francesca." She gave a somber sigh. "Your nonna's in mourning."

Aaaand let the guilt games begin, I thought as I rested the back of my arm on my forehead. "Mom, she's been in heavy mourning since *nonnu* died twenty-one years ago."

"Yes, but she's gone into deeper mourning now that you've turned thirty. She's started wearing a black veil around the house, and she's taken a vow of silence."

A vow of silence? That was both worrisome and wonderful—worrisome because my nonna lived to meddle, which she couldn't do if she wasn't able to talk, and wonderful because, well, she couldn't meddle or talk. "So, what's she doing, then?"

"Sitting on the couch, holding her rosary, and staring at the portrait of the Virgin Mary," she replied as maudlin as a martyr. "Your father's just sick about it too. It hurts him terribly to see his mother in this state."

"Mom," I began, annoyed that she'd played the sad dad card, "why don't you remind nonna that I have a terrific boyfriend who I've been dating for over a year?" I asked, referring to my banker beau, Bradley Hartmann.

"You know your nonna, dear."

Yes, I did. For her, the mere act of dating was equivalent to living in sin. Single young women were to be betrothed at a suitable age (by early twentieth-century Sicilian standards) and strictly chaperoned until the wedding, which was supposed to take place the minute the marriage banns went into effect. "Well, she can't expect me to have a two-week engagement like she did. That's just prehistoric."

"It's a little hasty, I agree. But you've been with Bradley for a year now, Francesca." She paused. "For your sake, I hope he proposes at dinner tonight."

I bolted upright, causing Napoleon's ears to do the same. "What do you mean 'for your sake'? It's not like being unmarried is an affliction. And besides, you can't put that kind of pressure on me—or on Bradley, for that matter."

"Now don't confuse me with Mother Nature," she said, lapsing into lecture mode. "She's the one putting the pressure on you. After all, your biological clock has been ticking for some time now."

I clenched my teeth, and a sharp pain shot through one of my upper molars. "Ow! Dang it."

"What's the matter, dear?"

I put my hand to my face. "My tooth hurts."

"You have to take better care of yourself, Francesca," she chastised. "You're not a young girl anymore."

"Mom, that's been made painfully clear to me today," I snapped. "Listen, I need to get going. I'm working overtime this weekend."

"Well, try to have a nice day, dear," she said as though it would be next to impossible.

"Right," I said, biting the inside of my cheek to stop myself from saying something I'd only halfway regret. I also managed to spit out a "love you" because I did love my mother, but not especially in that moment.

I hung up the phone and pressed my molar with my thumb. There was something wrong, all right. I wanted to believe that it was my sweet tooth telling me that I should never have given up sweets for Lent, because I could seriously go for a jar of Nutella right now.

Instead, I grabbed the bag of Hot Nuts and tossed a couple into my mouth. No sooner had I bit down than the pain jolted into my sinus cavity. This was no sweet tooth—this was a sign. On top of being husbandless and childless, I was destined to be toothless too.

~

"I'M BACK, FRANKI," my boss and best friend Veronica Maggio

called as she pushed open the door to her PI firm, Private Chicks, Inc., with a package under her arm.

I'd come to the office an hour earlier to escape the bad birthday juju at my apartment. Soon after I'd arrived and told Veronica about Glenda, my mom, and the saga of my nonna's vow of silence, she'd announced that she needed to run a few errands. So I had high hopes that she was going to right the wrongs of this morning's wayward well-wishers. "What have you got there?"

She saw me stretched out on one of the two opposing couches in the middle of the waiting room and stopped short. "Why are you lying down? Aren't you feeling well?"

I started to tell her that my tooth had begun hurting, but then I noticed that the package was a box from the Alois J Binder bakery on Frenchman Street, and I got a better idea. "I think I have low blood sugar," I rasped, going for a sick waif but sounding more like a steady smoker. "I haven't had any sweets since Mardi Gras, and that was over a month ago."

She smirked and placed the box on the reception desk beside the door. "Nice try, but I got you a plain croissant."

"Gah, Veronica," I said, pulling myself onto my elbows. "Sometimes you can be so cruel. Even my parents used to give me a birthday Lent reprieve when I was a teenager, and you know what strict Catholics they are."

"Yes, but you're not a teen anymore," she said as she looked inside the bakery box.

I scowled and lay back down. I should have known that Veronica would rain on my bedraggled birthday parade. When we first met in college, I thought that she was a bubbly blonde party girl, but I soon learned that she was all business and no pleasure. Case in point—she finished college and law school in about the same amount of time it took me to earn a bachelor's degree, and she did it with honors. "You know, you're the third person today to imply that I'm old, and it's only ten thirty."

Her smirk softened as she brought me the box. "I'm sorry you're having such a bad birthday. I don't know why you didn't take the day off."

"I could use the overtime pay, for one thing," I said, glancing pointedly at the lone dollar that hung from my shirt before taking the creamless croissant. "And I had to get out of that apartment. The baroque brothel décor was starting to remind me of an old funeral parlor, and with that creepy cemetery across the street, I felt like I was sitting around waiting to go to my grave."

Veronica rolled her eyes. "Oh, come on," she said, taking a seat on the opposite couch. "Turning thirty's not that bad. I did it six months ago, and I lived to tell about it."

"I know." I picked at the plain pastry. "Honestly, it's not the age that bothers me as much as the familial fallout from it."

"Well, look at the bright side," she said, pulling a vanilla cream napoleon from the box. "Now that your nonna has taken a vow of silence, you're going to get a much-needed break."

I shot her a skeptical look. With that delicious pastry in hand, she could afford to be optimistic.

The door swung open, and David Savoie, our part-time research assistant, entered, carrying two grocery bags. A junior at Tulane University, David could really put away the grub, but you'd never know it from his lanky frame.

"What've you got there, your lunch?" Veronica joked.

He flipped his brown bangs to one side. "Nah, Rouses Market donated this stuff for the food drive. It's mostly potato chips, pretzels, and pralines."

After swearing off sweets, I was so sick of savory snacks that I could just spit—except that I didn't have any saliva left because of all the salt. But my interest perked up at the mention of pralines. "What food drive?"

David placed the bag on his desk in the far left corner behind the couches. "My fraternity is collecting food for the poor for St. Joseph's Day."

I looked at Veronica to see whether she was as confused as I was. "Why is your computer science frat participating in a Catholic festival?"

"St. Joseph's Day isn't just a religious tradition in New Orleans, Franki," Veronica explained. "It's like St. Patrick's Day—the whole city celebrates it."

This was news to me. As far as I was aware, only Italian-American Catholics observed the day. "Okay, but why bring the food here?"

David sat on the back of the couch. "Veronica's letting me keep the donations in the conference room because my frat brothers keep eating them all."

"That's terrible," I said, resolving to slip across the hall to that conference room. I had no intention of stealing food from the poor, mind you. I just wanted to check those pralines—you know, to make sure they hadn't gone bad.

Veronica swallowed a bite of her pastry. "It's predictable behavior from a house full of hungry young men. That reminds me, David," she began, turning to hand him the open box, "I got you a little surprise from the bakery."

"A shoe sole! Dude, thanks," he exclaimed before shoving the sole-shaped pastry into his mouth. Then he retrieved the grocery bag, grabbed the conference room key from the reception desk drawer, and headed across the hall.

"Speaking of surprises, tell me what Glenda has planned for me," I ordered, giving Veronica my sincerest spill-it stare.

She licked cream from her finger in a ploy to avoid my gaze.

But I wasn't fooled. I was positive that she knew the score

because she lived in Glenda's fourplex too. In fact, Veronica was the one who'd convinced me to rent the ground-floor apartment across from hers, sight (and cemetery) unseen. And despite the world of differences between her and Glenda, they were as tight as Gwyneth and Madonna—before their unfortunate split. "I'm serious. Out with it."

She pursed her lips and took a deep breath. "You know I'm no spoiler—"

"Just say it," I commanded through clenched teeth.

"Glenda hired you a male stripper," she gushed.

I dropped the croissant. "Why in the hell would she do that?"

She shrugged. "She thought you needed a little cheering up. And in Glenda's world, that can only mean one thing."

Yeah, nude, hard-bodied men slathered in oil. Of course, there was a time and a place for that sort of thing, but not on the day that I had plans with Bradley. "Please tell me that the stripper isn't going to show up during my date. I'm finally getting to go to the Sazerac Bar, and I don't want to get escorted out."

Veronica shook her head. "I'm sure he'll come before then. Glenda would want you to enjoy him all on your own."

"What'd she get me?" I asked—just so I could be prepared, of course. "A carpenter? A fireman?"

She averted her eyes. "A cop."

"What?" Before joining Private Chicks, I'd worked as a rookie police officer in Austin, Texas, and I hadn't stood a fighting chance at that job. "How does she not know that I'd rather have any profession than a cop? Even a Wall Street executive."

"I told her that," Veronica replied, smoothing her blue Versace skirt. "But she said that you needed the authoritative type to bring you out of your funk."

I chewed my thumbnail. "Well, I hope this guy shows up soon. Because from the way things are going, that date is going to be the only bright spot of my day." *In addition to the Bloody Mary and the dollar.*

"Maybe this will help make your day a little brighter," she said, pulling an envelope from her purse. "It's a half day at the spa. I went by there on my way to the bakery, and they agreed to work you in at noon."

"You're the best, Veronica," I exclaimed as I jumped up from my sofa sickbed and wrapped my arms around her—bending my 5' 10" frame at the waist. "That's almost better than a pastry."

She laughed and shook her head. "Only you would prefer a pastry to pampering. Now, I have plans tonight, but I want to hear all the details in the morning—about the spa and the dinner."

"You got it." For the first time today, I was starting to think that I might have something good to recount.

"WHAT KIND of moron would leave their car running in the middle of the street?" I exclaimed to myself. I'd been standing outside Private Chicks for ten minutes, waiting for the owner of the neon orange Nissan Cube that was blocking my 1965 Mustang convertible. Because the firm was located on Decatur Street in the French Quarter, traffic was always an issue. And it didn't help that an Italian restaurant occupied the first two floors of the three-story brick building we were located in. I liked their pizza and pasta but not their patrons, who were prone to parking their cars in the street while picking up to-go orders.

I looked at the time on my phone as I paced the sidewalk. It was twenty till noon. If I didn't leave soon, I could kiss my spa appointment *arrivederci.*

A thirty-something guy holding a green beer and wearing a

matching T-shirt that read, "The leprechauns made me do it," approached from the other side of the street. "Hey, uh, is this the parade route?"

"Parade?" I repeated.

"Yeah." He wiped his nose with his wrist. "The parades for St. Patrick's Day and St. Joseph's Day start today at one o'clock."

I blinked. "They do?"

He took a swig of his beer. "They're always the Saturday before so everyone can get in on the action."

"You don't say," I said, narrowing my eyes at the Nissan. If a bunch of floats came down Decatur, I'd miss my massage for sure.

"Sorry to have bothered you," he said.

"No problem," I replied as I zeroed in on the real bother.

Without further ado, I marched to the driver's side of the Nissan and yanked open the door. As I settled into the seat and released the parking brake, I noticed an open box marked "Erzulie's Authentic Voodoo." Curious, not to mention a little concerned, I peered inside and saw around twenty see-through fabric bags containing incense sticks, candles, packets of white crystals, and little vials of liquid. The bags were marked "3-day ritual spell kits," and they were for everything from gaining wealth to garnering protection.

"What a wack job," I whispered as I pressed the gas pedal and pulled the car forward.

"That's my car," a gruff female voice cried.

I looked in the rearview mirror and saw the Nissan's middle-aged owner. How did I know it was her? My first clue was the teased, tangerine hair that was strikingly reminiscent of Endora from *Bewitched*.

"Help! Police!" She waved her purple-caftaned arms. "Stop that thief!"

I pulled up the parking brake and got out of the car just in time to see a thirty-something cop rounding the corner—and buttoning his shirt?

"Officer," she huffed, grasping his forearm, "this young woman was trying to steal my car."

His ice blue eyes looked through me as he fastened his top button. "Is this true, ma'am?"

I hesitated for a moment, not because I was guilty as accused but because a) I was annoyed by that "ma'am," and b) there was something weird about this cop. No officer I knew got dressed on duty, and he seemed uneasy in the uniform, maybe because it didn't fit him. His biceps were straining against the sleeves, and his pecs looked like they were going to pop out of his shirt.

Then it hit me. This was no street cop—this was the stripper cop.

Instantly annoyed, I shifted my weight to one leg and turned to the witchy woman. "Look, I'm late for an appointment, and your car was blocking mine. So I moved it, okay?"

The counterfeit cop cleared his throat. "Actually, it's not okay."

I gave a surly sigh. "I know, I know. I've been a very bad girl, and I need to be punished. But that's not gonna happen, because I'm going to the spa."

I opened the door of my Mustang and flopped into the seat.

"Ma'am," he began in a terse tone, "I need you to exit the vehicle."

I arched a brow. "Or what? You'll cuff me and teach me a lesson?"

He reached into his back pocket and flipped open his wallet.

My stomach tried to take off running as I stared at the New Orleans PD badge, which was as real as the regulation baton on his hip.

"You're under arrest for unauthorized use of a motor vehicle."

As he proceeded to read me my rights, my brain began to process the situation. To celebrate my thirtieth birthday, I wasn't going to the spa or to the Sazerac. I was going to the slammer.

2

"I'm taking you to the office so you can pick up your *own* car," Veronica quipped as we exited New Orleans's notorious Central Lockup at eight a.m. the next morning.

I clenched my jaw. She was clearly referring to my "unauthorized use" of the neon Nissan, but after spending the last twenty hours in a cold, cramped cell, I was in no mood for her sarcasm. "If you're thinking about a career in stand-up, forget it. You've got no comic timing."

She gave me a haughty look. "I wasn't trying to be funny, Franki."

We climbed into her white Audi in silence and fastened our seat belts.

"And I still don't understand how you, of all people, could've mistaken a real police officer for a stripper," she continued.

"I had a lot on my mind, okay?" I said as I rummaged through my bag for my sunglasses to shield my eyes from the harsh glare of the sunlight and the harsh reality of Central Lockup. "Besides, someone—and I'm not naming names—told me to be on the watch for a stripper cop."

She started the engine. "You're blaming me for this mess?"

I slid the sunglasses onto my nose. "There's plenty of blame to go around, starting with Glenda."

"She was just trying to do something nice for you," Veronica said as she peeled out of the parking lot. "There's no way she could've known that it would backfire like this."

I crossed my arms. "Maybe not, but she knew that I went to jail."

"What?" she exclaimed, hitting the gas so hard that both of our heads snapped backwards. "How?"

"After I called you and got your voice mail," I began, lowering my eyelids into a cold stare, "the officer agreed to let me try someone else. So, I called Glenda. When I told her where I was, she goes, 'I paid the young man extra for *hard time*, sugar. Enjoy the strip search,' and hung up the phone."

Veronica started to laugh but quickly turned the sound into a fake cough. "Well, look on the bright side. The woman whose car you moved dropped the charges. If I were you, I'd pay her a visit and thank her."

"I'm pretty sure 'that woman,' as you call her, is a witch—in both senses of the word. And because of her, I stood up my boyfriend and spent my birthday in the clink where a six-foot-five woman with a severe skin-peeling condition used my stomach for a pillow."

She put her hand over her mouth. "Oh my God, really?"

I nodded, as serious as a death sentence. "And to top it all off, this old prostitute ripped the dollar Glenda gave me right off my shirt."

Her eyes widened. "What did you do?"

"Nothing. She was a spitter." I searched my bag for my phone. "Now, I'd better call Bradley."

"Don't worry, Franki," Veronica said as she hooked a hard left onto South Rampart Street. "I explained everything to him after I got your message this morning."

I spun around in my seat so fast that my purse flew to the floor, and it wasn't because of that left turn. "You told him I was in jail?"

"He called me, frantic," she said, waving her hands in the air when she should have been steering. "What was I supposed to tell him?"

Now I was the frantic one. "Uh, not the truth!"

Veronica groaned and collapsed onto the steering wheel. "Here we go."

I glanced around the car. "Where? Off the road?"

She glared at me and straightened in her seat. "On a wild ride through your trust issues."

It was a well-known fact that I was kind of cagey where men were concerned. The problem was that I'd kissed more than my share of philandering frogs before meeting my persevering prince. But Veronica was wrong if she thought that I didn't believe in my boyfriend. "I already told you—I trust Bradley. I just haven't always felt the same about some of the people around him, like his snobby ex-wife and scheming ex-secretary."

"Uh-huh," she said, monotone. "If you trust him so much, then why didn't you want him to know that you spent the night in jail?"

I snorted in disbelief. "That has nothing to do with trust and everything to do with image. Bradley is a bank president. He needs a suitable woman by his side, e.g., one in a black cocktail dress, not an orange jumpsuit."

Veronica twisted her mouth to the side. "Are you saying that if you don't present the right image, you're afraid that he'll break up with you?"

"Not at all." I pulled off my sunglasses so that she could see my piercing look. "I'm saying that I need to be suitable, which I can't be if I'm behind bars. So, there's no way I'm thanking 'that woman' when she's the reason I got locked up in the first place."

"You're the reason you got locked up," she said, taking another sharp turn. "As an ex-cop, you knew that driving her car without her permission was a felony, so you need to thank her for saving you from a much lengthier stay in jail."

"All right, sure. I knew it was wrong," I admitted as I checked my seatbelt to make sure that it was securely fastened. "But in my defense, she started this whole fiasco by illegally parking her car."

"And if you'd simply reported her as opposed to moving the car, then she would've been the one in trouble with the law."

Of course, I realized that there was a grain of truth in what Veronica was saying—okay, a kernel. But the way I saw it, the woman should have apologized for blocking my Mustang instead of pressing charges and condemning me to spending the night with a skin-slougher.

I stared out the passenger window at a stretch of strip clubs on Bourbon Street. A platinum blonde in a gold lamé minidress and purple platform heels was pulling a small suitcase on wheels from the side door of Madame Moiselle's. I knew from Glenda that the club closed at four a.m., so the investigator in me wondered why a stripper would be leaving work so late.

Then a thought occurred to me. Veronica always worked late and was meticulous about checking her email and voice mail before going to bed. And yet, she didn't get my message until this morning. "Where were you last night, anyway?"

"I had a date with Dirk," she said in a quiet voice.

Veronica was famously private when it came to her personal life, so all I knew about her new boyfriend was that he was a gemologist, which made him a perfect match for my bedazzled bestie, and that his parents, Mr. and Mrs. Bogart, had made the surprising decision to name him "Dirk" after the late actor, Dirk Bogarde, rather than the obvious "Humphrey." "Wow, this is like your fifth date. Is it serious?"

The corners of her mouth tilted upward. "He's a keeper, like Bradley."

"Speaking of keeping Bradley, I'd better make that call." I retrieved my bag from the floor and resumed the search for my phone to no avail. I thought for a moment and remembered that the last time I'd used it was to check the time before moving the Nissan. "Oh, man."

She looked at me from the corners of her eyes. "What's the matter?"

I put my head in my hands. "I left my phone on the seat of that wacko witch's car."

"Looks like you're going to have to apologize to her now," she intoned as she pulled to a stop in front of 1200 Decatur Street.

I gave her my best stabby stare before exiting the Audi.

"And if I were you," she continued, "I would avoid calling her both wacko and witch. An officer at the lockup told me that her first name is Theodora, but that's all I know."

So, "Endora" hadn't been far off the mark. "She's either a customer or an employee of Erzulie's down on Royal Street, but since it's Sunday, they probably don't open for a few hours."

"Then you have plenty of time to shower off the jail germs," Veronica said as cheerful as a cheerleader. "You smell like a urinal."

I slammed the car door.

As I climbed into my Mustang, I wondered what in the hell I was going to say to the witch and what in heaven I was going to tell Bradley.

WHEN I STEPPED inside Erzulie's at eleven fifteen, over-caffeinated and under-rested, I thought that I'd entered the Age of Aquarius. Unlike the other voodoo and witchcraft shops in the French Quarter, which were fittingly dark and creepy, the shotgun-style store was a psychedelic mind trip of color. The walls were orange with purple trim, and pink paper lanterns dangled from the ceiling. Various tables and shelves were draped with turquoise and fuchsia glitter organza, and blue beaded curtains obscured a room in the back. Even the products on the shelves were colorful—yellow gris-gris bags, green spell candles, red voodoo dolls. The place looked like an LSD flashback to the 1960s, and thanks to the patchouli incense, it smelled like one too.

As I looked around the room for a sales clerk, my eyes were drawn to a portrait of a woman hanging above a purple mantel serving as an altar. She had a short, orange and green Afro, which matched her striped, strapless dress, and her right hand was placed in the middle of her chest. A lavender snake was coiled around her left arm, and a large, red heart was suspended from her right earlobe.

"That's Erzulie Freda, the Haitian Vodou goddess of love, sensuality, passion, pleasure, and prosperity," a regal female voice said.

I turned to see an attractive thirtyish brunette in a teal silk Mandarin dress. "Sounds like someone I need to meet." But then I remembered learning about a vindictive voodoo goddess with a similar name during my first murder case. "She's not any relation to Erzulie D'en Tort, is she?"

She smiled. "Erzulie D'en Tort is the Petro manifestation of Erzulie Freda. The Petro gods came from the New World and the West and are more aggressive than their benevolent Haitian counterparts." She gestured toward the altar. "If you like, you can get acquainted with Lady Erzulie by making her an offering. She prefers gifts of jewelry, perfume, flowers, cakes, and liqueurs."

"What a coincidence," I said in a joking tone. "So do I."

A corner of her mouth turned up. "Is there anything I can help you with?"

"I'm looking for someone named Theodora," I replied, approaching the cash register.

With a nod, the woman walked to the back of the room and slipped through the beaded curtain.

While I waited, I wandered around the store. Erzulie's didn't sell any of the typical voodoo and witchcraft wares, like severed gator heads and chicken feet. Instead, the merchandise consisted of more upscale items, such as goat milk spiritual soaps and jewel-encrusted skulls.

There were so many bright, sparkly items that I couldn't resist the urge to touch something. So I picked up a black-stained glass pentagram. Curious to see whether light would shine through the dark glass, I opened the door and held the pentagram up to the sun.

"You're not thinking about taking off with that too, are you?" a familiar voice asked.

I turned to face Theodora. She was wearing a yellow caftan with a necklace and earring set of green cat's eyes complete with slit pupil. Between her attire and her orange hair, purple eye shadow, and pink lipstick, she really blended in with the shop. "Don't worry," I said, returning the stained glass window to the display. "Pentagrams aren't my thing."

"I actually like them, and I'm not even a Wiccan." She leaned forward and shielded her mouth with her hand. "Nothing against the Wiccans," she whispered, "but I don't believe in organized religion."

"Ah ha," I said, taking a step backwards. "So, listen. I'm Franki and—"

"Theodora," she interrupted, grabbing my hand and giving it a shake. "How'd you find me? Are you clairvoyant?"

"Uh, no," I replied, suppressing a sigh. "I saw the box of spells from Erzulie's on your front seat and figured that you must be an employee."

"Oh, I don't work here. I'm a freelancer." She pulled a business card from a pocket in her caftan and pressed it into my palm.

I reluctantly read the card and saw that she was a "witchcraft consultant." Of course, I opted to ignore that little tidbit and focus on her lack of a last name. "Just Theodora, huh? Like Cher and Madonna?"

"No, they have surnames," she replied, toying with her necklace. "When I was born we didn't have last names."

I assumed a standoffish stance. I was a magnet for all the nutcases in New Orleans, and the last time I'd exchanged business cards with one of them, I'd ended up with a psycho psychic as my sidekick during a multiple homicide investigation at a plantation. "That's super interesting, but—"

"Aren't you going to ask how old I am?" she interrupted, blinking.

"U-um," I began, momentarily distracted by the discovery that her eyes were glowing green like her pendant, "my mother taught me never to ask a witch, er, *a woman*, her age."

"Well, I don't mind telling you that I had a milestone birthday last week." She raised her chin, striking a pose. "I turned three hundred."

And to think that I'd felt bad about turning thirty. "Wow," I exclaimed, searching for something sane to say. "You don't look a day over fifty-five."

She touched her teased hair. "That's what I hear."

I stared at the floor while I tried to wipe the stupor from my face. "So, aaanyway, I dropped by because—"

"I know." She held up a hand. "We got off on the wrong foot yesterday–your foot on my gas pedal, to be precise—and you want to make amends."

I scratched the back of my head. "Uh, about that—"

"No need to apologize," she said, giving my forearm a squeeze.

"Honestly, I wasn't—"

"Shht!" She flapped her caftaned arms like yellow wings.

I was starting to get annoyed. This witch wouldn't let me get a word in edgewise.

"The truth is, yesterday I was having a down day. I have SAD. You know, Seasonal Affective Disorder? And with spring around the corner, I'm prone to severe highs and lows."

Awesome. Of all the witches I could've run into, I had to go and meet the one with serious mood swings. "Hey, no need to explain," I said, trying to keep her spirits on the upswing. "I just came to get—"

"Help with the curse?"

I cocked my head to one side. "No, my phone."

"Well, why didn't you say so?" she asked, pulling my cell from her pocket.

I swallowed bile as I took the phone and shoved it into my bag. This witch was not only a wacko, she was also just plain willful. I knew that I should have left right then and there, but my curiosity got the best of me. "What did you mean by that curse comment?"

"It's obvious that someone has put a hex on you."

Even if you knew nothing about my life, the events of the past twenty-four hours were compelling enough evidence to support her argument, no matter how deranged it may have sounded. "It is?" I asked against my better judgment. "How do you know?"

She looked me up and down like I was the lunatic. "I'm something of an expert in these matters."

I shook my head, trying to knock some sense into it. "No offense or anything, but I don't believe in curses or witchcraft."

"If a witch had sent me to jail," she began in a droll tone, "I'd reconsider that position."

I shot her a steely stare. "I think we both know that had nothing to do with a curse. And besides, it's not like I have any witch enemies. The people I know are more the *malocchio*, or evil eye, types."

Her purple eyelids lowered. "You can put a curse on yourself, you know. If you wish someone harm, gossip about them, or call them names, those are curses that can boomerang back on you."

I'm not going to lie—I felt a stab of panic upon hearing this news. But then I got hold of myself. "If that's the case then I'm cursed for life, and no witch in the world will be able to undo it."

She crossed her arms, and her pupils turned to slits like the ones on her jewelry. "Try me."

I pulled my bag in front of my chest in a defensive posture. Were my eyes playing tricks on me? Or were hers? "Let me think on it," I gushed, making for the exit. "Now that I have my phone back, I need to make a long-overdue call to my boyfriend."

"Then know this," she said, pointing a yellow-lacquered fingernail at my forehead like a wand. "You'll never be able to have a healthy relationship until that curse is lifted."

I started to tell her that if she knew my family then she'd realize that I could never have a healthy relationship anyway—curse or no. But I didn't want to provoke her. Her mood had taken a turn for the worse, and I wasn't sure what this witch was capable of. "I'll take my chances," I said as I pushed open the door. "Thanks for returning my phone, though."

I hurried from the shop and turned down St. Ann where I'd parked my car, thinking about Theodora's eyes. That pupil thing had to be some kind of magic trick. I mean, what kind of sucker did that witch take me for? And as for the curse, the only thing to blame for my current wretched state was good old-fashioned bad luck—and my family and friends.

I pulled out my cell to call Bradley. The screen was black, so I pressed the power button. Nothing. The battery was dead.

Again, regular old bad luck. Right?

I shoved my phone back into my bag and proceeded down the street. Then an eerie sensation came over me. It wasn't an I've-been-cursed feeling, because I knew that was nonsense. It was more of an I'm-being-followed feeling. I glanced over my shoulder, but all I saw were a few tourists. Still, something didn't seem right. So, when I reached my car, I wasted no time getting inside.

And I told myself that the culprit was probably just the usual dark cloud hanging over me.

3

_____

"*Mannaggia a me*," I muttered as I plugged my cell phone into the car charger and contemplated how to explain my stint in the slammer to Bradley. Then a stunning realization hit me—I'd just said "damn me" in Italian, which qualified as cursing myself. I resolved to stop doing that stat.

The phone display lit up, and I scrolled through the list of missed calls. As I'd expected, most of them were from Bradley, and several were from my mother who was undoubtedly dying to find out whether I was engaged. But there were also a couple from Bradley's secretary, Ruth Walker.

It wasn't unusual for Ruth to call since our relationship pre-dated her position with Bradley. We met while I was investi-gating the murder of her previous employer, Ivanna Jones, and it was instant, well, appreciation. She had an abrupt, judgmental demeanor, but she had an eye for detail and a mind like a Rolodex, which made her an ideal assistant. She was also approaching sixty and quite plain, which made her an ideal assistant for Bradley.

Because I'd helped Ruth to get a job at Pontchartrain Bank,

she'd taken it upon herself to keep me informed of certain goings on, and I didn't object. It wasn't spying—it was more like safekeeping. And if you knew even half the stunts Bradley's last secretary, Pauline Violette, had pulled, you wouldn't blame me one bit.

My instincts told me to skip my messages and call Ruth ASAP. I slowed to a stop at the intersection of Dauphine and St. Peter and tapped her number. As a steady stream of tourists passed, I put the phone to my ear and spotted a salon called Vaxing for Vomen. Someone had obviously scratched off the first half of both *w*'s from the glass door. But still. The sign made the services sound more than a little harsh, especially for something like a bikini wax.

The phone rang once, and then someone picked up.

"I heard you went to the cooler," Ruth boomed without bothering to say hello.

"The cooler?" I repeated, imagining myself pulling a beer from an ice chest. Make that a bottle of Prosecco.

"You know, the dungeon? The hole?"

Now I knew what she meant. Unfortunately. "Why don't you just say 'jail'?"

She snorted. "I pretty much did."

I started to say something snarky but bit my tongue, because now I was more worried about whether word of my arrest was out at the bank. "Who told you I went to jail?"

"Who do you think?" she barked. "After you no-showed at The Sazerac, Bradley panicked and asked me to help him call the hospitals."

"Really?" Despite my guilt for making him worry, my heart swelled at the news of his concern. "That's so sweet."

"Well, Lord knows it's not like you to miss a drink."

That heart swell I mentioned? Shriveled right up.

"Anyhoo," she continued, "he called me this morning and

said you were in the pokey. Of course, I told him last night that we should've been calling the jails," she added in a lo-and-behold-I-was-right tone.

I floored the gas and sped around some tourists. Not only was I sorry that I'd phoned Ruth, I was also regretting ever recommending her for the job. "Is this what you were calling on a weekend to tell me?"

"Hell no. My weekends are too precious," she said as though mine weren't. "But there's some ugly business going on at the bank that we need to chat about away from the prying eyes and inquiring minds."

I heard the sound of ice clinking in a glass, and I wondered whether she was drinking. Ruth never touched alcohol—that is, unless you counted digestives (she didn't). "What's the ugly business?"

"You."

"Me?" I glared at the phone. She'd better hope that she'd been hitting the bottle. "I don't even work there."

"No, but your bank president beau does. And that new manager they transferred here from headquarters—Jeff Payne?" She gave a humorless chuckle. "Mark my words, he came to The Big Easy looking for more than a managerial position."

I gasped. "You mean, he's after Bradley's job?"

"Darn tootin'." She crunched a piece of ice.

"That weasel!" I exclaimed. "But what does this have to do with me? It's not like I have a say in the hiring."

"You could play a role in the firing, though."

"How about you dispense with the riddles, Ruth?" I flipped on my turn signal and mentally flipped her the bird. "Then maybe I can take part in this conversation."

She made a slurping sound followed by a sonorous swallow. "Do you even know what a bank president does?"

"Yeah, he...presides." Okay, so I didn't know the specifics of what Bradley did for a living, but in my defense, we didn't see each other very often because of our work schedules. And when we did get together, we had better things to do than discuss his job duties.

"There's a little more to it than that," she said as sarcastic as a classroom teacher at a home-schooling seminar. "The president is responsible for the financial well being of the bank and for its credibility with the community, staff, and board of directors."

"And Pontchartrain Bank couldn't have a more honest, upstanding president than Bradley Hartmann," I said, pulling up to a red light.

"I agree," she intoned. "It's his girlfriend that everyone is worried about."

My heart sank. "Why? What have I done?"

"Oh, I don't know...investigating the internal affairs of the bank, assaulting a bank employee, breaking and entering into the bank's security room, stealing bank information."

By this point, my heart had sunk so low that it was sitting on my stomach. "But, I did all those things to protect Bradley," I protested. "And the bank."

"The problem is that no one from the bank asked you to," she said, and I could practically hear the frown lines around her mouth permeating her pronunciation. "To make matters worse, Bradley didn't press charges that time he and the cop found you in the security room after hours. So now his credibility is in question."

A car horn sounded behind me, startling me from my shock. I took a quick left and asked, "How do you know all of this?"

She drained the rest of her drink with a loud straw-sucking sound. "I might have read a file on Jeff's desktop."

"Does Bradley know?" I whispered.

"He doesn't know that Jeff has a file about him on his desktop, but he's gotten the idea that you're a professional problem."

My heart stopped.

"Oh, blast and damnation," Ruth bellowed out of nowhere. "It's a quarter after twelve. I've got to get my popcorn popped and my Pimm's poured before the Judge Judy marathon starts. Meanwhile, you lay low, missy. Because if you get in trouble again, you could cost Bradley and me both our jobs. And if that happens," she began, lowering her voice like a guillotine, "Central Lockup's going to seem like a sanctuary."

The line went dead.

I dropped the phone and gripped the steering wheel. My worst fear was coming true, but it was even worse than I'd thought. Someone was trying to prove that I was unsuitable for Bradley, so much so that he could lose his job over me (as for Ruth, she could fend for herself).

Explaining my jaunt to jail suddenly got a whole lot harder.

As I pondered my predicament, I merged onto I-10 West. A green Nissan Cube cut me off, and Theodora's pupils popped into my mind.

And I started to wonder whether a person could actually be cursed.

Napoleon pawed at the pillow covering my face.

"All right, I'll call him," I huffed. "Can't a girl take an afternoon nap in peace?" I felt around for my phone on the nightstand.

Of course, I knew my dog had no conception of the fact that I was stalling on calling my boyfriend. But Napoleon could sense when something was bothering me, and recently he'd taken to hounding me, so to speak, until I started acting normally again. Like a total cairn terror.

After knocking the lamp and the alarm clock off my nightstand, I was able to find my phone. I pulled off the pillow and tapped Bradley's number.

The call went straight to voice mail.

I tossed the phone onto my hot pink duvet and stared at the matching canopy. My first thought was that the black, French bordello-style bed Glenda had picked out for my "boudoir" was so ugly that I seriously doubted whether a prostitute could get any action in it. And my next thought was that Bradley was so mad he was probably avoiding me.

The phone rang, and I rushed to answer.

"Before you say anything, Bradley, I want to apologize for—"

"Francesca Lucia Amato," my mother's shrill voice scolded from the other end of the line. "What did you do to Bradley this time?"

I pulled the pillow back over my face. Ever since the age of seven when I'd whacked my older brother Anthony over the head with his light saber for cutting my Totally Hair Barbie's long brunette locks, my mother had treated me like a delinquent. I'll admit that I could be combative, but it wasn't like I was a criminal—yesterday notwithstanding. "I didn't do anything to him, Mom." And that was the truth, but what I was about to say certainly wasn't. "Everything's fine."

She slammed the receiver onto what I knew to be the kitchen counter. "He didn't propose!"

"*È una zitella gattara a vita,*" Nonna wailed in the background, as if on cue.

According to my nonna's proclamation, I'd apparently earned two new distinctions since turning thirty: the first was that I was now a zitella *for life*, and the second was that I was also officially a zitella *gattara*, or old maid cat lady, even though I was allergic to feline dander and had only ever owned dogs. "Um, what happened to Nonna's vow of silence?"

"She's been forgetting about that vow quite often today," my mother grumbled.

"Give-a me a break-a, woman," Nonna cried. "I'm old!"

"Like just now," my mother added through what sounded like clenched teeth.

"Dad's not around, is he?" I asked, trying to hide the hopeful desperation in my tone. "He hasn't wished me happy birthday yet." Not that it would do any good, but at least it would get my mom off the phone.

The receiver hit the counter. "Joe! Get on the other line! It's Francesca!"

A blissful silence ensued as we waited for my father to pick up.

Then I heard my nonna praying loudly for a Savior—not Jesus, mind you, but a husband for me.

"Maybe Dad didn't hear you?" I pressed, anxious to get back to my own private hell.

My mother sighed. "It must be that wax buildup in his ears. I bought him a kit to clean that out, but does he listen to me?" She slammed down the receiver. "Joe! Could you stop playing black-jack on that computer and come wish your damn daughter a happy belated birthday?"

There was another blessed moment of serenity while my mom once again waited and while I tried to figure out how I felt about my dad's wax-encrusted ears and that "damn daughter" comment.

"What is that man *doing*?" my mother exclaimed. "Give me a minute, Francesca. I'm going to have to go find him." The phone hit the counter and then crashed to the floor. "Joseph! *Giuseppe!*" she added, as though my dad might not have recognized the Anglicized version of his name.

Nonna stopped praying. "*Madonna mia!*" she cried. "*San Giuseppe!*"

I wasn't sure what was happening, but either my nonna had just had some sort of revelation, or she was invoking the assistance of the Virgin Mary and the patron saint of Italy and the Catholic Church on my behalf.

Someone picked up the receiver. "Franki," Nonna began, her voice not unlike the Godfather's when he made someone an offer they couldn't refuse, "we have-a some hope."

"We *do*?" This was truly news to me.

"I just-a remembered," she rasped. "*La tavola di San Giuseppe*."

"What about Saint Joseph's table?" I asked, mildly intrigued. It seemed like everyone was talking about that festival lately.

"You know, the *limoni*."

"I don't know anything about any lemons, Nonna." Except for the fact that life was giving them to me by the bushel these days.

"It's a tradition, Franki. A *zitella* take-a the lemon from-a San Giuseppe's table, and by the next-a year she have-a the husband. But no one can-a see, or it's-a no gonna work."

"Wait. You mean, *steal* a lemon from the altar? To land a husband?"

"Of course," she replied, as though everyone knew that was how hard-up Catholic gals got their grooms.

"Whatever happened to 'thou shalt not steal'?" I asked, scratching my neck uneasily. The good sisters at my Catholic Sunday school had worked hard to instill psychosomatic disorders in us kids at the mere suggestion of committing a sin, so this conversation was making me itchy.

"It's-a like-a we say in *Italia*. All is-a permitted in-a war and-a love."

"All is fair in love and war," I corrected. "We say that in the US too."

"You see? The whole-a world-a can't be wrong."

I didn't bother telling her that Italy and the United States were not the "whole-a world-a" because I honestly didn't think that she'd ever heard of any other countries. Instead, I got down to brass tacks. "So, let me get this straight. You want me to steal a lemon from a Catholic altar devoted to Jesus's father that's intended to feed the poor?"

"You got a problem with-a that?" she asked, now sounding more like De Niro than Brando.

Before I could reply, someone picked up another line.

"I found your father, dear," my mother announced. "He's sitting on the toilet."

To my horror, I heard her handing off the receiver.

"Happy birthday, Franki," my dad said in an animated voice. "Did you have a nice time last night?"

I squirmed at the memory of the skin-slougher and at the image of my father talking to me from the john.

"Bradley didn't pop-a the question," Nonna replied from the kitchen phone.

"Sorry to hear that you didn't get that proposal," my dad said as though referring to a lost job offer. "Better luck next time, eh?"

"She'll have-a the luck," Nonna said. "The luck of the lemon."

"What's she talking about, Franki?" he asked.

"I'll let Nonna explain, Dad. I've gotta run." Then I remembered the toilet and instantly regretted my choice of terms. "Love you and talk to you soon."

I pressed *end* before they could object and held the power button down. I had no intention of talking to anyone else today —not even Bradley. And honestly, if I could've foreseen how these calls were going to go, I would have let that witch keep my stupid phone.

I slid off the bed and headed for the kitchen. Suddenly, I was craving lemon. And as the old saying goes, when life gives you lemons and your nonna tells you to steal one from a Catholic altar to snag a husband, make lemonade—or better, limoncello.

And then drink it.

MY PHONE WAS RINGING.

I opened an eye, and sunlight scorched my brain. I was lying face up on Glenda's antique bearskin rug in front of the fireplace. The back of my head was resting on the top of the bear's, and his right paw was wrapped around a half-empty bottle of limoncello. Now I understood why I felt like I was coming out of hibernation.

I rolled onto my hands and knees and pulled my cell from the bear's other paw, desperate to stop the noise. The display was dark, so I pressed the power button. Only then did it occur to me that my phone had been turned off.

The ringing switched to knocking, and I realized that the sound I'd been hearing was my doorbell. I made my way to the door holding my phone in one hand and my head in the other.

Still using the one eye, I peered out the peephole and saw slicked back brown hair.

Bradley? I opened the door.

But it wasn't Bradley. The man who stood before me looked like a young Nicholas Cage. And even in my semi-drunk state, I could see that his police uniform was made of cheap fabric similar to the kind used for Halloween costumes.

Glenda!

Stripper Cop Cage cocked a low brow and pointed a finger intentionally close to my breast. "According to a call that came over my police radio, ma'am," he began in an Elvis impersonator-like voice, "you've been evading arrest."

"Actually, I haven't," I said clenching my fists at that "ma'am." "I got out of jail just this morning."

He froze for a moment, and then his shoulders relaxed. "Well, now I'm going to have to do a full body search," he announced with his lip curling like that of The King. He pulled out a plastic baton and gave a lascivious smile. "Up against the wall, and spread 'em."

I ripped the baton from his hands and whacked him over the head, exactly like I'd done to my brother Anthony with that light saber.

"Ow," he said, rubbing his head. "Was that really necessary? I'm just trying to do my job."

My phone began to ring. I looked at the display and pressed answer. "Glenda," I ground out, "if you don't call off your cop, you're gonna have a homicide on your hands."

Stripper Cop Cage's low brow lifted to the top of his forehead.

"That's what I'm calling about, sugar," Glenda said. "I already do."

"Wait," I said, massaging my temple. "How do *you* have a homicide?"

She exhaled what was probably a puff of smoke. "There's been a murder at Madame Moiselle's, Miss Franki. An ex-house stripper named Amber Brown."

I thought of the blonde I'd seen leaving the club. "Did you know Amber?"

"Not well, but I'm friends with her ex-landlord, Carnie. I called her a few minutes ago, and I think she's going to need your services."

"I'll be right there." I ended the call and checked the time. It was three p.m., which meant that I hadn't burned off the near half bottle of booze I'd drunk two hours before. I grabbed my bag and headed for the door, but Stripper Cop Cage blocked my way and leered at my rack.

"Show's over," I said, referring both to my boobs and his striptease.

"Don't you want me to dance?" He did a sample Saturday

Night Fever-style spin and finished with a mimed hair-smoothing move.

"No, I want you to drive," I replied, pushing past him. "And if you even think about copping a feel in the car, stripper copper, the next place you do any spinning will be your grave."

As I tramped toward his tricked-out Trans Am, I had a bad feeling in my gut (related in part to the limoncello). I don't know why, but something was telling me to turn around—to go back inside my apartment and lock the door. But I didn't listen.

Because I was probably cursed, right?

4

———

My stripper chauffer skidded the Trans Am to a stop in front of Madame Moiselle's, and then *he* skidded to a stop and stared slack-jawed through the windshield at some skimpily dressed strippers gathered on the second-floor balcony. "Uh...you need an escort inside?"

"Nah," I said as I climbed from the car. Maybe it was the lingering effects of the limoncello, but just for kicks I bent down and added, "I'm really only here to see a dead body."

His slack jaw became even slacker, and then he peeled out with the passenger door still wide open.

I smirked and approached a blond police officer who looked like he was barely old enough to drink, standing guard at Madame Moiselle's red double-door entrance.

"The club is closed for the day, ma'am," he announced.

I processed that "ma'am" in disbelief. *Did a citywide press release go out about my birthday or something?*

Glenda leaned over the rail, her hair and breasts hanging down. "She's one of us, Officer, baby."

He looked me up and down and then narrowed his ice blue eyes like a poker player reading his opponent.

I matched his half-lidded gaze and gave him a how-dare-you glare. Not that I wanted to be taken for a stripper, but I sure as heck didn't want some cop who was practically a kid acting like I couldn't be one. After all, us thirty-year-olds could strip too.

"Wait on the second floor with the others," he said, stepping aside.

I mentally thanked Glenda for intervening on my behalf because the police were notorious for not wanting PIs puttering around their crime scenes. Before the officer could change his mind, I hurried inside.

And I experienced an immediate assault on my semi-drunk senses. Madame Moiselle's deep red décor and pink neon signage scorched my eyes, and the stench singed my nostrils. As a rookie cop I'd responded to calls at more than a few strip clubs, and they'd always looked and smelled the same—like sleazy cabarets that stunk of baby powder, stale sweat, spilled drinks, dirty money, and something male, possibly testosterone. This time, however, there was also a sweet, acrid odor that I couldn't put my finger on.

After my eyes adjusted to the redness, I scanned the rectangular room for the scene of the crime. To my left, five officers were gathered around a command post that had been set up at one of two small stages, which, except for the poles running through the center, looked oddly like dining room suites for twenty. Behind the stages, along the far-left wall, there were two men in suits, probably plainclothes detectives, who were conversing on a red, quilted, plush velvet couch that I wouldn't have touched with a ten-foot stripper pole.

I looked to my right and saw several crime scene investigators in white coveralls and Latex gloves standing on a much larger stage next to a full bar. I figured that's where I'd find the victim.

As I took a step forward, a hand gripped my shoulder and

pulled me back. I turned expecting to see the boy cop, but instead I came face-to-face with the bastard cop who'd kicked me to the cooler, to use Ruth's term. But this time he wasn't wearing an ill-fitting uniform—he was wearing a form-fitting suit. "What are *you* doing here?"

He crossed his arms. "I believe that's my line, Ms. Amato."

Sadly, the cop had a good memory. And as much as it pained me, I needed to get on his good side to have a shot at viewing the crime scene. So, I opted for the cooperative route. "I'm a private investigator, and I'm here on behalf of a prospective client."

He snorted and bowed his head. "A buddy of mine down at the station told me that your attorney friend said you were a PI." He grinned and shook his head. "He said you were an ex-cop too. But he was just pulling my leg, right?"

Well, I certainly didn't want to answer that question *now*. So, I turned the tables on him. "What's with the suit?" I forced a half-smile. "Don't tell me you just came from church."

The mocking grin disappeared from his face as he flashed his badge. "Detective Wesley Sullivan. Homicide."

"You're a homicide detective?" Okay, the compliant act was off. "Then what were you doing in uniform in the French Quarter yesterday arresting innocent people?"

"The only person I arrested was guilty," he said with a sardonic stare. "And we like to build up our police presence in the Quarter when the Irish and Italians have simultaneous street parties." His gaze bored into my eyes like a drill. "Because the Italians have been known to pick fights with the Irish."

I bristled at his comment. That was no stereotype—that was a veiled accusation. Now the gloves were off. "Spoken like a true Irishman, Detective." I grasped my chin in a pretend pensive pose. "Correct me if I'm wrong, but aren't the Irish the ones who are typically stereotyped as the fighters?"

He feigned a posture of his own, putting his finger on the

cleft in his chin. "Oh, that's right. The Italians are the drinkers. And while we're on the subject, is that alcohol I smell on your breath?"

Crap. I guess I should've taken an extra two minutes to brush my teeth before leaving the house. "That's my lemon mint breath spray?"

He pointed toward the door. "Out."

I blinked. "But I need to see the scene of the murder."

His pointed finger moved from the door to my face. "Do you really think I'm going to let a half-drunk PI with a flagrant disrespect for the law around my crime scene?"

The detective had a point. "Would it help if I told you that I was leaning more toward hungover than half-drunk?"

He put his hands on his hips, pulling back his suit coat in the process and revealing a set of handcuffs. "Would it help if I told you that I was leaning toward arresting you for disobeying an officer?"

"Given your track record? You bet." I spun on my heels and headed for the door. And to add insult to injury, my tooth started to hurt again.

Now *the alcohol decides to wear off.*

I exited the club and saw the officer on guard talking to a couple of scantily clad young women.

"You need to go straight to the second floor and wait with the other dancers," he said, gesturing toward the balcony. "An officer will question you shortly."

Seizing the opportunity, I waited for the dancers to enter Madame Moiselle's. Then I fell into step behind their six-inch heels and followed them to the pink neon "VIP Champagne Rooms" sign in the far-left corner of the club. They powered up the stairs in their platforms while I plodded along in my two-inch-heeled boots. Of course, I could've kept up with them if I exercised for a living like they did. Possibly.

"Is that you, Miss Franki?" Glenda called.

"In the flesh," I quipped, smiling to myself since I was the only fully clothed female in the joint. The smile faded when I caught sight of Glenda at the top of the stairs in an outfit that made me want to turn around and go back down. She was wearing red, cross-shaped pasties, a white ruffle that was failing miserably at passing for a skirt, a tiny red thong, and red fishnet thigh-high stockings with white go-go boots—naughty stripper–style, not Nancy Sinatra–style. All she needed was a nursing cap, and she'd look like a slutty go-go dancer for the Red Cross.

I reached the landing and shifted my gaze from Glenda to the décor. Everything was red—the walls, the ceiling, the woodwork, the couches, even the bar.

"Let's go into a VIP Room so we can talk in private." Glenda opened the nearest door, and I was instantly taken aback.

"Are they all glowing pink like this?" I asked, shielding my eyes from the neon *Veni, vidi, veni* sign.

"Sure are," she said, flopping onto a love seat. "The idea is that you go from the deep red outside to the vibrant pink inside to evoke lips opening into a mouth or labia opening into a vagina. That's why I decorated your living room in red and your bedroom in pink."

Great. Now in addition to thinking of my apartment as a whorehouse and a funeral parlor, I would forever envision it as a giant orifice.

"But forget the design scheme." She patted the seat next to her. "Come sit beside Miss Glenda so we can discuss the murder."

It didn't take an epidemiologist to know that there wasn't a sanitary surface in the place. "I'd rather stand, thanks."

"Suit yourself, sugar," she said with a shrug. "Now, did you notice anything unusual about the crime scene?"

"Oddly enough," I began, putting my hand on my hip, "I

didn't get to see it because the detective who arrested me last night—the one I mistook for the stripper cop you sent me?—he just kicked me out of the club."

She crossed her arms above her red-crossed breasts and looked at me like I was some kind of reprobate. "I can't imagine why."

I wanted to clench my jaw, but I had to protect my tooth.

"But never you mind, Miss Franki, because Miss Ronnie will be here any minute, and she'll charm the pants off that ornery detective. Then you'll be at that crime scene faster than you can say 'strip.'"

"Miss Ronnie" was what Glenda called Veronica. And she was right about her being able to charm Detective Sullivan, including the part about his pants. Veronica had a man-melting move that I'd named "the bat and twirl." All she had to do was bat her eyelashes over her cornflower baby blues while twisting a golden lock around her finger, and men's resistance dissolved. No matter how many times I'd tried to master it, I just looked like I had a nervous eye tic and a hair-pulling compulsion.

"Hey, so what time did you get here this morning to practice for your show?" I asked.

Glenda kicked her skinny legs across the back of the love seat. "What makes you think I came here to practice?"

I eyed her go-go nurse getup. "Well, it looks like you're going for some sort of saintly look."

"I told you, sugar. I'm a slut," she said, staring at me like I was one thong shy of a stripper costume. "And I came to the club because my manager, Eugene, called and said that the police wanted to question the employees about Amber."

I pulled a pen and paper from my bag. "Who found her body?"

"Eugene did when he came in early to let the cleaning crew in."

I made a note to question the manager. "What time was that?"

"Two o'clock," she said, stretching out a leg to pull up her stocking.

I glanced up from my pad. "Early? I thought you once told me that the club opens at noon for lunch."

"It does, but on Sundays we open at five since it's the Sabbath," she replied as though strip clubs routinely based their operations around religious practices.

I rolled my eyes and noticed a camera hanging from the ceiling, and a thought occurred to me. "Has anyone checked the security system video for evidence?"

"You'd have to ask Eugene about that, sugar."

"Glenda?" Veronica called. "Where are you?"

Without thinking, I opened the door and then stared at my hand in horror. "We're in here."

Veronica entered dressed in a red sweater and a pink skirt, and I wondered whether she was aware of the sex-laden symbolism of her outfit.

"Love the color of the room," she said. "It's so fresh and feminine."

If you only knew, I thought as I reached into my bag for hand sanitizer.

Veronica pulled her pink Miss Sicily bag into the crook of her arm. "Glenda, I heard from Carnie a little while ago. She made an appointment to meet with Franki and me tomorrow morning."

"Did she tell you why she wants to contract a PI?" I asked, rubbing the sanitizing gel into my hands. "It seems kind of odd when the police haven't even begun their investigation, much less questioned her about it."

"She was fairly vague on the phone." Veronica turned to Glenda. "I was hoping that you could tell us more."

Glenda fluffed her ruffle. "All I know is that when I called Carnie to tell her about Amber, she asked me if she had a necklace on. When I told her that she was wearing a chain with a flower on it, she said that she was going to need a private investigator."

"That's bizarre," I said, patting some sanitizer on my neck.

"I guess we'll have to wait until tomorrow for an explanation." Veronica began rummaging through her bag. "In the meantime, Franki, Detective Sullivan has granted us fifteen minutes to view the crime scene."

"Yes," I said with a fist pump. "What did it? The old bat and twirl?"

"A polite request," she replied, opening the door with a tissue.

I definitely dislike that detective.

"I'll call you later, Glenda," Veronica said. "I've got a business proposition for you."

"Ooh, Miss Ronnie," she exclaimed, squeezing her breasts together with her biceps and giving them a little shake. "That sent shivers down my spine."

Funny. It sent chills down mine.

On the way downstairs, Veronica handed me a bottle of Binaca. "Before we talk to the detective, spray this on that booze breath of yours."

"Jeez. All I had was a little limoncello."

"Well, I'm surprised at you, Franki," she said, crossing the club at a clip. "That stuff is loaded with sugar, and you gave up sweets for Lent."

I stopped and gave my mouth a couple of squirts and then jogged to catch up with her. "That's right—sweets, not alcohol. You can hardly expect me to give up liquor when I don't have dessert to comfort me."

Veronica shook her head and climbed the steps to the main stage.

I followed close behind her without paying much attention to my surroundings. But when I stopped and processed the scene in front of me, my breath caught in my throat. I'd never seen anything like it—not as a cop, not as a PI, not even as a devoted crime show watcher.

At center stage was a vintage pink claw-foot tub with a high back, like the one in my bathroom. It was filled to the rim with water.

And a human knee protruded from the surface.

I averted my eyes, perhaps defensively, to the three items on the stage beside the tub—a wooden incense holder with a consumed stick of incense, which explained the sweet, acrid odor that I'd been unable to identify, a purple candle that had burned down to the base, and a bottle of amaretto with the seal intact. It was a brand I didn't recognize, Amaretto di Amore.

Mustering up my courage, I walked over to the tub while Veronica remained rooted near the steps.

Amber was below the water, seemingly looking up at me, with her long, brown hair billowing around her head like a cloud. Her arms were across her chest, and the leg that was protruding from the water was leaning to one side, obscuring her pelvic region. It was as though she was hiding her own nudity even in death.

I looked away—this time out of respect.

"How did Amber end up in a bathtub on a strip club stage?" I asked, breaking the somber silence.

"No idea." Veronica moved to stand beside me. "But if she brought the tub into Madame Moiselle's, then she had help. Or it could've been a prop for the dancers. Glenda would know that."

I focused my gaze on the bathwater.

Veronica turned to me, her brow furrowed. "Are you okay?"

"Yeah," I replied, although I wasn't sure that I was. "It's just that the haze on the water looks like some kind of oil."

She sniffed the air above the tub. "It doesn't have a scent."

"Whatever it is, it makes me wonder whether Amber was taking an actual bath onstage."

She crossed her arms and rested her chin on her fist. Her eyes were fixed on the tub. "It could have been a romantic encounter."

"Or it could have been staged, quite literally, to look like one." I glanced again at the bottle. "I mean, why Amaretto di Amore?"

She cocked a well-groomed brow. "I'm not following you."

"Why not a common brand, like Disaronno?" I asked, gesturing toward the bar where a bottle of the famous almond liqueur was on display.

"Maybe this was her favorite kind?" she suggested in a questioning tone.

I pulled out my pad of paper. "Or maybe the 'amore' in the name is a sign from the killer."

"You mean to signal a love relationship."

"That or something we don't yet understand." I took a few notes and then knelt and smelled the candle. It was unscented, but the woodsy, vanilla odor from the incense holder was still strong. "Wait a second...I just realized that the incense is similar to the kind they always burn in places like Marie Laveau's and Reverend Zombie's."

Her blue eyes grew wide. "Do you think there's a voodoo connection?"

"We can't rule it out, not when incense and a candle are involved." I stood up and noticed that the CSIs were consulting with Detective Sullivan on the left side of the stage.

Veronica's eyes followed my gaze. "We should examine the body before they take it to the morgue."

I nodded and reluctantly looked into the water.

"When I spoke to Detective Sullivan earlier," Veronica began, "he said that it appears to be a pretty straightforward case of homicide by drowning."

I scrutinized the area around Amber's neck. There was some light bruising and scratch marks, either from the assailant or from Amber herself as she tried to break free. "There was clearly a struggle. The killer probably held her under the water."

"Ms. Maggio," Detective Sullivan interrupted.

"Speak of the devil," I remarked, my hackles rising at the sound of his voice.

"Can I talk to you for a minute?" he continued, ignoring my jab.

"Sure," Veronica said, going to join him.

My phone began vibrating in my bag. I pulled it out and looked at the display—Bradley. Without a second thought I tapped *Decline*. As much as I needed to talk to him, this just wasn't the time.

I shoved my phone into my bag and leaned closer to the bath water to study Amber's neck. My attention shifted to the gold chain that Carnie had been so concerned about. It was either really old or it had been treated to make it look antique. In the center of the chain was a gold filigree flower with a leaf and three gold loops beneath it. As I studied the design, I realized that something was missing.

Veronica climbed the steps to the stage, typing something into her phone. "Detective Sullivan asked that we not speak about the incense, candle, or amaretto to anyone. The police plan to keep them out of the news."

I nodded. "They should keep the necklace out of the news too."

She stopped typing and stared at me. "Why's that?"

I pointed at the gold filigree. "Because someone ripped a charm or a pendant from below the flower."

She held her hair behind her head and leaned closer to the water. "You're right. The middle loop is scratched and bent. I'll let the detective know. But are you thinking that this was some kind of robbery gone wrong?"

"There are so many different ways to interpret this scene, I haven't decided what to think," I replied.

But deep down I knew one thing for sure—Amber's murder was tied to something much more sinister than a simple robbery.

5

——————

"You're kidding me, right Veronica?" I asked, gripping my Krewe du Brew coffee mug for support. It was only eight forty-five on Monday morning, so I was hoping that this was some sort of poorly timed office prank.

She reclined in the armchair facing my desk and crossed her arms. "I didn't say that I was planning to hire a permanent investigator—just a temporary consultant."

"Don't get me wrong. I'm glad that Private Chicks is finally solvent enough to afford us some help, but..." I looked at my hands as I struggled to find the right words. "Why in the name of all that is rational would you hire *Glenda*?"

"It's just for this case, Franki." She stood up and clasped her hands behind her back, pacing like she used to do in court when she was presenting opening arguments. "Keep in mind that Glenda has worked at Madame Moiselle's off and on for close to fifty years. Not only does she know all the employees, she's also got a grasp of the inner workings of the club and the entire stripping industry. So, she can offer us a unique perspective on Amber's murder."

She most certainly can. "Okay, but can she investigate?"

Veronica stopped pacing and looked me in the eyes. "I don't think I need to remind you that she's had great insight about some of our hardest cases."

That I couldn't deny. Glenda might seem a little out there, but she was actually as sharp as a stiletto (the dagger, not the heel), and she'd bailed Veronica and me out of a serious jam when we were working our first homicide. But there was one thing I couldn't reconcile myself to—her potential PI outfits. Just imagine Charlie's Angels in their sixties and in stripper/birthday suits and you'll understand my concern.

The bell on the lobby door rang.

"I'll bet that's Carnie," Veronica said, retrieving her laptop from my desk.

I picked up my mug and followed her down the hallway to the lobby, and I was immediately transported to the 1940s.

Standing by the reception desk was a brunette with victory rolls so large they were practically the size of the World War II fighter plane exhaust that had inspired the hairstyle. To complete her vintage *Life* magazine look, she'd selected a navy blue dress with white polka dots, a beaded white clutch, and chunky white peep-toe heels.

But a pinup girl she wasn't. For starters, the woman was a forty-something-year-old man, and a big one too, at six foot four and three hundred fifty or so pounds. Not only that, she was built like the Abominable Snowman from *Rudolph, the Red-Nosed Reindeer*, and she was wearing enough cosmetics to make up the entire Broadway cast of *Priscilla, Queen of the Desert*.

"Hi, I'm Veronica Maggio, and this is Franki Amato. Are you Carnie?"

Her overdrawn lips à la Lucille Ball spread into a smile. "Why yes I am," she replied in a forced falsetto. "Carnie Vaul."

I mentally repeated the syllables. "As in 'carnival'?"

She eyed me warily from beneath her Mimi-from-The-Drew-Carey-Show eye shadow. "It's my drag name. I used to be a carnival clown."

That explained the creepy makeup. But what I couldn't understand was why a man dressed as a woman would want to associate with an institution known for its strong men and bearded ladies. "What's your legal name?"

"Ben Dover," she replied, smoothing a roll—on her head, that is.

I pursed my lips and then muttered, "You're not giving me much to work with."

"What did you say?" Carnie barked. Gone was the falsetto, and in its place was a brash voice that had a quack-like quality similar to that of the Aflac duck.

"She said that you'll be a pleasure to work with," Veronica intervened. She gestured to the lobby couches. "Why don't you have a seat, and I'll get you something to drink."

"Nothing for me, thanks," Carnie replied, giving me the stink eye as she sank into the sofa.

I, in turn, cast her a suspicious eye as Veronica and I took our places on the opposing couch. I'd been duped by a homicide client once before, so I had no intention of falling for any of this ex-clown's antics.

"Do you mind if I vape?" Carnie asked as she opened her clutch.

For a second I was worried that "vape" was some sort of variant of "vamp," but then I saw her remove an e-cigarette. "Have at it."

"Let's get started, shall we?" Veronica asked, opening her laptop. "Carnie, tell us how you knew Amber Brown."

"For the past two years she was my tenant and neighbor," she said, exhaling vapor. "She rented the other side of a duplex I own in The Marigny until about a week ago."

The Faubourg Marigny was an artsy, bohemian neighborhood next to the French Quarter. Tourists flocked to its jazz clubs and art galleries, but I went for the food. "Did she leave a forwarding address?"

She shook her head. "Nothing."

Veronica typed a quick note. "Were the two of you ever close?"

Her lips thinned, highlighting the exaggerated lines of her lipstick. "We were friends, but I wouldn't say we were close. I do drag shows at Lucky Pierre's, and when she was still at Madame Moiselle's we used to get home at the same time and have the occasional nightcap together. Then she quit stripping last year, and we didn't see each other as much."

I swallowed a sip of coffee. "What did she do for a living after she left the club?"

Carnie hefted one chubby leg over the other and draped her arm across the back of the couch. "She said she was leaving the sex industry, but I never saw her going to any job. Honestly, I thought she was hooking again because she'd told me that she used to make extra money that way."

Veronica and I exchanged a look. If Amber had worked as a prostitute, it would complicate the hunt for a suspect.

I crossed my ankle over my knee. "Did she ever bring men to the duplex?"

"Not that I was aware of," she replied with a shrug. "As far as I know, she didn't even have a boyfriend. Amber was a loner, and she didn't have any family."

It always made me sad to hear that someone was alone in the world. As crazy as my family was, I couldn't imagine life without them—well, most of the time. "When did you see her last?"

Carnie took a long vape and thought for a moment. "Friday at around two. I ran into her when I was leaving the duplex to run errands. She came by to pick up some mail. She said she was on her way to a dentist appointment, and since she didn't have a car I offered her a ride. But she opted for the bus."

Veronica looked up from her laptop. "Do you happen to know the name of the dentist?"

"We go to the same guy. Mitchell Lessler."

"Franki, when you talk to him about Amber," Veronica began, "you should make an appointment for yourself."

I rubbed my cheek, sorely regretting ever telling Veronica about my tooth. Now that she knew about it, she wouldn't let up until I had it looked at. And I liked dentists about as much as I liked gynecologists, which was to say not at all. "Did she have any enemies?"

Carnie arched a Bozo-the-Clown brow. "There was one—a platinum blonde from Madame Moiselle's. She used to get as drunk as a skunk and pound on Amber's door in the middle of the night, screaming at her for stealing her best client. I never found out her name, but she had a tacky tattoo of a stripper that covered her back." She scratched her five o'clock shadow. "So unladylike."

I thought of the platinum blonde I'd seen leaving the club, but I hadn't noticed a tattoo. "What did Amber do about it?"

"Well, she never opened the door. But the girl kept coming around, as recently as two weeks ago."

I twisted my mouth to one side. "That's weird, considering that Amber had stopped stripping."

"It's one of the reasons that I thought she'd gotten back into prostitution," she said with a knowing look. "Maybe the client wasn't interested in blowing his money on a stripper anymore when he could get straight up sex."

Veronica stopped typing. "Glenda said that you asked whether Amber was wearing a necklace."

She nodded. "That's why I'm here. A month ago I inherited

an antique necklace—a gold chain with a flower and an emer-ald-cut amber pendant—and it's missing. I showed the necklace to Amber when I first got it, and if what Glenda told me was correct, then I think she stole it from my apartment and was wearing it when she was killed."

I leaned forward with my coffee cup between my hands. "We saw the chain, but there was no pendant. That could either mean that she was killed for the necklace or that the killer took it as a memento."

Carnie frowned like a sad clown. "That's what I was afraid of. That amber was priceless, and I made the mistake of telling that to Amber."

"But amber is fairly inexpensive," Veronica said. "What was so special about this piece?"

She hesitated. "It was from the Amber Room, the one that the Prussian King Frederick William I gave to Tsar Peter the Great in 1716."

Veronica gasped, and her eyes lit up like amber in sunlight. "That's the room the Nazis stole from Catherine Palace during World War II."

"Yes, and it has never been found. Experts say that it's worth at least three hundred and eighty-five million dollars."

After I recovered my ability to speak, I asked, "If the room is missing, how did you get a piece?"

"My grandmother was from Russia, and she was a maid in the palace." She twisted a crown-shaped ring around her French-manicured finger. "When the Nazis dismantled the room, small pieces of amber broke off. They picked up every piece they could find, but they overlooked one that had been cut like a gemstone. My grandmother took it and intended to return it after the war, but her family fled the country. And then when the Soviets began work on a replica of the room in 1979, my mother had the amber made into a necklace."

I swallowed the last of my coffee and placed the mug on the table in front of me. "So, technically, that pendant belongs to the Russians."

Carnie's face flushed, and her bulbous nose turned as red as Ronald McDonald's. "My mother believed that the Soviets were evil like the Nazis, and she didn't trust them to return the amber to the palace," she huffed. "Besides, after the replica of the room was unveiled, it didn't seem as important."

"Just to clarify," Veronica began in a high-pitched, we-can't-afford-to-lose-this-client tone, "are you hiring us to find the pendant or to investigate Amber's death?"

"Both," she replied. "As soon as I report the theft of the necklace, which I intend to do today, I figure I'll become a suspect in her murder."

She figured right. I knew from my time on the force that she would be questioned, especially now that someone had ripped the priceless pendant from Amber's lifeless neck.

"And even though Amber and I weren't close," she continued, pressing a hand to her ample bosom, "I wouldn't feel right if I didn't have you try to find her killer. I inherited some money with the necklace, so I can cover your expenses."

"It's very admirable of you to honor Amber that way," Veronica said, her voice soft. "We'll do our best to see that the killer and the necklace are found."

I was thinking that we should do our best to find that three hundred and eighty-five million dollar room too. "Is there anything else we should know?"

Carnie bowed her head, causing her double and triple chins to bulge. "Amber felt like bad things had been happening to her since she'd quit Madame Moiselle's, and she was getting really paranoid and superstitious about it."

"Can you give us some examples?" I pressed.

"Nothing specific. But I noticed that she'd started carrying around good luck charms, wearing talismans, things like that."

Veronica nodded. "You've given us some great information. We'll start by questioning the employees at Madame Moiselle's, and we'll check with Dr. Lessler to find out whether he saw or heard anything unusual during Amber's appointment. We'll be in touch in a few days."

Carnie rose to her feet. "I've got a show in an hour." She offered her baseball mitt-sized hand, bending daintily at the wrist. "You've been so kind."

I noticed that she didn't extend the same courtesy to me, but no matter. Because as Veronica saw her out, my mind was already fixated on Amber's superstitious side. And I wondered what, if anything, it had to do with the bizarre murder scene at the club.

I STEPPED inside Madame Moiselle's at a quarter after eleven and stopped dead in my tracks.

Glenda stood before me dressed like a stripper Sherlock Holmes.

"Howdy, partner," she exclaimed, adjusting her deerstalker cap.

"You're wearing the wrong hat for that greeting," I said, trying to hide my inner panic as I took in the tiny cape cropped well above her magnifying glass–shaped pasties. "Is that tweed?"

"Yeah, and it's itchier than poison ivy on your privates, so I had to make a costume change." To my dismay, she spun around to reveal her bony buttocks protruding from the round holes she'd cut from the seat of her boyshorts. But on the bright side, she'd left the crotch intact.

"Well, I guess that about took care of it," I said, scanning the club to avoid checking out her cheeks. "Is the manager in yet?"

Mercifully, she turned back around. "Eugene? He's at the police station. Our bartender, Carlos, is in charge until he gets back."

I glanced to my right. "I don't see anyone at the bar."

"He's probably upstairs in the office. I'll take you up there."

Instead of leading me to the VIP Champagne Room staircase, Glenda led me past the main stage, and I noticed that the crime scene had been cleared.

Keeping my eyes fixed on the back of her head rather than on her backside, I asked, "Hey, do you know where the bathtub came from?"

"From the prop room," she replied, pointing to a door behind the stage. "It belonged to Lili St. Cyr."

"Who's that?"

Glenda turned and looked at me like I'd snapped her bra strap (if she'd been wearing one). "None other than the creator of bathtub burlesque, sugar."

As soon as she uttered the phrase, I wondered whether Amber had been recreating a sexy bathing routine for a lover who ultimately killed her.

"In the 1940s and '50s," Glenda continued, "Lili was as famous as Gypsy Rose Lee. Then she retired and ran a well-known lingerie business. Her deep plunge bra made Elvira a superstar. And on top of all that, she even got a mention in *The Rocky Horror Picture Show*."

"That's, uh, quite a list of credentials."

"You can say that again," she said, strutting toward a staircase in the corner. "When Lili passed in 1999, Madame Moiselle's started the 'Wash the Girl of Your Choice' service to honor her memory."

I started to say one of the usual clichés like "she would have been so proud," but I got distracted trying to envision how a client would wash a stripper when the club had a strict no-touching-the-merchandise policy.

Glenda pushed open a door marked *Strippers and Staff Only* and shot up the staircase in her gun-heel boots.

I climbed a few steps, and my message tone sounded. Grateful for the excuse to take a break, I pulled my phone from my bag and saw that the text was from Bradley.

"What's going on? Why didn't you return my call last night?"

My stomach did a belly flop. I should've called him back, but the past couple of days had been rough, to put it mildly. And after seeing Amber, I hadn't felt like talking. So, I sent a quick reply saying that I would meet him at the bank for lunch and explain everything—except for the part about me tarnishing his professional image, of course.

"Are you comin', Miss Franki?" Glenda called from above.

"Yeah, sorry." I shoved my phone into my bag, and when I finally reached the landing the tantalizing aroma of sausage teased my nostrils. "*What* is that *heavenly* odor?"

"That's Miss Eve cooking lunch for the girls."

"Wait," I said, holding out a hand to steady myself. "There's a kitchen? *And* a cook?"

She put her hand on her hip. "We don't call her a cook, sugar. She's a house mom. All the quality strip clubs have them."

I immediately began rethinking my career choice. Not that I was considering becoming a stripper. My parents and the Catholic Church had worked too hard to repress me for me to throw it all away by doing something as liberated as that. But an office with a house mom would be nice.

"C'mon," she said, gesturing for me to follow. "I'll introduce you to her."

As we walked down the hallway, I took note of the layout. There were two offices, one across from the other. Then came the kitchen on the left and the girls' dressing room on the right.

Glenda took me by the arm and pulled me into a sunny yellow kitchen where a short, plump woman in her mid-fifties was standing over a huge soup pot. "Miss Eve Quebedeaux, this is Miss Franki Amato, my private investigator partner."

"Well, hiii," Eve drawled, sounding remarkably like Blanche Devereaux from *The Golden Girls*. She wiped her hands on an apron adorned with peaches, possibly symbolizing the state of Georgia. "Miss Glenda's told me so much about yewww," she said, grasping my hands. "I'll bet you work up quiiiite an appetite doin' all that investigatin'. Can I git you some chicken Andouille gumbo and a slice of Bananas Foster piiie?"

I blinked and looked for the halo above her graying blonde curls. Then I sunk into a chair at the dining table and managed to utter a faint, "Yes."

"Uh-*uh*, Miss Franki," Glenda said, wagging her index finger (and, unintentionally, her boobs). "You can't have that pie. Miss Ronnie told me that you gave up sweets for Lent."

I shot her a seething look. I knew this hiring Glenda thing was going to be a big bust, and I wasn't referring to her breasts.

"We're actually trying to find Carlos," Glenda continued, planting her bare bottom in the chair across from me. "We've got to question him about Amber's murder."

"Oh, that poor girl," Eve lamented as she fixed me a heaping helping of gumbo. She placed the bowl in front of me and poured me a glass of milk. "I didn't get to know her all that well because she only worked here for two months, but I feel just awful about what happened."

"What was she like?" I asked and then inhaled a huge spoonful of the Cajun goodness.

Eve sat down at the head of the table. "She kept to herself, mostly. Some of the other girls thought it was because she was uppity, but I think she just didn't know how to act in a family setting."

I would've had a hard time seeing a strip club as a "family setting," but now that I knew they had kitchens complete with house moms like Eve, I was a believer. "I've heard that Amber was essentially an orphan. Did she ever mention any relatives to you?"

"Never." She rested her chin on her fists. "The only person I ever saw her with was her pimp."

I almost choked on a piece of chicken. "She had a pimp?"

"Uh-hu-h," she replied in three syllables. "He came here right before she quit the club."

So, Carnie might have been right about Amber working as a prostitute after she left Madame Moiselle's. "Do you know what he wanted?"

"He came to pick her up. And while Amber was changin' into her street clothes, I served him a plate of sauce picante, and we got to chattin'. He said his name was King, and I could see that deep down he was a nice man. So I encouraged him to repent his sins and let Jesus into his heart."

I smirked as I took another bite. The chances of a pimp finding God were about as high as Glenda joining the Cloister.

Eve touched my arm. "And would you believe that right after our conversation he became a minister?"

I lowered my spoon, openmouthed. "How do you know that?"

"Because when I'm coming to work I usually see him at the corner of Bourbon and Dumaine, preaching the gospel to passersby."

Eve's angel status just got elevated to saint, but I wasn't so sure about the status of the pimp preacher. I planned to find that out after lunch.

A Hispanic male who looked to be around twenty-five

entered the room and removed a bowl from a cabinet. "Are the girls ready to go, Eve?"

"Oh!" She jumped up from the table. "I'd better go see. Be right back, ladies."

"Carlos, this is Franki, my PI partner," Glenda said. "We wanted to ask you some questions about Amber."

He glanced in my direction. "You're talking to the wrong person. I barely knew her."

"Any information might be important," I said in an encouraging tone. "But could I ask what time you left on Saturday night? It would help to know when the doors were locked."

"Eugene would've been the one to lock up." His thick, black brows furrowed as he spooned gumbo into his bowl. "I had to leave at four fifteen when the club closed because Iris and I got arrested."

"Good grief, Carlos," Glenda exclaimed. "How'd you two end up in the hoosegow?"

He removed a spoon from a drawer and sat beside me. "Things got a little rowdy with some customers who didn't want to leave after last call. So we all went to the tank."

By this point, I was seriously starting to wonder if I'd missed the memo about using euphemisms for "jail." "Who's Iris?"

Glenda flipped her hair. "The bouncer, sugar."

This Iris must be a big girl. "When did you get out of jail, Carlos?"

He splashed Tabasco sauce on his gumbo. "At one o'clock yesterday afternoon after Eugene posted our bail."

So, he and Iris had airtight alibis. "Did you notice anything unusual before you got arrested?"

"Nah, it was business as usual," he replied, stirring his food. "And I haven't seen Amber around here in a few months."

I looked up from my bowl. "I thought she quit a year ago."

He took a bite and then shifted the food to one side of his mouth. "She did, but she came in sometimes for a drink."

On a hunch I asked, "What did she typically order?"

"The same thing she did when she was dancing here," he replied, resting his elbows on the table. "Amaretto, neat."

Glenda's two-inch false eyelashes opened wide. "It wasn't Amaretto di Amore, was it?"

He shook his head. "We don't carry that brand. Even though it's made here in New Orleans, it doesn't sell as well as Disaronno."

As I'd suspected, there was something weird about that bottle of amaretto beside the bathtub, but I still wasn't sure what. "Is that the kind Amber drank?"

"No, she used to tip me to keep a bottle of Lazzaroni Amaretto under the bar for her."

"Any idea why she wanted that particular brand?" I asked as Eve returned to her place at the table.

He smiled as though remembering something funny. "She liked it because it's the only kind made from an infusion of the Amaretti di Saronno cookies."

I memorized the name Lazzaroni, both because it was perti- nent to the investigation and because it was as close as I was going to get to cookies during Lent.

"What are the other amarettos made from?" Glenda asked, twirling her cape tie around her finger.

Carlos swallowed and wiped his mouth with a napkin. "Almond essence or apricot pits."

Eve rolled her eyes. "Amber definitely didn't like that kind."

My body tensed because I sensed that she was about to say something important. "Did she talk to you about amaretto?"

"No, but one time an anonymous admirer had a bottle of amaretto delivered to her here at the club. When she opened it, she got really mad and threw it across the kitchen. It took me hours to clean up the mess." She gestured toward the kitchen window. "And the worst part was that it ruined my chiffon curtains."

My pulse started racing. "Do you remember the brand?"

"Yes, because it was such a pretty name. A-muh-rhet-toe dee Uh-more-ay." Eve sighed and squeezed her shoulders together. "Doesn't it just remind you of a romantic trip to Italy?"

Actually, it reminded me of a senseless killing at a strip club.

And of a murderer with a message.

6

"You must have been starving," Bradley said as he topped off my champagne.

"Mm-hm." I chewed the last piece of a fourteen-ounce prime rib eye steak smothered in pepper-cream bourbon sauce. Of course, I hadn't been all that hungry since I'd eaten Eve's gumbo before coming to the bank. But Bradley had gone to the trouble of having Dickie Brennan's Steakhouse deliver lunch to his office as a belated birthday surprise, so who was I to disappoint him?

Dabbing my mouth with my napkin, I discretely scoured the room for any sign of the restaurant's famous creole cheesecake. "What's for dessert?"

He looked at me from beneath thick, dark lashes, and the corner of his mouth lifted into a sexy half smile.

I met his gaze, and a warmth spread through my body.

"I was going to order the praline chocolate mousse," he began in a husky voice, "but then Veronica called and told me you'd given up sweets for Lent."

That warmth turned as cold as Veronica's gelid heart. *Just who did she think she was, anyway? A Catholic cop?*

"However," he continued, his blue eyes twinkling, "I do have this for you." He pulled a rectangular box from his desk.

I covered my mouth with my hands. "What is it?"

"You'll have to find out," he replied, sliding the box in front of me.

I opened the lid and gasped. Inside was a gorgeous ruby and diamond necklace. The pendant was teardrop shaped, which, given that this was a thirtieth birthday present, seemed particularly appropriate. "It's stunning," I whispered. "Thank you."

"You're stunning," he said in an earnest tone. "Especially in red."

My chest swelled with happiness. Bradley and I had been dating for a little over a year, and even though I'd had reason to doubt him—actually, *two* reasons considering that he'd neglected to tell me he was married when we started dating and that he once broke up with me to hook up with his evil ex-secretary—it was times like these that I remembered why I was so crazy about him (and, obviously, when I found out that there were logical explanations for the above discretions). But as I gazed at him from across the table, I sensed that something was on his mind. "Is everything okay?"

His jaw tensed, and he glanced at his half-eaten steak. "The bank lost a couple of its biggest accounts last week."

"I'm sorry to hear that," I said, concerned. "Do you know why?"

"I don't." He rubbed his eyes. "I thought that I had a solid relationship with both of the clients too."

I hated to see Bradley upset. It always made me feel helpless, which I didn't like. "Have you tried contacting them?"

"They haven't returned my calls," he replied, depositing his napkin beside his plate. "But enough about business." He clasped his hands in front of his mouth. "Let's talk about you."

Just one more reason that he was the best boyfriend on the planet. "Well, I wanted to explain about—"

There was a knock at the door, and Jeff Payne, the over-ambitious bank manager Ruth had warned me about, entered without waiting for an invitation. With his brown brush cut and perpetual sneer, he looked more like a drill sergeant than a banker. "Sorry to interrupt your tête-a-tête."

I could tell from the smug look on his face that he wasn't sorry at all.

"What can I help you with?" Bradley asked in a polite but strained voice.

Jeff tossed a document on the table. "I need you to sign off on this loan contract."

Bradley turned and put the document on his desk. "I'll take a look at it after lunch."

Jeff's eyes narrowed, and he opened his mouth to say something. But then he turned and stalked from the room.

I looked at Bradley to see his reaction.

"You were saying?" he asked, picking up his champagne glass.

Following his cue to let the Jeff issue lie, I said, "I was just going to apologize for not calling you yesterday. Honestly, it was one of the worst days of my life."

He stopped in mid-sip. "What could be worse than going to *jail* on your birthday?"

There was something about the way he said "jail" that made me wish he'd used a euphemism like everyone else. "Oh, I don't know," I replied, irritated. "Seeing a young woman's dead body, having to investigate her death with Glenda..."

He frowned and put his glass on the table. "You're working on another murder case? And with *Glenda*?"

"Yeah, the victim used to strip at Madame Moiselle's." I almost added that I thought she'd been killed by a real freak, but

I stopped myself in time. Bradley worried when I worked homicides, and I didn't want him focusing on my safety when he had problems at work to deal with.

"Strip clubs can be dangerous places," he said, his brow knit with worry. "Do you have any idea why she was murdered?"

"I'm not sure," I hedged. "But listen, I need to get back to work. How about dinner at my place tonight?"

He leaned back and ran his fingers through his hair. "I'm flying to New York later today for an impromptu meeting with the board in the morning. What about tomorrow night?"

"Perfect." I forced a smile as I wondered whether the sudden meeting had something to do with the loss of his clients. Or with me.

Bradley's office phone began to ring. He stood up and glanced at the number on the caller ID. "I need to take this. It's one of the board members I'm meeting with."

"That's fine," I said, rising to my feet. "I'll see myself out."

He reached over the desk and picked up the receiver. "Hey, Bob. What's up?"

While Bradley listened to Bob on the other end of the line, I took one last look at my beautiful necklace before tucking it carefully into my purse. Then I drained my champagne, and Bradley pulled me into his chest with his free arm, and his mouth descended onto mine. It was a slow, probing kiss that made me want to lie down and keep kissing—for starters.

When Bob stopped talking, Bradley released me. "No problem at all," he replied into the receiver. "I'll have the report ready."

After a kiss like that, I needed a drink. So, I grabbed the half-empty bottle of champagne from the table and filled a go-cup. This *was* New Orleans.

Raising my drink as a farewell, I turned and opened the door.

Jeff recoiled in surprise as though he'd been eavesdropping and stepped quickly from the doorway.

But not quickly enough.

I tripped over his foot and went flying into Ruth's chair, spilling my drink on her desk in the process. When I regained my balance, I turned to give him a piece of my mind, but he was gone.

As I mopped up the spilled champagne with some tissues, my tooth began to throb. Although the sudden aching could've been a result of all the chewing I did eating those two lunches, I blamed Jeff for my pain. And now that I'd caught him listening at the door, I was certain that Ruth had been right—he wanted Bradley's job, and he struck me as the type who would do whatever it took to get it. What I needed to know was whether he'd had a hand in costing the bank those accounts to make Bradley look bad.

And I had every intention of finding out.

WHEN I EXITED Vieux Carré Wine & Spirits in the French Quarter a half hour later, I wasted no time unscrewing the cap from the bottle of Lazzaroni Amaretto I'd purchased. I hadn't had a dessert in weeks, so I couldn't wait to taste the liquid cookie liquor. Normally, I didn't drink on the job. But as long as I was working a case with Glenda, I had a feeling that I was going to stay semi-sloshed. So I tipped my head back and took a swig, and I understood why Amber liked the stuff. It was amaretto ambrosia.

Reluctantly, I replaced the cap and headed back to Madame Moiselle's. Then I remembered that King, Amber's pimp, preached near the club, and I decided to make a detour. Glenda didn't have to be with me every second of the investigation, especially if she was going to persist in wearing those stripper sleuthing suits. And with any luck I'd find King holding court on his corner, because it was time for the alleged pimp-turned-preacher and I to have a come-to-Jesus talk about Amber.

I hooked a left on Dumaine, and I caught a glimpse of someone darting from view behind me. Certain I was being followed, I stopped and backtracked a few steps, but the only person in my vicinity was a guy in a gator costume.

He must've thought that I was checking him out, because he lowered his snout and leered at me.

The animal. I turned around, and even though I knew that no one in their right mind would tail a person in a gator getup, I quickened my pace. This was Louisiana, after all.

A block from Bourbon, I heard the strains of a church organ, which was as out of place on the infamous party street as a harpsichord. It didn't take long to spot the source. Behind an electric keyboard stood a tall, thin man in a purple velvet suit with green silk lapels and a frilly gold shirt. Apart from his square white sunglasses and thick rope chain with a giant, jeweled crucifix, he either looked like a Mardi Gras pirate or Prince during the Purple Rain tour.

As I approached, he let out a scream worthy of James Brown.

I jumped backwards as his fingers crashed down on the keyboard.

"Temptation! Intoxication! Fornication! Pregnation!" He pointed at his audience of one, i.e., me. "Brothas and sistas, avoid damnation," he implored, sinking to his knees and raising his arms to the heavens. "God is elevation! So seek salvation at The Church of King Nation." He bowed before a fur fedora filled with cash. "Donations kindly accepted."

To use a *–tion* word, the man was a sight and sound sensation. Actually, "*sin*sation" was more appropriate, because I wasn't buying his religious bit for a second. "I take it you're King Nation?"

He sprung to his feet and smiled like a Cheshire cat, revealing gold front teeth engraved with the letters K and N. "At yo' spiritual service."

I held out my card, and he clasped my hand between his, both of which were adorned with three-finger rings that read "Lawd" and "Gawd," respectively.

Giving him a half-lidded look, I said, "My name's Franki Amato, and I'm a private investigator."

King dropped my hand like it was a counterfeit bill.

It was my turn to smile—like the cat that ate the canary. "I need to ask you a few questions about Amber Brown."

"God rest her soul," he said in a perfunctory tone. "I heard about that nasty biniss at Madame Moiselle's."

"Yes, well, speaking of nasty business," I began with a devil-may-care stare, "rumor has it that you were prostituting Amber."

He jutted out his lower lip. "I ain't seen her in over a year. And in case you couldn't tell, I quit the pimpin' profession. I'm a man of Gawd now."

I glanced at his outfit. "Judging from that suit you're wearing, I'd say you were still a pimp."

"Be easy." He gave me a sideways look as he tugged on his lapels. "The clothes don't make the man. What you cain't see is that I went through an inner transformation."

This I had to hear. "How so?"

"Six months ago, the good Lawd came ta me in a vision. I was in an alleyway, jus' waitin' on my friends and smokin' some grass when the street lamp went out. So I had me a drank ta calm my nerves, and the light done came back on. Then it happened agin —I had a smoke and a drank, the lamp went on and off—and that's when I knew that Gawd was showin' me the light."

Not to be a doubter, but I would've sworn on a stack of Bibles that drugs and a faulty light bulb had more to do with that vision than God. "Do you mind if I ask what you were drinking?"

"Crown Royal, the beverage fit for a King," he replied as his eyes shifted to my left hand.

I suddenly realized that I was talking to a pimp-preacher while holding a bag of booze. "Did you or anyone you know ever send Amber a bottle of amaretto?" I asked as I stuffed mine into my purse. "Amaretto di Amore?"

He grabbed a cane from beside the keyboard. It looked suspiciously like a pimp stick, thanks to the bejeweled voodoo god topper. "I don't know nothin' about no amaretto. My girls only drank the best—Hpnotiq."

I resisted the urge to roll my eyes as I pulled out my pad and pen. "Would you mind telling me where you were between the hours of four a.m. and two p.m. yesterday?"

His eyes narrowed to the size of coin slots. "At my church."

"You were there at four a.m.?" I asked, giving him a get-real glare.

He raised his chin. "I got there early ta write my Sabbath sermon."

Somehow I doubted that. "And where is this church, exactly?"

"You're standing in it," he replied, tapping the toe of his gold platform shoe on the sidewalk. "The streets are my pulpit."

I wrote "no church, no alibi" in my notes. "Okay then, do you have any idea who might've killed Amber?"

"It was the devil's doin'," he exclaimed with a flourish of his cane.

"Yeah, I got that part," I said drily. "I was thinking more along the lines of one of her ex-clients. Any chance you could provide me with a list?"

"No need." He crossed his arms on his crucifix. "They was all named John."

I set myself up for that one. "Do you know what Amber did for a living after she left your, uh, employ?"

He pulled a gold toothpick from the pocket of his jacket and slipped it into his mouth. "She tol' me she was tired of workin' fo' the money, so she was goin' clean."

"That doesn't make sense," I protested, resting the pen on my cheek. "Did she say anything else?"

"Tha's all I know. Now if you don't mind," he began, gesturing toward a lone wino sitting with his back against a nearby trashcan, "I need ta tend to my parishioners."

"Well, thanks for your time," I said, practically choking on the words. As shady as this King character was, I had to keep the lines of communication open.

He bowed and pointed to the fedora. "Donations kindly accepted."

My lips curled. I reached into my wallet for a five and tossed the bill into the hat. "You'll get more when I get more, *capisci*?"

"I dig," he replied and then raised his cane and whacked the wino, who was making a play for the fedora funds.

So much for Christian charity.

As I walked back to the office, I pondered King's comment about Amber "goin' clean." Of course, King was anything but trustworthy, but his story did line up with Carnie's recollection of Amber saying that she had wanted to quit the sex trade. So, if it was true that she hadn't worked for King or anyone else during the past year, then I needed to figure out how she could have come by money honestly without earning it. And the only way I could think of was that someone was giving it to her.

But who? And why?

~

"COME AND GET IT, MISS FRANKI," Glenda yelled as she threw open the dressing room door. "Miss Eve brought us a bucket of her buttermilk fried chicken."

My ears pricked up at the mention of the decadent Southern dish, and I rushed into the dimly lit white room. Long, black countertops and mirrors with vanity lighting lined the walls, and strippers in various stages of undress stood around a table attacking the meat like sharks at a feeding frenzy. As I gazed at the gory scene, the fourteen ounces of cow in my belly started kicking. "Thanks," I said, clutching my gut. "But I just ate. Twice."

"Well, while you were at the bank, I took the liberty of calling the girls who worked with Amber." She handed me a cardboard pantyhose insert with some writing on it. "I couldn't get ahold of one of them, but I started this list for the other two. It's got their contact information, alibis, and measurements."

Although I was impressed with Glenda's initiative, I was confused about that last item. "Why'd you give me their measurements?"

"To help you size them up!" she cried and then slapped her knee as she doubled over with laughter.

I stood there stone-faced until she got out her guffaws. When she finally recovered, I asked, "So, is Eugene back from the police station?"

"Not yet," she replied, wiping a tear from her eye. "But the two girls I called came in early for their shifts to talk to you."

I glanced at the list. Interviewee number one, Bit-O-Honey, was in the hospital on the night of the murder, and interviewee number two, Saddle, was working at a club in Las Vegas. "Do all the dancers use stage names?"

"If they don't, they should." Glenda flipped her hair. "We need to protect our identities, and the bottom line is that we can make more money with a name that appeals to clients. Personal-ly," she began, putting a hand over her heart, "I went for alliteration and romance with 'Lorraine Lamour.' But young girls today go for things like candy, liquor, and exotic locations."

"Then how do you explain 'Saddle?'" As soon as I asked the question, the answer came to me. "Never mind. I got it," I said, raising my hand in a stopping motion. "It refers to riding—but not horses."

Glenda put a hand on her hip. "It refers to the saddles she makes for a ranch supply store. Honestly, Miss Franki, you need to get your mind out of the gutter."

Yeah, because no one has inappropriate thoughts in a strip club. "That reminds me, what was Amber's stage name?"

She grimaced. "According to the girls, she never used one. They said she didn't care if anyone knew who she was."

I wondered whether Amber's openness had anything to do with the fact that she had no family.

Glenda turned to a chubby brunette who was sitting at the counter and gnawing on a thigh in nothing but a thong. "Bit-O-Honey, come talk to Miss Franki about Amber while I go get Saddle."

She choked down a chunk of chicken. "Yes, ma'am."

As Glenda left the room, I sat in the chair next to Bit-O-Honey and wished that she would put on a robe. "What was Amber like to work with?"

She stared at me, wide-eyed. "Um, she was a super dancer."

I gave her a reassuring smile. "No, I was talking about her personality."

"Oh." She wrinkled her mouth to one side and glanced up and down like a student wracking her brain for the right answer. "Um, she was super creative?"

I pursed my lips. This was going to be harder than I'd thought.

The door swung open, and Glenda returned with a long, lean black-haired beauty wearing a tan suede bikini and chaps complete with a whip. Judging from the cowgirl costume, this was Saddle.

"Was Amber superstitious at all?" I continued.

"She didn't have time for that nonsense," Saddle replied as she sat down and kicked her high-heeled cowboy boots onto the counter, revealing a crescent-shaped tattoo on her calf. "She was fearless."

"That's right," Bit-O-Honey agreed, shaking a chicken leg, among other things, for emphasis. "For her 'crazy as a polecat' routine, she wore a sexy straitjacket while she worked the pole."

"Wow," I said, trying to visualize that scene. "She must've had powerful legs."

"And labia too," Bit-O-Honey added with a round-eyed nod. "Even though she did put Mighty Grip powder on them."

I froze as an unusual image came to mind that I was sure couldn't be right. "Is that like extra-strength baby powder or something?"

Saddle shook her silky locks. "It helps you stick to the pole."

I knew I shouldn't insist, but I couldn't help myself. "Then why did she put it...down there?"

"She had to collect the clients' dollar bills somehow, sugar," Glenda intoned as she brushed her bottom with bronzer. "After all, her hands *were* strapped to her body."

My jaw fell open, and it took a long time to get it to close. "Uh, speaking of routines, did Amber ever use Lili St. Cyr's bathtub during a performance?"

"No one would dare because that tub is sacred to us strippers," Bit-O-Honey huffed, pressing a hand to her bare breast.

At this point I was willing to forgo the robe and take a pair of pasties. "Did she have any issues with clients?"

"She didn't like The Fly," Saddle drawled, "but it wasn't like they had a falling out or anything."

I paused. "Did you say 'The Fly'?"

"He's one of our VIP Room regulars," Bit-O-Honey gushed. "And he brings in a jelly jar full of flies and pays us to kill 'em with a fly swatter." She swung at an imaginary fly with her chicken leg as a demonstration.

This time my jaw dropped so low that it almost touched my neck. "Whatever happened to paying a stripper to dance?"

"Clients want all kinds of things in the VIP Room," Glenda explained as she checked out her bronzed behind in the mirror. "Dancing isn't usually one of them."

I shifted in my seat. Before this investigation was over, I had a feeling that I was going to learn a lot of things that I'd never wanted to know about the stripping industry. "Okay, so what about the other dancers? Did Amber have any problems or fights with them?"

The girls exchanged a look.

Saddle's lips thinned. "She had a Hatfield-McCoy-type feud with Curaçao."

For some reason I thought of the woman I'd seen exiting the club the morning after my arrest. "She's not a platinum blonde, is she?"

Bit-O-Honey gasped. "How'd you know?"

"Just a lucky guess," I muttered. "But where is Curaçao now? Did she quit or something?"

"She still works here," Saddle replied. Then she glanced at Bit-O-Honey. "At least, we think she does."

"She's the girl I wasn't able to get ahold of," Glenda said, brushing some bronzer on her cheeks (the ones on her face). "And, from what I hear, no one's seen hide nor hair of her since her Saturday night shift."

I looked from Glenda to the girls. "What about Sunday when the police had all the dancers come in for questioning?"

Bit-O-Honey threw her hands in the air, along with her chicken leg. "She never showed."

My gut lurched, and it wasn't from that kicking cow. "Has anyone reported her missing to the police?"

Glenda placed the bronzer brush on the counter. "Curaçao is known for her benders, Miss Franki. But I'm sure that Eugene told the police all about this today."

I leaned back in my chair. With Amber dead, Curaçao's disappearance could mean only one of two things. Either she didn't want to answer questions about her enemy's murder or she couldn't because she was dead too.

"Curaçao hasn't shown up for her shift, sugar," Glenda said, climbing onto the barstool beside me. "And she's still not answering her phone."

I took a sip of chicory coffee from Madame Moiselle's signature "mammary mug" as I digested the worrisome news. "Do we have an address for her?"

"That child is a free spirit," Glenda replied as though she were the epitome of conformity. "The last we heard, she was sleeping on some friend's couch. You'll have to ask Eugene if he knows who or where that is."

If he ever comes back. Eugene had been at the police station the entire day, and I knew why. Because he'd found Amber's body and had keys to the club, he was a prime suspect in the eyes of the law. The question was, did he deserve to be?

"In the meantime," Glenda continued as she hopped from the barstool in platform penny loafers, "the peep show must go on. Is it all right if I cover for Curaçao? Or do you need me to do some more sleuthin'?"

"It's six o'clock. The work day's over," I said, raising the mammary to my mouth.

"You going home?" she asked, tying her white button-down shirt into a knot beneath her bosom.

"Nah." I swiveled on my stool and leaned my back on the bar. "Bradley left town today, and Veronica offered to look after Napoleon, so I think I'll stick around tonight and observe—you know, see if I notice anything out of the ordinary." *For a strip club, that is.*

"Well, slap my ass and call me happy!" she exclaimed as she demonstrated the gesture. "I'm about to practice one of my acts for The Saints, Sinners, and Sluts Revue, so you'll finally get to see me dance."

I did my best to look enthusiastic, but seeing my sixty-something-year-old landlady strip was not on my bucket list—nor was slapping her ass. Besides, judging from her pigtail braids, micro-mini plaid skirt, and knee socks, I feared that she was about to reenact Britney Spears's "Baby One More Time" video. "You're a slut, right?"

"Yes indeedy, Miss Franki." She curtseyed, purposefully displaying boobs adorned with pasties shaped like crosses—the religious kind, not the Red Cross kind. "I'm a Catholic schoolgirl."

As she turned and strutted toward the stairs, I vowed vindication for present and former Catholic schoolgirls everywhere.

"Ride 'em, cowboy!" a female shouted.

Glancing toward the main stage, I saw Saddle galloping and cracking her whip as the song "It Wasn't God Who Made Honky Tonk Angels" began to play. "I don't care what Glenda says," I muttered, "that woman's name has nothing to do with making saddles."

I spun around to the bar to get one of Eve's honey-garlic chicken wings, but instead I came face-to-face with a turkey. From my up-close-and-personal viewpoint, I put him in his early forties. Apart from a noteworthy mole growing from his right eyebrow, his most distinguishing feature was his complete lack of fashion sense, i.e., baby blue bell-bottoms and a purple and white, floral-print shirt unbuttoned to his navel. If he'd been wearing a denim newsboy cap, he would've looked like one of the Wild and Crazy Guys.

"Hello, luscious. Didn't I see you at Hooters?" he asked, his eyes glued to my honkers.

I wasn't surprised by the lame line or the lascivious linger, but I was struck by the way he seemed to swallow his *l*'s. It sounded familiar, but I wasn't sure why. "Sorry to disappoint you," I began, blowing my honey-garlic breath in his face, "but I'm not looking to hook up. I'm here on business."

His eyes glinted like the gold medallion nestled in the fur rug on his chest. "You're in luck, lady, because I'm the manager," he announced, holding out his hand. "Eugene Michael."

Finally. Opting to skip the handshake, I said, "I'm Franki Amato."

"Amato, eh?" He moved his unshaken hand to his chin and rubbed his unshaven beard. "We could use a fiery Italian onstage."

I flashed a smart-aleck smile. "I'm sure you could, but it's not going to be this fiery Italian." I pulled a business card from my bag and placed it on the bar counter in front of him. "I'm investigating Amber Brown's murder."

He pulled a comb from his back pocket and ran it through his slicked-back hair, and I wondered whether he felt as cool and collected as he was trying to make me believe.

"You must be Glenda's friend," he said, returning the greasy comb to his pocket. "What can I do for you?"

"Answer some questions about Amber," I shot back.

He looked down and gave a frustrated sigh. "I met her the day she came into the club and asked me for a job, and I haven't seen her since she quit." He raised his head, and this time he looked me in the eyes. "So, I had nothing to do with her death, all right?"

Eugene was clearly on the defensive. The way I saw it, either he was tired of being questioned, or he was hiding something. "Do you know why she quit after only two months?"

"Strippers like to move around, look for better money, and in this industry it's easy to do," he said as he walked behind the bar. "You show up to a club, and if you've got good moves and the cash to pay the house fee, you can dance."

It didn't seem right that the women had to pay to work, but then there were a lot of things about this business that didn't seem right. "Carlos told me that you closed the club after he and Iris were arrested. What time did you leave?"

"At around five thirty," he replied as he browsed the bottles on the bar. "Then I went home to bed, and I didn't get up until Carlos called at noon and told me that his and Iris's bail had been set." He picked out a bottle of vodka. "And since no one can vouch for me, I'm evidently a suspect."

I remembered the surveillance camera that I'd seen in the VIP Room. "What about the video from the security system? If you had nothing to do with Amber's death, that could potentially clear you."

"There is no video because we don't run the system after hours," he replied, placing a highball glass on the counter. "Can I offer you a drink?"

"No, thanks." I wondered whether he was telling the truth about the video. If he was, Amber could've known that the cameras wouldn't be running since she'd worked at the club. But had the killer known this too? "Did Amber have problems with any of the clients?"

He laughed revealing discolored teeth, and my tooth gave a pang of repulsion. "The girls have problems with a lot of the clients," he said, pouring himself two fingers of vodka. "If I told you about some of our VIP Room regulars, you'd take me up on that drink offer."

After Bit-O-Honey's story about The Fly, I was inclined to agree with him. "What can you tell me about Amber's feud with Curaçao?"

"They had a few cat fights over one of Curaçao's regulars, a guy named Shakey." He took a swig of his drink and wiped his mouth. "Curaçao claims that he was going to propose to her and that Amber got wind of it and deliberately stole him."

If Curaçao had lost a husband to Amber, then she could've hated her enough to kill her. But until she surfaced, I couldn't rule out the possibility that she'd met with foul play too, maybe even at the hands of this Shakey character. "Do you think it's possible that Curaçao killed Amber?"

He gripped his glass. "As nuts as that chick is? Definitely."

"What about Shakey?" I pressed. "Do you think he could've done it?"

Eugene shot the remainder of his vodka. "I don't know anything about the guy except that he's a Texas oil man who wears a Stetson. But sure. Why not?"

I pulled out my notepad and jotted down the description, although I didn't hold out much hope of finding Shakey given that he sounded like a few hundred thousand other men in Texas. "Do you have any idea where Curaçao is? Some of the girls told me that she hasn't been seen since her shift on Saturday night, and I'm afraid she could be in danger."

"Don't worry," he said, pouring another drink. "Like I told the police, she parties pretty hard—alcohol, drugs, you name it. Sometimes she takes off for days at a time without telling anyone. But she always comes back."

If Curaçao had a substance abuse problem, she could be somewhere getting high or in withdrawal or worse. "Do you happen to know the name of the friend she's staying with?"

He drained his glass. "Maybe."

I blinked, wondering whether he was expecting a bribe for the information. "It's either yes or no."

"No, it's Maybe," he said, placing the glass on the counter. "That's her name. She danced here once or twice a couple of months back."

Now I wished that I'd asked for some of that vodka, because this case was going to give me a nervous breakdown. "You seem to know a lot about Curaçao. Were you ever intimately involved with her? Or with Amber?"

He moved in close and looked me in the eyes. "Honey, I stay as far away from these chicks as I can get."

A shrill whistle pierced the air followed by a strident "Yippee-ki-yay, y'all!"

I almost jumped from my stool. I glared over my shoulder and saw Saddle exiting the stage as Carlos the bartender pushed a fake altar up a ramp. Glenda must have been preparing to make her ungodly entrance, and that was my cue to look the hell away.

"Tell me something," I said, turning back to Eugene. "What do you think Amber was doing in that bathtub?"

He leaned on the counter with his forearms. "Probably getting it on with some loser who killed her for kicks."

I pretended to look at my notes while I recovered from my revulsion. "Did the police mention anything about a necklace?"

"You mean the amber?" he asked, arching the brow with the mole.

Apparently, he'd been questioned about the pendant even though Veronica had advised Detective Sullivan to keep its existence from the public. "Yeah, I'm curious about whether you have any thoughts on why the killer would steal it."

He straightened and hiked up his pants. "My first thought was that one of the girls killed Amber for the pendant."

I narrowed my eyes. "Why would you think that?"

"Because stuff goes missing around here practically every day," he said, opening his arms wide. "If it isn't nailed down or locked up, the girls take it. And they love sparkly things."

"So," I began, crossing my arms, "all strippers are thieves, huh?"

"Not all of them," he replied, raising a finger. "Just some."

For a second, I figured that he was trying to deflect suspicion from himself. But then I remembered that I had seen one of the girls, probably Curaçao, leaving the club with a suitcase containing Lord only knew what. "You mean, like Curaçao?"

"Primarily her," he replied with a pointed look.

"Eugene," Glenda called as she flounced up to the bar in her stripper schoolgirl uniform. "That darn sound system stopped working again." She gave a haughty flip of her braids. "I just can't work in these conditions."

It had to be divine intervention.

"I'll take care of it," he said, taking one last, lustful look at my breasts before exiting the bar.

Eugene was a creep, but I wasn't convinced that he was a killer. Curaçao, however, was a different story. From the sound of things, she had a healthy hatred for Amber and a strong motive to kill her on top of some psychological issues. I needed to talk to her ASAP.

I just hoped that I still could.

THE LEGS on the stripper-pole clock above the bar read ten p.m. I yawned and looked around Madame Moiselle's. After four straight hours of shaking, slapping, and sliding, I was spent. And I wasn't even doing the dancing. I was considering calling it a night because, as far as I could tell, everything was on the up and up at the club—thanks in part to the silicone.

My phone began to vibrate on the counter, and Ruth's name appeared on the display.

Eager for a break from the boobs and booties, I grabbed my phone and hurried through the hotbed of horny men toward the exit. But outside on Bourbon Street, it was almost as loud as the club. I tapped answer and covered my ear with my hand in an attempt to drown out the blaring jazz music and the din of the revelers. "Hey, Ruth," I shouted. "I'm glad you called."

"Where are you at?" she barked. "A damn rave?"

All right, maybe I wasn't so glad. "Madame Moiselle's."

A moment of silence ensued, followed by a gagging sound.

"Ruth?" I prodded worried that she was choking on an ice cube or something. "Are you okay?"

She inhaled sharply. "I told you to lay low," she rasped, "so first you come to the bank and get sloppy drunk, then you head straight to a titty bar?"

I grimaced as I realized that she hadn't been gagging, but raging. "Relax, will ya?" I huffed. "I'm here investigating a case. And I didn't get 'sloppy drunk.'"

She harrumphed. "Then why does my desk smell like a saloon?"

Annoyed, I collapsed against the exterior wall of the club—until a woman standing next to me pulled up her "I'm getting married, B*tches" t-shirt to flash some guys on the balcony across the street. "That was no well whiskey," I began, bolting away from the bodacious bride, "that was Dom Pérignon champagne, and it inspired a perfume, FYI."

"Yeah, for cheap tarts," she quipped. "Now what in the hell were you thinkin' drinkin' bubbly at my desk?"

I sighed. Compared to a conversation with Ruth, the strip club seemed like a spa. "Look, I spilled it on your desk because I tripped over Jeff when I found him eavesdropping at Bradley's office door."

"Well, well, well." She took a sonorous slurp. "And I found him alone in Bradley's office when I came back from my mammogram. The doc said my girls are doing fine, by the way."

My lips curled. I was up to my eyeballs in "girls" here at the club and on Bourbon Street, so I didn't need Ruth's old gals added to the mammary mix. "What was Jeff doing in Bradley's office?"

"He said he was looking for some loan contract, but we both know that was a load of bull pucky." She let out a boisterous belch. "So, I waited until he went home for the night, and then I broke into *his* office."

Panic gripped my chest. The last thing Bradley or I needed right now was Ruth getting arrested. "You didn't damage the door or anything, did you?"

"I want to keep my job, thank you." She popped the tab of some kind of can. "If you must know, I picked the lock. It's a skill I acquired in the Girl Scouts."

"For what?" I exclaimed. "The breaking-and-entering badge?"

"Let's just say that it was an inner-city troop and leave it at that."

As I processed her reply, something hit me in the head. I reached down to pick up the offending object—a set of Mardi Gras beads with a plastic penis pendant that said *Madame Moiselle's.*

"Sorry, Franki," Bit-O-Honey called from above.

I looked up to see her—and her bare breasts—leaning over the balcony as I rubbed the welt on my head. "Did you find anything interesting in Jeff's office?"

"You bet your patootie, I did," Ruth growled. "A receipt from Casamento's for two soft-shell crab loaves."

Casamento's was an old Italian restaurant on Magazine

Street that looked like a giant swimming pool inside because of the original owner's penchant for imported tile. "So what? I just ate pan bread and oyster stew there a week ago."

"I'll tell you *what*." She chomped a piece of ice. "It's dated the day before Martin Slater, one of those two clients Bradley lost, canceled his account. And according to Bradley's client files, that's not only Slater's favorite restaurant, it's his favorite meal too."

My jaw tensed, and I squeezed the plastic penis. It looked bad—for Jeff—but I needed to be certain that he was turning clients against Bradley. "We need hard evidence." I caught a glimpse of my hand and promptly dropped the beads. "Like an email or letter."

"I'm on it," she said. "Now I've gotta scoot. *The Best of Divorce Court* is coming on."

I knew better than to stand between Ruth and her armchair justice, so I hung up without further ado.

As I stood on the street pondering the situation at Pontchartrain Bank, a guy wearing nothing but a mesh shirt rubbernecked my rack. I laid a lethal look on him and entered Madame Moiselle's. It was cleaner inside the club.

"Club's closed! Everyone out!"

I bolted up on my barstool at the sound of Carlos's voice. The t & a show had gotten so tiresome that I must've dozed off.

Carlos removed some dirty glasses from the bar. "Glenda asked me to tell you that she was going upstairs to change."

"Thanks," I said. Although I couldn't fathom why she had to change when the costumes she wore at the club were the same as her street clothes.

As he began loading the glasses into a dishwasher, I scanned the room and saw the last of the patrons stumbling out the exit. Now that the club was empty, I wanted to search for any evidence that might've been overlooked.

"Hey, Carlos," I began, sliding off my stool, "when Glenda comes down would you let her know that I'm taking a look around the club?"

"Sure thing," he replied as he wiped the counter where my head had been laying.

Hoping I hadn't left behind a pool of drool, I headed for the prop room behind the main stage to check out Lili St. Cyr's claw-foot tub. When I pushed open the door and switched on the light, I gasped. Many of the items were larger than life so that a dancer could fit inside. There was a martini glass, a birdcage, a fishbowl, and a high heel, just to name a few. It looked like a giant was having a garage sale.

After a minute or so of searching, I spotted the bathtub in a corner to my right beside a three-tiered cake. For a moment, I forgot about the tub and gazed with yearning at the colossal confection. It had been so long since I'd had sweets that I seriously considered taking a bite.

Shaking myself from my dessert daydream, I approached the tub. But my foot got caught on the birdcage stand, and I went flying. Using my hands to break my fall, I bumped into a six-foot-long oyster shell, and the top opened to reveal an enormous fake diamond.

"Some stripper doesn't know her gemology," I muttered as I rubbed my aching wrists.

Since I was already on the floor, I crawled around the tub and examined the exterior. The epoxy was smooth except for a few chips on the lip. Next, I leaned into the tub and noticed scratches down to the cast iron right above the overflow face-plate. Upon closer inspection, I realized that the marks were a crude carving of a mermaid followed by several X's, all of which had circles around them except for the last one. I wondered whether the designs were made by Lili St. Cyr or whether they'd been done more recently, possibly even by Amber.

The sound of shoes scraping on pavement startled me from my thoughts. I looked up figuring that I'd find Glenda.

Instead, a bald man stood over me who was so massive that I halfway expected him to shout "Fee-fi-fo-fum!" Only, it wasn't his size that spooked me—it was his eyes. The irises were ice blue, but the whites were as black as coal. And in that moment, they held the same sociopathic stare as Malcolm McDowell's character in *The Clockwork Orange*.

They say that your life flashes before you when you die, but all I could see was Bradley's worried face as he told me that strip clubs were dangerous.

Then everything went as black as the scleras of the giant's demonic eyes.

8

———————

The pungent odor of hay assailed my nostrils, and something stabbed at the backs of my arms and legs. I tried to think—to remember where I was—but my mind was in a fog. *Am I back in Texas? In a barn?*

I opened my eyes a crack and saw a flesh-colored mass hanging over me. It was coming in and out of focus, but it looked like...*an udder?*

Okay. It was one thing to wake up in a barn, but it was quite another to be underneath a thousand-plus-pound cow.

Convinced that my eyes were playing tricks on me, I squinted at the mass. There were four teats all right, but two of them were covered with...*purple peace-sign pasties?*

"She's coming to," a familiar female voice said.

"Don't let her sit up," another added. "Wait until the whiskey comes."

I snapped my eyes shut. This was no Texas barn, and that was no udder—it was Glenda and Bit-O-Honey leaning over either side of me in the prop room.

While I pretended to be passed out, I had to wonder whether those pasties comprised the outfit that Glenda had changed into and whether Bit-O-Honey went through life topless until she had to put on a costume to perform.

Warm flesh pressed against my leg, and my eyes, understandably, flew open. Glenda had planted her bare bottom beside me on my sickbed, which I now realized was a big bale of hay, and she was coming at me with a feminine hygiene product.

All of the sudden, I longed to be beneath that cow in that barn.

"What shook you, sugar?" she asked, dabbing at my forehead with a thong panty liner.

The giant's face came back to me in a flash. "There was a huge man in here, and the whites of his eyes were black—like a zombie's."

"Oh, that's Iris," Bit-O-Honey bubbled as her boobs bobbed above me. "You know, our bouncer?"

"Wait. Stop," I said, shooting a pointed look in the direction of her breasts. "Iris is a man?"

"It's a nickname," she explained. "Because his eyes are so blue?"

I massaged my forehead—for so many reasons. "And no one thought the black parts were worthy of a reference?"

"Those are corneal tattoos, Miss Franki." Glenda flipped her hair and, unintentionally, a breast. "And Iris is sensitive, so we try not to comment on his appearance."

I closed my eyes instead of rolling them because it took less energy. If you asked me, any man who tattooed his corneas needed to have a thick skin, both literally and figuratively. "So, I take it that this hay is for one of Saddle's acts?"

"No, it's for The Wrangler," Bit-O-Honey replied.

Now my eyes were rolling because I felt a VIP Room story coming on.

"He's another one of our regulars, Miss Franki," Glenda said as she tamped down the edge of a protruding peace sign. "He likes the girls to neigh like horses and stomp around in hay while he tries to lasso them."

I snorted. "That's not degrading, or anything."

"It depends on how you look at it." Glenda leaned back on her hands and kicked her legs like a Rockette before crossing them. "Here at Madame Moiselle's, we subscribe to a feminist view of stripping."

I stared at her and wondered whether my ears were as woozy as my brain. "And what would that be, specifically?"

"We're exploiting our exploiters tit for twat," Bit-O-Honey explained as she took a seat on the lip of a large stoneware pot labeled "Winnie the Pooh."

I suppressed a smirk. These strippers might know their feminist theory, but they needed some serious instruction when it came to common objects and expressions. "You mean, tit for *tat*."

"No, sugar," Glenda said, batting her purple eyelashes. "She means tit for twat."

Bit-O-Honey nodded. "Amber used to say that we shouldn't objectify ourselves," she began, balancing with splayed legs on the honey pot, "and that men should pay us reparations for exploiting us for so long."

I looked at the ceiling and chewed the inside of my lip. Free money seemed to be a recurring theme where Amber was concerned, but the feminist aspect was new. I wondered again whether she'd found someone to fund her.

"Here's that whiskey," a mousy male voice announced.

I turned my head and saw Iris holding one of Madame Moiselle's signature "cock-tail" glasses, and I bolted up on my bale despite his Mike Tysonesque tone. But when my eyes crossed and his merged into a Cyclops eye, I had to lie back down.

"Iris, you gave Miss Franki quite a fright," Glenda scolded as she took the glass from his hand. "You've got to quit sneaking up on people like that."

"Well, I didn't mean to," he whined, twisting the bottom of his faded Marilyn Manson concert t-shirt. "She didn't see me when I came into the room before because she was looking at Amber's pictures."

I bolted up again, but this time only to my elbows. "Do you mean those etchings in the claw-foot tub?"

He opened his eyes wide. "Yes, ma'am."

I cringed at the "ma'am" even more than at the black scleras. "I didn't realize you knew Amber."

"I don't. Uh, I didn't," he stammered, rubbing his shaved head. "Another dancer told me that Amber did those drawings. Maybe."

"Well, did she, or didn't she?" I asked, pulling myself into a sitting position.

"She did." He gave a lizard-like blink. "That is, Maybe."

"Wait." I held out a hand. "You mean, *Maybe* Maybe?"

Glenda looked from me to Iris and then shot my whiskey. "I'm starting to think that we need to take both of you to the damn hospital."

"I'm fine," I said looking with regret at the empty glass. "He's talking about a dancer named Maybe. And according to Eugene, she's the friend that Curaçao is staying with."

Bit-O-Honey blinked. "Are you talking about Maybe *Baby*?"

I almost said, "Maybe," but I caught myself in time. "I guess."

"Well, I know *her*," Glenda exclaimed. "She lives over in The Marigny by Carnie."

"That's good, because we need to pay her and Curaçao a visit." I started the process of standing up. "But first I need to go home and take a hot bath and get a few hours of sleep."

"I'm with you, sugar," Glenda said, rising to help me. "Right now, I'm too pooped to pole dance, much less private investigate."

As we entered the club, a member of the cleaning crew turned on what the dancers liked to call the "ugly lights," i.e., the overheads that showed all of one's physical imperfections.

Angling a glance at Glenda's pasties, I asked, "Um, do you need to go upstairs and get your shirt?"

"Shirt?" she repeated as though it were a foreign word. "Now that you mention it, Miss Franki, I did forget something. I'll be right back."

Glenda strutted toward the stairs, and I leaned against the stage for support. I was half asleep and still kind of shaken up, which meant that I was in no condition to drive home. Deciding to let Glenda do the honors, I pulled my keys from my bag and promptly dropped them. When I crouched to pick them up, I saw a flash of light reflect off something between the wall of the stage and the pile of the red carpet. After a few minutes of searching, I found the culprit—a tiny glass tube covered in some kind of oil.

Sitting on my knees, I inserted the tip of my car key into the opening of the tube and lifted it to my nose. It had an earthy odor. As I examined it for branding, I noticed silver stilettos with a stripper-on-a pole heel in front of me.

"What'd you find, Miss Franki?"

I looked up to see Glenda in a white, floor-length feather boa. It wasn't a shirt, but it was a start. "Is this container from a product the dancers use?"

She leaned over and sniffed the tube. "That smells like dirt, sugar. We professionals stick to the basic man magnets—baby oil, cocoa butter, or vanilla perfume."

"That's what I was hoping you'd say," I said as I wrapped the tube in a tissue and dropped it into a zippered compartment in my bag. Because I had an idea of what it was. It was a long shot, but if I was right, it was going to add a whole new dimension to this case.

My Mustang skidded into oncoming traffic, and then Glenda swerved back into our lane.

"I might've taken that turn a tad too fast," she said, taking a deep drag off her cigarette holder.

I pulled a few of her boa feathers from my mouth and began feeling my head for knots. Because surely I'd suffered a brain injury when I fainted at the club, and that's what had prompted me to ask her to drive. "Would you please slow down and get your foot back inside the car? You're supposed to use it, you know, to *brake*?"

Her head retracted into a flock of feathers. "Well, who ever heard of using two feet to drive?"

"Only everyone who went to driving school," I snapped as I checked my seatbelt. "Where'd you get your license, anyway?"

"License?" she scoffed as she pulled the car to a stop in front of our fourplex. "What would I do with one of those?"

That explained the reckless ride. "Oh, I don't know. Abide by the law, use it for ID?"

"This is New Orleans, sugar." She exited the car and threw her boa around her neck. "Abiding by the law is a matter of personal choice, and everyone knows who I am."

She had me on both counts. I shook my head and climbed from the car, and I wondered why Glenda had parked on the street.

Then I glanced at the driveway, and the screechy-scary shower-scene music from *Psycho* pierced my brain like a blade.

"Glenda," I whispered, "please tell me that Veronica's boyfriend Dirk drives the exact same car as my mother."

She squinted and exhaled a cloud of smoke. "No self-respecting single man drives a station wagon, sugar."

I put my hand to my mouth. "I was afraid you'd say something like that."

We contemplated the maroon Ford Taurus in silence, and then I crossed myself because I didn't know what the hell else to do.

Glenda dropped her cigarette and stubbed it out with her shoe. "Family shouldn't stay under the same roof, Miss Franki. Do you want to sleep in my champagne glass?"

It was a tempting offer. I'd crashed in her glass once before after partying with some pirates, and it was a little cramped but not half bad. "Nah, I'd better go in and face the music," I said, thinking mainly of that *Psycho* soundtrack. "If my mother is here, then something's up."

"Whatever," she said with a shrug. "Just remember, my champagne glass is your champagne glass, sugar."

I watched with envy as she sashayed up the stairs, and then I slowly unlocked the door to my apartment and tiptoed inside. Even though I was thirty years old and had done nothing wrong, I felt like a teenager coming home past curfew—not that I ever did that, of course.

My mother was stretched out supine on the chaise lounge, snoring with her mouth wide open, and Napoleon was watching me warily from the bearskin rug. Clearly, my mother's unexpected visit had set him on edge too.

I turned and closed the door.

Napoleon growled like the traitorous terrier that he was, and my mother jerked awake. "Francesca Lucia Amato!"

A wave of guilt washed over me. There was something about hearing your mother say your full name that instantly elicited a sense of shame.

"Where have you been?" she scolded as she sat up in a nightgown that looked like it had come from the set of *The Golden Girls.* "It's—"

I waited while she slipped on her bifocals and looked at her watch.

"—six o'clock in the morning!"

"I was working," I said, clutching my bag against my chest as though I were hiding cigarettes or booze—not that I ever did that, either.

"All night?" she shrilled. "I thought that you wouldn't have to work the graveyard shift anymore after you quit the police force."

"I still work in crime, Mom," I said as I deposited my bag on the coffee table, "so I have to investigate whenever the need arises."

"Well I don't know how you're going to raise a family working these hours," she said as she adjusted the hairnet that protected her bouffant brown bob.

I almost replied that the only thing that was going to keep me from having a family was my family, but I held my tongue— between my clenched teeth. "How'd you get into the apartment, anyway?"

She slid her feet into dingy white slippers. "Veronica let us in."

My mouth formed a grim line. So, while I was busting my hump for Private Chicks, Veronica was probably busting a gut at the thought of me coming home to find my mom lying in wait like a lioness in my living room. "Why didn't you tell me you were coming?"

"We wanted to surprise you, Francesca," she said as she struggled to lift herself off the chaise lounge.

The *Psycho* screeching sounded again. "*We?*"

She pushed past me on her way to the kitchen. "Your nonna came with me, dear."

Of course, I couldn't see the expression on my own face, but I imagined that it looked a lot like Janet Leigh's did when Norman Bates pulled open the shower curtain dressed like his mother and wielding a knife.

"We had to share your bed since it's the only one in the apartment," she continued as she opened a can of Folgers.

There went the sleep I'd hoped to get.

"But your nonna kept me up half the night going back and forth to the bathroom, so I had to come out here." She pointed a spoon at me. "Then she woke me up at three a.m. and asked me to get her enema bag from the trunk. You know how backed up she gets before a big trip."

Aaaand there went that bath. "Yeah, so, what's the occasion for the visit?"

"It's a belated birthday present," she replied, spooning coffee into the filter.

The gift that keeps on giving.

"Also," she began, filling the carafe with water, "it's been a long time since your nonna returned to her old stomping grounds."

My nonna and nonnu had emigrated from Sicily to New Orleans and raised my father and my four uncles there. So, I'd long known that a visit from my nonna was inevitable, but I'd naively assumed that my parents would've given me a heads-up so that I could prepare—i.e., stock the refrigerator, buy an air mattress, attend a few therapy sessions.

"And the timing couldn't have been more perfect," she added, pouring the water into the coffee maker, "because your nonna can help her old church friends make the bread for the St. Joseph's Day table."

This time, instead of hearing the *Psycho* soundtrack, I felt Norman's knife stabbing into my flesh. Now I knew why my nonna was here—it was to make sure that I stole a lemon from that damn altar. "Mom, I'm not going to steal from a church."

She almost dropped the carafe. "Well, you most certainly are not, young lady."

To the world at large, I was now a "ma'am," but to my mother I would forever be a "young lady." Was there no end to the injustices? "Mom, I'm talking about the lift-a-lemon-snag-a-spouse tradition."

"Oh, that," she said, shoving the carafe into the machine. "It hardly counts as stealing, Francesca. After all, that food is there to be eaten. And besides, at this point, what've you got to lose?"

Only my last shred of dignity and possibly my spot in heaven. No biggie.

She flipped the switch to the coffee maker. "I've got to go get your nonna out of that bathroom so I can do my business." She pasted a smile onto her face. "And when I get back, we can all sip our coffee and have a nice mother-daughter-grandmother chat."

As my mother headed toward my bedroom, I visualized Janet Leigh sliding down the wall of the shower, slowly dying from the multiple stab wounds that Norman had inflicted.

"Carmela, come out of that bathroom," my mother demanded.

"It's-a gonna be a while," Nonna shouted.

A surge of adrenaline shot through my veins. I had to get out of my apartment while I still had some lifeblood left in me—and before my nonna opened that door.

I scribbled a quick note to my mom telling her that I just remembered an early morning meeting I needed to attend and snuck out the door. I started for the stairs to Glenda's, but then I got a better idea—I was going to give Veronica a piece of my mind for not warning me about the familial invasion.

Marching over to her door, I raised my hand to knock as a man dressed in black bolted from the side of my house. I spun around and saw that he was wearing a ski mask and gloves just as he jumped into a dark sedan parked in front of the cemetery across the street.

Because he came from the area of the kitchen window, my first thought was that he was a Peeping Tom who'd been checking out my mom in her granny gown.

But I knew that couldn't be right.

As the peeper peeled out and sped down my street, a more sinister thought occurred to me. I'd had the feeling that someone had been following me off and on for the past couple of days. Could he be the perpetrator? If so, who was he, and what did he want from me?

More importantly, he'd been to my house at least once—was he planning on coming back?

9

———

As I stumbled half asleep up the stairs to Private Chicks, I was about to curse the old building for not having an elevator when I remembered that weirdo witch's warning. I wasn't sure whether cursing an inanimate object could "boomerang" back on me, but I couldn't take any chances. Because in light of this latest "present" from the family, I now firmly believed that I was cursed.

I pushed open the door and glanced at the clock: five past noon. Instead of going to my office, I headed for the kitchen to make coffee. I'd gotten maybe three hours of sleep thanks in part to Veronica, who'd called the cops after my encounter with the masked man. But Glenda also bore some of the blame because before the officers could write up the report, she came down wearing a teeny stars-and-stripes-themed teddy in a "show of support for our men in uniform"—that turned into an actual show.

"Well, good afternoon," Veronica said as I entered the narrow kitchen. She was sitting at the two-seater table looking minty fresh in a pale green pencil skirt and crisp white blouse while nibbling on a salad.

"You know I worked late last night," I grumbled, feeling like wilted spinach next to her in my green button down shirt. "And are you seriously going to nag me after everything you've put me through?"

"I was just kidding, Franki." She stabbed her fork into a piece of lettuce. "And like I told you this morning, there was no way I was going to ruin your mother's surprise."

Veronica was wise to stay on my mom's good side, because the woman could swing a mean pasta spoon—and those things had spikes. "Did I miss anything this morning?"

She swallowed a bite of salad. "Carnie's on her way here. She's found something that might be relevant to the case, so I called Madame Moiselle's and asked Glenda to stop by."

"I can't believe Glenda's already at the club," I said, pouring some of Veronica's leftover French press coffee into my Italians Brew It Better mug.

"She had rehearsal for the revue. And by the way," she began, her eyes growing wide, "she told me what happened with Iris last night. You must've been pretty frightened to faint like that."

"I was, but then I went home," I said, shooting her an accusatory look. "Iris has nothing on the women in my family."

She giggled, but then her smile faded. "Speaking of scary people, I'm concerned about the man you saw at the house this morning."

"Don't be," I said as I reached into the fridge and pulled out my Baileys Bourbon Vanilla Pound Cake coffee creamer. "I've got bigger things to worry about."

She pointed her fork at the Baileys. "Like breaking Lent?"

"This is creamer, Veronica, not cake." I poured a half a cup of the dessert-like liquid into my mug. "And I was talking about my mom and nonna. Can you imagine what they'll do when I tell them about the masked man, not to mention their reaction when they get a load of Glenda's getups?"

She popped a crouton into her mouth. "I still can't believe they didn't hear the commotion outside this morning."

"I'm sure they couldn't hear it over the commotion inside about the bathroom." I took a sip of my coffee, which suddenly tasted bitter despite the creamer. "I'm also worried about something that's going on at Pontchartrain Bank between Bradley and the manager, Jeff Payne."

Veronica put her fork down. "Whatever it is, I hope you're staying out of it."

"I'm trying," I said, which wasn't really a lie since I was having Ruth look into the issue for me. "But Jeff is practically dragging me into it."

She narrowed her eyes. "How so?"

"Ruth says that he's after Bradley's job," I began, staring into my coffee, "so he's keeping tabs on any trouble I've caused at the bank because he's trying to convince upper management that I'm a liability."

"He sounds like a real jerk," she said as she carried her plate to the sink. "But you can't change the past, Franki. All you can do is make sure that you don't give this guy any new ammunition."

As Veronica washed her dishes, I thought back to my interactions with Jeff. The only thing I could come up with that might look bad was the champagne incident. But I doubted that he could hold that over me since it was a birthday gift from Bradley.

The lobby bell sounded.

"I'll go," Veronica said, drying her hands.

As soon as she'd left the kitchen, I topped off my coffee with more creamer and hurried into the lobby.

Glenda was talking to Veronica by the reception desk while suited up in a New Orleans Saints uniform that made the team's cheerleaders look like real saints. "I can't wait to find out what

Carnie has for us." She shimmied like a player who'd just scored. "I hope it's something scandalous."

"That reminds me," I said, trying not to gawk at her fishnet football pants, "why didn't you mention that Carnie was a man?"

She strutted to the couch in her brown pigskin boots and took a seat. "Because I treat my squirrel friends the same way I treat my stripper friends, Miss Franki."

I stared at her over the rim of my coffee cup. "'Squirrel friends?'"

She batted her game-day eyelashes and picked up a copy of *Woman's Day*. "Girlfriends who hide their nuts, sugar."

I was sorry I'd asked but glad I hadn't gone with the Baileys Hazelnut creamer.

"Oh, Franki, I almost forgot," Veronica began as she consulted a calendar on the desk. "I got you an appointment with Amber's dentist, Dr. Lessler. He had a cancelation for eight a.m. tomorrow."

My hand flew to my cheek. "But my tooth isn't hurting anymore."

Veronica scribbled something on the schedule. "Well, you might as well have him look at it since you have to go to his office anyway."

"Miss Ronnie's right, sugar," Glenda said as she flipped through the magazine. "You don't want to end up like The Tooth Fairy."

I was half tempted to ask what she meant, but I refused to bite.

"The Tooth Fairy?" Veronica looked up from the calendar. "I don't get it."

"He's an elderly gentleman who frequents our VIP Rooms," Glenda explained. "The poor man's got a full set of dentures, so he has a bit of an oral fixation. He pays the girls to brush with Crest and tips handsomely for their used dental floss."

I glowered at Glenda. The VIP Room stories were starting to set my teeth on edge.

The door opened, and Carnie paraded inside in a strapless, floor-length yellow-feathered number with a Marie Antoinette-sized wig and a Miss Universe-style crown. David stood behind her looking bewildered, and I could certainly empathize. It was disconcerting to see Big Bird dressed in drag.

"Uh, ladies," David greeted red-faced. He squeezed past Carnie and dashed to his desk.

"Lordy," Glenda exclaimed, fanning herself with the magazine. "Miss Carnie's serving up fish today."

"Fish?" I said, still thinking squirrels. "Are you having a dinner party or something?"

Veronica cleared her throat. "Franki, 'serving fish' refers to a drag queen who looks very feminine."

"And this ain't no trout, honey," Carnie said as she took a seat beside Glenda and frowned at my shirt.

No, more like a barracuda, I thought as Veronica and I sat on the opposite couch. "So, what have you got for us?"

"Amber's credit card bill." She pulled a sheet of paper from her breast feathers and handed it to Veronica.

I looked over Veronica's shoulder. "Anything interesting?"

"It's mostly groceries and gas," she replied, running her finger down the list of charges. "But there's also a purchase from etsy.com and one for Waxing Salon on Dauphine Street."

Glenda patted Carnie's beefy bicep. "Where'd you find this, Miss Carnie?"

"The mailman delivered it last night."

"And you opened it?" I asked, surprised.

"Of course I did." She adjusted her crown. "Amber's dead, and the bill did come to my house."

I shrugged. "It's still a federal crime."

"So's murder," she snapped in her man voice and then raised her chin. "And that's what we're here to solve, am I right?"

I declined to comment. This queen was too regal for my blood.

"And after what the police put me through yesterday," Carnie continued, returning to her falsetto, "I felt like I had no choice but to take the law into my own hands." She batted yellow feather and rhinestone eyelashes. "A lady-boy's got to defend her honor."

"Ain't that the truth?" Glenda said with a shake of her head.

This time I really wanted to comment, but Veronica silenced me with a don't-you-dare stare.

Veronica assumed her attorney air. "What happened with the police?"

"They questioned me for eight hours, using strong-arm tactics to try to get me to change my story." She held out a French-manicured finger. "But FYI PO-lice, this bitch don't budge."

I could attest to that.

"I'm glad you stood your ground," Veronica said. "Did you get a sense of where the police are in their investigation?"

"If they're focusing on me, then I'd say they're nowhere." Carnie turned and shot me a half-lidded look. "What about you? Got any updates?"

I decided to keep the glass tube to myself until I knew whether my hunch about its origin was right. "I've talked to Amber's ex-pimp, King, and everyone in the club who knew Amber except for a dancer named Curaçao."

"Curaçao?" Carnie cocked a Bozo brow. "Like the liqueur?"

"The Caribbean island," Glenda clarified.

Carnie put a hand to her feathered bosom. "How exotic."

Glenda nodded. "Precisely."

"Now that we've established that," I said with an eye roll, "I'm pretty sure that she's the platinum blonde you saw harassing Amber, but we don't have a picture of her to confirm."

"Well, when do you plan to talk to her?" Carnie huffed.

"When she finds her," Glenda replied. "We haven't seen or heard from Curaçao since Amber was murdered, and she didn't show up for work again today." She crossed her legs, flashing a fleur-de-lis thong. "That reminds me, Miss Franki, is it all right if I cover for her this afternoon?"

"Fine with me," I replied a tad too enthusiastically. "I'll head over to Maybe's house now. Hopefully, Curaçao's with her."

Veronica shook her head. "I don't want you going alone, Franki."

"I'll go with her," Carnie announced. "I'd like to have a word with this woman about Amber."

My enthusiasm waned. "Don't you have a show to do?"

"I can get someone to cover for me," Carnie replied. "My freedom's at stake."

"While you two are out," Veronica began, using the credit card bill to block her view of my imploring look, "I'll have David look into Amber's Etsy purchase."

David shot from his chair. "The dancer from Madame Moiselle's?" He ran over to retrieve the bill. "I'm all over that."

I started to tell him that anything Amber had bought from the artsy online market probably wasn't related to stripping, but I decided to let him dream. He was still young, after all.

Carnie turned to Veronica. "Franki and I could stop by that waxing salon afterward. And if we need to do it on the down low, I could pose as a client." She glanced at her lap. "I've been looking for a new esthetician."

I leaned my head on the back of the couch. It was one thing to investigate with Glenda, but going undercover with Carnie was a whole nother ball of wax. "I think it's best if we stick to the direct approach."

"Well, I'll leave you ladies to your business," Glenda said, rising to her feet. "I've got to go change out of this slut costume if I'm gonna cover for Curaçao." She pointed a gold fingernail at me. "Be safe out there, sugar. You don't want to attract the wrong kind of freak."

I mustered a wan smile. "I'll be careful."

As Glenda said her goodbyes, my thoughts drifted to the masked man. But I didn't want to think about why he'd come to my house or what he wanted from me. For the time being, I had to focus on finding Curaçao. She'd been MIA for three days and counting, and with every day that passed the likelihood of solving Amber's murder decreased. If I didn't find her at Maybe's house, I wasn't sure where I was going to look—or what was going to happen with this case.

"Yo, Carnie!" I called from the front porch of Maybe's Creole cottage. "Shake a tail feather, will ya?"

"I'm painting," she replied as she powdered her nose. "A queen has to look polished, Miss Thing."

My lips curled. She'd been sitting in my Mustang preening like a peacock for the past fifteen minutes, and yet somehow I was "Miss Thing." "Listen," I began, struggling to keep my cool, "I agreed to let you tag along for Veronica's sake, but if you're going to drag me down then you can leave."

She snapped her compact shut. "You be careful how you use the word 'drag' around me, honey."

I sighed and looked at the porch ceiling. It was going to be a drag of a day.

Carnie exited the car and adjusted the train of her dress. Then she strutted up the sidewalk like the cock of the walk, and I don't mean a rooster.

I turned and knocked on the door. I smirked when I realized that it had been freshly painted haint blue—kind of like Carnie's eyelids—while the white paint on the rest of the house was peeling. According to a Southern superstition, the blue-green color was believed to keep "haints," or evil spirits, from entering a house. I wondered how that had been working out for Maybe and Curaçao.

The door opened to reveal a tipsy-looking bleached blonde in high-heeled slippers and a sheer pink robe that left nothing to the imagination. She swayed slightly and shielded her eyes from the afternoon sun with a half-empty bottle of wine. "Yeah?"

I cringed at her high-pitched voice. "Are you Maybe, uh, Baby?"

"Who's askin'?" she squeaked.

"I'm Franki Amato, a local private investigator, and this is Carnie..." I hesitated because I'd about had it with the nonsensical names. "...Vaul. We're looking for Curaçao."

"I ain't seen her for a few days." She started to close the door, but Carnie shoved it open with her huge hand.

"We're going to need a few more minutes of your time," Carnie growled.

Maybe looked so shocked that you could have knocked her over with one of Carnie's feathers. I couldn't tell whether she was surprised because Carnie had blocked the door or because she was drunk enough to have initially mistaken her for a woman.

I held up one of my business cards. "I'm investigating the murder of a dancer named Amber Brown, and I have reason to believe that Curaçao is involved and maybe—I mean, *possibly*—even in serious danger. Can we come in?"

She was silent for a moment, then she waved us into the living room with the wine bottle.

I stepped inside onto a sea of dirty clothes that covered every square inch of the floor, and I held my breath just in case I was kicking up any airborne diseases. I figured the fewer times I inhaled the better.

Carnie entered behind me and glanced from the floor to a stained white couch. "If that's your only sofa, then I'll stand."

For once I had to agree with her. "I'll make this quick," I said, mainly because I wanted to limit my breathing. "Did you know Amber Brown?"

Maybe took a swig from her bottle. "Only what I heard from Curaçao, and she hated her."

Carnie's blue-shadowed eyelids lowered. "Was this because of that client Amber supposedly stole?"

Maybe took another swallow of wine. "The rich oil guy?"

Carnie shrugged. "I don't know. Maybe."

"What?" Maybe asked.

I rolled my eyes. "No, Maybe, she meant 'perhaps.' And yes, Carnie, he's a wealthy oil baron named Shakey. Which reminds me, Maybe, do you know his last name or contact information?"

"What do I look like?" she shrilled. "A dictionary?"

While I struggled to come up with a reply, Carnie pointed to a picture frame on a shelf beside a nesting doll. "That's the woman who was harassing Amber."

I followed Carnie's finger to a picture of a platinum blonde. She was the woman I'd seen leaving the club the morning Veronica bailed me out of jail. I turned to Maybe. "Is this Curaçao?"

She nodded. "The one and only."

"What's her real name?" Carnie asked.

Maybe tried but failed to arch her eyebrow. "That *is* her real name."

I started to take a deep breath and then thought better of it. "She was asking you for her legal name."

Maybe crossed one arm, but the other fell to her side. "Well, how should I know what she goes by in court?"

Once again, it wasn't the reply I was expecting, but it was clear enough.

"And I thought you said this was gonna be quick," she protested.

"Don't get your G-string in a knot," Carnie barked, "because Lord knows you need to put it on. Now, we just need a few more minutes."

Maybe groaned and flopped onto a blue beanbag chair in a position that my mother would have described as "extremely unladylike."

Carnie put her hands on her hips. "Guuurl, I can see your seafood platter. You need to sit up straight and clamp those legs shut tight like a clam shell."

Maybe pulled her see-through robe together as though that would have solved the problem. "You sound just like my mother."

"That's because I *am* a mother," Carnie said, brushing her curls back with her hand.

My head snapped up at that announcement.

"A *drag* mother," Carnie clarified as she shot me a sideways stare.

"What's *that*?" Maybe asked, her head tipping precariously to one side.

Carnie fluffed her breast feathers. "A mentor to young drag queens."

How I pitied those poor girls.

"Well, I hope you're not as controlling as my mom." Maybe put the wine bottle close to her "seafood platter" and picked at the label. "Or Amber's."

"Amber had a mother?" Carnie and I exclaimed in unison.

"Uh-huh," she replied, her head tipping in the opposite

direction. "Curaçao heard her talking on the phone to her mom a couple of times. She said she sounded like a total control freak."

I crouched beside the beanbag. "Did she happen to catch her name or the name of a town where she might live?"

Maybe's eyes seemed to cross as she tried to focus. "She said her name was Mama."

Carnie and I exchanged a look.

"Why did Curaçao think Amber's mother was controlling?" I pressed.

Maybe's head fell backwards onto the beanbag. "She said she could tell by what Amber was saying that her mom was telling her how to get rid of Curaçao."

"Get rid of her?" Carnie echoed, moving to stand in front of Maybe.

"You know, make her go away," she explained. "But Curaçao said she wasn't going anywhere until Amber paid her back for stealing Shakey."

"How could she do that?" I asked. "With money?"

"No, Curaçao didn't want that," she replied, waving her wine. "She wanted Amber's necklace."

My pulse picked up, and I glanced at Carnie. "Did she get it?"

Maybe chugged the rest of her wine. "Beats me."

Carnie leaned over the beanbag. "What did she tell you about this necklace?"

She dropped the empty bottle onto the clothes-covered floor. Then she plucked a feather from Carnie's dress and wiped her mouth with it. "Just that Amber stole it from some drag queen with serious RBF."

Carnie's eyes narrowed to slits and her cheeks turned blood red. And with her mad Mimi makeup and Dolly Parton 'do, she looked like she'd walked right off the set of the '80s horror flick *Killer Klowns from Outer Space*.

I looked at Maybe, whose face was frozen with fear. "What's RBF?"

"Resting Bitch Face," she whisper-whined.

Well, if the "drag queen" description hadn't been enough to identify Carnie, the "RBF" certainly had.

Before Carnie could flip her wig and Maybe could flood her basement (drag for "wet herself"), I yanked Carnie out of the house and wrestled her into the car.

As I sped from the duplex, I wondered how I was going to find Amber's mother, and where I was going to look for Curaçao next. Because I'd just learned one thing for sure. Curaçao had ripped that necklace from Amber's neck the night of the murder. What I needed to confirm now was whether she'd killed her too.

10

"What is this place?" Carnie squawked from the sidewalk. "A Soviet waxing salon?"

I pulled myself from the car and winced. I'd jacked up my back trying to get Carnie into the Mustang at Maybe's house, and it wasn't the only casualty of the scuffle. Carnie's feathers were ruffled—as in the ones on her dress—and a lot of them were broken. I just hoped that none of my vertebrae were. "What are you even talking about?"

"Guuurl, look at the door," she ordered. "Vaxing for Vomen?"

"That's weird," I said as I pulled Amber's credit card bill from my bag. "I drove by here a few days ago."

Carnie plucked her compact from the feather nest between her breasts and checked her crown. "I thought we were looking for Waxing Salon."

"That's the name on the charge," I replied, glancing from the bill to the sign, "but the address is a match. I guess whoever scratched off the other half of those *W*'s also removed the business name."

"Well, let's go in and get this over with." She pulled down her wig and yanked up her dress. "But from the sound of things, I'd best look elsewhere for my waxing needs."

As I pushed open the door, I felt a rush of gratitude for whoever had altered that sign.

"What'd I tell ya?" Carnie breathed as she entered the waiting room behind me. "It looks like Little Moscow in here."

She was right. The interior was a drab gray with chunky antique furniture, and the only decorations were a portrait of Gorbachev on the wall and a hammer and sickle flag in the pencil holder on the desk. Nevertheless, I found the austere, utilitarian atmosphere to be a vast improvement over Maybe's house.

A sixty-something woman with spiky, maroon-tinted hair and the body of a matryoshka doll emerged from behind a black curtain. "You vant vax?"

My eyebrows shot up. So now I knew that the other half of those *W*'s had *not* been scratched off. "Uh, no. I'm Franki Amato," I said, handing her my business card, "and I'm investigating the murder of a young woman named Amber Brown."

She scrutinized my card like a comrade checking papers at a Communist checkpoint and then slipped it into the pocket of her smock. "Nadezhda Dmitriyeva."

The second she said her name it occurred to me that she looked like Boris from the Rocky and Bullwinkle show but sounded like Natasha. "Are you the owner of this salon?"

Nadezhda sneer-smiled revealing a missing eye tooth, making me glad I had that appointment with Dr. Lessler. "I specialize in Brazilian and Sicilian."

She caught me off guard with that revelation. I'd heard of the Brazilian, but based on what I knew about Sicilian-American women, the practice of bikini waxing was as foreign as foot-binding.

"That's good to know and all," Carnie interjected. "But like the woman said, we're here to talk to you about Amber."

Nadezhda's dark eyes bore into mine as she jerked her head in Carnie's direction. "Who is him?"

Carnie gasped and drew a hand to her bosom. "Listen, Babushka. You've got a lot of nerve throwing shade like that with your Sharon Osbourne 'do."

I held my breath as I waited for the outburst, but the hair jab rolled off Nadezhda like vodka off a Cossack's back.

She pursed her lips and clasped her hands behind her. "What means 'trow shade'?"

"To criticize," Carnie replied, smoothing her feathers. "In this case, my lady look."

Nadezhda raised a well-waxed brow and turned to me. "Amber was regular client," she announced. "For one year."

Something about her sudden proclamation made me suspect that she'd been rehearsing her answers. I decided to put her honesty to the test. "When was the last time you saw her?"

She jutted out her lower lip. "Two weeks since today."

The timeframe corresponded to the charge on the credit card bill, but it was no guarantee that she'd tell me the truth about anything else. "Amber started coming to your salon at around the same time she quit a job at Madame Moiselle's Strip Club. She supposedly wanted to quit the sex industry and 'go clean.' Did she ever mention that to you?"

Nadezhda shook her head, but she was avoiding my gaze.

"What about her financial situation?" I pressed. "Do you happen to know where she was working this past year or if someone was giving her money?"

She walked to the reception desk and began unloading supplies from a cardboard box. "Not my business."

My instincts told me that Nadezhda made everything her business, so I tried another angle. "I know that clients often confide in their estheticians. Did Amber ever seem worried about anything? Or did she mention any problems she was having?"

"She had problem with her mama," she replied, pointing a package of waxing sticks at me. "Ze woman is Nazi."

"Talk about the Commie calling the Fascist black," Carnie intoned as she pretended to admire the Gorbachev portrait.

A pain shot through my backside that I was pretty sure had nothing to do with my injury. "Can you elaborate on that, Nadezhda?"

Her dark brow furrowed. "She call too much. Every time Amber come here, zey fight on phone."

I, of all people, knew that it wasn't unusual for mothers and daughters to argue, but I found it telling that Amber's mother had made such a bad impression on at least two people, and especially on a tough woman like Nadezhda. "Do you know anything about her mother? A name or an address?"

"*Nyet.*" She pulled a tub of cream wax from the box.

I swallowed my disappointment as I pulled my pad and pen from my bag. "What kinds of things did they fight about?"

She shrugged. "Sometimes money, sometimes her man friend."

"Wait." Carnie held up her hand in a stopping motion. "You mean Amber had a boy toy?"

She put her hand on her hip. "Zat's right, darlink. What else?"

"No need to get nasty, Nadezhda," Carnie replied, fluffing her curls.

I sighed and resolved to beg Veronica to free me from the cohort cross she was making me bear. "What can you tell us about this man?"

"Nusink," she replied, resuming her unpacking.

I wondered whether that was because she didn't know

anything or because she didn't want to tell me. "Do you remember anything about Amber's demeanor during her last appointment? Like, was she happy or depressed?"

Nadezhda took a seat behind the desk. "Her mama call," she replied in a low voice. "Zey have big argument about necklace."

"What about the necklace?" Carnie asked, rising to her feet.

"Her mama did not like." She shook her index finger. "She tell her not to wear."

Carnie gasped. "My mother designed that necklace, and it was fierce."

"Your mama design pentagram?" Nadezhda's lips curled. "Not surprise."

Carnie's clown brows rose to her wigline, and my mind flashed to the stained glass pentagram at Erzulie's.

"Nadezhda," I began, trying to keep a neutral tone, "do you think there was any special significance to the pentagram? Or was it a fashion statement?"

She looked me square in the eyes. "You tell me."

The door opened, and an elderly gentleman with hairy ears entered and did a double take when he caught sight of Carnie in all her yellow-feathered splendor.

Carnie held his gaze in a seductive stare and rubbed her hands down her Big Bird belly.

I rolled my eyes and grasped the door handle. "We'll leave you to your work," I said, hoping that the man was there to get his lobes weed-whacked. "But I'll be in touch."

The minute we got outside Carnie cornered me. "What do you make of that pentagram?"

"I'm not sure," I replied, heading for the car.

But that wasn't entirely true. Because if the pentagram necklace meant what I thought it did, then this case was about to take a dark turn.

"BRADLEY!" I exclaimed as he leaned over and planted a kiss on my cheek.

"I figured I'd find you here," he said as he slid next to me in the booth at Thibodeaux's Tavern, aka my home away from home thirty steps from my front door.

I snuggled up to him. "I thought you weren't going to be back until later tonight?"

"I caught an earlier flight." He winked at Veronica who was sitting across from me and held out his hand to her boyfriend. "Bradley Hartmann."

Dirk flashed a movie-star smile. "Dirk Bogart," he said with a handshake. "You're with Pontchartrain Bank, right?"

"For the time being," Bradley replied, slipping his arm around my shoulders.

I shifted uncomfortably. I couldn't tell whether that was a casual remark or an indication that something had gone really wrong at the board meeting, but I knew that it wasn't the right time to ask, especially if I was part of his "professional problem."

"I'm not interrupting, am I?" Bradley asked as his eyes searched my face.

"Actually, we both are." I glanced apologetically at Veronica. "I saw Veronica and Dirk through the window as I was pulling into the driveway, so I decided to pop in and say hello."

Veronica looked from my empty plates to Bradley. "That was an hour ago," she observed drily. "I guess you know that Brenda and Carmela arrived last night for an unexpected visit?"

"No, but I thought I recognized that Ford Taurus parked out front," Bradley replied with a twinkle in his eye.

For reasons I could never understand, he always looked amused when the subject of my family came up, which was pretty incredible given that when he'd met them last Christmas my mom and nonna had tried to "mafia-wife" him into marrying me. At least *he* could laugh about it.

"Anyway," Veronica began, "Dirk's a gemologist, and he was telling us about the Amber Room."

Bradley cocked a brow. "The room the Nazis stole from the Russians?"

"That's the one," Dirk replied with a nod. "Although the Nazis felt that Germany never should've given it to Russia, which is why they packed it up all six tons of it in '41 and moved it to Königsberg Castle."

I stirred my Campari and soda. "If they took the room back, then where did it go?"

Dirk ran his fingers through his reddish-blond hair. "That's the question politicians, researchers, and treasure hunters have been asking since 1945. The Nazis moved the room again when the Allies began bombing Königsberg, and no one has seen it since."

Bradley turned to me. "Why are you so interested in the Amber Room?"

I averted my eyes. Since Veronica and I were under orders from Detective Sullivan not to discuss certain details of the crime scene, I couldn't let on that this was connected to my case. "I don't know." I hedged, feigning an interest in my drink straw. "It's been in the news a lot lately."

Veronica cleared her throat. "Franki, Dirk says that before the Nazis made it to Catherine Palace, the Russian curator of the room tried to take it apart to hide it, but the amber was so brittle that it started cracking and splintering, so he had it covered with fake walls instead. He catalogued 28 amber shards that had broken off various parts of the room."

I looked up from my straw and met her gaze.

"I'm assuming that more pieces broke off when the Nazis took it apart too," she added with a slight nod.

I knew what Veronica was trying to tell me—that Carnie's grandmother could very well have picked up a piece of the Amber Room.

"Just think," Dirk said with a shake of his head. "We could all retire on what one of those shards is worth today."

"But isn't amber prehistoric tree resin?" Bradley asked. "I mean, how much could that be worth?"

"The history of this amber is what makes it priceless, and I'm not only referring to the mystery," Dirk replied with a knowing look. "It was a masterpiece of eighteenth century artistry that was widely considered to be the Eighth Wonder of the World. And, in fact, experts agree that the replica of the room the Russians unveiled in 2003 doesn't hold a candle to the 1716 version. Today at auction, a tiny piece of the original room could fetch millions."

I almost coughed up my Campari. Maybe had said that Curaçao wanted the necklace as payback for Amber stealing her man, and if Curaçao had even the slightest inkling of what the pendant was worth, it could've given her more incentive to kill Amber.

Phillip, the bartender, approached Bradley. "Yo, can I get you something, bro?"

He tapped his fingers on the table. "I'll take an Abita. Jockamo IPA, if you've got it."

"Coming right up." Phillip flipped his long, dirty-blond bangs to one side and headed for the bar.

Bradley turned his attention back to Dirk. "Isn't there supposed to be a curse on anyone who searches for the Amber Room?"

I stiffened. *Why was everything coming up curses?*

"That's the rumor." Dirk smiled and raised his eyebrows. "And considering the fate of some of the people who've looked for it, it would certainly give me pause."

I scooted closer to Bradley. "Um, what do you mean 'fate'?"

"The German museum director in charge of hiding the amber died under mysterious circumstances along with his wife, and their bodies vanished," Dirk replied, peeling the label off his beer bottle. "Then a Russian general died in a car crash after consulting with a journalist about the alleged location of the room." He paused to take a drink. "But the most famous incident involved a guy named Georg Stein."

Veronica opened her eyes wide. "What happened to him?"

"He was found dead in the middle of a Bavarian forest," Dirk explained. "Naked, with his stomach slit open by a scalpel."

I jumped and bumped my head into Bradley's jaw. "Ow," I said, turning to look at him. "Sorry."

He rubbed his chin and scrutinized my face.

Phillip returned with Bradley's beer, and I was grateful for the distraction. I couldn't help but wonder whether Amber had heard about the curse and whether she blamed it for the bad things that had allegedly been happening in her life. Of course, I also wanted to know whether the curse applied to someone trying to retrieve the stolen pendant, i.e., me.

"Does amber have any special properties?" Veronica asked.

Dirk put his arm around her and pulled her close. "Historically, people believed it could suppress bleeding and cure certain mental disorders, like hysteria and hypochondria."

Veronica glanced at me and then quickly looked away.

"But these days," Dirk continued, picking up his beer bottle, "the only thing I've heard of people using it for is to treat babies' teething pain."

My tongue went to my tooth, and I wondered whether I could suck on a piece of amber rather than going to Dr. Lessler in the morning.

Now Veronica was openly staring at me, and I shot her a what-the-hell stare.

Dirk swallowed some beer. "In Russian folklore, amber was thought to be a powerful deflector of the evil eye."

This caught my interest, especially in light of Amber's superstitious side. "What else can you tell us about amber?"

Dirk thought for a moment. "Most of it comes from the Russian town of Yantarny, which was named after the word for amber, *yantar*. And there are a few popular myths about its origin. The most well known is the one about a Lithuanian queen named Jurate."

I swallowed the last of my Campari. "Never heard of her."

"Well," he said, straightening in his seat, "legend has it that she lived in an amber castle beneath the Baltic Sea. And one day, she went to punish a young fisherman named Kastytis for depleting the sea of fish, but she fell in love with him instead. The god of thunder was furious that an immortal goddess had fallen in love with a mortal man, so he struck her castle, shattering it into millions of pieces."

"What did he do to the fisherman?" Bradley asked in a wry tone.

"There are a several endings to the legend," Dirk replied. "But according to the most popular version, the thunder god killed him, and Jurate still mourns him and weeps tears of amber."

Veronica snuggled closer to Dirk. "What a beautiful love story."

"Actually, it's kind of confusing," I said, stabbing at my ice with my straw. "I thought the amber came from Jurate's shattered castle, not her tears. Plus, she's not a real queen."

Dirk shrugged. "They call her a queen, but she's basically a sea goddess."

"A sea goddess?" I sat straight up, knocking Bradley in the chin for a second time. "Ow," I said, looking back at him. "Sorry."

He narrowed his eyes and took a sip of his beer.

I turned to Dirk. "Is Jurate by any chance a mermaid?"

"Yes," he replied, giving Veronica a squeeze. "She's the queen of all mermaids."

A shiver went down my spine as I thought about the mermaid that Amber had carved into the bathtub. It seemed like a long shot that it would be connected to a Lithuanian legend, but I was convinced that her drawing had some sort of significance to the case. On a hunch, I pulled my phone from my bag and googled *Queen Jurate*.

"It's getting late," Veronica announced, exchanging a look with Dirk.

"Right," he said, practically leaping to his feet. "Pleasure to meet you both."

Bradley stood up and shook Dirk's hand, and Veronica slid from the booth and gave Bradley a hug. "Night." She looked at me. "I'll talk to you tomorrow. After your appointment with Dr. Lessler?"

"Can't wait," I muttered, staring at the screen. I wasn't trying to be rude—well, okay, maybe a little after that dentist dig—it's just that I was surprised by the search results. The first link that came up was a Wikipedia entry about the myth of Jurate and Kastytis, and the second was an article in Forbes magazine titled "Mysteries of the Amber Room." It occurred to me that if Amber had done any research on the room at all, she might very well have come across the myth. What I didn't know was what that meant in terms of the crime scene.

Bradley slid back into the booth. "I don't know what you've gotten yourself into, but promise me that you're not thinking of looking for the Amber Room."

"Do I look like a treasure hunter to you?" I asked as I typed the phrase *Goddess Jurate* into my browser search field.

"I wouldn't put it past you," he muttered.

I turned and gave him a kiss on the lips. "You know me so well."

Bradley's eyes widened. "So, you *are* looking for the Amber Room?"

"Definitely not," I said tapping a link. "But if an international shipment of Nutella goes missing, I can't make you any promises."

He laughed and finished the last of his beer while I skimmed the first paragraph of "Jurate—the Baltic Goddess of the Sea." And I only had to read down to the second sentence to find what I was looking for—the mermaid queen was a "deity of healing."

I chewed my thumbnail as I thought about the bizarre assortment of items at the crime scene and the good luck charms and talismans that Carnie had seen Amber wearing.

Bradley nudged me with his shoulder. "Is everything okay, Franki?"

"Now that you're here, everything's great," I said as I wrapped my arms around his waist and rested my head on his chest. And I meant it, too.

There was just one problem I had to work out—whether Amber's death was a witchcraft killing or a ritualistic voodoo murder.

11

———

"What are you up to today, Francesca?" my mother asked way too brightly from the opposite end of the kitchen table.

I stared at her while I chewed the enormous spoonful of Cheerios I'd just shoveled into my mouth. She'd been sitting there watching me eat my breakfast for a good five minutes before she asked the question, so I figured she could wait for me to swallow. And besides, I knew that if I answered her with my mouth full, she'd chew me out.

I washed down the cereal with a sip of orange juice. "I have an eight o'clock appointment with a dentist about my tooth. And since he's involved in a homicide case I'm investigating—"

"You're going to a homicidal dentist?" she shrilled.

The spoon slipped from my hand and fell into the bowl. "Take it easy, Mom," I exclaimed. "He was the dentist of a stripper who was murdered."

She confiscated my napkin and mopped up a wayward Cheerio from the table. "You really should be more choosy when it comes to doctors, dear."

I fished my spoon from the chocolate milk. "Are you saying that he's a bad dentist because his client was murdered?"

"It's just so morbid," she replied, frowning at my wet fingers. "And you know what your nonna would say."

"Yeah, *porta iella*," I said, using the Italian phrase for *it brings bad luck*. "So, let's not tell her, all right?" The last thing I needed was a warning from my nonna about all the tragedies that were destined to befall me when things were already spectacularly craptastic.

"Fine with me." She sat back in her chair and resumed watching me eat.

Nonna entered the kitchen in her everyday wear—a basic black mourning dress accessorized with a cross.

"*Buongiorno*," she said, dropping her purse on the table with a thud that rocked some milk from my bowl.

"Morning, Nonna." I eyeballed her bag as I wiped up the spill before my mother could do it for me. My brothers and I had been wondering what she'd been carrying in that thing since we were kids, and I was beginning to think it was an anvil.

Nonna pursed her lips and patted the cushion of one of the Bordeaux-and-gold Dauphine chairs, which was the same height as her. "So, this-a Glenda..."

My body tensed, and I shoved a bite of cereal into my mouth as I waited for the other anvil to drop.

"...she has-a good-a taste."

I inhaled in surprise, and a couple of Cheerios flew down my windpipe, causing me to start coughing up a lung.

My mother sprung into action, slapping me repeatedly on the back. "This wouldn't happen if you'd chew each bite thirty times like I taught you."

Impervious to my pulmonary plight, my nonna continued to survey the apartment. "It look-a like the noble *palazzi* of-a Sicilia in here."

I made a mental note to scratch all Sicilian palaces off my future travel itineraries—that is, if I lived to take another trip.

My mother suddenly stopped slapping. "By the way, when are we going to meet Glenda?"

"She's..." I wheezed. "...working a lot." I coughed.

"That reminds me," she continued, "I noticed that Bradley didn't stop by last night." She shot me a probing look. "Nothing has happened between the two of you, has it?"

"No, I saw him last night." As soon as I'd said the words, I wanted to smack myself upside the head with my nonna's purse.

"Mah!" Nonna jutted out her lower lip.

When my nonna uttered the Italian sound of doubt, I knew the situation was dire. "Bradley had just flown in from New York, Nonna, so I told him to go home and get some rest. He'll come over tonight."

She tapped her finger on my chest. "If he no wanna see your mamma, he's-a no gonna marry you."

I knew that I needed to do something drastic to defend Bradley, otherwise he was going to get a ruthless reception when he stopped by. So I marched into my bedroom and pulled the ruby and diamond necklace from my jewelry box. Then I returned to the kitchen and dangled it in front of my nonna's face. "Would a man who isn't going to marry me give me this?"

"Eh, *sì,*" she replied with a combination shoulder shrug and hand flip.

I put my hands on my hips, bracing myself for the speech to come. "How do you figure?"

She crossed her arms and raised her chin like Mussolini standing on his balcony. "Because it's-a not a ring. And as-a the saying go, 'why buy-a the goat when you can have-a the milk for free'?"

"It's a *cow,* Nonna. A *cow,*" I stressed as I returned to my seat at the table. It might seem pointless to insist when neither animal painted me in an attractive light, but I didn't want to be compared to a goat because they had beards—like so many women in my family.

"A cow, a goat, an *ippopotamo*." She waved me away. "It-a no make-a the difference."

"It-a make-a the difference to me," I proclaimed, especially now that she'd thrown a hippopotamus into the mix. "Why can't you understand that Bradley and I don't want to rush into something as serious as marriage?"

"Rush-a?" she cried, throwing her arms in the air. "If-a two years is a rush-a, I'd-a hate to see you take it-a slow."

"She's got a point, Francesca," my mother said, cradling her purse like the grandchild I hadn't given her as she stared sadly at her lap.

Nonna clasped her hands in a pleading gesture. "Listen to your nonna, Franki. Take-a the lemon." She reached into the fridge and pulled out a plastic bag full of the yellow fruit. "And look-a! Your mamma she buy extra for *la tavola*. She make it-a so easy."

I stood up and practically threw my cereal bowl into the sink. "Aren't you two supposed to be cooking for the poor?"

My mother let out a stoic sigh. "We're going to bake bread at Santina Messina's house. But first we need to start loading up some groceries we bought last night and take them to the church."

Desperate to get them out of the house, I said, "I'll take care of that. A guy I work with is collecting food for the event, so I can bring it to the office and have him deliver it for you."

A flicker of interest flashed in my nonna's eyes at the mention of a male. "Who is-a this-a guy-a?"

I leaned against the kitchen counter. "Don't even go there, Nonna. David's a college student, so he's too young for me."

My mother looked at her watch and rose to her feet.

"Carmela, we need to get going. I told Santina that we'd be there by seven."

"If-a you want an older man, Santina's son-a Bruno is a catch-a," my nonna said as she retrieved her purse from the table.

I knew Bruno, and a catch he was not. In fact, the guy was as big a lemon as they came. He was a forty-one-year-old food stand manager who still lived at home with his mother. Not only that, when my nonna tried to fix me up with him a couple of years ago, he'd happily suggested that I cheat on Bradley with him. In other words, he wasn't exactly the kind of guy who swept a woman off her feet—unless you counted the fact that his reckless driving put his mother in a wheelchair.

"I hear Bruno's still single," my mother added in a singsong voice.

"I'm quite sure he is," I grumbled. "Anyway, if you guys don't mind," I began, pushing both of them into the living room, "I need to get ready for my appointment."

"Well, who's stopping you, Francesca?" my mother exclaimed in an exasperated tone as though I'd been stressing *her* out for the past hour. "Now, we'll be at Santina's until dinnertime," she said, pulling her keys from her bag. "We hope to see you then so we can have a nice meal together."

If dinner went anything like breakfast, I'd rather go on a hunger strike. And that was saying a lot coming from me.

My mother opened the front door, and I remembered my encounter with the masked man the morning before.

"Wait, Mom," I said, putting a hand on her arm. "You and Nonna be careful out there."

She closed the door and narrowed her eyes like Superman activating his X-ray vision. "What in the world would prompt you to say something like that?"

"Don't get all freaked out or anything," I began, "but some-one's been following me."

Nonna's eyes lit up like a prayer candle. "*Un spasimante?*"

I sighed and looked at the ceiling. "No, not an admirer. In the United States, men who follow women are called stalkers."

"The bastard had better not mess with my daughter," my mother growled to herself as she stared at the floor.

I felt sorry for the masked man if my mom ever caught him. When you messed with her kids, she exhibited another one of Superman's powers—heat vision, i.e., the ability to shoot red-hot beams from her eyes.

"Have you called the police?" she asked, her voice danger-ously low.

I nodded.

She put her hands on her hips. "What does Bradley think of all this?"

I glanced around the room, sensing that this was some kind of trap. "He doesn't know?"

"Francesca, honestly!" My mother threw open the door. "You're never going to have a meaningful relationship with a man if you don't confide in him."

Aaaand, I was right.

Nonna tilted her head back to look up at me. "You take-a the lemon. Or you start-a getting some cats."

"Don't waste your breath, Carmela," my mother huffed. "She's not going to listen to us." She motioned for my nonna to exit and then turned to me with a forced smile. "You have a nice day, dear."

After she'd closed the door behind her, I stormed off to my bathroom to get ready. I had no idea how my having a stalker had turned into an indictment of my ability to have a relation-ship, but I shouldn't have been surprised. With my family, sooner or later every conversation turned to my *zitella*hood.

The thing that bothered me most was actually my mom's comment about me not confiding in men. I'd been keeping a lot from Bradley lately—my suspicions about Amber's killer, the business with Ruth and my reputation at the bank, and the fact that I had a masked maniac following me around town. Did this mean Veronica was right when she said that I didn't trust Bradley? Or worse, did it mean my mother was right when she implied that our relationship was doomed to fail?

As I picked up a bar of lemon verbena soap, my mind drifted to the St. Joseph's Day lemons. Then I splashed cold water on my face and scrubbed my cheeks hard.

"GIVE IT TO ME STRAIGHT, Dr. Lessler," I said, looking up at the forty-something dentist from my reclining position in the dental chair. "How bad is it?"

He pulled the mask from his face, and his full lips constricted as though he was struggling to suppress a smile. "The pain you've been feeling is because of a crack in tooth 30," he explained, pointing with a sickle probe to my lower right first molar on the X-ray image, "and you also have a cavity in tooth 31."

My stomach spasmed like it had been hit by my nonna's purse. It figured that the bum tooth would be number thirty, and I could only surmise that the cavity in thirty-one was a sign of things to come. "How could I crack my tooth?"

Dr. Lessler handed the probe to a petite blonde hygienist. "Well, unless you got hit in the mouth, the usual culprits are grinding or clenching your teeth, or chewing hard things like ice, hard candy, or nuts."

Although I'd definitely had occasion to clench my teeth lately, I blamed the salty snacks I'd been eating since giving up sweets for Lent. Desserts wouldn't have done me this way. "So, what's the plan?"

He leaned back in his stool and crossed his muscular arms across his purple and gold Louisiana State University–themed scrubs. "I can fill the cavity today, but you're going to need a crown on that cracked tooth."

As soon as he said "crown," Carnie popped into my head—and I quickly kicked her out.

"My assistant could probably work you in for a temporary crown later this week," he continued, "but you'll have to come back when we get the permanent crown from the lab."

I laid my head back on the chair and sighed. Three dental appointments in two weeks were a clear manifestation of the curse, as were my rotting and breaking teeth. "I guess the filling involves a shot, huh?"

"Don't worry." He smiled, revealing two perfect rows of teeth. "I administer a topical numbing gel first."

That was a small consolation. But I didn't have time to stress because I had a more pressing concern—getting in a few questions about Amber before the lidocaine shot. "So, I mentioned before that I'm a PI."

"Mm-hm," he said distractedly as he took a Q-tip from the hygienist.

"I'm actually working a case involving one of your clients." I watched his face for a reaction. "Amber Brown?"

If he was surprised by my announcement, he didn't show it.

"Dana," he began, turning to the hygienist, "can you give us a minute, please?"

"Of course." She hurried from the room.

"I heard what happened to Amber on the news," he said, turning to lay the Q-tip on the tray next to my chair. "It's tragic to see a life cut short so young, especially when she was getting ready to start over."

I pushed myself onto my elbows. "What do you mean 'start over'?"

"She came in last Friday, the day before she died." His bright blue eyes looked into mine. "Anyway, she said that she was planning to get an associate degree in dental hygiene."

I couldn't help but wonder whether her decision had been inspired by VIP Room visits from The Tooth Fairy. "Any idea how she was going to finance it?"

"That I don't know."

It occurred to me that Amber could've been intending to sell Carnie's necklace on the black market to cover the costs of college. On the other hand, her mom could've offered to fund her degree. "Did she ever mention a mother?"

"Not that I remember." He crossed his legs at the ankle. "But I see a lot of patients, so it's hard to keep track."

"Right," I said, glancing at my dental bib. "What was her demeanor like that last visit?"

He rubbed his chin with his thumb and index finger. "She seemed excited. You know, about going to school."

From the way Dr. Lessler spoke, it was starting to sound like Amber had been in a good place when she died. "Had she been a patient of yours for long?"

He nodded. "A couple of years give or take a few months."

I realized that he would have known Amber both while she was dancing and after she'd quit the business. "Did you notice a change in her during that time?"

"Yeah." He locked his hands behind his head. "It really seemed like she was cleaning up her act."

His comment reminded me of Amber's plan to *go clean.* "How so?"

"She used to wear some pretty risqué outfits in here," he replied with a knowing look. "But she'd toned down the dress lately, even if it was a little dark."

"Dark?" I repeated. "Like, Goth?"

"No, but the last time I saw her she was all in black, even her nail polish." He paused. "And she was wearing this strange charm."

"A pentagram?"

He shook his head. "It was silver—a diamond shape with a ball in the middle on top of an upside-down triangle. Between the two shapes there were scrolls on either side."

Dana returned to the room. "Sorry to interrupt, Dr. Lessler, but we've got quite a few patients in the waiting room."

"Back to work," he said, picking up the Q-tip. "Open, please."

I lay back on the chair. While he dabbed anesthetic on my gums, I tried to think of any questions that couldn't wait until my next appointment.

He discarded the Q-tip, and Dana handed him a syringe containing the local anesthetic. "You'll feel a slight pinch, and then your jaw and lips will start to go numb."

I nodded and opened my mouth. There was a small sting, and then a warmth spread through my jaw.

He removed a latex glove. "While we wait for the anesthetic to take effect, I'm going to pop out and see another patient."

"Before you go," I began, already noting a tingling in my lips, "why did you think Amber's charm was a symbol and not just some random design?"

He rose to his feet and ran his hand through his blondish-brown hair. "Oh. Because I asked her what it was, and she said it was a *veve*."

I looked up at him. "What's that?"

His mouth twisted into a smirk-smile. "Supposedly, it's a religious emblem that acts as a conduit for a voodoo god."

I wanted to return his sarcastic grin, but I couldn't. Not only was I losing control of my lips, I was also struggling to keep control of my nerves. In a town like New Orleans, a voodoo candle and some incense were one thing, but a voodoo conduit was quite another.

WHILE I WAS HEADING for home to let the lidocaine wear off, my "Shake Your Booty" ringtone sounded. I wasn't planning on talking because my lips felt like lead, but then I saw David's name on the display. He usually only called if he needed a work assignment or had some information for me, so I tapped answer as I pulled up to a stoplight. "Hello?"

"Hey, Franki," David boomed into the receiver. "I finished that Etsy research, and Veronica told me to ask if there's anything you need me to do today."

Now that I'd finally questioned Dr. Lessler, the most pressing item of business on my agenda was finding Amber's mother. "I nee you oo look hor Ammmer's odder."

There was a moment of silence on the other end of the line.

"Uh, you need me to look for a whore and an udder," he repeated.

"No," I wailed, both because he was wrong and because I flashed back to Glenda and Bit-O-Honey's boobs bobbling over me. "I'll teksh you."

"Riiight." He paused. "You do that."

I was pretty sure that he hadn't understood me, but I figured he could just wait for my text. What I needed to know was what he had for me from Etsy about Amber's purchase. "Ut do you ha hor e?"

"Are you, like, speaking Italian?" he asked in a bewildered tone.

I slammed the back of my head into the headrest. Although the kid did have a point—I was using an awful lot of vowels. "No, Eshee."

"Yeah, so I'm good with programming languages, but foreign ones? Not so much. Anyway, this lady at Etsy emailed me a picture of what Amber bought. It's a necklace."

Given the significance of all the necklaces in this case, I was eager to get a look at that picture. "I nee duh icshure."

"Uh-huh," he said, clearly oblivious. "I forwarded the email to you, so, um... later."

"Anks." The light turned green, and I took the first right into the parking lot of Tulane University so that I could check my email. When I finally found the message and opened the picture, I gasped.

It was an exact replica of Carnie's amber necklace.

12

———

"It's Now or Never," I muttered, quoting The King as I climbed from my Mustang. It was ten thirty, and I'd been parked in front of my house for the past hour, dreading going inside. When I'd returned home from the dentist, there was no sign of the Taurus, but I found a flock of FIATs parked in and around the driveway. I knew instantly that my nonna had invited her friends over—after all, the FIAT was the Pope's preferred ride. So in the interests of self-preservation, I'd stayed in the car until the lidocaine wore off, because when dealing with a gaggle of Sicilian nonne it was imperative that you be able to speak.

As I strode up the walkway, my apartment door flew open, and Glenda darted outside like a prostitute fleeing a police raid.

"What were *you* doing in there?" I asked, not without a note of panic. I'd intended to introduce Glenda to my family gradually—you know, like when you add fresh pasta to a pot of boiling water.

She dragged off her cigarette holder like it was a lifeline. "I came here looking for you," she replied, exhaling smoke as she spoke. "But before I knew what'd hit me, the Lilliputians had tied me up in this straitjacket."

The "Lilliputians" were, of course, my nonna and her nonne friends, none of whom were over five feet in height. And the so-called "straitjacket" was an Italian-flag-colored bib apron that read, "If you like my meatballs, wait till you try my sausage." Obviously, the nonne had used it to cover Glenda's nudity but hadn't grasped the double entendre. "Sorry about that. I was getting a cavity filled at Dr. Lessler's office."

Her brow shot up and her hip jutted out. "*Mitchell* Lessler?"

I nodded and rubbed my jaw.

A sultry smile spread across her face. "That handsome hunk of man can fill my cavity anytime."

"Forget about Lessler," I said, because now I really wanted her to. "What are the Lilliputians doing in there?"

"At first I thought they were having a funeral, sugar, but they said that Miss Santina's oven broke." Glenda yanked at the halter of her apron as though it were a noose around her neck. "So your nonna brought everyone over here since there are three ovens."

The funeral part I could understand since the nonne were perpetually in mourning dress, but it took me a second to register what she'd meant by "three ovens." Then I figured it out —mine, Veronica's, and... "They're baking in *your* kitchen *too*?"

She took another deep drag off her cigarette. "They've invaded the entire fourplex, Miss Franki."

My jaw dropped, and I covered my mouth with my hands.

"Even your costume closet?" I whispered, referring to the forbidden fourth apartment, the sole purpose of which was to house Glenda's prized collection of stripper wear.

She shook her head. "I convinced them that the kitchen was out of commission."

"*Grazie a Dio,*" I breathed. Letting the nonne go inside Glenda's costume closet would've been like sending Santa's Elves to an S&M dungeon. "Where are my mom and nonna?"

"They took an extra bag of lemons to the church." She flicked some ash from her cigarette. "Do they serve lemonade at this St. Joseph's Day soiree?"

"Something like that," I replied, my tone as acidic as the yellow fruit.

The door to my apartment flew open again, and this time Santina Messina, Bruno's mom, appeared in the threshold. "Francesca!" she cried, clasping her hands. "*Figlia mia!*"

I was surprised to see her out of the wheelchair, but there was no time to comment. Instead, I assumed the customary limp position as she pinched my cheeks and smashed my face into her ample bosom, cutting off my air supply and cramming her cross necklace into my forehead. Thanks to the suffocating embraces of Santina and others like her, when I was a kid I not only frequently bore the sign of the cross on my skin, but I could hold my breath longer than anyone in my elementary school.

When she finally released me, I was excited to find that I could've held out another thirty seconds. I might be thirty, but I still had the lungs of a child.

"*Venite, venite,*" Santina urged, gesturing for us to follow her.

Glenda stubbed out her cigarette, and we went inside.

Thanks to a slew of twenty-five-pound flour sacks, endless crates of eggs, and a squad of not-so-lean but definitely mean nonne, my apartment looked and smelled more like an old world Sicilian bakery than a seventies brothel. I was kind of excited about the transformation, even though I was disappointed to see that the only thing the nonne were baking was bread.

Santina led us to the kitchen, and while I greeted the other nonne, she began filling the table with food—*grissini*, bread, an antipasti plate, *lasagne*, sardines, veal cutlets, eggplant, bell peppers, and a bottle of Nero d'Avola.

Meanwhile, Napoleon, who'd grown quite fond of the nonne and their food, assumed his begging spot beside the table.

"*Mangia!*" she exclaimed, shoving Glenda into a seat.

Glenda, who'd never been seen eating, grabbed a *grissino* and held the pencil-sized breadstick like she did her cigarette holder.

I, on the other hand, dug in with gusto, glad that my mouth was fully functional. And as I popped a piece of prosciutto into my mouth, it occurred to me that besides the food, the best things about nonne were that they called you "my child" regardless of your age, they thought you were wasting away no matter what your size, and they let you drink wine with pretty much every meal.

Santina pulled a bag of Swamp Nuts from her apron pocket and pressed it into my hand, beaming as though the Cajun-flavored corn nuts were nuggets of gold. "*Da Bruno.*"

I forced a smile at Bruno's untimely concession-stand gift.

"Pass me those nuts, sugar," Glenda said, showing a rare interest in an edible item. "Maybe if I have a few of these, Mitchell Lessler can do some drilling on me."

I rolled my eyes and, since we were in the presence of the nonne, tried to steer the topic away from sex. "How do you know Lessler, anyway?"

Glenda picked up the bag and began fondling it like a sex toy. "In the stripping business, we share doctors like we do body oil."

A rolling pin clattered to the floor as the nonne stopped baking and began furiously crossing themselves.

So much for a sex-free conversation.

"Was Mitchell able to tell you anything about Amber?" Glenda continued, contemplating the corn nuts.

I glanced at the nonne and leaned forward. "It seemed like

he thought that Amber was into voodoo, but her waxer implied that it was witchcraft," I replied in a low voice. "What I don't get is why Amber would need to resort to either one of those things if she was a tough, no-nonsense feminist like Saddle and Bit-O-Honey say."

"New Orleans has a long history of exotic dancing and an even longer history of mysticism and black magic, Miss Franki," Glenda explained as Santina deposited an empty plate in front of her and pointed at the food.

She locked eyes with Santina as she grabbed the *grissino* again, this time brandishing it like a bat, and then she turned to me. "I've seen girls come from as far away as Slovakia to dance here, and sooner or later they all do some kind of ritual before going onstage. And most of them will tell you that they don't do the ritual in any other city."

"A ritual I can understand," I said, pouring myself a glass of wine. "For example, I always put my clothes on in the same order."

"I'm not talking about OCD." She pointed the grissino at me. "I mean an honest to goodness ritual. I know this dancer from L.A. who buys an altar candle to gods and goddesses like Chango Macho or Oshun every time she comes here to help manifest her intention."

When she said "Chango," my mind drifted to Changos Taqueria in Austin. "I'm sorry," I said, shaking myself from my Tex-Mex trance, "but did you say 'manifest her intention'?"

"Stripping is all about bringing attitude, money, and intent, sugar, and strip clubs are dark places. To be successful, you have to bring light into the club. So a dancer may do a candle ceremony, anoint herself with oil, carry a gris-gris bag, chant a spell, or whatever else to set her intent for luck, money, or beauty."

I slipped Napoleon a slice of *soppressata*. "But some of those things are voodoo, and some are witchcraft."

Glenda hiked up her apron and crossed her glittered legs, provoking a "*Santo Dio!*," a "*Gesù mio!*," and an "*Oh, Signore!*" from the nonne.

"It's a matter of preference," she explained, immune to their exclamations. "But what it boils down to is this—there's a belief in the industry, and in the city at large, that the spirit of New Orleans has to bless you if you want to be here and do well."

"*Now* you tell me." I grabbed my wine and wondered if that was where I'd gone wrong on the curse front. "Do you think that's what Amber was doing in the bathtub?"

"It doesn't square up to me," Glenda replied, flipping back her hair. "She wasn't dancing anymore—at least not for strip-club patrons."

I looked up from my glass. "What do you mean by that?"

She shrugged and tugged at her bib. "Maybe she danced for the devil."

I gasped. "As in satanic worship?"

There was a clatter of bread pans as several of the nonne dropped to their knees and invoked the assistance of the Madonna.

"Just kidding," I announced, my face as red as the wine.

Glenda eyed the nonne over her shoulder as though *they* were devil worshippers. "All I meant was that maybe Amber crossed paths with a plain old psychopath."

I sat back and sipped my wine. After talking to Dr. Lessler and Glenda, I was more confused than ever about what had gone on inside Madame Moiselle's. What I needed was some clarity. "Can you do something for me?"

"Shoot, sugar," she replied, waving her *grissino* like a wand.

"Go to the club and talk to Saddle and Bit-O-Honey," I said, reaching into my purse for my wallet. "I want to know whether they ever saw or heard Amber doing any rituals, and what rituals the other dancers at the club do. Also, find out whether anyone has heard from Curaçao."

"Consider it done," she said, bouncing her crossed leg. "Where are you off to this fine morning?"

I pulled a business card from my coin purse. "I'm going to track down a warped witch."

"Was it necessary to meet in a graveyard?" I asked as I followed Theodora through St. Louis Cemetery No. 1, New Orleans's oldest burial ground and the final resting place for some of its most famous and infamous citizens. Between the creepy crypts and her black caftan, I was getting a bad case of the heebie-jeebies. "There's a CC's Coffee nearby, you know."

Her lips twisted like an old tree root. "I don't drink coffee. Besides, I have friends to see."

I started to tell her that as a three-hundred-year-old woman she might benefit from the energy boost, but I was too fearful of those "friends" she'd mentioned. "They're not coming to meet you now, are they?"

"They don't have to." She stopped in front of a crumbling gray mausoleum dated 1792 and patted the façade as though greeting an old pal. "They're already here."

A shiver shot through my spine like a spell from a sorceress's finger. As usual, this witch was weirding me out, and somehow it didn't help that she'd covered her crazy cat eyes with cat-eye sunglasses.

Theodora gave the ghoulish grave one last caress and resumed walking, her caftan billowing behind her like a shroud. "Why'd you summon me?"

I pulled the collar of my pea coat around my neck and stepped carefully along the cracked and broken concrete walkway. "I'm investigating a murder, and I need to know whether witches and voodoo practitioners ever borrow each other's methods."

She stopped dead in her tomb tracks. "Not on your life."

Like my nonna taught me, I pointed my index and pinky fingers down to cancel the curse she'd cast my way.

She cackled Maleficent-style. "What was that little gesture?"

I blinked, wishing that she hadn't seen my hand. According to Italian custom, there was an alternative to the gesture—men could tap one of their testicles, and women could touch iron. But that presented a problem for those of us who didn't know our metals. "It's called *scongiuri*."

"It's novices like you who mix witchcraft, voodoo, and hoodoo," she said, pointing at my forehead. "Around here they call that Old New Orleans Traditional Witchcraft."

I lowered myself a little—on the off chance that she could actually shoot spells from her fingertip. "Is that jazz-inspired or something?"

She sighed, and I would swear that I saw a puff of smoke come out. "It's the everyday kind of witchcraft that your great-great grandmother used to do, but with a touch of voodoo or hoodoo thrown in."

I was a little taken aback by her assumption that my *bis-bis-nonna* was a witch. But if my nonna was any indication, Theodora may have been onto something. "Can you elaborate on that?"

"It's just goal-oriented spell-casting."

"Oh, *goal-oriented*," I stressed in an it-was-as-obvious-as-the-wart-on-your-face tone. "As opposed to your regular, slacker spell-casting?"

She glanced over her shoulder, and for a split second it looked like her green eyes glowed behind her sunglass lenses. "It's the kind of spell work you do if you want something, like a job or a mate, but you need a little help to make it happen. It used to consist mainly of traditional supplies, but these days you can get more specialized items at Erzulie's and at Hex Old World Witchery down on Decatur."

Decatur Street was where Private Chicks was located, and as you can imagine, I wasn't wild about the news of the witchery.

"Look at the voodoo queen Marie Laveau's grave, and you'll see what I mean." She led me to an old, Greek Revival–style tomb covered with large x's.

I gasped. The marks were like the ones in Lili St. Cyr's bathtub—some were even circled. "What are those X's?"

"Years ago some fool started the rumor that if you want Marie Laveau to grant your wish, you have to draw an X on the tomb, turn around three times, knock on the tomb, and then shout your wish. If it's granted, you have to come back and draw a circle around your X and leave Marie a gift, like these," she said, leading me to the front of the crypt.

I looked down, and amidst lipstick tubes, Mardi Gras beads, coins, and various trinkets was a boa constrictor. "Sweet Jesus!" I shouted, jumping back. "Is that snake alive?"

"Shhht!" Her black arms flapped like the wings of a raven. "You'll wake the dead."

Like a psycho, I glanced around in case that was really a thing.

"It's clearly an animal sacrifice," Theodora said as though she were schooling a slow sorcery student. "Now, you can see from the burnt candles and incense that witchcraft was involved, but so was voodoo."

I looked again at the X's. "Have you ever heard of a mermaid queen named Jurate or any mermaids in the voodoo culture?"

She straightened her caftan collar. "I keep my distance from water women. They're a bitchy bunch."

I wanted to tell her that it takes one to know one, but I held my tongue for fear that she would take it and use it for some macabre magic. "What about amber?" I asked, opting to keep the necklace and its copy quiet. "Is it used in any spells?"

"All kinds," she replied, proceeding with her cemetery stroll. "For luck, love, protection, purification, prosperity, sexual energy, healing."

My ears pricked up at that last word because Dirk had said that Jurate was the deity of healing. Had Amber actually been invoking the mermaid queen? If so, what did she need to heal from? The possibilities were endless, not to mention obscure.

Theodora stopped in front of another mausoleum with a cracked, copper plate that read *Madame Lalaurie, née Marie Delphine Maccarthy, décédée à Paris, le 7 Décembre, 1842, à l'âge de 6—*.

I could make out enough of the French to know that it was the burial site of Delphine Lalaurie, a nineteenth-century socialite and sadistic serial killer of slaves. Despite being dead for over a century and a half, Lalaurie was still one of the most notorious killers in history—so much so that the TV series *American Horror Story* had created a fictionalized version of her for its "Coven" season.

Theodora dropped to her knees. "Madame Lalaurie, may I collect dirt from your grave?"

I didn't know what she was going to do with the dirt, but I took a step backwards nevertheless. It was wise to be wary of this witch.

She cocked her orange-red head to the side and nodded as though Lalaurie were speaking to her from beyond. Next, she pulled a spoon and a small wooden box from her pocket and began digging dirt from a crack in the concrete at the base of the tomb.

The dirt reminded me of Glenda's comment about the glass vial I'd found at Madame Moiselle's. I pulled the plastic baggie containing the vial from my purse. "Is this part of New Orleans witchcraft?"

Theodora opened the baggie and sniffed it. "Smells like a mugwort and dragon's blood blend I use in my spell work. Where'd you find it?"

I hesitated for a moment, remembering Detective Sullivan's request for discretion on the specifics of the case. But I seriously doubted that this witch was a snitch, and I hadn't used Amber's name, so I decided to give her some vague details. "Next to the crime scene. There was also a candle, some incense, and an unopened bottle of liquor."

"It could be a spell, except for the booze. That's a voodoo offering to some loa or other. I never can keep those damn gods straight." She returned to her digging. "And I can't understand why people leave food and drink for them. It's such a waste."

My sentiments exactly.

She put a spoonful of dirt into the box. "Where was the oil used?"

"Uh, in bath water," I replied evasively.

"Well, why didn't you say so?" she asked snapping the lid shut.

Before I could reply, she held out her hand to silence me. I watched as she dropped a dime in the hole and covered it with the remaining dirt.

"As I have paid you in silver, Madame Lalaurie, so shall you pay me in labor!" she shouted, staring at the crypt like she was spellbound.

At this point, I was *scongiuri*-ing left and right. I didn't know what this labor was that Lalaurie was supposed to do for her, but I hoped that she either couldn't or wouldn't do it right then.

"So anyway," Theodora said as she stood up and brushed off her caftan like she'd been gardening instead of grave digging, "your victim was probably doing some good old-fashioned bathtub witchcraft."

"*Bathtub* witchcraft?" I echoed. "Whatever happened to the cauldron? You know, 'double, double toil and trouble' and all of that?"

She lowered her sunglasses and laid her eerie irises on me. "You've been reading too much Shakespeare."

Honestly, I'd thought that the rhyme was from a Disney film, but I just went with it. "Do you have any idea whether that was a healing spell the victim was doing?"

"Nah." She walked toward another tomb. "That would've involved a lavender and vetiver blend. Based on the oil in that vial, it was most likely an anti-hex spell."

I looked up in surprise. It didn't make sense for Amber to invoke Jurate for healing if what she was after had to do with hexes. "So, does this spell ward off the evil eye?"

"It undoes a curse that someone has already placed on you. And if your victim bought the spell, then he or she was definitely fighting witchcraft with witchcraft." She stopped to scowl at a pyramid-shaped tomb covered in lipstick prints with the Latin inscription *omnia ab uno*, all from one.

I recognized the kissed crypt from the local news as the one the actor Nicolas Cage had bought for his eventual demise. Suddenly, I longed for a shot. "But how does the bottle of booze fit in?"

"Like I said, Old New Orleans Traditional Witchcraft is often a mix." She plucked a weed from the exposed bricks of a deteriorate mausoleum and popped it into her mouth. "Your victim could've included a voodoo offering for good measure, or the killer might have put it there to throw you off track. But either way, you need to start by finding the witch who put the spell on your victim."

My stomach bubbled like a cauldron at the sight of her chewing that weed. "And how, exactly, does one find a witch?"

She turned and headed toward the exit. "One looks for the signs."

"Like, a third nipple?" I asked hopefully. I mean, that wouldn't be hard to spot given the nature of this case.

She spun around and removed her sunglasses as her feline eyes flashed.

I flinched, halfway expecting her to turn me into a big boob.

"I was talking about a pagan tattoo or jewelry," she said between clenched teeth. "Like a triangle or a moon or a goddess."

My blood ran as cold as a witch's teat. All this time I'd been focusing on Curaçao as the possible killer. But now I was wondering whether I'd made a potentially costly mistake. Because I'd seen someone at the club with a crescent moon tattoo.

And that someone was Saddle.

13

———

When I walked into Lucky Pierre's, a Bourbon Street gay bar as famous for its 3-for-1 happy hours as it was for its drag and burlesque shows, the old wooden door groaned in protest.

"Can't you read the *closed* sign, Hunty?" a Lucy Liu lookalike shouted from behind the bar.

"Mind your manners, Miss Gaysia," Glenda said as she stood up from her stool in black thigh-high boots and a belted cutout romper that was more cut than not. "Miss Franki's with me."

"What's a 'hunty'?" I whispered, hiding my mouth with my hand.

"A combination of honey and the *C* word," she replied and then turned to the bitchy bar queen. "She'll have what I'm having."

Gaysia gave me a glacial glare and grabbed a glass.

Ignoring the drag diva's dis, I tossed my bag onto the transparent, liquid-filled bar counter and spotted a holster on Glenda's thigh. "What are you dressed as, anyway? A frisky FBI agent?"

She looked at me like I'd pulled a gun on her. "This is my private-investigating suit."

If anything, she looked more like a slutty spy than a private eye. "You're not actually packing heat, are you?"

"I'm just using this holster to hold my PI supplies," she replied, returning to her seat.

Prudently passing on asking about those supplies, I took a quick look around instead. Lucky Pierre's had once been a brothel, and it showed. The two-story structure had a wide stair-case that appeared custom-made for grand entrances, and it was decorated with sensual chandeliers, gilded crown moldings, sumptuous sofas, and a rainbow-shaped *Sinners* sign that served as a nod to the bar's *sexplicit* past and present. Thanks to the décor of my apartment, I felt instantly at home there.

Glenda scrutinized my face as she handed me the champagne. "You look like you've seen a ghost, sugar."

I took a sip and slid onto the stool beside her. "No, just a witch."

She didn't bat a feather false eyelash at my reply. "How'd you know where to find me?"

"I stopped by the club looking for Saddle, and Bit-O-Honey said you'd come here to talk to Carnie." I scanned the room and spotted a Céline Dion doppelganger at a table in front of the stage. "Where is she, anyway?"

"She'll be down in a minute." Glenda motioned to Gaysia for another glass of champagne. "She's getting ready to perform."

It was only one o'clock, and Lucky Pierre's didn't open until four. "It takes her three hours to get ready?" I asked. Then I remembered Carnie's fearsome five o'clock shadow. "Never mind. Are you here to talk to her about the case?"

"About arranging a funeral for Amber," she replied as she reached for her cigarette holder and lighter. "We entertainers take care of our own."

"Well, a few of the witnesses have said that Amber had a mother." I angled a glance at Gaysia expecting her to go off about the *no smoking* sign above the bar. "You might want to find out what her plans are."

"This is the first I've heard of any mother." She lit her cigarette and exhaled. "It seems odd that she hasn't come up before."

I had to agree. And it was even odder that she hadn't come forward despite considerable publicity about the case. "What'd you find out about the dancers' rituals?"

"So far I've only talked to the girls on the early shift," she replied as she adjusted a gadget on her belt. "Bit-O-Honey said that Amber used to light a candle before dancing, but that's all she remembers."

This was big news. If Amber had been into lighting candles, then doing a spell wasn't out of the realm of possibility. "What about the others?"

"The usual things," she said with a shrug. "Anointing themselves with oil, rubbing a dildo, carrying a lucky condom."

I had some questions about that condom, but it was better not to ask. My stomach was already queasy from the lava-lamp-like counter.

"Hello my lovelies," a falsetto voice crooned from the second floor. "And Franki," it added in a low, flat pitch.

I smirked and looked up as Carnie sashayed down the staircase like a coquette at cotillion. Only, with her Mimi makeup, wig cap, and the lifelike latex breastplate strapped around her neck, she looked more like the Bride of Frankenstein.

Glenda raised her glass. "Ladies and lady-boys, Miss Carnie Vaul."

Carnie sauntered over and placed a manicured hand on her faux flesh. "Do you have an update on the case?"

Her boobie-bib was more embarrassing than Bit-O-Honey's

bare bosom, so I was glad to have an excuse to turn away. "Gaysia, can you give us a minute?"

She gasped and stomped over to Céline, who was contouring her nose.

I started to lean in, but because of the boobs—live and latex—I opted to lower my voice instead. "After consulting with a local witchcraft expert, I think Amber was doing an anti-hex spell when she died." I shifted in my seat before asking the next question, realizing how silly it would sound. "Can either of you think of anyone who would've put a hex on her?"

"Curaçao, of course," Carnie said, putting her hands on her hoopskirt-sized hips. "I don't know if she was a witch *witch*, but she was definitely a witch *bitch*."

"Thanks for clearing that up," I said, shooting her a sideways glance. "I'll follow up on the witchcraft angle with Maybe."

"What about that Etsy charge?" Carnie asked. "Did you follow up on that?"

I tossed back the rest of my champagne. "It turned out to be for a copy of your amber necklace."

"That shady ho," she breathed. Then she stormed behind the bar and helped herself to a shot.

Glenda leaned back on her stool and kicked her lipstick-heeled boots onto the counter. "I'll bet Amber planned to swap the copy with the original."

"That's what I'm thinking," I said. "But I should notify the police in case there's more to it than that."

Carnie lurched forward, causing her bib to bounce. "So you're going to turn me in for opening her credit card bill?"

"Down, woman," I said, holding up my hands in case she hopped the bar. "I don't have to reveal my sources."

Her blue-shadowed lids lowered to half-mast à la Herman Munster. "You'd better hope you don't."

Unfazed by Carnie's behavior, Glenda blew a couple of

smoke hearts. "What makes you think this copy is relevant, Miss Franki?"

"Until we know where it is, I won't know whether it's relevant or not. What I need to figure out is whether the necklace is related to that mermaid on the tub." I turned to Carnie. "That reminds me, is there any chance that Amber was Lithuanian?"

"She was as Cajun as they come," she replied as she poured herself some Piehole whiskey. "Why?"

I put my forearms on the bar. "There was a drawing of a mermaid at the crime scene, and amber is associated with the legend of a mermaid who promotes healing."

"Amber wasn't sick or broken, okay?" Carnie said, pointing the bottle of whiskey at me. "Now I don't know why that mermaid was there, but we need to be clear on something—it didn't have a damn thing to do with fixing Amber."

I eyed the Piehole and wished that Carnie would shut hers.

"What about your necklace?" Glenda asked as she stubbed out her cigarette in the dregs of her drink. "Why do you think she was wearing it?"

Carnie slammed the bottle onto the bar. "Maybe she liked it, I don't know. But I can tell you this—she stole it because she wanted to sell it, not because she wanted to invoke some mermaid. That girl was about money and whatever it took to get it. End of story."

My sense was that she was right about the reason Amber stole the necklace. But because Theodora had confirmed that amber was used in witchcraft, I had to consider all the possible angles.

The door groaned, and a Dolly Parton drag queen in an Elly May Clampett costume flounced into the bar. She took a seat next to Glenda and tossed a roll of Tuck Tape into Carnie's outstretched hand.

Carnie gave her the once over. "Pure country realness."

"Well, you know what I always say," Drag Dolly said as chipper as a chipmunk as she fluffed her breasts. "It costs a lot of money to look this cheap."

"Truth, gurl." Carnie turned and eyeballed my ten-dollar Target turtleneck. "Speaking of cheap, if you don't have anything else for me, then I need to finish painting."

"By all means," I said. And I meant it.

Carnie placed her whiskey on the bar and exchanged air kisses with Glenda.

I glanced at the amber liquid, and a thought occurred to me. "You guys—I mean, ladies—wouldn't happen to know of a voodoo god that drinks amaretto, would you?"

"Oh, I would," Dolly replied, tightening the bow in her wig. "The patron of gays and trans just loves amaretto, but her favorite is pink champagne."

"Now that's a voodoo goddess I can get behind," Glenda said before tossing back the last of her bubbly. "Which loa is this, sugar?"

Dolly toyed with the frayed ends of her rope belt. "Erzulie Freda."

As soon as she said the name, I thought of the painting at Erzulie's Authentic Voodoo. The sales woman had said that Erzulie Freda was the goddess of love, among other things. But it didn't make sense to invoke a love loa during an anti-hex spell. And yet I knew that's what had happened because the bottle said it all.

Amaretto di Amore.

As I made my way up Canal Street to Pontchartrain Bank, I was met by an army of women in bodysuits, tights, and legwarmers. It was a terrifying sight, like an invasion of the '80s, but I forged through the fit females like a tank. All the talk about the goddess of love had made me want to see Bradley, and the fact that the goddess liked to drink had reminded me that I needed to invite him over to see my mom and nonna. If he didn't come there would be hell to pay, and my nonna would make sure that I was the one who paid it.

When I finally made it inside the bank lobby, I could see that Ruth was worked up about something. My first clue was the pursed look on her perpetually puckered mouth. The second was that the chains hanging from the sides of her black horn-rimmed reading glasses were swinging like swords at a fencing fight.

I eyed Bradley's closed door as I approached Ruth's desk. "Is everything okay?"

She tightened her gray-brown bun. "I've just been informed that I need to make last-minute travel arrangements for twelve board members—and during a national Jazzercise convention, no less."

That explained the warrior-like workout women.

"And I'll tell you what," Ruth said, pointing a letter opener at my gut. "If one more person comes in here and shakes their jazz hands at me, I'm gonna up and stab someone."

Given that I was ethnically inclined to gesture when I spoke, I took a step back. "Wait. Bradley just met with the board in New York. Why are they coming here?"

She bowed her head. "The bank lost two more big clients yesterday, and a third is threatening to follow suit. If I were a betting woman—which I'm not," she clarified with a flourish of her letter opener, "I'd wager that a certain bank manager named Jeff Payne was behind this business."

I happened to know that Ruth never missed Saturday night bingo at the Napoleon Room in Metairie and that she practically had a lifetime subscription to the Louisiana Lottery, but she called that "gaming," not "gambling," and I didn't dare disagree. "Why do you say that? Did you trace Jeff's restaurant receipt to Martin Slater?"

She put her hands on her thighs and jutted out her lower lip. "Mr. Slater's secretary confirmed that he had lunch with Jeff at Casamento's."

I was at a loss for words.

She grimaced, and the lines around her lips bled into her cheeks. "And that's not the worst of it."

I found my words. "Well, what is?"

"A few of the board members have been calling the clients who've abandoned ship." She paused and glanced around to make sure that no one was listening. "And apparently, every one of them has received the same anonymous letter."

I put my hand to my mouth. Anonymous letters abounded in the Sicilian culture, and they inevitably involved *le corna*, or bull horns, which were a symbol of infidelity in Italy. "What does it say?"

"No idea." She grabbed a peppermint from a candy dish and popped it into her mouth. "But that's still not the worst of it."

This time I took a step forward. "Would you just tell me what the worst of it is?" I asked through gritted teeth. "Or do I need to show *you* the worst of it?"

"Now don't go gettin' all pissy on me, missy." She sat back and raised her nose in the air. "I'm the one who's been trying to save your beau's behind while you've been out toodlin' around in a titty bar."

I clenched my fists one finger at a time. "How many times do I have to tell you that I'm working a homicide at Madame Moiselle's?"

"It's none of my never mind what a woman like yourself is doing in a gentlemen's club." She looked from side to side again and leaned forward. "But you should know that the anonymous mailer, aka Mr. Payne In The Rear, has also been sending out compromising photographs with that letter."

My mouth went as dry as her demeanor. "What do you mean by 'compromising'?"

Ruth threw her hands in the air. "Well, if I don't know what's in the letter, then I don't know what's in the photos, do I?" She arched an over-tweezed eyebrow and moved so close that I could smell her minty fresh breath. "But evidently they have something to do with Bradley."

"Bradley?" I shouted, wondering whether the type of compromising we were talking about was the *corna* kind. "What makes you think that?"

"Because the board is convening on Monday to discuss his future with the bank," she replied with a know-it-all nod. "That's what."

The news hit me like a pair of bull horns. If Bradley lost his job over a scandal, he'd have to leave New Orleans to find another bank position. On the other hand, depending on what was in those photographs, I might run him out of town myself.

Bradley walked out of his office, and I noticed that his face was drawn and pale. "Hey, babe," he said, sounding tired. "I thought I heard your voice."

I shook myself from my shock and forced a fake smile. I couldn't let him know that I knew the scoop. "You were right," I said as jolly as Drag Dolly at a square dance. "I'm here."

He pulled me into an embrace, and part of me wanted to hug him to make everything all better, but the other half of me wanted to hit him—just in case.

In the meantime, I locked eyes with Ruth over his shoulder. *"Get me that letter and those pics,"* I mouthed. *"ASAP."*

Bradley released me and brushed a lock of hair from my cheek. "You seem stressed. What's going on?"

I resisted the urge to reply, "That's the sixty-four-thousand-dollar question, isn't it?" Instead, I said, "It's Mom and Nonna. They're expecting you to drop by tonight, and you know they'll be offended if you don't."

"Of course." He ran his hand through his hair and glanced at his watch. "I have to take care of some things here first. Would eight be too late?"

"Not at all," I said, sickly sweet. Then I scoured his face for clues to the content of those photos.

Bradley narrowed his eyes, obviously suspecting that something was up. "Franki—"

My ringtone sounded.

"I'd better take this," I gushed, pulling my phone from my bag.

"Okay, but we need to talk later." He gave me a peck on the lips. "Right now I've gotta get moving if I'm going to make it to your place on time."

"See you tonight," I said, wondering just what it was that we had to talk about. Then I glanced at the unknown number on the cell display and pressed answer. "Franki Amato."

"Is this Franki Amato?" a female asked.

I rolled my eyes. "That's what I just said."

"This is Bit?" she said in an up-talker tone. "From Madame Moiselle's?"

"Oh, right," I replied, realizing for the first time that she was using "O'Honey" as a surname. "What can I do for you?"

"Miss Glenda said that you're to get down here right away," she said, her voice descending like a dancer down a pole.

Apprehension filled my chest. "Can you tell me why?"

"Because we have a situation," she replied, matter-of-fact.

For some reason I got a sudden mental image of her boobs bobbing about and was instantly irked. "What kind of situation?"

She cleared her throat. "A few minutes ago I asked Iris to pull the honey pot from the storage room for my performance today."

I waited for her to explain the "situation," but apparently, she thought she already had. "And?"

"It wasn't full of honey!"

I sighed. Getting information out of Bit-O-Honey was like pulling pasties from a stripper. "What was it full of?"

"Curaçao."

My heart took a nosedive. I felt bad for suspecting her, and now I had to face the frightening possibility that there were more murders to come.

"Um," Bit-O-Honey hedged, breaking the silence, "you know I'm not talking about the liquor, right?"

"Yeah, I gathered that," I grumbled as I headed for the lobby exit.

"Good," she said sounding pleased as punch. "Because that pot wasn't made to hold real honey or liquid. But anyway, Miss Glenda said that I was to tell you one more thing."

I waited, but she said nothing. "And what would that be, exactly?"

"Curaçao is wearing an amber necklace."

My stomach joined my heart in a tandem free fall. "I'll be right there."

I hung up and hurried onto Canal Street. As I jogged through the Jazzercisers, I wasn't worried about whether Curaçao was wearing the original necklace or the copy, nor was I thinking about witchcraft or voodoo. Because all I could think about was the curse that supposedly followed those who hunted the Amber Room.

Was the curse what had done Amber and Curaçao in?

14

"The cops are going to have to break the pot to get Curaçao out," Glenda said as I entered the prop room. "She's as stiff as a male member."

I shot her a you-didn't-just-go-there glare. "Couldn't you go with something predictable, like 'crystalized honey'?"

"I call it like I see it, Miss Franki." She struck a stripper pose. "And, child, I see a lot of it."

I knew for a fact that she did. "How do you know about the condition of her body? You didn't touch her, did you?"

"Lord, no," she said with a flip of her hair. "Iris tipped the pot, but she wouldn't budge."

I glanced around the room, and nothing seemed out of order. "Were you in here when he came to move it to the stage?"

"No, Bit-O-Honey was," she replied, taking a seat on the hay bale. "Eugene and I came in when Iris started to scream."

It figured that the burly bouncer would be the one to get emotional. "Has anyone else been in here?"

"Eugene kept the others out." She put her hands behind her and stuck out her chest. "And as you can see, the police are taking their sweet time."

That was okay by me, especially if Detective Sullivan was coming. He would kick me out of the club faster than Carlos could say, "closing time." "Did any of you notice anything unusual?"

"Just that." She pointed the toe of her boot toward the other side of the honey pot.

I walked over to where she'd been standing and saw an unopened pack of Pall Mall cigarettes beside a bottle of rum. There were whole peppers inside the bottle, and I would've bet my soul that there were twenty-one of them.

"It's an offering to—"

"Baron Samedi, the loa of death," I interrupted. In one way or another, the voodoo god of the underworld had been involved in all the homicide cases I'd worked since moving to New Orleans. I tried to remember where I'd seen his image recently but couldn't.

Glenda removed a flashlight from her PI belt and placed it in my hand. "Take a look in the pot."

Anxiety ate at my gut as I peered over the edge. Curaçao was wearing a crimson Juicy Couture tracksuit, and on her feet were beige Uggs. She was in a seated position with her knees drawn to her chest, presumably because of the cramped space, and her arms were hanging at her sides. The worst part was that her head was thrown back and her eyes were frozen with fear, and it seemed like they were staring straight at me. I switched on the flashlight and shined it on her chest. The amber pendant came to life as though emphasizing her demise—and the purplish marks on her neck.

"How long do you think she's been in there, sugar?" Glenda asked in a pensive tone.

I studied Curaçao's scratched arms and the porcelain skin of her legs. "I'm not a medical examiner, but I'd say at least ten to twelve hours. That's how long it takes rigor mortis to set in."

"Well, it's around three o'clock now," she said, checking the clasp on her handgun earring, "and I'm guessing that the murder took place when the club was closed. So it could've happened as late as five by your estimation."

I stepped away from the pot unable to stomach any more of the sickening sight and handed the flashlight to Glenda. "Will you find out who worked last night and who was here after closing?"

"I'll get right on it." She returned the flashlight to her belt and pulled a penis pen and pad from her holster. "Do you think she was strangled like Amber?"

"Most likely," I replied, massaging my temples after seeing that writing instrument. "But the crime scene is different. For one thing, Curaçao's not nude in a bathtub."

"But she *is* inside a stage prop," Glenda said, pointing at the honey pot. "And there's a bottle of liquor beside it."

"True." I stood up and started to pace. "And she's wearing an amber necklace or the copy. The thing that's missing is the witchcraft."

She scribbled a note on the pad. "What's that got to do with it?"

"Witchcraft was a big part of Amber's murder." I looked at Lili St. Cyr's tub. "The killer knew about the spell and brought a specific brand of Amaretto to complete the scene."

"Are you saying that you think Curaçao was killed by someone else?" she asked, toggling the penis pen back and forth between her fingers.

"It's a possibility." I sat beside her on the bale. "But what I mean is that this doesn't seem like a killer who's targeting a coven. The Amaretto di Amore suggests that Amber's murder had something to do with love, but Curaçao was probably killed because she witnessed the killing. After all, we know that she was here the morning it happened."

Glenda tapped the pen on her lip. "Then she went into hiding, and he found her."

My mind went to the masked man, and I shuddered as I wondered whether he'd been hunting me. "It looks that way, doesn't it?"

She chewed the tip of her pen. "But if he was just killing her to cover his bases, why the offering to Baron Samedi?"

I stared at the rum and cigarettes. "Maybe just to let us know that the crimes are connected."

Police sirens sounded in the distance, and I leapt to my feet. That was my cue to get some last-minute questioning done before they made their way through the bacchanalia on Bourbon Street, and I knew exactly where to start. "Is Saddle here?"

"She's in the dressing room." Glenda stood up in her stiletto thigh-highs. "Eugene told the girls to wait there until the cops came."

"Good, because Saddle's got some splainin' to do," I said as I exited the prop room.

As I climbed to the second floor with Glenda in tow, I could smell the aroma of Eve's cooking. And my stomach—which remained steadfast in times of sorrow, strife, stress, even sickness—reminded me that it hadn't eaten lunch.

"You should say hello to Miss Eve, sugar," Glenda prompted, sounding worried. "She's devastated about Curaçao, but she's staying strong for everyone else. I tell you, that woman is pure Southern steel."

Although I was pressed for time, I wanted to show my support for Eve. "I'll meet you in the dressing room."

I popped my head into the kitchen.

Eve had her back to me at the stove, and Iris was at the table with his head in his hands.

"Oh, I'm so glad you've come, Miss Franki," Eve said, turning to greet me. "Isn't it just awwwful? We haven't even buried Amber yet."

I put my hands on her shoulders and looked into her grief-stricken eyes. "I promise I'll do my best to find whoever did this to her."

"Thank yewww." She clasped her face. "I can't wrap my mind around the fact that she's gone."

Iris burst into tears, and Eve rushed to his side. "There there," she cooed as she patted his back. "It's gonna be all right. You just sit tight while I git you some Hoppin' John."

For a second I considered crying to get some of the spicy black-eyed pea and rice mixture, but I had a dancer to question, and quick.

"Here you go, hon," Eve said, preparing Iris's plate. She put the food in front of him and then pulled a lighter from her apron pocket and lit a white candle.

I couldn't help but smile as I exited into the hallway. It was just like a Southern woman to worry about table ambience at a time like this, even if the candle was shaped like a nude woman.

The door to the dressing room swung open, and Saddle stepped out looking like a pole-dancer Pocahontas in a skimpy suede number with Native American jewelry. "Glenda said you were looking for me?"

Time was of the essence, so I got down to turquoise tacks. "You told me that Amber wasn't the superstitious type, and yet Bit-O-Honey said that Amber always lit a magick candle before going onstage. How is it that you managed to miss that?"

She smiled, but her eyes didn't. "I come here to work. I don't pay attention to what the other girls are doing."

I nodded to make her think that I believed her. "From what I hear, it's common for dancers in New Orleans to perform some sort of ritual for luck before a show. I take it you don't subscribe to that sort of thing?"

She gazed at me as she toyed with her long, black braid. "That kind of BS is for the weak."

"Is that because you don't believe in it, or because you're into something more powerful?" I paused for effect. "Like witchcraft?"

Her lips parted. "What are you talking about?"

"That crescent moon tattoo on your calf," I replied, pointing to the area that was once again covered, this time by moccasin boots. "It's a pagan symbol popular with witches."

"It's also the symbol of my company logo, Crescent Moon Saddles," she said, her voice slick with sarcasm.

Glenda popped her head out of the dressing room. "Miss Franki, we need you in here."

I gave Saddle a long, hard look. "For your sake," I said as I stepped into the room, "I hope that business brand checks out."

Before the door closed behind me, I stole a glance at Saddle.

Her face was expressionless, but the suede fringe on her costume was shaking.

"Uh-uh. No. Not a chance," I said, staring at my reflection in the dressing room mirror.

"But it's the perfect solution, sugar." Glenda looked up from her kneeling position at my feet. "The Saints, Sinners, and Sluts Revue is tomorrow night, and you have Amber's coloring and height."

"I don't care if I'm her clone. There's no way I'm going to strip to lure a potential killer." I tried to think of a solid justification—other than the extra twenty pounds I was carrying around my waist—but nothing was coming to me.

"You might want to reconsider," Bit-O-Honey advised as she tied a halter-top fashioned from scarves at my back. "Tomorrow's St. Patrick's Day, and those Irish guys lay out a lot of green."

She met my gaze in the mirror. "You know I mean cash, not clover, right?"

"Yeah, I got that." I struggled not to roll my eyes and then seized on the holiday as my excuse. "But Catholics aren't allowed to strip on saint's days."

Bit-O-Honey leaned around my side, her bare breasts bumping into the back of my arm. "You should become a Unitarian. We can do whatever."

I fought off the urge to add, "like going topless in public, apparently." *I mean, I realized that I was in a strip club and all, but was it too much to ask for the woman to cover herself?*

"Shakey had a weakness for Amber, Miss Franki," Glenda explained as she wrapped an orange and black scarf around my hips. "If Madame Moiselle's advertises you as Amber's Texan cousin, Tiger Eye, I'm sure that would draw him to the club."

I didn't want to admit it, but her argument made sense. And now that I had a couple of homicide investigations under my belt I *was* starting to feel more comfortable in my own skin—but not so much so that I wanted to bare it onstage. On the other hand, I did need to question Shakey, especially since he'd been involved with both Amber and Curaçao. And if stripping could prevent another murder, I was in no position to refuse. "But I can't even dance. How could I perform a routine?"

"Don't think of it as dancing." Glenda inserted a pin into the fabric. "Stripping is a series of seductive poses set to music."

"Miss Glenda and I could teach you," Bit-O-Honey said brightly. "And since you've got the whole tiger thing going on, we could do a desert theme."

I didn't bother to correct her.

Glenda picked up her pincushion and rose to her feet. "This should give you an idea of what your costume will look like." She stepped back to admire her handiwork. "Keep in mind that I'll make a few adjustments when I sew it."

I stared at myself in the mirror. The skirt looked a lot like a loincloth, and based on the way my belly was bulging over it, I was glad that I hadn't had any of Eve's Hoppin' John. "Could you add a panel of fabric to cover my stomach? I look like a tubby Tarzan."

Glenda stuck out her hip and her lip. "Tarzan didn't have breasts like yours, sugar. At least, not the one on TV."

Bit-O-Honey giggled, and I looked from her to Glenda to get in on the joke.

"I was talking about one of our VIP Room regulars, sugar."

"Yeah, he's got big ol' man boobs." Bit-O-Honey cupped her breasts for emphasis. "But we call him Tarzan because he asks us to wear chimp masks and pound on our chests while he feeds us bananas."

My mouth fell open. If I didn't solve this case soon, these VIP Room escapades were going to drive me bananas.

Veronica opened the door. "Hey, ladies."

I covered my halter top with my hands. "What're you doing here?"

She looked at my loincloth and blinked hard. "Glenda called me. But the question is, what are *you* doing here?"

"That *is* a good question, Veronica." I glowered in Glenda's direction. "Why don't you ask the consultant you hired?"

"Never mind that now." Veronica motioned with her eyes to the hallway. "Detective Sullivan is outside, and he'd like to interview the dancers. Is everyone decent?"

"Let me check." Glenda inspected her posterior in the mirror.

Bit-O-Honey glanced at everyone's body but her own. "We're good."

"Speak for yourself," I said, reaching for my turtleneck.

Detective Sullivan entered and practically patted me down with his eyes. "Sorry to break up your little rehearsal, Amato, but

I need you in the hallway—*before* you change out of your Great Pumpkin costume."

He strode from the room, slamming the door behind him.

Stinging from the squash comparison, I yanked on my sweater, which happened to be burnt orange, and glared at Glenda. "Get to work on that stomach panel."

As I exited into the hallway, Detective Sullivan pointed a finger at my chest. "What the hell do you think you're doing playing dress up while there's a dead body downstairs?"

I couldn't tell him that I was preparing to set a trap for the killer, or he'd charge me with interfering in an investigation. Instead, I gave him my best blank stare.

"So that's the way it's going to be, huh?" His eyes locked onto mine like a pair of handcuffs. "Fine by me. Because I already have an idea of what's going on here. But for your sake, I hope I'm wrong."

A heavy-set officer came out of Eugene's office. "We're done with Stripper Sacagawea, Detective." He wrinkled his lips like he was suppressing a laugh. "Who's up next?"

Saddle pushed past the officer and flashed him a fiery look as she headed for the stairs.

"Bring in the manager. I'll be right there." Detective Sullivan turned to me. "You'd better be gone by the time I'm done with Mr. Michael, or I'll escort you to the door myself and maybe to jail."

I was so angry that I almost stormed from the club in my costume, but then I got a better idea. I had a couple of bargaining chips, and I intended to use them. "Before you do anything drastic, I suggest you hear me out. I've uncovered a couple of things that could be useful to you."

He studied my face like it was a piece of evidence. "I'm listening."

"Not so fast." I took a step forward to show him that I could play bad cop too. "I need some information from you first."

The detective's eyes did a Dirty Harry. "Such as?"

I swallowed and prepared to fire off a round of questions. "Eugene mentioned that the club doesn't use the surveillance equipment after hours. I'm assuming you verified this?"

"You assumed correctly." He crossed his arms.

"What about Amber?" I imitated his stance. "Have you been able to track down her last address?"

He pursed his lips. "She was living alone in a pricey condo in the business district."

So Amber *had* been getting money from somewhere, possibly her mother. Or Shakey. "What about her next of kin? And her ex?"

"We have reason to believe the ex-boyfriend's in town, and we've verified that she was orphaned at the age of thirteen."

The news that Shakey was in New Orleans was even more reason to submit to Glenda's stripping scheme, but I wasn't willing to dismiss Maybe and Nadezhda's accounts of Amber's controlling mom. "That's strange, because two witnesses reported hearing her on the phone with her mother."

"Could be a close family friend." He leaned a shoulder against the wall. "Now what do you have for me?"

Evidently, my question-and-answer session was over. "A small glass vial I found near the main stage."

He tilted his head. "How do you know it's related to the case?"

"A hunch," I replied, already bracing myself for his reaction to what I was about to say. "I'm almost positive it came from a witchcraft spell kit Amber was using for protection."

A sneer unfurled across his face like a roll of crime scene tape. "That's rich, Amato. What else you got?"

I didn't care that he'd laughed off the witchcraft, because

that only increased my odds of cracking the case before he did. Plus, I knew he'd take what I had to say next more seriously. "A credit card bill that links Amber to the purchase of a copy of the amber necklace."

His sneer faded. "I won't bother asking how you got that because I know I'd be wasting my breath." The steely glint in his eyes was menacing, like his tone. "But I expect you to turn it over immediately."

"It's at my place. I'll drop it by the police station with the vial." I paused as I thought of the pendant on Curaçao's neck. "Would you please do one thing for me?"

He snorted. "If you think I'm going to give you any more tips, you've flipped your jack-o-lantern lid."

I was pretty sure that my eyes flashed fire, and I imagined myself taking him down like I'd learned to do in police training. "Just keep the details of the necklace—and the copy—quiet from here on out."

Detective Sullivan raised his chin like he was prepping to punch a perp. "I told your colleague, Ms. Maggio, that my men and I would keep the pendant out of the investigation, and I've kept my word."

"That's great," I said. But it wasn't.

"Now you get out of here and bring me that bill within the hour." He shot me a cold, cop stare. "You understand?"

I nodded even though I hadn't heard a word he'd said. I was too busy trying to figure out how a suspect could've known about the amber pendant if the police hadn't mentioned it.

And any way I looked at it, it didn't look good for Eugene.

15

M y front door opened, and three white-haired women in black entered.

The nonne were increasing in number.

As Santina greeted the newcomers, I fed an *arancino* I'd plucked from a dinner platter to Napoleon and then looked across the kitchen table at Veronica. "How do you think Bradley's going to react to nine nonne under one roof?"

She tapped her cell display. "I don't know, but I wouldn't miss it for the world."

I scrutinized her bent head as I grabbed one of the fried stuffed rice balls for myself. Even though she was my best friend, it sometimes seemed like she had a serious case of *schadenfreude* where I was concerned.

"Crescent Moon Saddles looks legit." She held up her phone.

I leaned forward and studied the company's website on her browser. The brand image matched the tattoo on Saddle's calf to a T. "Well, it doesn't prove she's not a witch, but I have to admit that she doesn't strike me as one." I sat back in my chair. "And now that I know Eugene was aware of the pendant, I've shifted my sights to him. He doesn't have an alibi, and since he didn't run video surveillance after hours, he could've easily committed the murders."

She arched a blonde brow. "As a crime of passion?"

"For me, the Amaretto di Amore suggests that love was a factor, but he denies being involved with Amber or Curaçao." I bit into the arancino. "The thing I can't figure out is the part the necklaces play in all of this."

"What can I do to help?" She placed her phone on the table.

I wiped my hands on a napkin. "Do you know whether David has found anything on Amber's mother?"

She shook her head. "Not that I know of."

"Crap." I tossed the napkin on the table. "Then you look into the mom and have him pull any info he can find on Old New Orleans Traditional Witchcraft and the voodoo goddess Erzulie Freda."

"What about Baron Samedi?" she asked as she began typing a text to David.

For a split second, I almost remembered where I'd seen the Baron, but then the memory was gone. "I'm already way too familiar with him," I replied, chewing the rest of my rice ball as I grabbed another. "What I need to know is whether the amber had anything to do with the protection spell Amber was performing or with Erzulie."

"I may have to handle the research myself." She picked up a fork. "Your nonna's keeping David pretty busy."

I dropped my arancino and my jaw. "How the hell does she know David?"

Veronica piled prosciutto onto her plate. "Apparently, you told her about him and his fraternity."

My jaw fell open again. I was astonished at my ability to underestimate my nonna. I closed my mouth, but not before taking a bite of the arancino. "What's she having him do? Build a robot for me to marry?"

"He and his frat brothers are creating a computerized model of the St. Joseph's Day altar." She rolled a slice of the cured ham. "She wanted them to make it too, but they don't know how to build anything in real life."

That was hardly surprising. Comp-Sci geeks weren't known for their construction skills. "But the altar is usually just a bunch of card tables they push together. Why does Nonna need a special design?"

She picked at the prosciutto. "To make sure you have easy access to the lemons."

Rage rocketed through my body, and I squeezed the arancino so hard that tomato-sauce-coated rice, mozzarella, and peas oozed between my fingers.

"Um, not to change the subject," she said, looking at my hand with eyes as round as ravioli, "but have you had any more run-ins with the man in black?"

"As far as I know, I haven't been followed." I stood up and went to the sink. "Maybe he came back over here, and the nonne scared him away."

Veronica didn't laugh because that scenario was all too possible—probable, even.

The toilet flushed, and my nonna shuffled into the kitchen chewing on a toothpick. She kept one in her mouth whenever food was around to spear herself the occasional olive or cheese chunk. "Franki, did-a you see? Santina can-a walk again!"

I scrubbed my hands to keep them from strangling her. "How'd it happen? Physical therapy?"

Nonna shook her head. "Bruno tell-a her that he was gonna leave-a home since she no cook, and-a Santina, she stand up and-a make him a four course-a meal!" She crossed herself. "It's a miracle!"

I suppressed a sacrilegious smirk as I dried my hands. The "miracle" would be if Bruno ever left. He was what Italians called a *mammone*, i.e., a mamma's boy-turned-man who was content to live at home and let his aging mother wait on him for life.

"That reminds-a me," Nonna said as she stabbed a salame slice with her toothpick, "Bruno asked Santina about-a you."

I grimaced as I sunk into my seat. "I hope she told him I was still seeing someone."

Nonna munched on the meat. "She tell-a him you work at a strip-a club."

I put my face in my hands. Bruno would be all over that information like white on pasta.

There was a knock on the door, and Bradley entered. "Hello, hello!"

I stood up to greet him, but my nonna got to him first.

"*Benvenuto*, Bradley." She kissed him on both sides of his face in accordance with Italian custom and promenaded him into the kitchen.

He flashed a smile. "Evening, ladies."

The nonne gathered around as though they'd just been granted an audience with the pope.

"This is-a Franki's *fidanzato*," Nonna said, using the word for both *boyfriend* and *fiancé*. "But soon he gonna be-a much-a more than-a that. Eh, Bradley?"

His smile faltered, and my face turned as red as the ragù simmering on the stove. Before I could pull my voice from the pit of my sinking stomach, Santina approached Bradley and grabbed him by the cheeks.

"*Beddu comu lu culu de viteddu*," she cooed. Then she released his face and gave it a pat that was more like a slap.

Bradley rubbed his flushed flesh and looked at me. "What'd she say?"

Nonna beamed. "That-a you are as handsome as-a the ass of a calf."

He looked taken aback, but I put my hand on his arm to reassure him.

"It's totally a compliment," I said in a knowing tone. "Right, Veronica?"

When she didn't reply, I turned to look at her. She was grinning like a restaurateur who'd just booked an Italian family reunion.

"Can someone give me a hand?" my mother called as she entered the apartment carrying groceries.

Bradley rushed into the living room. "Let me get those bags, Mrs. Amato."

As soon as my mother's arms were free, she fluffed her hair. "Why, Bradley." Her shrill voice had taken on a breathy quality. "You know you can call me Brenda."

I rolled my eyes. Marilyn Monroe my mom was not.

"Of course, Brenda." He deposited the groceries on the kitchen counter. "Wow," he said, peering inside one of the bags. "That's a lot of lemons."

I gave my mom a sour look.

"Uh, Francesca," she said, averting her gaze to the plastic tubs of bread stacked against a wall, "have you shown Bradley the bread?"

He tilted his head. "What bread?"

I removed the lid from one of the tubs. "Since the altar is to St. Joseph, they bake bread in the shape of carpenter's tools, staffs, crosses, animals—"

"And hands," Nonna interrupted from the kitchen. "Like-a this one."

She hurried into the living room with a loaf that looked like a left hand. "Oh!" she exclaimed in mock surprise as she pointed to a bump in the bread on the third finger. "It-a look-a like an engagement ring! It's a sign from-a God-a!"

The other nonne gasped and scurried from the kitchen to see the holy hand.

"Carmela is right," one of the newcomer nonne agreed. "It's a *fede*."

Fede meant wedding ring and faith, something I was running short on at the moment. I grabbed a hand-shaped loaf from the open container and tore off a finger, fully intending on doing some stress eating. As I brought it to my lips, Bradley's eyes widened.

"Is that a...?" His voice trailed off as his eyes opened a little wider.

I realized how phallic the finger looked and dropped it, to Napoleon's delight. "Good Lord, no!"

My mom and nonna both cocked a brow, so I dragged Bradley into the kitchen before they could comment. I mean, in his defense, it was only natural that he'd think the finger was a penis since my nonna had once served him a pastry shaped like a boob.

"Hey, Bradley." Veronica shot him a sarcastic smile. "How's it going?"

He ran a hand (that the entire house now knew was glaringly wedding-ringless) through his hair. "Pretty good."

I could tell that he was trying to be a trooper, but work was clearly weighing on his mind. "Are things settling down at the bank?"

His jaw tensed. "Actually, no. Before I left I found out that Craig Burns is thinking about going with another bank. If he does, the board'll have my head."

My stomach almost upchucked the arancini. Craig was a construction magnate who'd hosted the party where Bradley took me on our first date (and where my lips puffed up like a couple of puffer fish after Craig taught me to suck crawdad heads Cajun style). "I can't believe it. You two are more than business associates. You're friends."

"That's what I thought too." He gazed out the window. "I just can't understand what's happening."

"Bradley," I began, preparing to tread on dangerous ground, "have you considered the possibility that someone from within the bank is sabotaging you?"

"Have you tried the arancini?" Veronica gushed, pushing the platter in front of Bradley. "They're a Sicilian specialty, and the name means *little oranges* because of their shape and color. Isn't that adorable?"

He looked from Veronica to me. "Franki," he said, his voice lethally low, "is there something you need to tell me?"

"Nooo," I replied as innocently as my Catholic guilt would permit. "I'm just surprised that Craig of all people would go to another bank. It makes me think that something else must be going on."

He shoved his hands into his pockets. "Well, if this were sabotage, I can't imagine what anyone would have on me. It's not like I've been negligent or broken any laws."

I stood statue-still as I remembered Ruth saying that Bradley knew I was a *professional problem*. My thinking was that if I didn't move, maybe he wouldn't remember it too and think that I was somehow responsible for this mess.

He gave me a small smile and kissed my cheek. "Don't worry. I'll deal with whatever's going on. As for Craig, I'm sure he has his reasons for wanting to leave."

And I knew exactly what those reasons were: Jeff and Payne. Evidently, the Machiavellian manager had paid Craig a visit like he had that other client Ruth told me about. The good news was that I knew Craig well enough to pay him a visit too—and to get to the bottom of this bank business.

My mother walked into the kitchen, tying an apron she'd brought from home around her waist. "Bradley, can Franki fix you something to eat?"

She gave me a serve-your-man stare, which I countered with a get-off-my-back glare.

"I'm good, thanks," Bradley said, sliding his arm around my shoulders.

A loud knock preempted my mother's protest about his refusal of food.

The shortest of the nonne opened the door and leaned her head back to see who it was.

"Evening ma'am," Detective Sullivan said. He had one hand on the doorjamb, and the other was in the pocket of his black, form-fitting suit pants. "Is Franki available?"

The baking ceased, and the nonne's eyes grew to the size of tortelloni. From their Old-World-Sicilian standpoint, the fact that a man had come to my home and uttered my name was tantamount to a declaration of undying love and also a sure sign of my betrayal of my not-yet-betrothed.

Stunned, the nano-nonna stepped aside and motioned toward the kitchen.

Detective Sullivan strode into the apartment and straight to my seat at the table. "I need a word with you outside."

The nonne's eyes darted from me to the detective and then fell on Bradley like a meat tenderizer on a veal cutlet.

"And you are?" Bradley asked, rising to his full six feet three inches.

I jumped up and knocked over my chair, which did nothing to allay his suspicions. "Uh, Bradley Hartmann, this is Detective Wesley Sullivan," I said as I picked up my seat. "He's in charge of the homicide investigation at Madame Moiselle's."

"Investigations, *plural*," the detective corrected, making no move to shake Bradley's hand.

Bradley looked at me. "There's been more than one murder?"

"Another dancer was killed this morning," I said in a hushed tone, hoping it would minimize the massive damage unfolding before me.

"*Madonna mia!*" the nonne shouted.

Bradley's face lost all expression, kind of like the calm before the storm. "And you didn't tell me about it?"

"Oh, Francesca!" My mother threw her arms into the air. "You really should confide in your boyfriends."

"Boyfriend, *singular*," I stressed. I wasn't surprised that my mom was more worried about my relationship than the homicide, but I was completely unprepared for her contribution to the "plural" party.

"Now everyone stay calm," I semi-shouted as I stomped around Detective Sullivan and headed for the door. "This is just business."

The detective followed me out, and the second we were alone on the porch I spun around to face him like a Tasmanian devil in a tornado. "What're you doing here?"

He squared his stance. "I came for the credit card bill and the vial."

I crossed my arms. "I told you I'd bring them by the station."

He leaned into my face. "And I told you I needed them within the hour."

I pointed at his pecs. "No, you didn't."

"Yes, I did." He gestured toward the door. "Now hurry up. I've got something you'll want to see."

I lowered my lids. I wasn't sure I trusted him to share evidence with me, but I needed all the breaks in the case I could get. "Be right back."

When I went inside, all nine nonne jumped away from the window, while Bradley, my mom, and Veronica pretended to be busy in the kitchen. Without a word, I ducked into my bedroom and pulled the plastic bags containing the items from my nightstand, and then I rushed back to the porch.

"Here." I thrust the bags into his hands. "This is everything

I've collected."

"Make sure you don't collect anything else." He turned and headed down the walkway.

"Hey!" I ran after him. "What do you have for me?"

"Right. My bad." He stopped and pulled a wad of fabric from his back pocket.

It took a second for my brain to register what it was. When it did, I felt my chest and realized that I was still wearing the scarf halter-top that Glenda had made for me at the club.

"Looks-a like you got-a some competition," my nonna announced from behind me.

A tightness wrapped around my torso like the bra I wasn't wearing as I turned and saw her and Bradley standing in the doorway.

Bradley's eyes were fixed on the bra dangling from the detective's hand.

I snatched the offending undergarment. "I can explain."

"Just business, eh?" Bradley said as he set off across the yard toward his car.

"Wait!" I yelled. "I know this looks bad—"

The door to his BMW slammed, and the engine roared.

I watched helplessly as he sped away.

"It may look-a bad to Bradley," Nonna said as she sized up Detective Sullivan, "but from-a where I'm-a standing, it's-a lookin' pretty good-a."

BRADLEY'S PHONE went straight to voice mail.

In the ten minutes that I'd been locked in my bathroom, I'd called him at least twenty times with no luck. Reluctantly, I opted to heed Veronica's advice and give him some space—but only until tomorrow.

To drown out the noise of the nonne, who were all abuzz about the *scandalo* that had gone down between Bradley, Detective Sullivan, and me, I put in my earbuds. Then I tossed back half of my highball of Lazzaroni Amaretto, desperately wishing that Lent were over so that I could top off my drink with a little chocolate cheesecake. In times like these, stress drinking alone wouldn't do. After all, I'd been trained to eat my emotions since birth.

With my laptop in one hand and my drink in the other, I climbed into the claw-foot tub fully clothed. I leaned my head against the back and felt something rubbery and cushiony, like an inflatable plastic bath pillow, so I settled in and got semi-comfortable.

Then it occurred to me that I didn't own a bath pillow.

I turned to take a look, and the screechy *Psycho* music went off in my head.

It was my nonna's enema bag.

After I'd scrubbed my hands for five solid minutes, washed and dried my hair, and lined the tub with towels, I got back inside and prepared to do some online research. Since sleep was out of the question and my nonna was monopolizing David's time, I decided to try to find out for myself whether the amber necklace was a component of the spell or the voodoo.

A half an hour passed. Various search combinations of *amber* and *Old New Orleans Traditional Witchcraft* and *New Orleans voodoo* produced nothing. Frustrated, I entered *amber amaretto* to see if I could find anything to connect the two items.

To my surprise, I got a hit—*Amaretto Amber.*

I clicked the link, and what I saw prompted me to drain my highball glass.

Now I knew how Amber had been making her money.

16

———

"Amber was *what*?" Veronica asked, her phone voice gravelly with sleep.

"Sugaring," I whispered into my cell, glancing across the dentist lobby at a twenty-something tech nerd absorbed in an issue of *Wired*. "You know, Lisa Ling, CNN?"

She was silent. "Did Dr. Lessler give you laughing gas?"

"I haven't even seen him yet," I replied, annoyed. "I was talking about a TV show on sugaring."

"Oh." A cabinet door slammed. "Is that the thing where young women date wealthy men for money?"

"Uh-huh." I picked at a crack in my thumbnail. "The women get rent or tuition or whatever, and in exchange the men supposedly get *companionship*, i.e., sex."

The man's head snapped up, as did his bushy brows.

I gave him a get-a-life glare, and his eyes lowered to his magazine.

"How do you know Amber was doing it?" Veronica asked over the banging of pots and pans.

"I found her profile on a sugaring website, sugarshack.org.

And get this—" I shifted the phone to my other ear and shielded my mouth with my hand. "She went by *Amaretto Amber*."

Veronica gasped. "Do you think that's why the amaretto was left at the crime scene? As a clue that she was sugaring?"

I scooted to the far end of the couch to get out of earshot of the gawking geek. "I still think the *Amore* part of the brand name is significant, but, yeah, I've been wondering if it was some kind of statement from a jilted sugar daddy."

The man peered at me over the top of his magazine, and I narrowed my eyes into an I-can-see-you stare.

"Wait a second." Silverware jangled as she closed what I assumed was a kitchen drawer. "Didn't Carnie say that Amber was leaving the sex trade?"

"I know what you're thinking—this sounds like prostitution." I paused and shot the man a preemptive dream-on smirk. "But in the eyes of the law it's not because both parties consider it to be dating."

"Yeah, that would be tough to prosecute." She yawned, and I heard water running. "Have you tried calling this company?"

"I can't because they don't have any contact info listed. I did a *Whois* search on the website, but nothing came up."

"They're using a masking service, obviously." The water sound stopped. "Your only option for information is to infiltrate the company somehow."

"If you're suggesting that I pose as a sugar baby, you can forget it." I crossed my ankle over my knee. "Stripping is as far as I'm willing to go."

The man's mouth dropped open and, to my dismay, stayed that way.

"Read your magazine, will ya?" I yelled, waving my arm Italian-style for emphasis.

He leapt up and left the lobby.

"I don't get it," Veronica said in a bewildered tone. "Why do you want me to read a magazine?"

"Never mind," I muttered. "Anyway, what would you think about me asking David to investigate the company? He could create a fake profile as a prospective sugar daddy to see what he can find out."

"I don't have any problem with that, but your nonna will if it interferes with that altar." She giggled.

"You let me handle her," I said, even though we both knew that I couldn't.

"Listen," she began, "have you talked to Bradley yet?"

I frowned at my broken nail. "No, but it's only seven thirty. If he hasn't surfaced by lunchtime, I'll call him."

Dana, the hygienist, entered the lobby holding a patient file. "Franki?"

I stood up, and my stomach fell. "They've come for me."

"Have fun," Veronica said as though I were redeeming her spa gift instead of getting a crown.

I was tempted to reply with a choice word or two, but I would've felt dirty swearing in front of a hygienist. So I tapped end—hard.

As soon as I was settled into the dental chair, Dana sat on a stool and clipped a bib around my neck. Then she rose to her feet and pulled a bleach wipe from a Clorox canister.

"Dr. Lessler will be here in a few minutes," she said as she disinfected the seat.

"Wow." I watched her swab the stool. "Now I get why they call you a hygienist."

She laughed. "Dr. Lessler's kind of a germophobe."

The doctor entered the room, pulling on a rubber glove. "I see how it is," he said in a joking tone. "I'm a few seconds late, and you two talk about me behind my back."

Dana's face turned a shade shy of the purple on the doctor's LSU scrubs.

I smiled as I semi-sat up. "We were discussing what a clean freak you are."

"Well, we see an awful lot of spit around here." He winked and pulled a surgical mask over his face. "How's that filling?"

"Fine, I guess." I reclined, resigned.

"Let's take a look before I start the crown." He took a probe from Dana's hand.

I opened my mouth and stared at a poster on the ceiling of a dolphin that was leaping carefree from the sea as if to mock me.

"How's the investigation going?" he asked, poking my tooth.

"Uh, ohay," I replied, mainly because it was the only thing I could safely say with a pick between my lips.

"I have some information for you." He prodded my gums.

My eyes widened. "Reary?"

He placed the probe on an instrument tray. "I just talked to my office manager, and she said that a woman called a couple of times over the past year to make sure Amber didn't have any outstanding bills."

I rose to my elbows. "Does she know her name or her relation to Amber?"

The corners of his mouth turned down. "The only thing she remembers was that the woman had a strong Texan accent."

At the mention of Texas, Shakey came to mind. It was possible that he had a secretary paying Amber's bills, but the woman could have also been an associate of a sugar daddy Amber had met through the website. Either way, someone had to be covering her expenses, especially the rent on that Uptown apartment she'd moved into. "Is there anything else you can tell me about Amber? Or about that necklace you saw her wearing?"

A memory dawned on his face. "I can't believe I almost forgot." He turned to Dana. "Can you give us a minute?"

She nodded and exited the room.

"Yesterday was my daughter's fifth birthday, and my wife gave her an Ariel doll. It reminded me that Amber had said something about the *veve* being associated with a mermaid."

I was so excited by this revelation that I almost forgot the reason I was in Dr. Lessler's office. If there was a voodoo mermaid, that would explain the one on the bathtub since the Lithuanian legend had never quite fit with the crime. "You might've just provided me with a missing link I needed."

"Glad I could help." He picked up a Q-tip.

"What's that for?" I asked, holding up my hand to keep his at bay.

His shoulders relaxed. "I have to anesthetize your tooth so that I can prepare it for the crown."

If I'd known about this part of the procedure, I would've anesthetized myself to prepare *me* for the crown. I sighed and gripped the arms of the chair. "All right. Let's get this over with."

He swabbed my gums with the topical anesthetic. "I take it you're not surprised that she was into voodoo and witchcraft given the, uh, sordid life she'd been living."

I turned my head to look at him. "You mean, the stripping?"

He gave an apologetic grimace. "I knew about the prostitution too. If her attitude hadn't given it away, her outfits would have." Dr. Lessler glanced at the clock and picked up the syringe. "I'd better get a move on. We've got a full schedule today. Ready?"

"No, but shoot." I opened my mouth but squeezed my eyes shut.

As the needle pierced my flesh, my eyes popped open. But it wasn't because of the prick. It was because I finally remembered where I'd seen the image of Baron Samedi.

It was on the top of King's cane.

～

I OPENED MY EYES, and a slack-jawed face came into focus. Fearing that the dude from the dentist had followed me to Private Chicks, I bolted upright from the lobby couch and knocked him in the nose with my noggin.

"Ooof!" His head flew back, and he pinched his nostrils.

I blinked and realized that he wasn't the nosy nerd but rather "the vassal," a fraternity brother of David's who'd earned the feudal nickname when he'd been appointed as a pledge to serve David the year before. "Sorry I hurt you," I said, rubbing my forehead. "But why were you staring at me like that?"

"You were breathing all weird, and then you stopped," David replied, removing a tissue box from the reception desk. "We thought maybe you'd died."

"I almost did," I muttered, recalling the horror of having my bad tooth filed down for the crown.

"Whoa." He handed the box to the vassal. "What happened?"

"The dentist appointment from hell." I touched my tongue to my temporary tooth. "Anyway, I have an urgent assignment for you."

David glanced at the vassal, who was inserting a tissue plug into his nostril. "But Standish and I are working on a St. Joseph's Day project."

I snorted. "Standish? Who's that?"

The vassal inserted a wad of tissue into the other side of his nose. "Mbe."

Trying not to peer at those plugs, I said, "First of all, you should stick with the vassal. And second, I know all about my nonna and that altar, but Veronica and I agree that the case takes priority. So, I need you to create a fake profile on a website for sugar babies."

The vassal's already Coke-bottle-lens-magnified eyes grew even larger. "I'm not allowed to eat caramel. Mother says dairy isn't good for me."

"It's not for the candy," I said dryly as I looked from him to David. "It's called Sugar Shack, and it advertises young women seeking platonic and sexual relationships with men in exchange for money or goods."

David doubled over, and the vassal exhaled so hard that the tissue plugs shot from his nostrils like rockets.

I curled my lips as I contemplated David's collapsed form. "Maybe you're not the man for the job."

He held up a hand. "Just...give me a second."

"No, now that I think about it," I said, shaking my head, "this won't work. To get the kind of info I'd need, you'd probably have to attend one of the meet-the-girls parties that prospective sugar daddies are invited to."

David's back seemed to give out, and he placed his hands on his thighs for support.

"And since you work for Private Chicks," I continued, "that could expose you unnecessarily."

The vassal clenched his fists at his sides and took a step forward. "I know how to party with girls."

I bit my lip. I'd been to a so-called "party" at the vassal's dorm the previous year, and the only women in sight were the ones on the surveillance video I'd brought for him to analyze. "I can't let you do that since you're not our employee."

My message tone chimed from my office.

"I need to see who that is." I pushed myself off the couch. "You two go ahead and work on that altar design, and then David, you get me anything you can find on a voodoo mermaid."

"Can't we at least do the profile?" David croaked.

He looked so broken that I decided to throw him a bone.

"Why not?" I said and then hurried down the hallway for my phone.

As I'd hoped, the text was from Bradley.

We need to talk. Can you come by my place at 8?

I started to confirm, but then I remembered that I had to strip at around that time. Of course, there was no way I was going to tell him that, so I opted for a kinder, gentler version of the evening's event.

I have a stakeout at the club. Is 10 too late?

While I waited for him to respond, I unlocked my lower desk drawer and pulled out my emergency bag of Elmer's Green Onion CheeWees *and* my crisis can of Zapp's Spicy Cajun Bean Dip.

I used a cheese curl to scoop a dollop of the dip and tossed it into the good side of my mouth. No sooner had I begun to chew than my "Shake Your Booty" ringtone sounded.

Tapping *speaker* to keep my hands free for snacking, I answered, "Hey, Glenda."

"Miss Franki." She exhaled what had to be a puff of smoke. "What are you doing right this minute?"

"Oh, just stress eating." I chewed another CheeWee. "Why do you ask?"

"Because we've got prep work to do before your performance."

I licked dip from my lip. Something in her inflection sounded ominous. "I've got to learn the routine, right?"

"Not only that," she said, sounding stressed. "I imagine we have quite a bit of waxing to do."

I almost choked on a cheese curl. "And why would you imagine that?"

"Are you or are you not Italian, sugar?"

"Not all Italians are hairy," I huffed, keeping it general. If I got into family specifics, I'd be busted for sure.

"Far be it from me to stereotype." She sucked in some more smoke. "But based on the way your front fluff filled out your panties during your costume fitting, I'd say you fall into the hirsute group."

I cradled the bean dip can for comfort. I didn't mind being outed by my underwear, but the implication that I had back fluff really stung.

"Now, normally I wouldn't concern myself with what grows in your grove," Glenda assured, "but for tonight, I need to make sure those pubes get pruned. Luckily, I was able to get you a noon appointment at Vaxing for Vomen."

I swallowed, stunned—not because I had to have my vagitation *vaxed* but because I didn't remember telling her about the salon or Nadezhda. "Why are we going there?"

"Because all the salons on Yelp were booked solid, and it was the only place I could find with an opening on such short notice."

Given its austere ambiance, that was certainly understandable. "If it wasn't on Yelp, how'd you hear about it?"

"I ran across Miss Nadezhda's card...at the club," she added evasively.

I dropped the dip. "*Where* at the club?"

"Don't tell Eugene," she said in a low voice, "but I found it when I was looking for a pen in one of his desk drawers. Why?"

That was exactly what I wanted to know.

"Could we at least leave a landing strip?" I pleaded, clutching my just-waxed inner thigh.

"Not with your tiger costume, sugar." Glenda adjusted her green, white, and orange feather boa to make sure that it wasn't covering her shamrock pasties. "That hairkini of yours is going Hollywood."

I got a visual of my vajayjay in bright lights. "What do you mean, 'Hollywood'?"

She raised her skirt and pulled her gold-sequined thong to

the side, and I stared at her hairless hoohah in horror. Now not only was my skin searing, my eyes were too.

To overcome the awkwardness, I asked, "What's that rainbow on your skirt got to do with St. Patrick's Day?"

She pursed her lips into a pout. "A leprechaun hides his pot of gold at the end of a rainbow, Miss Franki."

I rolled my eyes and then my head to the other side of the waxing table and watched as Nadezhda mixed the wax in the warmer. It occurred to me that she looked a lot like a witch stirring a cauldron.

She turned and ripped a muslin strip from my bikini line without warning. "I do mustache and goatee too. Yes?"

Glenda nodded, and I was in too much pain to protest.

Nadezhda looked at my upper lip and curled hers. "I get more vax."

As soon as she'd stepped out, I sat up and seethed. "FYI: I don't have facial hair—just a little peach fuzz. But we'll table that conversation for the time being, because we need to find out how the Wicked Witch of the Wax knows Eugene."

Glenda blinked eyelashes that matched her boa. "He could be one of her clients."

"How do you figure?" I whisper-shouted. "The guy's hairier than Tom Selleck in a gorilla suit."

"Well, I wouldn't know." She gave a haughty hair flip. "Maybe he's into manscaping."

"So, he tends the briar patch but leaves the weeds all over the rest of his body?" I asked in keeping with her gardening theme. "I doubt that."

She crossed her arms, covering her clover. "Then what do you suggest we do?"

"I don't want Nadezhda to think I'm questioning her, so when she comes back, get her talking about herself—you know, where she's from, what her hobbies are." I returned to my supine position. "Maybe she'll say something that'll help us connect her to Eugene."

Glenda tapped an Irish-manicured finger to her cheek. "This calls for some old-fashioned flattery."

Nadezhda entered with a block of wax and stole a sideways glance at Glenda and me as though she suspected that we'd been talking about her. She dropped the block into the warmer and began breaking it up with a wooden stick.

"Did you ever do any modeling, Miss Nadezhda?" Glenda asked. "You have such a striking face."

"Tank you." She gave a modest grin and touched her maroon spikes. "I was actress in Borscht Western."

I pulled myself onto my elbows. "A *what* western?"

Her grin turned to a grimace. "Like Spaghetti Western, only Russian."

"How exciting!" Glenda exclaimed, shaking her shamrocks. "Which one were you in?"

She did her signature sneer-smile as she turned up the heat dial on the warmer. "*Caviar Cowboy.*"

Glenda plopped down onto the waxing table, perching her pot of gold next to my face. "Did you have a speaking part?"

"I play saloon girl." Nadezhda put her hand on her hip and struck what I presumed was a seductive pose. "Larissa Lockhart," she drawled. "From Texas."

I tilted my head like Napoleon did when I said a word that sounded familiar to him. Only it wasn't a word that got me—it was Nadezhda's Texas accent. It wasn't good, but it wasn't bad either. In fact, unlike her English, it was pretty darn passable.

As she smeared wax around my mouth, our eyes locked. And even though I couldn't tell whether she was the woman who'd called Dr. Lessler's office asking about Amber's account, there was one thing I could detect.

Guilt.

Nadezhda was involved in the Amber Brown case, and I would've bet my bottom lip that Eugene was too.

17

———

"What the—" I flinched at my reflection in the dressing room mirror at Madame Moiselle's. And it wasn't because of the tiger-striped Lycra costume, the purple-and-gold platform pumps emblazoned with the LSU tiger, or even the tiger ears and tail. It was because of the big red bumps around my mouth and thighs. "Someone please tell me that you can't get herpes from a waxing salon."

Glenda squatted and scrutinized my crotch. "It's just a rash, Miss Franki."

"Or an allergic reaction," Bit-O-Honey added as she pressed the costume snap closed at the nape of my neck.

I bent over and examined my inflamed inner thighs. "No, it's a burn. I saw Nadezhda crank up the heat on that wax warmer, and she did it on purpose."

Bit-O-Honey pulled up one of the black thigh-high fishnet stockings of her sexy saint costume. "Why would she do something so cruel?"

"Because she knows I suspect her of being involved in the murders." I straightened and scowled at the redness around my mouth, which made me look a lot like a crazed clown. "Someone with a Texas accent called Dr. Lessler's office asking about Amber's bills, possibly this mother figure we've been hearing about, and it could've been her."

Glenda sealed the Velcro closures at my hips. "But why would she tell you and Carnie about Amber's mother if it was her?"

"Because Amber talked to the mystery mom on the phone in front of Maybe, too," I said, eyeing the Velcro with concern. "And if Nadezhda is this mom, she's probably trying to deflect suspicion from herself."

"Could be." Glenda stood up and checked to make sure that her apple-pastied breasts were still barely tucked inside her blue lace-up bustier.

"Hey, uh, I know you're a slut," I prefaced to preempt any protest. "So why would you dress as Snow White for The Saints, Sinners, and Sluts Revue?"

Her lips puckered into a playful pout. "She lived alone with seven men, sugar."

Now that I thought about it, that *was* suspiciously slutty.

"What do you think of your costume?" She stepped away from the mirror, and I got a full frontal of my tiger getup.

My first reaction was to suck in my breath—then my belly. Glenda had reduced the halter to the size of a string bikini top, and the skirt barely covered the thong I had on underneath. Even worse, the fabric panel she'd added to cover my gut consisted of an upside down triangle that essentially functioned as a giant arrowhead pointing to my lady bits.

"You call this 'a few adjustments'?" I asked, yanking my tail for emphasis.

She smoothed her yellow skirt. "Well, I had to sexy it up."

"Sexy it up?" I turned back to the mirror. "I look like a Mardi Gras tiger. With mange."

Bit-O-Honey snapped her fingers. "I know what you need. Tiger balm!"

I gave her a pre-pounce-on-the-prey gaze.

"There's no time for that. She's on in thirty minutes." Glenda pointed to a makeup case on the counter. "Get me the Dermablend."

I crossed my arms over my breasts. I didn't know what Dermablend was, but I already knew that I wasn't a fan of the spirit gum she'd used to glue on the pasties that the club required me to wear under my top.

"Relax, sugar," she said as she took a cosmetic tube from Bit-O-Honey. "It's body concealer."

"In that case, could you cover the spare tire I'm carrying around my stomach?" I leaned into her face. "Because that fabric panel isn't doing the trick."

"Oh, it won't cover fat," Bit-O-Honey gushed. "Just your rash."

I shot her a silent roar.

"A-anything else I can do to help?" she asked, pushing open the door as she backed away from me.

I caught a side view of myself in the mirror and winced. "Get me a stiff drink, will ya? And find out if Eugene is here yet."

Eugene appeared in the doorway as though he'd been standing outside trying to eavesdrop. He leaned against the jamb, striking a pose in his black-and-white Adidas tracksuit. "What can I do for you?"

"I need to speak to you privately." I tried to look him in the eyes, but they were otherwise occupied with checking out the exposed flesh in the room.

"We can talk in my office," he said coolly.

Glenda pointed the Dermablend tube at me. "You don't have time to talk, Miss Franki. You've got to be on that stage at nine o'clock sharp."

"This won't take long." I turned to follow Eugene, but I hadn't practiced walking in the six-inch heels yet. So, instead of the stealthy stride of a tiger, I had the spastic step of a chicken. By the time I got to his office, he was already seated behind his cheap metal desk.

"Guess I'm gonna get my wish," he said as he opened an Altoids tin.

I crossed my arms and frowned. "What wish is that?"

He dropped a mint onto his tongue. "To see a fiery Italian strip."

I was fiery, all right—as in angry and, if you counted the burning bumps on my mouth and thighs, on fire. But Eugene hadn't noticed those because he was focusing on the bumps on my chest.

"I gotta say..." His eyes traveled down my torso. "...based on what I know about your people, I'm surprised you didn't go for leopard."

I chose to ignore the Italians-wear-animal-print stereotype. I *was* wearing tiger stripes. "While we're on the subject of animals, I'm trying to figure out whether you're a wolf in sheep's cloth-ing." I glanced at his gold collar-style chain. "Make that dog's clothing."

His breathing seemed to stop. "What are you getting at?"

"Your relationship to Nadezhda Dmitriyeva." Now my eyes focused on *his* chest—specifically, on the hair tufting from his unzipped jacket. "And don't tell me you're one of her clients."

"Okay. I won't." He placed his hands behind his head.

I waited for an explanation, but one didn't come. "You might want to tell me how you know her, because right now it's looking like you two are accomplices."

"Accomplices in what?" he asked, sitting forward in his chair.

"Which one of you told the other about the amber necklace?" I shot back, trying to catch him off guard.

Anger erupted in his eyes. "Just what the hell are you trying to say?"

I bent over and rested my hand on his desk. "You knew about that necklace even though the police didn't make it public."

He opened his arms, feigning innocence. "They told me about it at the station."

"Not according to Detective Sullivan." I stood up and stared, waiting for his body language to betray him.

His arms relaxed at his sides, but his hands gripped the chair. "Well, he's wrong."

"I don't think so." I started to pace in my platform pumps but promptly abandoned that plan. "What I do think is that Amber told Nadezhda about the necklace, then Nadezhda told you. And the two of you decided to steal it."

He exploded from his desk like a Molotov cocktail, and I leapt backwards, stumbling slightly in my stilettos.

"Nadezhda was a friend of my mother's from the old country," he said through clenched teeth. "And since my mom died, she's been like a second mother to me."

My ears pricked up at the *mom* mention. *Had Nadezhda also been a second mom to Amber—one who betrayed her?*

Eugene and I faced off across the desk, and something told me to pursue the connection between Nadezhda and his mom. "Where, exactly, were they from?"

"Some small town," he muttered. "I don't know the name."

"You don't know where your own mother was from." I made it a statement rather than a question because I didn't buy it for all the vodka in Russia.

He looked down, and it wasn't because he was embarrassed. It was to hide the fear that flashed across his face.

And although Eugene claimed not to know the name, I had a feeling I did.

Yantarny.

Because anyone from the Russian amber-mining town would know about the Amber Room, its significance to the people of Russia, and, of course, its incalculable value on the black market.

"NO SIGN OF SHAKEY YET," Glenda said as she peered at the crowd through the curtains around Madame Moiselle's main stage.

"Welp, if he's not here, I guess there's no point in me dancing." I turned to go back to the dressing room—and I couldn't get there fast enough.

She grabbed my shoulder and spun me around. "We don't know that Shakey had anything to do with these murders, Miss Franki, so the show must go on. Remember, your dancing could help us catch the killer." She let go of me and reached for my cell. "Now give me your phone."

I pulled back and glanced at the display. Bradley had never responded to my text about meeting at ten o'clock, and I was worried that he'd had a change of heart about discussing the Detective Sullivan situation—just like I'd had a change of heart about the stripping situation. "Um, first I need to make a quick call."

"It's too late for that." She wrested the phone from my grip. "We hired a top DJ for this event, and he's about to announce you."

Bit-O-Honey bounced up and shoved a drink into my empty hand. "Carlos made you a tiger goddess."

"Thanks." I didn't feel like a tiger or a goddess—more like a combination of a chicken and a monster. But I chugged the drink, hoping it would give me a confidence boost.

It didn't.

"I can't do this." I thrust the empty glass at Bit-O-Honey and turned tail and ran—well, plodded, thanks to my platform pumps.

"You can, and you will." Glenda grabbed my arm and dragged me back. "Just remember your routine—crouch, roar, pre-pounce wiggle."

My legs started trembling so hard that my tail shook, but somehow in my hysteria I thought of another reason that I couldn't strip. "Wait! My costume doesn't fit with The Saints, Sinners, and Sluts Revue theme. I'll ruin the whole show."

"How silly of me," Glenda said in a blatantly false tone. "I forgot a key accessory."

I cocked a glittered brow. "What accessory?"

"One sec, sugar." She strutted to the prop room, and I seized the opportunity to peek through the curtains.

Madame Moiselle's was a zoo, and I was a caged animal. The club was standing room only, and there were so many men in green that it seemed like half of Ireland had flown in for the show. I scanned the room looking for a Stetson, but I spotted a Sullivan instead. And the dastardly detective was making his way toward the stage.

"Don't move," Glenda said from behind me. "I need to drape this over your shoulders."

I assumed she was referring to her Irish flag boa, but the accessory was heavy—and cold and slick. I looked down and froze. It was definitely a boa, but of the live constrictor variety. My eyes darted from the snake to Glenda, because I was too afraid to move anything else. "Wha...wha...wha?"

"St. Patrick drove the snakes from Ireland," she replied as though I'd formulated a complete question. "The idea is that the Irishmen in the crowd drive the snake—and the rest of your costume—from you."

I stared at her, stricken. Snow White wasn't only a slut, she was a *strega* too.

Morris Day and the Time's "Jungle Love" began to play, and my legs turned to jungle juice.

"Coming to the stage," the DJ intoned into a microphone, "Tiger Eye, the late, great Amber's Irish-Italian porn star cousin."

Porn star?

The crowd roared, and before I could strangle stripper Snow White with the snake, she shoved me onstage.

The lights were blinding, so I couldn't see the steps to exit. I couldn't faint, either, because I was too afraid of what the snake would do to me if I fell on it. So, I stood still and made like a jungle tree.

"Woo-hoo!" A man yelled. "Look at her shake that money-maker!"

Bewildered, I looked down and discovered that I was vibrating like Tina Turner on a treadmill.

"Come on, guys," the DJ boomed. "Make it rain for Tiger Eye —like in a rain forest."

"Crouch, sugar! Crouch!" Glenda yelled.

I inched sideways toward the sound of her voice, and then someone pulled my tail. My costume constricted, and a rush of air whooshed over my skin as the audience hooted and hollered.

Now I knew the reason for the Velcro and the snaps— Glenda had made me a tear-away tiger costume, and she'd just torn it off me.

"Reeeeemember, fellas," the DJ bellowed, "tip when they strip. If you want to see her flashin', you've gotta slide some cash in."

The snake, probably as annoyed by the damn DJ as I was, reared its horrifying head.

Terrified, I recoiled and fell backwards onto my hands, and the cheering turned to jeering.

"What the hell kind of move is that?" a man shouted.

"A crab walk?" another offered.

Ignoring the catcalls, I focused on the tasks at hand—getting myself off the stage and the boa off my boobs. Fortunately, in my crustacean position I was out of the glare of the lights. I glanced around for the exit and came face-to-face with another snake—Detective Sullivan.

He grinned and held up a five-dollar bill. "You might want to put this in the bank," he said as he slid the money into my thong. "Because it looks like your stripper career is going belly up, pardon the pun, just like your PI career."

A camera flash went off in my face, and when the light spots cleared my tiger's blood ran cold.

Bradley was making his way to the stage, and his eyes were darker than Iris's tattooed scleras.

I scuttled toward Glenda, but I slipped and collapsed. I watched in alarm as the snake slithered to the stage and as Bradley took a swing at Detective Sullivan.

The crowd went wild. Within seconds, green beer and top hats began to fly as a bar brawl broke out.

Iris swooped down and scooped up the snake and me and whisked us off the stage, depositing us in front of Glenda.

She crossed her arms and tapped a yellow-bowed stiletto. "Caught a tiger by the tail, didn't you, sugar? Too bad it wasn't the killer."

"THEY DON'T CALL us the Fighting Irish for nothing, eh, Sullivan?" A ginger officer joked as he loaded three handcuffed club patrons in shamrock suits into a paddy wagon outside Madame Moiselle's.

The detective laughed. "Ain't that the truth, Sean?"

I clutched my coat lapel to stop myself from going all *Raging Bull* on them and kept my eyes trained on the squad car that they'd loaded Bradley into fifteen minutes before. I hadn't spoken to anyone since he'd been arrested—not even to Bradley. And like the Irishmen in the club, I was fighting mad—at Glenda for suggesting that I strip, at myself for agreeing to the stupid scheme, at Bradley for coming to the club after I'd told him I had a "stakeout," and at Detective Sullivan for arresting him.

Sensing my animosity, the detective strode over to me. "Speaking of the Irish, you must have some of our luck. Otherwise, you'd be sitting in the back of that squad car with your boyfriend."

"This isn't about luck," I seethed as I rubbed my right fist, which was aching to punch him. "I didn't do anything wrong, and neither did he. You provoked him when you put that bill in my...uh...thong."

A corner of his mouth lifted. "Well, he's going to have to get used to that sort of thing now that you've taken up stripping. Fortunately for him, your business partner's an attorney, because he's going to need one." He paused and gave me a penetrating stare. "And you will too if you interfere in my investigation again."

He spun on his heel and climbed into the passenger seat of the squad car. Moments later, the engine roared to life. As the car pulled away, I watched numbly as Bradley disappeared into the night and, I feared, from my life. We'd been through a lot, but I wasn't sure how we'd survive this. Because when the bank got word of his arrest, heads were going to roll—his first and then mine. And the more I thought about it, the more I realized that it might be in his best interest if I rolled right out of his life.

"I thought we could use a drink," a squeaky female voice said.

I turned and found Maybe Baby standing next to me with two Hurricanes from Pat O'Brien's Bar. She was wearing a long, black nightgown with a fuzzy pink coat, a green wide-brimmed hat, and red heart-shaped sunglasses. Anywhere but Bourbon Street she would've looked conspicuous.

"Thanks." I took a go-cup from her hand and gulped down half of the red liquid. "But this won't take the sting off seeing my boyfriend get arrested."

"Gee, I'm sorry." She put a hand on my arm. "I didn't know."

I looked at my drink. "Then what's this for?"

She fished the cherry garnish from her cup and popped it into her mouth. "I saw you dance."

Tilting my head in concession, I raised my glass, and we made a silent toast to my epic stripping failure. I was no Blaze Starr, but for the record, I'm sure Blaze's landlady never slipped a snake on her seconds before she took the stage. "You haven't told me why *you* need a drink."

Maybe pushed stray blonde locks from her face with the back of her hand. "Somebody broke into my house last night, and I had to climb out my window in my nightie."

My gut lurched to alert me—in case my brain hadn't already—that this was probably no random break-in. "You haven't been home since?"

"Well, yeah." She gestured to her ensemble. "I went back this afternoon to change."

I glanced again at her gown and took another swig of my drink to prime me for the rest of the conversation. "Do you know who it was?"

"It could've been the maniac who killed Amber and Curaçao." Her brow furrowed as she chewed her straw. "Or my landlord."

My head jerked forward. "Does your landlord break into your house often?"

"Only when rent is due," she replied in a matter-of-fact tone.

Glenda was looking a lot better as a landlady—stripping, snake, and all. "What did the police say?"

Maybe looked at me and closed one eye, like she was trying to bring me into focus. "What've the cops got to do with this?"

"Um, their business is solving crime?" I suggested.

"You're funny, you know that?" She sat on the curb in the middle of the partying pedestrians and spread her legs.

Against my better judgment, I took a seat beside her on the filthy sidewalk—the partiers were known to puke, and who knew what else. As we sat in silence, I sincerely hoped her seafood platter wasn't showing. On a street like Bourbon, that would be like offering an open tab to a serious drunk, and I didn't need any more trouble. "So, did they take anything?"

She swallowed a half-gallon of her Hurricane. "Who?"

I sighed and stared at the pavement. "The person who broke into your house."

"Not that I could tell," she replied, swishing her drink in her cup.

That struck me as odd. But given Maybe's less than stellar housekeeping skills, I wasn't sure whether she would've noticed if an actual hurricane had blown through the place. Also, the intruder could've been scared away, especially if he or she hadn't expected her to be home. "What did they do? Jimmy the door?"

She put her drink down and frowned. "Who's Jimmy?"

"Oh, no one in particular." I pursed my lips and pondered how to rephrase the question. "What did this intruder do to actually get inside your house?"

"They broke the window in the room where Curaçao had been staying."

I bit my lower lip. Maybe was in serious danger, because the killer was looking for something, and my money was on the amber pendant. "Maybe, if Curaçao did steal that necklace from Amber, where would she have hidden it?"

She wrinkled her mouth and widened her eyes. "Your guess is as good as mine."

I folded onto my knees, thinking that the pendant might never be recovered. "Can you think of any reason that she would've been wearing the copy of the amber necklace when she died?"

"Beats me." She looked down at her clear plastic stilettos. "Curaçao told me that real amber would protect you since it was the stone of the mother goddess, but obviously that fake amber didn't do any good."

My back straightened. "What mother goddess?"

"It's got something to do with that hocus pocus stuff she was into," she replied as she grabbed her drink.

Shocked, I sat my cup on the sidewalk. "Why didn't you tell me about this the other day?"

Her fuzz-covered shoulders raised into a shrug. "Because I was drunk, I guess."

I gave her the onceover, marveling at the implication that she was sober.

"Also because I'm not sure how much she really believed in that witchcraft business." She drained her drink and wiped her mouth with her wrist. "Her mom is the one who got her into it."

"Her mom?" My gut was no longer lurching—it was doing a lap dance. "Do you know her name?"

She crunched a piece of ice. "Mama."

This time I wasn't annoyed with her reply. I was bewitched. "Maybe, what else can you tell me about Curacao's mother?"

She yawned and pulled her phone from her pocket. "Well, she wasn't her real mom," she replied, sounding bored as she checked her display. "Just some lady."

My head began to spin—but only partly because of the four

ounces of rum I'd imbibed. *Was there a witch acting as a mother figure to Amber and Curaçao? If so, was it Nadezhda?*

As hard as it was for me to imagine, she was like a mother to Eugene. Plus, she'd refused to answer my question about Amber being a witch that day at the salon. But if she had been a mother to the girls, I doubted that she would've let them call her by the Southern *mama*. Something about the affectionate term didn't jive with her harsh personality.

"You okay?" Maybe asked, nudging me in the side.

I nodded, even though I wasn't okay at all. "Can I use your phone?"

"Be my guest." She entered her passcode and handed me the device.

Out of curiosity, I pulled up her browser and googled the Russian word for mother. As I'd suspected, it looked somewhat severe—*мать*, pronounced *mought*. But what I hadn't expected to see was the more commonly used informal version of the term.

Мама, the pronunciation of which was all too clear.

18

———

"**F**rancesca Lucia Amato!" a deep voice bellowed.

I started to come to, still in a crab crawl position. *Why was I onstage again? And how did that guy in the audience know my real name?*

The boa constrictor began to slither on my belly, and my eyes flew open. I wasn't at Madame Moiselle's—I was lying in my claw-foot bathtub in my pajamas with my arms and legs hanging over the sides.

And the cord from my nonna's enema bag was on my stomach.

I hurled the bag across the room as I hopped from the tub.

But wait. I cocked my head to the side. *If that wasn't a strip club customer heckling me, who—*

The bathroom door burst open with a bang, and my mother marched in.

"Is it *true*?"

She had venom in her voice.

"Did you sss...sss...sss...?"

She even hissed like a snake.

"*Strip?*"

I was too terrified to move. When my mom was this mad, she was Medusa incarnate.

"Answer me, young lady," she commanded through clenched teeth.

I averted my gaze because, like her Greek mythology alter ego, I was pretty sure she could turn me to stone. "Mom, I'm investigating a case—"

"Don't try to deny it," she interrupted in a kind of low growl. "Bruno saw you."

My fear was replaced with contempt. The second I'd heard that Santina had told him I was working at Madame Moiselle's, I knew there'd be fallout. And thanks to that rat, I was backed into a corner—er, a bathroom—by a gorgon. "All right." I sighed, resigned. "I had to strip for work."

"*Mamma mia, che disgrazia!*" Nonna screamed from the doorway.

I started, unaware that she'd snuck up on us like that.

"Look at what you've done!" My mother gestured to my nonna, who chose that moment to fall to her knees and hold her hands up to heaven.

"*Che Dio ci aiuti!*" Nonna wailed, asking God to help us—for emphasis.

An assortment of supportive shrieks and laments ensued from the nonne in the kitchen.

"This is just great." I threw my arms in the air. "I'm a grown woman in trouble with her mom for doing her job. Tell me," I said, resting a finger on my cheek, "did Bruno get in trouble for going to a strip club to check out my semi-nude bod?"

My mother gasped as more cries came from the kitchen, and someone started moaning.

Nonna did the only thing she could do—whip out her rosary and begin to recite.

"He went there to try to talk you out of ruining your reputation and our family name," she rasped. "Get your mind out of the gutter, Francesca."

I was beginning to smell a double standard, which, in addition to garlic, was a common odor in Italian households. "Oh, of course." I sneered. "Because Santina's son is a saint."

It was no doubt my imagination, but I would've sworn that my mother's face turned a greenish hue. And I was halfway expecting snakes to sprout from her head.

"The fact that you would disrespect that nice man tells me that you're not the person I thought you were." She jabbed her finger in my chest as a preface to her classic closer, "Just wait till your father hears about this."

I sunk onto the edge of the tub as she stormed past my nonna, who stopped praying and glanced toward the kitchen. Then she clambered to her feet and rushed into the room.

"Franki," she whispered, "did-a that detective really give-a you a five-a dollar bill-a?"

"Uuuuhhhh," I uttered, wondering whether it was a trick question. "Yes?"

"*Evvai!*" she cheered with a fist pump. Then she retrieved her enema bag from the floor beside the sink and stepped into the hallway, making sure she was in full view of the other nonne. "You take-a your clothes off in-a public again," she said, shaking the bag at me for show, "and I'm-a gonna wrap-a this thing around your neck-a, *capito?*"

I stared blankly at the bag because, by this time, it had basically been all over my body. "I understand, Nonna."

With a satisfied nod, she tossed the bag into the sink and returned to the kitchen.

I closed the door and climbed back into the tub. My heart ached about the situation with Bradley, and my head ached from arguing with my mom—and from a hangover. After I'd collected my stripping money (twenty-four bucks counting the nineteen singles dropped during the brawl, which was better than that dollar I'd gotten for my birthday), I drowned my sorrows in a second round of Hurricanes with Maybe. Then I asked Glenda to let Maybe stay with her until the murders were solved, a decision I was starting to regret. Now I was going to have to deal with my Medusa Mom and Ninja Nonna until St. Joseph's Day was over, because the odds of me getting Maybe out of a giant champagne glass were slim to none.

The door burst open again, and I sat up in the tub.

Glenda ran into the room and latched the lock behind her. With a pink polka dot ruffled apron tied around her waist and another around her chest, she looked like something from a fashion-forward 1950s mag—except for the stripper shoes that said *Pay Me.*

"What's happened now?" I nestled back into the tub. "Did the Lilliputians tie you up in the kitchen curtains?"

"Miss Ronnie asked me to come get you because you haven't been answering your phone." The aprons rose and fell with her breath. "But right after I got here, Santina showed up with the strippergram, and the mood turned ugly in the kitchen. You see what happened to me," she said, gesturing to her apron dress. "So, you'd best shake a leg, sugar."

I shot her a look. "My shaking days are over."

She shot me a look right back. "I'm telling you, we have got to go. Besides, Miss Ronnie has news about Bradley."

My pulse perked up. "She's spoken to him?"

"It's 9 a.m., Miss Franki." She put her hand on her hip. "She's already been to the jail and had him released."

I sprung to my feet. "Let me change out of my pajamas."

"There's no time for that," she said, pulling me from the tub by the arm. "The way those women are slapping and pounding that dough makes me think that our buns are the next things they're gonna bake."

Glenda had a point. Nine nonne conferring in a kitchen about a fallen female family member was a recipe for disaster— in this case, mine. And I had an idea of the type of rehabilitation plan they'd cook up.

I grabbed her by the biceps in the grip of panic. "We've got to get out of here before they call in a priest for an exorcism."

THE PLAIN *PAIN perdu* seemed to mock me from my plate. French toast without syrup was like a life without love, which was what I was facing at the moment. "Sullivan's really going to press charges against Bradley?"

"I'm afraid so." Veronica pushed the butter dish toward me across her rattan kitchen table. "Battery against a police officer."

Glenda, who'd forgone French press coffee in favor of champagne, slammed her flute onto the glass tabletop. "How long a stretch in the jug are we talking?"

My head snapped in her direction. Sometimes she reminded me of Ruth—and of an ex-con.

"Typically, six months," Veronica replied as she pressed egg-battered bread into the skillet with a spatula. "But because an officer is involved, he could serve up to a year."

I put my face in my hands as I imagined Bradley back behind bars. *How would he hold up? How would I hold up? And what if he were cellmates with a spitter or a skin slougher? Or worse?*

"How was he supposed to know Sullivan was a detective when he was in plain clothes?" Glenda rose from her rattan chair. "And while we're on the subject, get me out of this bondage suit."

I untied the aprons and immediately understood why the nonne had covered her. She was wearing a red spaghetti strap dress that was all straps and no dress.

"Bradley knew who Sullivan was." I picked up my fork and stabbed my *pain perdu*. "The good detective came to my house the other night to collect some evidence—and drop off my bra."

Glenda gave me a shame-on-you smirk. "You little wildcat, you."

I was so mad that I could've mauled her. "I forgot it at the club when you were fitting me for my costume, which, incidentally, is what started this whole nightmare."

"Looks like you've forgotten your bra again," Veronica said with a pointed look at my pajama top.

"That's not fair. I just escaped from the nonne nuthouse." I stopped and shot Glenda a sideways glare. "And our seasoned stripper here forgot to tell me about pastie remover. So, like me, my boobs need a break."

Glenda, who'd also forgone food in favor of false eyelashes, opened a tube of adhesive.

I scooted my chair—and my pair—away from her. "Veronica, Bradley doesn't think I cheated on him, does he?"

She plated her *pain perdu*. "Of course not. But he does think Detective Sullivan is interested in you."

I breathed a sigh of relief—and two lungsful of eyelash glue.

"And, between us," she added as she took her place at the table, "he doesn't regret hitting him."

"*Roar*, sugar," Glenda said, elbowing me in the side. "Bradley's a tiger, just like you."

"Would you quit with the cat references?" I snapped.

She hissed and made a paw-swipe gesture.

I rolled my eyes and turned to Veronica. "Did you explain to him that Sullivan and I have a mutually antagonistic relationship?"

"I tried." She stirred Sweet'N Low into her coffee cup. "But he's convinced otherwise."

I dropped my fork and stood up. "Well, I'm going to go set him straight." *And maybe break up with him*, I thought. But I didn't say it. I wasn't ready to commit to the idea yet, much less communicate it.

"You'll do no such thing." Veronica narrowed her eyes. "Sit."

I stared at her, shocked, and did as I was told.

"As his attorney," she began, spreading a napkin in her lap, "I've advised him to lay low until after the bank board meets on Monday, and that includes staying away from you."

"What?" I grabbed my fork like a weapon. "Who are you, Jeff Payne?"

"I don't think you're a liability to Bradley, if that's what you're suggesting." She poured syrup on her food. "But for the time being, the only things he needs to worry about are staying out of jail and saving his job. Fortunately, the charge is just a misdemeanor, and the incident happened outside of work. But he can't afford to get into any more trouble."

"Oh. So you think I'm trouble, then." I shoved a forkful of dry French toast into my mouth to keep from saying something I'd regret.

She put the syrup down. "I think that right now you'd be a distraction."

"She's right about that, Miss Franki," Glenda said, gluing a red, spiked lash to her eyelid.

I swallowed so that I could snort. "Theodora told me I was cursed, and she was right. My boyfriend's going to jail, my family's ruining my life, and despite the fact that I gave up sweets for Lent, my teeth are falling out."

"Curses are nonsense," Veronica said as she cut her breakfast into bites.

"Are you sure about that?" I asked. And I was serious. "Look at Amber and Curaçao. There's a curse on people who hunt for The Amber Room, they both stole a piece of it, and they're dead."

She leaned across the table. "Franki, I'm not going to argue with you about this. I just need for you to let Bradley and me sort out his situation while you and Glenda focus on solving the murders. Okay?"

I stayed silent. I wasn't ready to make any promises.

"This case is getting scary," Veronica said, waving her knife. "We've gone from a murder to a possible serial or spree killing. Meanwhile, you're being followed by a masked man, and this morning Glenda told me that Maybe spent the night because the killer might be after her too. The way I see it, you can't afford to concern yourself with Bradley's problems because we have serious issues of our own."

She was right. I had to keep my head in the crime game. More lives might depend on it—possibly even my own. "Don't worry, I know. And we are making progress on the case. Last night I learned that both Amber and Curaçao were into witchcraft, and that Amber probably wore the necklace to invoke protection from some mother goddess."

"You mean, Erzulie Freda." Veronica took a bite.

"Actually," I said, reaching for my coffee, "since she was doing witchcraft, I think it's some pagan earth goddess."

She shook her head. "According to the research I've been doing, Erzulie's the mother goddess. Even witches conjure her."

I flashed back to Drag Dolly telling me that Erzulie loved amaretto. "That makes sense. Amber could've been summoning her for protection with the help of the amber necklace."

Veronica swallowed a sip of coffee. "I'm glad you understand it. There's a lot of information about the loas in the New Orleans context, but it's complicated because they all have so many different aspects. For instance, Erzulie isn't just a goddess of love. She's also a mother figure and a protector of lots of different groups, like children and prostitutes."

Dolly hadn't mentioned that, but the prostitute part fit in Amber's case. It also meant that she could've been appealing to Erzulie for assistance with an angry ex-john.

My cell began to vibrate on the table. David's name was on the display, so I put him on speaker. "Hey, man. Veronica and Glenda are here with me."

"Hello, ladies." He cleared his throat. "It's good that you're all there because I kind of have a situation."

Veronica frowned at the phone. "What's wrong?"

"Standish—I mean, the vassal—and I set up a fake profile on sugarshack.org for a twenty-five-year-old tech millionaire. And I found out this morning that he stayed up all night messaging with this chick from the site. I mean, girl." He coughed. "Woman."

"We get the picture," I said, trying to hurry him along. "What did he find out?"

"That this woman knew Amber." His tone sounded as astonished as Veronica, Glenda, and I looked. "She said Amber hooked up with the first guy she met at something called a sugar bowl party."

"Any chance she remembers the guy's name?" I prodded.

"I wish," he replied. "But I could tell the vassal to ask her to describe him."

Veronica furrowed her brow, probably calculating Private Chicks' legal liability. "This is great information, David, but we can't have him doing any work for us. Thank him and let him know that Franki will take it from here."

"But that's the situation," he said, his voice breaking slightly. "The woman invited him to a martini mixer at lunch today, and he's going. I told him it wasn't a good idea, but he's a man on a mission."

I couldn't help but smile. The sugar babies on that website were probably hotter than anything the vassal had seen since he'd been introduced to the Bunsen burner in high school science class. "Do whatever you have to do to keep him away from that mixer, you understand?"

He exhaled as though trying to stop the smitten Standish would be like taking on Mike Tyson. "I'll do my best."

I tapped *End*.

"Sounds like the killer could be Amber's sugar daddy," Glenda said, swirling the champagne in her glass.

"Or Nadezhda, or Eugene, or Shakey." I drummed my fingers on the table.

Veronica gazed at me over the rim of her mug. "What're you thinking, Franki?"

I looked her in the eyes. "That we might not figure out who the killer is until we make sense of the crime scene."

Glenda batted her lashes, looking like she was ready for a geriatric rave. "We already know what it means. It's an anti-hex witchcraft spell and a request to the voodoo goddess, Erzulie, for protection."

"Maybe. But there's one clue at the crime scene we haven't cracked—the mermaid that Amber carved into the tub." I glanced at the *Pay Me* message on Glenda's shoes. "And I think I know just the person to help me decipher it."

"IT'S JUST YOUR IMAGINATION," I said to myself as I looked into the rearview mirror of my Mustang. Ever since I'd arrived in the French Quarter, I'd felt like I was being followed. Of course, my paranoia could've had something to with the fact that Veronica had mentioned the masked man. Nevertheless, I couldn't shake the sensation.

I turned onto Bourbon Street and checked the mirror again. Still nothing.

"Told you so," I intoned as I searched for a place to park and seriously considered psychotherapy.

Across the street from King Nation's corner, I spotted a rare parking space. When I pulled up, I discovered that it was occupied—by the wino who'd tried to steal from King's tip jar.

"Excuse me, sir," I called as I leaned from the car window. "Could you please move to the sidewalk so I can park here?"

He lifted his head from the stuffed black trash bag that he was using as a pillow. "Can't you see I'm trying to sleep off a hangover, lady?"

I blinked. "Actually, I *can* see that."

He lay back on the bag, and I laid on the horn.

After jumping a good three feet in the air, he shouted out a string of obscenities that would've made Glenda blush. Then he did as I'd asked.

"Some people are so grouchy in the morning," I grumbled as I parallel parked.

My phone began to ring as soon as I stepped from the car. I bit my lower lip when I read Ruth's name on the display. If she'd heard about Bradley, then the wino's diatribe would seem pleasant in comparison to this conversation. But on the off chance she'd spoken to him, I tapped answer.

"Hey, Ruth. What's up?" I held my breath and waited.

Silence.

I looked at the display to make sure the call hadn't dropped and put the phone back to my ear. "Hello?"

Then I heard it—the sound of heavy breathing, bull-about-to-charge style.

Clearly, Ruth had found out about Bradley. But based on her

huffing and puffing, it didn't seem like the time to ask if she'd talked to him.

I glanced at King and saw that he'd started to roll up his red carpet.

Now, I knew that parishioners were hard to come by in the Quarter, not to mention at eleven thirty on a Friday morning. But judging from the way King was stealing sideways glances at me, I had a feeling that I was the reason he was closing up shop, i.e., church.

"Listen, Ruth. It's been great breathing with you," I said, keeping an eye on King, "but I've gotta run." I closed the call and crossed the street.

King saw me coming and rose to his feet, practically glowing in head-to-toe peach. In theory, his fruit-colored suit should've been an improvement over his purple, green, and gold getup, but the pastelness of it all would've taken even Ruth's breath away.

I strode up to him and stared into his gold sunglasses. "I guess you heard that another dancer was murdered at Madame Moiselle's?"

He frowned and clutched his linen lapel. "Shame about that."

"Her name was Curaçao," I added, watching his face for any sign of recognition. "I don't suppose she was one of your girls?"

"We was not biniss associates, no." He hoisted his keyboard. "But with a name like that, I could've made her a star."

Of the porno screen.

"Now, if you'll excuse me." He brushed past me. "I have an engagement elsewhere."

"Hold on a second." I started after him. "As a man of God, I know you'd want to help me find Amber and Curaçao's killer."

"You would think that," he said as he rounded the corner. "But the good Lawd doesn't want no misfortune ta befall me while I'm spreadin' his word." He stopped beside a Cadillac Seville that looked factory-made to match his ensemble, or vice versa, and popped the trunk.

"Wow." I shielded my eyes from the glare of his car and his gold teeth. "Someone's ready for Easter."

He stowed the keyboard inside the trunk and slammed it shut. "Peach is my favorite color."

"Huh," I said in a sarcastic tone. "I would've guessed green."

"Now that you mention it, I do enjoy green." He lowered his sunglasses so that I could see his eyes lower to my purse. "Particularly when I'm bein' pumped fo' information by a PI."

I could've kicked myself with one of his peach leather wingtips. I'd set myself up for that one.

"Without no cash, I've got to dash." He turned and headed back to his pulpit.

I trailed behind him and rummaged through my bag for my wallet, wishing I'd saved some of my stripping money to pay him off—and contemplating how sad that scenario sounded.

When we got back to his corner, he tossed the carpet over his right shoulder and grabbed his cane.

By some miracle, I found a twenty-dollar bill tucked in my coin purse—something that never happened when I needed money to spend on myself. I made sure King saw it, but I didn't want to hand it over until I'd asked a few more questions. "I noticed Baron Samedi on your cane. Do you practice voodoo?"

"Girl," he said, pulling down the brim of his peach pimp hat, "you been watchin' too many movies."

I was surprised that he would deny it, especially since it was common practice to mix voodoo with Christianity in New Orleans. I decided to offer him the cash to see whether that inspired some brotherly love.

When I held out the twenty, a breeze blew it from my hand. As I stepped into the street to retrieve the bill, a thought occurred to me. I turned and looked at King. "Amber learned voodoo from you, didn't she?"

His hands went to his face, and I read *Lawd* and *Gawd* on his rings at the same time I heard tires squealing.

Then I was down.

And out.

19

The first thing I saw when I opened my eyes was a large crucifix. I would have thought I was in heaven, but I was fairly certain that the crosses in paradise weren't encrusted with cubic zirconias.

I raised my eyes and realized that the crucifix belonged to King, who was stooped over me. With his wide-brimmed hat and distinct front teeth, he looked like the Mad Hatter, only in peach and gold. In that moment, I knew exactly where I was—down the rabbit hole.

"What's going on?" I asked, pulling myself onto my elbows.

He squatted beside me. "You done had yo' bell rung."

It all came flooding back—the twenty-dollar bill, the squealing tires. I looked around for a paramedic or a policeman, but the only people in sight were tourists. "Didn't you call an ambulance?" My tone reflected my anxiety. "I got hit by a car!"

He lowered his gold sunglasses. "There's no need for nervous postrations, now. That car didn't touch a hair on yo' head. But you did get a nasty bump when Apollo pushed you out the street."

Of course, I knew he wasn't referring to the Greek god, but I was kind of holding out hope for a fireman. "Who's Apollo?"

In reply, the wino walked up and waved.

Talk about a misnomer.

"Sorry 'bout that lump, lady," Apollo said, pulling his faded "Tales of the Cocktail" festival t-shirt over his exposed beer belly.

"No problem. Thanks for coming to my rescue." I felt the side of my head and looked at my hand. There was a trace of blood. "Did either of you get a look at the driver or any information about the car?"

The two men exchanged a look that I'd become all too familiar with since moving to New Orleans—one of a complicit silence that reined supreme among the Kings and Apollos of the city.

"It happened so fast." King spread his hands in a helpless gesture.

Apollo pushed matted brown hair from his puffy face, presumably so that I could see how honest he was trying to look. "And we were worried about you."

"Tha's right." King tipped back his hat. "After you hit yo' head, Apollo carried you ta safety. I couldn't do it myself, you understand, because this suit is dry clean only."

Apollo nodded as though saving the suit was the logical concern.

"Uh-huh." Clearly, I wasn't going to get anywhere with these guys. But if the driver of the careening car was the masked man, he was going to get away with attempted murder.

As I pulled myself to my feet, both men offered their hands. After weighing the two options, I took King's hand, albeit with reluctance. When he let go, I wobbled.

"Hold on ta this." He handed me his cane.

The Baron Samedi topper glinted in the sunlight, and I

remembered what I'd asked King before losing consciousness. "We still need to talk about Amber and voodoo."

He turned to Apollo. "Why don't you get the lady somethin' ta calm her nerves? You'll find a selection of beverages in my Caddy."

Apollo's eyes lit up like a neon bar sign, and he hurried around the corner.

Although I couldn't see King's eyes through his dark lenses, I stared straight into them. "I was right about you teaching Amber voodoo, wasn't I?"

"F'true, but it wadn't no big thang." He adjusted his suit coat. "Tha's jus' how we do in New Awlins."

He was right about that—voodoo was an integral part of the local culture. "What did you tell her about a mermaid voodoo goddess?"

"La Sirène?" He pulled a gold toothpick from his pocket. "She's the goddess of the sea and all its treasures. But she's also the goddess of love, motherhood, and protection."

I remembered my earlier conversation with Veronica about Erzulie's three aspects. "Are you sure you're not talking about Erzulie Freda?"

"La Sirène *is* Erzulie," he said, pointing the toothpick at me.

My head was starting to throb—both from the accident and from this conversation. "I don't get it."

He sucked his teeth. "You know how tuna is the Chicken of the Sea?"

I blinked, unsure if he was really referring to the fish or if that bump was getting the best of me. "Uh, I guess?"

"La Sirène's like that." He slipped the toothpick into a corner of his mouth and smiled. "The Erzulie of the sea."

Okay, so it wasn't the bump. "Is it possible to appeal to the gods for more than one thing at the same time? Or maybe to use witchcraft to ask for one thing and voodoo for another?"

His lips protruded. "It's not advisable, no. You got ta put all yo' energy into a request for it ta work. Plus, if you axe fo' mo' than one thing, the gods might think you bein' greedy."

That corresponded to my suspicions about the crime scene. Amber hadn't left that amaretto—the killer had. "If someone is invoking a god, can another person undo it with their own voodoo?"

"F'sure." He nodded. "It's called red magic."

The color red got my attention since the Amaretto di Amore label was red and even the amaretto was a reddish-amber. "Not black magic?"

"Tha's Hollywood." He clutched his bedazzled cross. "In real voodoo, we don't have no black nor white."

I hated to mention the amaretto to King, especially since I'd already asked him about it once before, but he was the best chance I had of deciphering the killer's message. "What if a red magic practitioner gave La Sirène a bottle of amaretto?"

"She'd drink it." He collapsed with laughter and slapped his knee.

While King cracked himself up, I glanced around for Apollo, wishing he'd hurry up with my drink. In the meantime, I decided to try another tack. "If I wanted to ask La Sirène for help, how would I do that?"

He rubbed his eyes beneath his sunglasses. "Lots o' ways— pray to her image, light a candle, hold her *veve*, or jus' take a baf."

I leaned forward. "A what?"

"A baf. You know." He lowered his lenses and winked. "Rub-a-dub-dub?"

I tightened my grip on the cane both because Amber had been taking a bath with La Sirène's image etched into the tub and also because I wasn't sure what that wink was about. "What does her *veve* look like?"

"It's shaped like a diamond about yay big." His rings sparkled as he approximated the size. "And it sits on top of an upside down triangle—"

"With scrolls on each side?" I interrupted.

"You seen it?"

"No, but I've heard about it," I replied, recalling my conversation with Dr. Lessler about the *veve* Amber had worn.

"Tha's good." His head bounced up and down as he straightened his suit coat. "Because you don't want ta mess around with La Sirène."

I thought about Erzulie D'en Tort, Erzulie Freda's Petro manifestation. "Does she have a vindictive side?"

"Her Petro nation aspect is La Baleine, a whale disguised as a nice piece o' tail." He broke into a glittering gold smile. "Like what I did there? The rhyme and the tail thang?"

I wrinkled my lips. It was as close as I could come to faking a smile. "Why does she disguise herself?"

He snorted. "To trick the ones that offended her. She lures 'em inta the deep and drowns 'em."

The drowning didn't quite fit with Amber's murder. Even though she was in the bath, she didn't drown—she was strangled. And Curaçao wasn't anywhere near water when she was killed.

Apollo rounded the corner carrying a black chalice that looked a lot like a pimp cup—except for the word *preacher* written in rhinestones. "This'll make you feel better."

"Is it wine?" I asked as I took the cup from his hand. I wanted to know because I was worried that it had come from Apollo's personal stash.

He smiled, revealing purple-stained teeth. "It's red drink."

"Ah." Red drink was the local name for Barq's Red Creme Soda.

"I tol' you to get her somethin' ta calm her nerves, and you get her creme soda?" King pulled the hat from his head and whacked the wino who stepped backward and knocked the *preacher* cup from my hand.

"Boy!" King stomped a peach wingtip on the sidewalk. "Now look what choo done."

I watched with dismay as the red liquid trickled into the gutter. Make no mistake—I was glad that I didn't have to drink it. But as it drained away, I felt like my hopes of understanding the meaning behind the Amaretto di Amore were draining away with it.

ONCE I WAS SAFELY in the Mustang, I pulled a bottle of aspirin from my purse. The headache from my hangover was kid stuff compared to the post-accident migraine assailing my brain.

While I wrestled with the child safety cap, I glanced at my phone. Bradley hadn't called, but Ruth had. Twelve times. I wondered if she'd ever calmed down enough to find her voice, but I didn't really want to find out.

When I finally got the cap off the bottle, Ruth brought the call count to unlucky thirteen.

I put her on speaker and placed the phone on the center console. "You still mad at me?"

There was no heavy breathing, just a series of choking noises.

"I'll take that as a yes." I popped four aspirin and started to chew. Now I had two reasons to need pain relief.

The gagging turned to gurgling.

"Maybe try saying just one word," I suggested as I gingerly laid my head against the headrest.

"Jeff," she gasped.

My head shot up, along with my pain level. "What about him?"

Silence.

"Speak, Ruth," I urged. "You can do it."

"Acting president," she said through clenched teeth.

I grabbed the phone. "Was Bradley fired? Spit it out, woman!"

"On leave."

More choking noises followed, but this time I was the one making them. Jeff might've gotten Bradley's job temporarily, but if he thought that he was going to keep it, he had another thing coming—from me.

Gripping the steering wheel, I ground out, "Get me Craig Burns's phone number ASAP."

AFTER CONVINCING Craig to meet Ruth and me at ten a.m. the next morning, I was on my way home to treat my head wound and wash my hair. Craig had been reluctant to agree, but luckily Ruth had told me that his favorite restaurant was Cochon Butcher on Tchoupitoulas Street. It had taken considerable coaxing—the promise of a Le Pig Mac and a Cajun Pork Dog as well as a vow of silence if his health-conscious wife ever got wind of the forbidden feast—but in the end his hankering belly had beaten out his hesitant brain.

I could understand why Craig wouldn't want to meet his banker's girlfriend and secretary for breakfast, but there was one thing that I couldn't wrap my hurt head around—he hadn't once reminded me about my lips blowing up like two blowfish at his crawdad boil. And if you knew Craig, then you knew that he was the guy who was going to jokingly remind you of that thing you'd rather forget every time you talked to him for the rest of your life. And his silence about that sensitive subject spoke volumes. Craig was upset with me.

But why? Did he think that I was a professional problem for Bradley too? If so, where would he have gotten such an idea? No matter how upset Bradley got with me, he would never talk about me behind my back. And Ruth wouldn't betray me, either —not because she was loyal to me, mind you, but because she wouldn't want to jeopardize her job. The obvious source was Jeff. But what could he have told Craig about me that would cause him to sever his friendship with Bradley and pull his money from Pontchartrain Bank? Was it about me breaking into the bank's security room the year before and those other minor incidents that Ruth mentioned? Or was it something else?

As I pondered this puzzle, my phone began to ring. To my relief, it wasn't Ruth. But it wasn't Bradley.

With a sigh, I pulled up to a stoplight near Tulane University and pressed answer. "Hey, David. Whaddya got for me?"

"An epic fail."

My gut tensed. David didn't use gaming terms lightly. "This isn't about the vassal and that sugar baby, is it?"

He took a couple of deep breaths, frat-boy-prepping-to-chug-a-forty style. "They hooked up at the martini mixer."

I slammed my fist on the dashboard. "I thought I told you to stop him from going?"

"I tried," he whined. "But he had, like, meta strength. I stood in front of his door to block him, but he picked me up and moved me out of the way."

My eyes almost popped from my head. The vassal was at least a foot shorter than David, and thanks to a lifetime of computer programming and video games, he had the muscles of a newborn babe. "Where is he now?"

"In his dorm room." He cleared his throat. "That's where I'm calling from."

The tension in my belly relaxed somewhat. "So what's the problem?"

"Yeah. About that." He paused. "He wants to clean out his college account to pay for the sugar baby's boob job."

My stomach bounced like a silicone breast implant on a strutting stripper. Not only was the vassal jeopardizing his own future, he was also laying Veronica's and mine on the line because his parents would surely sue. "This time you've got to stop him."

"Uh, I have," he said in an uncertain tone. "But I don't know how long it's gonna last."

That didn't sound good. "What have you done to the vassal, David?"

"Oh, uh, me and a couple of his dorm mates tied him to his Emperor Palpatine throne with a fifty-foot Ethernet cable."

The light turned green, and I hooked a U-turn. "I'll be right there."

"Open up!" I yelled as I stood outside the vassal's dorm room in Tulane's Monroe Hall. I was in a hurry to get inside—not so much because I was worried about the vassal, but because the hallway smelled like dirty socks.

The door opened to reveal a pasty-faced boy that I recognized from the first time I'd come to the dorm. Actually, it wasn't so much him that I recognized as his orthodontic headgear. "What's your name again?"

"Shorty." He was as solemn as a soldier as he stepped aside.

The room was so jam-packed with computer equipment and video consoles that it smelled like a Best Buy. But compared to the hallway, it was like perfume to my nose.

As I crossed the threshold, I spotted David sitting beside the vassal's *Star Wars*-themed throne. "Untie him this instant."

"But he'll try to escape," he protested as he rose to his feet.

I strode over to the throne and spun the vassal around to face me. Despite the stress of being bound, he still had his usual slack-jawed stare. "We can trust you to stay put, right Vassal?"

"Honestly," he began, "I'm probably going to make a break for it."

I bowed my aching head. *Why were men so difficult?*

"I know how to handle this," Shorty announced. He reached for the crystal-studded Godric Gryffindor sword hanging on the exposed brick wall above the gaming console.

"Slow down, Shorty." I pulled him away from the sword by the back of his Dumbledore's Army of Tulane t-shirt. "There's no need for weaponry. Now is there, Vassal?"

He shrugged. "Well, if I'm gonna run..."

I pursed my lips. By this point, I was pretty sure that I was getting a headache on top of my migraine.

David looked from the vassal to me. "What should we do?"

"Don't worry. I got this." Resting my hands on the throne armrests, I bent over and leaned into the vassal's face. "You can't throw away your college degree on this girl because you're going to need a lucrative career to keep her in breast lifts. Trust me when I tell you that those implants are eventually going to drop." I straightened and added, "Not that I would know anything about that."

His magnified eyes blinked behind his thick lenses. "You make a valid point."

"All righty, then." I patted him on the thigh. "David's going to untie you, and then we're going to have a chat about the martini mixer. And if you try to run, or if you blow your college money on breasts at any point after I leave here today, then I'm going to get that Ethernet cable, hog-tie you with it, skewer you with your sword, and roast you over a spit like we do in Texas. Sound good?"

His slack-jaw slackened, and Shorty slipped from the room.

David dropped to his knees and began untying the cable at the vassal's feet.

I took a seat on the vassal's twin bed and opened a pizza box. I hadn't eaten a thing since the *pain perdu*, and seeing the vassal tied up like a roast reminded me that it was well past lunchtime. "What's this girl's name, anyway?"

"Sugar Cherie." The vassal sighed. "She's really sweet."

"I'm sure." I bit into an ice-cold slice of pepperoni. "So," I began, covering my full mouth with my hand, "did this, uh, Cherie give you any more info about Amber's sugar daddy? Like a name or a description?"

He shook his head, which was the only part of his body that he could still move. "She never saw the guy because she wasn't at the sugar bowl party Amber went to. Cherie only heard about him after the fact when she ran into her at the mall."

"Crap." I gnawed off a piece of crust.

David began to work a knot behind the vassal's knees. "Didn't she tell you that the guy turned out to be someone Amber already knew?"

The vassal started, as though coming out of a Sugar Cherie–induced stupor. "I almost forgot. Amber said that her sugar daddy was a man she'd known for a while. Apparently, she wasn't aware that he'd been in the market for a sugar baby."

It wasn't much of a lead given that Amber had regularly come into contact with men who spent money on her, but Shakey did come to my mind. "Did she tell you anything else about him? Any little detail?"

The vassal rubbed his freed knees. "Only that he rented her an expensive apartment."

So, the apartment was courtesy of the sugar daddy, and not the mystery mom. "Did you learn anything at all about how the business works?"

"Not really." He stood up so that David could untie the cable at his wrists. "You create an account, and then you can browse the sugar babies' profiles and exchange messages with them. Plus, they have the parties."

"Cherie invited you to the mixer today, right?" I popped a piece of pepperoni into my mouth.

"Yes, but I also got an email invite from the owner—some guy who goes by the name Peach."

I started choking on the pepperoni, and the vassal, whose hands were now free, whacked me on the back, knocking the food from my throat. Personally, I suspected that he was paying me back for my earlier threat, but I couldn't worry about that at the moment.

Because all I could think about was King and his favorite color.

Peach.

It was a long shot, but it wasn't out of the realm of possibility that the preacher was the owner of the sugaring service given his pimp past.

Was it?

20

"If you ask me, Craig escaped through the bathroom window," Ruth said, looking in the direction of the men's room at Cochon Butcher where Craig had gone a good fifteen minutes before.

"Well, I didn't ask you." I rested my elbows on the butcher-block table and massaged my temples. After doing some fleeing of my own—from my family—and spending the night on a couch at Private Chicks, my migraine was gone. But breakfast with Ruth was bringing it back.

She slurped through her straw and jabbed it in the ice. "You probably ran him off with the way you've been beating around the bush about the business at the bank."

I glared at her through my hands. "That's ridiculous, and you know it. He just overdid it with the meal."

The old-world market-style restaurant was a butcher shop, sandwich counter, and wine bar, and within forty-five minutes of arriving, Craig had taken liberal advantage of all three.

I glanced at Ruth's empty whiskey glass—the third of the morning. "That cherry bounce is alcoholic, you know."

"Oh, pshaw." She shooed me and swayed slightly on the tall metal stool. "It's made from cherries."

"Uh, and brandy." I widened my eyes for emphasis.

"And that's made from grapes, which makes this a fine fruit punch." She raised her glass in a salute. "It was one of George Washington's favorite drinks. He used to make it all the time."

"That explains the cherry tree—and the false teeth." I looked around the renovated warehouse and spotted Craig en route to our table.

I turned to Ruth. "Here he comes. Remember, I'm doing the talking."

"All right, but if you don't find out why he's closing his account in the next five minutes..." She made a slicing motion across her neck with one of her plastic cocktail swords.

I rubbed my sweaty palms on my jeans as Craig took his seat.

"I thank you ladies for the nice meal and the pleasant company." He pulled a handkerchief from the pocket of his beige button-down and wiped sweat from his brow—courtesy of the pint of Covington Pontchartrain Pilsner and side of hot boudin sausage he'd had for dessert. "Now why don't you tell me what it is that you need my help with?"

"Actually..." I paused and licked my lips. "Bradley's the one who needs your help."

Craig looked from me to Ruth. "Are you sure this is about him?"

That was an odd question. "Of course I am." I hesitated as I weighed whether to mention Jeff, but then I decided that it was best to be vague in case he and Craig were friends. "Someone at the bank is intentionally sabotaging Bradley."

"And outside the bank too." Ruth pointed her sword at me.

I was tempted to kick her, but it was too much of a risk. She wasn't known for keeping her lips locked, especially when she was liquored up.

"Franki, I don't think anyone at the bank has it in for Bradley." Craig folded his hands. "If he's in trouble, he's either brought it on himself or..." His voice trailed off.

"Or what?" I pressed.

"Well, maybe Ms. Walker's right." His normally booming tone had grown subdued. "Bradley's troubles could be due to someone outside of work."

Ruth grinned behind her glass.

Of course, I suspected that he was referring to me, so I decided to turn the tables on him. "If you're referring to long-time clients like yourself taking their money elsewhere, then yes, his problems stem from the outside."

He pursed his lips. "That's not what I mean."

My eyes narrowed. "What exactly *do* you mean?"

Craig looked down at his empty plate. "A man in Bradley's position needs—"

He stopped short as the bald, bespectacled bartender hand-delivered Ruth's fourth cherry bounce.

When the bartender had left, I asked, "Needs what?"

"A good secretary behind him," Ruth replied, raising her glass and drinking to herself.

I snorted and rolled my eyes.

"You laugh," Craig said in an admonishing tone. "But Ms. Walker's onto something."

"Ain't that the truth, Ruth?" She cackled and drank to herself again.

It took me a second to figure out what he was getting at, but it soon became painfully clear. What Bradley needed wasn't a good secretary—it was a good woman. And, apparently, I wasn't one. "Why don't you just come out and say it, Craig?"

His ruddy complexion turned as red as Ruth's cherry bounce. "You know I've always liked you, Franki—"

"But what?" I interrupted as I crossed my arms.

He slid off his stool and pulled a manila envelope from the side pocket of his briefcase. "It's only right that you know. I got these pictures in two emails—the most recent came last night."

My hands were shaking as I took the envelope and pulled out the pictures. As I flipped through them, so many things began to make sense, starting with the reason I'd been followed. Based on the images, I gathered that the photographer could've also been the driver of the car that had almost clipped me and possibly even the man in black.

There were seven photos in all—me being released from Central Lockup, holding a pentagram at Erzulie's Authentic Voodoo, drinking booze from a bag in front of Vieux Carré Wine & Spirits, hanging out with a preacher who looked like a pimp on Bourbon Street, wrestling with a drag queen outside a drunk stripper's house, stripping with a snake at Madame Moiselle's, and, the coup de grace, lying unconscious in the arms of a wino.

With each picture, Ruth's breathing had grown heavier.

But I refused to look at her—or at Craig, for that matter. Instead, I took a minute to fight back the angry tears stinging my eyes. I couldn't imagine what I'd done to deserve such a hateful attack, or how I was going to undo the damage to Bradley. Because even though I could explain the pictures, they were still proof enough that I was a professional and personal problem that Bradley needed to wash his hands of if he wanted to save his job and salvage his career. It was time for me to walk away so that Bradley could make things right at work and move on.

When I finally had my emotions in check, I looked at Craig. "I'm assuming that the sender of those emails was Jeff Payne?"

He bowed his head in reply.

Ruth bowed her head too, but she wasn't mad. She was as juiced as a jackrabbit on a wheatgrass farm.

~

Glenda opened her apartment door strutting her stuff to the RuPaul song "Supermodel (You Better Work)." Even though it was past noon, she was still in her pajama pasties. "Hello, Miss Franki." She shook her *Playboy* bunny tail. "Do we have investigating to do?"

"It's St. Joseph's Day, so I'm calling it a mental health day," I replied, fully conscious of the fact that I had to carry out the lunatic act of stealing a lemon from a church that night. "But I was hoping to talk to Veronica. Is she around?"

"She went to lunch with Dirk, sugar." Her eyes narrowed as she scrutinized my face. "Why don't you come in so we can chat?"

I really wanted to vent to Veronica about what Jeff had done, but if I had to choose between talking to Glenda and the nonne, it was a no-brainer. "Okay, but are you having a party or something?"

"A few of the girls from Lucky Pierre's are here," she replied as I stepped inside. "And Miss Carnie's on her way."

That explained the music selection.

Glenda closed the door behind me. "We're cooking for Amber's funeral tomorrow. And between you and me," she said in a low voice, "those women are slave drivers. I've worked on my feet, knees, and hands for years, and I can barely keep up with them."

Probably because they're really men. "Hey, where's Maybe?"

"Still asleep." She gestured toward the giant champagne glass in the center of her all white living room, and I could make out Maybe curled up in faux fur blankets inside.

"Must be nice," I muttered, thinking about my bedtub and that blasted enema bag as I followed Glenda into the kitchen.

After days of seeing the nonne baking in black at my house, the scene at Glenda's was disorienting. With Céline in a sheer Cher-style number, Dolly in a crystal country costume, and

Gaysia in a geisha-inspired gown, I felt like I was backstage at Cirque du Soleil—or The Grand Ole Opry—instead of in a kitchen. "Hey guys, er, gals. What're y'all making?"

"A chocolate-cherry piecaken," Dolly chirped as she stirred cherries in a saucepan. "It's a drag dessert."

I opened the cabinet and got a champagne flute—the only glassware Glenda kept in the house. "How is that drag?"

Céline cocked a silver-glittered brow as she kneaded dough. "Because it's a pie baked inside a cake."

"Okay?" I turned on the faucet and filled my glass.

Glenda lit a cigarette in a pink holder. "It's all in the imagery, Miss Franki. Think of it as beef cake but with cherry pie."

For the first time I was grateful that I'd given up sweets for Lent. I took a sip of water and pulled out a chair, but there was raw poultry on the seat cushion. "Ugh! Who put these chicken cutlets here?"

Gaysia turned off the mixer and picked them up with her bare hands. "Uh, *hello*, Hunty! It's not like they're the kind you eat."

"What other kind is there?" I asked, bewildered.

"The kind you make boobies with," she replied, stuffing them into her bra.

I poured out my water and grabbed an open bottle of champagne.

"What's eating at you, sugar?" Glenda sat on the kitchen table trucker-girl-mudflap-style. "Are you having more man troubles?"

"You could say that." I flopped into the chair. "Jeff Payne, the manager at Bradley's bank, has been sending pictures of me in compromising positions to the bank clients."

Glenda gave me a half-lidded look. "You took nudie pics?"

"Werk it, girl," Céline said as she rolled out the piecrust.

Gaysia licked chocolate cake batter from her finger. "Sounds like Ms. Cheesecake could teach us a thing or two in the dessert department."

"It wasn't like that." I filled my champagne glass to the brim. "Out of context the pictures look incriminating, but they're not."

"Mm-hmm," the queens intoned in unison.

"I'm serious," I protested. "Jeff set me up so that he could get Bradley fired and take his position as president."

Dolly stopped stirring. "Now why in the heck would this man sabotage you to get your beau's job?"

"Because women have been exploited by men throughout herstory," Gaysia replied, jabbing the mixer at an invisible enemy.

Céline shook her rolling pin. "Someone needs to make this Jeff guy RuPaulogize."

"He'll get what's coming to him, girls." Glenda took a deep drag off her cigarette. "'Whatsoever a man soweth, that shall he also reap.'"

My jaw dropped as my injured brain wondered whether it had hallucinated that Bible quote. If it hadn't, then forget Cirque du Soleil and The Grand Ole Opry—Glenda's kitchen was *The Twilight Zone*.

As if to reinforce my theory, Carnie entered the room sporting a blonde pixie wig and a shift dress with long, puffed sleeves covered with pink, yellow, and orange daisies. She looked like the 1960s model Twiggy, only trunky.

"Sorry I'm late." She spotted me and put a hand on her chest. "Well, look what the tiger cat dragged in. I haven't heard from you in so long that I thought you'd run off to the jungle to live among your kind—the snakes."

I sighed. Carnie was no hippie at a love-in, no matter what her outfit implied. "Um, I saw you three days ago, and I've been working on your case ever since."

She sniffed and eyeballed my champagne. "Doesn't look like you're working now."

"It's Saturday, Miss Carnie." Glenda gave her a reproachful look. "Miss Franki's taking a well-deserved day off."

Carnie glanced at her mod Mary Janes and managed to look quasi-contrite. "I was shocked when I saw the news about Curaçao's murder. Glenda said she was wearing an amber pendant. Do you think it was mine?"

"I'm no Dirk, but I'd say it was the fake," I replied. "Real amber doesn't sparkle the way that pendant did when I shined my flashlight on it."

Céline placed a platter of pigs in a blanket in front of me and winked. "The weenies are tucked extra tight."

"Awesome," I said, because it seemed like the appropriate reply.

"You know," Carnie began as she took a seat, "I can't say I'm surprised that Commie waxer is a killer."

"We don't know that Nadezhda killed anyone." I helped myself to a pig in a blanket. "Eugene is still a suspect, and so is Amber's ex-pimp."

Glenda exhaled a puff of smoke. "This is the first I've heard of you suspecting King. What gives?"

I blew on the piping hot pig. "Yesterday I found out that he might be the owner of the sugaring company Amber was working for."

Carnie shrugged her psychedelic shoulders. "So, he found a new way to exploit her. That doesn't make him the killer, either."

"I know, but preaching for tips on Bourbon Street has to be the world's worst way to make a living—second only to begging at a homeless shelter." I pulled the pig from the blanket and popped it into my mouth. "He needs another source of income, and your necklace could've set him up in suits for a long time."

Glenda stubbed out her cigarette. "Miss Eve did tell us that

King has been upstairs at Madame Moiselle's, so he knows his way around the place."

"Right." I swallowed and bit into the blanket. "I just have to verify that he goes by the nickname Peach."

"Peach?" Carnie echoed. "Gurl, I heard Amber talking on the phone to someone by that name about a month ago. That's why I thought she was hooking again."

I almost choked in mid-chew.

"Why?" Glenda slid seductively off the table. "What did she say?"

Carnie pressed flower-power fingernails to her pixie. "She said something about not being able to take on another client while she was in school. I figured it had to be a regular john."

I swallowed. "Or a second sugar daddy."

Either way, it was time to pay another visit to the pulpit.

SEMI-CONVINCED that I was being punked, I glanced in the rearview mirror and then turned to stare at my mother from my Mustang window. "Are you guys seriously going to watch the St. Joseph's Day parade from Madame Moiselle's balcony?"

"Well, what do you expect us to do, Francesca?" She flailed her arms like a drowning woman. "Santina just started walking again, and your nonna doesn't like crowds. It's the perfect place."

Sure, except for the nude women, the horny men, the simulated sex acts, the excessive drinking, the foul language, and the occasional fist fights. "Uh, does this mean that you're okay with me stripping there?"

My mother's lips grew as thin as a switchblade. "I didn't drive all the way from Houston—with your nonna, no less—to have you smart off to me. Drop the attitude before you get back from parking the car."

"So much for the mental health day," I said as I pulled away from the curb, and I didn't care if she'd heard me. I wasn't big on parades, especially after I'd gotten arrested at the last one. And now not only did I have to go to a parade, but I had to watch it with my mom and the nonne from lap dance chairs on the balcony of a sex club.

If I ever made it back, that is. The parade was due to start at six, which wasn't for another hour. But the Quarter was already packed, and I had to make it the mile to the Private Chicks parking lot.

As I inched my way up Burgundy Street, I started to think about Bradley and the fact that he hadn't called. Attorney's orders or no, he should've contacted me by now, and I couldn't understand why he hadn't. He wasn't the type to blame me for his own actions, so the only thing I could guess was that he was embarrassed about punching Detective Sullivan. *Or...*

My blood ran so cold that icicles pierced my heart.

...Jeff had sent him those pictures.

I shuddered and shook off the thought. Even though it didn't matter if he had seen the pictures since I was planning to break up with him, I couldn't go there, not now. To distract myself, I looked out the window at some members of the Italian-American Marching Club who were standing by their traditional ATV-drawn chariots. I took one look at their signature black tuxedoes with flashy red and green bowties and stacks of matching Mardi Gras beads around their necks, and I swerved onto St. Ann.

Forget the freakin' parade, I had a pimp-preacher to call on.

It took twenty minutes to travel the two short blocks to King's corner, but I was rewarded for my travail. He was standing in the pulpit in a silk dollar-bill suit—not with bills pinned to the fabric like Glenda did to me on my birthday but with solid dollar-bill print fabric.

And on the subject of bills, a buxom fifty-something woman in a bodacious blue spandex minidress was in the process of handing him a wad of them. It was too much to be a donation for a street sermon but enough to be a payout from a long day of hooking.

King looked over his shoulder when he pocketed the cash, as though making sure no one had seen him. By chance, our eyes locked through the windshield, and he broke into a run.

On autopilot, I whipped into a customer-service zone and hopped from the car. As I gave chase, he dashed up the street and darted to the right.

When I rounded the corner, he ducked into the last place I would've expected—Cathedral Academy, an old convent chapel that served as the site of St. Louis Cathedral's altar to St. Joseph.

I ran inside and saw David and the vassal standing by the altar as King hoofed it up the aisle on the right side of the building.

"Stop that preacher!" I yelled as I pointed at King.

Not known for their physical prowess—unless sugar baby boobs were at play—David and the vassal began pelting King with lemons, presumably those that my mom and nonna had bought to ensure my engagement.

At least they're serving some purpose, I thought, *because my engagement odds aren't looking good.*

King stopped running and shielded himself with his arms, and I shoved him stomach-down to the ground.

"You're Peach, aren't you?" I ground out as I straddled his back and twisted his arms behind him.

"What choo talkin' 'bout, woman?" he demanded with one side of his face pressed to the floor.

"You own the sugar baby company that Amber signed up with. Admit it," I ordered as I gave his wrists a twist.

"Ow!" He kicked his leopard-spotted shoes. "I don't own no damn comp'ny."

"Then what was that woman paying you for?" I leaned close to his ear. "And don't try telling me it was for a sermon, because if you do, you'll be preaching that song and dance to the police."

His body went slack. "I cain't be arrested. I'm in a sanctuary."

That explained the choice of the chapel. I turned to David and the vassal. "Arm yourselves."

"That won't be necessary, now." King drew a deep breath. "If you mus' know, I'm often called upon by the female doubters in my congregation to help them find the divine—through sacred unity."

"I don't understand."

He grinned revealing his gold teeth. "I help them find Gawd with sex."

I cocked a brow as the reality of what he'd said dawned on me—and as I tried to comprehend how any woman could get past his suits. "You're a *gigolo*?"

"If you don't mind, I prefer the term *spiritual escort.*"

I climbed off of him. "No more questions."

King stood up and straightened his pink dollar-sign tie. "I'd like to say it was a pleasure, but instead I'll wish you all a blessed day." He looked at me and winked. "And may the Lawd be with you."

For once, the vassal wasn't the only one with a slack-jawed stare. David and I watched equally open-mouthed as the pimp-turned-preacher-gigolo strolled from the chapel like a king leaving his castle.

"We'd better pick up those lemons," I said as I noted the whispers and scowls of a few churchwomen. "What're you guys doing here, anyway?"

David scratched his head. "Uh, your nonna said we had to test out the altar before you guys got here from the parade."

I rolled my eyes. "Thank God it's finally St. Joseph's Day so I can get back to my life, and you can get back to working on the case."

"Oh, I have something for you." He pulled a piece of paper from his back pocket. "I looked up Old New Orleans Traditional Witchcraft, but it's, like, lame."

"Why do you say that?" I asked as I bent over to retrieve a lemon.

The vassal pushed up his glasses. "Because the practitioners rely mainly on different colors of the same candle for all their witchcraft needs."

"Huh?" I stood up and looked at the color printout in David's hand, and my face turned as white as the image he was pointing to.

It was the candle of the nude woman that I'd seen in the kitchen at Madame Moiselle's on the day Curaçao's body was discovered.

The one that Eve Quebedeaux had lit.

21

"Why did we have to visit this altar again?" Glenda asked as she wrestled with the blue and white tablecloths that the nonne had draped over her. "I'm sweatin' like a whore in church in this getup."

I refrained from commenting on her second statement given that a) the Cathedral Academy was owned by the Catholic Church, and b) she was dressed like the Virgin Mary. "You heard the nonne—because we're stripper sinners, you need to eat, and I have to steal a lemon."

"Oh, for heaven's sake." She grabbed a grissino off the table, bit off the tip, and chewed it like she was eating a dead cricket. "There." She choked down the breadcrumbs. "I've eaten. Now I'm heading back over to Madame Moiselle's."

I grabbed her by the garments. "Not without me you don't. You're my ticket out of this hell."

She rolled her eyes. "Then swipe a damn lemon already."

By this point, I was more than ready to steal a lemon if it meant getting my mom and nonna on the road back to Houston. The problem was that people were milling around all three tiers of the altar. "I have to wait until no one's looking."

Glenda frowned at a fig pie next to a platter of lemons. "Then you might want to gouge out the eyes on this pie."

The only eyes I wanted to gouge out were Bruno Messina's, because they'd been glued to my chest ever since he'd arrived with Santina to see the altar. "That's a St. Lucy's eye pie," I explained as I gave Bruno a go-to-hell glare. "They put eyes on it because she was blinded for refusing to renounce her Christian faith."

She blinked blue lashes. "That's an odd tradition."

What could I say? Obviously, since I was about to steal a lemon from the church to get a husband, the oddities in the Sicilian-American culture abounded.

"And what does '*prega per noi*' mean?" she asked, referring to the words written in crust on the pie.

"'Pray for us.' And frankly, I could use some prayers right now." I looked longingly at a bottle of Pinot Grigio on the altar. "Between my crazy family and this case, I don't think I'm going to make it to thirty-one."

As though reading my mind, Glenda picked up the bottle and popped the cork. "Well, your mom and nonna are leaving the day after tomorrow, and you're making progress in the case. You've practically ruled out Saddle and King as suspects."

"But I've added Eve, I think." I picked up a wine glass. "I mean, she's the house mom, so it makes sense that she could be Amber's mother figure. I just can't believe she's a witch. She seems so normal."

Glenda filled my glass. "Appearances can be deceiving, Miss Franki."

"I'll say." I glanced at her Virgin Mary look. "The thing is, Nadezhda could be a witch too."

"Why don't you call Witchiepoo?" she asked as she poured herself a drink.

I almost gagged on my wine. "Theodora?"

"No, sugar," she replied drily. "The witch from *H.R. Pufnstuf*."

I looked at her like she'd lost it. "Why would I want to call that whacked witch?"

"Because she might be able to tell you whether Eve is a witch." She tipped her glass toward me. "And Nadezhda too, for that matter."

As much as I wanted to avoid Theodora, I knew she could help. After all, she was a *witchcraft consultant*, according to her business card. "I guess I could ask her to stop by Amber's funeral in the morning. I'm sure Eve and Nadezhda will be there."

"Perfect." She took the wine from my hand. "Why don't you go pick your fruit and then give her a call?"

"All right. Here goes nothing." Glancing from side to side, I approached the lemons. When I reached the table, the platter raised to the level of my hand. Astonished, I looked around and spotted my nonna—holding a remote control.

Now I knew why she'd had David and the vassal design the altar.

"Franki, baby!" Bruno shouted from behind me.

I jumped as though my hand had been in the collection plate instead of the lemon platter.

He lowered his mirrored shades. "Or should I call you *Tiger Eye*?"

As smooth as his slicked back hair, I thought. "You don't call me anything after throwing me under the bus to your mother."

"Hey, it was nothing personal." He straightened the black collar of his *Saturday Night Fever* shirt. "I had to tell her something after she found a receipt from the club in my pants pocket."

No doubt when she was doing your laundry.

"By the way, Mamma said you liked those peanuts." He gave a self-assured sneer. "Consider them a belated birthday gift."

I rolled my eyes. The peanuts reminded me that I still had to go back to the dentist to get my permanent crown, which was yet another reason to dislike Bruno. "Yeah. Thanks."

He nudged me with his shoulder. "I hear you're gonna swipe a lemon."

"Why would I do that?" There was no way I was going to let this creep think I was looking for a proposal.

His beady black eyes widened. "Because you're not getting any younger, and I've seen you strip."

Before I could react, Glenda stepped between us and pointed at a platter with twelve whole fried trout, symbolizing the twelve apostles.

"Move it on along, mister, or you'll be sleeping with the fishes." She picked up a loaf of bread shaped like a cross and held it like a club. "You got me?"

Bruno backed away and ran to his mother.

"Now's your chance, sugar." Glenda pointed the cross at the altar. "Go get yourself a lemon."

I saw my nonna and a short, dark-haired woman headed in our direction. "I can't. My nonna's on her way over here with someone."

Nonna shuffle-strutted up wearing a tricolored sash that one of the parade marchers had bestowed on her, as well as the "Kiss me, I'm Italian" beads that she'd wrenched from the grip of a Swedish tourist. With her black mourning dress, the red and green accessories made her look like Miss Elderly Italian-America.

"Glenda," Nonna began as she took her by the arm, "my friend-a Mary, she want-a to meet you."

I smirked and wondered if it was because of Glenda's Virgin Mary garb.

"How nice." Glenda smoothed her tablecloths.

"She say you bake-a the best-a man hands she's-a seen," Nonna said with an approving nod.

Mary put a hand on her bosom. "The detail! I don't know how you do it."

Oh, I did. Glenda had intimate knowledge of the male hand.

Mary turned to me, wide-eyed. "If you haven't seen her work, you really should take a look at it."

"Eh, she's-a no gotta time for that." Nonna shoved me toward the altar. "She's-a gotta get a lucky fava bean. Right, Franki?"

Of course, lucky fava bean was code for lemon. But, I figured I could use a fava bean too since it was supposed to give you good luck in the coming year. "Sure, Nonna." I sighed. "Whatever you say."

While they continued to talk man hands, I made my way around the altar looking for a bowl of the beans. I passed the *pasta milanese* topped with *mudica*, which was browned bread-crumbs representing Joseph's sawdust, the fried *pignolatti* pastries reminiscent of the pine cones that Jesus played with as a child, and, my favorite, the *pupa cu l'ova* bread baskets baked with dyed eggs inside as a reminder of the coming of Easter.

I found the fava beans next to the *cucchidati* fig cookies at the base of the life-sized statue of St. Joseph holding the baby Jesus, which was on the main tier of the altar. I pocketed a bean, hoping that it would undo the effects of the curse I'd been living under.

Thinking of the curse reminded me of the one allegedly on those who hunted for the missing Amber Room. Logic told me that the people who had died searching for the priceless trea-sure had probably been killed by accident or by the hands of greedy individuals, and not because of any curse. Was that what had happened to Amber and Curaçao? Had they been killed for the amber pendant? Or were their murders tied to a love gone horribly wrong, as the bottle of amaretto suggested?

And where was the pendant? I had a hunch that whoever

had broken into Maybe's house had been looking for it. But was it there?

I gazed up at the statue of St. Joseph and the baby Jesus. As I looked to them for divine inspiration, something whizzed past me and knocked a statuette of the Virgin Mary to the floor. Startled, I looked down.

It was a lemon.

I looked back at St. Joseph as another lemon shot from between his feet and hit me hard on the arm.

Then I clenched my teeth. Either St. Joseph was trying to tell me that the answers to my questions lay in finding a husband, or Nonna had David and the vassal put an air cannon underneath the statue that she was now using to pelt me with lemons.

Clearly, it was the latter.

Crouching into my old softball outfielder stance, I caught the next lemon and slipped it into my pocket. Then I turned and looked around. Incredibly, no one seemed to have noticed.

Cursing my nonna all the while, I knelt to pick up the statuette and saw that it had broken. I was pretty sure that breaking an image of the Virgin Mary negated the effects of the lemon and the fava bean and ensured more years of bad luck than a broken mirror. But hey, I'd been living this way for thirty years. What was ten or so more?

The statuette had broken in half, and it was hollow. I fit Mary's upper and lower half together to see whether they could be glued, and I flashed back to another hollow figurine I'd seen.

A jolt went through me as though God were striking me down. And no, I hadn't been hit by another lemon. I'd been struck by a shocking realization.

I knew exactly where the amber pendant was hidden.

FROM MY STOOL at the Madame Moiselle's bar, I rubbed my eyes and looked at the stripper pole clock. It was ten forty a.m., and I'd spent a sleepless night thinking about Bradley and the case. Now everyone I'd questioned was gathered near Amber's casket in front of the main stage—Carlos, Iris, Bit-O-Honey, Saddle, Maybe, Eugene, Nadezhda, Eve, King, and even Dr. Lessler. It felt like the culminating scene in an Agatha Christie novel. I just wished that Miss Marple or Hercule Poirot would show up and solve the murders.

Other guests included Detective Sullivan, who, like me, was keeping an eye on the situation. He was seated at a table in the middle with his men, as was Carnie with hers. My mother was sitting in the back with the nonne. She'd insisted on attending to show her support since Amber didn't have any immediate family. And the nonne had come because that's what little old Italian ladies did in their spare time.

One thing that struck me was the mood in the room. No one was sad, and everyone was tense. The dancers didn't know what to make of the cops being there, the cops didn't know what to make of the drag queens being there, and none of them knew what to make of the nonne being there. But the nonne didn't seem bothered by the odd assortment of people. They were too busy trying to cover all the exposed flesh with their shawls, and I, for one, was grateful that they'd bundled up Bit-O-Honey and her boobs good and tight.

Out of the corner of my eye, I spotted Glenda coming downstairs from the dressing room in a black cage dress and a matching mourning hat with a veil. She paused and placed her hand on the closed casket and then strutted up to me. "Is Glinda the Good Witch here yet?"

"Pfff," I scoffed. "She's more like Elphaba with a healthy dose of Endora. And I left her a voice mail, but I haven't heard back from her."

Glenda slid onto a stool. "Well, I hope she flies in on her broom soon, because we have to start at eleven o'clock sharp. The jazz band has another funeral after this."

I took a sip of the obituary cocktail that Carlos had prepared for me. "What's the agenda?"

"We'll process with the hearse to the cemetery for the burial, and then we'll process back to the club for the food and stripper-oke." She pulled a pair of black funeral gloves from her bag. "You know, a proper funeral."

I tilted my head to one side and then the other, unsure where to start. "What's stripperoke?"

"Karaoke with strippers," she replied as she pulled a glove onto her hand. "They strip to try to distract the singer."

By this point, I knew better than to question Glenda's logic, but I had to ask. "How is that proper at a funeral?"

She slipped on her other glove. "Amber was a stripper, sugar. And the mourners need some form of release."

Oh, they'll get it, I thought as I took another drink of my cock-tail. "Any word from Shakey?"

"Not so far." She lit the cigarette in her *Breakfast at Tiffany's*-style holder and exhaled. "But he's still got fifteen minutes."

Someone tapped me on the back, and I turned to see Nonna and Santina armed with shawls.

"Ciao, Franki." Nonna turned to Glenda. "I see you got-a your face all-a covered up." Her gaze lowered to the straps that barely covered her body. "But it look-a like you forgot-a your dress again."

Santina shoved a shawl at Glenda. "*Dai, prendilo!*"

"She's telling you to take it," I explained in an apologetic tone.

"No ma'am." Glenda gestured to her cage dress with one hand while holding her cigarette with the other. "This is proper attire for strip clubs and jazz funerals. I draw the line at a habit."

Nonna raised her chin, and Santina lowered her lids.

Sensing a Sicilian storm on the horizon, I said, "They're not habits. They're mourning dresses."

Glenda forced a smile. "I'm not saying I don't like them. In fact, I think they're...well...*convenient.* You didn't even have to change for the funeral."

"You know us-a," Nonna said, pointing a thumb at herself and Santina. "At-a our age, we're always-a mourning something!" She chuckled as though enjoying her grieving status. And from the way she talked about my late nonnu, I was pretty sure that she was.

Santina nudged my nonna. "*Il limone.*"

"Oh, that's-a right!" Nonna turned to me. "Show us the lemon that you stole-a last night."

Refraining from an eye roll, I fished the fruit from my purse and noticed that it was bruised.

Nonna planted her hands on her cheeks with a smack. "*Oddio!* You stole a *lemon* lemon?"

A bitter taste filled my mouth like I'd just bitten into the bad lemon. "Is that a problem?"

"Sorry to interrupt," Carnie boomed as she bounced up in a black Elizabethan bustle dress and a hat with a bulky black bow. "But we need to chat."

I glanced at my nonna, anxious for her reply. With my luck, the bum lemon meant that Bruno would be the one to propose to me instead of Bradley.

"*Pronto,*" Carnie pressed, yanking me from my seat to the end of the bar.

Prying my arm from her manly grip, I huffed, "What's the matter with you?"

She crossed her big biceps over her bigger bosom. "Glenda says you know where the pendant is, so I'm wondering why I don't have it. Are you trying to squeeze a few extra paychecks out of me or something?"

"No one wants to squeeze you." *Least of all me.* "When you hired me for this case, you said you wouldn't feel right if you didn't try to find Amber's killer. I think I have a way to do that."

The muscles in her jaw relaxed. "I'm listening."

Even though she seemed calm, I took a few steps back to keep a safe distance between us. "Since the funeral is closed casket, you start the rumor that your amber pendant has been found, and you say that given the tragedy now associated with it, you've decided to let Amber be buried in the necklace. Then we wait and see who tries to open the casket before it goes into the ground, and we have our killer."

"It's morbid, but I like it." She put her hands on her hips. "Is there someone specific you want me to tell?"

"The queens," I replied without missing a beat.

Her blue lids dropped like metal shutters. "Are you implying that we're gossips?"

"Yes, I am."

She nodded, and the bow on her hat did too. "Fair enough."

I exhaled as she turned and bustled back to her table.

When I returned to my stool, a tiny, forty-something man dressed in a dark green suit, black boots, and a black Stetson entered the club.

I patted Glenda's shoulder. "Is that western-style leprechaun Shakey?"

She turned and lifted her veil. "Sure is, sugar. I've never met him, but I've seen him around."

Shakey's spurs jangled as he approached the bar. "Miss Glenda O'Brien?"

"The one and only." She extended a gloved hand, and he didn't have to bow to kiss it.

"Pleased to make your acquaintance," he drawled in a high-pitched voice. "Milton Presacco, but my friends call me Shakey."

Glenda gave a sly smile. "As in, *The Shakiest Gun in the West*?"

"With all due respect, ma'am," he replied, removing his hat, "there's nothing shaky about my gun."

She cocked a brow. "Duly noted, cowboy."

"Um," I interjected to break the awkward sexual-weapon vibe, "why do they call you Shakey?"

He placed his Stetson on the bar counter, which was as tall as he was. "Because I used to own a chain of Shakey's Pizza Parlors. Now I'm in olive oil. Got a grove outside o' Austin."

Texas oil baron, my eye. "Well, my name is Franki Amato, and I was contracted to investigate Amber's murder with Glenda."

He ran a hand through his reddish wisps of hair. "I heard through the grapevine that Miss O'Brien was working with a PI, so I wanted to tell y'all what I told the police."

"You have information about the case?" I asked as I reached into my bag for a pad and pen.

"Indeed I do, ma'am." He straightened his bolo tie. "Like I told that detective, Amber got mixed up in some bad business on account o' her mama—not her real mama, mind you, but kinda like a stepmama."

I glanced at Glenda. "What kind of bad business?"

"She went and got herself a sugar daddy," he said in a low tone.

Glenda crossed her legs. "We know all about that, Shakey."

"Hang on, though," I said, holding up my hand. "What does her mother have to do with the sugar daddy?"

He tucked a thumb inside his silver-buckled belt. "She had a rough view of relationships. Told Amber that all women exchanged their bodies for money, even wives with their husbands. Said she might as well get a man to pay her bills and keep her freedom."

Precisely the kind of thing I could imagine Nadezhda saying. "Do you know anything about her mother or her sugar daddy?"

Shakey scratched his clean-shaven cheek. "I can't say I know anything about the man, but her mama goes by the name o' Peach."

I sunk onto my stool.

Amber's mother owned the sugaring company.

22

────────

"Did you see that?" Gaysia shrieked as she stood in the cemetery with her hands pressed to her wig cap. "That hoochie mama ho pulled off my hair!"

The jazz band abruptly halted their rendition of "The Stripper" as Saddle waved Gaysia's black-and-blonde wig like a handkerchief.

"*Your* hair?" Saddle laughed like a coyote. "You got this fur piece off a German Shepherd."

Gaysia gasped and swiped at Saddle with panda-adorned claws.

A scuffle broke out between the queens and the dancers. And as Detective Sullivan and his men set about breaking up the brawl, feathers and sequins began to fly.

"So much for a 'proper' funeral," I said under my breath, although nothing about it had been proper. Before the procession had gotten underway, the dancers announced that they would be the "first line," traditionally reserved for family, and that the queens would be the "second line," reserved for friends and passersby. A catfight ensued, and rather than "processing" to the cemetery, the strippers and queens had scratched, slapped, and shoved each other the entire way—that is, when they weren't voguing and vamping for onlookers.

"I've had enough of this nonsense," Glenda huffed as she high-stepped onto a tomb in black stripper shoes that said *Pay Your Respects*. "Ladies! Where are your manners? We're in a place of rest."

The scuffling ceased.

Gaysia retrieved her wig from the ground and arranged it on her head. "I know Amber was a stripper, Miss Glenda, but we queens feel that the strippers should walk in the second line on the way back to the club." She smoothed her mofuku kimono. "We belong in the first line because we have style." She turned to Carnie. "Except for you, Lady-boy Macbeth. With those garage doors, you belong in the second line."

"Garage doors?" Carnie's face turned purple. "This blue on my eyelids is a blend, not a single shade."

King stepped between the querulous queens. "There's no need ta fight, ladies..." He turned to Carnie and her crew. "...and gentlemen. Cuz, like our Lawd and savior hisself, King Nation is here ta save the occasion." He grasped the zebra-striped lapels of his black velvet suit. "If it's style y'all want, then I'll lead the procession back ta the club."

I halfway agreed with him. He *was* wearing red leather shoes reminiscent of a previous pope—but his were crocodile, not cow.

"You and I need to talk," Detective Sullivan growled over my shoulder. "Now."

Although I had no intention of speaking to the detestable detective, I followed him down a path, away from the gossip-prone guests. "Until you drop the charges against Bradley, I've got nothing to say to you."

"Well, I have something to say to you." He placed a hand above his holster. "There's a rumor circulating that the missing pendant is on the body. You wouldn't know anything about that, would you?"

As a former cop, I knew that he would be obliged to open Amber's casket if I didn't tell him the truth, and I didn't want it to come to that. "I started the rumor to flush out the killer."

His ice blue eyes turned stone cold. "And you have no idea where the amber is."

I hesitated, and he stepped forward.

"Save your breath," I said, holding up my hands. "I'll tell you where the pendant is when the funeral's over."

Glenda strutted down the pathway with her cigarette holder. Scowling at the detective, she flicked her ash and turned to me. "The service has started, Miss Franki."

"We'll resume this discussion at the end of the ceremony, Amato." He straightened his tie and stalked off toward the gravesite.

She thrust out a hip. "You all right, sugar?"

"Yeah, thanks for coming to get me," I said as we headed back. It wasn't that I didn't want to deal with the detective—I just didn't want to miss the eulogy. Bit-O-Honey had obtained ministry credentials online for Amber's funeral, and it wasn't every day that you got to see an ordained stripper minister.

As we made our way back, Theodora emerged from a burial vault like a zombie from a grave.

I swallowed a scream to avoid causing a scene.

Glenda gave her the onceover. "You must be the witch."

"My name's Theodora." She brushed dirt from her black caftan. "It means God given, which is kind of ironic, don't you think?"

On a couple of levels. I cleared my throat. "Uh, we need to get back to the service. Theodora, I'll point out the two women I left you the message about."

"Sounds like a plan." She extracted a root protruding from a broken crypt and took a bite.

My belly began to bubble like a cauldron. "Do you have to eat here?"

"Yes, we're serving pigs in a blanket and piecaken after the service," Glenda said in a helpful tone.

Theodora spat, and it was red from the root—at least I hoped that's what it was from. "I can't come to the club." She wiped her mouth with her wing-like sleeve. "Tonight's a full moon."

Not wanting any details of her lunar exploits, I hurried toward the attendees and started scouring the seating area by the casket for Nadezhda.

The first two rows of folding chairs were occupied by my mom and the nonne, who'd convinced Shakey to sit with them not only because he was their same size but also because he was now their olive oil contact in the "new country." The strippers were in the last two rows, and King had planted himself among them since they comprised a whole new crop of women that he could help to "find Gawd." The queens stood behind the seating area, this time voluntarily taking a backseat to the strippers, because it meant they were with all the men.

I spotted Nadezhda near the queens, leaning on a mausoleum topped with a stone cross. And I was surprised to see that she was deep in conversation with Drag Dolly, who was presumably spreading the necklace rumor. "That's one of the women right there."

Theodora lowered her sunglasses and fixed her feline eyes on Nadezhda.

Unaware that she was being watched, Nadezhda sidled up to Eugene and whispered something in his ear.

My heart raced when I saw Eugene's gaze lock onto the casket. Even though I was unable to prove it, I was positive that the pair had plotted to steal the pendant.

Theodora pushed up her sunglasses. "That one's a witch, but the kind that starts with a *b*."

At least I'd been right on that count.

"Where's the other woman?" she asked, scanning the crowd.

"Over there." I pointed at Eve, who was standing by a tree to the left of the seating, red-faced, and wringing her hands.

Theodora removed her sunglasses and chewed on the tip. "There's something earthy about her, yes."

I scrutinized Eve, who'd been getting more distraught as the day progressed. "Why do you think that?"

"Have you missed the fact that I'm a witch?" she snapped, pointing her creepy pupils at me.

"D-definitely not," I stuttered, moving backwards a step.

She turned and looked at Eve. "Did you notice that she's wearing amber?"

My head jerked in Eve's direction. Sure enough, it looked like she had an amber pendant around her neck, but it was round, not rectangular like the missing piece. "Maybe in honor of Amber?"

"Or to invoke the mother goddess." Theodora narrowed her eyes like a cat contemplating a mouse. "She seems like an amateur. Is she from New Orleans?"

I shrugged. "Her last name is Cajun, but I just assumed from her accent that she's originally from Georgia."

"Hm." Theodora's red-stained teeth bit her lip. "A Georgia peach."

I froze at the reference. And then I remembered seeing peaches on one of Eve's aprons.

Eve was Peach—Amber's mother and the owner of the sugaring website!

I looked toward the tree, but Eve was gone. Frantic to find her, I glanced around the grounds and realized that she was standing right in front of the casket.

"Farewell, Amber," Bit-O-Honey said as the coffin began to lower into the ground. "We'll see you in that big strip club in the sky."

A murmur of disapproval arose from the queens, most likely because of the strip club reference.

An anguished wail followed.

"You can't take my girl!" Eve screamed and threw herself on the coffin.

A murmur of approval arose from the nonne, since casket diving was a thing among elderly Italian women.

Detective Sullivan rushed to the casket and pulled Eve to her feet, while the ginger officer I'd seen the night of Bradley's arrest began to handcuff her.

"Eve Quebedeaux," the detective announced, "you're under arrest for the murders of Amber Brown and Curaçao."

She gasped. "You can't be serious." As the detective read Eve her rights, she looked from him to me. "Miss Franki, you're an investigator," she shouted over him. "Tell them I didn't murder those girls! You know I could never do such a horrible thing."

I stared at her, unsure what to think. It wasn't clear whether the officers had arrested her because they thought she was making a play for the necklace or because they had evidence against her that I was unaware of. Nevertheless, when Detective Sullivan stopped reciting, I approached her and put my hand on her shoulder. "It's all right, Eve. If you're innocent, you have nothing to worry about."

"I loved Amber," she explained. "Curaçao too, although I did *not* like her behavior. That's why I told Amber to do the spell— to undo the hex that Curaçao had cast on her." She began to sob. "I wanted to make things riiight."

So, it had been an anti-hex spell. I was tempted to ask Eve about the Amaretto di Amore and Amber's sugar daddy, but I couldn't risk compromising the investigation or her defense. She'd said too much already.

Detective Sullivan looked at the ginger officer. "Let's get her to the squad car."

"I loved those girls like they were my own," Eve shouted as they led her away. "I was trying to help them. Why, I even found men to take care of them so they could get out of the stripping business. You have to believe me."

The funny thing was, I did believe her.

But if Eve hadn't killed Amber and Curaçao, who had?

VERONICA SIGHED into the phone receiver. "I feel awful that I missed Amber's funeral because of work. I might have to go ahead and hire a part-time investigator."

I shot straight up in the dental chair. "Swear on your life that it won't be Glenda," I practically shouted into my cell. I lay back down and then sat up again. "Or anyone associated with the Amber Brown case."

"Don't worry, Franki," she breathed. "I swear on my life that if and when I hire someone, it'll be a professional PI."

Still vaguely unsettled, I clutched my phone and scooted deeper into the dental chair.

"Anyway," she continued, "judging from what I've seen on the news this morning, it was quite a ceremony."

"Veronica, even if Federico Fellini, Wes Anderson, and Tim Burton were all directing the same film, they couldn't have created a scene like that." I shook my head at the memory. "When I get to the office, I'll fill you in on all the outlandish details."

"Oh, I'm still at the house." She slammed a cabinet door. "What time will you be in?"

I glanced at the clock and saw that it was already seven thirty. "I thought I'd be out of here by eight or so, but Dr. Lessler's hygienist called in sick, and his receptionist is running late, so he's having to make some calls to try to find a sub. No telling how long that'll take."

"It's a Monday," Veronica said. "While you're there, I'll call my contacts at the police station and try to find out whether there's any chance of Eve being granted bail."

"I would give my eye teeth to be able to question her right now." I glanced at the dental instruments on the tray next to my chair. "On second thought, no I wouldn't."

A knocking sound came from the other end of the line.

"I think your mom and nonna are here to say goodbye," Veronica whispered. "I'll let you go."

"Make sure they actually leave, will you?" I urged, but she had already hung up.

Still holding my phone, I looked at the poster on the ceiling. Seeing the dolphin frolic among the waves made me think of the sea goddess, La Sirène. Even though King had laughed off my question about La Sirène and the amaretto, I still suspected that there was information out there somewhere that could help me connect the liqueur to the crime—and maybe even clear Eve's name.

"Sorry about the wait," Dr. Lessler said from behind me.

From my reclining position, I looked back and saw him in the doorway in his LSU scrubs.

His blondish-brown brow furrowed. "I'm going to call a temp agency for dental hygienists, then I'll be right with you."

"No problem, doc." I held up my phone. "I can do some case research while I wait."

"Great." He flashed his dazzling dentist smile. "Be right back."

Once he was gone, I opened my browser and googled La Sirène. After scrolling through several links, I clicked one that had an alphabetical list of the various voodoo gods and their functions. Baron Samedi was at the top, and the first thing it said was that he was called upon to heal sexual diseases.

I curled my lips. *That explains why King has the Baron as his cane topper.*

The entry for La Sirène referred the reader to the entry for Erzulie. I scrolled up and discovered that the entity known as Erzulie was actually a family of voodoo goddesses divided into four categories, one of which caught my eye—Petro Manifestations. The woman at Erzulie's Authentic Voodoo had implied that Erzulie D'en Tort, who sought vengeance for wronged women and children, was Erzulie Freda's sole Petro aspect. But according to this article, there were three others—Erzulie Mapiangue, who protected newborn babies, Erzulie Toho, who aided those who were slighted in love, and Erzulie Yeux Rouges, who took revenge on unfaithful lovers.

The unfaithful lovers line got my attention. I'd suspected all along that love was a factor in Amber's murder given the bottle of Amaretto di Amore at the crime scene. I figured that either she had some boyfriend who'd found out about her sugar daddy, or she'd cheated on the sugar daddy with someone she really cared about. What I needed to know was whether Erzulie Yeux Rouges was so evil that her acts of revenge included cold-blooded murder.

As tension mounted in my gut, I performed a search on the vengeful Erzulie. And I discovered that when Erzulie Freda's desires as the goddess of love weren't met, she turned into the fierce and fearsome Erzulie Yeux Rouges, which was French for Red-Eyed Erzulie. Apparently, the red eyes referred to crying and anger. And not only was she merciless, but her wrath knew no bounds.

I chewed my thumbnail as I contemplated the reference to the color red. Was there a connection between Erzulie's eyes and the label on the Amaretto di Amore? It was tenuous, but I had to try.

With my heart in my throat, I typed *Erzulie* and *amaretto* into the browser. It took a few minutes, but I located a source in Italian, of all languages, that confirmed what I'd suspected.

Erzulie Yeux Rouges preferred gifts that were red in color, and like Erzulie Freda, she loved to drink amaretto.

"All right," Dr. Lessler said with a clap of his hands.

I jumped at the sound.

He laughed as he took a seat on his stool. "You know, I'm used to people being scared of me, but I've never had a patient jump when I entered the room."

"Oh, it wasn't you. I guess I got spooked by some information I came across." I put my phone beside my left leg and lay back in the chair. "Did you find a hygienist?"

"Ugh." He threw his head back. "The agency's sending someone over, but she won't be here for at least an hour. So, I'll have to go it alone with your crown. Speaking of which," he said, holding up a tooth with a gloved hand, "this is a porcelain-fused-to-metal crown. Pretty cool, huh?"

"I guess," I said, unaffected by his enthusiasm for a fake tooth. "What I'm really interested in is the shot situation."

He smirked and placed my crown on the tray. "Most patients are fine with a topical anesthetic, but if you experience any pain I can administer a local."

I hid my disappointment at the needle news as he placed a bib around my neck.

He pulled up his surgical mask and selected a tool from the tray. "Open, please."

I did as I was told and felt him prodding my gums.

"That was quite a funeral yesterday, wasn't it?" His eyes met mine as he sat up and reached for another tool.

"Uh-huh." I looked at the dolphin to avoid further eye contact.

"I'll tell you what," he said as he began working the tool between my gums and the crown, "the last thing I expected was to see the murderer arrested at the ceremony."

"I O," I replied, which was dentalese for, "I know." Of course, I didn't think that Eve was the killer, but I couldn't tell him that.

He snorted. "Did you believe all that stuff she was saying about loving Amber and Curaçao like they were her own children?"

"I O O," I said, which was the negative, "I *don't* know."

"If she did love them," he said as he tugged at the crown with his fingers, "she sure had a funny way of showing it."

My tooth felt cool, and I watched as he tossed the temporary crown onto the tray.

"Now I'm going to remove the cement." He picked up another instrument. "Let me know if this hurts, okay?"

I nodded and opened wide.

"The part that got me was when she said she had Amber do an anti-hex witchcraft spell," he said as he scraped the surface of my tooth. "What a psycho."

Prior to this case, I would've agreed with his assessment of Eve. But after my crazy encounters with Theodora, Eve just struck me as a sweet but naïve woman who grasped at whatever straws she could—namely, spells—to try to control the uncontrollable.

Dr. Lessler returned the tool to the tray and grabbed a Q-tip.

I focused on the dolphin as he dabbed the anesthetic on my tooth.

He gave a sardonic laugh. "Only in New Orleans."

"Ut?" I asked, the meaning of which was obvious.

"This is the only city I know of where even the witchcraft involves alcohol." He tossed the Q-tip into the trash. "Like the amaretto."

"Oh," I said.

Then my eyes dropped from the dolphin to the doctor.

And the room seemed to rock like I was seasick.

Because the only way Dr. Lessler could have known about the amaretto was if he'd been at the crime scene.

23

———

Dr. Lessler's bright blue eyes turned icy gray, like two frozen lakes. "You're going to need that shot now."

A chill spread through my veins like a lethal injection. He and I both knew that I wasn't in pain and that the shot would be my death sentence. "If I die in your office, it'll be obvious you killed me."

With his gaze glued to me, he reached for a packaged syringe. "Not if I make it look like an accident during oral surgery. Patients do occasionally die in the dental chair."

Something I'd suspected since I started going to the dentist. "But I'm just here to get a crown."

He smirked as he removed the syringe from the plastic. "I'll say that I convinced you to let me remove your wisdom teeth too."

There was no point in protesting—Dr. Lessler was diabolical. My fingers felt for the phone I'd left by my leg, and I tried to buy some time. "Why'd you do it?"

He shrugged. "Simple. Amber had become an expensive nuisance, and I wanted out of the spit business."

The word expensive reminded me of the vassal's conversation with Sugar Cherie about Amber meeting a man she'd already known at the sugaring party. "You were her sugar daddy."

His full lips thinned. "Among other things."

I located the home button on my cell. "The two of you were emotionally involved?"

"Let's just say that I'd availed myself of her professional services and leave it at that," he replied drily.

"Okay." I needed to distract him, because I couldn't make a call without looking at my screen. "But why become her sugar daddy if all you wanted to do was steal the necklace?"

"She tried to sell it to me to cover the cost of school, and I told her I wasn't interested in buying stolen property, especially amber that belongs to Russia. Next thing you know, she came up with the idea of sugaring to pay her bills while she looked for a black market buyer." He grimaced and shook his head. "Amber was such a disappointment. She'd said she was going clean, but she was never going to be anything but a whore and a thief."

I didn't dare point out his hypocrisy. It would have been lost on him, and it might have accelerated his plan to kill me.

"I figured that if I set her up in an apartment for a month or two, I could find out where she was hiding the necklace." He picked up a small vial marked Ketamine HCl. "So I signed up with the Sugar Shack under an assumed name and went to a so-called sugar bowl party. The rest is history."

As he inserted the needle into the vial, I pressed the *Home* button.

"I don't understand," I said as I glanced at my cell screen to orient my fingers. "Why didn't you just steal the amber from the apartment, then?"

He thumped the side of the syringe and continued to extract the clear liquid. "Because I realized I could get the necklace and get rid of her when she told me about the witchcraft spell."

"How did that come about, exactly?" I tapped the Emergency icon.

"Curaçao told Amber that she'd put a hex on her back when they were working at Madame Moiselle's." He lowered his eyes from the syringe to me. "And Amber was stupid enough to believe in that witchcraft crap."

In light of that comment, I felt like a fool for thinking that I was cursed myself—although my present situation sure seemed to support the idea.

"Amber was convinced that the hex was the reason she hadn't been able to get her life together since she'd quit the club." He removed the needle and scrutinized the liquid in the barrel. "And she was afraid she never would—that is, until Eve recommended that she do an anti-hex spell on the spot where the hex had been placed."

My fingers froze when my eyes set sight on that syringe. "So, you snuck into the club while she was doing the spell and strangled her, but Curaçao came in before you could take the necklace."

"Right." The corners of his mouth turned down. "Somehow she found out when Amber was going to do the spell."

Based on what Carnie had told me, I guessed that Curaçao had been eavesdropping on Amber or Eve. "But why would Curaçao try to sell you the necklace after seeing you kill Amber?"

"She didn't see me," he replied like he was talking about spotting a friend at the cinema. "While I was choking Amber, I heard a sound and hid in the prop room. I watched through a crack in the door as she ripped the pendant from Amber's neck."

The casualness of his tone as he talked about killing gave me the mental kick in the rear I needed. As he returned the vial to the tray, I glanced at the numbers on my phone.

"And you didn't kill her and take the necklace?" I asked as I tapped 9-1-1.

"That was the plan." With the syringe in his hand, he smoothed his bangs. "But someone started unlocking the front door, so she ran to the back exit. Before I could do the same, the stripper mom came in."

My surprise at learning that Eve was at the crime scene made it easier to do what I had to do next. I sat up and started to cough to cover the sound of the 911 operator's voice.

He slammed me back into the chair with his left arm, and my cell hit the floor with a clatter. "Well, look at that—your phone." He stood up and pressed his left hand to my neck, and he kept it there as he walked around the back of the dental chair and smashed my phone with the heel of his shoe. "Try that again," he growled as he made his way back around, "and I'll make this as painful as possible."

I swallowed hard and wondered whether the call had made it through, although I wasn't holding out hope. I hadn't heard the 9-1-1 operator answer, and I wasn't even sure that I'd dialed the number correctly. "I-I wasn't trying anything," I lied. "I just didn't expect you to tell me that Eve was there."

The tension on his face relaxed as he released my neck and sat down. "That caught me off guard too. Until I saw her at Madame Moiselle's, I only knew her as the Texan lady that owned the sugaring company."

Now I understood why he'd said that a woman with a Texas accent had called his office about Amber, but I wanted to clarify that he was talking about Eve, and not Nadezhda. "You mean, Georgia."

He rolled his eyes. "Same thing."

Yeah, like honey and molasses. "After you saw Eve there, you decided to frame her for Amber's murder."

A conceited smile spread across his lips. "Actually, you gave me that idea when you asked about her mother. If I would've mentioned Eve before, it would've been too obvious that I knew more about Amber's life than I wanted to let on."

"Why didn't Eve report you to the police?" I asked, keeping an eye on the syringe still in his right hand. "Even if she didn't know your real name, she must've recognized you from the sugar bowl party."

He leaned back on his stool and crossed his arms. "She never saw me. When she noticed Amber onstage, she dropped the grocery bags she was holding and started screaming, 'Curaçao, what have you done?'"

So Eve had covered for Curaçao even though she thought that she'd killed Amber. Protecting her girls no matter what.

His lips curled with contempt. "While she was in hysterics, I slipped out the back entrance too."

I realized that the morning Veronica drove me home from the police station, I'd probably missed seeing Dr. Lessler leave by mere seconds. "How did Curaçao come to contact you, of all people, about buying the necklace?"

"She was one of my patients," he said with a flick of his hand. "After she stole it, I had my secretary call and schedule a cleaning appointment. When she came in, I casually mentioned that I was looking for an exotic gift for my wife for her birthday, and she fell right into the trap."

My blood began to boil at the mention of his wife because it reminded me that he had a young daughter too. But I had to keep a lid on my anger. Otherwise, my goose was cooked.

"We met at her place when her roommate was out." He laughed and shook his head. "She tried to play me by telling me that she had other buyers—a couple of Russians who supposedly knew the value of the amber and were willing to pay big bucks."

Eugene and Nadezhda.

"I pretended to go along with it, agreeing to beat the Russians' offer." He stopped and scowled. "But then she showed me a pendant that was obviously a fake, so I got pissed and offed her."

I squirmed in the chair. He was so cavalier about killing. "And you took her body to the club to make it look like Eve had killed her too."

He cocked a brow to match the cocky twist to his lips. "Pretty clever, huh?"

I didn't reply. We'd reached the end of his story, which meant that my story was about to end too.

He glanced at the clock, and the self-satisfied look left his face. "I've got to get a move on before that temp gets here and my next patient shows up."

"Wait," I breathed, winded from fear. "You don't know where the amber pendant is, and I do."

He slapped his knee. "As luck would have it," he said in a mocking tone, "Curaçao told me that she'd hidden it in that pigsty she called a house right before I wrung her naïve little neck."

For a moment, I thought that the dental chair had dropped a foot, but it was my stomach falling.

"I went there to get it, but her roommate was home, and then the cops started watching the place." He gave an apologetic smile. "Now that the killer has been arrested, though, you're the only thing standing in the way of me and that pendant."

Desperate for more time, I half-shouted, "Hold on. I still don't understand the Amaretto di Amore. Did you love Amber?"

He ran his hand over his lower face and jaw as though wiping a bad taste from his mouth. "I thought I did once. But after she left the club she cheated on me with one of her ex-johns."

Amber's death had been related to infidelity, after all.

"There's no such thing as love, anyway." He snorted. "It's like that bottle of amaretto."

"What do you mean?" I pressed, trying to keep him talking in case the police had gotten my call.

The corner of his mouth turned up, and he almost seemed sad. "You can give it a romantic name, but it's just plain old booze."

"Then why did you leave it at the crime scene?" I scanned the vicinity, looking for something I could use as a weapon.

"Lots of reasons." He sighed and rubbed his thighs. "For one thing, to remind Amber of what she'd thrown away."

I thought about the bottle Eve had seen Amber launch across the kitchen, and I knew it was from him too.

"And, you don't know this," he said, tilting his head toward me, "but my *grann* was Creole. She taught me to pay my respects to the voodoo *loa*, so I know better than to risk the wrath of Erzulie Yeux Rouges."

I marveled at the discovery that Dr. Lessler practiced voodoo, even though he'd said that witchcraft was "crap." *When was I going to learn that anything was possible in New Orleans?* "Were those your only reasons?"

"Not quite." He scooted his stool closer to my chair. "I knew that Amber's pimp had taught her voodoo, so I was trying to raise your suspicions about him too. The more suspects, the merrier, right?"

Slowly, I began to slide away from him. "That explains why you alluded to Amber's past as a prostitute and told me that she'd been wearing a mermaid *veve*."

"And it's the reason I left the rum and cigarettes for Baron Samedi, besides paying my respects, of course." He put his thumb on the end of the syringe. "But I'm going to have to skip the offerings this time since I have to kill you here in the office. I hope the loa don't mind."

I recoiled into the armrest. "If I were you, I wouldn't gamble on the gods."

His mouth turned down, as though annoyed by my impertinence. "You'd say anything to get out of a shot, wouldn't you?"

Especially one that was fatal.

He reached for my forearm. "As much as I hate to kill a fellow LSU fan—"

"A *what*?" Even on the brink of death, the Texas Longhorn in me was outraged.

"I was there when you stripped in those LSU tiger shoes, trying to lure the killer to the club." He sneered. "And now that I think about it, after that performance you deserve to die."

Since the day of my birthday, I'd endured countless injustices and humiliations—starting with turning thirty. But I was damned if I was going to continue to deal with the fallout from Glenda's stripping scheme.

Gripping the armrests, I kicked the dental tray as hard as I could, and it went flying into Dr. Lessler, instruments and all.

He shielded himself, giving me time to shove him away and leap from the chair. On the off chance that a patient had entered the lobby, I screamed, "Help!"

"Francesca?" My mother's voice was as shrill as a dental drill.

My head jerked toward the door from the shock of hearing my mom.

Dr. Lessler gripped my forearm with Superman-like strength and inserted the needle into my vein.

Stunned, I shot him a questioning look.

"Rock climber." He grinned.

The horror of what had happened hit me so hard that I fell backwards into the chair. Figuring that I had seconds to live, I knew what I had to do. "Mom, run! Dr. Lessler's the real killer!"

But even as I said those things, I knew that she wouldn't

listen. When you threatened my mother's kids, she was half mamma bear and half mafia boss.

She rushed into the room and rose to her full five feet four inches with her claws and fangs bared. "What's happening?" she rasped like Vito Corleone. "What have you done to my daughter?"

Dr. Lessler turned to face her, and I cold-cocked him with the hanging light.

We sunk to the floor.

Nonna stormed the examining room holding her handbag like a club. "I can-a take-a him, Brenda!"

From a supine position, I watched as she pounded Dr. Lessler with her purse while my mom punched a number into her cell. Despite the chaos, I looked up at the dolphin poster and felt at peace.

The ketamine was taking effect.

My mother leaned over me and pressed the phone to her ear. "I told you that you should be more careful when choosing a doctor, Francesca!"

Then my appointment abruptly ended.

24

———

"**G**et the hell up," a male voice demanded.

In my semi-conscious state, I realized I wasn't dead, but I knew Dr. Lessler wasn't done with me yet.

The peaceful feeling was replaced with primal fear as I remembered my mom and nonna coming to my rescue. *What had he done to them?*

I tried to open my eyes, but I couldn't. *Did he inject me with a paralytic drug?*

Two powerful hands gripped me by the biceps and shook me.

Summoning my strength, I forced my eyes open. Then I let out a hair-raising scream.

Carnie was standing over me in the Private Chicks lobby, her face practically purple with rage. And in her black strapless dress and spiky white wig, she was the spitting image of Ursula, the half-human, half-octopus villainess from *The Little Mermaid.*

"The police just held another press conference," she huffed with her hands on her hips. "It seems that my amber pendant has been found."

High heels came clattering down the hallway from Veronica's office.

"Are you okay, Franki?" Veronica asked as she and Glenda rushed to my side on the lobby couch.

"Divine." I pushed myself into a sitting position. "But get Ursula off my back, will you?"

Carnie's blue lids lowered and her red mouth frowned. "You'd best be talking about Ursula Andress, or you'll wish you were back in that dentist's chair."

Glenda swallowed a sip of the celebratory *sleuthing* champagne she'd been drinking since Dr. Lessler's arrest the day before. "What's the matter, Miss Carnie?"

She pointed a red-lacquered fingernail at me. "Your partner in cracking crime here gave my family heirloom to Detective Sullivan."

"I didn't *give* it to him," I protested. "He figured out that I knew where the pendant was at Amber's funeral."

Carnie raised a McDonald's Golden Arch–shaped brow. "Then how the hell did he end up with it?"

I massaged my temples in preparation for the headache she was about to give me. "When he came to interview me in the ER yesterday, I cut a deal to let him find it in exchange for dropping the battery charges against Bradley."

Carnie gasped. "I paid you to find the amber for *me*!"

"And I did!" I threw up my arms in an I-give gesture. "It's not my fault that it's evidence in the case against Dr. Lessler."

Veronica smoothed her skirt and took a seat beside me. "Franki was legally bound to inform the police about the pendant, Carnie. So it's nice that something good came of it, don't you think?"

In reply, she looked at Veronica like she was considering biting her with her venomous beak.

"There, there," Glenda said, patting one of Carnie's massive shoulders, "you'll get it back after the trial."

"But that could take years!" Carnie cried as she collapsed onto the opposing couch.

I wanted to tell her not to get her padded panties in a knot, but I held my tongue. After narrowly escaping the clutches of one madman, I wasn't willing to get caught in the tentacles of another.

Glenda sat next to Carnie and kicked up her heels. "Where was the pendant, Miss Franki?"

As I got ready to relive the events of the past twenty-four hours, I pulled a cushion into my lap for comfort. "In a matryoshka doll on a shelf in Maybe's living room."

Carnie, who'd turned her head away to sulk, stole a glance in my direction. "How did you know it was in a nesting doll? Did it have something to do with that nasty Nadezhda?"

I smirked as I shook my head. "It was partly because of Glenda and partly because of the nonne. When we were at the St. Joseph's Day altar, the nonne covered her up like the Virgin Mary. Then when my nonna was shooting the lemons at me, a statuette of the Virgin Mary broke in half, and it reminded me of the nesting doll because it was hollow inside and because the doll depicted a stripper. Since Curaçao was a stripper and the amber was Russian, I just knew that was where she'd hidden it."

Glenda winked. "Glad to know my body could be of service, sugar."

I took a deep breath as I prepared to say something that I never dreamed would pass my lips. "Your near nudity was a huge help. Thank you."

She raised her flute in a salute. "Speaking of naughty matryoshkas, what's going to happen to Nadezhda?"

"At the initial press conference yesterday, the police said

others would be indicted." Carnie fluffed her odd updo. "You know that Russki's one of them."

Veronica cleared her throat. "I'm sure they'll charge Nadezhda and Eugene both if they can prove they conspired to steal the necklace."

The creases in Glenda's brow deepened. "And Miss Eve?"

"She confessed to withholding evidence, so she'll face prosecution." Veronica looked down at her lap and shook her head. "If she'd told the police that she'd seen Curaçao at the crime scene, they would've taken Curaçao into custody—and she might still be alive today."

Regardless of what she'd done, I felt bad for Eve. In trying to protect Curaçao, she'd more than likely contributed to her demise. And I knew that was the last thing she would have ever wanted to do.

Carnie shifted and crossed her ankle over her knee, despite her dress. "What I don't understand is why that dentist knocked you out instead of killing you."

I shot her a long look—making sure to avoid the area below her torso. "According to Detective Sullivan's theory about what happened, Dr. Lessler needed to make it look like I'd died under anesthesia."

My story stopped as I made the sign of the *scongiuri*. Given everything I'd been through, I wasn't completely cured of my curse conviction yet.

"So he gave me ketamine, which is what dentists usually use for oral surgery, but just enough to knock me out for fifteen minutes or so. In that time he could've hooked me up to an IV to make it look like the drug had been administered normally and then cut off my air supply." I shuddered at the thought—and at the fact that I still had to get my permanent crown done.

"What a sick, twisted man," Glenda said, staring at her glass.

"I'll say," I muttered. "But then, he's a dentist."

The office phone began to ring.

"That's probably my mom calling to tell me they're leaving." I rose to my feet, and the room began to spin. "Whoa!"

Veronica stood up and placed her hand on my back. "I wish you would've taken the day off."

"You know I couldn't do that." I sunk back into the couch. "My mom and nonna said they were going to stay until they were sure I was all right. And after *getting* to share my bed with my nonna last night," I grumbled, "I'm more then ready for them to go."

"You owe your life to your nonna, Franki," Veronica chided as she walked to the reception desk. "If she hadn't insisted that your mother bring her to that office…"

I grimaced. The fact that my nonna's meddling had not only helped me find the amber but had also saved my life was a particularly bitter pill to swallow—and one that would keep coming up over and over again, both literally and figuratively.

When Veronica reached for the phone, it stopped ringing. She brought the receiver to the couch and placed it on the coffee table.

Glenda drained her glass. "Why *did* your nonna want to stop by Dr. Lessler's, sugar?"

"She never told me." I chewed the inside of my cheek. "But if I had to guess, it was to try to marry me off to the man."

The phone started ringing again.

"I'll get it." I grabbed the receiver. "Private Chi—"

"Why haven't you been answering your phone?" Ruth growled.

I squeezed the couch cushion. "Well, apart from the fact that it was crushed by a homicidal dentist, I've been kind of busy fighting for my life. Maybe you saw something about it on TV last night?"

"If it's not on *Nancy Grace*, I don't know about it."

That was worrisome news.

"Now, as much as I'd love to sit here and chit chat about the ups and downs of your day," Ruth snarked, "I have work to do. This is a courtesy call to let you know that Jeff Payne just resigned from Pontchartrain Bank thanks to your sweet grandmother."

As shocked as I was to hear that Jeff had resigned, I was even more astonished that my nonna had anything to do with it—and that she was "sweet." "Are you sure it was *my* grandmother?"

"Yes, ma'am," she crowed as she popped what sounded like a cork from a bottle. "About fifteen minutes ago, she burst into the board meeting with your mother. I didn't catch everything she said because she speaks like a female Father Guido Sarducci."

That was Nonna, *all right.*

"But I did hear her likening Jeff to a *mafioso*." She took a slurp of something. "Then she started passing out the compromising pictures."

"Hang on." I shot forward in my seat. "My nonna had compromising pictures? Of Jeff?"

Veronica and I exchanged a freaked out look.

"Did. She. Ever," Ruth syllabified. "She said she'd gotten them from 'the Madonna,' but I'll tell you what—the Virgin Mary don't know nothin' about the kinds of things going on in these pictures, even if she is looking down from heaven."

"What are you talking about?" I wheezed as the air left my lungs. "What was in the pictures?"

Veronica put her ear to the receiver, and I bowed my head to listen.

"Well, he was drunker than Cooter Brown on the 4th of July, but that ain't no big whoopty doo to a bunch of boozehound bankers," she said in a teetotaler tone. "What got them was that he was all tarted up in a stripper costume, performing for a gaggle of drag queens."

My head shot up, and I glanced from Glenda to Carnie—both of whom averted their eyes.

"And he was at a real swingin' cathouse, too," she said with relish, "because some of the pictures were taken in an all-pink room with a loveseat, others were in an all-red room with a small stage, and there was even one in an all-white room with a giant champagne glass."

My eyes zeroed in on Glenda.

Her lips spread into a slow smile. "Men find it hard to resist a free coupon for the VIP room, sugar."

"Actually, Ruth..." I paused and broke into a grin. "I'm friends with a Virgin Mary who knows all about those sorts of things—because she's anything but a saint."

As I slowed the Mustang to a stop in front of my apartment, I eyed my Mom's Ford Taurus. For the first time in days, the *Psycho* soundtrack was gone. It had been replaced with "When the Saint's Go Marching In"—the Louis Armstrong version. And when I got out of the car and headed up the driveway, I was mentally high-stepping and twirling a baton as I led the brass band playing in my head.

Although I had a newfound appreciation and respect for my mother and nonna after they'd defended me from the deranged dentist, and I loved them more than words could express—English, Italian, or Sicilian—I was oh-so ready to see them go. Now that the case was over, I needed some rest and relaxation before getting back to the grind. And I wasn't going to get any of that by sleeping in my bedtub.

I also needed some space to work out what had happened between Bradley and me. I'd planned to call him if he hadn't contacted me by Tuesday. But now that the day had arrived, I wasn't sure whether I wanted to talk to him. I understood that he'd been under attack at work, not to mention under orders to lay low, but I was hurt that he hadn't contacted me after I'd nearly been killed. Surely he'd seen the news, unlike Ruth?

When I reached my front stoop, the door opened.

"What are you doing home, Francesca?" my mother asked, swinging her purse onto her shoulder as she exited. "Aren't you feeling well?"

"I'm fine, Mom." I wrapped my arms around her and considered asking her about what had happened at the bank, but I decided to leave it alone. After all, everything had ended as it should. "I just wanted to come and say goodbye."

Her face was flushed as she reached up and brushed a strand of hair from my face. "Well, aren't you sweet."

My nonna appeared in the threshold with her big, black weapon on her arm. "*Bella mia!*"

"*Ciao,* Nonna." I hugged her hard, breathing in her garlicky aroma and wondering for the nth time what made her purse so heavy. I could've asked, but I decided to let that go too. Some things were better left a mystery.

"I'm-a glad you're here," Nonna said while we walked arm-in-arm to the car. "There's-a something I forgot-a to tell you. *Un piccolo dettaglio.*"

I opened her passenger door while my mother climbed into the driver's seat. "Is this 'small detail' what you came to Dr. Lessler's office yesterday to talk to me about?"

"Don't even speak-a his name, *quel criminale.*" She waved her hand as though brushing away the doctor's memory and got into the car. "It's about-a the lemon." Her eyes darted to my front door. "And you need-a to know it-a now."

My brow furrowed. *Was it bad news about the bum lemon? And why did she look at my apartment? Was Bruno lying inside in wait?*

Nonna fastened her seat belt and then stared straight ahead through the windshield. "When-a you steal a lemon from-a the altar of *San Giuseppe,* there is another thing-a that can happen."

I didn't have to know what this "thing-a" was to know that it wasn't good, especially because she wasn't looking at me. "O-kay..."

She gripped the handle of her purse. "Instead of a husband, from-a time-a to time, you get a *bambino.*"

The *Pyscho* music screeched in my head.

"But-a either way, it's-a win-a win-a, eh Franki?" She turned and winked at me, and for a split second, I could've sworn that she had cat pupils.

My mother started the engine, shaking me from my shock.

"I hope we see you before Christmas, dear," she said, getting in one last guilt trip before their car trip back to Houston. "I assume you still know our address."

I rolled my eyes. "I'll be home this summer, Mom," I replied, resuming my usual defensive tone. "You guys drive safe."

As she backed the Taurus out of the driveway, I thought back to my conversation with Theodora about Old New Orleans Traditional Witchcraft being a kind of everyday magic that great-great grandmothers used to do. And it occurred to me that the lemon tradition and all the other bizarre customs I'd grown up with could be considered a type of witchcraft that nonne do.

But whatever. Since I was planning to break up with Bradley, the odds of my having a bambino out of wedlock were zilch.

I turned toward the house and stumbled over something, hitting the ground with a thud. I looked back and saw Glenda's stripper garden gnome.

The Virgin Mary.

Jumping to my feet, I rushed inside to call Theodora about an anti-hex spell—just in case. But I was distracted by the aroma of Italian food. My apartment smelled like my mom and nonna had made some meals for me before they'd left. I walked into the kitchen to see what they'd prepared.

There stood Bradley, holding a dozen yellow roses and a glass of Prosecco.

Our eyes met as he handed me the glass, and I drank it all in —not the Prosecco, the romantic atmosphere. The curtains were drawn, and there were lit candles on the kitchen table, which had been set with fine china and crystal that definitely didn't belong to me. Napoleon was even wearing a bowtie. And although I was furious with Bradley, I had to admit that he looked handsome in his dark blue suit—so much so that I understood why my nonna had told me about the other lemon legend.

He cleared his throat. "Can we talk?"

"It depends on what you have to say." My tone was frosty, like my heart.

He pulled out a chair. "Would you like to have a seat?"

I swallowed a sip of Prosecco. "I'll stand."

"Fair enough." A muscle worked in his jaw. "I'd like to start with how sorry I am that I let the pressure at work come between us."

"That's a good place to start." I crossed my arms. "But skip ahead to why you didn't call me after you punched Detective Sullivan."

"I wanted to, Franki. I really did." He tossed the flowers on the kitchen counter and ran a hand through his hair. "But Veronica insisted that I not contact you until I knew where I stood with the bank. My gut told me not to listen, but as my attorney and your best friend, I figured she knew what was right for both of us."

Although I wouldn't have admitted it to Bradley, I had to agree that Veronica was usually the wiser one in a crisis. But still. "So, like Jeff, you thought I'd be a professional problem for you. Because I am, you know."

He winced. "That's not true, Franki. My job is dependent on me, and me alone. And it wasn't Jeff or my job that I was worried about. It was you."

My cold heart began to thaw, but just a little. "How so?"

He turned as though he wanted to pace in the tiny kitchen. "I can go home to Boston and get a job any time I want, but I didn't think you'd want to go with me."

"What?" I practically gasped the word. "This isn't about Detective Sullivan, is it?"

"No, but that son—" He bowed his head for a moment and put his hand on his hip. "That *detective* got what he had coming to him after dangling your bra in front of me and putting a dollar bill in your G-string."

"It was a five, but go on," I said, deadpan.

"Look." He sighed. "Boston is a long way from New Orleans, and from Houston, for that matter. I didn't want to have to ask you to leave your family and friends or your work for me."

My heart continued to defrost. It was considerate of him to take my needs into account, but something didn't add up. "If you were so worried about me and my wellbeing, why wouldn't you call me after I was almost killed?"

His eyes looked anguished as he took a step forward. "I did call—over and over again."

I bit my lower lip. My cell phone *had* been destroyed.

He looked at me from under his lashes. "So, I came over to make sure you were okay."

"You did?" I asked, taking a step forward myself.

"I stayed here all night," he replied, his voice soft.

My heart warmed but promptly sank. *My nonna's enema bag.* "You didn't sleep in the bathtub, did you?"

He tilted his head. "No, I sat at the kitchen table, drinking coffee and talking to your nonna first, and then when she went to bed, to your mom."

Now *that* was devotion.

"I kissed you on the cheek before I left for the board meeting, but you didn't wake up." He shoved his hands in his pockets. "I wanted to skip the meeting, but your mom said that it was important that I go."

My heart had not only risen back into my chest, it was practically bursting. I put my glass on the counter. "I swear to you, Bradley, I had no idea that they planned to crash the meeting, and I had nothing to do with those pictures."

The corner of his mouth lifted. "I know. Your mom and nonna explained everything. They're quite a pair, those two."

I snorted. "You can say that again."

"Just like someone else I know." The smile faded from his face, and his gaze bore into mine. "Can you forgive me?"

I nodded, and he crossed the distance between us. As he cupped my face in his hands as his lips pressed against my forehead, my eyelids, the tip of my nose, and finally, my mouth I knew that there was nothing in the world that could make me break up with him.

My knees weakened, and I wrapped my arms around his neck.

And I thought of that damn lemon.

I stiffened and pulled away.

Bradley gave me a searching look. "What is it?"

Of course, I could hardly tell him about the lemon I'd lifted and the "small detail" my nonna had laid on me before she left. But I wasn't ready for this magical moment to end.

My mind raced as I tried to conjure up a way to ward off the lemon's adverse effect. Obviously, I wasn't a great-grandma or grandma, but I *was* thirty, so I figured I had some witchcraft in me too. Making the sign of the *scongiuri* behind my back, I whispered, "Nothing. Everything is perfect."

He flashed a dazzling, eye-twinkling smile. "Good, because I've been thinking about that tiger costume you wore at the club." His lips nuzzled my ear. "And I was hoping you'd show me some of your animal moves."

BOOK BACKSTORY

Amaretto Amber was inspired by two events in my life—a nine a.m. bathroom stop at Big Daddy's strip club on Bourbon Street (the club was closed, and the bathroom turned out to be the strippers' dressing room with an "open-air" toilet) and my first ever drag show, "RuPaul's Drag Race: Battle of the Seasons," at Austin's Paramount Theatre (Bianca Del Rio and Ivy Winters were fierce!). Those strippers and drag queens forever changed my life.

When I started planning *Amaretto Amber*, I decided that it would be fun to incorporate some reader suggestions into the plot; specifically, requests to have Franki's nonna show up in New Orleans and to make Bradley pay for what he'd put Franki through with Pauline in *Prosecco Pink*.

In terms of the plot, I would like to thank Daniel Joseph Gomez for patiently answering a slew of questions related to the entertainment industry, and to K'Tee Bee, a fan and great friend, for suggesting that I have Franki's meddling *nonna* visit the French Quarter. That idea formed the basis for this entire story, and I shudder to think of what the book would've been without it.

Speaking of fans, I'd also like to say how much I appreciate the support of the Sardis Library Book Club Ladies and the NBPLRomance Readers. Thank you for all that you've done for me—your emails, book clubs, Facebook posts, pictures, and tweets—and for authors and readers everywhere. I have always loved libraries and the people who run them!

As for the technical stuff, I owe a huge debt of gratitude to Detective Ruben Vasquez and pathology expert Dr. Judy Melinek for their professional expertise. I would also like to thank Dana Brown for helping me with the dental references in *Amaretto Amber* and Dr. Michael Lessner, my absolute favorite dentist of all time (go see him—without fear!).

If you couldn't tell from my books, I'm fascinated by foreign language and by names. So, when Suzie Gaspard Quebedeaux joined my street team, I told her that I was going to use her awesome Cajun last name in a book. Suzie, I finally did it, so thank you! I also borrowed the entire name of one of my favorite ex-Italian students, Carlos Del Rio, because it just belongs in a book. And Cherie Havard, don't get mad at me for how I used your first name—it was such a perfect fit that I had no choice!

Last but not least, a big *grazie mille* goes to my family for their love, support, and patient proofreading.

Cin cin (Cheers)!

Traci

COCKTAILS

AMARETTO AMBER CRANBERRY KISS

Franki loves amaretto, especially when it's mixed with vodka. She's particularly fond of a good kiss too, but she prefers that it come from Bradley—or Hershey's.

Ingredients
    1 cup cranberry cocktail juice
    1/2 cup vodka
    1/4 cup amaretto
    1 and 1/2 tablespoons orange juice

Mix all ingredients in a cocktail shaker with ice, and strain into a martini glass. Add an orange slice for garnish.

ITALIAN SUNSET

This sunny cocktail reminds Franki of her college-study trip to Italy—and of a certain Carlo she met there. Every time she drinks it, she dreams of going back to Rome one day. Maybe a mystery will take her there?

Ingredients
    2 ounces amaretto
    3 ounces pulp-free orange juice
    3 ounces club soda
    dash of grenadine

Pour the amaretto into a highball glass with crushed ice. Layer the remaining ingredients in the order listed above. Finish with a dash of grenadine. Don't stir, or the sunset will disappear.

FREE MINI MYSTERIES OFFER

Want to know what happens to Franki after *Limoncello Yellow*?
Sign up for my newsletter to receive a free copy of the *Franki Amato Mini Mysteries*, a hilarious collection that contains "Prugnolino Purple" (Franki #1.5) and five other fun short mysteries. You'll also be the first to know about my new releases, deals, and giveaways.

Here's the blurb for "Prugnolino Purple:"

It's springtime in New Orleans, and Franki Amato's BFF and boss, Veronica Maggio, has dragged her to an art auction at one of the city's historic house museums. Up for sale, a provocative, not to mention peculiar, painting of their sixty-something ex-stripper landlady that is anything but priceless. Franki thinks the only crime at play is the image on the canvas until a cocktail waitress is found unconscious in front of an empty easel. After Franki finds a purple splotch on the presumed weapon, she and Veronica spring into action to ID the attacking art thief and locate the missing painting. But Franki's biggest surprise isn't the culprit—it's the "blooming idiot" who bought the portrait before the auction started.

And don't forget to follow me!

BookBub
https://www.bookbub.com/authors/traci-andrighetti

Goodreads
https://www.goodreads.com/author/show/7383577.
Traci_Andrighetti

Facebook
https://www.facebook.com/traciandrighettiauthor

ALSO BY TRACI ANDRIGHETTI

FRANKI AMATO MYSTERIES

Books
Limoncello Yellow
Prosecco Pink
Amaretto Amber
Campari Crimson
Galliano Gold
Marsala Maroon
Valpolicella Violet
Tuaca Tan
Nocino Noir
Sambuca Scarlet (coming in 2025!)

Box Sets
Franki Amato Mysteries Box Set (Books 1–3)
Franki Amato Mysteries Box Set (Books 4–6)
The Franki Amato Mysteries Big Box Set (Books 1–7)

Short Stories

Franki Amato Mini Mysteries
(short mysteries free to newsletter subscribers only)

Franki Amato also investigates with the sleuths of Leslie
Langtry, Arlene McFarlane, and Diana Orgain in the

KILLER FOURSOME MYSTERIES

Books
4 Sleuths & A Bachelorette
4 Sleuths & A Burlesque Dancer
4 Sleuths & A Barnstormer

DANGER COVE HAIR SALON MYSTERIES

Books
Deadly Dye and a Soy Chai
A Poison Manicure and Peach Liqueur
Killer Eyeshadow and a Cold Espresso

ABOUT THE AUTHOR

Traci Andrighetti is the *USA Today* bestselling author of the Franki Amato mysteries and the Danger Cove Hair Salon mysteries, and she is a co-author of the Killer Foursome mysteries. In her previous life, she was an award-winning literary translator and a Lecturer of Italian at the University of Texas at Austin, where she earned a PhD in Applied Linguistics. But then she got wise and ditched that academic stuff for a life of crime—writing, that is. Get news of Traci's upcoming books and latest capers at www.traciandrighetti.com.

Speaking of capers, Traci and one of her Killer Foursome co-authors, Diana Orgain, take published and aspiring authors on writing retreats to Italy through LemonLit. If you're up for an Italian adventure, then *andiamo*! But be careful. Traci and Diana are a lot like their sleuths, so you never know what—or who—might go down on the trip...

SNEAK PEEK

If you liked these Franki Amato mysteries, read the first chapter of:

CAMPARI CRIMSON
Franki Amato Mysteries Book 4

2018 Mystery & Mayhem Award Finalist

by
Traci Andrighetti

CHAPTER 1

"That vampire is staring at me." I clenched my jaw and tipped my head at a fanged female standing among parade-goers at the gates of Jackson Square.

Veronica Maggio stood on tiptoes and gazed over the crowd. "The one with the curls and blue dress?"

"Uh-huh." I pulled up the collar of my peacoat. "Every time I look at her, she's ogling my throat."

She gave a get-a-grip gasp. "Franki, she's barely twelve years old."

No matter how hard I tried, I could never convince my best friend and employer that danger was a daily concern. Sometimes it seemed like she clung to her perky-positive Elle Woods worldview to spite me, and the proof was in her *Legally Blonde*-inspired pink Playboy Bunny costume. "Go ahead—scoff. But she reminds me of Claudia, the blood-thirsty kid Kirsten Dunst played in *Interview with a Vampire*."

"Well, this little vampirette isn't going to bite you, especially not at a Halloween parade."

I looked to the voodoo doll beside me for support, but she looked away. "How does that make any sense?"

Veronica shot me the side-eye. "You're one to talk about making sense. I don't know why you're always so suspicious of people."

"Uh..." I blinked, incredulous. "Because we're private investigators, and we're in New Orleans?"

"We both know vampires aren't real." She turned toward Decatur Street, resuming her wait for the first float. "And no one comes to the Krewe of BOO! parade to bite anyone. They're here to have fun."

Judging from the way the buzzed Betelgeuse to my right had been baring his teeth at me, I wasn't so sure about the biting part. "Maybe, but as soon as Glenda gets here, I'm heading home."

She glanced at her phone. "It's six-thirty, so I'm expecting them any minute."

If I hadn't been sufficiently spooked by the vexing vampiress, the realization that my sixty-something ex-stripper landlady was bringing a companion did the trick. "*Them?* I thought it was *her*."

"Carnie's coming too."

Dread filled my veins like a bad transfusion. As her stage

name implied, Carnie Vaul was a carnival-clown-turned-drag-queen friend of Glenda's who once hired me to investigate a homicide involving her priceless amber necklace. And even though I technically worked for Veronica's PI firm, Private Chicks, Inc., Carnie had thrown her weight around—all three hundred fifty pounds of it. The worst part was that I'd solved the case six months before, but she was still hanging around like an albatross from my neck—or a big boobie-bib. "I would've appreciated a heads-up."

"You just got one." She stood on her tiptoes and scoured the crowd. "Try not to pick a fight with her, okay?"

"Me?" I said, shocked. "That devious diva has targeted me from day one."

"She's difficult, I know. But you played right into her hand."

I snorted. "Maybe it's because her hands are so huge."

The crowd gave a collective gasp followed by cheers, and Veronica and I strained to see the float.

"Oh." She covered her mouth. "It's Count Dracula."

The old phrase, "I vant to suck your blood," came to mind. With a grimace, I turned to eye my toothy little friend but came face-to-face with Glenda.

"How do you like me, ladies?" She struck a pose in a floor-length black feather dress and matching cabaret shoulder collar. "Miss Carnie and I decided to go as each other this Halloween season."

"Local celebrities trade places," Veronica said as Carnie waddled into view. "What a cute idea."

"Creepy" was a better term. Glenda looked like an old crow with clown hair, and Carnie, in a white, plus-sized halter-top and boy shorts, bore an unsettling resemblance to the New Orleans Pelicans' King Cake Baby mascot in his giant bib and diaper—except for the platinum wig and cigarette holder.

"You know me." Glenda flapped her two-inch purple feather lashes. "I love an excuse to dress in costume."

I suppressed a smirk. Glenda O'Brien, in art Lorraine Lamour, had worn a stripper costume every day since she'd started dancing some fifty years before. And everyone in The Crescent City was acutely aware of it.

"Franki likes costumes too," Carnie said in a fierce falsetto. "And hers is so realistic—a worn-out working girl who's given up on her looks and her life."

A float of Chucky and his axe-wielding bride came into view, which was appropriate since I was feeling stabby.

"I'm not wearing a costume because I was working." I straightened my coat. "I had to finish my notes for an employee theft case."

Carnie's eyes lit up like a jack-o'-lantern. "What did he steal? Your femininity?"

That burned, especially coming from a queen.

Glenda gave a raucous laugh. "If you need a costume, Miss Franki, you know I'll do you right."

Wrong. Glenda was an avid stripper costume collector who'd provided me with outfits for a couple of cases. And thanks to her creations, I'd had wardrobe malfunctions that made Janet Jackson's Super Bowl nip slip seem demure. "I don't need a costume, thanks." I hit Carnie with a direct stare. "But now I need a drink."

Veronica pulled some cash from her bunny suit. "I'll buy us a round."

Before I could refuse, she took me by the arm and led me across the street. We walked along the gutter to bypass the partiers, and the Chucky float pulled up beside us.

Glenda looked at its krewe. "Throw me something, Monster," she shouted, using the Halloween variant of the Mardi Gras cry, *Throw me something, Mister.*

A zombie chucked a painted oyster shell, but it sailed over Glenda and conked me in the head.

"Ow!"

The zombie looked dispirited. "Sorry, lady!"

Carnie cackled as I checked for blood—and did a quick scan for the canined kid. Once I'd located her, I turned to take on the float. "You guys should stick to soft throws like Aunt Sally's Pralinettes."

"Let's get you to safety." Veronica ushered me into Big Easy Daiquiris, and maybe it was the possible concussion, but I could have sworn I saw her smiling.

Despite the crowd outside, there were only a handful of people in the shotgun-style establishment.

"You have a seat," Veronica said as she, Glenda, and Carnie approached the bartender.

Following her advice, I sat at the bar and glanced at the TV hanging in the corner of the room. There was a *Breaking News* banner at the bottom of the screen, and it was clear from the gold New Orleans PD shield behind the empty podium that the police were about to hold a news conference.

Glenda pulled out the barstool beside me and hiked her dress to her thighs before sitting down. "You going to meet your banker beau tonight, sugar?"

The mention of my boyfriend, Bradley Hartmann, made my lips pucker—and not for a kiss. The day before he'd surprised me with the news that he was going on a two-week trip to New York for Pontchartrain Bank. The trip had been a surprise to him too, so I didn't blame him for the late notice. What I did blame him for was not inviting me to come with him, not even for the weekend. "He's wrapping up some things at the office."

She patted my knee. "I used to be like him, you know."

I couldn't wait to hear how.

"Hustling twelve-hour days, seven days a week."

"It must be tough being a stripper," I said to commiserate. "And a bank president."

She gave a grave nod. "One day I realized that all of this"—she pointed to her body—"was no good to my clients if I wasn't good with myself. So I made time to live a little."

Based on the stories she'd told me about her stripping days, she'd lived a little *a lot*. "Bradley can't always control his own schedule. He just found out that he has to leave town tomorrow for work."

"And he's not making time for you before he goes?" Carnie put a hand to her bogus bosom. "How telling."

I hit her with a don't-go-there stare. "We're meeting for brunch in the morning."

"Sounds about as sexy as a date at a grocery store." She flopped onto the stool next to Glenda.

Although I knew better than to fall victim to one of her jabs, it still hurt. I was sensitive enough about Bradley not inviting me to New York, so I didn't need her picking apart our plans. "He has to be well rested for the trip."

"Well, you can hardly expect him to catch up on his beauty rest during a three-hour flight, can you?" Carnie had raised her falsetto an octave to sound innocent.

I lowered my voice an octave to sound incensed—which I was. "He can't sleep on the plane because his secretary's going with him."

Glenda and Carnie exchanged arched brows.

"It isn't like that," I protested. "Ruth Walker's at least sixty years old."

One of Glenda's eyelash-wings lowered to mid-flap.

"I think someone's throwing shade at mature women, Glenda," Carnie said, using drag speak for *insult*.

"'Sixty' and 'sexy' are practically the same word, Miss Franki. You'd do well to remember that."

I gave a three-second sigh. With Glenda's feathers all ruffled and Carnie's boy shorts in a bunch, I would've been better off at the parade with the vampire. "I wasn't 'throwing shade' at anyone. All I meant was, Bradley's not into older women."

Glenda flipped her Bozo hair, but it didn't budge. "His loss, sugar."

Veronica walked up behind me as the bartender delivered our drinks. I started to compliment his Captain Jack Sparrow costume, but then it occurred to me that it might be his normal look.

"Three Zombifieds and one Vampire Bite," he announced, placing orange-colored drinks and a blood-red concoction on the bar.

I didn't have to ask which one was mine. I frowned at Veronica, who raised her fleur-de-lis–shaped cup in a toast, and wished I'd gone home as planned.

"Look, Miss Carnie." Glenda pointed at the TV. "It's that handsome hunk of man meat, Detective Sullivan."

Carnie licked her Lucille Ball lips. "Gurrrl, you know I'd like to take a bite of that beefsteak."

I dosed myself with my drink and glowered at the screen. The superintendent of police and the chief were on either side of the podium, and Detective Wesley Sullivan was right where he liked to be—front and center. I knew because I'd made the mistake of getting in the way of his glory while working on Carnie's case. And because his ego was as inflated as his biceps, he'd done everything he could to sideline me, starting with throwing me in jail.

I made eye contact with the bartender, who poured a daiquiri from one of the machines. "Could you turn up the sound, please?"

"F'sure."

Veronica looked at the TV. "What's going on?"

"I'll bet it's about the blood bank, Miss Ronnie." Glenda held her straw like a cigarette holder.

The cold, red liquid I'd sipped took on a ghastly chill in my mouth. I held it there for a second and then swallowed, hard. "Blood bank?"

The bartender aimed a remote control at the TV, and the murmur of reporters chatting in the background became audible.

"As you may know," Detective Sullivan said, quieting the crowd, "last night there was an attempt to break in to The Blood Center on Canal Street at eleven forty-five p.m. We believe the culprit or culprits were scared away by officers responding to an unrelated call near the scene."

"Send those officers my way, Detective. I don't scare easily." Glenda arched her back to emphasize her sex, not her strength.

Detective Sullivan shot a somber look at the camera, matching my mood exactly. "The security camera outside the building was disabled. Fortunately, a security camera across the street captured an image of a suspect, who we'll show to you now."

Video footage of a caped figure aired.

"A *cape*?" I was dumbstruck—and disturbed. "A guy goes to steal blood from a blood bank and wears a *cape*?"

Veronica shrugged. "Who said it was a guy?"

"Um, the point is the cape?" I glanced around the bar, surprised that no one else was freaked out by the suspect's choice of outerwear. "It's awfully vampiric, don't you think?"

Veronica bit her straw and turned away.

"It's too much clothing." Glenda scowled at the screen. "The public doesn't want to see that."

"And capes are out of style," Carnie chimed. "They need to put the camera back on that delicious detective."

Detective Sullivan reappeared, and Glenda and Carnie clinked cups.

"If you know this individual, or if you have any information about the break-in, you can call us at the number on the screen." He read from a sheet of paper on the podium. "If you'd rather remain anonymous, you can call Crime Stoppers, send them a text, or leave a tip online."

"What about your phone number, Detective?" Glenda cooed.

As Sullivan left the podium, a young male reporter appeared on screen. "Do you have any active leads?"

The detective looked annoyed. "We're following up on some tips, but at this time we do not have a suspect." He nodded at the gathering of reporters. "Yes, Bill."

An older man stepped forward with a notebook. "Do you have any reason to believe this attempt is related to the break-in at the Metairie blood bank last month?"

"I'm not at liberty to discuss that." The detective pointed to someone off camera. "Ann?"

"Do you have any idea what the motive would be for stealing blood?" she asked.

The superintendent leaned into the microphone. "I'm afraid we're out of time. This concludes the press conference."

I glanced at Veronica. "The superintendant skirted that question, didn't he?"

"Yeah." She sat on the stool next to me. "I wonder why."

"I'm not sure I want to know." I reached for my Vampire Bite but then decided to leave it be. "Had you heard about the break-in at the Metairie blood bank?"

"M-hm." Her pretty pout thinned. "They wiped out their entire supply of B Positive."

My blood type. I scratched my neck. "Bizarre."

Glenda plucked a few feathers from her breast area. "Stranger things have happened in New Orleans, sugar."

After a year and a half in the city, I knew that was true. "But why would anyone steal blood? And only one type?"

"I say it's a fetish." Glenda pulled a cigarette holder from the heel of her stripper shoe. "When I was dancing at Madame Moiselle's back in the '90s, we had this VIP room regular we called The Podiatrist. He took pictures of our feet with a Polaroid." She laughed and slapped my leg. "Then he rubbed the pictures between our toes before putting them in individually marked plastic baggies."

I pulled Veronica's drink from her grip and took a gulp.

Carnie, nonplussed by The Podiatrist, leaned back on her barstool. "Maybe it's a wounded criminal in hiding."

A mobster or a drug lord was a possibility—one I didn't want to consider.

Veronica twisted her ring, staring into space. "Or maybe it's for voodoo or witchcraft."

That was my cue to leave, or rather, flee.

"Whatever the reason, I'm glad it's Detective Sullivan's problem and not mine." I hopped from the barstool and, without thinking, chugged the rest of my Vampire Bite. And when I put the glass on the bar, I had a bitter taste in mouth, but not because it reminded me of blood.

It was because something told me that I'd jinxed myself and that the blood bank problem was about to be mine.

I awoke, shivering. The temperature in my bedroom had dropped at least ten degrees since I'd gone to bed. Too exhausted to open my eyes, I rolled onto my back and reached for the hot pink velvet duvet, pulling it over the sheets. Then I waited to drift back to sleep.

A blast of hot air hit my neck.

And another.

In my semiconscious state, I realized the blasts were coming in rhythmic bursts.

Like breathing.

In a flash I was alert, frozen with fear. It was ludicrous to think of vampires and blood bank thieves, but I did.

As well as deranged drag queens.

I couldn't get my gun, because it was in the nightstand. My only option for taking on the intruder was the self-defense training I'd received during my year on the Austin PD.

Corralling my courage, I opened my eyelids a crack. And the blood drained from my body.

A hairy face hovered at my throat.

Was it a big bat? A werewolf? An unshaven Carnie?

The creature's mouth opened, as though in slow motion, revealing pointed teeth and emitting a putrid odor.

The smell of death.

I whimpered, and it...barked?

My body went limp.

The creature was my cairn terrier, Napoleon.

"Bad boy," I shouted, supine. But I was madder at myself than at my dog. I didn't know what had gotten into me—all I knew was that I wanted it to get out.

He barked again.

"Ugh." I raised my head. "What do you want?"

In reply, he jumped off the bed and trotted to the doorway. Then he turned and looked over his shoulder.

"This had better be important business." As soon as I'd said it, I thought of Bradley's trip, and then I was doubly annoyed.

I dragged myself from the black bordello-style bed and grabbed my gut. I'd been in a bad state before hitting the sack, so I'd gone out with a bang—an alligator sausage Dat Dog and crawfish étouffée fries topped off with a quarter jar of Nutella. The problem was that the alligator and the crawfish sought revenge, swimming in the muddy swamp of my stomach.

Lumbering Bride-of-Frankenstein-style through the living room, I reached the front door and peered through the peephole. Satisfied it was safe, I opened the door. "Shake your tail fur."

Napoleon darted into the yard, and I lost sight of him in the darkness. I wasn't sure what time it was, but it was after two a.m. because the lights were off at Thibodeaux's tavern across the street.

A cat howled from the cemetery next to the bar, and Napoleon growled.

"Stay," I commanded, although I still couldn't see him. "You go in there, and you're on your own."

The ghoulish graveyard had been the bane of my existence ever since Veronica had talked me into renting the apartment next door to hers on the first floor of Glenda's fourplex. Because I lived in Austin at the time, my best friend had mailed me the lease. And she'd stayed as mum as a corpse about the macabre tombs, crypts, and mausoleums across the street. Otherwise, I would've run for my life. Even the locals knew how disturbing their aboveground cemeteries were, which is why they'd nicknamed them *cities of the dead*.

And, as far as I was concerned, there was nothing uplifting about living by the dead, especially in one of Glenda's apartments. Veronica described the décor as bordello chic, which was fitting since Glenda had furnished the place from brothel fire sales, but it also had a disturbing funeral parlor feel. When the day came that I could afford to move out, I was going to write a book about the experience—*The Little Whorehouse of Horrors*.

The cat started caterwauling, and I heard my cairn "terror"

tear across the grass to save the cemetery from the feline infiltrator.

"Damn dog never listens to a word I say," I muttered, slipping on my soccer sandals.

The alligator and the crawfish switched from the freestyle to the butterfly the second I set off for the cemetery. When I got to the gate, I cursed whoever had left it open. The musty scent of decay assailed my nostrils, and I covered my nose and mouth. There was no way to know whether the odor was from the damp earth and thick carpet of dead leaves—or from something else.

"Napoleon! Come. Here. Right. Now."

Nothing.

As I debated whether to enter, a gargoyle glared at me from atop a tomb. Gritting my teeth, I took a step forward and stopped.

The leaves were rustling—a lot.

"That's a big cat," I said to the gargoyle, shifting my weight to the other foot. "Like, lion-sized."

A hiss sounded, and a yelping Napoleon dashed past me with his tail between his legs.

I cracked a smile at his cowardice and glanced in the area of the cat commotion.

And what I saw scared the smile from my face.

Moving among the mausoleums was a caped figure—like the one on the press conference video.

Following Napoleon's lead, I turned tail and ran to the apartment in Olympic time.

After checking on Napoleon, who was holed up beneath the zebra-striped chaise lounge, I peeked through the gold fringe of my drapes.

There was no one in sight, but I wasn't about to relax because I finally understood why I'd been so spooked. I'd lived in New Orleans long enough to know that people and things were connected in this city in ways they weren't anywhere else. In unthinkable and unknowable ways.

The vampire, the press conference, the caped figure—the uneasy feelings they'd given me had been no accident. One way or another, they'd come back to haunt me during Halloween.